PRAISE FOR *RUSSIAN SPRING*

"Spinrad's best novel in years—intelligent, detailed, well-constructed, and emotionally compelling."
—*Chicago Sun-Times*

"An impressive achievement . . . A welcome addition to those science fiction books that seriously attempt to show what the future might be like."
—*The Washington Post*

"It's moving. It's inspiring . . . I don't cry that easily over my reading, but I cried for Jerry and his family several times."
—*San Diego Tribune*

"Using the techniques of future extrapolation to comment so movingly on our current world situation, [*Russian Spring*] does what science fiction and only science fiction can do: It shows us where we might be headed and offers thoughts on how we can make the best possible real future with the tools we have."
—*Omni*

NORMAN SPINRAD
RUSSIAN SPRING

SPECTRA™

BANTAM BOOKS

NEW YORK · TORONTO · LONDON · SYDNEY · AUCKLAND

For Mikhail Gorbachev,
who made it necessary,
and
N. Lee Wood,
who made it possible

RUSSIAN SPRING
A Bantam Spectra Book

PUBLISHING HISTORY
Bantam hardcover edition published October 1991
Bantam paperback edition / October 1992

ISBN 0-553-29869-0

Published simultaneously in the United States and Canada

Bantam Books are published by Bantam Books, a division of
Bantam Doubleday Dell Publishing Group, Inc. Its trademark,
consisting of the words "Bantam Books" and the portrayal of a
rooster, is Registered in U.S. Patent and Trademark Office and in
other countries. Marca Registrada. Bantam Books, 666 Fifth
Avenue, New York, New York 10103.

PRINTED IN THE UNITED STATES OF AMERICA

RAD   0 9 8 7 6 5 4 3 2 1

Author's Introduction

When I began writing *Russian Spring* in August 1988, I had just returned from an international writers conference in Budapest, and by the time the hardcover edition was published in October 1991, the August coup attempt in Moscow had just failed. Between the novel's conception and its completion in 1991, the story went through many revisions, reflecting the revolutionary changes taking place during those three years that so transformed the world. At this writing, February 1992, the final outcome of those changes remains entirely in doubt, so much so that the only safe prediction is that there will be yet more such changes before you can read what I am writing now in October 1992.

Many of the changes I foresaw during the writing of the book actually took place before the final draft was finished —democratic elections in the Soviet Union, the dissolution of the Soviet Eastern European empire, the reunification of Germany, the end of the Cold War, the beginnings of American military disengagement in Europe—and the final version reflected them in altered detail.

Others occurred after the novel was committed to production. Some of these, while not quite occurring as predicted in time frame or detail, eerily followed the novel in broad outline and inner meaning—the American economic malaise, the new steps toward a transnational Confederal Western Europe, the resurgence of tribal nationalisms in Europe, East and West, and the unfortunate results.

Still other predictions would presently seem to have turned out to be wrong. The Soviet Union is no more, and the Communist party would seem to have no place in the future unfolding in the former territories thereof, and their economies are in a state of collapse.

And yet, who knows? The fine details of future history, captive as they are to the rise and fall of personalities, random occurrences, coups, disasters, the winds of chance, may be impossible to predict with accuracy, but the broader and deeper economic, technological, and geopolitical imperatives that underlie the destinies of peoples and nations are another matter.

In 1968, in *Bug Jack Barron*, I presented a vision of American presidential politics twenty years or so in the future, entirely subsumed and subverted by the power of television. Now, twenty-four years later, while the specific political details may not have come to pass as predicted, the larger and more general prediction has proven to be all too true. In 1987, in *Little Heroes,* at the height of the so-called Reagan Boom I foresaw the economic decline of America in the 1990s, not all that hard to do, given the economic and social realities beneath the hype of the moment.

So too, while some of the details of *Russian Spring* may have been superseded by cataclysmic events, the larger forces shaping the future toward which the world is moving remain. The E.E.C. is moving inevitably toward something like the Common Europe of the novel, its economic dominance is already a fact, and the nations of Eastern Europe are moving toward membership. The United States has indeed become the military overlord of the planet, an American-dominated Western Hemispheric Common Market is already in the process of formation, and the first elements of the Strategic Defense Initiative will soon be deployed. And the debt-driven decline of the American economy is already a sad fact of life.

But what of the Commonwealth of Independent States, the former Soviet Union? Riven by ethnic chauvinisms, their economies in a state of collapse, can these republics really come back together in some coherent framework and rebuild their economic lives to the point where they are capable of merging with the E.E.C. to revive Gorbachev's vision (and my own) of a "common European house," a prosperous and democratic union of peoples from the Atlantic to the Urals, and beyond?

I still believe that they can. Because the economic and geopolitical realities still say that they must.

The Soviet Union, the successor to the Russian empire, was a transnational state a thousand years in the building, and the economic and geopolitical environment that evolved down through all those centuries has not vanished with the collapse of the Soviet state.

There are still over a hundred separate peoples within the territories of the fifteen republics of the former Soviet Union, and they are still thoroughly intermingled. Scores of millions of Russians still live outside the boundaries of the Russian Federation—Estonia is forty percent Russian, for example, and so is Kazakhstan, and there are millions of

Russians in Ukraine, Latvia, Lithuania, Moldavia. Armenian enclaves in Azerbaijan, Azeri enclaves in Armenia, Ukrainians in Russia, enclaves within enclaves within enclaves. The Russian Federation itself is just that, a mosaic of scores of ethnic groupings.

Without some form of confederal structure, without a common citizenship and centrally guaranteed internal minority rights, there are only two possible outcomes—continuing ethnic warfare and permanent chaos, no stable outcome at all; or a series of puppet states independent in name only and ruled from Moscow by the demographically, economically, and militarily dominant Russian plurality.

So too have the centuries welded the republics of the former Soviet Union into a single economically interdependent union whether the governments or the peoples thereof like it or not. Ukrainian wheat feeds Russian oil field workers, who supply the energy that fuels the economies of all. Baltic milk cannot be bottled without Russian machinery. Ukrainian factories must have parts made in Russia, and vice versa. Uranium produced in Central Asia feeds the generators in Russia and Ukraine that supply power to a transrepublic grid. Gas and oil pipelines, roads, railnets, all have been long since laid out and constructed without regard to internal borders.

The results of the attempts of the republics to function as independent economic entities are all too apparent—empty food stores, fuel and power shortages, the debasement of all currency, the precipitous decline in industrial production, economic collapse.

It is no coincidence that this collapse followed on the heels of the Soviet Union's demise. Far from it; the destruction of federal coordination *caused* the economic collapse. For while the Communist central planning bureaucracy may have been responsible for much of the former Soviet Union's economic ills, in hindsight it can be clearly seen that, whatever its faults, it was certainly better than no economic coordinating authority at all.

So while *Russian Spring* may no longer be an accurate prediction of the near-term course of events in the lands of the former Soviet Union, it remains a vision, a hopeful vision, in general terms perhaps the *only* hopeful vision, toward which the peoples of that land must evolve if their destiny is not to be generations of poverty and endless bloody strife.

Will it, against what presently seem like long odds, come to pass?

That is where detached prediction ends and hopeful engagement begins. Barring further catastrophes, by the time you read this, *Russian Spring* will have been published in Russia itself. Where I can only hope it will play some small part in the continuing struggle to roll back the chill of the winter's despair and bring about that new springtime of which it speaks.

Norman Spinrad
Paris, February 1992

PART ONE

AMERICAN AUTUMN

Secretary Goddard: "Sooner or later, Bill, we're going to have to face the unfortunate fact that Latin America simply isn't capable of standing alone."

Bill Blair: "Standing alone against what, Mr. Secretary?"

Secretary Goddard: "Standing alone on its own two feet. Successfully managing modern economies with stable currencies, feeding its own people, and maintaining some semblance of stable democratic government. They certainly aren't doing it now, and history is no cause for optimism. A passive role is an abdication of responsibility."

Bill Blair: "You mean we should intervene openly in the affairs of Latin American countries whose internal policies are not to our liking?"

Secretary Goddard: "I mean we should do whatever we have to do to establish stable democratic governments capable of joining with us to form a Western Hemispheric Common Market that will prevent this hemisphere from turning into another Africa! And if that's your idea of gunboat diplomacy, well then I'll be proud to have you call me a gunboat diplomat!"

—*Newspeak*, with Bill Blair

STAGGERING TOWARD DISASTER OR JUST TAKING CARE OF BUSINESS?

The Americans seem to be staggering into yet another mini Vietnam in Latin America, and outraged but impotent European opinion seems to be stumbling once more into the wishful conclusion that it will be a disaster like all the others.

But what if the wise men have been wrong all along? Certainly this latest intervention seems like a disaster for the poor Costa Ricans, and certainly it seems likely to involve the United States in yet another endless military quagmire.

But what if the Americans have been applying different

lessons all along? For them, after all, the Vietnam War was a long period of domestic economic prosperity. And the Gulf War taught them that no other nation on earth could hope to successfully oppose their high-tech might, establishing the United States as the impoverished military overlord of the planet.

"If you've got it, flaunt it," goes an old and currently quite ominous American aphorism. And if you don't have much of anything else, is nakedly flaunting your de facto military overlordship really a mistake in the amoral world of political and economic realpolitik?

What if keeping their military involved in endless little military quagmires in Latin America is precisely what the American economic establishment has intended all along?

—Libération

AMERICA FOR THE AMERICANS

The condemnation of our efforts to rescue Costa Rica from far-left fanatics and outright chaos by the Common European Parliament, led by self-righteous German Green Socialists, and the threat of economic sanctions implied, should finally convince even the most Europhilic skeptics that half a century of American generosity has been cynically betrayed in the service of Common European economic hegemonism.

When we saved Europe from the Nazis, we were hailed as heroes. When we rebuilt their shattered economies with Marshall Plan aid, we were praised as benefactors. When we stood with them against Soviet imperialism, we were staunch allies. When we preserved their oil supplies in the Gulf with our arms and our treasure, we saved their economic prosperity at no little cost to ourselves.

When the reunited Germany was hardwired into a tighter confederal Common Europe, there was loud cheering on both sides of the Atlantic that the so-called German Question had at long last been solved. The Soviets pulled their troops back behind their own borders in return for untold billions of deutsche marks in grants, loans, and joint venture capital, and the United States was able to bring its troops home at last.

Now we see how we have been repaid for preserving European freedom and prosperity for half a century and more.

We find ourselves frozen out of the largest economic market the world has ever known. We find ourselves facing a Common Europe, dominated economically by the German colossus, determined to sabotage our efforts to establish a Western Hemispheric Common Market.

We have an enormous overseas debt to the very beneficiaries of our generosity and goodwill, a staggering economy, and an unholy alliance meddling in our own hemisphere, led by a swaggeringly self-righteous Germany, with the Soviet Union cheering it on from the sidelines.

America stands alone. And in sad retrospect, we can see that it has always been so. When our aid was needed, the nations of Europe were our friends. Now that they have long since gotten what they wanted from us, they will not even leave us to tend our own front yard without their interference.

We have been had. We have no other alternative. We must build and preserve an economically free and integrated America for all Americans, North and South. We must make whatever sacrifice is necessary to insure that overwhelming European economic power is counterbalanced by absolute American military impregnability.

We must stand up to Common European hegemonism, bite the necessary bullet, and deploy Battlestar America at long last, whatever the cost.

—*Washington Post*

Defense stocks, particularly anything aerospace related, which have been in the doldrums for a decade, have already exploded. The early bird does indeed get the fattest and freshest worm.

But there's still plenty of upside left in secondary and particularly tertiary issues. And even at today's sharply risen prices, there's still more upside left in the big aerospace conglomerates in the medium run than the pessimists think. Contrary to popular opinion on the Street, we believe it's still not too late for smart investors to cash in on the Battlestar America bonanza. We believe that the best is yet to come. Think independent subcontractors.

—*Words from Wall Street*

METHOD IN THE AMERICAN
MADNESS?

Conventional wisdom has it that the decision of the American Congress to fund deployments of major elements of the so-called Battlestar America nuclear defense shield was an act of collective madness. But in truly ruthless realpolitik terms, from the American point of view, maybe not.

Against whom is Battlestar America supposed to defend? Against a Soviet Union which presents no military threat? Against a peaceful and prosperous Common Europe in the midst of an economic boom? Against hypothetical Third World madmen eager to commit national suicide by launching a puny nuclear assault against the planet's only military superpower as some naive apologists sincerely contend?

This, of course, is a question without a rational answer. But it may not be the right question. For if one asks instead what the Americans have to gain by deploying Battlestar America, however flimsy the official excuses may be, the answers become all too clear.

By deploying Battlestar America, the United States props up a sagging defense sector without which its already staggering economy would fall into a deep structural depression.

By deploying Battlestar America, the American politicians validate the billions they have poured into its development over the decades.

By deploying Battlestar America, the United States serves notice on the republics of Latin America that American force reigns supreme in the Western Hemisphere, that no matter what interventionist excesses the Americans may descend to, no one will ever have the will or the power to oppose them in their own self-proclaimed sphere of influence.

Long ago, Mikhail Gorbachev promised to do a terrible thing to America. "We will deprive you of an enemy," he proclaimed, and lived up to his words.

And now we see the American response. Having been deprived of the enemy whose existence propped up their economy and rationalized their foreign policy for half a

century, the American government has simply gone out
and nominated a replacement.

If Germany and Common Europe had not existed to
serve this purpose, they no doubt would have been
forced to invent us. And indeed, in a certain sense, they
have.

—*Die Welt*

I

With a leaden thump, a protesting squeal of rubber on concrete, and a disconcerting groan of tired metal, the old 747
hit the runway, popping open half a dozen overhead luggage
bins as the thrust-reversers roared, and the plane shuddered, and the lights flickered.

It had been a truly ghastly fourteen hours from Los Angeles in this aerial cattle car, what with a thermostat that
seemed incapable of maintaining a constant temperature,
and two lukewarm and pasty TV dinners, and a movie machine that didn't work, and a seat that wouldn't recline all
the way, and bad vibrations from the left inboard engine,
but somehow the plane had made it, and Jerry Reed was in
Paris, or anyway officially on French soil.

For a born-and-bred Californian space cadet whose only
previous experience with foreign intrigue had been limited
to picking up hookers in Tijuana, it was a long way, my son,
from Downey.

Eight weeks ago, Jerry had been planning to spend his
three-week vacation backpacking in the Sierras. He hadn't
even *had* a passport. Now here he was, taxiing toward the
terminal at Charles de Gaulle, and heaving a great sigh of
relief that he had made it to Common Europe without having it lifted.

"No, no, but of course not, there is nothing at all illegal
about it," André Deutcher had assured him. "The worst
thing that can happen is that they refuse to let you board
the airplane."

"And confiscate my passport."

André had smiled that worldly smile of his and blown out a thin pout of smoke from one of his ten ECU Upmanns. "If they confiscate your passport for trying to leave the country, then it was a document of no value in the first place, n'est-ce pas, Jerry?" he said.

"True enough," Jerry admitted bitterly. "But if they slice my clearance for trying it, I'll never work in the Program again, like poor Rob."

"Rob is finished, Jerry, it is a sad thing, but it is true," André Deutcher said much more coldly. "And because people like Rob Post are no longer welcome, so is your American space program. . . ."

"With our heavy lifters and our shuttles and our sat sleds, our basic logistic technology isn't that far behind. . . ." Jerry protested wanly, sounding sad and foolish even to himself.

"While the Soviets are building three more Cosmograds and going to Mars and we are building the spaceplane prototype."

"When the politics change here, all the Battlestar America technology will give us—"

"Jerry, Jerry, take my offer or not as you like," André said, fixing him with those ambiguous gray-green eyes of his, "that much is the representative of ESA speaking. But do not delude yourself as all the people at this party must in order to face their shaving mirrors in the morning. This is what happened to Rob, n'est-ce pas, I would not wish to see the same happen to you, and this is a new friend speaking, a friend who has dreamed the same dream, and who knows all too well how he would feel had he been unfortunate enough to be born American instead of French at this hour in its history. Battlestar America is the problem, and can never be the solution. Rob knew this in his heart, yes, and thought he could fight it from within. Do not let this happen to you."

Jerry had only known André Deutcher for three weeks now, and indeed had met him at Rob Post's previous party. André had been introduced, by Rob himself in fact, as an ESA engineer spending his vacation time in the United States seeing the sights and meeting like-minded American space people for his own pleasure.

Jerry, of course, had not believed this for a minute, had assumed that the Frenchman was some kind of industrial

BUSINESS REPLY MAIL

FIRST CLASS   PERMIT NO. 137   BOULDER, CO

POSTAGE WILL BE PAID BY ADDRESSEE

US NEWS & WORLD REPORT
SUBSCRIPTION DEPARTMENT
P.O. BOX 52136
BOULDER, CO 80321-2136

APPROVED
FOR 74%
DISCOUNT

spy, and had immediately begun to kid him about it. André had countered that the American civilian space program, being all but nonexistent, had no industrial secrets worth stealing, and that he was really working for French military intelligence. The bullshit had flown back and forth, and somehow a spark of friendship seemed to have been lit.

Jerry took André to the original Disneyland, showed him Forest Lawn, and managed to take him on a circumspect tour of the open areas at the Rockwell plant in Downey, and the Frenchman had in turn wined and dined Jerry on the ESA expense account at restaurants that he hadn't even known existed.

And then tonight André had committed the California faux pas of lighting up a big cigar in the middle of the crowded living room, handing Jerry another, and insisting he do likewise.

There was an unseasonable marine layer rolling in and a foggy chill in the air, so that when Rob's wife, Alma, had shooed them outside to smoke their noxious Havana weeds, as André had known she would, the deck of the Posts' rotten-rustic hilltop house in Granada Hills—all that Rob had managed to salvage of the good old days—was empty.

And once André had gotten Jerry out into the chilly privacy of the foggy Southern California night, he finally dropped his cover, or so at least it seemed, and admitted what his trip to America was really about.

André Deutcher was nothing so sinister as an agent of French military intelligence or even an industrial spy. He was simply a headhunter for the European Space Agency.

"You are someone I think ESA might be interested in, Jerry," André had told him. "Not that this is yet anything like an offer of employment, you understand. But you have told me you have a three-week vacation coming up, and I am authorized to invite you to spend it as the guest of ESA in Paris, meet some interesting people, learn more about our program, and let us learn more about you."

He shrugged. He smiled. "At the very least, you will have a free first-class vacation in Paris, which, I may assure you, is hardly a fate worse than death, n'est-ce pas?"

It had always seemed that André really *was* hiding something behind his series of phony secret identities, but now, looking into his eyes out here in the chilly damp, with the lights of the San Fernando Valley far below just barely glowing beneath the bank of fog, it seemed to Jerry that André Deutcher was at last speaking from the heart. André might still be trying to sell him something, but Jerry could not deny that everything André had said was the bitter truth.

If he stayed with what was left of the Program, sooner or later, one way or another, what had happened to Rob Post was going to happen to him. If it hadn't happened already.

Inside, the party was starting to run down, guests sitting listlessly around the guttering fireplace, leaning up against walls with half-filled paper cups hanging in their hands.

Running down. Like Rob Post himself, blearily surveying the detritus from the kitchen doorway, like the Program itself, facing the endless morning after.

Rob Post had been a friend of his father's since before Jerry was born, and Jerry's most potent early memory was of being rousted from bed by Daddy in the middle of the night, handed a huge bowl of chocolate ice cream swimming in dark gooey Hershey's by Rob, and then sitting between them on a dusty old couch in a darkened living room, watching the TV with the ice cream bowl in his lap, gobbling it up with a big serving spoon and smearing it all over his pajamas —a bleary four-year-old suddenly wakened into an unreal hog heaven.

"Sandy's gonna really read me out over this, Jerry, and you're not gonna understand till you're grown up," Daddy said. "Do you have any idea why I'm letting you eat all the chocolate ice cream with syrup you can handle tonight?"

"Because you love me, Daddy?" Jerry said, blissfully digging into it.

Daddy hugged him and kissed him on the cheek. "So you'll remember this moment all of your life," Daddy said in a silly solemn voice. "You're too young to understand what you're going to see tonight, but you're not too young to understand a whole pint of Häagen-Dazs."

"It's an experiment, Jerry," Uncle Rob told him. "The greatest moment in human history is about to happen and you're alive to see it, but you're too young to remember it with understanding. So what your Dad and I are trying to do is implant a sensory engram in your long-term memory so that when you grow up you can call it up and be here now with your adult consciousness."

Uncle Rob giggled. "And if you eat so much you puke, so much the better for your future recall," he said.

Jerry didn't puke, but he did remember. The bittersweet cold softness and double-good hit of chocolate syrup over chocolate ice cream still never failed to time-warp him back to that couch in the living room, watching the Moon Landing with Daddy and Rob.

He had been hooked on chocolate ice cream ever since, to the detriment of his endless battle against the scale, but he could sit there in the body of a blissful four-year-old and watch Neil Armstrong set foot on the Moon in real time with his adult consciousness, transforming the memory of somatic joy into the deeper joy of true understanding.

The strange pearlescent television-gray lunar landscape coming up under the lander camera to the laconic crackle of far-off voices from Houston . . . The hollow descending hiss of the retrorockets through the metal bulkhead . . . "The Eagle has landed." And then the bulky figure descending that ladder in slow motion . . . And Armstrong's hesitant voice blowing the scripted line as his foot came down on the gray pumice and changed the destiny of the species forever. "That's, uh, one small step for man, uh, one giant leap for mankind."

Oh yes, as a boy Jerry had only to taste chocolate ice cream to be transported back to the moment whose memory would shape his whole life, and later, he had only to *imagine* the taste of chocolate ice cream covered with Hershey's bittersweet chocolate syrup to replay the Moon Landing through an adult perception that could thank Dad and Rob from the bottom of his heart for the best present any four-year-old could ever have, for giving his adult self this clear and joyous memory, for the dream they had knowingly and lovingly implanted within him.

That was how much the space program meant to Dad and Rob, and while Dad never did much more than join the L-5 Society and the Planetary Society and every space lobby in between, Rob Post had followed the dream and given it his all.

He had joined the Program fresh out of Cal Tech and landed a job as a glorified draftsman on the Mariner project. He was at best a mediocre engineer, but as he worked his way up the ladder, it became apparent that he had a certain talent for project direction, for getting better engineers than he could ever be to work together toward a common goal. He believed in mankind's destiny as a space-going species with an ion-blue purity, he could translate that passion into belief in the project at hand, and when he was on, he could infect a team with that same passionate innocence.

He got to work on Voyager and on the shuttles, and he gave up smoking dope when the piss tests came in and he had to, and he took long backpack hikes in the Sierras and worked out every day, for he was still under fifty and he had accumulated clout, and if Mars was out of the question, he certainly had a good shot at a Moonbase tour if they got one built before he turned sixty and if he kept his nose clean and his body in shape. Or anyway that was the fantasy upon which his whole life was focused before the Challenger explosion.

With a father who had turned him loose in his vast, untidy collection of musty science-fiction magazines, paperback books, and model spacecraft before he was old enough to read, and Rob Post for a favorite "uncle," Jerry knew what he was going to be when he grew up before he was old enough to know what growing up meant.

He was going to be an astronaut. He was going to float out there, weightless in the vasty deep. He was going to walk the pale gray pockmarked lunar surface, and search for remains of life on Mars. He was going to the asteroids and Titan, and who knows, it was not entirely beyond the realm of possibility, he was young, the Program was moving fast, life extension loomed on the horizon, he just might live long enough to be among the first to set foot on a planet circling another sun.

"The Moon maybe, Mars, if I'm incredibly lucky, but that's as far as an old fart like me is going to get, kiddo," Rob would tell Jerry in the days when he was beavering his way through high school. "But you, hey, you were lucky enough to be born at the right time, Jerry. You crack those books, and by the time you're out of college, we'll have a lunar base. Mars before you're thirty. Titan before you're fifty. You could live to see the first starship launched. You could even be on it. You're going to live in the golden age of space exploration, kiddo. It's up to you. You can be one of the people who makes it all happen."

So Jerry ground his way through high school, and, with his good marks and an effusive letter of recommendation from old grad Rob Post, got into Cal Tech, where he majored in aerospace engineering.

Jerry busted his balls his first three years at Cal Tech. Almost literally. The work was hard, but he was a practiced student by now and a totally committed one, and he aced his way to the top 5 percent with little difficulty.

But he knew that he had to do more than make the top of his class to get into astronaut training. He had to get himself into physical condition, and for a nerdish grind with no interest in sports, a naturally endomorphic body, and an addiction to chocolate ice cream, that wasn't easy.

Rob Post was there for him then too, and a good thing, for Dad was the quintessential couch potato. Rob introduced him to long backpacking hikes in the Sierras. He bought him a set of weights for his birthday. By the middle of Jerry's sophomore year, he had shed his blubber, built himself a set of muscles, and was doing better with girls than he ever had in his life, learning to get his endorphins charged via sex and sweat instead of chocolate.

And then, during his junior year, the Challenger exploded, and took the civilian space program with it, or rather the long hiatus between the Challenger disaster and the next shuttle launch exposed and finalized what in retrospect could be seen to have already happened.

The bright future in space that had seemed inevitable when Jerry was a four-year-old never happened. No space station by 1975. No lunar base by 1980. No Mars by 1985. Oh yes, the 1970s and early '80s were a golden age of unmanned space exploration, with the incredible pictures from Mars, and the Jovian moons, and the rings of Saturn, but the *real* space program—the manned space program, the actual raison d'être, the evolution of humanity into a space-going species—essentially sat there spinning its wheels for the decade between the last Apollo and the long-delayed advent of the space shuttle.

And by that time, Ronald Reagan was President, and military budgets were soaring, and Star Wars started gobbling up space funding, and the Air Force already had its hooks deep into the shuttle, into NASA, and about 40 percent of the payloads were already military even before the Challenger exploded.

Those in the know, like Rob Post, knew damn well that the Challenger had been destroyed by political pressure to launch outside the shuttle's safe-flight envelope, or as Rob had put it at the time, "Give me a thermometer reading fifty degrees Fahrenheit, and I'll gladly get on one tomorrow."

But it took a two-year hiatus of bureaucratic ass-covering for NASA to finally work up its courage to launch Discovery, and by that time the Agency's spirit was broken, and its administrative structure had been thoroughly militarized, and there was a huge backlog of military payloads, and the civilian space budget had been cut to the bone and then some, and the doom of any visionary American civilian manned space program had been quite thoroughly sealed.

When the dust cleared, endless Star Wars pilot-study funding had been so cunningly hardwired into the budgetary process that it had a life of its own. Even the disappearance of the Soviet Union as a credible bogeyman made no difference, especially after Saddam Hussein conveniently allowed the Pentagon to nominate the entire Third World as a replacement. The idea of a career as a civilian astronaut had become pathetically ludicrous by the time Jerry graduated.

Rob Post was there to offer Jerry advice and aid again, but now it was of a sadly different sort. By this time, Rob had advanced into the upper middle-management levels at Rockwell, a spacecraft project manager with a good track record at a time when contracts for civilian projects were becoming virtually nonexistent.

During Jerry's senior year at Cal Tech, Rob had held his nose, sighed, and taken the job of manager on the Advanced Maneuverable Bus project. "It's that or join the army of the unemployed," Rob insisted wanly. "Besides, it's not as if the damn thing doesn't have potential civilian applications. . . ."

The AMB was typical of the myriad low-profile cheap projects that kept Star Wars alive during the scaled-back "Bright Pebbles" hiatus before European outrage at the Latin American interventions finally gave the defense industry what it needed to push its deployment through Congress as Battlestar America. The AMB was basically an upscaling and redesign of the MX fourth-stage warhead bus, supposedly to be used to deploy scores of cheap little orbital interceptors, at least as far as Congress was concerned.

But what the Air Force had really commissioned behind that smoke screen was a platform that could be launched into Low Earth Orbit with a variable mixed payload of at least twenty reentry vehicles and/or boost-phase interceptors. It had to be able to station-keep for a year without refueling, change orbits up to a point, juke and jerk to avoid satellite killers, and launch its payloads with a high degree of accuracy.

"Shitcan the warheads and interceptors, give it a big fuel tank and corresponding thrusters, mount a pressure cabin on it, and you've got yourself a space jeep to take you from LEO to GEO," Rob would muse dreamily.

When Jerry graduated, Rob was able to hire him on as an entry-level wage slave on the AMB project. But even a naïf like Jerry could see what Rob was doing once he got to Rockwell. Everyone on the project knew it. Everyone was collaborating in the deception, knowing, of course, that it was Rob Post who would take the flak if and when the Air Force copped to what was going on.

What was going on was that Rob Post, like the Air Force itself, was pursuing his own hidden agenda. He was using the Air Force funding to design a Low Orbit to Geosynchronous Orbit ferry with the capability to take crews to a GEO space station that didn't exist in the guise of giving them their Advanced Maneuverable Bus.

The thrusters were far bigger than anything a warhead and interceptor bus needed. The so-called refueling collar was being designed to take a large fuel tank neatly balanced along the long axis to handle a 1 g thrust. The bus platform itself was being designed to accommodate forty interceptors so that a pressure cabin would have room atop it. And so forth.

Perhaps this had something to do with the fact that Rob was smoking grass again, or perhaps vice versa. Though he had stopped when the piss tests came in, he had started again sometime during the early stages of the AMB project, coming home to Granada Hills, toking up, sitting down at the computer, and designing, on his own time, the pressure cabin, and the expanded fuel-tank module that would turn the AMB into a space ferry that could take ten people from LEO to GEO.

Eventually, of course, the inevitable happened.

The Air Force gave the design a thorough going-over before the AMB went to prototype, and some bright boy realized what was happening. Early one bleary Monday morning, the piss patrol showed up in force and had everyone working on the project urinate into test tubes in plain view.

Such snap mass random testing was not quite unheard-of, but when they took blood samples to nail down the evidence of any infraction of the purity regs, everyone knew that the plug was about to be pulled.

Somehow Rob Post's piss tested out pure, but they caught him with borderline traces of cannabinol in the blood sample, which might or might not have washed him out of the Program for life if he had chosen to fight a dismissal in court. So instead of trying to nail him directly, they got cute about it.

They canceled the AMB project prior to prototype, which cost Rockwell big bucks, and they made it quite clear that Rockwell's chances of landing the replacement program would be slim and none if Rob Post was still on their payroll. What was more, he must not be permitted to resign, he had to be forthrightly fired for mismanagement of Air Force funding.

This the Rockwell management was far from reluctant to do, when they toted up how much the cancellation of the AMB had cost them. Rob Post was rather loudly fired, and Rockwell got the sat-sled contract.

Rob, as they say, never worked in the Program again, or at least not directly, eking out a precariously unpredictable if not exactly penurious living as a technical consultant on various non-Program projects via his many connections in the California high-tech and space communities. Meanwhile, he threw these parties every month or so to maintain his sad and forlorn connection to people like Jerry who were still in the Program.

Such as it was.

Jerry looked away from the tired party scene behind the glass balcony doors, away from André Deutcher's knowing eyes, and up into the Southern California night sky. But the stars were hidden by the bank of offshore fog and were nowhere to be seen.

Jerry finally looked back at André, who lounged against the deck railing, staring him down and puffing out a long, languid plume of rich Havana smoke that melted into the fog.

"It is a sad time here for people like you and Rob, oui, a sad time for all of you," André said, nodding toward the scene in the living room beyond the glass, which Rob was crossing in their direction. "Do not think I do not understand, Jerry," he said with an air of worldly commiseration. "You are an American, but you believe in something that your country no longer does. . . ."

"Yeah, well at least I'm still in the Space business," Jerry drawled in a phony Groucho Marx voice, waving his cigar and blowing out about five dollars' worth of contraband Havana in what even he realized was a futilely foolish attempt to ape André's panache.

For that matter, he didn't really like the taste of tobacco smoke; for him smoking this cigar was what passed for a small act of defiance of the national purity regs under which most of the people at this party, himself included, were constrained to exist if they wished to remain employable. Tobacco still wasn't on the piss list, but *Cuban* tobacco still had the tiny thrill of safe danger that pot must have had in the old days when a trace of it in your urine didn't mean you were out of the Program for life, like poor old Rob.

Oh yeah, he was still in the Space business, all right. He still had a job at Rockwell, ironically enough with the team developing the propulsion and maneuvering systems for the sat sleds, which had replaced the canceled AMB. And to turn the screw a little further on Rob Post, it was Rob's unauthorized upscaling of the AMB design that had put the sat-sled bug in the Air Force's ear, though of course no one would ever admit it.

Why *not* go right to something capable of taking payloads from LEO to GEO that could also do the AMB's job in the bargain? Rob's design for the refueling collar and the big mother fuel tank proved quite usable. Just add big throttle-able stop-and-start thrusters, a maneuvering and control system, a platform just big enough to hold the whole thing together, and a clamp-on system for payload modules.

Voilà, the sat sled, which could not only deploy warheads and interceptors in Low Earth Orbit, but which could maneuver killer satellites at high speed and ferry spy satellites to GEO, and at a price not much greater than that of procuring the single-purpose AMB.

And now, with the Congressional purse-strings pried wide open again, they were already talking about a scaled-up second generation of sat sleds, capable of clamping onto a shuttle and taking it to Geosynchronous Orbit, or, more to the Air Force's Battlestar America point, of boosting huge mirrors, monster lasers, high-speed interceptors, and particle-beam accelerators out there to GEO where they would be all but invulnerable to attack, making America the military overlord of Geosynchronous Space itself, master of the ultimate global high-ground.

Poor Rob had had some starry-eyed pipe dream of turning the AMB sword into a space-going plowshare, but he hadn't bargained with the Pentagon's superior ability to do precisely the reverse.

And now here Jerry was, out on Rob Post's deck on the outside looking in at the party, though from another perspective he was on the inside looking out, and here came Rob out onto the deck, looking more than a little stoned, on the outside looking in, as he had been for too many years.

"That tobacco in those ropes, or are you guys holding?" he said by way of greeting.

Ever since Rockwell had canned him, Rob had made a bigger and bigger thing out of his dope-smoking despite the real risk of serious jail time, grown his hair even longer than it had been in the late '60s, taken to blue jeans and workshirts, hidden his bitterness behind a false façade of ancient burned-out hippie. "Why not?" he would say when Jerry called him on it. "What've I got to lose that I haven't lost already?"

"The best Havana," André said, whipping out his cedar cigar case, pulling one out, and offering it to Rob.

Rob glanced around in mock paranoia. "Alma'll kill me," he said, but he snatched it up anyway and let André light it with his fancy silver Dunhill, and the three of them stood there leaning against the railing of the redwood deck in the foggy fragrant chill, sucking in expensive carcinogens in awkward silence.

It was Rob who had introduced Jerry to André, and it was Rob whom ESA should be trying to recruit if there was any justice in the world, at least the way Jerry saw it. But as André had said, Rob was finished, at least as far as ESA was concerned.

What Jerry really wanted to do was ask Rob's advice about André's offer. Would he be risking his career by merely accepting a freebie to Paris?

But he was prevented from doing this twice over; first because he didn't know how André would take his blowing his cover to Rob, second because he feared it might break Rob's heart to know that it was Jerry and not him who had a chance to work in the ESA program.

Unexpectedly enough, Rob Post was there for Jerry one more time when he needed it. "So, kiddo," he said, brandishing his Upmann, "you think you could at least smuggle a box of these back for me when you go to Paris? Some primo Afghani, I know, would be out of the question."

You know?" Jerry blurted, looking back and forth from Rob to André. "You told him?"

"But of course," André said, "or rather it was Rob who recommended you as a possibility."

"But then why not—"

"Go myself?" Rob said. "They're hardly interested in over-the-hill project managers who haven't worked in the Program for years. They want innocent young blood, it's only natural. . . ."

He sighed, he turned to stare out over the ravine that led down the slope of the Santa Monica mountains toward the fog-obscured floor of the San Fernando Valley, a million little lights glowing faintly through the glistening mist, took a quick puff on his cigar, and slowly sighed out the smoke.

"Besides," he said, "I'm pushing sixty, and even in the ESA program, I'm just too old already to ever get my chance to go into the old up and out; that dream's finished for me, kiddo, and I know it. And somehow along the way, I fell in love with this country, not the old US of A or the pinhead government in Washington, but California, the Sierras, the redwoods, these hills. . . . I've lived here all of my life, and I'm a part of this land by now, and it's a part of me, and even if I were offered the choice . . ."

He shrugged, he turned back to Jerry, laughed a little laugh. "The bad news is that no one's offering me the choice," he said. "The good news is that I don't have to make it."

"You're telling me I should go?" Jerry said.

Rob Post looked back at him with bloodshot, deeply shadowed eyes. His long gray hair was thinning now. There were deep lines around his mouth and the corners of his eyes and finer ones all over the tanned skin of his face, upon which a few liverish spots had begun to appear. Jerry noticed all this for the first time, really noticed it.

And for the first time he realized that the hero and patron of his childhood and young manhood was growing old.

That Rob Post was going to age and grow frail and finally die without ever getting to set foot on Mars or the Moon, or even to float free of gravity up there in the starry dark for one bright, shining moment at his life's end.

Jerry's hands balled up into fists, tears began to well up in his eyes, and he had to take a long drag on his cigar and cough out smoke to cover the wiping of them.

"Hey, kiddo, I'm not telling you anything," Rob said. "What the hell do I know, I've never even been to Europe. I don't even know what they may end up offering, if they end up offering anything. But if you want my opinion . . ."

"I *always* want your opinion, Rob. You know that."

Rob smiled, and in that smile the ghost of a younger face seemed to fade back in over the aging mask of defeat. "Well, if you want my opinion, Jerry," he said, "my opinion is . . . what the fuck?"

"*What the fuck?* What the fuck *what?*"

"What the fuck, all it is is a free three-week vacation in Europe," Rob said, pacing back and forth in front of Jerry in a little elliptical orbit.

"You're saying I should do it?"

Rob laughed. "What the fuck, why the fuck not? What kind of red-blooded American boy would refuse a free trip to Paris? What kind of red-blooded space cadet would refuse a peek inside the ESA program?"

"One who doesn't want to lose the clearance to work in *ours,*" Jerry said.

"There *is* that," Rob said much more somberly.

André Deutcher, who had been leaning back quietly against the deck railing smoking his cigar during all this, finally spoke. "The matter can be handled in what we would call a fail-safe manner," he said. "You apply for a passport. They either give it to you or not, n'est-ce pas? If they do not, then the matter is quietly forgotten without any argument from you. It will hardly endanger his clearance to simply ask for a passport, will it, Rob?"

"I don't see how. . . ."

"He then applies for a thirty-day Common Europe tourist visa through an ordinary travel agency and simply gets on a first-class Air France flight to Paris with me when—"

"Uh-uh," Rob said. "That dumb, they're not. He better

fly alone, and on an American carrier, not a Common Europe airline, and no first class, or they'll suspect he's flying on someone else's plastic, and just may not let him on the plane."

André shrugged. "I'm afraid he's right," he told Jerry. "Best you fly with the peasantry in coach." He smiled, he winked. "But not to worry, Jerry, we will begin to atone for this unfortunate piece of necessary tackiness and then some the moment you are safely in Paris, I can promise you that, and first class on Air France on the flight back."

He paused, blew out another plume of smoke. "If there *is* a flight back," he said.

"Well, I'm glad you two guys have gotten it all decided for me," Jerry snapped. But there was little vehemence in it. For after all, Rob was right.

What the fuck, they weren't about to lift his clearance for applying for a passport. What the fuck, he could always play innocent if they didn't let him on the plane, couldn't he? All he would be doing would be taking a vacation in Paris, as far as they were concerned.

And as if a sign had been granted, there was suddenly a distant roar, and a bright point of light became barely visible, burning its way skyward through the mist at unreal speed, accelerating as it rose like a glorious ascending angel.

"Alors!" André Deutcher exclaimed. "Qu'est-ce que c'est?"

Jerry's eyes met Rob Post's. They both laughed wanly, and somehow, in that moment, the decision was made.

"Nothing to get excited about, André," Rob said.

"Yeah, it's just another ground-based reentry phase interceptor test from Vandenberg."

And a strangely similar roar, but louder, and closer, blasted Jerry out of his time-zoned reverie, and he found himself all but pressing his nose against the cabin window in a futile attempt to see.

"My goodness, what was that?" the old lady in the seat beside him exclaimed.

"An Antonov 300 boosting off the runway," Jerry muttered, for he knew that no other civilian aircraft made such a godawful noise on takeoff.

Until the ignition of the Antonov's rocket-trolley had

abruptly jolted him out of it, Jerry had been dozing along in airline space, where the interior of one plane was the interior of every other, and one great amoeboid airport seemed to connect the spaces between, and any connection to actually being in a country other than America had been quite unreal.

But now the ancient Pan World 747 was taxiing up to the main terminal at Charles de Gaulle, and Jerry could see two more Antonovs sitting there on the tarmac connected to the terminal building by jetways and surrounded by trains of baggage carts as if they were ordinary Boeings sitting on the ground at LAX—one painted in the red, white, and blue of British Air and the other actually bearing the winged hammer and sickle of Aeroflot—and he knew he was no longer in technological Kansas.

The Antonov 300 was the plane that had finally given the Russians a real piece of the world market. They had taken their old shuttle transporter, itself a monster upgraded from an older military transport by adding on two more engines, and turned the world's biggest airplane into the world's biggest airliner.

With a full load of fuel in its gigantic belly tanks, it could carry one thousand coach passengers and their luggage 10,000 kilometers at about 800 kph in somewhat dubious comfort, and as much as a hundred more in spacious first-class luxury in the add-on upper deck that replaced the shuttle pylons, making it the most profitable airplane in the world to run in terms of fares versus cost per passenger mile.

It was also a ponderous mother that required a runway longer than most commercial airports had to groan its way up to takeoff speed and then leave the ground-effect envelope.

In their typical straightforward, brute-force manner, the Russians had solved the problem by mounting a fall-away trolley aft of the main landing gear and equipping it with a battery of solid-fuel throw-away rocket engines apparently adapted from old short-range missiles.

The Antonov was a joke at Rockwell, where they built hypersonic bombers that could give you "The Ride of the Valkyries" in multiphonic sound on their state-of-the-art automatic disc decks on your way to ground zero.

But up close, there was something somehow loveable

about this piece of time-warped technological Victoriana. It was something that Jules Verne and Rube Goldberg surely would have admired.

It had the elephantine grandeur of the Spruce Goose that Dad had taken him to see in Long Beach—the sheer splendor of being the largest of its kind, indeed of being larger than its kind's natural envelope.

The old 747, itself once the world's largest airliner, was sidling up to the gate now, right beside the Aeroflot Antonov, which dwarfed it as the Boeing had dwarfed the short-hop wide-bodies on the ground at LAX fourteen hours and a world away.

It's like some cartoon version of Russian technology, Jerry thought as the Pan World 747 docked with the jetway. Huge, and brutal, and powerful, and cobbled together from a dustbin of obsolescence with chewing gum and baling wire.

Yeah, but it's cheap, and it works, he reminded himself. You could laugh at the way the Russians did it, but *they* were laughing all the way to the bank.

If America could build hypersonic penetration bombers, then why couldn't Rockwell or somebody build a scaled-up airliner version and recapture the long-haul market with speed and elegance?

Why was he working on sat sleds instead of manned propulsion systems? Why were the Russians mounting a Mars expedition while the U.S. was still studying a Moonbase? Why was it ESA who was building the prototype spaceplane and not Rockwell or Boeing?

Of course, to ask those questions was to answer them in the two words that were the bane of Jerry's existence.

Battlestar America.

That was where the lion's share of America's high-tech R&D budget had been going for the better part of two decades under one guise or another, and one story that Rob Post had told him years ago, when Jerry was a sophomore in high school and the Program was still called the "Strategic Defense Initiative," told it all.

"I was sitting around half-crocked at a party with a bunch of aerospace engineers, and they were all bullshitting about the contracts their companies were landing for SDI studies. X-ray lasers powered by fusion devices, orbital mirrors, rail-guns, the whole ball of wax. Hey, I said, thinking I was being funny, what about a tachyon-beam weapon? Sits up there in orbit and waits for the Russkies to launch, and then sends tachyon beams back in time and zaps their birds on the pads twenty minutes earlier. Some of the guys laughed, but a couple of them working for Lockheed get this weird look on their faces. Yeah, one of them says, I think we could get about 20 mil for a preliminary study. And about a year later, I find out that they actually did. The Pentagon put about 100 million dollars into it before they realized they were being had."

America was becoming the world's best-defended Third World country, and the best and the brightest were collaborating in the process and pissing into bottles for the privilege while the Russians went to Mars and sold their Antonovs and Common Europe dreamed of luxury hotels in Geosynchronous Orbit.

But don't get me wrong, Jerry thought sourly as the seatbelt light winked off and the passengers all crowded toward the exit, I still love the space business.

Jerry snatched up his flight bag from beneath the seat in front of him and stood there in the crowded aisle with the rest of the sardines waiting for the exit door to open.

Finally, after the usual inevitable stifling, sweatstinking eternity, the door finally opened, and Jerry found himself slowly shuffling off the crowded plane in the endlessly clotted human stream, out through the jetway, and onto a long people mover past hologrammic advertising images babbling at him in incomprehensible French while displaying an amazing profusion of bare-breasted pulchritude, and finally into a jam-packed chaos of a reception area, where more people movers were disgorging yet more passengers from other gates into the hub of the radial terminal.

At the far end of the reception area, barely visible through the godawful mob scene, stood a line of customs booths, a customs official in a fancy military-looking uniform in each. Signs in French and English above the line of booths designated "Common European Passports" and "All Others." There were four of the former, where people flashed their passports and sailed right through, and only two of the latter, where long lines of people were already queued up, and where the customs guards seemed to be checking every last passport through computer terminals.

Upon being greeted with this anti-American outrage and

realizing it would be about an hour before he could clear passport control, after which he would have to play baggage-carousel roulette and then probably stand on an even slower and longer line with his baggage to clear customs, Jerry found the zone, and the sleeplessness, and the fatigue, and the babble of incomprehensible tongues finally catching up with him with a vengeance. His knees dissolved to rubber, his mouth, he realized, tasted like copper, his head was bonging, and to make matters worse, amazingly enough, half the people in the reception area seemed to be lighting up noxious cigarettes that filled the air with acrid, choking smoke.

"Welcome to Common Europe," he muttered miserably under his breath, and numbly elbowed his way through the mob to the end of one of the long, crawling lines.

"Monsieur Jerry Reed, Monsieur Jerry Reed, presentez-vous à la caisse spéciale à la gauche de la salle. . . ." said a female voice over the P.A. system, barely audible over the tumult, and in incomprehensible French at that. "Jeez, now what am I supposed to—"

"Mr. Jerry Reed, Mr. Jerry Reed, please report to the special-handling booth at the left of the room. . . ."

Jerry broke into a cold sweat. Good Lord, did the long arm of the Pentagon extend *this* far, just when he thought he was home free?

Woodenly, fearfully, Jerry bulled his way through the crush toward the left side of the room, drawing angry scowls, more than one elbow in the ribs, and getting pinked on the forearm with a lit cigarette.

"Jerry! Jerry! Over here!"

It was André Deutcher's voice calling out to him. Jerry swam through the crowd toward him, where he stood beside yet another customs booth that Jerry hadn't noticed before. There was a man inside it who was not wearing a uniform, and a man standing with André who was, although this one was plain black with no insignia; but there was no line of waiting passengers.

"Welcome to France, my friend," André said. He looked around the reception area with a moue of aristocratic distaste. "Would you please let me have your baggage claim and your passport so we can remove ourselves from this mêlée?"

Numbly, Jerry handed them over. André handed the baggage claim to the uniformed man, who disappeared with it through the customs booth. "Marcel will see to your baggage," André said. He handed Jerry's passport to the plainclothes customs official, who stamped it immediately, handed it to Jerry, said, "Bienvenue à Paris, Monsieur Reed," and actually gave him a little salute.

André whisked him along a corridor and into a little elevator which speedily deposited them in a hallway that led directly through a private exit to a curb outside the terminal, where a vaguely elliptical black Citröen limousine sat gleaming in the eye-killing bright morning sunshine, all low-slung sweeping, stylized Deco pseudo-streamlining and smoked glass, looking like a Frank R. Paul version of a Martian Mafia don's flying saucer.

"Super bagnole, eh?" André said, as a liveried chauffeur in a uniform matching Marcel's emerged from the driver's seat, and opened the back curbside door for them smartly. "Fuel cell version; we are 90 percent nuclear these days in France, and we have electricity to burn."

The rear seat was a softly upholstered couch done in deep navy velour, and the carpeting was of the same material, as were the tiny cushioned ottomans upon which to rest one's feet. Tiny adjustable overhead halogen spotlights bathed each of them in a soft pool of ersatz sunlight. The compartment walls were covered with pastel blue leather set off with chrome brightwork that might actually have been silver plate. Below the sealed window separating them from the front seat, an incongruously cheap-looking little screen and keyboard were built into the plush seatback.

There were sets of dual controls built into each passenger's armrest. André fiddled with one set, and some kind of subdued electronic pseudo-oriental symphony began playing mellowly in the background. He did something else and laughed when Jerry did a take as a compartment in the seatback before them popped open, revealing the inside of a small refrigerator containing two glasses and a cold bottle of champagne, then snapped shut again.

"Is this thing *yours*, André?" Jerry exclaimed.

André Deutcher laughed. "Don't I wish!" he said. "Actually, it's a diplomatic limousine lent to ESA by the Foreign Ministry for the occasion. After the way you were forced to travel here, we were able to convince them that the honor of France demanded it."

Amazingly enough, less than ten minutes later, while André was showing him how the videotel in the seatback was both videophone and computer terminal—connecting the car with the phone system, the teletel public data net, and, via access code, with the ESA mainframes too—Marcel appeared with Jerry's luggage on a little trolley; how he was able to retrieve it with such speed was a bit of magic that somehow impressed Jerry even more than the sail through passport control or this state-of-the-art automotive palace.

"Avanti," André shouted into thin air as Marcel climbed into the front passenger seat, and the car pulled away from the curb with hardly a lurch and no sound at all that was audible above the low background music.

Soon they were out of the airport and on a highway slicing through verdant green countryside interspersed with fields of dry brown cropped stubble, and it was then it really hit Jerry Reed that he was truly in a foreign country, and not just because the cars and trucks on the road all looked subtly alien and barreled along at incredible high speeds or because the road signs were all in French.

For there was no roadside ticky-tacky at all, no Burger Kings, no Golden Arches, no car lots, no shopping malls and parking lots, no sprawling cheap housing developments, none of the endless suburban crudscape that marked the ride from the airport to any major American city.

And when the Parisian suburbs finally started, it was all at once, as if the car had suddenly crossed a frontier; godawful, they certainly were, but godawful in a way quite different from anything Jerry could have imagined. Blocks of huge apartment houses with balconies from which actual laundry hung drying, gray grim concrete, a lot of it, but a lot of it painted in truly garish pastel colors, sometimes in two or three hideously clashing hues of green and pink and powder purple. And then this gave way to industrial buildings, gasworks, and railyards that might have been anywhere save for the French lettering on the walls, and the billboards that began to appear, flashing bare tits and asses huckstering unknown brands of ambiguous products.

And then the car took a sweeping turn across a bridge,

and there it was, faintly visible in the far distance above the ticky-tacky, the unmistakable pinnacle of the Eiffel Tower.

"Et voilà!" André exclaimed, and popped open the refrigerator again, this time withdrawing the champagne bottle and peeling off the gilt foil.

"A little early for me, André," Jerry muttered in a daze.

"Mais non!" André exclaimed gaily. "For you, it is still late at night in Los Angeles!"

But he waited until the car had turned off the highway and was careening across a huge traffic circle jammed with cars zigging and zagging every which way before he popped the cork. The champagne bubbled up out of the bottle and frothed down it and onto the carpeting. André shrugged and paid the mess no mind. "Good for the carpet as you say in America, oui?" he declared.

And Jerry found himself sitting there in the back of a limousine—careening along through streets packed with traffic, past sidewalk cafés and massively ornate nineteenth-century architecture, sidewalks thronged with people, a city alive with a life and energy he had never experienced before —exhausted, zoned, half asleep, but nevertheless having a high old time getting royally drunk on champagne at eleven o'clock in the morning.

By the time the limousine finally pulled up at the hotel, he was barely able to stand.

"The Ritz," André told him, as they exited the car amid an absolute swarm of doormen and bellmen. "Hemingway and all that, a bit theatrical, peut-être, but we thought you might find it amusing."

It was the understatement of Jerry Reed's life. He was ushered into a reception area that seemed like a palace set for an old Cecil B. DeMille movie, into an elevator out of the same film, and into a room . . . into a room . . .

"Holy shit. . . ." Jerry sighed as André tipped the bellman and closed the door behind them.

The room was enormous. There was a brass bed, and a lavishly furnished sitting area separated from it by brocaded curtains. There was a table heaped with baskets of flowers and fruit and trays of petits fours and a silver tray holding a crystal bowl of caviar with all the fixings. There was a fully stocked bar with a refrigerator and a sink. The ceilings were covered with plaster floral-work painted in garish full color, and the moldings were all gilt braid, and the walls were papered in red and gold and blue velvet flocking, and hung all over with original oil paintings in heavy complicated frames. "My God, I feel like I'm sneaking into some royal bedroom. . . ." Jerry muttered.

André Deutcher laughed. "I know what you mean," he said. "Nothing exceeds like excess. See a movie, be a movie, as someone once said."

He went over to the floor-to-ceiling windows, drew the drapes, and opened them vertically like a pair of doors, and with a little bow, ushered Jerry out through them onto a little balcony. "However," he said, "*this* is the real Paris."

Jerry stepped shakily out onto the balcony into the warming morning sunlight. From this vantage he could see far out across the low rooftops of the city to the shining waters of the Seine beyond the treetops of some intervening garden. Traffic buzzed across ornate stone bridges. Bright sunlight through an occasional dappling of shadows from fleecy white clouds illumined the famous Left Bank like a picture postcard of itself, and way off to the right the Eiffel Tower proclaimed the fabled cityscape's identity.

It was a view that everyone in the world had probably seen a thousand times, a cliché landscape of a cinematic city. But there was a subliminal music in the air and a subtly alien heady perfume wafting to his nostrils that told his backbrain that, no, this was no painting on black velvet, this was no picture postcard, this was no movie.

This was utterly unexpected. This was overwhelmingly beautiful and overwhelmingly real. He could smell it, and taste it, and hear its song calling to him.

"It is said," said André Deutcher, "that every man has two hometowns. The place he was born and Paris."

In a way that he doubted André could fully understand, Jerry Reed, American, space cadet, stood there drinking in the marvelous unexpected alien wonder of it all, and knew, somehow, that it was true, dangerously and wonderfully true.

And knew as well in that moment that this would be no mere three-week freebie vacation. Knew that there were temptations here that could change his life forever.

Knew somehow that it had been changed already.

Turning to the business news, in Munich today, Red Star announced the purchase of 35 percent of the Löwenbrau brewery empire. "This will not only give the Soviet consumer ready access to good German beer, thereby diminishing our nikulturni reliance on rotgut vodka, it will give us a ready market for surplus grain and establish a major hops industry in the Ukraine," declared Valery Zhores, Red Star's Chairman.

"And we're not paying for it in valuta, either," he added. "The deal is being financed by furnishing Löwenbrau with grain at 50 percent of world prices over the next ten-year period."

Score another Hero of Socialist Entrepreneurship Medal for the Big Red Machine!

—*Vremya*

LONDON INVADED BY THE RED MENACE!

They're young, they've got money to burn, and they seem bent on turning London tits for asses! As our granddads used to say of the Yanks, they're overpaid, oversexed, and over here! Of course we're talking about the self-proclaimed Red Menace, the charmingly horny Eurorussians who have made the club scene here part of their weekend circuit.

They're the barkeeper's delight and the bouncer's bane, they've all got AIDS vaccination certificates, and they're giving it away at a rate that's got half the hookers in Soho on the dole. From me according to my ability, to you according to your need, that's the party line these days, and the Comrades have dutifully become Stakhanovite party animals!

Check out the scene at Ivan the Terrible's or The Electric Samovar and see some red-hot glasnost in action!

—*Time Out*

Thank God or Marx or Gorbachev or whomever passed for the patron saint of the children of the Russian Spring for this vacation, Sonya Gagarin thought as the TGV sped her across the unheeded French countryside at 300 kph, away from Brussels and Red Star and her boring job and Pankov the Human Octopus, toward Paris and two weeks of freedom.

There were times—such as this last week at the office, slaving away at editing particularly boring AI translations of stock prospectuses and stat sheets into humanly comprehensible French and English and fending off Pankov's moist and pathetic advances—when it seemed to Sonya that she had spent her whole life with her nose to the grindstone waiting for the fun she had so richly earned to finally begin.

On the other hand, there were also times, such as every Friday at 1730, when the office closed and the weekend began, such as right now, sitting in a high-speed train approaching Paris and washing the taste of the workaday world out of her mouth with a passable Côtes-du-Rhône, when she knew full well how lucky she was, or more fairly, how well the scenario she had worked out for her life had played thus far.

Brussels might be *Belgium* and Red Star might not be the foreign service and her job might not be much more than that of a glorified secretary, but she was young, and she was Russian, and she was actually living in *Europe,* and how many people could say at the age of twenty-four that they had achieved their girlhood dream?

Not that it had been exactly handed to her as a birthright! Not that she hadn't earned it by her own diligent efforts!

Sonya Ivanovna Gagarin was no relation to the famous first cosmonaut—though as a Pioneer and a young Komsomol member she certainly did nothing to disillusion peers, teachers, and youth leaders who might think she was.

Glasnost or not, perestroika or not, family connections and prestige still counted for as much in the New Russia as they did in the Decadent West, or anywhere else on Earth if truth be told, and a daughter of a trolleybus driver and a cashier at the GUM growing up in a two-room flat on the tenth floor of a grim housing block in Lenino, barely inside

Moscow, with no real connection to anyone with connections for as far back as her ancestry was traceable could hardly afford to toss away the only aura of connectedness she had in the fanatical service of the total truth.

Of course, if she was asked point-blank if she was a relative of the heroic Yuri she would admit she was not, nor did she ever exactly claim she was, for that would be an actual lie, one that would speedily enough be uncovered if told to teachers or youth leaders and inscribed accordingly in her kharakteristika with exceedingly unfortunate consequences. But if they or her schoolmates chose to entertain such fantasies without her assistance, who was Sonya Ivanovna Gagarin to smash their rosy illusions with excess candor?

If she was going to be one of the favored few to live in the West, she needed all the advantage she could get, and—aside from her dark good looks and precocious breast development and her willingness to work hard—her name was the only edge she had.

Sonya Ivanovna had grown up dreaming longingly of life in the West. When had it started? When she was a toddler watching the *Vremya* coverage of the opening of the French Disneyland, where girls just like herself cavorted with Donald and Mickey? When her father brought home a cassette of *Roger Rabbit* for her sixth birthday?

It was as old and as deep and as innocently nonpolitical as all that. It started with Mickey Mouse and Donald Duck and Roger Rabbit and travelogues and progressed through picture postcards into stamp collecting and an interest in geography to pen-pal programs and a knack for grade-school English and French, via Eurovision broadcasts and foreign music videos and magazines, to a career scenario that had been formed long before Sonya knew what a "career" or a "scenario" was.

It was still the time of the Troubles, before perestroika had finally begun to deliver the goods when it came to filling the stores with earthly delights, and intellectual freedom and the official approval of foreign exotica were desperately being offered up to the Soviet people in lieu of same.

So Sonya had never been told that her enthusiasm for the marvelous worldwide Disneyland outside the borders of the Soviet Union was in any way unpatriotic or reactionary. Far from it! Her father encouraged her stamp collecting and her interest in geography and her mother helped her with the correspondences with pen pals in England and France. All this had been encouraged by a sharp Pioneer leader who had seen that with proper channeling this young girl's passion for things Western might serve as a locomotive for her academic pursuits.

As it did. Sonya was a diligent student and threw herself enthusiastically into any Pioneer activity with even a tenuous connection to the world outside. By the time teachers and parents and Komsomol leaders had begun to broach the question of higher studies and career choices, Sonya had already formulated a firm and resolute answer and was ready to forthrightly enlist their assistance in the attainment of her chosen goal.

Sonya Ivanovna Gagarin was going to become an officer in the foreign service. How better to secure a life of abundant travel in the West? Indeed, considering that she had no family connections, no talent for sport or the arts or science or theater or dance or music, how *else* for a young Soviet citizen to trip the life fantastic through the wide and wonderful world?

Yes, even her fifteen-year-old decision to join the foreign service was blithely nonpolitical, though she knew enough to construct the persona of an idealistic young Komsomolya seriously aspiring to eventual Party membership and seeking to channel her natural abilities in the patriotic service of the Motherland.

Glowing recommendations from the Komsomol, combined with her high grades in everything not having to do with science or mathematics, got her into Lomonosov University, where she majored in English, French, world history, comparative and pragmatic economics, and met for the first time a crowd of congenial young people in many ways much like herself.

Everyone here whose family lacked connections had arrived at Lomonosov University by a process similar to her own. Thus the composition of the student body represented the realistic triumph of Soviet egalitarianism. The children of Party officials, bureaucrats, academics, and other members of the inevitable national elite might have a leg up by virtue of the luck of their birth, but at least the real sons and daughters of workers and peasants could earn their way into their company without regard to parental fortune as long as they made their grades and took care to present a whole-some enough image to teachers and youth leaders.

Those in the Golden Circle for the most part kept to themselves, and the "Workers and Peasants," as Sonya's crowd sardonically dubbed themselves, had little use for those they referred to as the "Children of the Damned."

"Meritocracy" was one of the buzzwords of the period when perestroika really started taking bites out of the flabby buttocks of all the entrenched bureaucracies, meaning that the children of the Golden Circle were far less likely to inherit anything from their apparatchik parents save an odi-ous reputation, and the Workers and Peasants, the Mer-itocrats, were far more likely to be the beneficiaries of the new age as the true Children of Gorbachev.

This might be said to be Sonya's first awakening to politi-cal consciousness, if of a rather careerist sort, an awakening, such as it was, greatly enhanced during her last two years at Lomonosov University by her relationship with Yuli Vladi-mirovich Markovsky, her first really serious boyfriend in more ways than one.

Unlike Sonya, who as a Muscovite was constrained to live at home with her parents, Yuli, as a student from the prov-inces, had the right to a bed in an on-campus dormitory. This he scorned, choosing instead to rent a tiny room out in Nikulino, which he could barely afford, and which put him three Métro stops from the university. He pretended that this was some sort of ideological statement, when actually it was more of an open invitation to the hordes of Moscow girls living with their parents while they attended the univer-sity, to whom the possibility of any kind of overnight tryst at all was enough to make them less than particular about with whom. Even when it came to sex, Yuli was something of a romantic careerist.

Like Sonya, Yuli sought a career in the foreign service. But unlike Sonya, Yuli wasn't just interested in foreign travel. He saw entering the foreign service as the first step on his long march to the post of Foreign Minister, from which vantage he could best serve the interests of both the Soviet Union and himself, living the high life of a top gov-ernment official with all the helicopters and first-class world travel it implied while fulfilling the emerging Eurorussian vision.

The thing about Yuli that charmed Sonya was that with him this was no mere sophistry. He really believed it.

"The twenty-first century will be the Century of Europe, one way or the other," he would often declare by way of grandiose post-coital pillow talk, "and if we do not gain entry into Common Europe, the Germans will dominate everything, and the Soviet Union will become a Third World state. On the other hand, a Europe that *included* the Soviet Union would inevitably become the dominant center of a new world order in which *we*, not the Germans, would be first among equals. Those Pamyat muzhiks call themselves Russian nationalists, but like the dimwits they are, they fail to understand that Russian destiny will be most gloriously served leading Europe from the inside, not standing outside the sweetshop window looking in."

And then, just when Sonya was thoroughly convinced that he really *was* a totally pompous ass, he would laugh, and take a swig of the raw Bulgarian cognac that was the best he could afford, and become the other Yuli, the one who had grown up as the son of a steelworker in Sverdlovsk, who had fought his way to the center, and who was determined never to be relegated to the periphery again.

"From me according to my enormous ability to fulfill our national destiny," Yuli would declare. "To me according to my equally enormous need for a Black Sea dacha and a whole floor on Tverskaya Street and a helicopter and a chauffeured Mercedes-Benz!"

"What a perfect hypocrite!"

"No one is perfect," Yuli would say, rolling over onto her, "but admittedly, I do try."

And he certainly did, in bed and in the classroom and in the Komsomol, and in what went on at the right school parties, where Eurorussian-minded professors and outside intellectuals mingled with the favored students. And he took Sonya with him. By their final year they were considered "little Pioneers," who would become "Komsomolya" when they got engaged upon graduation and eventually take the nuptial vows of "full Party membership."

While Sonya was not yet quite ready in her own heart to tie her fortunes to any man before she had even tasted the unknown worlds of Europe, she went along with this illusion, for despite all the enlightened socialist feminism in intellectual circles these days, this was still Russia, where the power of the patriarchy was bred in the bones, and where the paternal regard for the favorite son of same could be easily enough spread to his future choice of wife.

Sonya had the grades to get into the foreign service academy, even if they weren't quite up to Yuli's, and her kharakteristika was exemplary if unexceptional, but when push came to shove, and especially for a woman, it paid to be an adopted favorite daughter of the Eurorussian intellectuals who were trying to clean out the foreign service bureaucracy from the bottom on up by installing a like-minded new generation, even if it was by putative marriage. And indeed both she and Yuli were formally admitted a few weeks before graduation.

Sonya was content, if, strangely enough, not quite ecstatic. She was three steps away from achieving the life's ambition of the little girl who had so wished to go to the French Disneyland. Two more years of schooling to gain entry into the foreign service, a year or two at a desk in Moscow, a first posting to some nikulturni disaster area like Bangladesh or Mali, and with any luck, she'd get a chance to serve in Common Europe before she was thirty.

This was the scenario she had been following all along, but what she had not counted on was Yuli Markovsky's place in it. It was not so much that she resented entering the foreign service academy with the aid of his connections, but that she now found herself tied to a man, as she had found herself in the Pioneers and the Komsomol, without having the chance to make the choice of allegiance, as a result, somehow, of the collective will of others.

And that suddenly began to rankle a bit for the first time.

It wasn't so much that she didn't love Yuli as that somehow she had been robbed by pragmatic circumstances of ever really being able to tell whether she loved Yuli or not. On the one hand, it was hard to really love him because loving him was clearly so expedient, and yet on the other hand, perhaps that was the only thing that actually kept her from loving him, in which case she was being a perfect idiot not to love him. . . .

And so forth, until the thought finally occurred to her that once they were both in the foreign service academy, things would have a chance to sort themselves out naturally, even if they did become engaged Komsomolya as she knew Yuli wanted.

Because, after all, she would have two years to decide whether she really wanted to be the wife of Yuli Markovsky, and when she did, the choice would be that of the heart alone.

As it turned out, she was quite wrong.

Two weeks before graduation, she was summoned out of class to the provost's office. Fearing the worst without being able to imagine what sin she possibly could have committed, she made her way through the endless corridors and elevators of the vast central university building with her heart in her stomach.

But instead of receiving a dressing-down, she was handed a telephone over which she was told by a secretary that a meeting with her was being requested by Vitaly Kuryakin, personnel director for the central branch of Red Star, S.A. If she was presently available, a Red Star car would pick her up outside the main entrance.

Sonya muttered her uncomprehending consent and stood out there on the steps before the huge and hulking old Stalinist-Gothic university building in the soft spring sunshine waiting for the car to arrive and trying to collect her thoughts.

Sonya had studied all about Red Star, S.A., in her course in pragmatic economics, for there was no Soviet economic enterprise more aggressively pragmatic than what some Common Europeans nervously called the "Big Red Machine."

Red Star, S.A., was the corporate child of the Russian Spring, and the new vision of "One Europe from the Atlantic to the Urals," beloved of the Soviet external propaganda machine.

It was cunningly incorporated in Common Europe, not as a Soviet corporation, but 60 percent of the stock was owned outright by the Soviet government. The rest traded openly on the Bourse, so as to allow the legal pretense that it was a true European transnational.

And so did Red Star, S.A., itself. It sold Russian wheat, oil, minerals, furs, furniture, heavy machinery, caviar, medical equipment, satellite-booster services, declassified aerospace technology, and some even claimed hashish from Soviet Central Asia. It shipped half the proceeds home in the form of consumer goods and reinvested the rest in Common Europe, gobbling up shares in Common European cor-

porations the way the Japanese used to gobble American
real estate. The political entry of the Soviet Union into
Common Europe might be one of Yuli's dreams of the future, but the Soviet Union already owned a controlling interest in one of Common Europe's biggest and fastest-
growing conglomerates.

If in the West it was known as the Big Red Machine, here
in Moscow it was dubbed USSR, Incorporated, and for
much the same reason—it was a capitalist transnational corporation, but it had the capital resources of an entire nation
squarely behind it whenever it made a move, a diabolically
successful example of socialist entrepreneurship that had,
some said, saved perestroika from the Troubles by starting
to fill the empty shelves, and made a semi-convertible ruble
possible.

What on earth could Red Star, S.A., possibly want with
the likes of her?

It did not take Sonya long to find out. In less than twenty
minutes, a sleek export-model Zil limousine pulled up beside her, of a type usually sold to the modest government
elites of better-run impoverished Third World countries,
only painted a quite outrageous primary red.

This unlikely vehicle sailed down the drive out of the
Lenin Hills like a Czar's carriage, fairly bulldozed its way
through the downtown Moscow traffic, and soon enough
deposited her in front of the equally unlikely Red Star
Tower on Marx Prospekt overlooking the Kremlin and the
river beyond.

This was a thirty-story office block in the old Bauhaus
mode, Russified by rose-tinted glass walls, a neo-Stalinist
black marble ground-floor façade replete with abstract versions of heroic statuary, and a red-and-gold-striped onion-
dome cupola topped by a huge red star outlined at night in
neon. It looked something like a refugee from Tokyo and
something like a *Krokodil* cartoon of its own bad taste, and
yet there was something rather engaging about it, an almost
punk sensibility that seemed to be thumbing its bright young
nose at the massively stodgy old government palaces among
which it arose.

Vitaly Kuryakin's office on the twentieth floor, when
Sonya finally reached it, was more of the same, with a big
window looking out over the ancient Kremlin and Red
Square—those suddenly archaic-seeming old emblems of

Russian power—from on snobbish high. Its sleekly modern decor of chrome and polished teak and black leather and computer terminals proclaimed its distance from the symbology of the center of Mother Russia far below and its kinship with any such corporate office anywhere in the developed world.

Kuryakin himself seemed quite at home as a creature of this transnational corporate venue. He looked to be somewhere between his late thirties and his mid-fifties, with light brown hair pinstriped with silver and expensively styled into an earlobe-length conservative rakishness. He wore a sharply tailored powder-blue suit and a white silk stylized peasant blouse with a gold embroidered choker in lieu of collar and tie. He sported an antique clockwork Rolex and rimless swept-back eyeglasses tinted a subtle gold.

He was, in his way, beautiful and awesome, that fabled creature of which Sonya had heard and dreamed of becoming herself—a true Eurorussian, a sophisticated and elegant Soviet citizen of the world.

Kuryakin himself democratically poured them glasses of tea from the old silver samovar that was the only item of Russian tradition in the whole office and then came right to the point.

"Red Star is expanding rapidly and we have an immediate need for entry-level personnel," he told her. "A profile of the ideal recruit was constructed by our department, and when we ran the school records and kharakteristikas of the current crop of university graduates through it, your name popped out in the top 25 percent. Congratulations, Sonya Ivanovna! You are privileged to be offered an entry-level position in Red Star, S.A."

"But . . . but . . . but I have already been accepted into the foreign service academy and—"

"The foreign service!" Kuryakin exclaimed disparagingly. "It will take them another decade to root out all the old dinosaurs, and it would take you at least that long to get anywhere in that bureaucratic mess. Red Star, not the foreign service, is the place for a bright young woman, let me tell you!"

"But . . . but . . . I'm engaged to be engaged, in a manner of speaking—"

"Your personal life is your business if you come to work for Red Star," Kuryakin said airily. "The bottom line is the bottom line as far as we're concerned, you perform your job well and you can screw the whole Red Army chorus on weekends if you want to, or marry an orangutan."

"But Yuli . . . My career. . . ."

"Come, come, don't be an idiot!" Kuryakin declared. "It will take you two more years of schooling before the foreign service will even hire you at a salary a third less than what we're offering you right now, and in *valuta,* Sonya Ivanovna, not rubles!"

"Valuta?" Sonya said sharply, her mind snapping suddenly back into focus at the sound of the word.

Valuta was hard convertible currency—dollars, ECU, yen, Swiss francs—that could be spent freely by anyone in the West, unlike the ruble, which was convertible to the ECU only on an official international accounts level. Anyone who dreamed of traveling in the West, dreamed of doing so, somehow, with a satchelful of valuta, since the alternative was a penurious stipend through the Outourist misers.

"Yes, of course, valuta, it's one of our main tasks to turn rubles and Soviet goods into the stuff, and so naturally we're swimming in hard currency," Kuryakin told her. "Besides, there's our image to maintain. We can hardly have our employees slouching around Common Europe like the worst Western stereotype of the impoverished Russian, now can we? Surely you can keep from embarrassing us with the Belgians on a salary of 5,000 ECU a month!"

"Belgians? 5,000 ECU a month?"

Kuryakin eyed her confusion most strangely. "Haven't you been listening to a word I've said?" he snapped irritably. "I'm a busy man, Sonya Ivanovna, I've interviewed at least fifteen people today already, and I've got no more time to waste. Do you want the job, or not?"

"But you haven't even told me what the job is, Comrade Kuryakin," Sonya pointed out.

"I haven't?" Kuryakin said. He groaned, his eyes rolled toward the ceiling behind his glasses, he threw up his hands and gave her an apologetic smile. "You're right, I haven't," he said. He shrugged. "I've recruited so many people so fast today that you're all starting to blur, and I'm starting to get ahead of myself!"

He got up and refilled his tea glass from the samovar without bothering to offer the same to Sonya or even noticing the rudeness, took a long sip that looked like it should have burned his tongue, sat down again, and then seemed to slip back into his smooth man-of-the-world persona.

"We're offering you the position of French and English translator in the Brussels office—5,000 ECU a month to start plus one month's signing bonus for relocation expenses, going to 5,500 the second year, after that on merit. All medical coverage of course, Common Europe holidays plus May Day, Lenin's birthday, and the Anniversary of the Revolution."

He reeled it all off rapidly and diffidently like an American politician reading off a TelePrompTer into a television camera.

"Two weeks' paid vacation the first year, going to three after two years, four after five, an extra day for every year of seniority thereafter. The right of free travel within Comecon and Common Europe on your days off with a permanent travel visa from the Foreign Ministry on your passport. Free lunches at the commissary, wine or beer extra . . ."

He paused, sipped more tea, seemed to downshift into a lower gear. "Well, I think that about covers it," he said. "You *do* want to take it, now don't you?"

"Yes, of course!" Sonya exclaimed without thinking.

It was all like some fabulous dream, like something happening to the heroine on some American soap opera cassette, like a jet to Disneyland West. Brussels! Common Europe! 5,000 ECU a month in valuta! Unlimited and unencumbered travel in Europe on weekends and holidays and vacations and the hard ECU to pay for it!

"But . . . but . . ." she stammered in the next moment as the reality began to sink in. Yuli . . . the foreign service . . . engagement . . . marriage . . . the whole life scenario that she had carefully constructed and worked for . . .

"But what?" Kuryakin snapped in annoyance. "I thought it was all settled."

"But I've never even thought of being a translator," Sonya said, playing for time in which to collect her wits. "I can read and write English and French fluently, to be sure, but I have no training in—"

"No problem, no problem," Kuryakin said expansively, with a dismissive wave of his Rolexed hand. "Translation is AI augmented these days, three weeks at our seaside training school in the Crimea, and you will know enough information technology to begin. We have a hole to fill immediately, and we don't expect a graduate from the foreign languages institute!"

He glanced at his watch. "Well, what do you say, yes or no?" he demanded. "I've got another interview scheduled in five minutes, and with all the tea I've been drinking today, I really *would* like to have time to go to the toilet first."

"Can't I have a few days to think about it?"

"No, you cannot," Kuryakin said flatly. He leaned back in his chair, sipped his tea, swirled the glass in front of her face, and regarded her more sympathetically. "Look, I know this is a big decision to make right now, on the spot," he said, "but the fact is that I've got twenty-eight positions to fill in four days, and I've got at least ten possible candidates for each, so I can't afford to wait around while one of them decides what to do."

He smiled, he shrugged. "Or think of it as a test," he said. "We're socialist entrepreneurs here at Red Star, we deal with high-speed capitalist jet-setting wheelers and dealers, and we have to be able to wheel and deal just a little faster than they do. We deal in options and currency-rate fluctuations and the electronic economy, where if you stop to think too long you've already blown it. We don't want the kind of obsolete Russian who thinks slowly and carefully and paranoically, as if the KGB is watching every moment. We want the *new* Russian, Sonya Ivanovna, the Eurorussian— worldly-wise, decisive, instinctive, even a little impulsive."

He stood up and peered down at her with the big window at his back looking down on the Kremlin and Red Square and the river and southern Moscow beyond, all small and unreal from this vantage in the cloud-dappled bright sunshine, like a diorama of a toy city illumined by spotlights from above in a children's palace.

"Yes or no," Kuryakin said. "Brussels or the foreign service academy? The New Europe or the old Russia? Rubles or valuta?" He laughed. "If you find *that* a difficult decision to make, you're certainly not for us!"

Put that way, what *could* Sonya say? It wasn't as if she was so in love with Yuli that she really wanted to spend the rest of her life as his wife, she had never been sure she loved him, and if she couldn't be sure, it must mean she really didn't, and if she didn't really love Yuli enough to throw away the instant fulfillment of the dream of her lifetime for him, then what other reason was there for stupidly turning down such a golden opportunity?

"You have a point, Comrade Kuryakin," she said, "and you have hired yourself a translator for Brussels, and you still have time to visit the toilet."

And in the end, it was as easy as all that after all.

Though telling Yuli was another matter.

Sonya's stomach tightened as the memory of that night rose up unbidden, and she took a quick swallow of Côtes-du-Rhône, and tried to concentrate on the countryside whipping past the train window.

But the TGV was slicing through the awful, banlieue housing blocks northeast of Paris now, huge monolithic towers of workers' apartments all too reminiscent of the arrondissement she had grown up in, in Lenino, and there was nothing quaint about that, only another reminder of the past, and even the taste of Bordeaux wine in her mouth seemed to conspire against her, for, she suddenly remembered, she had brought two bottles of château-bottled Médoc to his room and insisted they polish off the first one before she told Yuli the reason for this unprecedented extravagance.

When she had finally had wine enough to blurt it all out, Yuli carefully placed his wineglass on the floor and just sat there across the bed, staring at her in immobile stony silence.

"Well, aren't you going to say something?" Sonya demanded.

"What would you have me say?" Yuli said woodenly.

"That you hate me? That I'm a coldhearted self-centered careerist bitch?"

Yuli managed a little laugh. "I've always said I'm not a *perfect* hypocrite," he said, breaking her heart with his gallantry. "Which I would be if I pretended that *I* would give up my life's ambition for *you.*"

"True," Sonya said, strangely enough loving him more in that moment of cynical admission than she ever had before.

"And of course, this always has been your real life's ambition, Sonya, hasn't it?" he said in a harder voice. "Life in the West with a nice supply of valuta, that's always been enough for you. Everything else, your studies, the foreign service, has always just been a means to that end. . . ."

"Not you, Yuli," Sonya moaned miserably.

And his expression softened again just as suddenly. "Of course not, Sonya," he said, touching a hand to her cheek. "In some ways, we are real soul mates. If I had to choose between my dream and love, I'd choose my destiny too, which would not mean that I didn't really love you either. On that level we truly understand each other, and there is no blame, Sonya Ivanovna."

"Yuli—"

"But in other ways we are quite different," he said, snatching up the second bottle of Médoc. "For you the dream is merely personal, but I serve a vision. I too am a careerist and an individualist, but I am also an idealistic Communist, or will be when I am admitted to the Party."

He opened the second bottle with the corkscrew, refilled their glasses, slugged half of his down as if it were cheap vodka rather than a noble imported French vintage. "You seek only personal gratification, whereas I identify my own personal gratification with the good of Mother Russia."

"What's good for Yuli Markovsky is good for the Soviet Union!" Sonya snapped back, swilling an unseemly gulp of wine herself.

"What's good for Yuli Markovsky is the satisfaction of sailing the ship of Soviet state into the safe harbor of Common Europe," he declared grandiosely, and Sonya, through her own growing barblement, realized that he had become quite drunk.

"And living the luxurious life of a globe-trotting diplomat in the process!" she said.

"But of course! The New Soviet Man is no socialist monk!"

"I'll drink to that!" Sonya declared, and she did.

"And so will I," said Yuli, pouring himself another.

"You don't hate me for doing this, Yuli?" Sonya muttered, feeling her head starting to spin, feeling herself becoming quite maudlin.

With what seemed like a mighty effort, Yuli held himself bolt upright and stared with bloodshot eyes unwaveringly into her own, and through the drunken haze, or perhaps via its instrumentality, a crystal moment of clarity seemed to pass between them.

"I don't hate you, I pity you, Sonya," Yuli said. "There is a dimension of life you are blind to, a passionate color your eyes don't see, the joy of true dedication to a vision of something greater than yourself, without which, without which . . ."

"Ah yes, Yuli Markovsky, the selfless servant of the people, and next you will be quoting Lenin on socialist idealism, no doubt!" Sonya shot back. But there was something in his eyes, something behind his words, that made her want to get even drunker, though the room was already beginning to whirl, and she swilled down another gulp of wine, without, however, being able to avert her gaze.

"Nothing of the kind," Yuli said. "These are great days to be young and Russian and part of a great adventure. This is to be our hour in the center of the stage, to push against the world and feel it move, to ride the wild stallion of history, to hold the reins in your hands and bend destiny to your will to serve the greater good. . . ."

"Great days to be young and Russian and be living in Common Europe, that is the great adventure, Yuli," Sonya shot back, clawing her way back from the edge of something pulling her down into his wild bloodshot Rasputin eyes, something she feared to fathom, something that was beginning to make her feel small and foolish and lost.

"You don't understand what I'm saying, do you?" Yuli said, and then at last he broke the intense eye contact, and slugged down another drink. "You have no sense of destiny at all, mine, or your own!"

"Don't patronize me!" Sonya snapped.

"Oh I wouldn't think of it," Yuli said, lurching across the bed in her general direction.

Sonya managed to catch him in her arms as the room really began to reel. "You're completely drunk!" she declared.

"And so are you!"

"Who am I to deny it?"

"In that case," Yuli said, rolling her over under him and fumbling at her breasts and his pants at the same time, "let us not spend our last night together yammering like feckless intellectuals. Let us fuck ourselves good and senseless like honest drunken peasants!"

And so they did.

Under the circumstances, it seemed the only thing to do. They screwed and screwed and screwed without either of them coming until they passed out in each other's arms.

And when Sonya awoke in the morning with an awful head-ache and a sour taste in her mouth, she knew it was over.

Three weeks later, she found herself at the Crimean sea-side, swimming in the Black Sea before breakfast, studying "information technology" until five, another swim before dinner, and more often than not uncomplicated sex on the beach afterward with someone she knew she would never see again.

It was a perfect transition. The weather was balmy, the food was good, the alfresco sex was bracing and athletically unemotional, and the studies not at all taxing when compared to what she had long been used to in the university, consisting mainly of familiarization with computer hardware and software, with a perfunctory pass at actual programming.

Three weeks after that, there she was living her new life in Brussels, with a studio apartment all her own that might not be much by local standards but which seemed immense compared to her room in her parents' flat in Lenino.

True, her job as "translator" had proven to be mostly deadly tedium, as day after day she sat there before a screen and keyboard in a big boiler room with ten other "transla-tors," rewriting a grammatical AI babble into decent English and French, enlivened only by the occasional random humor emerging from the translation software.

True too that she was endlessly fending off the drippy advances of her supervisor, Grigori Pankov, a timid old goat who *would* take no for an answer, but who doggedly insisted on submitting himself to the humiliation of her coy rejections on a regular basis just the same.

But there was no homework, no mandatory Komsomol meetings, no worries about black marks on her kharakteris-tika, no parents. For the first time in her life, Sonya's non-working hours were entirely her own.

Brussels was not exactly London or Paris or even Amster-dam, but by plane or even cheaper high-speed trains, it was a weekend jaunt from everywhere that was anywhere, which was to say that she was indeed in *Europe,* and it was spread out before her, and it was everything she had dreamed of and more as she tripped the weekend life fantastic.

She learned to ski in Zermatt and water-ski in Nice. She gambled in Monaco and went to an actual orgy in Berlin. She partied in Paris and went to the theater in London and got disgusted at the Oktoberfest in Munich and went to the races at Le Mans and the bullfights in Madrid and smoked hashish on a canal boat in Amsterdam and drank retsina in the Plaka in Athens, and, yes, even went to Disneyland, and contrived to do most of it at someone else's willing expense.

For she was young and attractive and openheartedly eager to give herself freely to simpàtico companions in fun and adventure, and she was a member in good standing of the Red Menace, the tide of liberated young Eurorussians like herself rolling through Common Europe, an innocent sort of wild bunch who hadn't gotten to party like this for a hundred years and were determined, in their wide-eyed and charming enthusiasm, to make up for it at once. Her major ambition in life, a common obsession of both Red Menace sexes, was to collect lovers of every European nationality as she had once collected stamps, and there were girls at the office who actually stuck pushpins in a map.

Only at rare moments like this, alone in a train or a plane in a hiatus of transition, with too much time to think, and a random resemblance of a face across the aisle, or an overheard snatch of political passion in Russian, or the taste of Bordeaux wine in her solitary mouth calling up an old memory of Yuli Markovsky, of the road not taken, of the way they had parted, did she give any thought to the possibility of any morning after.

But those shadows passed as quickly as clouds across the Spanish sun, as quickly as the sidewalks of St.-Germain refilled after a summer cloudburst, as quickly as the TGV sped through the banlieue and outskirts and showed her a quick vision of central Paris in the hazy distance beyond the ticky-tacky before plunging into the underground approach to the Gare du Nord.

From this distance, Paris was a picture-postcard diorama, reminiscent, in a way, of the view of central Moscow she had once seen through the window of Vitaly Kuryakin's office in the Red Star Tower.

There she had looked down from on high on the red-brick battlements, cathedral, and gardens of the Kremlin compound, the gaily colored domes of St. Basil's, the broad main avenues converging on Red Square, and across the sweeping blue curve of the river meandering through its city not unlike the Seine, knowing all too well that Moscow looked much better from this perspective than from down there in the quotidian streets of the real city, where life was all too prosaic and familiar and hardly a romantic fantasy even in the melting snows of the Russian Spring.

But here, however, she was left with the image of the Paris skyline floating like a shimmering mirage above her as the train descended into the darkness of the tunnel, the white dome of Sacré-Coeur, the lacy Victoriana of the Eiffel Tower, the monolithic Tour Montparnasse, shining distantly in the sunlight like the fairy castles of the Magic Kingdom, and, like the signature skyline of the Disneylands and quite unlike the view from the Red Star Tower, promising carnival and magic in its enchanted streets.

Oh yes, of all the cities Sonya Ivanovna had frolicked in in her year in Europe, Paris was the best of all, and not just because she spoke the language, for neither London nor Geneva nor Brussels nor even Nice so lifted her spirit as the City of Light.

It was the greatest cliché of every tourist guidebook in the world, but nevertheless it was true. It was not just the side-walk cafés and the gardens and the wonderful promenades along the Seine and the restaurants and the clubs and the museums, and certainly not the climate (which was quite inferior to Madrid or Athens or Rome), nor even the enticing food aromas everywhere.

It was the Métro honeycombing the city with instant access to everywhere and the oceans of wine and the intimate scale of things—the neighborhood market, the brasserie on the corner, the shops ringing every little square, and the way the streets were filled into the wee hours of the night, and the madhouse street fair surrounding the Beaubourg and the tawdry grandeur of the Boule Mich, the sheer compression of a city constructed on such a human scale, a city seemingly designed on the one hand completely for pleasure and on the other hand, bustling with the electric energy of Common Europe's wheeling and dealing economic metropole.

Paris made Moscow seem like Siberia, Vienna seem like a museum piece, London seem gray and glowering, Geneva like an old folks' home, and Brussels like, well, as the French would say, like *Belgium*.

By the time the train slid out of the underground darkness and into the cavernous grimy vastness of the Gare du Nord—noise, and bustle, and huffing passengers lugging baggage, and polyglot babble, and the mingled aromas of ozone, greasy fried merguez, dark tobacco smoke, petrol, and travel-sweat—Sonya's atavistic moment of nostalgic Slavic melancholia had vanished back into the cold eastern steppes of memory from whence it came.

It was summer, it was party time, it was two weeks of freedom to do with as she willed. She was young, the sun was shining, and it was Paris, and never could the little girl who had sat before the TV in a two-room flat in grim old Lenino, longing to dance down Main Street in the new French Disneyland with Mickey and Donald, have truly believed that one day this moment really *would* arrive, nor wished for anything more.

Representative Sigmunsen: "We can't simply sit back and watch lunatic Marxists turn Peru into an American Lebanon. If we don't step in and restore order now, these maniacs will spread their subversion to Colombia, Bolivia, even Brazil, and who knows, someday we may even find them at the Rio Grande. My mail tells me that my constituents are overwhelmingly in favor of dealing with the situation now."

Bill Blair: "You're suggesting that we send ground forces into Peru too?"

Representative Sigmunsen: "Only to establish and protect bases for helicopter gunships and tactical fighters. A major air commitment should be enough to enable the Peruvian freedom fighters to gain the operational initiative."

Bill Blair: "And if it doesn't?"

Representative Sigmunsen: "Well, Bill, as Caesar said at the Rubicon, we'll just have to cross that bridge when we come to it."

—*Newspeak*, with Bill Blair

AIDS VACCINE STILL NOT
REACHING AFRICA

"While the Western world enjoys its so-called Second Sexual Revolution, millions are still dying in Africa, and the number of new cases is only now beginning to decline slowly," Ahmad Jambadi, Secretary General of the World Health Organization declared at the United Nations today after a ten-day fact-finding tour of the African continent.

"The World Health Organization simply does not have the funds to begin to deal with the problem," he said, "either in terms of hiring the manpower needed, or securing an adequate supply of the vaccine at current prices. The Western drug companies simply must donate what is necessary out of the enormous profits they're making in their domestic markets. The fact is that the cost of manufacturing a dose is a tenth of what they're charging. Now that AIDS is no longer a major problem in the developed world, there is no further civilized excuse for not dealing with the African situation in the only way possible, as a global community."

—*Le Monde*

|||

It took Jerry Reed about twenty-four hours to get unzoned, with André Deutcher walking him through it.

André let him crash out for a few hours, then appeared in his room at about 2:00 P.M. with a room-service waiter and a pot of powerful black coffee. He drew open the curtains to wake Jerry with a golden bath of bright sunlight, handed him a cup of coffee and a handful of pills, which Jerry regarded blearily and dubiously.

"Two hundred units of B-complex, a gram of C, five hundred milligrams of kola extract, three hundred milligrams of phenylalanine, all perfectly legal," André assured him.

"Though if you want something stronger, that too could be arranged. ESA does not consider it dignified to require people to piss into bottles, let alone stick its nose into the odious results."

The pills, two cups of coffee, and a long steaming shower in a bathroom the size of an ordinary hotel room later, Jerry was feeling almost human.

"So," said André, as he emerged in the thick blue terrycloth robe provided by the Ritz, "while you are dressing, let us discuss important matters. What shall we have for lunch? Would you prefer cuisine minceur, cuisine bourgeois, fruits de mer, perhaps Provençale?"

"Uh . . . maybe you know a place where we could get some eggs Benedict?" Jerry muttered in an attempt to sound sophisticated.

André Deutcher was archly scandalized. "Come, come, Jerry, be serious!" he exclaimed. "A man's first meal in Paris must be an event to remember, anything less would be an insult to the honor of France, not to mention the ESA expense account."

"Then you choose, André," Jerry told him. "To tell you the truth, I wouldn't know cuisine bourgeois, whatever that is, from Taco Bell."

Outside the hotel, instead of the Citröen limousine, a sporty little red two-seat Alfa-Peugeot convertible waited at the curb with the top down, a noisy, head-snapping, old-fashioned gas-powered demon that André told Jerry was his own car. "Ecologically atavistic, peut-être," André admitted as he peeled rubber away from the Ritz, "but I prefer a bagnole, as you Americans say, with some crash."

And as if to prove it, he took Jerry on a crazy alfresco ride during which crashes seemed to be averted by a whisker every other minute—down a traffic-choked side street to a main avenue running between a park on one side and a crowded arcaded shopping sidewalk on the other and into a huge square where hundreds of cars careened across each other's paths every which way at once like a monstrous demolition derby in which no one managed to score a hit, across a bridge over the Seine, down another boulevard, through an impossible maze of back streets, another boulevard, more back streets, then onto a riverside avenue going the other way for a couple of blocks, to a parking space, such as it was, that seemed squarely athwart a crosswalk.

By the time they had parked, Jerry was wide awake—how could he not be?—and by the time André had led him up three flights of steep, rickety old stairs to a strange sort of rooftop restaurant redolent with enticing aromas, he realized that he was now quite hungry.

"Le Tzigane," André told him the place was called, not that it purveyed Romany cuisine, whatever that might be, Jerry was assured.

Formally set tables with white tablecloths were set out in the open air under a moveable canopy, rolled halfway back now to afford most of the tables sun. Waiters in traditional black and white moved in and out of a mysterious tent at the back of the rooftop as a similarly clad maître d' who seemed to know André showed them to a choice table at the front with a truly magnificent view across the river at the Gothic gingerbread spires and buttresses of Nôtre-Dame.

"A gypsy restaurant indeed," André told him, as they were handed menus in ornate handwritten French that Jerry found about as comprehensible as Arabic graffiti. "No fixed address, it moves around Paris with the months and the seasons, here for a while, the Luxembourg Gardens, a riverboat, Montmartre, one never knows where it will appear next when it folds its tents—unless one is on the mailing list —they refuse to even list the new location on the minitel. It is intimated that master chefs from other restaurants rotate through its portable kitchen, though that too they insist upon mystifying."

André ordered for them, and it was all quite delicious. Tiny raw oysters in little individual nests of fried buckwheat-sesame noodles topped with shredded wild mushrooms, green onions, and roasted peppers in rice-wine vinegar, washed down with a hearty white wine. Thin slices of wild boar in a fresh raspberry sauce served with thin green beans stir-fried with cumin, cayenne, and turmeric; roasted onions glazed with Stilton; tiny baked potatoes soaked in some tangy caraway-flavored butter and garnished with caviar; and a truly powerful Bordeaux. Little soufflés in three flavors—chocolate, orange, and walnut—with three different sauces. Cheeses. Roasted pecans. Coffee. Cognac. One of André's Cuban cigars.

By the time they were back on the street, Jerry had a wonderful glow on, though what with the small portions of everything, he did not feel at all stuffed. Nevertheless, he readily enough agreed when André suggested they "take a little stroll along the Seine and St.-Germain to walk it off," for by now he was quite eager to finally explore a bit of the city afoot.

The "little stroll" turned out to be a meandering promenade that lasted something like three hours, with time out for three leisurely pit stops people-watching at sidewalk cafés, two for coffee, and then another for a blackberry-flavored wine drink called "kir."

For a native Southern Californian like Jerry, whose only previous acquaintance with real pedestrian street-life had been a dozen or so blocks of Venice and Westwood, Tijuana sleaze, and San Francisco, the Left Bank was like a city on some exotic alien planet, though somehow it also managed to seem like a place familiar to him from half-remembered dreams.

Or more likely from endless TV shows and movies, for so much of this part of Paris had been used as locale for so many shows down through the decades that it was familiar to Jerry in the same way that Hollywood Boulevard or Mulholland Drive or the Ventura Freeway was to people throughout the world who had never been within six thousand miles of L.A.

However, seeing a movie set in Paris was one thing, and *being* in one quite another. Paris had its own characteristic aroma, something too subtle to quite register as a smell, but something that sank into the backbrain and told Jerry on a level that vision never could that he *really was* in a foreign land.

And the girl-watching was something else!

Not that the women on these Parisian streets were any more physically stunning than the fabulous starlets and surfer girls and hookers of Los Angeles, where feminine pulchritude was a major item of commerce at every level.

But all these tantalizing creatures were *right out there on the street,* displaying themselves at sidewalk tables, promenading by when Jerry and André sat down for a drink, dozens of them, hundreds of them at every turn; the unfamiliar density of it all was overwhelming, creating the impression that meeting them would be so easy, given the sheer law of averages, given the compacted human environment of the St.-Germain streets.

On the other hand, everyone *was* speaking French.

Not that Jerry hadn't expected it, of course, but he had always associated the sound of tongues other than English with people on the outside looking in, immigrants, foreigners, and street-sleaze.

Here, however, *he* was the one on the outside looking in. There they were, all these French guys making easy conversation with all these beautiful girls, leaning from one café table to the next, walking down the street, making it all seem so easy, as for them it probably was, as it could be for him too, if only it wasn't all going on in *French*.

Before Jerry had too much time to reflect on his linguistically frustrated horniness, André had walked him to the banks of the Seine, where they descended an old stone ramp to the quay, and boarded a tour boat a good deal smaller than most of the angularly glassy behemoths plying the river, though just as crowded.

"Hopelessly touristic, oui," André said with a shrug as the boat warped out into the river, "but one must get these things out of the way nevertheless, no?"

And so they did. They cruised around the St.-Louis, back into the main channel under the Pont Louis behind Nôtre-Dame, westward down the Seine under ornate bridges and past the Tuileries and the Louvre and the Musée d'Orsay, to the Trocadéro, across from the foot of the Eiffel Tower, where the boat made a one-eighty back upriver to the dock at Pont-Neuf.

After that, André took him on another crazy ride, this time to the Eiffel Tower to watch the sun go down and the lights come out from on high, sipping another kir that began to turn Jerry's knees a wee bit rubbery.

"I think I'm beginning to fade, André," Jerry said when they got back to the car. "Maybe I should just go back to the hotel and crash, after all, I've only had about three hours' sleep. . . ."

"No, no, no," André insisted, "it is not even eight o'clock, you must stay awake till midnight, or you will take days to get unzoned, trust me! It is a bit early, but we can proceed to dinner."

"I'm not really all that hungry. . . ."

"Something light, peut-être. . . . Ah, of course, bouillabaisse at Le Dôme, it is still the best in Paris, and at this hour, we should be able to get in without reservations!"

Another drive through the streets of the Left Bank, five

minutes of driving around back streets looking for a place to park, and then a four-block walk on rubbery legs to the Boulevard Montparnasse, a big bustling nightlife avenue not unlike St.-Germain, and into Le Dôme, brightly but warmly lit, somewhat cramped but still congenial, all old wood and brass, but somehow modern and airy too, opening out onto its own sidewalk tables.

It was noisy in a not unpleasant way, it picked up the energy of the streets without being washed over by it, and once Jerry was seated and inhaling the heady odors of the spicy seafood stew, he found himself perking up a bit. Though by the time he had finished the bouillabaisse, and half a bottle of white wine, and a raspberry mousse in chocolate sauce, and the snifter of Cognac that André *insisted* he must have, he was fading out again.

"*Now* can I go back to the hotel?" he asked plaintively when they got back to the car.

André checked his watch, shook his head. "Two more hours, mon ami, and then you will sleep like a rock and wake up naturally on Paris time in the morning, ready for some *real* fun."

"I don't think I can stay awake that long. . . ." Jerry moaned.

"We go to La Bande Dessinée, that should keep your eyes open if anything can," André said, and off they drove again, with Jerry beginning to nod out even in the open sports car, so that the trip passed in a timeless blur as if he had been teleported to he knew not where, and then a short wobbly walk through a genteelly sleazy neighborhood full of neon marquees with nude photos and sex shops and loud bars, floating just about out on his feet past a doorman and into . . . and into . . .

Oh God, a sleazy TJ sex-show bar!

In the middle of the bar, and lit from above by a rose-colored spotlight, was a round central stage upon which quite a stunning nude redheaded woman and a sleekly muscled black bodybuilder type were screwing away to an electronic version of an ancient burlesque bump-and-grind rhythm on a red velvet couch, she atop and blowing kisses to the patrons. Around three walls of the roughly circular room ran a brass and polished-wood bartop, with stools, mirrors behind, and bartenders in candy-striped shirts and handlebar mustaches. Between the stage and the bar, little café tables were serviced by topless waitresses in stylized French-maid miniskirts. A thick rosy mist, compounded no doubt of tobacco smoke and reddish lighting, seemed to fill the air and soften the edges of everything.

"Jesus, André, you've gotta be kidding," Jerry said as they took one of the few available empty tables, about halfway back from the stage. "I come all the way to Paris, and you take me to a Tijuana sex show?"

André laughed. "Things are not always quite what they seem," he said.

"Huh?"

"Observe the customers."

Jerry did as André ordered something from a passing waitress. The place was pretty well packed, but not with the horny sleazoids and middle-grade hookers one would have expected. There were as many women as men, but it seemed to be mostly couples, not a pick-up scene. Most of the people, men and women, were rather fashionably dressed in one way or another; younger people rakishly modish to be sure, but quite a few conservatively dressed older couples. There was indeed something peculiar about it.

"So it's a lot of trendy people slumming," Jerry finally said as the waitress returned with snifters of what looked like straight vodka.

André laughed again. "Drink," he said, lifting his glass. "Watch," he said, nodding toward the stage.

Jerry drank. The clear liquid was at room temperature, it had the kick of vodka with absolutely no sweetness but it tasted like pears. Wow! He could get used to this stuff.

On the stage, the black man had somehow removed himself while Jerry wasn't looking, and the redhead lay back on the couch in the big shaft of rosy light stroking her breasts lubriciously, awaiting a new partner—

—who suddenly seemed to drop into the spotlight from out of nowhere to the opening bars of the theme from the *Superman* movie, and oh no, it was indeed some muscular dork poured into a full Superman suit, red cape and all, who stood there with his hands on his hips above her, and then, what the—

A penis sprouted from the crotch of his costume, silvery and throbbing, and as the customers in the bar cheered, grew, and grew, and grew until it was about the size of a baseball bat. As the *Superman* theme played louder, and louder, and louder, the Man of Steel somehow managed to plunge the full length and width of it into the woman on the couch and began humping away.

Jerry took a fiery slug of his drink, not really knowing what he was doing, and certainly not comprehending the impossible thing he was seeing!

Superman humped and humped, and the redhead thrashed and thrashed, and then they both came. You could tell because sparks and stars and smiling sperm shot out of her ears and Superman was propelled backward off of her and out of the spotlight by the billowing red blast of a dick which had metamorphosed into a booster rocket complete with ornate Flash Gordon tailfins.

The girl on the couch turned a sleek shiny black, her nipples glowed bright neon red, her ears grew and rounded, her eyes became wide white circles with central black dots, and yes, there she was, a lusciously buxom Minnie Mouse, rolling her eyes, grinning her wide cartoon smile, and ready for action.

And here came Pluto, the canine klutz, scampering into the spotlight with a foot and a half of bright red tongue lolling out of his mouth, which he proceeded to apply between Minnie's legs. . . .

"Holy shit!" Jerry finally exclaimed. "It's all a hologram!"

"Better than anything in any of the Disneylands, n'est-ce pas?" André said dryly. "A triumph of French technology!"

And so it was. Mickey Mouse dislodged Pluto, found himself being buggered by Donald Duck. Woody Woodpecker made it with Jessica Rabbit, the Michelin Rubber Man displayed an awesome flexibility, Daffy Duck, Porky Pig, Mr. Natural, Batman, and Wonder Woman, all joined in the general orgy.

It was even more impressive when Humphrey Bogart and Marilyn Monroe and the American President and Adolf Hitler and James Dean and the Pope began to join in the action, along with a whole panoply of others, who from the jeers and hoots and laughter they drew from the crowd must have been famous French show-business personalities or politicians—for they must have done such stuff by holoanimating two-dimensional film library material, even black-and-white stills, and that took wizard programs and gigabytes of memory.

And then the show metamorphosed again, into something

that drew Jerry's attention out of the bits and bytes of what
he was seeing and into a marvelous and beautiful erotic
reality.

The crazy-quilt orgy melted into an equally crowded Indian erotic temple frieze, stonework turned sinuously and
sleekly subtle to the drone and driving rhythm of sitar and
tabla, breasts and thighs and legs and lingams and yonis
moving in and out and around to the rising beat like a living
arabesque of intertwined sensuality. . . .

Becoming a classical Greek version of the same sexual
tableau, pale white marble flesh, finely delineated muscula-
ture, rounded nippled breasts, strong thighs and clean athletic arms, noble visages under flowing ringlets, idealized
realistic bodies moving against each other like gods and
goddesses to the music of flute and lyre . . .

And in turn transforming into a living painting of the high
Renaissance in full rich oil tones and dancing chiaroscuro
modeling, with violas and woodwinds, with fauns and full-
fleshed nymphs of rosy-fleshed cheeks and tremulous buttocks . . . a Flemish realist version to a cerebral Bach
fugue . . . a French Romantic version, all swirling bodies
and Beethoven bombast . . . softening into the perpetual
sunset and shimmering eroticism of Maxfield Parrish Art
Deco damsels and fey swains to the accompaniment of
Spanish guitars . . . an orgy scene in the Japanese floating
world style . . . Impressionist etherealism . . . the heavy
dark-skinned Polynesians of Paul Gauguin . . .

A truly smoky Weimar Republic version, all net stockings
and fancy brassieres and high heels and leather to down-
and-dirty jazz, transformed itself into a Haight-Ashbury
love-in to the electric guitars and synthesizers of acid rock,
girls with long swirling flower-bedecked hair, young long-
haired men in paisley and velvet, the colors and the flesh,
and the wildly flowing hair, all melting into an abstraction of
themselves, into a dance of pure erotic shapes and motions,
of light, and tone, and interpenetrating movement that exploded into stained-glass shards to the climax of Ravel's
Bolero . . .

Leaving a round central stage lit from above by a rose-
colored spotlight upon which a nude redheaded woman and
a sleekly muscled black bodybuilder type were screwing
away to an electronic version of an ancient burlesque bump-
and-grind rhythm on a red velvet couch, she atop and blow-

ing kisses to the patrons, sophisticates all, who seemed to be resuming their previous conversations as if nothing really extraordinary had happened.

"Vive la France. . . ." breathed Jerry Reed.

"Welcome to Europe," said André Deutcher.

Jerry Reed dozed in and out of Parisian dreams on the drive back to the Ritz, and by the time André got him to the hotel, it was indeed after midnight, and he had just about enough strength left in him to get to his room, get out of his clothes, and crawl into bed before passing out and sleeping like a brick for a solid nine hours.

He awoke the next morning feeling rested and not at all hung over. He had a little trouble ordering a room-service breakfast—the woman spoke good English but couldn't get the concept of sausage and eggs somehow, so he had to settle for a ham-and-cheese omelette—and by the time he had showered, shaved, and wrapped himself in the fluffy terrycloth robe, it had arrived. He was just finishing a croissant with raspberry preserves and his second cup of coffee, when, as if on cue, the phone rang.

It was André Deutcher, down in the lobby. It was time for him to get back to work at his ESA job, so he had brought along "Jerry's guide for the next few days" to make the introductions, they'd be right up.

Jerry hesitated. Should he try to get his clothes on before they got there? He probably didn't have time. As it turned out, he was right, but he found himself wishing he had tried anyway, for there was a knock on the door in about three minutes, and when he opened it, standing there with André was a woman who snapped his prick to instant attention, a rather embarrassing occurrence with him clad only in the bathrobe.

"Good morning, Jerry," André said, as Jerry closed the door behind them, hunching over and twisting to one side as best he could to hide his erection. "This is Nicole Lafage, who will be your companion for the next two days or so."

Nicole Lafage was certainly one of the two or three most stunning women Jerry had ever seen in the flesh.

She was just about his height and carried herself like an athlete, long leanly muscular bare thighs and calves displayed above tight leopard-skin boots, a rakishly cut black skirt, longer on the right side than the left, that belled out at the bottom but seemed painted on her hard, rippling ass, some kind of silky black sheer T-shirt that displayed tantalizing glimpses of small jiggling breasts with frankly visible nipples beneath a short, unbuttoned leopard-skin jacket. Long wavy black hair fell to her shoulders in artful dishabille. Thin dark eyebrows and long black lashes framed bright green eyes above a full-lipped little mouth with a subtle built-in pucker, and the aroma of sensuality coming off her went directly to Jerry's backbrain.

"My . . . uh . . . companion . . . ?" he stammered, dropping down into the nearest chair so as to conceal what was threatening to poke right through the cloth of his robe.

"I'm arranging a tour of our facilities for you," André said, "but it will take a couple of days to organize, and besides, it is best that you have some time to enjoy Paris before we get serious, and of course, you can do this better with Nicole than with the likes of me, n'est-ce pas?"

Jerry sat there blinking. Nicole Lafage gave him a little smile that flashed a quick pink tongue tip. "Pleased to meet you, Jerry," she said in a husky voice, in perfect English lightly flavored with a certain Gallic syncopation. She perched lightly on the edge of the chair across from him, and leaned forward just far enough for her jacket to hang open, displaying her free-swinging breasts.

"Well, I have much work to do before lunch, so I will leave you in the capable hands of Nicole," André said with a sly little grin, and with that, he left, leaving Jerry naked beneath his bathrobe and alone with this incredible creature.

"Uh . . . you work for ESA, Miss Lafage . . . ?"

"Occasionally. . . ."

"*Occasionally?*" Jerry said. "What kind of aerospace work can you do *occasionally*? Are you a consultant? An independent contractor?"

Nicole Lafage stared at him incredulously. "This is not an American joke?" she said. "You are serious?"

"Joke? I said something funny?"

Apparently he had, for she burst out laughing. "I do not work in the aerospace industry," she managed to say. "I am, of course, a prostitute."

Jerry's mouth fell open.

"You do not believe me?" Nicole Lafage said. "Voilà, I demonstrate!"

And so saying, she sprang forward onto her hands and knees, crawled across the few feet of floor between them, parted his bathrobe, and without further ado proceeded to give him the most incredible teasing, lingering, and ultimately explosive blowjob of his entire life.

Afterward, he slumped back in his chair in a daze, while Nicole sat there at his feet, gazing around the incredibly luxurious hotel room, at the canopied brass bed, and the paintings on the walls, at the antique furniture, and finally back up at Jerry with the silliest grin on her face.

"I am hired for your pleasure, Jerry," she said, "but nevertheless I would ask a favor. . . ."

"Anything . . . ," Jerry said dreamily.

Nicole giggled. "I have never been in the Ritz before, so you must say something for me," she said. "You must say, 'Why is a nice girl like you in a place like this?' "

"Aw come on!"

"Please, please, you must say it for me!" she begged, like a little girl for a candy.

"All right, all right, 'Why is a nice girl like you in a place like this?' "

Nicole ran her eyes slowly around the hotel room again, then looked back at Jerry with an expression of utmost avidity. "Why else?" she said with a stage Gallic shrug. *"For the money!"*

And they both broke up laughing.

"To fuck for money is really not such a bad job, Jerry," Nicole told him after she had done just that for the second time in his hotel room that night. "I am young, I am beautiful, I am well educated, I speak good English, passable German, and some Russian, and I know Paris well, so this puts me at the top of my profession. I only accept corporate assignments, I am paid very well, I can choose who I will and who I will not accept as a client, and I demand good use of the expense account."

She snuggled up against him in a friendly fashion and poured herself another glass of room-service champagne as if to demonstrate, sipped at it, gave him a sly little grin. "You have enjoyed today, no?" she said.

Jerry sighed contentedly. "It's been wonderful . . . ," he said.

And indeed it had been. Nicole had taken him on the grand tour of Paris during the day, by taxi, by bus, on foot, even by Métro, shifting from one to the other according to whim and convenience.

They spent a mere hour wandering around the Louvre, strolled through the Tuileries garden and across the Seine to the Musée d'Orsay, where they meandered about for another hour, went down into a convenient Métro station, caught a train, changed once, and came out through a station beneath a gigantic enclosed shopping mall close by the Centre Pompidou, yet another museum, a truly garish structure—all naked piping and scaffolding and industrial bric-a-brac painted in weird primary colors—that reminded Jerry of a cross between an oil refinery, a nuclear power plant, and the Beverly Center.

Here they did not even bother to go inside. Instead, they just wandered around the amazing monstrosity, through the crowded streets of rather tacky bars, restaurants, and souvenir shops surrounding it, and paused for a bit to take in part of a fire-eating street act that was going on in the plaza it fronted on.

"The Louvre, the Musée d'Orsay, the Pompidou, these are the most famous museums in Paris, and now you can say that you have seen them all," Nicole said. "Later, if you wish, you can view favorite individual works of art, you let me know, and I will find them for you, I am well versed in the Flemish Realists, and the Impressionists and the Surrealists and Cubists, also Japanese and Pop, but the Renaissance I do not so much care for, and the French Romantic period, this is kitsch, no . . . ?"

"Oh, I couldn't agree more . . . ," Jerry said, and since he had almost no idea of what she was talking about and even less interest in painting, this was technically the truth.

"You have been to the top of the Eiffel Tower, yes, you have taken the boat ride down the Seine, you have seen Nôtre-Dame, okay, we will go to Montmartre for lunch, it is very touristic, but a fine view, after which we will have taken care of the obvious, and then I will show you the real Paris. . . ."

A long taxi ride north to the foot of the Butte Montmartre, quite a hideously congested tacky tourist area, narrow streets clogged with people and sleazy greasy spoons and souvenir shops. Then up a funicular running beside a kind of terraced vertical park with endless flights of stairs and up to the top of the big hill or small mountain to Sacré-Coeur, a big whitish domed church that looked more Moslem than Catholic even to Jerry's untutored eye. And, as promised, a magnificent view from the terrace in front of it out over the entire city.

They wandered off into the maze of ancient streets around Sacré-Coeur, and ended up in a dark and tiny Moroccan restaurant, where they sat Arab-style on floor cushions around a low brass table, and ate a truly incredible couscous with fingers and dabs of flat bread, feeding each other morsels of fish and lobster and shrimp and spicy sausage, drinking heavy red wine, Nicole stroking Jerry's crotch all the while with her free hand, until he was so inflamed that he feared he would lose it then and there.

But she was indeed professional, and it never happened, though by the time the meal was over and the bill paid from a huge wad of ESA money that Nicole pulled out of her purse, he was quite dizzy from the exquisite torture.

"You poor boy," Nicole said with a giggle, when they were back out in the street, running a fingernail slowly up the bulge beneath his fly. "We must take care of this at once. . . ."

And she took him by the hand and led him up a dank and secluded alley between two ancient patinaed walls of old stone blocks, slightly redolent of must and decayed organic matter and time. She pressed herself up against him, unzipped his fly, lifted her skirt, pulled down her panties, and guided him into her.

Then she cupped his buttocks with both hands, thrust forward with her pelvis, and ground him back against the wall, fucking him with gentle roughness as she teased his ear with her tongue, an unexpected and delicious role reversal that drove him quite wild, that shortly brought him to a tremendous orgasm that left him gasping for breath and leaning languidly against the cool stone for support.

"And now we resume our guided tour of quaint old Paris," Nicole said dryly. And they did.

They wound their way down the steep little streets of Montmartre and came out into the entirely unexpected sleaze and sex-show neon of the Place Pigalle, which Jerry recognized as the area where André had taken him to see the hologram show less than twenty-four hours and what now seemed half a lifetime ago.

They took a cab back to the Seine, and spent the long afternoon mostly out-of-doors in the warm sunlight, walking along the stone quays looking at all the houseboats and jackpotting about what it might be like to live on one.

They had a few kirs at a sidewalk café, then took the Métro to the Trocadéro, a huge semicircle of concrete and statuary on the Right Bank just across the Seine from the Eiffel Tower with a grand view out over the city, then Métroed to the Place de la Concorde and walked the full length of the Champs-Élysées to the Arc de Triomphe, pausing in the middle for yet another kir at yet another sidewalk café.

They took in sunset atop the Arc de Triomphe, and then it was time to wander off to a dinner of roast duck with olives at the Tour d'Argent, a stiff, haughty, formal, and rather touristy place on the Seine that made Jerry feel somewhat nervous, but which Nicole told him with no little pleasure was about the most expensive restaurant in town as she gleefully ran up the ESA expense account.

After dinner, Nicole took him on a tour of a few of the most famous cafés, and by the time they got back to the Ritz, it was well past 1:00 A.M., and Jerry was quite wiped and ready to crash.

Or so he thought.

But when they got back up to his hotel room, Nicole produced a vial of white powder which she assured him was pure cocaine of the highest quality. Jerry, who had had to cope with the piss police all his working life, had never even thought of trying cocaine before and had to be talked into it. After all, this was Paris, this was his vacation, she told him as she did a long slow striptease. After all, the last traces would be out of his system long before he returned to Los Angeles, he told himself, as he realized how willing was his spirit and how exhausted his flesh.

And indeed, after one line, he was actually able to make love again. And after another, to do it one more time.

Enjoyed today?

"It's been the best day of my life, Nicole," he told her quite truthfully as he wrapped his arm around her. "And you, did you enjoy it?"

"Of course I have enjoyed it. This is the whole point of

being a prostitute, at least on my professional level where one can pick and choose, to spend one's time enjoying oneself with pleasant company, and make huge amounts of money doing so. . . ."

She laughed. "Alors, Jerry, if *you* could make 5,000 ECU a day by fucking reasonably attractive women and showing them and yourself an expensive good time on a corporate expense account, would *you* not prefer to be a whore?"

You could say I already am, Jerry thought somberly, a whore for the Pentagon, only I don't get to enjoy it.

"You are sad, Jerry?" Nicole said, touching a hand to his cheek. "I have said something that bothers you?"

"No, no," Jerry told her, "it's nothing, this is the happiest day of my life." And to show her it was true, as after all it was, he leaned over to kiss her.

Nicole stopped him by laying an admonitory finger to his lips. "No, no, mon cher," she told him gently. "You must not kiss a prostitute. I am beautiful, yes, and I am expert at sex, and expert as well at showing you a good time, so you must not kiss me, else you forget I am a professional, and start to fall in love with me. And this would be a disaster for you, yes, for I like my life as it is, Jerry. . . ."

She laughed, and gave his flaccid prick a friendly tug to destroy the somber moment. "A disaster for me too," she said. "They would throw me out of the prostitutes' union!"

"I wouldn't want that to happen," Jerry said, and found to his peculiar delight that he was able to laugh back and mean it.

"That is much better," Nicole said, snuggling back against him. "I am not for falling in love with, I am for enjoying like the great work of art I am. But I am a work of *performance art,* mon cher, to be experienced like a play or a dance or a symphony, not possessed and collected like a painting or a piece of sculpture. Do you understand?"

"I do believe I do," Jerry said truthfully.

"And it does not make you sad?"

Jerry thought about it. "No, it doesn't," he said. "Why should it?"

"Et voilà, you see, you have become a man of the world," Nicole said. "Bienvenue à Paris!"

Ah yes, my son, he thought as he drifted off to sleep, it is indeed a long way from Downey!

They slept late the next morning, made love, had a petit
déjeuner of croissants, coffee, and champagne with orange
juice, then strolled down to the Seine through the Tuileries,
crossed the river to the Quai d'Orsay just in front of the
museum, where they boarded a strange little catamaran riverboat with a flat deck and a funky wooden deckhouse.

They took seats in the sun up at the front of the boat,
which warped away from the dock, sailed eastward past Île
de la Cité and Île St.-Louis, up a lock and through the Bastille boat basin, and then the boat entered a long tunnel
beneath the city, ancient vaulted stonework punctuated at
regular intervals by big round gridwork manholes through
which circles of sunshine filtered like Victorian arc lights,
transforming the tunnel into a magic reality of dusky twi-
light and cool misty shadows.

The boat finally emerged from the tunnel and moved
slowly up the Canal St.-Martin, a channel rimmed by a long
thin park and running straight through a residential part of
the city, through a series of ancient locks that took forever
to negotiate. It was more like spending the early afternoon
sitting on a park bench than a boat ride, watching the gray
stone buildings, the shops and cafés, the traffic circles and
the pedestrians while slowly moving by at the pace of a
walking man.

And if Jerry Reed had indeed become enough of a man
of the world to understand the foolishness of allowing himself to fall in love with someone like Nicole, by the time the
boat had docked at the Parc de la Villette, he certainly had
allowed his feelings to generalize themselves, which was to
say he saw no reason not to fall in love a little with Paris,
with a city at once timeless and energetically modern, a city
happily rooted in its own past while it boogied forward into
the future.

And that was the Parc de la Villette in spades, a vast and
sprawling collection of museums of science, industry, music,
and cinema, of amusement rides and slick restaurants, surrounded by a futuristic quarter of hotels, restaurants, and
fancy condo buildings that looked like downtown Mars—a
kind of Disneyland of the future done right, and with a
French accent.

They ate lunch at a sleekly modern Chinese restaurant

and then spent a long afternoon taking in the exhibitions. This was Jerry's kind of place, and he would have felt entirely at home if only it hadn't all been in French, or even if Nicole had had the technical background to translate it all properly for him. Instead, she did her best to translate the words into English, and Jerry tried to make all the technological wonders comprehensible to her, and in the end quite enjoyed it, for here, at least, *she* was the innocent, and *he* got to be the tour guide, and he suspected that, professional that she was, Nicole had planned it just that way to please him.

By unstated mutual agreement, they left the European Space Agency exhibit for last, for somehow Jerry knew that it would signify the last act of their time together, and the first act of something else, the something else that had brought them together, that had brought him to Europe in the first place, and something he had not given a thought to these past two days, nor cared to.

But finally, fortified by Cognac at the museum bar, they went inside.

There was a short history of space travel told with models and holograms. There was a whole Ariane booster rocket and a mock-up of a Hermes space shuttle you could crawl around inside. There were satellites and deep-space probes and space suits and an EVA maneuvering system you could play with yourself. The usual stuff.

But then they went into the Géode, the 360-degree surround theater, where an ESA promotional film shot in full-circle high-definition Dynamax video was being shown, and that wasn't the usual stuff at all, that took Jerry's breath away, and, in the end, almost made him want to cry.

The full-surround HD Dynamax video process warped him immediately into the reality the moment the film started as no color hologram could, for while the image might not be truly three-dimensional, you weren't looking at it, you were inside of it, it filled your entire field of vision no matter how much you craned your neck around like a spectator at a tennis match, and the sound had been disced from a central point in each setup, giving the sound track quite perfect 3-D reproduction of reality.

He stood at a departure gate looking out on a busy airport which Nicole told him was Charles de Gaulle. And taxiing slowly past him, decked out in conventional red, white, and blue Air France livery like an ordinary commercial airliner, was the Daedalus, the European spaceplane that was about to enter prototype production.

It had the sleek proportions of the old Concorde or the American B-1 bomber, but it was twice the size, with a payload of a hundred passengers in this configuration. Like the B-1, it had swing wings, extended now for takeoff and atmospheric flight. There was a huge intake under the nose aft of the cockpit for the main engine and two much smaller ones where the wings joined the fuselage for the auxiliary turbojets, and a weirdly recurved exhaust bell at the rear.

As a voice babbled in technical French which Nicole was at a loss to translate, the Daedalus taxied past the terminal, turned onto the runway, lit its turbofans, and somewhat ponderously took to the air.

The scene abruptly changed. Now Jerry was riding in some impossible magic helicopter way up above a fluffy white cloud bank as the Daedalus rose through it toward him, its wings swinging back halfway into the fuselage as the main Rolls-Royce engine took over with a shattering roar and a long gout of thin blue flame, burning liquid hydrogen and atmospheric oxygen compressed by the speed of passage into the main intake like a conventional ramjet.

Up, up, and away like Superplane, the Daedalus rose, far faster than any so-called speeding bullet, with the magic helicopter tracking with it from above, as the sky deepened to violet, to black, and the Earth below showed a curve, and the wings retracted completely into the fuselage, and it was burning its fuel with internal liquid oxygen, like a rocket.

Then the rocket cut out, and the spaceplane was matching orbits with a rather Russian-looking space station, ungainly globular Cosmograd modules cobbled together awkwardly and painted a dim dingy green. Four space-suited figures maneuvered the most ungodly version of a scaled-up sat sled into position below the Daedalus and fixed it there with rather ridiculous magnetic clamps—a silly ungainly mess with rocket nozzles out of a cheap old science-fiction movie that would have torn the Daedalus to pieces if actually fired up in that position.

But in the HD Dynamax video version, the klutzy thing worked, of course, and the spaceplane blasted off toward Geosynchronous Orbit on a tail of unrealistic orange flame.

The view changed again. Jerry was standing in another

weirdly prosaic airport arrival gate, with crowds of people, jetway doors, newsstands, souvenir shops, and a men's room door behind him.

Weirdly prosaic because the airport crowd was swimming around in the middle of the air, and the jetway doors, and newsstands, and souvenir shops were all plastered at impossible angles to the walls of a circular waiting room with no up or down, an ordinary waiting room in a *spaceport* in zero gravity somewhere up out of the gravity well.

Without the feel of his buttocks nailed to his seat by gravity, the illusion would have been quite complete, as he seemed to swim toward a modest-sized circular viewport and watched the Daedalus rise toward him from the globe of the Earth on a trail of pale orange flame.

Perspective shifted again, and Jerry was space-walking himself—they even dubbed in the chuffing sounds of EVA thrusters—looking down on a truly bizarre Geosynchronous space station. Domes and passageways and clunky Cosmograd modules stuck together every which way like a model of a complex organic molecule put together from the contents of a junkpile. A big slab of a metal deck jutted out under a kind of marquee like the formal entrance to the Century Plaza Hotel and indeed emblazoned on it in blue neon the words "Méridien d'Espace."

And with that, the show was over, and a few minutes later, Jerry was outside in the golden sunlight of late afternoon with Nicole, blinking his way back into Parisian reality.

"You are all right, Jerry?" Nicole said, peering at him with some concern. "You look as if you are still out there in outer space. . . ."

"Yeah, I'm okay, just got to adjust my eyes to the sunlight again," he told her.

But the truth of it was that something had indeed changed. All through the long cab ride back to the center of Paris, Jerry was indeed in outer space, trying to remember all he had read about the Daedalus project. The Rolls-Royce engine had been on the drawing boards for decades, and rumor had it that they had actually built one before the Thatcher government canceled the project. ESA was building a prototype Daedalus now, but it was supposed to be a combination of a replacement for the Hermes space shuttle and suborbital hypersonic airliner, as far as he had heard.

Commercial flights to a hotel in GEO? It seemed like one of Rob Post's visionary pipe dreams.

On the other hand, if you *did* have the spaceplane, you *could* get it to GEO with some kind of sat sled, though hardly the silly thing he had seen in the exhibition hall. You'd have to have it firing directly along the plane's long axis somehow, and you'd have to have the exhaust well clear of the fuselage, maybe a beam arrangement aft, or . . .

It was more of the same during dinner, a wonderful meal in the Jules Verne restaurant high atop the Eiffel Tower. Jerry ate his food, drank his wine, took in the fabulous view, managed to make small talk with Nicole with a corner of his mind, and even maintained a hard-on as she groped him under the table, but his mind was centered elsewhere.

The whole idea was crazy, decades away if feasible at all —commercial airliners to orbit, spacetugs to take them to GEO, a hotel when they got there, a series of improbabilities that reminded him of some hoary old science-fiction film—but if the notion was mad, it was, alas, just the sort of divine madness that had gone entirely out of the American space program.

And technically speaking, at least, it all *was* doable. The Daedalus *was* under construction, you *could* cobble together some kind of half-assed hotel out of Russian Cosmograd modules, and you *could* get it all to GEO with modified versions of the military sat sleds he himself was working on back in Downey.

And once you had a logistical system in place capable of supporting a hotel in GEO, a real lunar colony would be a snap, and even Mars could become a tourist run within his own lifetime. . . .

When they got back to the Ritz, there was a message waiting at the desk from André Deutcher. He would pick Jerry up at 11:00 the next morning to take him to a meeting at ESA's Paris headquarters. Jerry showed Nicole the note in the elevator up to his floor.

"This will be our last night together then, Jerry," she told him.

"Why do you say that, Nicole?"

She averted her gaze. The elevator stopped. They got out and walked down the hall to his room.

"That was the arrangement all along?" Jerry said as he opened the door.

Nicole nodded. "Your friend André Deutcher is a wise man," she said. "It is better that such things end before parting becomes too much of a sadness. You must never fall in love with a prostitute, Jerry."

"Yeah, I know, remember, I'm a man of the world."

She laughed. She gave him a warm smile that nearly broke his heart. "I am not so sure," she said gaily. "Sometimes I think you are a man of other worlds, yes? Mars, peut-être, or better yet Venus, the planet of love, n'est-ce pas?"

Jerry had to resist the temptation to sweep her up into his arms and kiss her.

Instead, he ordered a bottle of the most expensive champagne on the room-service menu, and a double order of the best caviar. After it arrived, they sat there for a long time, eating caviar, drinking champagne, and saying very little, for what indeed was there to say?

At length, indeed at considerable length, long enough for them to have reached the bottom of the champagne bottle, Nicole stood up.

"Perhaps it is better that I go now, yes?" she said.

Jerry sat there in his chair looking up at her and not knowing quite what to say. Then, he took both of her hands in his, stood up, and looked deep into those bright green eyes, and realized that she was right, that there was really nothing left to say or do, that in a sense it had all really ended somehow back there in the Parc de la Villette, in the Géode, ended, as he was now sure, in the way that Nicole in her professional wisdom had meant it to end, in the way that would hurt him the least.

"A man of the world should not kiss a prostitute," Nicole said waveringly.

"But surely," said Jerry, "a woman of the world can kiss a friend good-bye."

And she laughed, and let him take her in his arms, and kissed him gently on the lips. And then, without another word, she was gone.

Jerry Reed stood there alone for a long time after she had left, trying to understand what he felt. Something told him that he should feel sad that Nicole Lafage had gone out of his life forever, that a long golden moment had come to an end, and yes, he felt a certain wistful nostalgic glow for what had been, but he was also somewhat bemused to realize that he was happy.

Was this what it *really* meant to become a man of the world?

Was this the parting gift that Nicole had left him?

Jerry opened the big windows and stepped outside onto the little balcony and looked out over Paris as he had on that first golden morning a mere three days ago.

It was night now, and the cityscape was alive with the night lights, and the red and amber streamers of the bustling traffic. The Eiffel Tower glowed like a beacon in the distance, and along the darkened Seine, the brilliant white spotlight beams of a tour boat played along the quayside buildings.

And not only the time of day was different from that first vision of Paris, for the eyes that looked out upon the city had changed too; Jerry Reed knew what was down there beneath the picture-postcard view now. He had a feel for the city, he had lived in those streets and felt their rhythms, and now, in some small way, he felt a part of it, felt it speaking to him, though what it was saying he could not quite yet fathom.

He looked up into the clear night sky, quite washed out by the city's brilliance. Only a sliver of crescent moon, a few first- and second-magnitude stars, Mars, and Jupiter were visible up there above the City of Light.

But then, as his eyes adjusted, a few fainter points of light appeared, and some of them were moving slowly and deliberately through the darkness. Soviet Cosmograds. The American space station. And beyond, invisible out there in GEO, spy satellites and communication satellites and the-Pentagon-knew-what. And still farther out, the Soviet Moon lab, a permanent base on another world.

There was a dance of lights going on up there that spoke to him too, of dreams that had been, and dreams that had been lost, and dreams that might be again.

He remembered what Rob Post had often told him too. "You were lucky enough to be born at the right time, Jerry. You're going to live in the golden age of space exploration, kiddo. It's up to you. You can be one of the people who makes it all happen."

For a long time now, all that had seemed lost, destroyed by the Challenger explosion, and SDI, and Battlestar America. But Rob's words had a new, and yes, somewhat terrifying meaning now too, for all at once they were true again in a way that Rob had probably never imagined or intended.

There *was*, after all, a golden age of space exploration aborning up there right now, and tomorrow he was pretty damned sure he would be given the chance, his last chance, to be one of the people who would make it all happen.

And he remembered something else Rob had once told him, on a day when Jerry was feeling down and discouraged, the words of a great Grand Prix driver named Stirling Moss.

"I do believe I could learn to walk on water," Moss had told an interviewer. "I'd have to give up everything else to do it, but I could walk on water."

A TRUE EUROPEAN HOUSE

The overtures from the British and the French, however vague and crafted for deniability they may be, do indeed merit the serious discussion that is currently taking place in the Supreme Soviet.

The economic advantage to the Soviet Union of membership in Common Europe is readily apparent, and the ruble now seems solid enough to be merged into the ECU common basket without ruinous domestic inflation.

True, reconciliation of legal systems and modes of economic organization, as well as certain defense matters, present serious problems. True too that the Soviet Union, as the largest independent nation in the world, with the largest population on the European continent, not to mention the most powerful military forces, can hardly be expected to simply apply for membership under the present structure like a second-rate power.

But despite the tentative nature of the feelers, it is clear that Britain and France, not to mention the many other member states they seem to be representing, have as strong a self-interest in Soviet membership as we do, and may very well be willing to negotiate the changes in the

Common European constitution and legal systems needed to meet our requirements for entry.

For as things stand now, neither Britain nor France, indeed not even the two of them together, can serve as a political counterbalance to German economic power. Only the entry of the Soviet Union, with a population triple that of Germany, with a GNP almost as large, with its leadership in space, with the prestige of its Red Army, can prevent Common Europe from inevitably evolving into a de facto Greater German Co-Prosperity Sphere.

Only a Common Europe that includes the Soviet Union can long remain a true fraternal house of equals.

—Pravda

GAINES TESTS DOMESTIC MARKET

After considerable success with consumer acceptance of the product in the pilot marketing study in Haiti, the Gaines Company has announced that it will begin marketing Gaines People Chow domestically. Sales of the nutritionally balanced basic foodstuff, manufactured from soy flour, linseed oil, and a proprietary secret recipe of vitamins, minerals, and artificial flavorings, will at least at first be institutional. Contracts have already been signed with prison systems in Arkansas and Rhode Island.

People Chow will provide nutritionally balanced meals at a small fraction of the cost of conventional prison catering programs, and Gaines hopes to penetrate this market rapidly.

Direct consumer sales, at least for now, will be limited to selected Latin American countries, where famine situations can be counted upon to overcome problems with taste and texture, which do not affect the nutritional content.

Meanwhile, Gaines is experimenting with new flavor formulas and packaging concepts to gain entry to the domestic consumer market, including sugar coating, and synthetic chili gravy.

—U.S. News & World Report

Pierre Glautier had an apartment on Rue St.-Jacques in the heart of St.-Germain, he had family money from something to do with meat packing about which he preferred not to speak, he was darkly handsome with long black hair and patrician features, he was a good lover, as a journalist he had access to a lot of good parties, and he and Sonya Ivanovna Gagarin had an arrangement.

They had met at a party in Monaco, ended up in bed together about two hours later, shared a room in Tignes for a skiing weekend, hosted each other in Brussels and Paris, all without ever falling into anything like love or a serious relationship, and now they were friends and occasional bedmates.

Staying with Pierre was like sharing an apartment with a lover and a good girl friend at the same time, for in his way, Pierre was both to Sonya. They could escort each other to parties, leave with others if they felt like it, and compare erotic notes afterward.

Several of her circle of Red Menace girl friends, like Tanya and Lenya and Katrinka, had similar arrangements with understanding gay men in Paris or Munich or London who found it mutually convenient, but it seemed to Sonya that this was much better. For one thing, Pierre was a good lover and always willing if no one else interesting showed up, and for another, she didn't end up being dragged to a lot of clubs and parties where all the men were only interested in each other.

Sonya took a cab to the apartment, was let in by the concierge, with whom Pierre had left a set of keys, and didn't see him until he returned somewhat bleary-eyed but not without a cold bottle of champagne at 11:00 the next morning.

"Have a good time last night?" Sonya said after the quick kiss hello in the entranceway.

Pierre shrugged, waved his raised hands somewhat deprecatingly as he marched into the kitchen. "A pleasant enough little Hungarian," he said airily as he peeled the tinfoil from the champagne bottle. He grinned at Sonya as he popped the cork and poured the champagne into tulip glasses. "*This,* however," he said, "is Moët & Chandon Brut, ma petite."

They clinked glasses, walked around the breakfast bar and into the rather bizarre living room. There was no real furniture as such and no floor in a conventional sense either. A conversation pit, a raised dais full of electronic equipment, toadstool-shaped tables, bookcases, cabinets, lamps, all seemed to flow and grow out of each other in organic curves and soft carpeting. A big picture window looked out on an inner courtyard, and two walls were mirrored, giving the place a strange feeling of boundlessness. It was an ideal venue for parties, even orgies, and it had seen plenty of both, at least to hear Pierre tell it.

"So, what are your plans for the big vacation?" Pierre said, plopping himself down in the padded conversation pit.

"I am here, am I not?" Sonya said, sitting down beside him, but well outside his body-space.

"You plan to spend two weeks in Paris with me?" Pierre said dubiously, or perhaps nervously, for the truth of it was that they had never spent more than four days at a time together.

"You are not flattered?" Sonya said with wide-eyed innocence.

"Ah, well, but of course I am *flattered,*" Pierre stammered uneasily. "Mais, this I had not exactly expected or planned for, chérie, I mean, since you have not had two whole weeks of freedom for a year and will not again for another, I had assumed you would wish to travel about, have adventures, meet new people, not that I am not pleased, you understand, but I had thought, I mean, I am not the sort to, comprends . . ."

"Oh, Pierre, you are so transparent!" Sonya said as she burst out laughing. "Who is she? When does she arrive?"

"In five days," Pierre said, grinning with relief.

"And what does she have that I do not?" Sonya demanded good-naturedly.

Pierre took a sip of champagne. "You are not going to believe this," he said.

"Coming from you, I will believe anything."

Pierre leaned forward, licked his lips, and smiled dreamily. "She is a porn star from London!"

"A *porn star?*"

"Well, peut-être, perhaps not quite a *star* as yet, I met her last month when I was doing that piece on the made-to-order underground-sex-disc business in England, and some of her footage was quite incredible, what she can do with her mouth and a few simple props, oo la la, and—"

"And you persuaded her that with your connections you just might be able to break her into real films in Paris."

Pierre laughed. "You are right, ma petite, to *you*, I *am* transparent, but to *her,* well . . ."

"It is obviously necessary for her to come to Paris and give a private demonstration of her talents so that perhaps you will write a feature story on her for *Actuel.* . . ."

"Actually, I said *Paris Match* or peut-être *Spiegel,*" Pierre said. He shrugged. "It's not as if I have never sold anything there. . . ."

"What a creature you are, Pierre Glautier!" Sonya exclaimed, toasting him with her champagne glass.

"You are not angry with me, then?"

"Don't be silly," Sonya told him. "I was only playing with you. Of course you were right, I do not wish to spend my whole two weeks with you in Paris. A few days, a few parties—"

"I go to three in the next four days—"

"—and then off to who knows where with whoever I meet."

"That's my Sonya!" Pierre said happily, obviously mightily relieved. "I promise I will do my best to help you find someone interesting, an Englishman perhaps—"

"Too obsessed with boring fetishes!"

"An Italian?"

"Hopeless phallocrats!"

"A rich German?"

"Please!"

"Ah, yes, I know you Russians, you collect nationalities! You would prefer one you have never had before. . . . A Romanian, maybe?"

"I had one in Vienna, like a cross between an Austrian and an Italian."

"An Israeli?"

"In Nice."

"Dutchman?"

"I've been to Amsterdam three times."

"Irish?"

"Madrid."

"Spaniard?"

"Back home in Brussels."

"Japanese?"

"Once in Rome, and never again, thank you!"

"You are not making this easy," Pierre complained. "What nationalities *do* you need to complete your collection?"

"Albanian, Cuban, Afrikaner, Chinese . . ." Sonya said with a grin, ticking them off on her fingers.

"Be reasonable!"

"Maltese, New Zealander, Andorran . . ."

"Andorran!"

"According to my latest information, there are 180 member states in the United Nations, and this does not include the constituent republics and autonomous regions of the Soviet Union or the states of India," Sonya told him. "I have experienced a mere 21 nationalities, which leaves me 159 to go at minimum, so surely the odds are on my side in such a cosmopolitan city as Paris, and with Pierre Glautier as my spirit guide, n'est-ce pas!"

Pierre laughed. "I'll do my best," he said, sidling closer to her. "In the meantime, how about a Frenchman to tide you over?"

"A Frenchman?" Sonya exclaimed with a giggle. "But they all think they are God's gift to women!"

"But of course we are," Pierre said, flinging himself upon her. "On the other hand, I would be the last to deny that the reverse is equally true!"

To an American space cadet who had seen NASA headquarters in Houston, the Paris headquarters of the European Space Agency was rather underwhelming. Tucked away on a little side street off the Avenue de Suffren close by the École Militaire and the grandiose curving sweep of the UNESCO building, it was a low, dingy-white institutional-modern building surrounded by larger and older and richer-looking apartment houses, with no unobstructed view of anything. Were it not for the national flags festooning the plain façade above the entrance, it could easily enough have passed for a medium-sized high school in the San Fernando Valley.

Indeed, a Valley high school would have had its own parking lot; here, however, André Deutcher was constrained to park on the street.

Once inside, they took an elevator to the third floor, where André ushered Jerry into a windowless conference room where three men were sitting around a black steel table. One wall was a big video screen and the others were adorned with big full-color blowups of the Hermes space shuttle, the Earth as seen from low orbit, and a Super-Ariane booster blasting off from a launching pad in Kourou.

The three of them stood up as Jerry and André entered, and offered their hands in turn as André introduced them. Nicola Brandusi was a tall, dark Italian in an elegant light tan suit. Ian Bannister was a rumpled and slightly overweight Englishman. Dominique Fabre, like André, was a Frenchman, but darker, with a hint of Arabic ancestry.

Fabre was introduced as the executive in charge of something called "Project Icarus," Bannister was the hands-on project manager of the same thing, and Brandusi was from the personnel department. All of them spoke good English, which, Jerry was assured, was the working language of ESA when it came down to actual international engineering work forces.

"And how have you been enjoying Paris, Mr. Reed?" Fabre said when they were all seated. "André tells me this is your first visit. I hope he's been showing you a good time."

Jerry smiled at him. "Pas problem," he said, essaying one of the handful of French phrases he had picked up from Nicole Lafage. Fabre smiled back. André chuckled.

"Shall we get down to business, gentlemen?" Bannister said.

"By all means, Ian," said Fabre. "You are more or less familiar with the Daedalus, Mr. Reed?"

Jerry nodded. "I've read the literature and I've seen the film at Parc de la Villette," he said, wondering just whose idea it had *really* been for Nicole to take him there yesterday.

"It's the next giant step into space, Jerry—if I may Jerry you, Jerry—so to speak," Bannister said. "Not as glamorous as the Russian Mars mission, maybe, but in the end much more important. As things stand now, the only way to get people up out of the gravity well is *still* atop great big bloody primitive rockets, which, runway reentry vehicles or no, still means huge expensive launch complexes and pathetically damn few of them. But with the Daedalus, we'll be able to

fly directly into orbit from any major airport in the
world. . . ."

"Commercial space travel will finally become a reality, at
least for those who can afford it," Fabre said. "The problem,
of course, is that there's no place to go that makes economic
sense. . . ."

"We've had the bloody engine design for decades and the
airframe is just a matter of materials and engineering," Bannister said in a rather exasperated tone of voice. "We'll be
able to roll out a prototype in less than two years."

"But we can't get the financing to go into production,
Jerry," André Deutcher said. "The Common European Parliament has authorized three Daedaluses as a matter of
prestige, but they'll have to be configured primarily as satellite launchers, which is a total waste, and with a production
run like that, they'll be ridiculously expensive."

"Makes no sense," Bannister said. "Not when we could
produce them for 30 percent of the unit cost on a production line, like airliners."

"Well, why not?" Jerry said. "Surely there's a market for
a plane like that!"

"You'd think so, wouldn't you?" said Bannister. "But all
the bankers see is the cost per passenger mile. They just
laugh at us, look what a disaster the Concorde was, they say.
Three times as fast as the 747, but a complete commercial
flop nevertheless."

"They want us to scale the plane up to carry 250 passengers and lose the orbital capability," André said. "Now we
do have a compromise design, a version capable of flying
175 passengers as a suborbital liner that could take about
seventy-five people or a nice cargo load into Low Earth
Orbit, given extra fuel and life-support oxygen. . . ."

"But to get a good production run of the compromise
version financed, we have to give the full orbital capability
an economic justification," Fabre said.

"Which presently doesn't exist," said Bannister. "We're
between a rock and a hard place. We can build three smaller
Daedaluses with orbital capability on the ESA budget, or we
can get the financing for a fleet of bigger hypersonic airliners with no orbital capability. . . ."

"Or find some way to justify the compromise version,"
André said.

"The Geosynchronous space station!" Jerry exclaimed, finally getting the drift of it.

"Right, Jerry," André said. "The Méridien people have already agreed to finance 20 percent of it with a resort in GEO provided we first guarantee them a transportation system that can get the customers there. We have interest from several companies willing to invest in the project in order to build retirement communities for the elderly rich and zero-g hospitals and convalescent homes. It will be an ideal base from which to launch and service communication satellites."

"And it will be the logistical base needed to make a real Moon colony viable," Bannister said.

"Which can be expanded using lunar material at less than half the cost of boosting it from Earth . . ."

"Making it possible to assemble large ships able to support a permanent settlement on Mars . . ."

"And bring back iron asteroids from the Belt . . ."

"Eventually water ice from the Jovian satellites . . ."

"You're talking about building a real city in space!" Jerry exclaimed. "You're talking about opening up the whole solar system!"

Ian Bannister's eyes bored right into him with an intensity that Jerry had not seen for years, a fire of engineering passion he had long since thought had gone from the world, and for a moment, it seemed as if Rob Post's eyes from long ago were looking back at him over a big bowl of Häagen-Dazs chocolate ice cream swimming in Hershey's chocolate syrup, and a thrill went through him as Bannister spoke in a hard, cold, determined voice.

"You're bloody damned straight we are, my lad," he said.

"Of course all that will be the work of decades," Fabre said.

"But we know how to do it, Dominique," Bannister insisted. "No major breakthroughs are required. All we've got to do is roll up our sleeves and get to work!"

"And put the financial package together, Ian," André Deutcher pointed out. "Which brings us to Project Icarus, Jerry."

"The missing piece in the puzzle," Fabre said. "Ian . . . ?"

"What we need is a means for getting the Daedalus from Low Earth Orbit out to GEO," Bannister said. "Something like one of your bloody military sat sleds writ large. Take off from an airport runway, fly into LEO, then attach a propulsion module to take it to GEO, you've seen the presentation at Parc de la Villette . . ."

"*That's* Project Icarus?"

Bannister nodded. "Well?" he said.

For a long moment everyone was silent, as Jerry felt the pressure of all their eyes turned on him. "Well what?" he finally said.

"Well, what do you think, lad!" Bannister snapped.

Jerry looked in turn from Bannister to André to Fabre and back to Bannister, wondering just what to say.

The vision that they had opened up before him was enormous, exhilarating, the return of the long-gone dream that had set his boyhood spirit soaring, and he felt an energy in the room, a connectivity, a passion, and a hope, that left him feeling like a little boy with his nose pressed to a pastry-shop window, and he longed to return that enthusiasm with a positive reply that would admit him to this charmed circle.

The truth, however, was something else again, and with a nervous little sigh, Jerry Reed at last opted for it.

"It's shit for the birds," he said.

The silence was deadly. The stares were unwavering. Jerry stared straight into the Englishman's eyes. Bannister didn't give him a clue. There seemed nothing for it but to go on.

"Any magnetic clamps strong enough to take the acceleration would screw up your electronic systems royally," he said. "Where you've got the sled clamped, the rocket exhaust will fry the vehicle. If the thrust isn't directly along the center axis of the Daedalus, your chances of controlling the thing are slim and none."

He shrugged. "I'm sorry, Ian," he said, "but there you are. No one's ever tried to build a sat sled to move a payload that massive before, but it *is* essentially scaled-up sat-sled technology, and I've been working on it for years, and I do know what I'm talking about. What can I say? The whole design is fucked."

Jerry braced himself for the inevitable explosion.

But it never came.

"We know that, lad," Bannister said softly. "And we also know, as you have just proven, that the Rockwell sat-sled team is years ahead of us. We know that you have what it takes to help us turn that bloody sword into a marvelous plowshare."

The expense-account holiday, the Ritz, Nicole, all the money ESA had lavished on him, it all suddenly began to make sense to Jerry. They weren't just recruiting a bright young engineer; the bad luck that had landed him in the lousy sat-sled program had, through a brighter turn of fate, made him someone special, someone with access to the key piece of technology to make this whole wonderful scheme work. What delicious irony that the job he hated was the very thing that had dropped this sweet plum right into his lap!

The Italian, Nicola Brandusi, had said not a word during all this tech talk, sitting back in his chair as if it were all Greek or worse to him, but now he leaned forward, smiled at Jerry, and all at once became the focus of attention.

"We are prepared to make you an offer now, Mr. Reed," he said. "Ten thousand ECU a month, plus full social benefits, with annual salary reviews. A fifty-thousand ECU relocation bonus provided you sign a three-year contract, and of course the full resources of ESA in helping you find suitable quarters here in Paris."

"To work on my team, Jerry," Bannister said. "What do you say, lad?"

"It sure is tempting," Jerry blurted, for of course it was, nor was it entirely unexpected, for André Deutcher had made it clear from the very beginning that this was the purpose of ESA's beneficence, though the financial terms were quite a bit juicier than Jerry had imagined. Then again, the sat-sled technology that was *his* end of the deal made it a bargain in their terms at twice the price.

Still, now that the offer was actually on the table, he found himself in something of a state of shock.

"Take your time, Mr. Reed," Brandusi said. "We realize that this is not a step to be taken lightly."

"By all means, take your time, enjoy Paris," Bannister said good-naturedly, "there'll be time enough for me to work your arse off later!"

"We can talk about it over lunch, Jerry," André Deutcher suggested. "There is quite a decent little Moroccan place not far from—"

"If you don't mind, I think I'd just like to go back to the hotel," Jerry muttered. "I'm not very hungry right now, and I need some time to think. . . ."

And indeed, he found himself lost in his own thoughts

already, even as the meeting broke up in smiles and hand-shakes.

What the Europeans were planning was grand indeed, and if they succeeded, it would be in significant measure because of the spacetug they were asking him to help design, and his fantasies were already racing ahead to the next step, to something they had apparently not yet thought of, for if you linked the tug technology to the American shuttle tanks that were now being wasted with every launch, why you could cobble together spaceliners capable of taking tourists as far as the Moon, and maybe even Mars, and if he was instrumental in getting *that* built, he could surely promote himself a berth on it, and . . .

All his life, he had been waiting for a chance like this, waiting for a chance to be, as Rob Post had said, one of the people who made the golden age of space exploration happen, one of the people who would live to set foot on the Moon, on Mars, even beyond, and all his life he had known that when that chance came, he would take it without a moment's hesitation.

But that it would mean leaving everything and everyone he had ever known to do it . . .

That he would even consider doing such a thing . . .

That he would even consider *not* leaping at the chance . . .

He could walk on water.

He would indeed have to give up everything else to do it.

But he *could* walk on water.

Sonya Gagarin was beginning to wonder how long it was going to take for her luck to change. This was the second party Pierre Glautier had taken her to, and from the look of things, it was going to be the second party she left with Pierre. Not that she minded, but his London porn star was going to arrive in two days, and if Sonya didn't connect up with someone interesting by then, she'd have to make plans for the rest of her vacation on her own.

Pierre would take just about any journalistic assignment he could hustle up—from rock-music coverage and low-down items like the English sex-disc-to-order business, to lightweight popular treatment of subjects as serious as the election of a new Pope or the Common Europe space program, meaning that one of the charms of partying with Pierre was that you could never predict the sort of scene you would find yourself in next.

But it could become rather exasperating too. Last night's soiree had been the launch party for a magazine called *La Cuisine Humaine,* dedicated to transnational gourmandizing, and had featured an incredible buffet of the most diverse and delicious dishes from around the world that Sonya had ever stuffed herself silly on.

Unfortunately, most of the men at the party were well into early middle age, more of them than not were in attendance with their wives, and not only seemed boringly obsessed with the free food and drink they were greedily cramming down their throats, but clearly displayed the results of their primary passion around the waist and buttocks.

Pierre had promised her that tonight's party would be much more interesting, but he hadn't exactly made it clear that he was dragging her to a reception being given by a fashion and photographers' model agency for the purpose of displaying their pulchritudinous wares to attendees of an international advertising convention.

Pierre was supposedly covering this event for *Paris par Nuit,* or so at least he claimed to all the models he had been trying to "interview" for the past three hours, while Sonya fended off the advances of drunken advertising executives who assumed that any woman there must be willing to sleep with the unwholesome likes of them in the foolish expectation of landing a lucrative assignment. The only thing that kept her from being quite furious with Pierre was the same thing that kept the party from being a total bore, her amusement at watching the models inflict upon him the punishment he so richly deserved.

Pierre would sidle up to a beautiful model, begin to engage her in small talk. She would flash him a stunning smile of professionally inviting warmth, thinking he was an advertising executive or art director who could hire her, and then shut it off like a flashlight beam and give poor Pierre the cold shoulder when she realized he was only a journalist trying to come on to her.

"Poor Pierre," Sonya cooed at him sarcastically, as she came up behind him after the latest one had cut him dead. "You can look, but you can't touch. . . ."

Pierre turned with the most frustrated look on his face,

but almost immediately regained his savoir-faire and gave Sonya his best insouciant smile.

"Oh come, come, chérie, surely it is obvious to you that I have not really been trying," he said. "I realized as soon as we got here that there would be no men of interest for you, and so I was not so ungallant as to entice any of these creatures to my lair even though I could have easily enough had my choice. . . ."

"How thoughtful of you, Pierre," Sonya said dryly, and then could not stop herself from giggling.

"Bien sûr," Pierre replied, cracking a silly grin himself. "I'm glad to see you appreciate the enormous restraint I've been exercising."

"Oh, certainement," Sonya said, taking his hand and kissing him lightly on the lips, "and I'll be happy to show my appreciation back at the apartment if you're ready to get out of here."

"That's the best offer I've had all night."

"That's the *only* offer you've had all night," Sonya said, and they both burst into good-natured laughter.

"Ah well, pas problem, tomorrow is another day. And tomorrow night is another party."

"I hope it's more promising than the last two," Sonya said. "I haven't forgotten that Miss Magic Mouth from London is arriving the day after."

"Miss Magic—?" Pierre slapped his forehead with the heel of his hand. "Merde!" he exclaimed. "Would you believe it, *I* had forgotten!"

"Not really," Sonya muttered.

"Not to worry, chérie, not to worry," Pierre assured her. "Tomorrow's party will be truly transnational. Englishmen, Italians, Dutch, Germans, Belgians, who knows, perhaps an Albanian, a Maltese, a New Zealander, or even the legendary Andorran to add to your collection!"

Jerry Reed was lost, not quite thoroughly lost, perhaps, but lost enough, as lost as he had set out to be.

As long as he could find north, which was easy enough from the time of day and the position of the sun in the sky, he could find the Seine, from whose banks he could easily enough find the Louvre and the Tuileries, at the other side of which was the Place Vendôme and the Ritz. For that matter, all he really had to do was hail a cab and tell the driver "Hotel Ritz" and he'd be delivered effortlessly back to the hotel.

But that would be cheating. That would be violating the whole purpose of this little excursion into the maze of little back streets between the river and the Boulevard St.-Germain.

André Deutcher had dropped him back at the hotel after the meeting two days ago and then left him to his own devices until dinner to ponder the ESA offer.

André had brought Ian Bannister along with him when he showed up at about eight, and the three of them had dinner at what Bannister declared to be a perfect simulacrum of an authentic English restaurant: leek and potato soup, roast beef with Yorkshire pudding, Stilton cheese, fruit trifle, port served with roasted walnuts and huge Havana cigars, polished dark wood and brass, crotchety old waiters in ill-fitting tuxedos, the whole thing somehow reminding Jerry of something on La Cienega's Restaurant Row in Los Angeles.

All during the long leisurely dinner, Bannister assured Jerry that living in Paris wouldn't really be that much of a problem for an English-speaker; he himself didn't speak much French, English was the main working language of ESA, most of the "frogs like friend André here" had the good sense to learn how to speak it, and if one got lonely for hearing the Mother Tongue spoken properly on the street, why Victoria Station was a mere three hours from the Gare du Nord by Eurotube!

The next day, André took him to lunch with Nicola Brandusi at a quite acceptable sushi bar off the Champs-Élysées, though hardly up to LA standards, after which Brandusi took him around to a series of apartments that ESA had already lined up for his perusal.

That night André took him to dinner again, this time to a Chinese restaurant up in the northeast somewhere in a place called Belleville. Jerry was given to understand that another prostitute could be his for the asking, but in some weird way, this seemed like a betrayal of something special he had shared with Nicole, as well as a subtle insult to his manhood, so he settled for a few after-dinner drinks with André at a café overlooking the Place de la Bastille, and then called it a night.

And today, when André Deutcher called him after breakfast, and started discussing where they would go for lunch, and singing the praises of someone called Marie-Christine who would be his companion at dinner and accompany him to an ESA reception tonight, Jerry had finally cut him short and asserted his own independence for the first time since the 747 had dropped him in Paris.

"Hey, André, thanks, but no thanks," he said. "I want to go out and see if I can manage lunch on my own today. You can pick me up at the hotel for dinner, but no more hookers, okay? If we're going to go to a party tonight, I want to see how I can make out on my own for a change, if you get what I mean. . . ."

"Bien sûr," André said suavely over the telephone, "pas problem, je comprends. . . ." And then, in a much more real, more honest tone of voice, "Yes, that's a real good idea, Jerry."

And so Jerry had gotten dressed, and walked across the Place Vendôme and down through the Tuileries, along the right bank of the Seine toward St.-Germain.

He had already been in this area in the company of André and Nicole, it was jam-packed with tourists, there seemed to be hundreds of little restaurants, many of them with menus posted in Russian and Japanese and German and English as well as French, so Jerry had figured that this was as good a place as possible for his first solo excursion into the mysteries of Paris.

He wandered east along the river bank, crossed to Nôtre-Dame, stuck his nose inside for a few minutes just to say he had done it, walked clear around the cathedral, looking up at the gargoyles, then crossed the Pont St.-Michel into the Left Bank and onto the Boulevard St.-Michel, by which time he had worked up enough of an appetite to consider the adventure of ordering his first meal at a real French restaurant.

The Boulevard St.-Michel was a wide street lined on both sides with clothing stores, fast-food joints, bookstores, disc shops, and school-supply shops catering to the hordes of students and college-age tourists swarming along it, reminiscent of a combination of the Venice boardwalk, Hollywood Boulevard, and Westwood on a hot Saturday afternoon.

There was, however, what looked to Jerry to be a real French brasserie on the corner of St.-Michel and St.-Germain, a big place with lots of little tables right in the middle of the street scene, so he screwed up his courage and sat down at one of the few empty tables, next to a pair of neat-looking young girls in jeans and halter tops, who sat there sipping long drinks and babbling away to each other in a language that didn't seem like French.

After a good long while, a waiter finally appeared and dropped a plastic folding menu on his table. It was in French, but with translations in smaller type in Russian, Japanese, German, and broken English, and there were full-color pictures of featured dishes that reminded him of the bill of fare at any Denny's.

So, alas, did what was featured—burgers, pizzas, sausages, sandwiches, sundaes—but there was a little card attached, hand-lettered in French, obviously the specials of the day.

Jerry didn't know what any of it meant, but he was damned if he was going to order any of the fast-food junk with English subtitles, so when the waiter reappeared, he pointed to the first item, and essayed a pronunciation. "Uh . . . the cassoulet, si voo play . . ."

When the waiter nodded and wrote it down on his pad, Jerry was encouraged. "And . . . uh . . . wine . . . uh . . . vin, vin rouge . . ."

The waiter cocked a lofty and inquisitive eyebrow. "Uh . . . Côtes-du-Rhône . . ." Jerry said, which was the only French wine name he could think of.

"Pichet? Demi?"

"Huh?"

The waiter smiled perhaps somewhat condescendingly. "Grand?" he said, holding his hands apart. "Ou petit?" And he brought them closer together.

"Uh . . . petit . . ."

"Bon," the waiter said, writing it down, and then he departed, leaving Jerry proud enough of himself to smile at the girls at the next table, who had been stealing glances at him and giggling.

While he waited for whatever it was he had ordered to arrive, Jerry surveyed the street scene. There was just nothing like this in all of his previous experience, all these thousands of people crammed together on the street, this compression of possible random human contact that just didn't exist in car-bound Los Angeles, where there was hardly any street scene at all. Jerry realized that this too

would be his if he took the ESA job, this feeling of the
infinite possibilities of human and sexual adventure cramming the streets, this entirely different level of existence. . . .

If only the French had had the good sense to adopt English as their national language, the decision would already
be made for him!

The food, when it arrived was, well, a little weird, though
not entirely inedible when washed down with red wine from
a brown-glazed ceramic pitcher—a crock of some kind of
white beans baked in a savory sauce with pieces of two or
three kinds of sausage, some kind of greasy dark-meat poul-
try on the bone, and a disgusting slab of what looked like
the world's fattiest bacon.

Jerry kept stealing glances at the girls at the next table as
he picked his way carefully through the edible bits of this
stuff, and was rewarded with an occasional glance back. Finally, when he was sitting back sipping the last of his wine,
one of them ventured to say something to him in a babble of
incomprehensible guttural syllables.

Jerry could only smile, shrug, and throw up his hands.

More babble.

"Uh . . . no parlay-voo français . . ."

For some reason, the two of them thought this was quite
funny.

"Uh . . . do you speak English?"

Now it was *their* turn to goggle at *him* in incomprehension.

"Sprichst du Deutsch . . . ?" one of them ventured.

Jerry shook his head in frustration.

One of them, the prettier one at that, gave him a look of
eager anticipation. "Russki?" she said hopefully.

"Shit no!" Jerry snapped indignantly.

"Amerikanski?" the other said, with the strangest little
wrinkle of her nose.

And when Jerry nodded, that ended that, as, for some
unknown reason, the two of them frowned, pointedly turned
their backs on him, and went back to their gibberish conversation.

"Well, screw you too, and the horse you rode in on!"
Jerry shot back in futile indignation. And he hailed the
waiter on his next pass, handed him a 500 ECU note,

counted the change, calculated what the check had been, left a 15 percent tip, pocketed the rest, and departed.

The crap he had gotten from the two girls had soured his sense of accomplishment somewhat, but the sun was bright and warm, his belly was full, he had a slight buzz on from the wine, and he was not about to let two snotty little teenagers ruin his game plan for the day, which was to order and eat a real French meal at a real French restaurant all by himself, and then stroll around without paying much attention to where he was going until he was pleasantly lost and then see if he could find his way back to the Ritz without having to take a taxi.

Jerry couldn't exactly tell himself why, but he knew that this little game was somehow an essential part of his decision-making process.

If he had any politics at all, it was no more than his loathing for the Battlestar America projects he would have to work on for the rest of his life in order to stay in the Program, for what had destroyed both Rob Post's career and the hope of any visionary American space program.

His true allegiance was to the dream of space itself, the dream that ESA, not NASA, was now passionately pursuing.

So he could certainly take the ESA offer with a clean conscience; his personal goals and his idealistic passion perfectly coincided, and they both told him he would be a total asshole not to kiss off Rockwell in favor of Project Icarus.

Face it, he had told himself as he wandered off the Boulevard St.-Germain into the unknown back streets of Paris, the only thing that kept you from taking them up on it right there on the spot was the fear of being alone in this city.

After all, he had no real friends in Paris, didn't really know anyone in all of Europe, and he didn't speak French.

Paris tantalized him and intimidated him. He longed to be a part of it, to be able to explore it like a native, to taste its infinite complexities.

But no two streets ever seemed to meet at a right angle, all the street signs bore French names he had difficulty even remembering, and now here he was, in this tangle of back streets filled with beautiful women he couldn't talk to, restaurants he couldn't order a meal in, bars where he would have trouble even getting a beer, lost indeed, and in more ways than one.

Which, he reminded himself, had been his intention all

along. If he couldn't even find his way back to the hotel by himself, he certainly had no business thinking about becoming a Parisian!

Having gotten himself fairly good and lost, Jerry now set about trying to find his way back to the Seine, from which it would simply be a matter of following the river away from Nôtre-Dame and toward the Eiffel Tower until he saw the Louvre and then the Tuileries on the other side, after which it would be a simple enough matter to proceed north across the gardens to the Place Vendôme.

Okay, so the Seine is north of here. . . . So which way is north . . . ?

As Jerry wandered around growing more and more confused, a certain panic began to set in. Every little street began to seem like every other. He could swear he had been on the same street three or four times. The people strolling by seemed to be inhabiting another reality, and the babble of French and the incomprehensible street signs began to assume a certain sinister character.

He forced himself to stand still and think. Sooner or later, after all, a cab would come by, and all he had to do was say the magic words "Hotel Ritz" and he would be rescued.

His panic subsided. This was, after all, just a game he was playing with himself.

So let's try and win it.

How do you solve a maze?

You go to a wall, and follow it by making every right turn that comes along until you get out.

Jerry began walking up the narrow street. He made a right on the next cross street, and the next, and the next, and the next. This stupid little maze was bounded on two sides by the Boulevard St.-Germain and the Boulevard St.-Michel and on a third by the Seine. Sooner or later he would have to intersect one of them and the maze would be solved.

And sure enough, he soon found himself standing on the Boulevard St.-Michel, indeed with the spires of Nôtre-Dame in full sight to the north, and the brasserie in which he had eaten lunch clearly visible not three blocks up the street.

All he had to do now was walk up St.-Michel to the river, hang a left on the bank of the Seine, follow it past the Louvre to the Tuileries, cross the bridge, cross the park, continue on up to the Place Vendôme, and he'd be back at the hotel.

So why didn't it smell like victory?

Why did he feel as if he had somehow cheated?

Or been cheated.

Winning the game was supposed to make him feel more like a sophisticated prospective Parisian, but the way he had won it had somehow left him feeling even more like a stranger in a strange land.

The hell with it! he thought sourly.

There was a line of cabs sitting at a taxi stand just down the street on the other side. It was getting late, there was a party tonight, and there was nothing to be gained by pigheadedly trudging all the way back to the hotel on foot to prove a point he had already made to his own dissatisfaction.

"Hotel Ritz," he said, getting into the taxi at the head of the line, and letting it carry him across the Seine and back onto the old magic red carpet ride.

But no more hookers, he promised himself. At least until I've really tried to get laid on my own.

That, at least, was a game a guy always knew whether he had won or lost!

LET GERMANY LEAD THE WAY

Amid all the current cries of outrage at even the suggestion that the Soviet Union be admitted into Common Europe in order to balance so-called German economic hegemonism, it may seem quixotic, even unpatriotic, for Germans to support such a proposition.

True, every German, from the greenest of Greens to those throwbacks who secretly embroider swastikas on their underwear, can only be offended by what it implies about our true standing in the hearts of our fellow Europeans.

True too that we have earned our present economic

predominance through hard work, skill, and positive cultural values, rather than as the outcome of some dastardly plot. True as well that we have neither the preponderance of votes in Strasbourg nor the military power to translate it into anything more sinister than our own prosperity.

But alas, it is also true that we have given our European brothers abundant historical reason to fear us. And if that fear may no longer have a rational basis, its emotional reality must be dealt with.

And sometime soon we may be presented with the opportunity to at long last exorcise the ghost of the Third Reich for all time.

Let Germany not stand in the way of Soviet entry. Let us even support it. We would only be placing ourselves on the side of a long-term historical inevitable, and by so doing, proclaim to the peoples of Europe that we have not only foresworn military power, but are willing to surrender our unquestioned economic dominance in order to create a more balanced union.

Germany may be far from ready to contemplate such a selfless act in its present state of wounded outrage, but in the end we must finally ask ourselves what we really have to lose by Soviet entry.

We are already the Soviet Union's largest trading partner, large amounts of German capital are already invested in co-ventures with the Soviets, we do not now dominate Europe politically or militarily in any case, and so, in real terms, rather than in terms of national pride, we stand to gain much and lose nothing.

That is the future Europe Germany should seek. A Europe in which Germany and the Soviet Union can stand side by side, feared by no one, and truly accepted by all as fraternal and moral equals.

—*Die Stern*

V

"This should really be quite a party," Pierre Glautier had assured Sonya in the taxi. "The European Space Agency is having a reception for potential launch customers, there should be people there from all over Common Europe, the Middle East, and Africa too, maybe. Scientists and media barons and who knows what else. They're trying to convince as many people as they can to book launch services on their Daedalus spaceplane, which apparently doesn't even exist yet, so you can be sure that everything will be strictly first class and plenty of it!"

Well, Pierre had certainly been right about the lavish style! The party was being held up on Avenue Foch in the 16th, in what had apparently once been the parlor floor of the private mansion of a true plutocrat of the old school but which was now rented out for corporate functions such as this.

There was an immense eighteenth-century salon, with two much smaller rooms done up as more intimate living rooms on either side. The main salon had brocaded cloth wallpaper in red and gold, high ceilings with gilded rococo plasterwork and hanging crystal chandeliers, antique chairs scattered about. The kitschy and murky French Romantic portraits and landscapes and battle scenes in heavy gilt frames that one would have expected in such a setting had been replaced by huge and stunning photographs—the rings of Saturn, great Jupiter, spiral galaxies, and of course, the inevitable portrait of the living Earth entire from on high.

A long bar had been set up along one wall, from behind which a team of tuxedoed bartenders served quite decent champagne, considering the volume, and mixed drinks to order. Along the other long wall an immense buffet table had been set up, with whole precarved roast geese and ducks, sliced hams and charcuterie, great platters of raw oysters and cracked crab and lobster meat, smoked salmon, huge bowls of Russian caviar, canapés and crudités and breads of every description.

The centerpiece of this enormous buffet was as impressive as the food—an ice sculpture about three meters long of a sleek aircraft in the act of roaring skyward on a trail of frozen fire.

True too that this reception had an impressively transna-

tional cast, with Germans and Spaniards and Englishmen
and Dutch; and Portuguese, Belgians, and Arabs; and even
a few Turks and Japanese and who knew what else liberally
sprinkled in amid the French. And the men here were of
every age, shape, and form, and outnumbered the women at
least four to one.

But what Pierre hadn't bothered to tell Sonya was that all
of these people seemed to be here to do business or discuss
arcane technical matters beyond her comprehension or interest.

Pierre, as usual, had left her to fend for herself while he
flitted about the salon sniffing after potential material for
popular journalism. Sonya found herself wandering aimlessly around, drinking champagne, eating from the buffet,
and waiting for interesting men to try and chat her up.

She was wearing a tight white leather skirt cut diagonally
from left to right so that her left thigh was quite exposed
while her right leg was covered to well down below the
knee. She wore a contrasting black silk blouse asymmetrically cut the other way, exposing her right shoulder and the
top of her right breast, a red sash tied around her waist, and
a fashionable sprinkling of stardust in her long dark hair.

Even Pierre had remarked on how stunning she looked,
and in all honesty she did not think she was being conceited
in believing there was not another woman in the room
nearly so attractive. Men should have been swarming all
over her.

But they weren't. Most of them seemed more interested
in talking to each other, and the only woman in the salon
surrounded by a retinue of admirers was a plain-looking old
woman who must have been at least sixty holding forth on
the subject of "wormholes," which, apparently, had more to
do with outer space than with spoiled apples from what
Sonya overheard.

A few men indeed had tried to make small talk with her,
mostly in French, one in English, and another in largely
incomprehensible German, but they were odd types, physically acceptable for the most part, but somehow sexually
quite unappetizing, perhaps because they were simply boring, with their inept and primitive comments on the cuisine,
and their technobabble about launch vehicles and landsat
sensors and transponders and GEO and LEO, whoever they
were, by way of small talk.

Sonya was becoming exasperated, and she was also getting a bit nervous. Pierre's London porn star would be showing up tomorrow, which meant Sonya would have to make other arrangements, and here she was at a party with something close to two hundred men from all over the world, or at any rate from all over Common Europe, and nothing was happening.

Surely there must be at least *one* man here worth at least *flirting* with!

And then she saw him.

He was about her age, decently built, not quite handsome, though more than good-looking enough, but what Sonya found instantly attractive was his attitude.

He was standing by himself with his back up against the bar and a champagne glass in his hand, surveying the scene with the most charming glazed look of world-weariness. Here at last was a man who obviously found this party as terminally boring as she did! If nothing else, it was an undeniable sign of good taste. At the very least, here was someone who might indeed be worth talking to. . . .

Maybe it hadn't been such a good idea to forego André Deutcher's offer of a paid companion for the evening, Jerry Reed thought unhappily as he stood there by the bar, very much the English-speaking wallflower. At least she probably would have spoken enough English to stick with him and translate, although, come to think of it, it might take some doing to find a prostitute who was technologically literate in both languages.

Be that as it may, while Ian Bannister might still be right about English being the working language of ESA when it came to design and engineering teams, at this party French was what was being spoken, Bannister wasn't here for some reason, André had disappeared into one of the other rooms to try to sell satellite boosts to some Algerians and Senegalese, and so Jerry had been left all by himself for at least an hour to eat food, drink champagne, and wish he knew enough French to take part in what he was sure was the high-powered and fascinating conversation going on all around him.

"C'est une soirée un peu gris, hein, beaucoup de cuisine et très bien aussi, et la boisson aussi, mais les gens . . ."

"What?"

Oh Christ, what surely must be the most beautiful girl at the party, a terrific brunette with stardust in her hair, wearing an outrageous black-and-white asymmetric outfit that promised as much as it revealed and revealed as much as it promised, with the most inviting full lips and the biggest green eyes, had walked right up to him with a great big smile and started babbling in French! What exquisite torture!

"Uh, no parlay-voo français. . . ."

"*Je ne parle pas français,* that's the way it goes," she said. "You are English?" In English!

Jerry hesitated. He had heard that Americans were pretty damned unpopular in Europe these days, something about what was going on in Latin America, and trade balances and the national debt or something, but he hadn't thought much about it until those girls at the brasserie had turned up their noses at him. Now he wondered whether it might not be a good idea to pretend to be British or Australian or Canadian. But this girl might speak really good English, and he was hardly good enough at accents to get away with anything.

"Nope, American," he admitted, flinching inside as he waited for her smile to fade.

"An American!" she cried, and Jerry was surprised and delighted to see her smile widen and her big green eyes light up like emerald lasers.

A real live American! What incredible luck! American lovers were as exotic as . . . as Andorrans in Common Europe these days, and all the more so if you were a Russian. What a coup this could be!

The United States was limiting American investment in Common Europe and even more so European investment in America, had let the dollar drop like a stone against the ECU in order to try to devalue its enormous external debt, was reinvesting its capital and excess military capacity in Latin American adventures and Battlestar America, and loud voices in the American Congress and elsewhere had started clamoring for debt renunciation and even expropriation of Common European holdings in the States, none of which exactly assured Americans a warm welcome in the metropoles of Common Europe.

Besides which, with the dollar so far down against the ECU and all the currency restrictions on American tourists, they could no longer afford to inundate the Continent, so most of the Americans one saw in Europe these days were either rich capitalists with ECU incomes or businessmen on corporate expense accounts, neither of whom had much use for the Russians who were in the process of supplanting them as Common Europe's favorite foreigners.

"My name's Jerry Reed," he said. "And you?"

"Son—" On impulse, without thinking, Sonya choked it back. "Samantha Garry, ducks, from London," she said in what she hoped was a good imitation of a lower-class English accent. "And I haven't the bloodiest of what I'm doin' at this bloomin' frog party!"

Well, why not? She'd probably have no chance of getting him into bed if she admitted she was a Russian—all Americans *hated* Russians, everyone knew that—and besides it would be an interesting challenge to see if her command of English was really good enough to keep an American convinced she was British until breakfast.

"You're not involved in the space business?"

"Space business!" Sonya said off the top of her head. "The only space in *my* business, luv, is the one between me legs!"

"Huh?"

Well, in for a penny, in for a pound, as Samantha Garry, London porn starlet, might herself say, for this English lady had to be *somebody*, so why not Pierre's hot little crumpet from London? It would serve him right.

"The old pooter-tooter, you know, me snatch, though actually me star turn's more of a skin-flute recital if you get my drift, cobber."

"What on earth are you talking about?"

"Why me profession of course!"

"Which is?"

"The old in-and-out, so to speak."

For some reason that didn't go down very well. "Oh no, not another hooker!" Mr. Jerry Reed moaned.

"Hey, luv, you got me wrong!" Sonya said. "I ain't no bloody hooker! I'm in *show business!*"

"Show business? What kind of show business?"

"The show business of showing me business," Sonya said. "On disc, you know, porn TV to order, luv, eatin' the old banger's my speciality."

"You're a *porn star?*" he exclaimed.

"Well, not exactly a star yet, ducks," Sonya told him. "That's why I'm over here in bloody Frogland. This French journalist fed me the old shitty bitty about getting me some real parts in Paris, but the only parts he's gotten me so far is his own privates, and now he's dragged me to this party and pissed off with his froggy mates to powder his nose so to speak."

Sonya grabbed Jerry Reed by the arm with one hand and patted his buttock with the other. "So what say you and me piss off too, hey mate?" she suggested. "You can tell me all about Outer Space, and I'll see what I can do about a bit of your hard vacuum, better than a poke in the eye with a sharp stick, now innit . . . ?"

And watched him break into a sweat while trying manfully to keep his tongue from dropping down below his knees. Oh yes, win, lose, or draw, this was certainly going to be more fun than she had had since she got to Paris!

For an apparently uneducated girl from London, to judge by her accent, Samantha Garry seemed to speak good French, though on the other hand, all the French she babbled so freely to waiters and bartenders and cabdrivers could have been as weird as her English for all Jerry could really tell. There was something humiliating about that; if a porn starlet like Samantha could cope with the language, then why the hell couldn't *he?*

She really knew the city too, or at least the sort of down-and-dirty parts that hadn't been on André Deutcher's or Nicole Lafage's versions of the grand tour.

She took him to a weird bar in some back street not far from the Champs-Élysées, where half the clientele, male and female, had shaved heads and elaborate skull tattoos, the music ran to complex synthesized neo-African percussion tracks, and the drinks were served with complimentary amyl nitrate poppers.

"Zoo Zombies, luv," she told him. "Used to be one meself back in London, it never really caught on, but I've got a freakin' lizard face on me head under the hair, and Elvis likewise on me bush."

"Are you pulling my leg?"

"Am I?" she said, reaching under the table and giving his prick a sudden sharp yank. "That's not yer leg, now is it?"

Samantha let him give her one deep long kiss in the taxi on the way to the next stop, an Arab-style nightclub somewhere toward the east, where they sat on cushions, drank some incredibly strong milky-white stuff that tasted of licorice, and where, as a teenaged-looking belly dancer wriggled her crotch within about six inches of Jerry's nose, Samantha gently placed his hand on the inside of her own bare thigh.

They left the Arab place and went to a disco in a cellar not far away called, appropriately enough, "London," where the decor was wood-and-cordovan clubby, and the music was ancient punk metal stuff out of the 1970s, and the middle-aged bartenders all wore black leather jackets, tinted spiked or Mohawk hairdos, and phony pins through their cheeks, and there was nothing to drink but bitter beer or gin and tonic, and the air was so thick with some kind of oily artificial fog that Samantha probably couldn't even see what a terrible dancer he was when she dragged him out onto the floor.

When they got back to the bar, she pressed her body close to his, and draped a bare arm across his shoulder. "Hey, ducks," she whispered throatily in his ear, "are you game for some of the *real* down and dirty?"

"What did you have in mind . . . ?" Jerry replied eagerly.

"Not what you think, luv, not just yet anyway, but don't worry, you'll get yours when we're good and ready, wouldn't want you to think I'm too cheap a date, now would I?"

And from there, she took him to a truly sleazy dive up in Pigalle, "the most puke-awful sex show in gay Paree, ducks," she promised in the cab, "but everybody should see everything once, as the vicar told himself with his arsehole up against the mirror."

She wasn't kidding. In an otherwise undistinguished bar, a cage was set up on a crude pedestal.

In it, as they entered, a small male dog was fucking a large female cat.

"Jesus Christ!" Jerry exclaimed. "I see it but I don't believe it!"

"Cute stuff, innit?"

"How do you *find* these places, Samantha?"

"Oh, I've been goin' to Paris since I was a sixteen-year-old with my thumb out in Dover givin' it away for a ride to Frogland, it's just next door, innit?"

Jerry had never thought of it that way before, but it was quite true, London was closer to Paris than LA was to San Francisco, even if they were in different countries and the people didn't even speak the same language!

"That's how come you speak French?"

"You have a better time if you speak the local blabble, now don't you? I got a bit of the old Deutsch too."

"You've been to Germany also?"

Samantha laughed. "Hey, Yank, this is Europe, innit! With a big thumb and a short skirt and an improper attitude, a schoolgirl can go anywhere on her holidays; beats hangin' around in Brighton all the time, donnit?"

"Yeah, I guess so," Jerry said, wondering jealously what it would have been like to have grown up like her, a teenager on the loose all over Europe.

One round of overpriced drinks later, the dog and cat were replaced by a duck and a chicken.

"How do they get them to do it?"

Samantha shrugged. "You're the scientist, ain't you, Jerry, you tell me!"

Jerry thought about it. "Well, if you saturated each species with the other's pheromones, and shot them up with the right biochemical cocktail, that might do it, as long as the parts fit, I suppose . . . ," he told her. "On the other hand, it could all be holograms. . . ."

"Holograms . . . ?"

The duck-and-chicken show was replaced by a small pig and a scrofulous monkey.

"You think this is weird?" Jerry said with a world-weary leer. "Hey, I can show you *really* weird if I can find the place, and I think it's right around here somewhere. . . ."

They left the bar, and wandered around in Pigalle looking for the place that André Deutcher had taken Jerry to that very first night in Paris before Jerry managed to remember that it was called "La Bande Dessinée" and got Samantha to ask someone for directions.

They got seated just as the clown in the Superman suit

was dropping down onto the stage where the naked red-headed woman lay waiting on the couch for his advent.

"Hey, luv," Samantha said with a little sneer, "should I stop you if I've seen this act before?"

Jerry said nothing. He just sat there smugly waiting for her reaction when the Man of Steel grew his huge silver cock, nor was he disappointed as her jaw fell open, and she goggled at him with much the same look of wide-eyed amazement he must have given André Deutcher.

She squealed when Superman climaxed and rocketed backward off the redhead, she broke up when the woman turned into Minnie Mouse, she kept laughing through the whole cartoon-character orgy, and she gave Jerry the strangest look of perplexity when Humphrey Bogart and Marilyn Monroe and Hitler and the rest showed up for some live action.

"Holograms . . . ," he whispered to her, "all done with holograms."

"Fuck a duck!"

"That was the last place," Jerry reminded her, and they broke up into laughter.

But when the orgy of the media images faded into the sexual phantasm of the living Indian temple frieze, she grew quiet, and when Greek gods and goddesses began making love, her hand found his, and by the time the erotic holograms had metamorphosed into the penultimate psyche-delic love-in, her thigh was pressed against his, and after it all ended, the dirty-talking porn star from London sat there staring at him with the tender-eyed innocence of the little girl even she must once have been.

"That was wonderful, Jerry," she said simply and quietly, snuggling against him. "Shouldn't we go someplace quiet now, maybe? Someplace simple and romantic where we can just sit and talk?"

"Funny you should ask," Jerry said. "I know just the place."

Sonya had heard of the Hotel Ritz but she had never been inside the place before and she didn't need much acting talent for "Samantha Garry" to go all goggle-eyed, for this monument to nineteenth-century rococo-plutocrat opulence and excess made the Czar's Winter Palace and Versailles seem almost like modest understatement, all the more so because the Ritz was a place where people actually paid enormous sums of money to stay, not a museum. It was places like this that made her understand the French Revolution and made her proud to be reminded that she was a citizen of a socialist country.

And at the moment, that was about all she had to feel proud of, for while Jerry Reed still maintained his enthusiastic belief that she was a porn starlet from London, the whole Samantha Garry act was by now wearing rather thin on her conscience.

Back there at the ESA party, what seemed a long, long time ago, Jerry Reed had been just an abstraction, a relief from boredom, an opportunity to bed her first American, and a chance to test the limits of her command of English in the bargain. She had created "Samantha" out of bits and pieces of movies she had seen and books she had read and her catty concept of what Pierre's London sexpot would have to be like, and she had dragged Jerry Reed around to hideous places out of an article Pierre had written called "Sleaze-Pits of Paris" just to see how badly a dirty lady from London could shock the archetypal naive American.

But she had forgotten that the archetypal naive American was also supposed to be what they called "a good sport," which Jerry had certainly been, and she had not at all expected him to take to a creature like Samantha with such openhearted good humor, and she had certainly not expected to be so charmed herself by the way he so gallantly refrained from crudely hustling such a lewd and loose lady.

Nor had she at all expected to feel what she had felt when he took her to La Bande Dessinée and concluded their crawl through the low spots by showing his dirty lady from London a moment of truly moving erotic beauty. If this had been meant to seduce her, it had succeeded beautifully and fairly, and if it had all been innocently playful, why that was even more endearing. One way or the other, Sonya very much wanted to make love to this man now.

But the problem was that she wanted to make love to him as herself, as Sonya Ivanovna Gagarin, not Samantha Garry, and she could see no way of revealing herself without losing him, without making him feel naive and stupid and outraged at being made to play the buffoon by a treacherous Russian.

The Hemingway Bar was at the other side of the hotel,

and considering the overripe grandeur one promenaded through to reach it, the place was unexpectedly tiny and modest, with a little bar and a single bartender, a few stools, a handful of small tables, a bust of Ernest Hemingway, and ancient black-and-white photos of the American writer on the walls. The only people in the bar at the moment were two elderly couples seated together in the far corner.

It was an entirely unexpected, perfect quiet place for intimate talk. Once again, Jerry Reed had managed to surprise and delight her.

"So luv," she said, when they had ordered themselves some Cognac, "how's about you tell me a bit about yourself before we get to the old in-and-out? I've told you all my own down and dirty. . . ."

Which was the biggest lie of all, of course, but there seemed nothing for it now but to stay in character as Samantha and encourage him to do the talking, for the truth of it was that she found herself really wanting to know more about this man, and not just because she had never before met an American. There was something about Jerry Reed that did not compute. He seemed like a naive American tourist, but the currency problem had banished that species from Europe. He didn't seem rich, and he didn't seem like a corporate type, and yet here he was in Paris anyway.

"I'm not sure what you mean . . . ," Jerry said.

Sonya gave him a Samantha laugh. "Well, ducks," she said, "to begin with, what's a nice boy like you doing in a place like Paris?"

Jerry laughed. "I'm being seduced," he told her.

Samantha placed a hand on his thigh under the table. "I mean aside from tonight, luv," she purred at him. "What's brought you to Paris?"

"I told you, I'm being seduced. By headhunters."

She goggled at him. "You've got a bit of crumpet from New Guinea with a bloody bone through her nose stashed somewhere and you haven't told me!"

Jerry laughed again. "Not by cannibals," he said, "by headhunters from ESA, from the European Space Agency."

"Do tell. . . ."

"You really want to hear this?" Jerry said dubiously. "I

mean, I can't explain without getting kind of technical, and I don't want to bore you. . . ."

Samantha worked her hand deeper into his crotch and stared straight into his eyes, gave him the sweetest little smile, and all at once seemed unexpectedly serious. "Don't you worry your sweet little buns about that, luv," she said softly.

Jerry stared back at her for a long silent moment, as something began to open up inside him. Looking into her big green eyes, he realized all at once how alone he had really been here in Paris, how much had happened to him, how momentous a decision he would soon be forced to make, how much he really needed someone, anyone, to talk to.

"Go ahead, Jerry," Samantha said, "tell me all the secrets of your soul."

He sighed, he shrugged, and he did.

He told her about his job at Rockwell. He told her about Project Daedalus and he told her about meeting André Deutcher back in Los Angeles. He told her about the job they were offering, and the salary, and the apartments they had showed him.

And as he sat there sipping Cognac and talking and she sat there listening raptly without saying a word, the strangest and most wonderful thing began to happen. It all started to come out, not linearly and sequentially, but hologrammically, spiraling inward from the peripheral mundanities toward the center of his heart, toward the core of his being, as he found himself speaking of things he had never spoken about to a woman before, things he had never found a woman who would sit still and listen to before, and thought he never would.

He found himself telling a porn-film starlet from London about Rob Post and the death of the American civilian space program, about his father's science-fiction collection and a four-year-old boy watching the Moon Landing over a huge bowl of chocolate ice cream. He told her about his lost dreams of going to the Moon and walking on the surface of Mars. He told her of his frustration at being born out of his proper time, of knowing he would die long before man's starships would reach out into the wide galactic main to discover the unthinkably advanced civilizations that must surely be out there somewhere on planets circling far-distant suns.

He spoke for a long, long time, or so it seemed to him, forgetting where he was and who he was talking to, and even the touch of her hand on his cock and what he had hoped was to come, as he relived his own life's journey from the moment the Eagle landed to the decision it had brought him to now.

And all the while, Samantha Garry just sat there wide-eyed and listening, leaning ever closer to him, so that by the time he had wound down, her face was inches from his across the little table, and he could feel the soft breeze of her breath, and somehow, by some magic, sense the slow, even beating of her heart.

And just when he felt quite finished, she leaned even farther forward, and bridged the final distance, placing her palm against his cheek, and kissing him long and gently on the lips.

"That was quite a lovely story," she said, "and you are quite a lovely man, Jerry Reed."

Jerry screwed up his courage, placed his hand on hers beneath the table on the quick of him, and squeezed it hard. "Shall we?" he said.

"Oh indeed we shall, luv, I wouldn't miss it now for the world."

The hotel room was quite incredible, and under ordinary circumstances Sonya would have marveled at its grandeur and probably laughed at its baroque excess, but these were hardly ordinary circumstances, for this was hardly an ordinary man, and so she paid the setting of the magic moment little mind.

Sonya had known many men, and she had enjoyed the company of most of them, and some of her lovers, like Pierre Glautier, had even been her friends. But there had really been only one man in her life who had ever caused her to ponder seriously the question of whether she might really be in love, and that had been Yuli Markovsky, and though at one point she had planned to marry Yuli, she had given him up for life in the West when push came to shove, and truth be told, had seldom looked back with regret.

But as she sat there listening to Jerry Reed, she found herself remembering Yuli, remembering his passion, remembering what he had said to her that awful last drunken night in Moscow.

"There is a dimension of life you are blind to, a passionate color your eyes don't see," Yuli had told her angrily, "the joy of dedication to a vision of something greater than yourself. . . ."

What Yuli had told her in anger then, she hadn't understood or wanted to, but after listening to Jerry pour out his own passionate dreams so sweetly and so innocently, she understood it now.

There was a lot of Yuli in Jerry, but Jerry had something more—and something less too that somehow made him a finer and sweeter man.

Like Yuli, Jerry knew the joy of passionate dedication to something greater than himself, but unlike Yuli, Jerry had no burning desire for fame and fortune and personal power. Jerry truly *was* dedicated to something greater than himself; if he too wanted to push against the world and feel it move, it was not to hold the reins of the wild stallion of history in his hands and bend destiny to his will, but simply to be one of the people who made his vision of a golden age happen for the innocent joy of living to inhabit the world of his dreams. And if that vision itself was not one which Sonya could share, Jerry, unlike Yuli, drew a sweetness from its possession which she could feel, which in some way her heart could share, with which she could fall in love.

If indeed that was what this unknown feeling of aching tenderness really was, as she gathered him up in her arms and drew him down with her onto the big canopied bed.

Jerry Reed had not quite imagined what it would be like to fuck a porn-film starlet; he had expected it to be some kind of ultimate sexual experience, but none of his fantasies had been anything like this.

She had taken the lead and thrown him on the bed, and that he had expected, and she had undressed him with sure and frank hands, and that he had expected too. But when she stood up to undress for him, there was something so sweet and strangely tender and gentle about it, no cheap porn-disc striptease but the unhurried unfolding of a bud into full rosy flower, a sweet revelation just for him, as if she had never revealed those hard-nippled little breasts, that secret pubic triangle, for the eyes of all those anonymous unknown strangers.

Nor had he imagined that they would stare at each other silently and not touching for such a long moment. Or that it would finally begin with a simple kiss.

They kissed, and she opened her mouth and reached for his tongue with hers as he had imagined she would, but then she demurely withdrew and seemed to open herself to him.

And before he quite knew what was happening, all those thoughts of fantastic blowjobs and arcane perversities were quite gone from his head, and he didn't feel cheated at all, he didn't regret it a bit, and she simply reclined beneath him, and took his cock in her hand, and guided him into her, and wrapped her legs around him.

It felt just fine with his cock snugly fitted inside her cunt in the most basic position there was, it felt right, and clean, and somehow like home.

And if at first he felt rather intimidated to be fucking a woman of such experience, if in the first few moments he almost came in his excitement and feared that he would fail her, that all passed as she paused and slowed his rhythm, and he found himself in control of himself, seeking to please her, falling into a steady, easy, rolling motion that brought her easily to her first orgasm after an unhurried while.

After that, he simply kept going in an even, measured pace, fucking, no, making love, with a confidence and grace he had never known before, forgetting all his fears, losing himself in her cries of pleasure, finding himself in possession of skills he had understood but had never quite mastered before, until finally she smiled up at him, and, stroking his balls gently, whispered, "Let it go, luv, come inside me now."

And almost at once, looking right into her eyes, he gratefully and peacefully did, and collapsed dreamily down onto her soft breasts, into her waiting arms.

Sonya Gagarin lay there awake for a long while with Jerry Reed asleep in her arms before finally drifting off to sleep.

She had made love with many men, with men of twenty-two nationalities now by current count, and if in the tender afterglow some romantic impulse wanted to convince her that Jerry had been the best, she was not quite capable of that level of self-deception.

She had had Italians who were far more conventionally romantic, and Germans with twice the athletic endurance, and Frenchmen who had more savoir-faire, and a Swede who had read her better, and Pierre Glautier knew techniques that poor dear Jerry had probably never dreamed of.

But if Jerry Reed was not the best lover of her life, and this had not been her best sexual experience, still, love-making had never before *felt* this good. Jerry had been so sincere, so careful of her own pleasure, that it seemed he had had to seek her permission to enjoy his own. He was such a little boy at heart. And perhaps there was something more.

There was a sweetness to him that was not quite innocence, for after all this *was* no naive little boy, but a man with a vision, a man who quite sincerely and openly sought to change the world, indeed who dreamed of building whole new worlds in space, worlds that had never been, of traveling to unknown lands circling foreign suns.

And in some strange way, she sensed that this made him a brother in spirit to the little girl in Lenino who had dreamed of traveling to the bright unknown worlds of adventure in the mysterious and wonderful West. And with Jerry in her arms, that girl still lived.

Was it this, not military might or economic power or technological skill that had once made Americans the envied darlings of the world? Was it this that had taken them to the Moon? Was it this that had made Russians seek their acceptance in their heart of hearts even as they feared and hated the Yankee imperialists?

Was it this that she was falling in love with?

Sonya Ivanovna Gagarin gently stroked the hair of her American lover. He stirred in his sleep, but did not awaken, and she was grateful for that as a chill went through her.

Yes, Sonya, you are falling in love, she admitted to herself. But in a very real sense, this man does not even know that you exist.

How ever will you tell him the truth when the morning comes?

"The Animal Liberation Front today claimed to have been responsible for yesterday's explosion at the Agromax Labs in Nebraska. 'Beakless chickens that mature in three weeks and giant trout that could never survive in the wild are obscene enough,' their faxed manifesto declared, 'but the cows that Agromax has turned into insensate meat-factories are mammals just like us. How long before the Dr. Frankensteins of genetic engineering turn their beady eyes on the human genome?' "

—CNN

V I

"You're really a *Russian?* But . . . but Samantha Garry . . . that *accent* . . ."

"You think Russians cannot do accents? Besides which, ducks, having never been to Old Blighty, how do you know whether this isn't the old phony baloney out of the movies, eh mate?"

Jerry Reed laughed. He had been awoken with a kiss and a confession.

The kiss had come from his porn starlet from London of the night before, and the confession had come from another woman, who had sat up in bed after the kiss with the strangest expression of trepidation on her beautiful face, and babbled it all out nervously to him in English of quite a different accent—American almost, or Canadian, with only the slightest hint of a foreign flavor in its rhythm.

"I really do not know how to tell you this, Jerry, I've been lying awake here for an hour trying to think of something clever, but there isn't anything clever to say, I've been far too clever already, so all I can do is tell you the truth and get it over with one way or the other, and the truth is that my name is Sonya Ivanovna Gagarin, not Samantha Garry, and I am not a porn star, just a translator for Red Star, S.A., *in Brussels,* and I am from Moscow, not London, and I am Russian, not English, and I was bored at that party, and you were the only interesting man there, and it started as a joke, but now I do not think it is a joke, though I am not saying I am falling in love with you, you understand, and so there you have it, and I'm sorry, which is not to say it wasn't fun. . . ."

And, having spat it all out in a single lump, she had crossed her arms over her bare breasts and heaved a great theatrical sigh of relief. "There, now that is over," she had said in the same accent, but in quite a more confident tone of voice, the confident tone of the apparently nonexistent Samantha Garry. "So what do you think? Do you want to throw me out of your bed, or should we make love again?"

Jerry hadn't known what to think. Indeed, she had hit him with it before he was awake enough to think at all, before he was even awake enough to *consider* being pissed off.

And now that she had made him laugh by becoming for a moment the Samantha Garry of the night before, it was pretty hard to work up any anger at her, especially when she was feeling him up under the bedclothes and looking at him with those big green eyes.

"I guess I've got to admit you did a pretty good porn starlet," he said.

She licked her lips and snuggled closer to him. "For a tool of the Pentagon," she said, "you weren't so bad yourself."

"Tool of the Pentagon?"

"Don't you remember? You told Samantha Garry everything last night. All about your job in California building satellite sleds for Battlestar America, and how ESA wishes to hire you away to work on—"

"Oh my God!" Jerry moaned. He remembered all right now. He had told this woman the whole story of his life thinking she was a British porn star, and now it turns out that she's a *Russian!*

Sonya Gagarin laughed. "Shall I tell you what you are thinking?" she said. "You are thinking, what if this woman is a Russian spy."

Jerry blushed. "It sounds kinda dumb when you put it like that . . . ," he had to admit.

"Why, not at all, Jerry," Sonya Gagarin said slyly. "After all, I had you completely fooled last night, now didn't I, so I could be fooling you now too, yes? For all you know I could indeed be an agent of the KGB. . . ." She gave him a little wink. "Or worse still, of the CIA! In which case . . ."

"In which case . . . ?"

"In which case, it's far too late for you to do anything about it, now isn't it, luv?" she said, stroking his cock teasingly. "So, as they no doubt say in the porn business, you might as well lean back and enjoy it."

"You're not really a Russian spy, now are you?" Jerry Reed said over the grotesquely expensive lunch of lobster bisque, raw oysters, Sevruga caviar, and champagne they had put on the room-service tab after the long morning's love-making.

"Of course not, Jerry," Sonya said seriously. "I am who I told you I am, just a girl from Moscow with a job in Brussels, halfway through a two-week vacation, and out to have fun. . . ."

"There's got to be more to you than that."

"Does there?" Sonya said somewhat wistfully.

"Sure there does," Jerry said.

"Why?"

"Because there's more than that to everyone."

They had made love all morning, and when the room-service waiter had arrived, Sonya had gone into the bathroom and Jerry had put on his robe to let him in. Now they were seated across the little dining table from each other, Jerry in his robe, and Sonya naked, and all at once feeling quite exposed.

"Not to me . . . ," she said, suddenly feeling rather depressed without quite knowing why. "Not really. I'm not like you, I don't have a vision of the way things ought to be, I don't want to change the world. . . ."

"No girlhood dreams?"

"Well of course! But nothing very grand, nothing that I haven't already achieved. . . ."

"Tell me about it."

"There's really not very much to tell."

Jerry winked at her. He stood up, took off his robe,

dropped it on the floor. "Come on, Sonya," he said. "I've shown you mine, now you show me yours."

Sonya laughed. Jerry sat down again, leaned back, picked up his glass of champagne, swirled it around, looked straight at her. "Come on, luv, as yer friend Samantha would say," he said in a truly dreadful British accent that touched her heart, "tell me all the secrets of your soul."

And so she did, such as they were.

She tried to tell him what it was like growing up in Lenino, and what traveling in the Disneyland of the West had meant to her, how this selfish little dream, so petty and egoistic beside his own, had shaped her whole life, had made her aspire to a foreign-service career. . . .

And then she paused, poured herself another glass of champagne and drank it down for courage, and found herself telling this naked man, this stranger of the night before, this American, about Yuli Markovsky, about how she had turned her back on him, on love and her chosen career, on everything else that mattered to her, when Red Star held out the offer of life in the West *right now*.

"And do you know what the worst thing about me is, Jerry?" she said. "The worst thing about me is that I don't regret it! I've gotten what I wanted, and it turned out to be everything I thought it would be! I'm *happy* with my decision. I'd do it all over again!"

She sighed, she picked aimlessly at an oyster shell with a fork, and averted her gaze from him. "That's what a shallow creature I really am . . . ," she said much more softly.

Jerry Reed got up from his chair, walked over to her, put one hand on her shoulder, lifted her chin with the other so that she was looking right into his eyes, so that she could see his soft little smile.

"Hey, lady, you managed to pick yourself up maybe the one guy in Paris who really understands just how shallow that's *not*," he said.

Sonya cocked her head at him in total incomprehension.

"I grew up dreaming of going to the Moon and Mars, and you grew up dreaming of traveling to the West," Jerry Reed said. "I've spent my whole life looking for a way to get out there to the worlds of my dream, and now, if I'm brave enough, maybe I can get to do it, sort of. . . ."

Jerry's eyes were shining down at her so glowingly that somehow she found her depression melting away like a cool spring morning's mist under a warm rising sun, even if she did not quite understand why. "I don't think I follow you . . . ," she said.

"I told you about my 'Uncle' Rob last night, didn't I?"

Sonya nodded.

"Rob told me a line he had read somewhere that stuck with him, and I've never forgotten it either," Jerry said. "You can learn to walk on water. You'd have to give up everything else to do it, but you could walk on water."

"So . . . ?"

"So that's what I've got to find the guts to do now," he said, and the way he looked at her seemed absolutely radiant. "But you, Sonya, you've *done it.* You've given up everything else to do it, but that little girl from Moscow has walked on her water already."

Sonya's eyes quite filled with tears.

"Jerry Reed, you are a beautiful man," she said, "has any woman ever told you that before?"

"No," he said quite seriously, "no one ever has."

And then they were in each other's arms.

And so it began.

So it truly began.

They spent the afternoon just walking and talking. They talked about growing up in Moscow and growing up in Los Angeles. They talked about movies they had seen. They talked about Paris. They talked about food. They talked about what it might be like to live in one of the houseboats tied up along the Seine.

Jerry Reed was falling in love, which was a thing that had never really happened to him before, but he didn't really want to talk about that, because he didn't know how, and in any case saw no need.

Instead he talked about space. He babbled on and on, and Sonya Gagarin let him talk, and smiled, and never called it "space babble," as other women had, and she never ever told him it was boring her to tears, and she asked him the occasional technically naive but intelligent question as if to prove that she was sincere, and held his hand, and told him with her eyes that she really *was* entranced, that if she didn't understand a lot of what he was talking about, she was willing to learn, for she understood entirely what it all meant to him.

And that, somehow, was the most magical thing of all.

Late that afternoon, they went back to the Ritz, opened the French windows of the hotel room wide, moved a table and two chairs halfway out them onto the balcony, and Jerry ordered more champagne to sip as they watched the golden Parisian sunset.

"It's all like some kind of old Hollywood movie," Sonya said dreamily. "Sipping champagne up here on our balcony overlooking the Seine, and this hotel room, good Lord, what it must cost . . ."

Jerry clinked glasses, raised his in a toast. "To the European Space Agency!" he said. "To the people who are paying for it all!"

"They must really want you very badly," Sonya said, and a thought like a shadow drifted across her mind, namely that there was something a bit peculiar for ESA to be spending *this* kind of money to recruit someone like Jerry, someone who by his own description was no senior engineer or scientist, someone not much older than herself.

Jerry shrugged. "It's probably all a tax write-off anyway," he said. "It's not as if anyone were spending their *own* money!"

No doubt that was it. Sonya had encountered this strange capitalistic attitude before, if never on this lavish a scale. She wondered just how far it might be pushed. . . .

"I've got an idea," she said, "I've got eight days' vacation time left, and all you've seen of Europe is Paris, so why don't we take a trip together, a kind of mini grand tour, yes? London, Baden-Baden, Vienna, Budapest perhaps, certainly a bit of the Greek islands, Rome. . . ." She shrugged, she laughed. "Let's not even plan it, let's just hop on trains and planes and get off where we feel like. . . ."

Jerry's eyes lit up. "Wow, that's great!" he exclaimed. He frowned. "But also monstrously expensive, do you have that kind of money? I certainly . . ."

He paused in mid-sentence, looked at Sonya. She clinked her champagne glass against his, grinned, nodded. "To the European Space Agency!" she said.

"Do you really think . . . ?"

Sonya shrugged. "The worst they can do is say no," she pointed out. "Even in the Soviet Union it's been a long time since anyone was shot for just trying. . . ."

"Pas problem, I am sure, Jerry," André Deutcher told him on the videotel when Jerry had nerved up enough courage to explain the situation and broach the outrageous idea. "I will call Nicola Brandusi right now. . . ."

Twenty minutes later the videotel chimed. It was Brandusi. "What a wonderful romantic notion, Mr. Reed," he said, his videotel image positively beaming. "I almost wish I was going with you, but of course that is the last thing you have in mind, eh! The best thing is a Gold Eurocard, it is good everywhere, and you can get cash out of automatic tellers, and they will just bill ESA. Of course this will take some time to arrange. . . ."

"Uh, we only have eight days, Mr. Brandusi. . . ."

"Nicola, Nicola, please, Jerry!" Brandusi said effusively. "Not to worry, not to worry, we will messenger it to your hotel tomorrow. Have un petit déjeuner, make love, have a nice lunch, and it'll be there for you by fifteen hundred hours, in time for you to catch dinner in London or Madrid. And don't worry about your room, it will be there when you get back. Arrivederci, Jerry, have a good trip, kiss the lady for me where it counts, eh!"

And sure enough, when they arrived back at the hotel from lunch the next day, the magic piece of plastic was there waiting, and in an elegant little goatskin case too.

"Well then, where should we have dinner tonight, Sonya?" Jerry said gaily, waving the card under her nose.

"It's your Eurocard, Jerry, you choose."

"Let's go to London, then," he said, "it's the only place where I know anyone. . . ."

"I thought you'd never been there."

"I haven't," Jerry said, laughing. "But I met this English porn star, see . . ."

Sonya had heard that the Savoy Hotel was the British equiv-alent of the Ritz, so they checked into a room there that was almost as big and even more expensive than the one they had left in Paris, and after a full British breakfast the next morning that left them both groaning, she took Jerry on the obligatory whirlwind tour of the standard sights—Westminster Abbey, the Houses of Parliament, Buckingham Palace, Hyde Park Corner—all of which were in walking distance of the hotel.

They had dinner in an incredible Indian restaurant Sonya had heard about, which featured curries and tandooris of venison, quail, partridge, bear, rattlesnake, and even elephant, hippo, and lion, or so the menu claimed, and then they crawled through the pubs of Chelsea and Bayswater before reeling back to the Savoy.

The next day, Jerry quite surprised her by playing tour guide himself. He dragged her around to the famous high-tech toy stores on Tottenham Court Road, fed her lunch in a random pub, bought her an expensive ostrich-skin purse in Harrods, took her sailing on the Serpentine in Hyde Park, something he had seen in a movie, and to the London Zoo, which he had heard was almost as good as the one in San Diego.

Eurocard or not, Jerry insisted on fish and chips for dinner, because, he said, he wanted some real English food. Sonya felt like sinking through the floor when he asked the Savoy desk clerk to recommend the best fish and chips place in town.

But the desk clerk smiled and recommended a place in West Kensington called "Poisson avec Pommes Frites" which, he said, was certainly the best fish and chips restaurant in the world.

And so it was. There, in a salon done up like an elegant private club, waiters in full evening dress served them succulent nuggets of salmon, sturgeon, halibut, tuna, eel, and boned trout; bits of lobster and langoustine; whole clams and oysters and snails, enrobed in the most delicate tempura batters spiced with saffron and basil and cilantro and fried in sesame, walnut, and olive oils, served up with light-as-air fried slices of potato and yam and a whole trayful of exotic flavored vinegars, washed down with a truly noble Czech beer.

It was certainly the strangest day Sonya had ever spent in London, and in its way the most charming, for her unworldly American from California had somehow contrived to show her the city anew through his own innocent eyes.

That night, she showed her appreciation, and in the

morning they were off via hydrofoil to Normandy, where they had moules and cider for lunch, took a TGV to Bordeaux and a local train to Bayonne, where they spent the afternoon at a bullfight, hopped a plane to Madrid, and watched the sun go down from a sidewalk café over tapas and a bottle of Rioja, checked into a hotel, made love, had a seafood paella, crashed out about midnight, then got up about ten, took another TGV to Barcelona, where Sonya hired a taxi, showed Jerry some of the fantastic organiform buildings erected there by Gaudi, which Jerry said reminded him of nothing so much as certain crazy movie-star homes in Bel-Air, then caught a first-class luncheon flight on Air France to Nice.

They lazed away the afternoon sipping Americanos on the beach in front of their hotel and swimming in the Mediterranean under azure skies, made love under a beach blanket in the middle of a crowd, and then rented a huge old Rolls convertible, which Sonya drove that evening under the starry skies along the bas-corniche past the luxury homes of Cap Ferrat to Monaco, where Jerry managed against all odds to win almost enough at blackjack to pay for the lobster thermidor and Pouilly-Fuissé they had at a quayside restaurant, after which Jerry declared grandly that the true Angeleno learned as a teenager to drive from anywhere to anywhere drunk out of his mind, and against all odds proved it by somehow managing to drive the Rolls back to their Nice hotel.

They collapsed in each other's arms and slept till nearly noon. They had lunch in town, then caught a flight to Rome, where they spent the day seeing the standard sights, gorged themselves on tournedos Rossini and pasta, caught a quick flight to Brindisi, which was truly ghastly, and slept that night on a ferry to the Greek isle of Corfu.

Kerkyra, the major town on Corfu, was a tourist nightmare that Jerry said reminded him of nothing so much as Tijuana, but it did have an airport, so they caught a flight to Athens in time for a lunch of moussaka and retsina in a taverna high up in the Plaka, after which they reeled rather drunkenly up the Acropolis to wander around the crumbling ruins.

Athens itself, below the monuments to its own great past, was a smoggy, noisy, smelly nightmare, and so Sonya decided that the best thing to do was catch a flight to Munich, have a fairly early dinner there, hop on a train to Baden-Baden, rent a cabin outside the town, and make love in front of a fireplace in the Black Forest, with the odor of pine surrounding them, and the gentle night breezes whooshing through the tree crowns.

Sonya sighed as she drifted slowly off to sleep afterward, in the cozy feather bed, with Jerry warm and toasty beside her, and the glowing embers of the fire the only light in the smoky cabin bedroom. If only this could go on forever, she thought. If only I didn't have to be back to work in Brussels in three days. . . .

Somewhere in the distance an owl hooted lugubriously, like a faroff pleasure train already receding from her into the depths of the nostalgic past.

You sound like I feel, she told the mournful night bird inside her own head. And then she was forced to laugh silently at herself.

Poor Sonya! How unfair of the world to refuse to ice your cake with chocolate mousse forever and not continue to drop organically grown eggs in your fine German beer! You have found the love of your life, and you have been privileged to have a princess's vacation all expenses paid, and now you are outraged at the thought that you must soon go back to work!

She snuggled closer to Jerry. Yes, this magic time must soon end, but not our time together, luv. We may soon lose our magic piece of plastic, but there's no reason we have to lose each other, Brussels is not so far from Paris, we can be together most weekends, and surely you can make ESA give you the same vacation weeks as mine. . . .

The owl hooted again, but this time it did not seem to be mourning the recession of their short golden present together into the night of things past. *This* train seemed to be pulling into the station, and its destination was the bright future, and there was no real reason that Sonya could see why the two of them could not climb aboard.

How weird and wonderful it was to be crawling along in a cab through the streets of Paris in the rush-hour traffic in the golden late-afternoon sunlight toward the Hotel Ritz on the Place Vendôme with his Russian lover at his side and the uncanny feeling that he was coming home.

Which, in a satisfyingly science-fictional time-warped sense, Jerry Reed realized he was, for by now it was all quite decided, and he was ready to sign the ESA contract in blood if need be.

It was amazing to realize that they had only been traveling for about a week, that all they had seen and done had transpired within the geographic bounds of an area that could just about have been fitted between the California coast and the Mississippi River. Country after country, each of them with an incomprehensible language, strange sights, sounds, and smells, utterly different things to eat, rooted in its own unique ancient stories, just like all those alien worlds in Dad's old science-fiction magazines.

You could spend the rest of your life visiting these worlds and still not exhaust their newness and strangeness. Oh yes, now he *truly* understood how Sonya's girlhood passion for travel in Western Europe was on the deepest level *exactly* like his boyhood passion to walk the lands of far-off planets circling alien suns!

And if that boyhood dream was fated to remain forever a fantasy, if the man he had become knew that he would never live to see the dawn of that great star-faring age, that man had been presented with the opportunity to become in some small way one of the people whose life's work would one day surely have helped to bring that age about.

And in the bargain to have the next best thing—the alien worlds of Europe to explore with a woman who truly understood his heart.

Which, this trip together had convinced him, Sonya Ivanovna Gagarin surely did. Indeed there were times when it seemed she knew him better than he knew himself. For after their whirlwind tour from London through Munich, she had wisely slowed things down, taking him to a quiet cabin in the Black Forest for the night, and then they had spent half the next day just walking in the green woods and talking before taking a leisurely train ride to Vienna for a romantic candle-lit dinner, after which they went to their hotel, made love, talked far into the night, and then caught a luncheon flight back to Paris.

"Yes, yes, Jerry, I know, I know, we have not been to Budapest or Amsterdam or Brussels or Geneva, or Lake Como or the Alps," she kept telling him during these last two days whenever he started complaining that they were wasting time. "But they are not going anywhere, and if you try to see too much too fast, you will miss everything, like the mountains the train is passing through now—look out the window, is this not beautiful?"

And of course she was right. Europe was not going anywhere, Sonya was going no farther than Brussels, and he didn't have to leave either. By the time their plane from Vienna touched down at Charles de Gaulle, they had figured it all out and planned their convergent futures.

Jerry would take the job with ESA, of course, and he would have to do the preliminary apartment-hunting by himself, since she had to be back in Brussels next Monday, but she would fly back to Paris next weekend to have a look at the choices he was presented with and help him decide, since she would be spending plenty of time in his apartment, and the weekend after that she could come back again and take him furniture-shopping on the Rue du Faubourg-St.-Antoine, where, she assured him, most anything could be found at decent prices.

After that, why, they were young, they had their weekends and holidays, and of course, Jerry must make sure that his vacation time coincided with hers, and if it was a great nuisance that they had to live in different cities for work reasons, why there was nothing really to be done about it, now was there? It wasn't as if they were planning to get married or something—after all, they had *years* ahead of them to travel around and have a good time, and they had known each other hardly more than a week!

Jerry smiled and gave Sonya a big hug when the taxi finally pulled up in front of the Ritz. "Welcome home," he said, as the flurry of doormen and bellhops descended upon them. "I almost feel like carrying you over the threshold."

"If you try it, you're likely to provoke a strike by the doorman's union," Sonya told him dryly. "Besides, we'd better not get too used to this place. Soon enough, I'll be back in my studio in Brussels, and you'll have your own apartment in Paris, and neither of us will be able to order champagne and caviar from room service. But in the meantime . . ."

"In the meantime," said Jerry, "how about some Sevruga and Dom Perignon when we get to the room for soon-to-be-old-times' sake?"

Sonya laughed. "You're learning, Jerry, you're learning!"

When they got to the room, Sonya was delighted to see that champagne and caviar, even if only Moët & Chandon and Beluga, were already waiting with a card that said "Compliments of your friends at ESA."

But waiting also was a phone message in an envelope that had been slipped under the door. And when Jerry picked it up and read it, the laughter suddenly stopped.

"What's the matter?" Sonya asked. "What is it?"

Jerry tried to give her a diffident shrug. "Nothing much," he said, but his expression told her better. "Just a phone message asking me to call the American Embassy."

Actually what the message said was:

> Mr. Jerry Reed:
> The American Embassy called. You are asked to return the call as soon as you arrive. Please ask for Doris Steiner.

It seemed innocent enough, but there was something about the tone of it that Jerry found quite disturbing. Perhaps it was the part about "call as soon as you arrive." That gave him a sinking feeling in his stomach, the kind you got when a messenger showed up with an unexpected telegram.

"What's wrong?" Sonya said, coming to his side.

"Nothing, I hope," he said. "At least I hope not. . . . My father . . . my mother, Jesus . . . I hope nothing's . . ."

Sonya took his hand and squeezed it. "Whatever it is, it's best to get it over and not torture yourself. . . ."

Jerry nodded. He thumbed on the videotel and got the hotel operator. A minute later he had an operator at the American Embassy, voice only, behind the Great Seal of the United States.

"Doris Steiner, please?"

"Who's calling?"

"Jerry Reed returning her call."

"Hold the line."

He was then treated to what seemed like half an hour of

recycling Muzak but which was probably no more than three or four tense, sweaty minutes, before the Great Seal was replaced by the bored-looking face of a middle-aged woman with short iron-gray hair.

"Doris Steiner," she said in a diffident Midwestern voice.

"Jerry Reed."

Doris Steiner stared at him blankly. "So . . . ?" she finally said.

"So I'm returning your call," Jerry said nervously.

"You are? Lemme punch up my log. . . ."

About ninety seconds of agonizing silence.

"Oh yeah, here it is, you got an appointment with Lester Coldwater at eleven tomorrow morning."

"I do?"

"That's what it says here."

"Who the hell is Lester Coldwater?"

"Assistant commercial attaché. . . ."

"I don't know any Lester Coldwater, I never made any appointment with anyone at the Embassy, and—"

"Didn't say you did," Doris Steiner said in her obnoxious flat voice. "It's Coldwater that wants you in his office at eleven sharp, it says here."

"And if I don't feel like seeing him?" Jerry snapped.

"Hey, don't give *me* a hard time, okay?" Doris Steiner shot back at him, scowling. "I just work here, okay?"

"Don't *you* give *me* a hard time, Ms. Steiner," Jerry told her, about fed up with all this. "I'm an American taxpayer, and my taxes are paying part of your salary, and I'm asking you a reasonable question, and I think I'm entitled to a straightforward answer. What happens if I don't show up for this appointment?"

Doris Steiner's face grew ice-cold, and her voice became clipped and hard. "This is France, Mr. Reed, so we can't send a couple of Marine guards over to arrest you. But the flag in your file clearly states—"

"What flag? What the hell do you mean *my file?*"

"—that failure to appear at the Embassy within half an hour of the requested time of the appointment will result in the immediate suspension of your passport."

"What the hell is going on?" Jerry shouted into the videotel receiver.

"How should I know?" Doris Steiner told him. "It's not

my job, Mr. Reed, I'm just a C-3 messenger girl, and you
better keep your voice down. . . ."

"Keep my voice down! You listen to me, you—"

"Good-bye, Mr. Reed," Doris Steiner said with a truly
poisonous smile. "Have a nice day." And she hung up.

NATIONAL SECURITY ACT
UPHELD BY SUPREME COURT

By a vote of 6 to 3, the United States Supreme Court
has upheld four controversial sections of the amended
National Security Act, ruling, in effect, that the waiver of
Constitutional rights implied in the acceptance of employment requiring a security clearance, being a matter of civil
law between the two contracting parties, is therefore voluntary and does not constitute an act of the federal government prohibited by the Constitution.

In a dissenting opinion, Associate Justice Carl Waverly
declared that "this is a dark day indeed for liberty and this
distinguished court. By allowing such sophistic logic to pre-
vail in the name of national security, the Court has violated the spirit, if not the letter, of the Bill of Rights, and
opened the door to future and even more egregious
abuses."

—*New York Times*

FROGS CLOSE EUROTUBE

A wildcat strike by maintenance workers on the French
side closed the Channel Tunnel for six hours today, caus-
ing massive rail traffic jams clear back to Paris and London.

"Bomb? Who said anything about a bomb?" François
Deladier, unofficial spokesman for the workers, said
archly. "All we are saying is that we cannot guarantee the
safety of trains traveling through the Tunnel for six hours
today. With a 5 ECU an hour wage increase, we might be

motivated to make an effort to insure that such a situation is not repeated."

Irate travelers nearly came to blows with French workers on several occasions. "If me mates was with me," declared a supporter of Manchester United attempting to return home after a Continental weekend who asked not to be identified, "we'd bloody well do to these lazy frogs what our lads did to the micks last Thursday!"

—*News of the World*

VII

Sonya simply could not fathom Jerry's blithe attitude. He had been quite upset after yesterday's phone call with the American Embassy, but even then he had been angry rather than afraid, and now he was actually making jokes about it on his way out the door!

"They probably think you're a spy," he said, giving her a chaste little kiss. "They probably think that all Russians are spies."

"That's not so funny, Jerry!"

"Oh come on, Sonya!"

"I don't like it, Jerry, perhaps you should not enter the American Embassy, I have heard stories—"

"Right, on Russian TV spy shows, I'll bet," Jerry said. "Don't be silly, Sonya, these guys aren't the KGB, they're *Americans*." He laughed. "What are they gonna do, kidnap me and ship me off to Siberia for falling in love with a Russian? Don't worry, I'll be back in time for a late lunch."

He laughed again, gave her another little kiss, and then he was gone.

Sonya went back to the breakfast table and poured herself another cup of coffee. Don't worry?

Jerry seemed so naive about these things. These satellite sleds he had worked on seemed like a piece of technology that the Soviet Union would probably find quite valuable, and what was valuable to the Soviet Union would also be valuable to the Americans. Were Jerry a *Soviet* citizen possessed of such knowledge, he would never have been permitted to leave the country in the first place.

The thought that the CIA might drag Jerry back to America was terrifying, and the hollow emptiness she found herself feeling at the thought that she might never see him again convinced her as nothing else quite had that she had indeed fallen in love. And the knowledge that she had to be back at work in Brussels in forty-eight hours with all this going on was the final turn of the screw.

On the last count, as it turned out, she needn't have worried. Jerry had been gone for five minutes when there was a rather tentative knock on the hotel-room door.

When she opened it, her mouth fell open, and her heart skipped a beat, and her flesh began to crawl.

For there in the doorway stood her *boss,* Grigori Pankov, Pankov the Human Octopus, stooped over at the shoulders, wringing his hands nervously, beads of unwholesome sweat on his balding head, as if he had been waiting in the lobby all along for Jerry to leave, which, from the look of him, he probably had.

Jerry Reed didn't get in to see Lester Coldwater until 11:40, and not because he didn't reach the American Embassy in time. First he had to wait on line to be frisked by a Marine guard and gone over with a metal detector. Then the reception clerk let him cool his heels for about five minutes while he yammered on the telephone. When Jerry was finally directed to an office on the third floor, a secretary who did not even offer coffee kept him sitting in the outer office for another twenty minutes with nothing to read but back issues of *The Wall Street Journal* and *Barron's* before Coldwater deigned to see him.

Coldwater's office was painted a nauseating institutional lime green and was floored with institutional tan carpeting. His desk was more of the same; a big steel model humanized with tacky wood-grained plastic veneer, with the inevitable computer terminal sitting on it. One wall was bookcases in the same style. There were two overstuffed-looking armchairs in front of the desk, upholstered in cheap brown Naugahyde. The only items of decor were an American flag beside the desk and a photo of the President behind it.

Lester Coldwater himself looked to be about fifty, slightly overweight in a blue pinstriped suit, with somewhat unruly graying hair, and watery-looking blue eyes behind modish swept-back glasses.

"Sit down," he said by way of greeting.

Perhaps it was the decor, which reminded Jerry of nothing so much as his high school guidance counselor's office, perhaps it was the hurry up and wait, perhaps it was Coldwater's vibes, but whatever the reason, by now Jerry was good and pissed off and it was loathing at first sight.

He dropped down into one of the chairs across from the desk, and folded his arms across his chest. "So?" he said.

Coldwater punched something up on his computer console. "So, Mr. Reed, it is my duty to inform you that you may be about to commit a violation of the amended National Security Act recently signed into law by the President."

"How so?" Jerry said, beginning to get a little nervous, but damned if he would give anything away to this guy.

"You are familiar with the terms of the amended National Security Act, Mr. Reed?"

"No," Jerry said. "I'm no lawyer, and I have no interest in politics."

Coldwater punched something else up on his screen. "According to our information, you have received a formal offer of employment from the European Space Agency—"

"How did you find that out?" Jerry blurted, then instantly regretted it.

"Not my department, Mr. Reed," Coldwater declared diffidently. "Do you care to deny it?"

Jerry thought about it for a moment. Obviously they knew all about the offer, probably down to the salary and fringe benefits. There would be no point in getting cute, or, on the other hand, in offering anything.

"No," he said. "Is that a crime?"

"Not unless you accept it," Coldwater said. "Since you have had access to a medium-security military project, you are forbidden by the amended National Security Act to accept employment outside the United States or for a foreign company inside the United States. Should you do so, it may be construed as espionage and prosecuted accordingly.

Since such an offer has been formally made by ESA, you are now required to sign an affidavit that you will not accept it, in order to retain a valid American passport."

He reached into a drawer, pulled out a document, slid it across the desktop at Jerry, then took a ballpoint pen out of his breast pocket and put it down beside the paper.

"And if I refuse to sign?"

"Then I am required to request that you hand over your passport."

"And if I won't?"

Coldwater sighed. He shrugged. "Not my department, Mr. Reed. Suffice it to say that you will not be permitted to leave the Embassy with the document in your possession."

Jerry stared at the affidavit. He was beginning to get frightened, but he'd be damned if he'd sign anything without knowing what he was doing. "I don't have to sign anything without the advice of a lawyer," he told Coldwater. "That's my right as an American citizen, now isn't it?"

"Not under the terms of the amended National Security Act," Coldwater told him. "By accepting a medium-security clearance when you went to work on satellite sleds at Rockwell, you waived your right to counsel in such matters."

"What! But that was years ago—this amended National Security Act didn't even exist then."

"Indeed," Coldwater said. "That was why Congress, in its wisdom, made Section 12 retroactive."

"That's got to be unconstitutional!" Jerry snapped, his head reeling. "I'm not signing something I don't understand without legal advice!"

"As you wish," Coldwater said blandly. He thumbed on his intercom. "Would you please ask Al Barker to come down here to discuss Mr. Reed's situation with him?"

Coldwater stood up, checked his watch conspicuously. "It's getting to be lunchtime," he said, moving toward the door. "I might as well let you and Barker use my office. . . ."

"And what is this Al Barker's *department?*" Jerry asked.

Coldwater opened the door, looked back at Jerry patronizingly. "Let us not be crude, Mr. Reed," he said, stepping through the door, then closing it behind him, leaving Jerry alone and feeling very much like an errant high school student waiting in the guidance counselor's office for the principal to arrive.

Pankov took forever to sleaze up to the point. He mopped his brow with the back of his hand, he asked for a cup of coffee, he complained about the flight from Brussels. He glanced furtively at the unmade bed, then at Sonya, and sat down primly on a chair without making even a perfunctory pass or so much as an off-color remark, and that, somehow, was the most ominous part of it.

"What on earth are you *doing* here, Grigori Mikhailovich?" Sonya finally demanded when she could stand it no longer.

Pankov grinned at her most nervously. "Much as I would like to be able to say that this is a matter of romantic ardor, Sonya Ivanovna," he said, "alas, the fact is that I am here in your boudoir at last on official Red Star business. . . ."

"I do not understand. . . ."

Pankov seemed to be staring right through her as he reeled off a stammering little speech that sounded like something he had memorized on the plane and probably was.

"We are on the verge of completing a deal with Common Europe worth scores of billions of rubles. ESA, you are no doubt aware, due to your, ah, liaison, shall we say, with Jerry Reed, is in the process of building prototypes of its spaceplane, the so-called Daedalus. . . ."

"Why are you telling me this?" Sonya demanded. "What does it have to do with—"

"Patience, patience, Sonya Ivanovna!" Pankov said. "I am a bit over my head here myself, to tell you the truth, so please do not interrupt, or I will start to forget everything!"

He was starting to sweat again. He mopped his brow with a napkin from the breakfast table and took a gulp of tepid coffee before continuing. "Where was I . . . ? Ah yes, ESA and a European consortium wish to purchase Cosmograd modules in order to assemble some sort of hotel, improbable as it may seem, in Geosynchronous Orbit, in order to make the Daedalus economically viable, though how this is to work, I do not quite—"

"Yes, yes, they will build a space station in order to give their Daedalus someplace up there to go to, so that they can justify its cost to the bankers," Sonya said irritably. "Jerry has explained all this to me. . . ."

"He has?" Pankov said, staring at her in some perplexity. "Well then perhaps you already know that they also want to purchase Energia rockets, which they would use to place large tanks of fuel into orbit in order to fuel up tugboats which will somehow pull their Daedalus to their space station. . . ."

Pankov groaned. "Modules! Space hotels! Tugboats!" he cried. "Does any of this make any sense to you?" he asked plaintively.

"Everything but why you have come all the way from Brussels to babble about this to me!" Sonya snapped, by now entirely exasperated. "Will you *please* come to some sort of point, Grigori Mikhailovich?"

"Point? Point? Ah yes, the point! Well the point is that Red Star refused to sell them the Energia rockets, insisting instead on selling them the fuel in orbit, since that would be much more profitable, and the Europeans refused to go along with this, since it would make their space station dependent on the price of Soviet fuel F.O.B. Low Earth Orbit. . . ."

"The point, Grigori Mikhailovich, the point! Will you please get down to business!"

"Business? Well, yes, that much I do understand. After a lot of what I am told was extremely hard-nosed negotiation, Red Star hammered out a compromise with the Common Europeans. We sell them the Cosmograd modules and the Energia rockets and use the proceeds to purchase 49 percent of a transnational consortium to build the Daedalus spaceliners. A sweet deal for Red Star, is it not?"

"Wonderful! Ingenious! Marvelous! But what on earth does it have to do with me! What are you *doing* here?"

"Yes, yes, I was getting to that," Pankov said, and his voice became calmer and surer, which did not reassure Sonya the least little bit.

"You see, the key item is the tugboats, without which ESA cannot get its spaceplanes to its hotel, or build it either. But ESA does not have the technology to build such tugboats, and neither does the Soviet Union, though I am told our military would indeed very much like to have it, and without them the whole deal is dead, hundreds of billions of rubles, or so I am told. . . ."

"Only the Americans have this technology, with their satellite sleds . . . ," Sonya said slowly. "And that is why ESA is spending all this money to persuade Jerry to work for them!"

Pankov heaved an enormous sigh of relief and gave her an immense smile that would have fairly been called "winning" had it not been plastered across the face of such a slimy creature. "Yes, yes, exactly, Sonya Ivanovna, thank God you *do* understand!" he exclaimed.

"Understand *what?*" Sonya said, but her perplexity this time was unfortunately somewhat feigned, for despite herself, she was all too afraid that she was finally beginning to get it.

"Why we are extending your vacation time with full pay for the duration," Pankov told her.

"For the duration of *what?*" Sonya asked him, knowing all too well what this was coming to, but determined to make Pankov sweat as much as possible by way of futile vengeance.

"Must I?" Pankov said miserably, wringing his hands.

Sonya simply gave him a stare of silent incomprehension.

"This is not my doing at all, you understand, Sonya Ivanovna," Pankov whined. "I have been ordered to transmit this request by Sergei Dakolov, who was informed by *his* superior, who was informed by the Red Star Tower back in Moscow that high Party circles . . . ah . . . find it desirable that you . . . uh . . . continue your liaison with this Jerry Reed until he defects and that you do everything in your . . . er, power, to persuade him to do so. . . ."

"Defect!" Sonya exclaimed. "Who says Jerry has to *defect?* And to whom? It's all just a matter of accepting a job offer, isn't it?"

Grigori Mikhailovich Pankov, having at last delivered himself of the entire unwholesome message from his superiors, seemed finally to pull himself together well enough to revert to his normal petty-bureaucratic persona.

"No, it is not," he said in his pompously authoritative office manager's voice. "As to whom, ESA will no doubt secure him a Common European passport. As to who says he has to defect, that, of course, will be the Americans. After all, what is required of him is that he aid ESA in developing their own version of a key piece of Battlestar America technology. The Americans will do whatever they can to prevent this from happening short of violating French sovereignty, which means they will most certainly not allow him to remain in Common Europe on an American passport when he signs an employment contract with ESA."

"*If* he signs an employment contract with ESA. . . ."

Pankov gave Sonya a look that she knew all too well. "It is your duty as a loyal employee of Red Star, S.A., and a patriotic citizen of the Union of Soviet Socialist Republics, who, I might add, has been blessed with an unlimited travel visa for Western Europe on her passport, to see to it that Jerry Reed goes to work for ESA," he said in his best officialese.

"And if I refuse to have anything to do with this sleazy business?"

Grigori Mikhailovich Pankov shrugged. "If you refuse to cooperate with the wishes of high Party circles, while there may no longer be a gulag," he said, "Red Star *does* have a position vacant for a clerk-typist in Vladivostok."

This time they didn't let Jerry Reed stew in his own juices for very long. It couldn't have been five minutes after Coldwater left before Al Barker more or less burst into Coldwater's office, and if he didn't quite slam the door behind him, he certainly shut it with a thunk of crisp authority.

Barker was a black man of medium height and wiry build, wearing a very well tailored dark green suit, which on him somehow managed to convey the aura of a uniform. He had high cheekbones, close-cropped hair salted with gray, and cool hard eyes that looked used to command. He strode crisply across the office without introducing himself, sat down behind Coldwater's desk, bolt upright on the swivel chair, put his forearms on the desk, fixed Jerry in an unwavering gaze, and came right to the point.

"I'll give it to you straight, Reed," he said in short clipped syllables. "You have been a perfect asshole and you are in deep dark shit. You are in mental possession of classified Battlestar America material, and you may rest assured that the cretin who let you out of the country with a Common Europe visa on your passport will never be in a position to make such a stupid mistake again."

Barker steepled his fingers, pursed his lips, and regarded Jerry with a sort of sour resignation.

"Now one could say that was not really your fault, Reed," he admitted. "After all, you were offered a free vacation by the ESA headhunters, you didn't play cute and hide your destination, somebody fouled up and let you out of the country, and the worst that could be said was that you were an avaricious jerk."

"How . . . how did you know about—"

"How did we know about ESA's game?" Barker snapped. "Jesus Christ, Reed, what sort of incompetents do you think we are? You show up here and ensconce yourself in the goddamn *Ritz* and start pissing away money like there's no tomorrow, and we're not supposed to notice? You show up at a big ESA reception with *André Deutcher,* and we're not supposed to be bright enough to count to two?"

Jerry was reeling under this verbal assault. "All right, all right, so ESA paid my way to Paris and made me a job offer," he said. "Is that some kind of crime?"

Barker shrugged. "It *could* be construed as conspiracy to violate the National Security Act if we were really reaching for something to nail your ass with," he said. "But we don't have to reach that far to nail you if you force us to, Reed. Oh no, you had to go and make it easy for us by shacking up with a Russian agent!"

That was finally too much for Jerry. "That's ridiculous!" Jerry snapped. "Sonya's no spy!"

Barker rolled his eyes toward the ceiling. "I see, Reed," he said, "you know that for a fact, do you? Why I'll bet the lady even told you so herself!"

"She's a translator for Red Star in Brussels," Jerry insisted. "You could check it out."

"Are you for real? You really think we *didn't* check her out?"

"So then—"

"Jesus Christ, Reed, what do you think the Russians do, pin signs on their agents' asses that say 'Fuck me, I'm the KGB'?"

"You have proof that Sonya works for the KGB?" Jerry demanded.

"We don't need proof, Reed. Use your head. Her *cover story* is that she works for Red Star! Don't you know what that means?"

"Uh . . . it's some kind of Russian trading company, isn't it?" Jerry said.

"Yes, Reed, it is indeed, as you say, some kind of Russian trading company," Al Barker told him in the weary, exasperated voice of a teacher confronting yet one more unprepared student. "It is, in fact, *the* Russian trading company and an arm of the Soviet government whose mission is to penetrate, buy up, and subvert as much of the Common European economy as possible and to move technology East. Whether it is a KGB subsidiary on Moscow's organizational charts these days or vice versa is a moot point."

"So just because Sonya works in their Brussels office that makes her an agent?" Jerry snapped. "I think maybe you've been reading too many spy novels. The whole idea's silly anyway. I mean, what would a Russian spy want out of me in the first place?"

"What does *ESA* want out of you, Reed?"

"They want me to go to work for them, that's all. . . ."

"On Project Icarus, isn't that right, Reed?" Barker said quietly.

"How did you know—" Jerry caught himself short. "I guess that's a stupid question, isn't it?" he said in a much smaller voice.

Al Barker favored him with a wintry little smile. "That's the smartest thing you've said so far, Reed," he said. "Your job will be to help them build a spacetug that will take their Daedalus to GEO using your sat-sled experience. . . ."

"Well, yes," Jerry admitted, "but it's not a military project, and there aren't any Russians—"

"You know that for a fact, do you?"

"Well, no, not exactly, I mean . . ."

Barker got to his feet and started pacing in small circles, forcing Jerry to crane his neck to follow him. "Would you say that you're a patriotic American, Jerry?" he said in an abrupt change of tone.

"Well, yeah, sure. . . ."

"Know much history?"

"Some."

"Well then maybe you know that the United States saved Western Europe's goddamn ass from the Nazis and then protected the ungrateful fuckers from the Communists for fifty years until they were ready to stand on their own two feet," Barker said. "And when they were good and ready, when they had their Common Europe together, when they held trillions of dollars of American debt that we ran up protecting them, they made their sleazy deal with the Russians and froze us out in the economic cold."

"I don't understand what all this has to do with—"

"It's really quite simple, Jerry. We're way ahead in space-weapon technology, and they're trying to play catch-up in their usual manner by stealing the technology from us."

"What does all this have to do with me?" Jerry protested disingenuously, but beginning to become all too aware of where this was going.

Al Barker sat down behind the desk again, his little history lesson over, and resumed his previous persona. "Everything," he said. "Forget your goddamn love life. Because even if Sonya Ivanovna Gagarin really *is* the innocent little translator you think she is, we *still* can't let you stay here, because we can't let you help transfer any sat-sled technology to ESA either. They coo like doves now, but do you really expect us to hand stuff like that over to *any* potential adversary?"

"That's why you're insisting that I sign the affidavit that I won't take the ESA offer?"

Barker shook his head. "You lost that option when you made Coldwater call me in," he said. "I'm not willing to trust you that far, Reed. The bottom line now is that you must return to the United States within forty-eight hours or face the consequences."

"What consequences?" Jerry demanded.

"Permanent loss of passport. Revocation of your security clearance and the dead certainty that you'll never be able to get another even at the lowest level, meaning you'll never work in any space program ever again. Criminal prosecution under the National Security Act."

Something inside Jerry Reed snapped. He had listened to Barker call him a jerk and an asshole and call the woman he loved a spy, and he had never been allowed to catch his breath long enough to even defend himself coherently. But now Barker was *really* insulting his intelligence, and that somehow finally loosened Jerry's tongue.

"What're you trying to do, Barker," he blurted without thinking, "*force* me to defect?"

The word seemed to burn his tongue even as he uttered it. Oh my God, what have I said? he thought. But Al Barker seemed at least as taken aback as he was. "What are you talking about, Reed?" he said in a worried tone, and all at once it seemed that he was on the defensive.

Perhaps it was love that made Jerry brave. Perhaps it was the look on Barker's face. Perhaps it was that things had slowed down long enough for him really to consider the dreadful logic of the situation.

"You're telling me that you'll lift my passport if I don't go back to the States within forty-eight hours—"

"It's no longer a valid document now, Reed, as far as we're concerned—"

"—but you're telling me that I'll be prosecuted if I do."

"Hey, hey, don't get me wrong," Barker said quickly, "you forget all this ever happened and be a good boy, Reed, and there won't be any prosecution."

"And you'll guarantee that in writing?"

Al Barker squinted at him owlishly. It seemed to Jerry that there was another new expression on his face, perhaps one of grudging respect this time. "Okay, sure, why not?" he said slowly. "I think we can go that far. . . ."

"And what about my security clearance?" Jerry said.

"What about it, Reed?"

"Will you guarantee in writing that I can keep it?" Jerry said, knowing all too well what the answer had to be.

Barker studied his face with an unreadable expression and said nothing.

"Well . . . ?"

Barker shrugged, and for the first time averted his gaze. "I'm afraid I don't have that authority," he admitted very quietly. "But I'd be willing to recommend it to the people who do."

"Yeah, sure," Jerry said. "I thought so."

"Thought what, Reed?"

"I've got two real choices, right? I can turn in my passport and go back to the States, where my security clearance will be lifted, and where I'll be fired by Rockwell and never be hirable for anything connected with the space program again. . . . Or I can . . . stay here, take the ESA job, and . . . and . . ."

"Defect," Barker said, staring right at Jerry now. "Because make no mistake about it, Reed, if you accept employment with ESA, that *is* what you'll be doing. Don't kid yourself. You won't be able to change your mind. You'd be arrested the moment your foot hit American soil."

"Shit," Jerry sighed.

Something in Barker's expression softened. He leaned forward across the desk, shook his head, and for a moment it seemed to Jerry as if the man were about to reach out to touch him.

"Look, son," Barker said almost tenderly, "you don't really want to do that, now do you? You don't really want to betray your country. You don't want to spend the rest of your life in exile. You don't want to never see your native land again. You don't want the folks back home to call you a *traitor*, now do you?"

"No," Jerry whispered miserably.

"I thought not," Barker said softly.

"But . . . but if I go back now, what will I be going back to?" Jerry said plaintively. "I'll never be able to work in the space program again, will I?"

Barker studied the plastic wood-grain of the desktop. "With your background, you'll be able to get a decent job, Reed. Civil aircraft design, maybe, or the auto industry. Hey, you know, I've got an old buddy pretty high up at Piper, might even be able to do something for you there. . . ."

"You don't understand, Mr. Barker, you really don't understand. . . ."

"I understand one thing, Reed," Barker said, not entirely unsympathetically, or so it seemed to Jerry. "You've put yourself in a position where you've got to choose between your career and your Russian girl friend and your country. You're stuck with it, son. I don't envy you, but there it is."

Jerry nodded slowly. "There it is," he whispered.

Al Barker rose slowly from behind the desk, came around to the other side, and actually laid a paternal arm across Jerry's shoulders. "Tell you what," he said. "I'm gonna do something I shouldn't. I'm gonna let you walk out of here with your American passport in your pocket even though I'm really not supposed to. I'm going to give you five days to decide instead of forty-eight hours."

He took his arm off Jerry's shoulders. He shrugged. "I'm really leveling with you now, Reed," he said. "We can't drag you back to the States by force, and I will indeed catch a certain amount of personal shit if you do defect, you better believe it. But believe this too, Jerry—I don't want to see an innocent kid like you turned into a traitor to his country by these conscienceless European degenerates, I don't want to see you forced into a decision you'll regret till the day you die."

All at once the walls of the windowless room seemed to be closing in on Jerry, and the air seemed to congeal in his throat, and everything seemed to funnel down into Al Barker's eyes boring squarely into his.

"Do you believe I'm being straight with you, Reed?" Barker said. "One American to another?"

Jerry looked back at him and felt like crying. "Yeah," he found himself forced to say through the horrible lump that seemed to have bloomed in his throat like some noxious fungus. "Yeah, I do believe I do."

It was well past lunchtime before Jerry returned to the hotel room, and by that time Sonya was about a third of the way through the bottle of Russian potato vodka she had ordered from room service in order to nerve herself up to tell him about Pankov's visit.

There really had never been any question of simply not telling him, for she was going to have to explain the magical extension of her vacation time one way or another. Pankov, in his sweaty amateur incompetence, had failed to provide her with a plausible cover story, and she was not about to do his work for him by dreaming up some stupid lie herself. These things, she had actually found herself thinking after the first drink, are better left to the professionals of the KGB.

Besides, there really was no reason not to tell Jerry the truth, now was there? she had decided after the second drink. For after all, he had decided to do exactly what those high Party circles wanted him to do anyway for reasons of his own heart. After the third drink, it seemed to her that the only real problem for anyone was the problem that Pankov had created by coming here in the first place, and after the fourth, she had narrowed the problem down to constructing an opening sentence that would loosen her tongue. By the time Jerry had arrived, she even had the first half of it figured out: "Isn't it wonderful, Jerry, my boss has extended my vacation time because . . ."

But all of that was forgotten when Jerry burst into the room. He didn't seem to notice that the bed was still unmade. He didn't seem to notice the bottle of vodka in the ice bucket. He didn't even seem to notice that Sonya was well into it. His eyes were wild and his face seemed ashen, as if *he* were the one who had gotten drunk, and that sobered Sonya up fast.

"You look horrible, Jerry," she said as he flopped down into the chair across the table from her. "What happened at the Embassy?"

Jerry hooked the vodka bottle out of the ice bucket, poured himself a stiff one, and slugged it down like some muzhik, as if it were the most natural thing in the world. "They won't let me take the ESA job, Sonya," he said.

"What do you mean, 'they won't let you'?" Sonya demanded. "How can they stop you?"

"They'll prosecute me under something called the National Security Act."

Sonya stared at him narrowly. "You are not making sense, Jerry," she said. "If you are working for ESA in Europe, how can the American authorities prosecute you for *anything?*"

"Well, I guess they can't . . . ," Jerry muttered. "But I don't want to be a traitor. . . ."

"Traitor to *what?*"

"To my country, goddamnit!"

"What about *me?*" Sonya demanded. "What about *us?*"

Jerry shook his head and gave her a look of perfect agonized befuddlement.

"Poor baby, they've got you all confused, haven't they?" Sonya said, touching her hand to his cheek. She poured both of them fresh drinks. "Let's have one together, and you can tell me all about it from the beginning."

Jerry nodded, took a sip of vodka, seemed to shake some clarity back into his mind with a convulsive shrug of his shoulders and a jerk of his neck, and he did.

"That is monstrous," Sonya said when he had quite finished. "But I really don't see what the problem is."

"*You don't see what the problem is?*" Jerry moaned. Hadn't she understood a word he was saying? "If I go back to the States, I'll never see you again, and if I don't, I'll never work in the space program again!"

"But Jerry, you just told me that they will never give you security clearance to work in the American space program again even if you *do* go back!"

Jerry took another sip of vodka and forced himself to

calm down and think. She was making sense. The horrible fact of the matter was that *whatever* he did now, he was already as dead in the Program as Rob Post.

"You're right, Sonya," he said sadly. "I'm finished. I'm washed up. Oh God, oh Christ, oh shit. . . ." Tears began to well up in his eyes, a terrible void seemed to open up in his gut, and he began to tremble. Is this what it feels like to be Rob? he wondered. To feel this emptiness inside for twenty, thirty, forty years . . . ?

Sonya rose rather shakily from her chair, came around behind his, and started massaging the tense muscles at the back of his neck.

"Oh no, Jerry," she said softly, "you're not washed up at all. The best part of your life is just beginning. Don't you see? You've got a fine job ahead of you at ESA doing the work you love. You've got all of Europe to taste and explore." She leaned closer, put her arms around his neck, whispered in his ear. "And you've got me. . . ."

Jerry sighed. All that was true. What was there for him back in the States anyway? Even if none of this had ever happened, all he had had to look forward to was an eternity of slaving away on stupid military contracts. Here in Europe, he had love, and hope, and work that mattered waiting, work he believed in. But . . . but . . .

"But if I do that, I'll be a traitor to my own country!" he cried.

Sonya came around the chair to face him. She stood there with her hands on her hips, weaving back and forth woozily but with the fire of more than vodka in her eyes.

"Traitor to what?" she demanded. "Traitor to the Battlestar America program which destroyed your dream and the life of your friend? Traitor to a country which will not even let you pursue your dream elsewhere? Which will not even let you remain with the woman you love? Which requires you to give up everything in return for nothing? Who is betraying whom, Jerry?"

"Now you're talking like a Russian Communist!" Jerry shouted back at her.

"I am a child of the Russian Spring!" Sonya proudly declared. "And we have at long last learned what you Americans once knew better than any people on Earth but have now, it would seem, forgotten—a nation only thrives when its people are free to follow their own hearts!"

And there she stood, the woman that he loved, the woman who loved *him* as no woman ever had before, drunk out of her mind or not, livid, enraged, impassioned, and utterly magnificent.

In that moment, he would have given up anything for her. In that moment, he would have followed her anywhere. In that moment, he wanted to take her in his arms and hug her to him forever.

But before he could do anything, Sonya Gagarin had sunk to her knees before him, and her fingers were on his fly. "Do not leave me for empty words and stupid politics, love," she pleaded, as she freed his tremulous cock. "Can you give up *this* in the name of patriotic chauvinism?" she said as she took it in her tender loving mouth.

And she gave him an object lesson in just what it was that he would have to give up in the name of patriotism besides the chance to finally work for a space program in which he could believe.

And when, after a long, long tender time, he let himself go, let himself find release at last in a willing lover's mouth, he knew that there was a limit to how much a man could be expected to give up for his country, a limit which the demands of his country had long since surpassed, especially when that country offered nothing in return but the death of a dream.

Afterward, and yet another round of vodka later, Sonya at last found the courage to tell Jerry about Grigori Mikhailovich Pankov's visit, and why she would not be going back to Brussels on Monday after all, for by that time she was quite thoroughly drunk, and the thought of secrets between them entirely unbearable.

"Then all that stuff about being free to follow your own heart was complete bullshit!" Jerry shouted woozily, for by this time he was not exactly sober either. "You really are working for the KGB!"

Sonya rose shakily to her feet. "I love you!" she cried. "I want you to stay here with me! Fuck the KGB! Fuck the CIA! Fuck politics! Sonya Ivanovna Gagarin follows her own heart!"

She looked down at dear Jerry, still sitting there on his chair with his pants around his ankles, and never had he looked more precious to her. "Is it my fault that what is in my heart happens to happily coincide with the long-range interests of the workers and peasants and space cadets?" she said, and burst out laughing.

Jerry looked up at her, then down at his own dishabille, and he too could not contain his laughter. "Yeah, well, speaking as a tool of the capitalist imperialists and a lackey of the good ol' bottom line," he said, "I think maybe the workers and the peasants and the space cadets oughta sweeten the deal a tad. . . ."

"What did you have in mind?"

Jerry managed to rise to his feet. "If your bosses at Red Star are so fuckin' hot for this deal to go down, then they gotta transfer you to Paris to be with me, or you say that I say 'no way, José!' "

"Oooh, Jerry, I never knew you could be so *political!*" Sonya squealed in delight. "And why not a raise as well, as long as we're about it, and a more interesting job with some real advancement potential, and no Human Octopus with his hands on my ass!"

"I'll drink to that!" Jerry declared, and reached for the vodka bottle.

But he never made it. Instead, they both somehow fell forward and collapsed into each other's arms.

HOOLIGANISM IN THE SUPREME SOVIET

An unseemly display of hooliganism occurred at today's Supreme Soviet session when Ukrainian and Russian delegates actually came to blows over a resolution introduced to establish a nationalities quota system for the Red Army officer corps.

Russian delegates shouted down the attempt of Ivan Smolents to read the resolution, and several Ukrainian delegates responded with pushes and shoves, and, at least according to some of those present, with fists.

This is carrying the attempt to emulate Western legislatures a bit too far. Such brawls are best left to the Israeli Knesset, where the antagonists prepare by showing up in shirtsleeves, or the United States Senate, where fistfights have an ancient and honorable tradition.

—*Moscow Morning Sun*

Larry Krugman: "There's nothing they can really do about it, is there? It's like a sweet spin-off from all the taxpayer's dollars we've been shoveling into a high-budget space-epic that'll never gross a dime. Now that the FCC says we can do it, the Porn Channel's satellite will be watched over by good old Battlestar America. There's nothing to stop us from hitting every home satellite dish from Lisbon to Moscow with our twenty-four-hour hard-core format."

Billy Allen: "You really think you can get ratings with moldy old stag films?"

Larry Krugman: "Moldy old stag films? We've got the world's biggest library of films from the golden age of the American Erotic Cinema, including many such acknowledged classics as *Deep Throat, Behind the Green Door,* and *Debbie Does Dallas,* and we've already sold out 90 percent of the first year's commercial time for top ECU. A lot of high-grade advertisers over there obviously believe our format will appeal to upscale European consumers."

Billy Allen: "If you're right, the good old US of A is finally gonna start giving those government-subsidized highbrow European channels some pretty stiff competition!"

—*No Biz Like Show Biz*

V I I I

Reasonably early, if not exactly bright, the morning after, Sonya put in a call to Grigori Pankov at the Red Star offices in Brussels, reasonably certain that he would not be there yet to receive it. When she was told he was out of the office, she asked to be put through to Alexander Katchikov, the Regional Director himself, knowing full well that the operator would not be likely to disturb such an august personage with a call from a lowly wage slave in the translation section. However, it was enough to get her on the line to one Dimitri Belinski, a middle-aged, balding man who identified himself as Katchikov's assistant, no doubt not *the* assistant, but the assistant in charge of deflecting nuisance calls such as this.

"This is Sonya Ivanovna Gagarin," she told Belinski. "I am calling from Paris to confirm the matter of the indefinite extension of my vacation time."

Belinski goggled at her woodenly for a long silent moment. "Are you sure you have not had too much vacation already, Comrade Gagarin?" he finally said tiredly. "You are not making any sense."

"Comrade Katchikov will know exactly what I am talking about," Sonya told him.

"Comrade Katchikov will have my ass if I disturb him with such ravings."

"Well then you had better take this up with the KGB liaison," Sonya said. "He will know exactly what I mean."

"KGB liaison?" Belinski exclaimed with a great show of innocence. "Surely you know that Red Star, S.A., is in no way answerable to the KGB!"

Sonya sighed and decided it was time to play the card she had not really used since she was a teenager in Lenino. "You will deliver my message to either Katchikov or the KGB and you will deliver it accurately, to wit, that Sonya Ivanovna . . . *Gagarin* wishes to discuss matters connected with the indefinite extension of her vacation time with the proper authorities," she said frostily. "If I am forced to call a certain number in Moscow in order to transmit it, which I will do if my call is not returned within the hour, you will have occasion to learn personally the extent to which Red Star employees are or are not answerable to the KGB."

And before Belinski had time to digest *that,* she gave him the phone number and hung up.

"Do you think that's really going to work?" Jerry asked, still lying in bed and nursing his hangover.

"I think I have about enough time for a nice hot shower,"

Sonya told him, which, considering the state of her own head, might not be such a bad idea.

And indeed, she was just toweling herself off from a very long and very hot shower when the phone rang and Jerry's voice called out from the other room. "It's for you! Someone called Katchikov!"

Sonya kept Katchikov waiting for a couple of minutes while she dried herself thoroughly, and then for the sake of devilment, emerged from the bathroom stark naked, killed the video, and took the call on the videotel handset, voice only, luxuriating supinely atop the bedclothes next to Jerry with her left hand in his crotch for good luck.

"Katchikov," said a deep male voice on the other end of the line. "The American is in the room? Just say yes or no."

"Yes."

"Can you get rid of him?"

"No."

"Well then why—"

"Comrade Katchikov," Sonya interrupted, "I did not call you to play telephone games. I called to give you good news, which is that the mission I have been assigned has been almost accomplished. Jerry Reed is about to accept the job offer from the European Space Agency—"

"*He is?* But . . . And you're saying all this right in front of him?"

"More or less," Sonya said gaily, snuggling into the crook of Jerry's arm. "There is no reason for secrecy, since I have already told Jerry everything."

"You have done *what?*" Katchikov shouted.

"I have done what was required to fulfill my orders, which happily enough coincide perfectly with the dictates of my own heart," Sonya told him. "One could call it a perfect vindication of the new Communist ideal, could one not? Socialist patriotism, not only with a human face, but with a romantic ending as well; what could be more perfectly Russian?"

"I suppose there is no arguing with results . . . ," Katchikov admitted grudgingly. "One might say your country owes you its thanks, if I did not suspect that you have acted out of something other than pure socialist idealism."

"One might say that my country owes me a *concrete* expression of its gratitude," Sonya said. "Which is to say,

Comrade, that there are certain minor details to be ironed out."

"Details? Why do I not like the sound of this?"

"Jerry has attached certain conditions to accepting employment with ESA—"

"*Conditions?* That is for them to deal with, not us!"

"You will forgive me for contradicting you, Comrade Katchikov, but that is not exactly the case," Sonya said. "You see, Jerry wants very much to take this job, but the problem is that he is an American, he speaks nothing but English, he knows no one in Europe but me, and so naturally he is fearful of succumbing to loneliness and homesickness and even romantic despair were he to be left here in Paris all by himself. . . ."

"I believe I am beginning to get the drift of this . . . ," Katchikov said slowly.

"Fortunately, it is well within Red Star's power to overcome this minor obstacle to the achievement of what we all want," Sonya said. "It is simply a matter of transferring me to the Paris office. . . ."

There was a dry little laugh on the other end of the line.

"Then it is done?" Sonya asked, holding her breath.

"I have no problem with your transfer," Katchikov told her. "But I have no authority to hire for the Paris office. That will have to come from them, by way of Moscow, assuming that Moscow accepts my recommendation, and it may take some time."

"The Americans have given Jerry only five days to decide, which is to say that if he is to return to the United States at all, he must do it by then, or they will ship him to their gulag if he tries to return."

"I understand the situation," Katchikov said. "You will hear from either me or the Paris office before then. And may I say, Sonya Ivanovna, that you have demonstrated that you have an interesting future with Red Star, whether here or in Paris; it has been entertaining negotiating with you."

And with that he hung up.

"Should you have told that guy that?" Jerry said.

"Why not? It will speed things up, you do not know our bureaucracy as I do, this way Moscow will not permit the Paris office to hem and haw forever to demonstrate its bureaucratic independence."

"If you say so," Jerry said, giving her a quick kiss. "But in

America, when we buy a house, we don't like to tell the salesman we need to close the deal by next Tuesday 'cause the landlord's about to kick us out."

"Not to worry, Jerry," Sonya said, patting his cheek. "In Russia we have a saying: 'A frozen bureaucratic ass melts quickest over a hot stove.' "

Jerry laughed. "You made that up, didn't you?" he said. "I hope you're right, Sonya, because we've got a saying in America too, and this one isn't my invention: 'Shit flows downhill.' "

As it turned out, they were both right, and they were both wrong, in a way that neither of them could have imagined.

It seemed to Jerry Reed that it was taking forever, and indeed by objective measurement, he *was* nursing his third kir, and Sonya *still* had not emerged from the Tour Montparnasse.

Despite Sonya's belief that she had lit a fire under the bureaucratic ass of Red Star, S.A., the phone call they had been waiting for hadn't come until this morning, four long days later, and only twenty-four hours before the now-or-never deadline that Al Barker had set for him, four days that they had spent eating, sleeping, making love, wandering fecklessly around Paris, and putting off André Deutcher and Nicola Brandusi, but mostly just nervously killing time while the Russians let them sweat.

When the call finally came and Sonya got off the phone, she was beaming.

"Good news?" Jerry said.

"It's got to be. That was the Paris office in the Tour Montparnasse, and they want me there at three o'clock. If they were turning me down, the call most certainly would have come from Brussels."

Jerry had insisted on accompanying her as far as the Montparnasse Métro stop so as not to be kept in suspense any longer than necessary. He had taken a streetside table here at this big and somewhat overpriced café right by the Métro, and here he had sat ever since, breathing the fumes of one of the busiest intersections of Paris, watching the crowds of pedestrians swirling by, from time to time ordering another kir in order to keep his seat—though the waiter here never gave him the evil eye when his glass was dry as an American waiter would—but mostly staring up the avenue in the direction of what he was told was still the tallest building in Paris and waiting for Sonya to reappear.

When at long last she did finally come sauntering down the street toward him, she certainly seemed to be taking her own sweet time, and when she finally sat down at the table, she had the most peculiar and unreadable expression on her face, definitely not depressed, but somehow not elated either. Bemused might be the word for it.

"Well?" Jerry demanded.

"Well, as I believe you say in America, there is good news and bad news," Sonya said, her mouth smiling but her eyes somewhat glazed over with some unreadable emotion.

"Well for chrissakes, spit it out, Sonya!" Jerry cried.

"Just a minute," Sonya said, and she crooked her finger at the passing waiter. "Champagne, s'il vous plaît, la bouteille le meilleur de la maison!"

"You're ordering champagne?" Jerry said, much relieved. "Then what's the *bad* news?"

"The champagne is for the *bad* news, maybe," she said enigmatically. "But first the good news. The good news is that I had a meeting with Vladimir Moulenko, the head of the economic strategy department, and we hit it off quite well even though he was apparently being told what to do by Moscow, and they're willing to transfer me to Paris and give me a job in Moulenko's department with a raise of five hundred ECU a month. . . ."

"That's wonderful!" Jerry cried. "But . . . but . . . but then how can there be any bad news?"

The waiter arrived with a silver ice bucket on a stand, a bottle of champagne, and two glasses. He set the glasses down before them with a little flourish and started to peel back the foil on the bottle.

"Non, non, pas maintenant, s'il vous plaît, peut-être après," Sonya told him, holding up her hand. The waiter shrugged, put the champagne in the ice bucket, and departed.

"What did you do that for?" Jerry asked.

"I said this champagne is for the bad news, if that's what it is," Sonya told him. "We'll open it after I tell you if you want to."

"Will you stop playing games and tell me already!" Jerry moaned.

"The bad news, if that is what it is," Sonya said, with a strange little smile and a shrug of her shoulders, "is that first we have to get married."

"*What!*"

"There was another man at the meeting, name of Sasha Ulanov. He introduced himself as a public relations expert from Tass, but he could have been KGB. Apparently someone in Brussels or Moscow or possibly Paris has figured out a way to protect you from the wrath of the Americans and score a public relations coup in France in the bargain. If we get married, the Americans will have to go relatively quietly according to this Ulanov, or face a propaganda disaster, seeing as how the romantic Russians will have already announced that they are more than willing to transfer their socialist Juliet to Paris to be with her American Romeo. The French will love it, and whatever the Americans do or say, the matter of the sat-sled technology will be lost in all the juicy copy about star-crossed lovers."

Sonya cocked her head at Jerry, gave him a fey little smile. "Ulanov says Tass will even pay for the wedding," she said.

She reached out and put her hand on the champagne bottle. "So what do you say, Jerry, do we now open this bottle?"

"Is . . . is that a proposal . . . ?" Jerry stammered, quite dumbfounded.

"I do believe it is," Sonya said. "I mean, what real choice have we? After all, if it doesn't work out, we can always get divorced later."

"That's not very romantic," Jerry said.

"Is that an acceptance . . . ?"

"We *don't* have much of a choice, do we?"

Sonya reached across the table, squeezed his hand, and for a moment, at least, her smile was properly radiant. She reached into the ice bucket, pulled out the bottle, uncorked it, and let it foam all over the table, and her dress, and his pants before she poured it.

"Look at it this way, love," she said, "it is, after all, summer, and we are young, and in Paris, and celebrating our betrothal with the best bottle of champagne in a Montparnasse bistro, and by so doing, thwarting the bureaucratic killjoys of East and West and achieving both our hearts' desires in the bargain. . . . How much more romantic can you get? Do we really need Gypsy violins and flowers?"

Jerry laughed, and clinked glasses, and in that very moment realized how truly in love with this woman he really was, how right what they were doing was in some crazy fashion, if for all the wrong reasons.

"I'll drink to that!" he said, and they raised their glasses high with a dramatic gesture, drained them dry messily, reached across the table, embraced and kissed with the empty glasses still in their hands.

And as they did, Jerry heard a spattering of hand claps, and when he looked, he saw that all around them patrons of the sidewalk café had risen to their feet and were smiling and applauding.

"If only they knew . . . ," Jerry murmured, blushing happily.

"Ah but they do, love, they do," Sonya declared gaily. "We *are,* after all, in Paris."

Sonya laughed. She had heard of this before, but she really didn't believe it. "You really insist on doing such a thing, Jerry?" she said.

"I sure do," Jerry told her, "it's a romantic old American custom."

"What a strange phallocratic notion of romanticism," Sonya said as he unbolted the three locks to the apartment they had finally chosen, on the third floor of an old building on the Île St.-Louis.

Twenty-four hours after the proposal of marriage that had really come from Moscow, they had found themselves making it legal in front of a French magistrate, that evening there had been a little dinner party in a wedding palace high atop the Eiffel Tower, attended by Pierre Glautier, her new boss Vladimir Moulenko, Sasha Ulanov, three of Jerry's colleagues from the European Space Agency, and half again as many reporters, and then off for five days of honeymoon in a quiet little hotel way up in the Scottish Highlands, a welcome contrast to everything that had transpired in the past two weeks to put them there.

And now, here they were, at the door of their new apartment, about to begin married life together, without really having had time to catch their breath!

"Okay," Jerry said, pushing open the door, "here goes!" And with a little grunt, he actually managed to snatch her up off her feet and carry her shakily across the threshold, through the little entrance foyer, and into the bright noonday sunlight of the parlor.

"Well, here we are," Jerry said, dropping her back on her feet, "that wasn't so bad, now was it?"

The furniture they had ordered from several different establishments along the Rue du Faubourg-St.-Antoine would not begin arriving for hours, and the parlor, like the rest of the three-room apartment, was quite bare. But the walls had been freshly painted a pristine white, and the cobwebs had been swept from the high exposed beam ceiling, and the big windows freshly washed, and the floor waxed to a warm woody glow, and everything smelled of paint, wax, and cleanser.

It was hot and stuffy in the sunny room, and Jerry went to open the windows. "Wait a minute, love," Sonya said, "smell this place with me for a moment as it is now."

Jerry gave her a peculiar look, but came away from the windows and put his arm around her waist. "Take a good deep breath before you open the windows," Sonya told him. "Can you smell it?"

Jerry wrinkled his nose. "Smells like paint and ammonia to me," he said.

Sonya laughed. "Some romantic you are, Jerry Reed!" she said. "Take another breath! Doesn't it smell like *newness?* Doesn't it smell like a whole new life together? Doesn't it smell like *the future* waiting to happen, Mr. Urban Spaceman?"

Jerry laughed. He squeezed her waist. He smiled at her and gave her a little kiss.

Sonya kissed him back, stood there a little longer, smelling the magic odor of this frozen moment that she knew could never quite come again, and wondered why her happiness was spiced with just a frisson of fear.

But then, with a little sigh, she shrugged it off. "All right, love," she said, "open the windows wide and let it in!"

Jerry Reed stood there before the wide-open windows of his Parisian apartment, with his arm around his Russian bride, looking out across the Seine at the stonework quay and the strangely French buildings of the Right Bank, inhaling the foreign odors blowing in on the warm breeze, and for a moment it all seemed quite unreal, as if he were not really himself, but a character in some science-fiction story, standing atop the air-lock gangway of his spaceship setting eyes for the first time on an unknown alien world.

As in some sense, he thought, I am.

The American Embassy had indeed lifted his passport, but had made no move to revoke his citizenship; once the deed was done they controlled the damage as best they could by more or less holding their peace. ESA had gotten him a peculiar sort of Common Europe passport that required no renunciation of his American citizenship, so in a legal sense, his nationality had not really changed.

Still, as he stood there looking out on the river, he suddenly seemed to be moving down it, standing high on the bridge of a ship that was the Île St.-Louis, pulling away from the shore of all that was familiar, and out to an unknown sea.

And although this was a feeling that he had in some way spent his whole life pursuing, he found that in the real world, the beginning of such an adventure did not come without a certain formless dread.

But then a big glassed-in tour boat came plowing up the river past him and he heard the distant tinny voice of the guide babbling through the P.A. system in windblown incomprehensible French, and the illusion was shattered, and the Île St.-Louis was no longer moving beneath his feet, and he was back in the living room of his apartment with Sonya, with the woman with whom he had shared so much, and Paris was just Paris, and all was right with the world.

"A ruble for your thoughts," Sonya said quietly beside him. "No, make that an ECU, since we are now both Common Europeans together."

Jerry laughed. "Oh, nothing much," he said. "I was just thinking how standing here with you right now is like the storybook ending of some romantic novel. . . ."

"So it is, so it is," Sonya said, snuggling up against him. " 'And they both lived happily ever after.' "

PART TWO

RUSSIAN
SPRING

Representative Carson: "Just talking out loud what most of the mealy-mouths in this town are thinking privately, you understand, Billy, but we gotta do *something* about the mess the Peens and the Japs got us into, don't we? They tricked us into borrowing all that money like a gang of sleazy loan sharks, didn't they? And now they own more of this country than we do!"

Billy Allen: "But in every movie I've ever seen, the loan sharks *break your kneecaps* if you try to stiff them!"

Representative Carson: "What are they gonna do, send the Red Army up Pennsylvania Avenue to collect what we owe them?"

Billy Allen: "Well, when you put it that way, Harry . . ."

Representative Carson: "If Brazil and Argentina could do it, why can't we?"

Billy Allen: "But we *didn't* let them get away with it!"

Representative Carson: "But *they* weren't sitting on enough nukes to turn the Eastern Hemisphere into a parking lot, now were they? And they didn't have Battlestar America, now did they?"

Billy Allen: "If you got it, flaunt it, hey?"

—*Newspeak*, with Billy Allen

I X

It wasn't quite raining when Jerry Reed left the family apartment on Avenue Trudaine, but as usual for one of these Greenhouse Februarys, it looked as if it might, billowy gray clouds hanging low over Paris under a thin cool mist that turned Sacré-Coeur into a ghostly white specter.

The climate, like the city, hadn't changed much from year

to year, not so that you could notice it happening, but on a morning like this, with twenty years of his life about to pivot on this single meeting, Jerry found himself in a rare retrospective mood as he walked through the familiar neighborhood toward the Pigalle Métro station and realized, perhaps for the first time, that the winter weather of Paris had come to resemble nothing so much as his dim recollections of San Francisco.

The borderland between the 18th and the 9th had slowly and imperceptibly evolved too. Back when he and Sonya had bought the place on Trudaine, this had been a relatively cheap and sleazy area, and they had been considered something of urban pioneers for daring to move up here with two young children.

Then the real estate agents had taken to calling it "Montmartre Bis," and the prices went up, and the grungy stores started to be replaced with fancy boutiques and pâtisseries and sleek brasseries, and the produce in the open-air market improved, and the Place Pigalle got a modern hotel and a refurbished Métro station and expensive restaurants, and the crummy sex shops and porn houses gave way to an ENO and an FNAC and a thematic mini-mall version of themselves, and without being able to figure out quite when it had happened, Jerry and Sonya and the kids found themselves living in a fashionable neighborhood.

Life in Paris seemed to go like that. The climate got imperceptibly warmer, the neighborhood slowly gentrified, his French gradually improved, and voilà, here he was without quite knowing how he had gotten here, known at the pâtisserie, and the fruit market, and the dry cleaner's, and the corner brasserie, and the father of two teenaged children, sauntering down the boulevard like a comfortable old Parisian.

Or so at least it could seem in moments like this, out on the street in the penumbra of the Butte Montmartre, away from the endless sniping between Bob and Franja, away from Sonya and her political blathering, and for the moment, at least, not yet immersed again in the politics that had poisoned his career.

Politics! Politique politicienne! Why couldn't people just be left alone to "do their own thing," as they used to say in California half a lifetime ago?

They *had* let him do his own thing all during the Project

Icarus design phase. Ian Bannister was a hands-on engineer who ran his équipe on a strictly pragmatic basis, he appreciated Jerry's sat-sled experience, and Jerry had been happy as the proverbial clam.

Politique politicienne hadn't intruded until the design phase was completed, the prototype spacetug certified for production, and the design team disbanded.

There had been a big party with lots of champagne out at the Le Bourget atelier to celebrate the completion of the project. The bar was set up on sawhorses in front of the prototype itself, there were many toasts to the fruit of their long labor, and everyone was pleasantly high by the time Nicola Brandusi thanked them all for a job well done and announced their new assignments. Bannister was awarded the assistant project manager's post on the Spaceville preliminary design team. Kurt Froehmer got the job of overseeing the design of the tanker upper stage of the Energia boosters. Brizot got the tanker maneuvering systems. Constantine got the tanker docking collar.

Jerry waited with pleasant anticipation as Brandusi went down the list, an anticipation that grew tenser, however, with every promotion that Brandusi announced. Everyone on the Icarus équipe, down to the junior engineers, seemed to be getting a choice slot on the Spaceville Project or the tankers, and indeed they all deserved it. But what was going to be left for him?

"Alain Parmentier has been named chief engineer of the Icarus propulsion and maneuvering system ground-testing crew, and Jerry Reed will be his assistant, a promotion which comes with a five-hundred-ECU-a-month raise. . . ."

This outrage was announced with a fatuous smile as if it were some choice plum, while Jerry stood there like a fool with his mouth hanging open as Brandusi quickly passed on to the next name on his list.

Ground-testing! Certifying existing hardware! It wasn't fair! It was an insult! He was a designer, not a glorified quality-control tech! Without him, the maneuvering and propulsion systems wouldn't even exist!

For long minutes after he had finished speaking, Brandusi tried to avoid Jerry and tried to brush him off when Jerry braced him at the bar. But Jerry was having none of it, and when Brandusi saw that the alternative was going to be an ugly public scene, he finally let Jerry drag him off into a quiet corner and vent his wrath.

The Italian just stood there taking it with infuriating urbanity as Jerry chewed him out, looking not so much at him as through him, letting Jerry rant and rave until the nonresponse finally wore him down.

"Come, come, Jerry," Brandusi said when Jerry was good and finished, "for you it will be excellent and necessary experience. Parmentier is a bureaucrat, so you will really be in charge in the lab, and it will be your first chance to prove yourself as a supervisor, as well as hands-on experience with the actual hardware."

"Running quality-control tests on hardware I designed myself!"

Brandusi gave him a fatuous smile. "Hardware you *assisted* in designing," he corrected.

"Without me—"

"Without you, it would have taken a few more years, your contribution was indeed significant," Brandusi said. "Which is why your salary was higher than that of anyone else in the project of comparable age and experience. . . . But now . . ." He shrugged. "Now that the . . . special circumstances are over, well, you are still making more money than people with quite a bit more seniority, and I have to consider the, ah, shall we say, *social equity* of the situation, you understand. . . ."

"And what if I refuse to go along with this bullshit?" Jerry demanded.

Brandusi shrugged, threw up his hands, and that was the end of the conversation. Sonya had just given birth to Franja, there was no place else for Jerry to go, Brandusi knew it, and he knew that Jerry knew that he knew it too, the bastard.

There was only one hope. He had spotted André Deutcher at the bar, and André these days had long since emerged from his shadowy role as a headhunter and "technology transfer expert" and was involved in the Soviet-European consortium that was building and marketing the Daedalus, which the press had promptly rechristened the "Concordski." He might not be Brandusi's superior, but he did move in higher circles. Surely Jerry's old buddy André could do a little leaning on his behalf.

But when he finally cornered André Deutcher, André fidgeted, shook his head, gave him the old Gallic shrug. "I am long out of that particular circuit, Jerry. I'm not even in the ESA chain of command."

"Chain of command, my ass, André! You're way up there with the big boys now! You do some leaning, and Brandusi will feel the weight!"

André frowned. "You are forcing me to be painfully honest with you, Jerry. . . ."

"At least a little honesty would be a novelty around here!" Jerry shot back.

André sighed. "I'm afraid that you're the victim of larger considerations," he said. "Soviet technology is already being intimately integrated into the cutting edge of the ESA program. . . ."

"So what?"

André gave him a somewhat furtive and embarrassed look. "It might unduly disturb our partners to give someone like you too intimate an access to Soviet space technology. . . ."

"What do you mean, *'someone like me'?*"

"You know," André said uneasily.

"No I don't!"

André Deutcher sighed. "An American . . . ," he said. "One who has already been involved in, shall we say, a bit of gray technology transfer in the opposite direction. . . . Someone who the Americans might just have willingly given up in order to plant a mole in the ESA program. . . ."

"That's ridiculous!"

"You know it, and I know it," André said, "but the Russians . . ." He shrugged. "C'est la politique," he said.

"Politique *politicienne!*" Jerry shot back. His French might still have been pretty primitive at the time, but he knew enough to make the uniquely French distinction between legitimate political necessity and bullshit bureaucratic backstabbing. "C'est la merde!"

But he was in it.

That had been a long time ago, but "politique politicienne" was still Jerry Reed's contemptuous conversation stopper whenever anyone tried to justify the way ESA had treated him all these years in terms of the petty maneuverings in Strasbourg, or the endless negotiating of the details of the Soviet Union's entry into Common Europe, or what the United States was presently doing in Venezuela.

But Jerry had inevitably found himself involved in another sort of politics, at which he had become something of a grudging adept, and which, he earnestly hoped as he trotted down the stairs of the Pigalle Métro station, would finally, at long last, pay off today.

When he sobered up that next morning, he had realized that he had no choice but to accept the inevitable, and later, accepted Parmentier's old post too, when his superior was promoted, even though it meant the same tedious old thing at a higher salary.

Once again, there was no real choice. Bob was already a year old, the place on the Île was just too small, and the raise was just big enough to let Sonya and him swing a three-bedroom apartment near Pigalle by mortgaging themselves up to the eyeballs.

Two years after that, he made second assistant head of all ground testing, then first assistant, and finally section chief. From there, he became chief engineer in charge of prototype fabrication, realizing other people's designs for Spaceville construction equipment.

Finally, they had made him chief project engineer on the LEO to GEO freighter project, merely scaling up the spacetugs and designing big freight pallets for them to ferry to the Spaceville construction site.

And there he had languished for the last five years. Space was farther away than ever, they hadn't let him work on the cutting edge since Project Icarus, and maybe, just maybe, they would have finally made him a project director before he retired if they could have found something trivial enough to trust to an expatriate American.

What had kept Jerry going through all those long dark days was the vision that had come to him at the very beginning, back when he first left Rockwell and sat sleds to work on Project Icarus for ESA.

As it had been obvious to Rob Post that the Rockwell Advanced Maneuverable Warhead Bus could be upscaled into a LEO-to-GEO space jeep, so had it been obvious to Jerry that the Icarus spacetug technology could be developed into something like a real spaceliner, no doubt because he had seen how Rob had done his clandestine redesign of the AMB.

The idea, after all, was quite similar.

Scale up the propulsion system. Attach it to the end of a

long boom extending through the midline of a great big mother of a balloon fuel tank. Sling a simple framework with lock-on clamps to the balloon tank and you could carry any configuration of freight and passenger modules you chose.

It could take a hundred passengers from Low Earth Orbit to Spaceville or even the Moon fast and in comfort. With a big enough balloon tank it could go to Mars with enough payload to make permanent colonization possible. Since there was no limit on the size of the fuel balloon, you might even be able to configure it to support expeditions as far out as Jupiter. It would be a great leap forward into space, using nothing more arcane than scaled-up available technology.

While he was still working on Project Icarus, Jerry hadn't done anything with the notion, assuming that after the spacetug became operational he would be promoted into some position where he could persuade his superiors to get an official preliminary design study funded, with himself as the head of the team.

When that didn't happen, he started working on the design at home, knowing that no one would listen to a mere test engineer, that even if they did, the project would be taken away from him. The time to surface the concept would be when ESA moved him back into the design end.

When they made him ground-test chief instead, Jerry started talking about upscaling the spacetug around the atelier. He might be merely in charge of testing hardware, but at least he *was* a chief engineer, meaning he had younger people working under him who would be eager to listen to their boss's babble, or at least pretend to be.

Soon enough, he had members of his équipe fooling around with the designs, speculating on how the hardware they were testing might be modified for use in the fantasy project, and the thing started to take on a life of its own, especially since ESA had nothing beyond Spaceville on its drawing boards to capture the visionary imagination of its younger engineers and workers.

One day, one of the brightest of the young engineers working under him, a Belgian named Emile Lourade who was rather taken with his American boss, put a bug in his ear.

"This little fantasy of ours, it is becoming talk in ESA

outside our équipe, Jerry," Emile told him. "It becomes a small Agency legend, you must be careful. . . ."

"Careful of what, Emile?"

They were sitting at a small table in the crowded commissary together, speaking in English amid a multilingual cacophony that was nevertheless, like ESA itself, rather dominantly French. Emile leaned closer and ran his eyes around the room with exaggerated furtiveness.

Jerry laughed. "Yeah, I know that you Belgians are the Polish jokes of France," he said, "but—"

"You Americans are a lot worse than a joke, and not just with the French, surely you know that . . . ," Emile said.

"Yeah, well . . ."

The early talk about Soviet entry into Common Europe was already in the air, Washington was making vague threats, the dollar had been devalued again to the discomfort of European holders of American paper, Battlestar America was just about fully deployed, and "Festung Amerika" was a buzzword in the European press. Americans were about as highly thought of in Common Europe these days as Europeans were in the United States.

"Someday, this spaceliner idea of yours is going to be taken seriously by ESA," Emile told him. "And if you do not take care to see to it that it does not simply seem to arise out of the ESA bureaucracy itself, what chance do you really think there is that they will let an *American* play a major role in the project, let alone be the chief of the design team?"

"Slim and none . . . ," Jerry had muttered, quite touched by Emile's concern.

But what to do about it?

Sonya was rising steadily in the Red Star bureaucracy by this time, already earning a larger salary than he did, and Jerry seldom discussed his career dissatisfactions with his wife anymore, it was just too painful, and productive of nothing but strife. But this time he did. And for once Sonya was sympathetic.

"This friend of yours is absolutely right!" she declared forcefully. "You must take steps to protect your position at once. It is the iron law of bureaucracy—cover your ass!"

"Great, just great. And how am I supposed to do that?"

"Attach your name to this idea in the press."

"Yeah, maybe I should give an interview to your friends at Tass," Jerry snapped sarcastically.

"Too political . . . ," Sonya said quite seriously. "I have a much better idea."

And she did. She set him up with an old friend of hers, a journalist named Pierre Glautier. Glautier wrote a piece called "La Grand Tour Navette," part popular science and part personality profile, which was published in a French popular science and science-fiction magazine called *Esprit et Espace,* and voilà, the project had a sexy name in French, and his name was epoxied to it.

The ESA bureaucracy was not amused—particularly since there was already grumbling in the ranks over the fact that the Spaceville Project was eating up so much of the Agency's budget that nothing half as visionary as the Grand Tour Navette was even in the design-study stage—and, as Jerry had expected, Nicola Brandusi called him on the carpet.

But this time it was Brandusi's turn to rant and rave impotently at a fait accompli and Jerry's turn to smile blandly when he was done.

"Gee, Nicola," he said ingenuously, "I thought you'd be pleased. I mean, it's good P.R. for the Agency, isn't it? Shows we're still looking to the future, especially with the stuff you're starting to hear about how ESA's so bogged down with Spaceville that it's conceding the rest of the solar system to the Russians. . . ."

Brandusi seemed to buy this display of naiveté. "Employees of ESA are not supposed to discuss Agency projects with the press without authorization, surely you know that, Jerry . . . ," he said with the exaggeratedly patient tones of someone talking to a dimwit.

"Well sure I know that," Jerry said sweetly. "But I thought the Grand Tour Navette was just my own crazy idea. Now you're telling me it's an official ESA project?"

"No, it is *not* under official consideration!" Brandusi snapped.

"Well then where's the harm in my talking about it?" Jerry said. "I mean, if you put a lid on it now, won't it look like an ESA project instead of my own little hobby?"

"No! Yes! Arrr!" Brandusi rolled his eyes skyward in exasperated frustration, but as Jerry well knew, there was really nothing he could do, for the cat was already out of the bag, and any attempt to stuff it back in would only make the noisome creature that much more conspicuous. They couldn't shut him up now, nor could they fire him.

Of course, they could, and did, take bureaucratic vengeance.

While Jerry became a hero to the lower scientific and engineering echelons of the Agency as the "Father of the Grand Tour Navette," the powers that be kept him on as chief testing engineer long after most of his original équipe, including Emile Lourade, were promoted up and out.

And his eventual promotion to chief engineer of the prototype fabrication section was mainly the result of internal pressure from people like Emile, who were now chafing rather loudly at the budgetary policy that was turning ESA into little more than an arm of the consortium building Spaceville, which these "Space Cadets," as they had already begun to call themselves defiantly, saw as draining the lifeblood out of the Common Europe space program.

Jerry found himself drawn deeper and deeper into the Space Cadet movement, speaking at unofficial seminars, appearing from time to time at science-fiction conventions, giving the occasional press interview, becoming the point man for the Grand Tour Navette Project, if not entirely against his will, then certainly against his hope of career advancement.

For the more the Space Cadets agitated for a commitment to the project against the will of the bureaucracy, the more that bureaucracy took out its displeasure on the most obviously available target, the adopted godfather of the Space Cadets and father of the Grand Tour Navette, the American in their midst, Jerry Reed.

Finally, when Space Cadets like Emile Lourade, Gunter Schmitz, Franco Nuri, and Patrice Corneau began percolating into upper middle management, the movement had enough clout within the Agency, if not to ram through a Grand Tour Navette design study, then at least to get their mentor into the design end again at last.

But the higher-ups put a nasty little spin on it, making him chief engineer on the LEO to GEO freighter project, where, with an irony that was lost on no one, he was constrained to spend his time and energies essentially *scaling down* the visionary Grand Tour Navette concept into mere automated freighters to ferry construction material from Low Earth Orbit to Spaceville.

Perhaps they thought this would get him to resign from the Agency in terminal disgust, perhaps this was merely their symbolic means of slapping down the Space Cadets and their pet project, but either way, Jerry had no place to go, so once more, he accepted the inevitable, hung in, hunkered down, and waited.

And now, it appeared, his endless patience was finally about to be rewarded.

The negotiations between the Russians and Strasbourg had ripened to the point where the entry of the Soviet Union into Common Europe had become inevitable, and all that was left was the thrashing out of the details.

One of which was the extent to which the Soviet and Common European space programs would be merged and who would contribute how much to what kind of budget. And the Russians were being sticky about it.

ESA had plenty to gain from the Russians. The Soviets had four large Cosmograds in Low Earth Orbit. They had a new generation of Heavy Lift Vehicles with twice the payload of the old Energias. They had a permanent scientific base on the Moon. They fielded repeat expeditions to Mars and were talking about a permanent base.

What Common Europe could offer in return was not very much. The Soviets were already co-producers of the Concordski. The orbital tankers were modified Russian hardware, Spaceville was being cobbled together from the same, leaving the Soviets understandably reluctant to participate in a project from which they had nothing to gain in the way of new technology. About the only thing Common Europe had to offer was a merged space budget under which the Soviet end of the program would be the net financial gainer, and that went over like a ripe fart with the Common European Parliament.

Then Emile Lourade made his mysterious trip to Strasbourg.

Emile, by this time, had risen to director of the advanced planning section, the highest any of the Space Cadets had gone, but something of a hollow position, since there were no advanced projects on the drawing boards and still no hope for any in the budget for years to come.

No one knew what had really happened. Emile had apparently made the trip on his own. He had stayed in Strasbourg for a week. He had testified behind closed doors to Parliamentary committees. He had had meetings with Ministers.

When he came back to Paris, everyone had expected the Agency Director, Armand Labrenne, to fire him for insubordination. Instead, to the amazement of everyone, a week later Labrenne announced his sudden retirement for "health reasons," and Emile Lourade was named Director of the European Space Agency.

And now his old protégé and friend Emile had summoned Jerry Reed to a meeting only two days after his appointment.

It was raining as Jerry arrived at ESA headquarters, but the weather couldn't dampen his spirits, for while he could not quite conceive of what Emile Lourade had said to the politicians to make himself Director, he was quite sure he knew what *this* meeting was about.

That one of Emile's first acts as Director was to summon the father of the Grand Tour Navette to his office could mean only one thing. Indeed, that a Space Cadet like Emile Lourade had replaced Labrenne so suddenly after whatever had happened in Strasbourg was a loud, clear declaration that *his* Space Cadets had been put in charge of the Agency to change its direction.

At long, long last, the Grand Tour Navette was going to become an official European Space Agency project.

And of course, Emile was going to make him chief project engineer, or perhaps even project director.

That his dream was about to come true was only just, but that his old friend Emile should be the man to give him the good news, ah, that was the chocolate syrup on his bowl of Häagen-Dazs.

"Dimitri Pavelovich Smerlak had harsh words today for those who would allow petty national chauvinisms to intrude themselves into the treaty negotiations.

" 'The national allocations of Soviet seats in the Common European Parliament cannot and will not be a subject of discussion between the Soviet government and Common Europe,' the President declared. 'The spectacle of Ukrainians and Kazhaks picketing their own embassy in Geneva is shameful. They are only resorting to such obstructive tactics because they have no hope of gerrymandering national quotas in the democratically elected Supreme Soviet. And we will never consider allowing internal Soviet election laws to be subject to review by the Common European Parliament.' "

—*Vremya*

Heads nodded and faces smiled as Sonya Gagarin Reed came bustling through the data pit on the way to her office, late again after breaking up yet another breakfast shouting match between Franja and Robert.

"Good morning, Sonya."

"Good morning, Comrade Gagarin."

The computer slaves called her "Sonya" if they had been there long enough and "Comrade Gagarin" if they were still wet behind the ears, for Sonya had long since taken to calling herself "Sonya Ivanovna Gagarin" at work, as if that were going to solve her problems with the elusive Moscow Mandarins.

Once, you could have pointed an unambiguous finger at Party commissars or the KGB, and once, they would have made their wishes bluntly obvious and the penalties painfully clear. But this was the Russian Spring, and it simply would not do to remind anyone of the governmental nature of Red Star, S.A., or for the KGB to be caught transmitting diktats to its employees in the West.

Thus the Moscow Mandarinate, the nebulous level between official government circles and the upper management of Red Star. Officially, of course, it did not exist. Officially Red Star was an independent corporation chartered under Common European law whose majority stockholder just happened to be the government of the Soviet Union. Officially its decisions were made by its own board of directors.

But in the real world, Red Star was an organ of the Soviet State, connected to the policy level by the interconnected and interpenetrating bureaucracies of the Party and the government. You could never quite focus on who or what back in Moscow pulled which strings, but the Moscow Mandarins

had no trouble at all passing their displeasure down the line
to *you.*

Sonya disappeared into what she still thought of as her
new office, closed the door behind her, and sank into the
swivel chair behind her desk. There was an electric espresso
machine on the desk as well as a smart videotel, and an
untidy mess of correspondence and printouts, and she
thumbed the coffee maker on and waited impatiently for
the ninety seconds it took to cough up the day's first cup.

Red Star might have built its very own building here on
the newly trendy Avenue Kennedy in the always-chic Trocadéro end of the 16th, but the assistant head of the economic strategy department didn't rate a major office with a
real view. Still, this little office *did* have a window peeking
around the edge of the neighboring Sony building on her
own tiny slice of the Seine, and at least it *was* finally hers.

It had certainly taken her long enough to get here! If she
was not quite in disfavor, she knew full well that she had
long been skating on thin bureaucratic ice, for she had only
finally acceded to this position by plodding bureaucratic seniority, which was not the way things usually worked in the
Red Star meritocracy at all.

By rights, she should have been *department head* long ago;
she had been in the economic strategy department longer
than anyone, she knew France far better than any of the
timeservers they had brought in from Russia above her, and
it was only Jerry who had kept her from advancing as she
should have.

That had once more been made painfully clear when they
had brought Ilya Pashikov in from Moscow to be department head above her two months ago instead of giving her
the job when Gorski left for the London post.

Indeed Pashikov himself had seemed rather embarrassed
at their first meeting in the big corner office. He had admitted with rather engaging forthrightness that she should have
been seated behind the big old walnut desk instead of himself. "But under the circumstances . . . ," he had said,
without quite meeting her gaze. And she had not been
crude enough to force him to amplify.

For she knew only too well that she was in political purdah. Oh yes, they had given her her Party card or she would
never have even gotten this far, but her kharakteristika had

plenty of good-sized gray marks, if not quite any great big black one.

She had never worked in the Soviet Union. She had secured this coveted Parisian posting in a politically shady manner, which, while it spoke favorably for her negotiating abilities, made her political loyalties slightly suspect.

More to the point, she was married to an American, who, while he might be considered a traitor by Washington, was still perversely American enough to refuse the benefits of Soviet citizenship to her own children.

She had ranted and raved at Jerry for weeks after Pashikov had come in over her, but he would have none of it. His eyes would glaze over, and he would mutter "politique politicienne," and he would disappear back into outer space.

The coffee came whooshing and foaming into the cup, and Sonya gulped half of it down. Why couldn't he understand? It could be so *easy*. It wasn't as if she was asking him to renounce his own American citizenship. All he had to do was let Robert and Franja become citizens of the Soviet Union, as was their right under Soviet law.

But no—

The intercom buzzed. "Ilya here, Sonya, where have you been, I've been—"

"I'm sorry, Comrade Pashikov, the children—"

"Yes, yes, well, will you please come to my office right now—"

"If you'll just give me a few minutes to get together the daily—"

"Never mind the daily update for now, we can go over that after lunch," Pashikov said, "this is about another matter."

Sonya somehow didn't like the sound of that, and when she reached the Director's office, she didn't like the look on Ilya Pashikov's face either.

She and Pashikov had developed a peculiar relationship, somewhat strained on the one hand, yet on the other less strained than it could have been under the circumstances.

Pashikov was a few years younger than Sonya, with elegantly coifed long blond hair very much à la mode, clear blue eyes, and dramatically chiseled, almost Tartar features, and he wore his expensively tailored clothes like a model and moved like a dancer. He was one attractive male animal, Sonya could not help but find him attractive, and oh yes, he knew it.

It would have been insufferable if he had acknowledged this, but Ilya Pashikov was very much the suave Eurorussian man of the world; indeed, since this was his first assignment outside the Soviet Union, he worked hard at it.

Pashikov was clearly one of the Moscow Mandarinate's favorite sons; what for Sonya was the long-denied apex to an ordinary bureaucratic career was for him only a way station on a fast-track rise to the top of the Red Star hierarchy, and perhaps beyond. Ilya Pashikov was undeniably *connected*.

If Sonya was overqualified to be his assistant, Pashikov was a bit underqualified to be director of the economic strategy department, and one of his charms was that it seemed to embarrass him, at least in her presence. He relied upon her to put together the reports and strategy papers which he delivered to the Paris director as his own and let his embarrassment at that show too from time to time.

Pashikov looked embarrassed right now, but there was something squirmy and furtive about it, which had never at all been Ilya's style.

"Problems with Robert and Franja again?" he said as he poured her a glass of tea from the samovar.

Sonya shrugged. "The usual big sister, younger brother business," she said, "you know teenagers!"

Pashikov shrugged. "I'm afraid I do not," he said, "single as I unfortunately am. . . ."

"Yes, I know," Sonya said dryly, "and you find it a great hardship."

Ilya laughed. "I manage to survive, with a little help from my lady friends," he admitted.

"Surely we are not here to discuss my children or your love life, Ilya Sergeiovich. . . ."

Pashikov frowned. "As you know, I am not one to meddle in your domestic affairs," he said, "but . . ."

"But?"

Pashikov drummed his fingers nervously on the desktop. "This is not my idea, you understand, I find this rather embarrassing. . . ." he muttered, avoiding her eyes.

"There is an old Russian proverb which I have just made up," Sonya told him. " 'When you find yourself with a turd in your mouth, it is best to either swallow it immediately or spit it out at once, considering the flavor.' "

Pashikov laughed. "It's about the new Director of the European Space Agency. . . ." he blurted.

Sonya cocked her head at him expectantly.

"Emile Lourade . . . ? He is an old friend of your husband, is he not?"

Jerry is meeting with him right now, Sonya's instincts kept her from saying. "In a manner of speaking . . . ," she said instead.

"Something very peculiar is going on at the European Space Agency, surely being married to Jerry Reed, you know that much . . . ," Pashikov said slowly.

"You mean about the way Emile Lourade suddenly became Director?"

Pashikov nodded. "He goes to Strasbourg, it would seem not at all under orders from Armand Labrenne. He talks privately with delegates and Ministers. He testifies to Parliamentary committees at closed meetings, which the KGB is unable to penetrate. When he comes back to Paris, Labrenne resigns for so-called health reasons, even though his medical records, which the KGB *was* able to access, show nothing of the kind, and Lourade becomes Director. . . ."

"So?" Sonya said.

"So you tell me. . . ."

"Tell you what?"

"What happened?"

"I don't understand. . . ."

"Neither do we," Pashikov told her. "That's the whole point."

"I don't mean to seem dimwitted, Ilya Sergeiovich, but I do not get the point," Sonya said. "What does any of this have to do with Red Star?"

Pashikov drummed his fingers on the desktop again. "Red Star may not be officially involved in the negotiations for the Soviet Union's entry into Common Europe, but as you know, from time to time we are . . . asked to assist with information by various agencies. . . ."

"Like the KGB?"

"Not this time," Pashikov said quickly. "This request comes from the Space Ministry, they are the ones handling the negotiations that will determine the nature and contractual terms for the merger of the Soviet and Common Europe space programs when we enter Common Europe. The negotiations have reached a rather sticky point over budgetary shares, and now . . . *this!*"

"Now *what?*"

"That's exactly what our negotiators would like to know as quickly as possible!" Pashikov exclaimed.

"Surely that sort of thing is a matter for the KGB, not our economic strategy department. . . ."

Pashikov shrugged, and the furtiveness which had evaporated during all this came rushing back. "Ordinarily that would be true," he said. "But under the circumstances . . ."

"Under what—" Sonya caught herself short.

"Oh," she said much more quietly.

Ilya Sergeiovich heaved a great sigh of relief. He shrugged again. "To put it delicately," he said, steepling his fingers, "the Space Ministry has officially requested a report from this department on the matter of Emile Lourade's sudden ascension, with particular emphasis on any policy changes involved that may affect the negotiations. . . . It has been suggested that . . . you prepare this report personally . . . considering the . . . unique resources at your command. . . ."

He paused, looked down at the desktop, then looked her straight in the eye for the first time during this whole séance. "We *do* understand each other fully, do we not, Sonya Gagarin . . . *Reed?*" he said softly.

Sonya stared right back. "I'm afraid we do, Ilya Sergeiovich Pashikov," she said in the same tone.

"I cannot order you to do such a thing, Sonya," Pashikov said more breezily. "There will be no official repercussions if you refuse, of course, but . . ."

He shrugged yet again, threw up his hands in quite a Gallic gesture. "But speaking as your friend," he said, "all you are really being asked to do, after all, is report a little family table talk for the good of your country, really just using what you happen to be in a position to know when you write your report, da?"

Sonya continued to stare at him. "And if I do this thing?" she said with a coldness that quite surprised her.

"It will look very good in your kharakteristika, I can promise you that much," Ilya Sergeiovich Pashikov said, "and that is your superior in the bureaucracy talking. But speaking as your friend, Sonya Ivanovna, we both know how much you need it."

FIRST HINT OF EXTRATERRESTRIAL CIVILIZATION?

An official spokesman for the astronomy section of the Soviet Academy of Science downplayed the hasty conclusions leapt to in the popular press over the anomalies reported in observations of the recently discovered fourth planet of Barnard's star by observers on Cosmograd Copernicus.

"Yes, it definitely is a solid body, not a miniature gas giant, and yes, the nightside glow is clearly from surface sources, and yes, there certainly is a suspiciously regular halo of medium-sized bodies in perfect Geosynchronous Orbit," said Dr. Pavel Budarkin. "But to announce that we have discovered an extrasolar civilization on such circumstantial evidence would be quite premature at this time."

—Tass

Emile Lourade's office was a mess. There were half-unpacked cardboard boxes all over the place, shelves heaped with as-yet-unorganized books, journals, and discs, his desk was piled with more of the same, as were the three chairs before it, and there were half a dozen framed pictures still lying on the conference table waiting to be hung. The new Director of ESA sat there in his shirtsleeves with the air of someone who didn't have the time or inclination to get his office organized before getting down to serious business.

But Jerry grinned when he noticed the one item of personal decoration that Emile had managed to get hung on the wall—a big framed blowup of the lead illustration from the old article in *Esprit et Espace* which had introduced the Grand Tour Navette to the world all those years ago.

"Sit down, Jerry, sit down," Emile said, "just throw some stuff on the floor and don't worry about it."

Jerry laughed, cleared himself a chair, sat down on it. "So here I am," Emile Lourade said, with a wry grin and a little shrug. "A long way from the quality-control atelier, n'est-ce pas?"

"A long way from where you were a few weeks ago, is what everyone is saying, Emile," Jerry told him. "What on earth did you do in Strasbourg?"

"I took the chance of a lifetime, Jerry, I risked everything," Emile said much more seriously. "And I won."

"Obviously," Jerry said dryly, "or Labrenne would have had your ass instead of a sudden attack of ill health. But what the hell did you say to the damned politicians?"

"That I knew the only way to get the Russians to put more money into the merged space budget than they were going to take out for their own projects," Emile said.

Jerry glanced at the rendering of the Grand Tour Navette that was the only thing hanging on the walls of the new Director's office, then looked back at Emile Lourade, his spirit soaring.

Emile nodded. "What else?" he said. "As far as the Russians are concerned, Spaceville is just something that allows them to make money at no financial risk by selling us Cosmograd modules and obsolescent old Energia boosters. They think we're crazy for pumping most of our space budget into the thing, and they certainly want no part of it themselves."

He shrugged, giving Jerry a wry smile. "And who are we Space Cadets to deny that they have a point?" he said. "The only reason their space people are even talking about a joint budget is that the politicians on both sides are requiring that they cut a deal with us as part of the deal for the Soviet entry into Common Europe. Space is only a small part of something much more important as far as both Moscow and Strasbourg are concerned, and if a deal is not made between our space agencies on its own merits before the treaty is ready for signatures, the politicians will simply force their own terms upon both of us. . . ."

"Politique politicienne," Jerry muttered.

Emile Lourade frowned. "That was Armand Labrenne's attitude too," he said. "And that is why I am here and he is not. One must learn to speak the language of the politicians. And one must also learn to factor their equations."

A change seemed to come over Emile Lourade, or perhaps it was merely that Jerry was finally recognizing a change that had long since occurred. For this was not the young Emile who had worked under him; this was the Director of the European Space Agency.

"Labrenne was demanding that the Russians fund 50 percent of a merged space budget," Lourade said. "This would mean a significant bailout of what Spaceville is costing us. The Russians have been standing firm for 25 percent, meaning that Strasbourg would instead be financing a big piece of their advanced programs. In a few weeks the treaty will be ready, and Strasbourg simply will not allow this minor detail to hold it up. If the Soviets just sit still and stonewall us, they know they will have things more or less their way."

Lourade curled his lip contemptuously. "Labrenne was a fool for believing he could wait the Russians out, they have had asses carved out of stone since Gromyko and Vyshinsky," he said.

"And this is what you told the politicians in Strasbourg?"

Lourade nodded. "What I told them is that what we needed was a new bargaining chip *right now,* and fortunately enough we had one, just waiting to be funded. . . ."

"The Grand Tour Navette. . . ."

Emile Lourade grinned. "The GTN is something the Russians will really want, something they can be forced to fund heavily as a joint venture. What is more, as part of a joint program, the project will finally make economic sense, as it never really has for us. . . ."

"What?" Jerry exclaimed. "But you always agreed that—"

"That it was a visionary program that was man's next step out into the solar system," Lourade said coldly. "But for ESA, it would be Spaceville all over again, and worse! Why do you think we've never been able to get it funded? Because the politicians are all imbeciles?"

"The thought had crossed my mind from time to time . . . ," Jerry said dryly.

Lourade sighed. "You really always *have* been naive, haven't you, Jerry?" he said. "What would we *do* with Grand Tour Navettes? We already have the Concordskis and the Icarus and the automated freighters, which is to say we have a complete logistical system in place for Spaceville—"

"Are you crazy, Emile?" Jerry snapped. "With the GTN, we could have our own Moonbase, colonize Mars, go to the Belt, and Jupiter, and Titan—"

"And how are we supposed to *pay* for all that after we've sunk most of our budget for years into the GTN itself?"

Emile Lourade demanded. "What return could we show on the enormous costs?"

"I never thought of that . . . ," Jerry muttered.

"Well they certainly have in Strasbourg all these years!" Lourade said harshly. "Labrenne was never against the GTN as a program. How could anyone who cared about the future in space enough to work in the Agency fail to fall in love with it? But neither Labrenne nor anyone else who understood the real world dared to present it as a budget item because everyone *knew* the politicians would never buy it."

"Until you, Emile. Until now."

Emile Lourade leaned back in his chair, clasped his hands behind his head, and gave a smile of self-satisfaction. "Not even me until the negotiations with the Russians reached this impasse," he said. "Then I realized that the merger of the Common Europe and Soviet space programs would change everything. The GTN fits into *their* program perfectly. *They* already have a scientific base on the Moon that they want to turn into a real colony. *They* have already gone to Mars and have plans to establish a permanent base. And dreams of going to Jupiter. And a preliminary feasibility study for bringing back ice with shaped nuclear charges from the Jovian moons to terraform Mars. For *them*, the numbers come out. The Grand Tour Navette can give them the solar system."

"*This* is what you told them in Strasbourg?" Jerry exclaimed, his head reeling.

"Of course," Lourade said. "Next week, a supplementary appropriation will be passed by the Common European Parliament, and the Grand Tour Navette will become an officially funded design study, and since, thanks to you, the results of such a study already exist, our negotiators will present them to the Russians as our dowry, as it were. And if they want the marriage to go through, as they surely will, they will have to agree to fund at least 40 percent of the joint space program, or the GTN will stay on the drawing boards. That will be our final offer, they will know it, and they will have to take it."

"Jesus Christ," Jerry moaned. This was the dream of his lifetime about to be funded into hardware; why this sinking feeling in the pit of his stomach?

Emile leaned forward and peered at him in puzzlement.

"What's the matter, Jerry?" he said. "This is what we've been dreaming of for years!"

"Well yeah, but . . . but . . ." Grand Tour Navettes of his design opening up the solar system, going to Mars and Jupiter and Saturn, a city on the Moon, a colony on Mars, all he had ever dreamed of and worked and hoped for . . . but . . . but . . .

"You're going to give it all to *them?*" he cried.

"Them?" Emile said ingenuously.

"The fucking Russians!" Jerry exclaimed.

Emile Lourade peered at him narrowly. "Don't you even read the papers, Jerry?" he said. *"Them* is *us,* or soon will be! We're not going to take our petty old national chauvinisms out into the solar system, we're going to build the future out there together as *Europeans!"*

"We . . . ?" Jerry said slowly. *"As Europeans?"*

Lourade shrugged. "As the human race, then," he said rather offhandedly. "Mon Dieu, Jerry, *you* were the one who believed enough in this dream in the first place to leave America to work for it here! Surely after all you've gone through, you're not going to tell me you don't want to be a part of it now that it's about to really happen because it means sharing our dream with the Russians! It wouldn't be happening without the Russians. You're *married* to a Russian! All of a sudden you're going to tell me you've turned into a Yankee chauvinist?"

"No . . . ," Jerry muttered sadly. "Of course not, I'm your man, Emile."

No, it was not anything he felt against the Russians that made him feel like crying in his hour of triumph. He was going to build his Grand Tour Navettes, and they were going to go to the Moon and Mars, and the moons of Jupiter, and the grand adventure would truly begin.

That soaring vision filled his mouth with the taste of Hershey's chocolate syrup over Häagen-Dazs chocolate ice cream, and the memory of chocolate on chocolate brought another vision to his mind's eye, the grainy video image of the onrushing lunar landscape.

And he could hear the glorious words of long ago through the years and across the vacuum and over the static: "The Eagle has landed."

And he knew it was not himself he was crying inside for. For the first time since he had left its shores in the service of the very vision which now was to be fulfilled, Jerry Reed found himself weeping inside for what had once been America.

"Are you okay, Jerry?" Emile Lourade said in a much softer tone, and for a moment the Director of ESA was the young Emile again, peering at his mentor with friendly concern. "You *do* want in?"

"Of course I do, Emile," Jerry said quickly. And in ways, he thought, that a European like you can never quite know.

"Good," Emile said, "it just wouldn't be right without you." And he was the Director again, thumbing on his intercom and speaking crisply. "You can send in Patrice Corneau now."

Jerry rose to greet Corneau as he entered the office, and allowed Patrice to kiss him on both cheeks, French-style, a casual European gesture that he had gotten over being embarrassed by, at least when it came from someone who was more than a mere acquaintance, as Patrice Corneau certainly was.

Corneau was another of Jerry's original Space Cadets, whose first job with the Agency had been under Jerry in the testing atelier, and he had worked under Jerry in the prototype équipe too, before climbing on the fast track. He had been a tall, gangling, sloppily dressed young engineer type in those days, with a mop of unruly black hair and a holder full of pens in his shirt pocket. Now he was assistant project manager on Spaceville, his hair was expensively coifed and streaked with gray, and he wore an elegantly tailored lime-green suit.

"You will be working with us on the Grand Tour Navette, of course, Jerry?" Patrice said as they seated themselves.

"Us?" Jerry said. "You're moving over from Spaceville, Patrice? But I thought you were in line for the project manager's job over there. . . ." He was quite touched that Corneau was apparently willing to give up such a career opportunity to work under him on the Grand Tour Navette.

Corneau gave Lourade a surprised look. The Director gave him a furtive and uncomfortable-looking glance back.

"You haven't told him, Emile?" Patrice said.

"Told me what?"

"I've appointed Patrice project manager on the GTN, Jerry," Emile Lourade said evenly.

The words hit Jerry like a sock in the gut. For a long

moment he just sat there frozen, staring silently and wood-enly into the Director's eyes. Emile Lourade stared just as fixedly back, with no readable emotion on his face.

Time seemed to lapse into slow motion as Jerry's mind wrestled with his emotions. Lourade, to his credit, just sat there giving him time, and that, more than anything else, finally allowed Jerry to assess the reality with cold clarity and pull himself together before he finally spoke.

"Well, I can't honestly tell you I'm not a little disap-pointed, Emile," he finally said, and then managed a wan little smile. "But I suppose you're right. I'm a designer and hands-on engineer, I'm no administrator, never have been, and I guess I never will be. . . ."

He turned to face Patrice Corneau. "Pas problem, Pa-trice," he said. "Who cares if I was once your boss? I'll be happy to work under you as chief project engineer, I mean that sincerely." And he held out his hand.

And as Patrice Corneau took it somewhat hesitantly, Jerry found, to his own surprise, that he did mean what he said. After all, he would not really enjoy hassling budgets and dealing with subcontractors. Designing the spacecraft and supervising the construction of the hardware was where the true joy of it all lay for him.

In a way, Jerry thought, I should be feeling sorry for *Patrice*. He gets to deal with all the crap, and I get to have all the fun.

"I'm afraid not, Jerry," Emile Lourade said sadly.

"What?"

"I'm afraid I can't make you chief project engineer ei-ther," the Director of the European Space Agency said, staring down at his desktop, not meeting Jerry's eyes. "You've got to understand my position. . . ."

"I've got to understand *your* motherfucking position!" Jerry shouted.

"I'm afraid I don't understand either, Emile," Patrice said. "If you think I'll have any trouble working with Jerry, you're quite wrong, I *want* him as my chief engineer, he's the only logical choice."

"You can't have him," Emile Lourade said.

"Why on earth not?"

"Two reasons, Patrice. First and foremost because Jerry would not be at all acceptable to the Russians in such a high position in the project. Not an *American*, renegade or not, and certainly not someone whose . . . political unreliability was demonstrated when he betrayed the American sat-sled technology to us. . . ."

"Son of a bitch!" Jerry shouted.

"C'est la merde, Emile," Patrice Corneau said.

Emile Lourade shrugged. "La merde peut-être," he said, "but that is the politics of the situation, and I am forced to deal with them. And with one thing more—the Soviets in any case will want a Russian in the job."

Corneau pursed his lips, frowned, nodded. "Of course," he said.

Jerry found himself on his feet shouting, madder than he had ever been in his life. "Where the fuck would this project be without me? Where would *you* be without me, Emile? If you hadn't had *my* project to sell out to the fucking Russians, you wouldn't be sitting in that chair now in the first place! You make me want to puke! You were my friend, Emile! When did you turn into such a piece of shit?"

Patrice Corneau seemed quite aghast at this outburst, shrinking back in his chair with his eyebrows raised and his eyes bugging out. But the Director of ESA just sat there quietly and took it, waiting till Jerry was finished before he spoke. And when he did, it was in a quiet voice, leached of all anger or recrimination.

"You had a dream, Jerry," he said. "It was a worthy dream, and you gave it to me, and to Patrice, and to many others like us. You had to leave your own country to do this, and unjustly enough, endure indignities and discrimination, and a certain amount of contempt here precisely for having done the right thing. That is the price *you* had to pay. . . ."

Emile Lourade shrugged. "This is the price *I* have to pay to make that dream a reality at long last," he said. "I have to betray an old friend to whom I do indeed owe much, I have to endure your hatred, and I have to endure my own disgust. In order to make the Grand Tour Navette a reality, I must commit a great injustice against an old friend whom I deeply admire. I ask you to forgive me, Jerry, knowing I have no right to do so, but knowing also that in terms of what we both believe in, I am doing the right thing. The only possible thing. And you know it too, do you not?"

Jerry collapsed back into his chair, totally deenergized. Even his rage was gone. For of course, Emile was right. If the Soviets would not swallow Jerry Reed as chief project engineer, then even if Emile had tried to appoint him, all it could have done was killed the project.

"Yeah, Emile, I know," he said tiredly. "In your position I'd do the same disgusting thing."

"Ah, but this is quite intolerable!" Patrice Corneau declared. "We need Jerry on the project. I must have him working with me and the devil take the Russians!"

"I quite agree," said Emile Lourade.

"You do?" said Jerry.

"I have a proposal to make to you, Jerry, the proposal I intended to make all along," Lourade said, "knowing that you would surely have refused before . . . before the unfortunate circumstances were made bitterly clear. . . ."

"Which is . . . ?"

"I could appoint you to the position of 'maneuvering system design consultant' on the project. . . ."

"*'Maneuvering system design consultant'!*" Jerry snapped. "What the fuck is that?"

"A useful fiction," Emile Lourade said. "Something the Russians could not object to. . . ."

"I'm supposed to let myself be demoted from chief project engineer on the freighter to . . . *maneuvering system design consultant* on the GTN?" Jerry said bitterly. "I've got a wife and two kids and a mortgage, Emile. . . ."

"I'll promote you to senior engineer at the same time," Lourade said.

"Senior engineer? I never heard of any such thing. What the hell is that?"

Emile managed a little smile. "Something I just made up so I could raise your salary to that of a project manager," he said. "I *am* the Director, after all, and I can bend things that far for an old friend. . . ."

"What the hell is a 'maneuvering system design consultant' supposed to do on the project?"

Emile Lourade's smile widened. "Whatever the project manager wants him to, of course," he said.

"Génial, Emile!" exclaimed Patrice Corneau.

"Let me get this straight," Jerry said slowly. "What you're really saying is that I'll have a project manager's salary and more or less of a chief designer's job while you hide me behind this phony shitass title. . . ."

"Something like that," Emile said.

"While some damn Russian has the title and struts around taking the credit . . . ?"

Emile shrugged. "There you have it, Jerry, that's the best I can do under the circumstances," he said.

"That's pretty lousy," Jerry muttered.

"It could be worse, Jerry," Patrice pointed out.

Emile Lourade got up from behind his desk and pointedly walked across his office so that he was standing under the framed blowup of the artist's rendition of the Grand Tour Navette, the illustration for the magazine interview that he himself had caused Jerry to give all those years ago, when Emile was a very junior engineer, and the whole project was nothing but an impossible dream.

"Remember, Jerry?" he said. "Remember when we were all just crazy Space Cadets together and the Grand Tour Navette was just your dream? Well, now it's going to happen, Jerry, with you or without you. It all comes down to this—what really counts, the lives of the dreamers, or the dream itself?"

Jerry Reed sat there staring at the old artist's conception of the dream he had spent all these years pursuing. And once more he could taste chocolate syrup over chocolate ice cream, the bitter and the sweet. And hear the voice of Rob Post speaking to him across the years, "You're going to live in the golden age of space exploration, kiddo. You can be one of the people who makes it all happen. It's up to you."

You can walk on water. You'll have to give up everything else to do it, but you can walk on water.

Jerry sighed. He shrugged. "You got me, Emile," he finally said. "And you knew it all along."

The Director of the European Space Agency looked back at him with actual tears in his eyes, and nodded. "Yes, old friend," he said, "I did."

GOSPEL FOR THE BARNARDS

The Reverend Ike Ackerman announced today that he was consulting with other leading evangelical ministers for the purpose of chartering a nonprofit nondenominational corporation to raise funds to beam the Gospel to Barnard's Star.

"If there really are intelligent beings on the fourth planet, they too must be children of God, with souls in need of saving," he declared. "If the Russians can send them their message, so can we, and not just here we are, but here Jesus Christ has been also, hear the Good News, and rejoice in the Lord."

—*Valley News*

It was frayed around the cuffs from obsessive wear, the lining had been restitched around the armholes twice, and the original zipper had had to be replaced, but the blue-and-white satin Los Angeles Dodgers team jacket that his father had given him for his sixteenth birthday was still Robert Reed's fondest possession. He wore it on hot summer days, he wore it over bulky sweaters in the dead of winter, he wore it in the rain, wore it despite Franja's taunts and his mother's pleas, and he still wore it to school even though it got him called "gringo."

He loved the jacket as he loved his father for ordering it for him all the way from far California. For there on the left breast, in fancy white embroidery mirroring the style of the team logo on the back, was the name "Bob."

Ever since he could remember, Robert Reed had wanted to be called Bob. But this was a sound that did not exactly slide trippingly off the French tongue, and it was an aggressively gringo name besides, as bad as Joe or Tex or Al, and so his teachers insisted on Frenchifying his full name into "Robaire," as did the kids in school whenever they wanted to bait him, for they knew that he hated it.

His mother called him "Robaire" too when she spoke to him in French, which was usually when she was pissed off at him, otherwise it was Bobby. What friends he had called him "Bob-bee," which was the path of least linguistic resistance to the French palate. That was also what Franja called him, but she had a way of putting a whining accent on the second syllable even in English when she was needling him. He even called *himself* Bobby inside his own head when he wasn't watching what he was thinking.

Only from Dad did he get a good old American "Bob." Only Dad understood what it meant to him. Only Dad understood what a bum-out it was to be an American in Common Europe.

America had been an object of contempt in Europe since long before Bobby was old enough to understand why. Dad had tried to explain it to him as best he could when Bobby first began to realize there was something different about him, something that made kids he had done nothing bad to, sometimes kids he really didn't even know, hate him, and tease him, and call him nasty names.

"Are you a gringo, Dad?"

"I'm an American, Bob. 'Gringo' is a bad word people call Americans when they don't like us, like we used to call people niggers and spicks and frogs back in the States. Nice people don't use words like that."

"Am I an American?"

"Not exactly, Bob, but when you're old enough to decide for yourself, you can be one if you want to."

"Is it bad to be an American?"

"No, Bob, it isn't bad to be an American, it isn't bad to be a Frenchman or a Russian either, but . . ."

"Then why don't people like Americans?"

Dad got the strangest faraway look on his face. "Because . . . because sometimes the United States of America does bad things, Bob," he said.

"Do other countries do bad things too?"

"Oh yeah, other countries have done some really bad things, worse than anything America has done, much, much worse. . . ."

"Then why don't people hate *them* the way they hate us?"

Dad peered at him really weirdly and didn't answer for quite a while. "That's a damned good question, Bob, and I wish I had a good answer for you," he finally said. And then his eyes got all teary and it looked like he was going to cry.

"Everybody loved America once," he said. "America saved Europe from some very bad people. America forgave its enemies and rebuilt ruined countries with its own money. And Americans did the most wonderful thing, Bob, we were the first people to go to the Moon. They loved us, they admired us, we were the light of the world. . . ."

Dad rubbed at his eyes before he spoke again. "And then . . . and then something happened to America, and . . . America stopped doing all these wonderful things and . . . started doing bad things . . . no worse than what other countries did, maybe, but . . . I don't know, Bob, I'm not really good about these things. It's like . . . it's like everyone loves Père Noël, so if one Christmas instead of giving out presents, he was to get drunk and beg money on the streets instead . . . well, that would be worse than if it was someone else doing it, wouldn't it?"

"I don't understand, Dad. . . ."

And Dad had just shrugged his shoulders and given out a great big sigh. "Neither do I, kiddo," he said, "neither do I."

Dad always used to buy him models of classic American spacecraft when he was a little kid, one corner of his room was still a dusty and forgotten museum of them, the Apollo, the Saturn V, the Eagle, the space shuttle Columbia, and all the rest. Bobby had never really been into this stuff, but he loved his father, and when he was ten, he took the bulk of the money he had saved up from his allowance and bought Dad a really neat model of the Terminator hypersonic bomber for his birthday, all metal, retractable landing gear, swing wings, and even fully detailed spring-loaded missiles that fired from their pod when you pressed down on the cockpit.

Bobby had burst into tears when Dad unwrapped the gift and started cursing. "You don't like it . . . ?" he wailed.

Dad gathered him up in his arms and dried his tears. "It's a beautiful model, Bob," he said, "and the damned real thing is a beautiful piece of hardware too, you've got to give the bastards that. And I love you very much for buying it for me. But . . . but maybe you're old enough now to understand . . . about what I do and why I'm here and why I got so upset when I saw your present. . . ."

And Dad told him. About watching the first men landing on the Moon, about watching *Americans* landing on the Moon, as a little kid. And his Uncle Rob. And the Challenger disaster. And Battlestar America. And how it had somehow turned the wonderful country that had gone to the Moon into something bad. About how the Terminator could have been a *real* spaceplane like the Concordski instead of a weapon. About how he had moved to France to work on real spacecraft. And the great idea he had for a spaceliner that they wouldn't let him work on because he was an American.

There was an awful lot of it that the ten-year-old Bobby didn't understand, but his ten-year-old heart understood what counted.

Once, Americans had been the greatest people on Earth and done a wonderful thing, and Dad had tried to help America do even more wonderful things. And then something or someone called Challenger or Battlestar America had tricked America into doing bad things instead, things that hurt his Dad so bad that he had to leave America to do his work, and so he came to France to build spaceships, but they wouldn't let him do that because they hated Dad for being an American.

It was Bobby who gave his father a great big warm hug when he was finished. "I hate America too, Dad!" he declared. "America is bad! Why don't we become French people? Or . . . or we could become Russians, just like Mom!"

"No, Bob," Dad told him firmly, "you shouldn't hate America. Don't you ever forget that it was once something special and wonderful to be an American. We were the first humans to set foot on another planet, and no one can *ever* take that away from us. *We're* the real Americans, you and me, kiddo. When we forget that, the bastards that killed the dream win again."

That was when Dad started giving him old American science-fiction novels and sent away for baseball cards from the United States and bought him a bat and a ball and a glove. Dad got him subscriptions to American sports magazines and brought him discs of old American movies. He got him the *Visual Encyclopedia Americana* on disc for his computer and game programs for baseball and American football. And a marvelous software atlas of the United States that windowed full-color pictures of almost any point in America at the touch of a mouse.

Bobby's room filled up with Americana, with a wall map of the United States, and a Statue of Liberty rug, and a star-spangled bedspread, with posters and picture cards of ballplayers he had never seen, with untidy stacks of American sports magazines and old comic books, with models of classic Cadillacs and old Buicks, with bits and pieces of Harley chic, to the point where his mother began fighting with Dad about it.

He overheard them arguing about it once when he was about thirteen.

"It's unnatural, Jerry, you've got him living in some kind of fantasy America out of your own adolescence, twenty years and more out of date, an America that even then never was."

"It's his heritage, Sonya, what about all that Russian stuff Franja is into all the time?"

"Those are books and magazines and discs that are really teaching her something, not a roomful of obsessive old Russian pop-cult kitsch! His mind's been filled with too much of this stuff to get rid of the obsession, perhaps, but if he's doomed to be obsessed with America, at least let me give him some things that will give him some historical perspective on the United States, instead of this random collection of old junk, of—how would you have been saying it twenty years ago—'golden oldies.'"

"Just as long as it isn't a bunch of anti-American propaganda!"

"Oh, really, Jerry!"

So Bobby's Russian mother began giving him things to read about the United States, and if none of it was anti-American propaganda, none of it was the rabid anti-European power fantasies spewing out of Festung Amerika these days either. There were novels by Twain and Melville and Salinger and Kerouac and Mailer and Robert Penn Warren. Biographies of Lincoln and FDR and Malcolm X and Martin Luther King, Jr., and Eugene V. Debs. Histories by de

Toqueville and Halberstam and Rattray. Treatises by Jefferson and Paine. Discs of old American films like *Abe Lincoln in Illinois, PT-109, All the President's Men,* and *Born on the Fourth of July.*

Bobby gobbled it all up and went back for more on his own, plowing through *Naked Lunch, Electric Kool-Aid Acid Test, I Reach for the Stars, Profiles in Courage, Bug Jack Barron, Less Than Zero,* and anything else he could lay his hands on at the English used-book stores. He dug out ancient tapes of *Easy Rider, Candy,* and *Dr. Strangelove, American Graffiti,* and *Beach Blanket Bingo.* He collected moldy old copies of *Time* and *Playboy* and *Rolling Stone.*

So Bobby grew up with a peculiar montage image of America as seen from afar, compounded of his father's vision of an America which had had a golden age that put men on the Moon and then sold it out for a mess of military hardware, his mother's reading list, what he learned in a French school, and the random results of his own packrat curiosity.

By the time he was about fifteen, he thought he had it all figured out.

America had indeed once been the light of the world. It had given the world democracy and modern industrial technology and the telephone and the airplane and movies and the phonograph and jazz and rock 'n' roll. It had fought a terrible war to save Europe from the Nazis. It had rebuilt Japan and Western Europe after the war with its own money and protected the shattered countries from Stalinist Russia with its own troops and atomic bombs. Without America there would be no Common Europe now, and maybe there would never have been a Gorbachev or a Russian Spring either. Once it had been a great and wonderful and prideful thing to be an American; the people of the world had loved America, and not without good cause.

But it all started to slide downhill when the CIA assassinated John F. Kennedy.

Kennedy was the father of the American space program. He had promised to put an American on the Moon before 1970, and America did it. But it was the last great thing that America did.

The CIA and the Pentagon and the Military-Industrial Complex hated Kennedy. The CIA was in the drug-running business in Southeast Asia, the Pentagon was pissed off because Kennedy wouldn't let them invade Cuba, and the Military-Industrial Complex wanted to make a lot of money selling weapons, so they all wanted the little war in Vietnam to turn into a big one that would last a long time. They knew that JFK wouldn't allow this, that he wanted to spend the money on a space station and a Moon colony and an expedition to Mars instead, so they had him assassinated.

They got their nice long war, but a generation of Americans not much older then than Bobby was now had seen through the jingoistic propaganda, they were listening to their own rock 'n' roll, which was telling them a different story. They refused to fight, and they marched against the war, and in 1968 they hounded Lyndon Johnson out of office. They would have ended the war that year and saved America's economy and its honor by electing JFK's brother Bobby, but the Military-Industrial Complex wasn't having that either, so they had Bobby killed too.

The hippies tried to start a revolution in Chicago and Kent State and Woodstock. The military put it down easily, but it made the country paranoid enough to elect Richard Nixon, the biggest paranoid of all, who almost succeeded in making himself dictator.

The war finally ended after Nixon was overthrown, but by that time America was broke and no longer the light of the world, and all that was left of the civilian space program was the shuttle. And then because the Ayatollah Khomeini wanted to destroy the United States economically, he held American hostages during the whole election campaign while Jimmy Carter was tortured and humiliated on television, and so the Military-Industrial Complex was able to elect its own President again, a professional actor named Ronald Reagan who was *very* good on television.

Reagan did what he was elected to do. Even though the Vietnam War was over and he wasn't able to start a new one, he still managed to buy lots of expensive weapons, but because the country was broke from Vietnam, he had to borrow huge amounts of money to do it and kill the civilian space program, which was why the American economy was still such a mess after all these years that no one knew how to keep it going without a war somewhere, and why Dad had to come to Common Europe to work for ESA.

Meantime, Common Europe had been formed, and America got shut out of what was the world's biggest market, and had to keep devaluing the dollar to stiff its European creditors and fight the Forever War in Latin America to keep the crumbling U.S. economy afloat.

And now that the Soviet Union was talking about entering Common Europe, the United States was trying to stop it by threatening to abrogate its overseas debt in Europe if that happened, rather than enrich the people who sold out democracy to the Communists.

And that was why Dad couldn't work on his spaceships and why *he* was catching such shit from the real French kids for being a gringo, and from Robert Reed's fifteen-year-old perspective, it had become hard to blame them.

That was the year that Bobby went through his brief anti-American phase. He took to calling himself "Robaire" and speaking French exclusively, even to his father. He tried to learn to play soccer. And when the United States invaded Panama again, he even marched in an anti-American demonstration.

When Bobby came home from that one and monopolized the dinner table with an endless incoherent anti-American tirade, that was finally too much for his father, and Dad sat him down at the dining room table afterward for a man-to-man.

"Look, Bob—"

"Ro*baire!* Et en français!"

Dad actually seized him by the shoulders and shook him. "We're *Americans,* damn it, *Bob,*" he said, as angry as Bobby had ever seen him, "and we will damn well discuss this as Americans, in *English.*"

"I was born in France," Bobby told him sullenly. "When I'm eighteen, I want a Common European passport and French citizenship!"

"Look, Bob, I'm not very good about this political crap," Dad said much more gently. "But . . . let me show you something. . . ." And he led Bobby out of the dining room, through the living room, and down the hallway to his own room.

Despite his current anti-American phase, Bobby had never bothered to redo his room. It was all still there—the Statue of Liberty rug, the star-spangled bedspread, the models of American spacecraft in the corner bookcase, the piles of *Rolling Stone* and *Playboy,* the books, the huge baseball-card collection, even the big wall map of the

United States, marked up with little scrawled baseballs for major-league cities, rocketships at Cape Canaveral and Vandenberg, routes of his fantasy trips traced along the road networks, peace signs drawn over San Francisco and Chicago and Woodstock and Kent, Ohio.

"How come you haven't gotten rid of all this stuff, Bob?" Dad asked.

Bobby shrugged. "Je ne sais pas. . . ."

"I'll tell you why, son," Dad told him. "Because you collected all this stuff and put it together over your whole life, ever since you were a little kid. It's . . . it's a model, like one of those spacecraft, but what it's a model of is the inside of your head, and it didn't come as a kit, you built it from scratch. It's the America inside you, Bob. Battlestar America, the invasion of Panama and Peru and Colombia, the dollar devaluations, what the Pentagon did to me and Rob Post, Vietnam, piss tests, debt abrogation, economic blackmail, all that crap, that's *politique politicienne,* and it's right to hate all that. . . ."

Dad paused. He waved his arms as if to encompass the whole room. "But don't start hating *this,* Bob!" he said forcefully. "Don't hate Project Apollo and the High Sierras, don't hate the Los Angeles Dodgers and the Statue of Liberty, don't hate the Boston Celtics and Highway One, and Mardi Gras, the redwood forests and Mulholland Drive and Donald Duck, don't hate three hundred million fucked-over people with the same stuff inside their heads as you have. That's the real America, Bob, and if you start hating *that,* you're gonna end up hating *yourself.*"

Dad's passion subsided and he looked directly into Bobby's eyes with a much softer expression, sad, and lost, and a little confused. "I'm not real good at this stuff, Bob," he said with a little shrug. "Do you understand what I'm telling you, kiddo?"

"Yeah, Dad," Bobby found himself saying. "I do believe I do."

And so he did. From that moment on, America wasn't the wonderful time-warped Disneyland version of itself that he had never seen, or the evil and paranoid "Festung Amerika" of the French media; it was neither, and it was somehow both.

It was a *mystery,* and that mystery, Bobby realized from that moment on, was inside of him as well. And from that

moment on, he knew that he had to go to America to solve
its mystery for himself. For it was in some way the mystery
of himself, and he knew he would never know who he really
was, let alone what he wanted to become, until the mystery
within confronted its mirror image without on the American
shore.

And that was the beginning of his campaign to go to college in America. He had announced it at the dinner table
about three weeks later. Franja had sneered, but Franja
sneered at everything he did or wanted to do, of course.
Mom had been noncommittal, she didn't really take it seriously at the time. But Dad had nodded, and let him know he
understood.

"I hear Berkeley and UCLA and Cal Tech are still pretty
good schools," he said.

"You can't really be serious, Jerry. . . ."

"What're you going to study in America, Bob-*bee?*"
Franja whined. "Baseball?"

"What're you going to study in Russia, spacehead, zero-
gravity pipe-jobs?"

"Robert!"

"*I'm* going to be a cosmonaut! What are you going to be
in America, an imperialist blackmailer or just more cannon
fodder?"

"Franja!"

And so it went. Franja ragged him mercilessly about it,
Mom tried not to take him seriously, but Bobby persisted,
and Dad encouraged him, and Bobby's marks even began to
improve. And on his sixteenth birthday, Dad gave him the
Dodgers jacket.

"You'll need this when you see your first ball game in
Dodger Stadium," the enclosed card said.

The Dodgers jacket had been his emblem and his battle
flag ever since, and ever since he had first put it on, the
battle had turned serious, had become more and more of an
open conflict between Dad and Mom.

"We can't let our son waste his college education in some
backwater school in the United States," Mom would declare.

"We're going to let our daughter study in the Soviet
Union," Dad would counter, for by now Franja was quite
serious about cosmonaut school.

"That's different!"

"What's so different about it?"

"It's *Yuri Gagarin,* Jerry, it's a very prestigious place!"

"It's a *Russian* school, that's what you mean, isn't it?"

"Do you really want your son to have a third-rate education?"

"In a third-rate *country,* isn't that what you mean, Sonya?"

"You said it, Jerry, I didn't!"

"But you thought it!"

"Well, isn't it true?"

"How would you know, Sonya, you've never been to the United States."

"And neither have you, for almost twenty years!"

"So neither of us can tell Bob anything at all about what America is all about. That's why he has a right to see for himself!"

It had gone round and round like that for two years now, with neither of them giving ground, but now that Franja had actually gotten into cosmonaut school, Bobby was becoming confident of victory.

For Franja needed Dad's signature on her admission papers, and Bobby had long since persuaded him, or so at least he hoped, not to sign them until Mom agreed that he could go to college in America. It was only fair, now wasn't it?

And this morning, when he looked in the mail, there was a big packet of papers for Franja from the Yuri Gagarin Space Academy in the Soviet Union, which could be only one thing.

If he knew his older sister, and by now, alas, he certainly did, Franja would waste no time in presenting the admission papers for the necessary parental signatures, meaning at dinner tonight.

Bobby went to his closet and took the Dodgers jacket off the padded hanger where he always carefully placed it when he finished wearing it. He laid it out on the bed, sprayed the satin with the special cleanser, wiped it off with a chamois cloth, put it back on the hanger, and hung it on the edge of the bookcase, where he could see it while he played an ancient Bruce Springsteen chip and waited.

Dinner was not exactly a formal event in the Reed family. But Robert Reed was going to dress for it tonight.

UNCLE JOES GET PIE IN THEIR
MUSTACHES—AND WORSE!

It was quite a scene on Saturday afternoon in Gorky
Park when Pamyat hooligans tried to break up an outdoor
picnic of the Moscow Socialist Feminist Society. The ladies
had anticipated just such a Bear attack, tipped off the police, and armed themselves with what must have been at
least three hundred cream pies. While police and militia
stood by laughing uproariously, they pelted the aggressors
with them.

Several police and militia persons had brought their
own pies, eager to take it out on the Uncle Joes who have
long since become their number-one headache.

No custard-cream humor for these earthy guardians of
the public order, however. Their pies were filled with pig
manure.

—*Mad Moscow*

Franja Gagarin Reed had not quite gone to the point of
calling herself Franja Gagarin, even though her mother *did*
use her own famous Russian name professionally. Reed
might be a loathsomely American name, and an American
name might be a burden, but Jerry Reed had made that
burden an honor too, and she loved him for it.

Anyone who wanted to go to Mars and beyond as passionately as Franja did could hardly be ashamed to have
Jerry Reed for a father, a father who not only shared, but
served the same dream.

It was Bobby, of course, his personal favorite, whom Father had tried to give the dream to when they were both
small, Bobby who got the expensive models for his birthdays
and Christmases, while Father got her stupid dolls and his
weird concept of little girls' clothing, Bobby whom he told
his best stories to, Bobby whom he fed all that chocolate ice
cream.

But there had been a certain rough justice built into the
universe of her childhood, and not just because Mother
made Franja her favorite, her little confidante, her fellow
Russian in willing exile, sharing as much of her work life as
Franja could understand, spinning tales of her girlhood in
an awakening Soviet Union, even hinting at a previous life
as a notorious member of the legendary Red Menace.

For Bobby, despite Father's ardent wishes, refused to become the little space cadet that Father longed for. The little ingrate blew it.

When she was about twelve, and had learned enough from Mother about the art of bureaucratic manipulation to take matters into her own hands, and even Father had begun to face the fact that his efforts with Bobby were hopeless, she began to ask her father questions about space. Intelligent questions. Questions she studied to prepare and framed carefully. Questions designed to pique his attention, to show him that he at least had a *daughter* to pass the torch along to.

"Do you think the Barnards have starships, Father?" she asked him one day. "Do you think they might mount an expedition when they get our message?"

Father looked at her peculiarly. "Starships?" he muttered.

"It would seem that there are artifacts scattered throughout the Barnard system, large ones too, as if they've built something like the old O'Neil colonies. Wouldn't that imply the technology to take the next step? A generation ship expedition, or at least an automated probe?"

Father got a distracted faraway look in his eyes, the one Mother called his outer-space stare. "We'll both be gone before anyone knows the answer to that," he muttered.

"Maybe not. Maybe they'll answer our message. If they do, I'll still be around to hear it. And if they *do* answer, by that time, won't *we* be ready to mount an expedition to *them?*"

"You're probably right," Father said. "They do seem to have occupied more of their solar system than we have, and we probably could mount an expedition thirty or forty years from now."

"With a little luck, we could both live to see it!"

Father laughed. "I'm afraid I'd need a lot more than a little luck to last that long," he said. "But you, Franja . . ."

He had looked at her with new eyes then, with a new awareness; he was deep into his outer-space stare, but now it was focused intently on *her* for the first time. She could feel things shifting. She could feel the world changing.

"You, Franja . . . ," he said again.

"Me, Father," Franja said softly, outer-space staring back at him, measure for measure.

And after that, it was Franja who got the telescope, Franja whom Father encouraged to pursue a career in space, Franja to whom Father poured out what Mother called his space babble, father and daughter who found each other through a shared vision.

"We're like the ancient Polynesians sailing our first little outrigger canoes from island to island across the unknown Pacific," Father told her. "And one day one of our tiny little boats is going to sail into the harbor of some galactic city a million years of evolution grander than anything we could have dreamed. And you could be on it."

Franja believed that, she really did. She did more than believe it. She set it up before her as the shining goal of her lifetime, and she worked to fulfill it. She studied hard. She became something of a grind. She watched her nutrition carefully and kept herself in shape with long hours of swimming, which also, she had heard, was the best exercise to prepare her reflexes for zero-gravity locomotion.

She was going to get there. She was going to be a cosmonaut. She would do what she had to to get into Yuri Gagarin, the only real space academy in the world, where Russians who had been to the Moon and Mars trained what was by far the largest cosmonaut cadre in the world.

But when she finally proudly told Father of her intentions, she was stunned by his reaction.

"You don't want to go to Yuri Gagarin," he told her. "You don't want to end up stuck in the Soviet program. Not when ESA is someday going to open up the whole solar system with my Grand Tour Navettes. ESA's the place for you, Franja, where I can help you, where someday you can go to Mars on a ship that I built. Won't that be something? Who knows, I might even get to ride along."

What could she say to that? Certainly not the bitter truth, she knew even then.

"But Father," she told him instead, "Soviet cosmonauts are going to Mars already! Who knows when ESA will really build Grand Tour Navettes? It's the Soviet Union that has the *real* space program. Tell the truth, Dad, if you could, wouldn't *you* become a Soviet cosmonaut right now?"

But Father refused to believe that the Soviet space program had been a visionary one from the start, as far back as Tsiolkovsky's dreams of exploring the solar system and Yuri Gagarin himself, a thing of the romantic Russian heart.

The Americans had gone to the Moon for political prestige, and then their space program degenerated into a militarist nightmare. Common Europe could think of nothing grander to do than expend all its energies on building a glorified *resort hotel* for senile plutocrats. The Japanese cared for nothing but orbital factories and power stations.

But the Soviet Union had had a vision all along. Why couldn't Father see that it was his vision too? Of exploring for life on Mars, or on Titan, or even in the superheated sea beneath the Uranian ice. Of eventually extending the search to the stars. And of building in the meantime a solar system—wide civilization that would be worthy of sailing its canoes into the galactic main as equals.

Why couldn't Father accept that as good enough reason to go to Yuri Gagarin and not tempt her to cruelty?

Surely Father knew the bitter truth that Mother had explained to her in words of many painful syllables. Surely Franja could have won this argument once and for all by forcing him to acknowledge it.

Surely she could never do it, no matter how frustrated with him she became, no matter how sorely she was tempted.

How could she tell her own father that being his daughter would be the political kiss of death to her at ESA?

She couldn't. She didn't. She couldn't stoop to winning the endless argument with that any more than she could rid herself of her American family name by calling herself Franja Gagarin at the cost of what was left of her father's pride.

Not that she exactly made a point of using her family name these days, either. An American name did not exactly endear anyone to the powers that be in the French educational system, nor was it worth the risk to be caught lying about her father being English when his name appeared in the back pages of the newspapers at unpredictable intervals.

At school, she was Jerry Reed's daughter, and she was stuck with it, and if that meant a certain pointed pronunciation of her name from time to time, she had to admit that there were also times when it was a badge of honor.

But when it came to her social life, what there was of it, being Franja Reed was quite another matter.

Franja was a good Russian name, and it was a fine thing to be young and Russian and in Paris. Not only was the

Soviet Union greatly admired, Paris was embracing styles
and trends and things Russian, and the French were eager
to embrace what Russians they could find, in every sense of
the word.

The sons and daughters of Embassy staff and Red Star
personnel who formed the core of her small circle of friends
joked about it among themselves, and made a wry point of
doing so in thick Russified French, but that didn't stop any
of them from dressing up in stylized cossack gear and playing the second coming of the Red Menace for appreciative
French audiences.

Oh yes, it was fun being a Russian named Franja in Paris!

Being an American named Reed was something else
again.

There were boys who eyed her from afar, only to flee in
the other direction when they learned her full name. There
were self-styled men of the world who professed not to care
until their parents forced them to end it. There were cretins
of both sexes forever trying to force her into the position of
actually defending the loathsome policies of the United
States so they could vent their wrath upon a convenient
target.

The old Russian solution would be to substitute the patronymic whenever possible, but "Franja Jerryovna" was
hardly an option.

It was the rising tide of socialist feminism that rolled in
with a *modern* Russian solution.

In the Soviet Union, a fashion arose among the enlightened youth of the Russian Spring for giving yourself a new
patronymic of your own choosing; as a declaration of gener-
ational perestroika if you were a socialist feminist chafing
under the linguistic yoke of tired old Slavic phallocracy, and
if you knew what was good for you when paying court to
same, even if you were a hairy unreconstructed phallocrat
among the boys.

One chose the name of someone one admired, someone
famous, someone you were telling the world you wished to
emulate. For Franja, of course, the choice of a pop patronymic was obvious and perfect.

Who could deny that Yuri Gagarin was a worthy exem-
plar of socialist virtue and Russian pride? Who better per-
sonified everything she wished to become?

So she chose to call herself "Franja Yurievna Gagarin

Reed," "Franja Yurievna" period, when she could manage, and if there were those who called her "Franja Yurievna Gagarin" let them make of it what they would, and preferably to her advantage; she did not encourage it, now did she, and she had never used anything but her full legal name on any document.

Including the application for admission to the Yuri Gagarin Space Academy.

And there it was in full, "Franja Gagarin Reed" all over the admission forms that had arrived in the mail this morning.

Not that she could have hidden behind any pop patronymic with the Yuri Gagarin Space Academy. Jerry Reed might be an American, but he was still her father, and under Soviet law, she could no more attend Yuri Gagarin without her father's written consent than she could claim her Soviet citizenship without it until she reached her legal majority.

And Father, who had every reason to want to sign these papers, who had encouraged her career so strongly, who wanted so much to see his daughter go where he could not, was being manipulated by Bobby into withholding his permission until Mother agreed that her brother could go to college in his beloved America.

As far as Franja was concerned, ruining his life by getting a third-rate education in a country that was loathed by the civilized world would only be what Bobby deserved. Let them draft him into their Foreign Legion and ship him to some Latin American jungle if that's what he wanted.

But with all the scruples and honor of the devious paranoiacs in Washington who were trying to sabotage the Soviet entry into Common Europe, Machiavellian little Bobby had weaseled himself into a position where he held her admission to the Soviet space academy hostage.

If she had a right to go to Yuri Gagarin in the Soviet Union, then he had a right to go to college in America. That was the way Bobby saw it, and that was the way he had manipulated Father into seeing it.

Father would never pretend to be balking at letting her go to Gagarin if Bobby hadn't persuaded him that linking the issues was the only way to persuade Mother to let Bobby go to America.

What Father would really do if Mother called his bluff, Franja didn't want to think about.

"Dinner is ready," Mother's voice called from the kitchen.

Franja grimaced, and not just because Father and Mother had been in the kitchen together by themselves since they came home, which usually meant a private argument and a truly revolting concoction on the table, for she had the feeling that the dinner conversation was likely to be even more unpalatable than the battleground cuisine.

When Franja walked down the long hallway past Bobby's room, the door was ajar and the room was empty. Just like him to make sure he got there first, as if . . . as if he had sneaked a look in the mailbox this morning before she got there and seen the packet from Moscow.

And indeed, he was already seated at the dining table when she arrived, greeting her with a fatuous smile and knowing eyes that told her that was exactly what he had done.

It was not like Jerry Reed to come staggering home from work drunk like some nikulturni muzhik, so Sonya did not have to be a Pavlov Institute psychic to guess that his meeting with Emile Lourade had not exactly been a triumph.

She was in the kitchen cutting up the beef when he arrived and plunked down a bottle of some dreadful-looking Barolo on the long wooden counter under the window, his acumen clearly adversely affected by what he had already drunk before purchasing it at some Felix Potin instead of their regular caviste.

"Somehow I sense that the news was not exactly good, Jerry?" she said as he began cutting onions off the string beside the spice rack with a paring knife as if this were the most normal day in the world.

"Well, as the famous old American saying goes, there's good news and bad news," Jerry said sardonically, angrily slicing off the ends of onions as if they were the heads of enemies. "The good news is that the Director of the European Space Agency had a few drinks at the corner brasserie after work with the newly appointed project manager of the newly funded Grand Tour Navette Project. . . ."

"Why that's marvelous, Jerry!" Sonya exclaimed, and moved down the countertop to give him a hug.

"The bad news is that I was there too," Jerry told her,

freezing her in her tracks. "Does that answer your question?"

"La merde, Jerry, what *happened?*"

As Jerry stood there cutting up onions and spitting it all out through the sniffles and tears, the dreadful realization came over her that she was in the process of acquiring precisely the information that Ilya Pashikov was after for the Space Ministry without having decided whether she wanted it.

Knowing what Emile Lourade had cooked up now would probably allow the Space Ministry to hammer out a deal on a combined space budget about 10 percent better than what they'd get if Lourade controlled the timing of its revelation to them.

What had been done to Jerry was appalling, though in retrospect hardly surprising. But what was somehow at least as appalling was the *pettiness* of the moral quandary she had now been put in.

If she told Pashikov what she now knew, it would save the Soviet Union about 10 percent of the combined space budget, a modest bureaucratic coup that would look good on her kharakteristika and make the economic strategy department look good, and not much more.

If she kept this to herself, she might not be blamed for being unable to come up with the information, but it would not exactly enhance the confidence of the Moscow Mandarins in her political loyalty. Nor would it exactly enhance her working relationship with Ilya, who would lose bureaucratic points with the Moscow Mandarinate too.

Under the circumstances, she was not about to tell Jerry about her day at the office with Ilya Pashikov and the bureaucratic vengeance they could take on Lourade, since as far as he was concerned Lourade was not the villain, but the more Jerry blamed it on Soviet pressure, the angrier she became at the treacherous Emile Lourade, and the sweeter the opportunity to deal him a little justice seemed.

It was in these dissonant but equally distracted moods that the two of them had cooked dinner, and she didn't need Franja's turned-up nose as she put the tureen down on the table to tell her that the linguini à la Romanoff showed it. The pasta had been overboiled into a sticky mess while they weren't watching it, and the crème fraîche had been simmered long enough to fall apart into a runny goo, in which floated slices of overcooked beef and undercooked lumps of raw tomatoes.

But with Robert dressed in his ludicrous baseball jacket, always a bad sign at the dinner table, and with Franja fingering the packet of papers on her lap nervously, Sonya had the awful feeling that it was somehow going to be fitting fare for tonight's table talk.

THE AMERICAN BLUFF

Despite the current posturing in Washington, it is hard to find anyone in the City who seriously believes that the impending entry of the Soviet Union into Common Europe will really result in a so-called unilateral junk bond rescheduling of the American overseas debt.

They simply can't do it, so the smart thinking goes. Even if they suspended interest payments entirely, the American Federal Budget would still be deeply in deficit, and the need for overseas borrowing would still be there. And who would be willing to lend more money to a nation that had totally destroyed its financial credibility?

The United States would in the end only be committing financial suicide, and while the current American administration may indeed be foolish enough to do almost anything, the American financial and industrial establishment, which would be left to face the grim consequences as its overseas financing quite dried up as well, will never permit the politicians to carry their self-defeating policies to such a terminal extreme.

When the discount on American paper reaches 40 percent, institutional bond traders are set to leap into the market and gobble it up.

—*Financial Times*

Mother put a horrid-looking meal on the table that Franja recognized all too well—a huge dish of overcooked spinach pasta and a tureen of beef and mushrooms stewed in a tomato and crème fraîche sauce that she called "linguini à la Romanoff."

Father emerged from the kitchen with the wine, plunked it down on the table, collapsed into his chair, and then just sat there leaning on his elbows staring into space with the most desolate look on his face. His eyes were bloodshot, and there were deep circles under them.

There was an unspoken rule at the dinner table that no one was to discuss anything but culinary matters until everyone had food on their plate and wine in their glass. Since what Mother had placed on the table appeared to be something that no one wanted to pay any more attention to than necessary, the loathsome linguini was dished out in silence while Franja squirmed in her seat, impatient for an opportune moment to present her papers for parental signature and get things over with.

But brother Bobby wasn't going to allow that.

"What've you got there, Franja?" he said, as soon as everyone had begun the distasteful task of getting this ruined dinner down. No doubt he was just delighted to see Father in some kind of funk, under the circumstances, it would make it all that much easier for Bobby to play on his emotions.

"What are you talking about, Bobby?"

"The papers on your lap," Bobby said disingenuously. "You're not careful, you're gonna spill sauce on them, why don't you just put them on the table."

"What *do* you have there, Franja?" Mother said, and now there was nothing to be done but go through with it as planned.

Jerry Reed stared at the packet of papers that Franja had laid out on the table as if they were a pile of dog turds. "Jesus Christ, Franja," he moaned after she had finished her little speech, "why do you have to hit me with this stuff at a time like this?"

"At a time like *what,* Father?" Franja said, furrowing her brow.

And now he had gone and done it! Now he was going to have to tell his *kids* about what the damn Russians had done to him! Well, he was going to have to tell them sooner or later, and now at least, he thought as he took a huge gulp of wine, I've got a head start on getting drunk enough to do it.

"Those sons of bitches!" Bobby exclaimed when Dad was finished. "You can't let them get away with that, Dad!"

"What am I supposed to do, Bob, call up the American Embassy and ask for a Terminator sortie against Moscow?"

"Maybe you *should* call up the Embassy," Bobby found himself saying. "Maybe they'd let you build your own Grand Tour Navettes for America, so the Russians won't end up owning the solar system. . . ."

"Bobby, Bobby," Dad said in a little sad voice, "the people running the United States these days aren't interested in exploring the solar system. Besides, the way they see it, I'm the guy who gave Common Europe American sat-sled technology. If I show up in Downey asking for my job back, they'll ship me to Leavenworth and throw away the key."

"Then why can't you understand that Yuri Gagarin is the place for me, Father?" Franja butted in.

"Merde, Franja, how can you still be thinking about sliming into the Russian space program after what the bastards have done to your own father!" Bobby snapped at her.

"Because it's obvious that being the daughter of Jerry Reed is not exactly going to open doors for me at ESA!" Franja shouted back.

"Franja!" Mother shouted. Not that she had to, for Franja was regretting the words almost in the act of shouting them, furious at Bobby for having goaded her into it.

But Father just sat there waving his wineglass woozily, nodding his head slightly, and looking at her with only sadness in his eyes.

"No, Sonya, she's right," Father said. "I can't even open the door to the men's room at ESA. . . ."

"Dad . . ."

"Jerry!"

"Then you *will* sign my papers?" Franja said, reaching into a pocket, pulling out a pen, and laying it down on top of the packet.

Jerry Reed stared at the papers before him in somewhat Scottish befuddlement.

Why had he really been against his daughter going to Yuri Gagarin anyway? With his dream of being Franja's fairy godfather at ESA shattered, Jerry had to admit that Gagarin *was* the place for Franja. The two programs *were*

going to be merged anyway in some fashion, and Common
Europe had nothing like Yuri Gagarin; careerwise Gagarin
graduates *would* have the fast track.

He reached down somewhat clumsily and picked up the
pen.

"Wait a minute, Dad," Bobby blurted, "what about *me?*"

Dad's pen hand froze in midair. "What about *you*, Bob?"
he said, staring at Bobby perplexedly.

"It isn't fair! Why should Franja get to go to school in
Russia if I can't go to college in the States?"

"Oh no, not *that* again!" Mom moaned.

"Yes, *that* again, Mom! It isn't fair! If Dad's gonna let
Franja go to Russia, you've got to let me go to the United
States!"

"Have you been putting him up to this again, Jerry?"
Mom said, looking at Dad, not at him.

"Putting him up to what?" Dad said confusedly.

"It's Bobby who's been putting *Father* up to it!" Franja
whined.

"Shut up, Franja!"

"Shut up yourself!"

"Shut up everyone who *says* shut up!" Dad roared at the
top of his lungs. He shrugged, threw up his hands. "Including me," he added in a much smaller voice. And he led the
laughter at his own expense.

And all at once, Bobby could see that Dad had taken
charge of the table, not by outshouting everyone, but by
making them laugh. And in the act of so doing, seemed to
have recovered his full faculties.

"It seems to me we've had this discussion a few million
times before," Dad said.

"But not with Franja's admission papers handed over to
be signed, Dad," Bobby told him, and then he found himself
telling an inspired lie, which he would certainly turn into the
truth tomorrow morning. "I've already written away for applications to Berkeley and UCLA, because if I want to get
in for next fall's term, I've got to apply before this one is
over. . . ."

"He's got a point, Sonya," Dad said. "We're going to have
to decide where he goes to school sooner or later, so it
might as well be now—"

"So that the two of you can blackmail me with Franja's admission papers to Gagarin?" Mom said angrily.

"That isn't fair, Sonya. . . ."

"No, Jerry, it certainly isn't! You never *really* objected to Franja's going to Gagarin. It's been a bluff all along! You'll sign Franja's papers no matter what I do, because you love your daughter too, and you're not mean enough to destroy her life as an act of vengeance against me."

Dad shrugged. "You *do* know me," he said.

"Dad!" Bobby cried, feeling it all starting to slip away.

"Your mother's right on this one, Bob," Dad told him. "You really wouldn't want me to ruin Franja's life to punish her for your not getting what *you* wanted, now would you? How would you feel if you were in *her* shoes?"

"Just like I feel now," Bobby moaned miserably.

"Well, I'm going to give you a chance to feel a little better, Bob," Dad said, picking up his wineglass and sipping at it lightly, but never taking his eyes off Bobby's. "I'm going to leave it up to you. *You* tell me whether to sign Franja's papers or not. I won't sign them until *you* give your permission—"

"Jerry!"

Dad held up his left hand for silence, but he didn't even look at Mom. His bloodshot eyes kept staring into Bobby's until Bobby felt that his father was staring right down into the center of his soul.

"It's simple, Bob. Would you feel better doing what those Russian bastards just did to me or would you rather feel like an American?"

Bobby stole a sidelong glance at Franja, and for a moment their eyes met. There was nothing he could read in his sister's eyes but the intensity of their focus on him. What must she be thinking? Cringing inside knowing that now he had his shot at vengeance? Fear that he was going to take the dream of her lifetime away from her?

That he was going to do to her what Mom was doing to him?

Bobby sighed. Franja had tormented him for as long as he could remember and certainly had never done anything noble for him. Was it really possible to love such a sister?

But that wasn't the point, was it? Nor was vengeance, however sweet, however richly deserved.

Dad was teaching him a hard, loving lesson about himself that he would never forget.

Clean vengeance was one thing, but a deliberate act of naked injustice was just something he couldn't make himself commit.

"Sign the papers, Dad," he muttered unhappily.

"Spoken like a man, Bob," Dad said, gathering up Franja's admission papers. He turned his gaze on Mom for a long silent moment. "Spoken like a *real* American."

Never before had losing felt like having won.

Sonya sat there marveling at her husband as Jerry signed the papers. After what had been done to him today, he was still able to see his way through to the fair thing and make Robert show it to himself in the bargain!

During the last few years of travail and conflict and career stagnation, she had in her darker moments seen Jerry as a lead anchor, whom she had somehow had to marry to get transferred to Paris.

But moments like this reminded her that she really had married Jerry Reed because she loved him, for they reminded her of *why*. This was the Jerry Reed who had left his country for love and a dream. This was the Jerry Reed who had kept his faith all these long years of bitter disappointment.

And understanding that anew, she also knew that Emile Lourade was indeed Jerry's friend, that in a sense he had understood Jerry better than she had lately. He might be too much of a bureaucratic infighter to make a futile gesture that would endanger his position, but he had given Jerry the only thing he could, the chance, at whatever cost to his pride, to work on the dream of his lifetime.

And knew too that she could never report tonight's conversation to Ilya Pashikov, though she couldn't quite fully understand why. Did she really care that much about betraying Lourade, when all it would do was change some figures in a treaty by a few percentage points? Because it would be a betrayal of Jerry even though it did him no harm?

Or was it for the same reason that Jerry had put the decision to sign Franja's papers in Robert's hands? The same reason that made Robert tell him to sign them? She was sure that was true.

But she couldn't quite put her finger on what that reason was.

Nevertheless, she knew she had to act on it anyway, even though it was going to make trouble with Pashikov and put her even further out of favor with the Moscow Mandarins.

Sometimes even a professional bureaucrat had to follow her own heart.

Franja couldn't help herself from stealing a glance at Bobby while Father was signing all the forms. No, he didn't look any different. He was still wearing that idiotic jacket, and a halo had not magically appeared in the air over his head.

She couldn't for the life of her see what he had hoped to gain by doing what he had done. She found it hard to believe that he had done it out of a suddenly developed sense of brotherly love.

That left only one other possibility that she could think of, no matter how improbable it seemed. He had done it because even Bobby knew damn well that it was the right thing to do.

Was it possible? Was Bobby really capable of violating his own petty self-interest to do the right thing like a true Socialist Idealist?

She glanced at him again. Well, yes, all the right features were in all the right places, she had to admit that they were members of the same species, members of the same family, when you came down to it.

Maybe it *was* true.

Maybe her little brother *was* a human being after all.

Jerry Reed put the pen back in its holder and slid the papers back across the table to Franja. "Now it's Bob's turn to have his college plans finally decided," he said, looking at Sonya, on whose face he was surprised to see a radiant smile of a sort she hadn't turned on him in years. "He's certainly earned the right to go to America as far as I'm concerned."

Sonya's smile turned to a hectoring frown. "It's not that I'm not very proud of Robert for what he's just done, and it's not that I have any intention of denying him a right to choose," she insisted. "If he doesn't want to go to the Sorbonne, he can go to any university in Common Europe that will admit him, and if he wants to study in English, there are much better schools in Britain than anything in the United States."

"Britain!" Bob cried. "Everyone there talks like they've got a pencil up their nose! And they play *cricket* instead of baseball!"

"I wasn't aware that you were planning to major in baseball, Robert," Sonya said dryly.

"You know damn well that I'm gonna major in history, Mom!"

"And the British are very good indeed at teaching that. And no place is better than the Sorbonne."

"American history, not a bunch of crap about dead kings and who conquered what when!"

"I simply cannot agree to let my own son receive an education in a country where the history presently being made is which Latin American country needs to be invaded next! You can't seriously expect to learn anything about history in a country that won't even remember history long enough to pay its own debts."

"Very funny, Mom."

"I'm serious, Robert. You can't get a decent education in an atmosphere like that, and what's more, it may be dangerous. There's quite literally no way of predicting what the madmen in Washington might get it into their heads to do next."

"What do you think is really going to happen to me in America, Mom? Am I gonna be drafted into the Army or lynched by rednecks or eaten by alligators in the swamp? You really think I'm going to be in physical danger?"

"No, but—"

"Brainwashed by the CIA? Turned into a Republican?"

"He's got a point," Jerry said. "What *are* you afraid of? The only reason you've given for not letting Bob go to college in America is because *you* don't like its politics!"

"No rational person likes its politics!" Sonya snapped back at him. "Do you?"

"Screw politics!" Jerry told her angrily. "I didn't let *politics* stop me from signing Franja's papers to go to school in goddamn *Russia*, did I? And Bob didn't let *politics* stop him from doing what was right."

Jerry stared into his wife's eyes and wondered who was looking back now. The Russian? The career bureaucrat? The girl who had called herself Samantha Garry on a wild tour of Paris all those years ago? All of them? What was she seeing now? The man she loved? A failure? An American who wanted to turn her son into one of *them?*

"You know why Bob and I did that, Sonya?" he said. "Because it was the right thing to do. The fair thing. The *American* thing to do. Being an American used to mean that too, Sonya. Maybe to some people it still does. Maybe some of that's still alive over there. . . ."

"And if it isn't?"

"Then I have a right to find that out for myself, don't I?" Bobby said.

"What about a little of the famous romantic Russian spirit, Sonya?" Jerry said. "What about a little of the socialist justice they're supposed to have these days in Moscow? Or are we Americans the only ones who know anything about it?"

"*Now* who's playing cheap chauvinist politics, Jerry Reed!"

Franja had tried to disappear into the meal before her as Father and Mother argued over Bobby's fate, but the congealed mess on her plate did not exactly invite careful attention, and what was being done to Bobby made it hard for her to just sit there in the glow of victory.

It just wasn't right. Having just won her own freedom of choice, she could not avoid knowing all too keenly how she would have felt if Father had refused to sign those admission papers, meaning that whether she liked it or not, she could not avoid knowing precisely how Bobby felt now.

Against her will, despite her better judgment, and to the further erosion of her appetite, Franja found herself taking the side of her brother inside her own head.

Bobby, after all, had just been *her* ally for the first time in his life. And now it was costing him.

It just wasn't fair.

Maybe all that stuff about being a real American was jingoistic blather, but Bobby had believed it, and believing it had actually made him act like a real brother for the first time.

Maybe such a thing as an American concept of virtue was actually possible. Maybe it really wasn't that much different from the concept of socialist morality, from the idea that the community existed to promote the welfare of the people through the bonds of fraternal solidarity among its individuals as a family of equals.

And if that were so, socialist morality, honor, and simple human decency, which was what this was really all about, demanded that she stand up for justice for her brother now.

After all, she told herself unconvincingly, you'll forever be in the little monster's debt if you don't, and that would really be unbearable.

"Father's right, Mother," she found herself saying. "You're wrong. Bobby has a right to live his own life too. And you have no right to stop him."

Sonya gaped at her daughter in astonishment. "Et tu, Franja?" she cried.

Franja stared straight into her eyes, and in that moment, she somehow seemed more like a sister to Sonya than a daughter, an adult equal in every sense of the term.

"Aren't you the one who taught me that a society only thrives when its citizens are free to follow their own hearts?" that adult equal told her firmly. "Where's our Russian Spring if we act like unreconstructed old Stalinists with our own family? Doesn't socialist morality begin at home?"

Sonya looked away from this new Franja, looked at Jerry, who was smiling like the doubly proud father now. She looked at Bobby, who had manfully sacrificed his own pragmatic advantage to do what was right for the sister he had seemed to despise, Bobby, who was looking at that sister now with a new respect, with as much love for her as he was capable of.

Finally, she looked back at Franja, at this daughter who presumed to lecture her on socialist morality.

And she saw that the same spirit united the three of them in a way that it never had before.

She felt proud. She felt defeated. She felt ashamed. She felt very much on the outside looking in. Her mind could not be changed, but in the end her heart could only be melted.

She sighed, she shrugged her shoulders, once, twice. "I

still think we are making a terrible mistake," she finally said. "But clearly I have been outvoted. So I guess I really do have to accede to the will of the majority, don't I? Because I have no right to do anything else. Merely the power. That's what it's all about, isn't it?"

"Yeah, Sonya," Jerry said softly. "That's what it's all about."

"Well then you have my permission, Robert," Sonya sighed. "It's not so easy to admit that your child has a right to a will of his own. Do you understand that, Robert? Do you understand how I feel?"

Bobby looked back at her and smiled a tender little rueful smile. "Yeah, Mom," he said, "I do believe I do. I think we all do."

There was a long moment of silence, but there was nothing awkward about it; Sonya felt it as a moment of grace, a moment of completion, a moment of familial unity she had never quite experienced the like of before, a moment so tender as to be almost embarrassing.

Sonya came blinking out of it looking at what was on the dinner table before them and found herself surveying a loathsome uneaten mess of congealed pasta covered with thoroughly decomposed crème fraîche sauce and forlorn bits of cold, tough meat.

"We are going to poubelle this stuff and go down to Le Magnifique," she declared. "It may not be exactly the best brasserie in Pigalle, but even they can do better than this. And this decision, at least, will *not* be subject to a majority vote of the Supreme Soviet!"

Representative Carson: "Hell no, Billy, we're not bluffing. We're going to go into joint session as the Common European Parliament votes, there's a ton of legislation in the hopper, and believe me, we're not going to adjourn until we've given the President what he needs to really kick some European butt. We'll show them who's been bluffing! They've got our paper, but I'd just like to see them try and collect on it! We may not have exactly built Battlestar America with this in mind, but it's nice to know it's about to pay off a big fat extra dividend. The Russians and the Peens have been sneering at 'Festung Amerika' for years, now we're gonna see who laughs last!"

Billy Allen: "Speak softly and carry a big stick, eh?"

Representative Carson: "Speak softly, my ass! We're gonna let them know it loud and clear, or my name isn't Harry Burton Carson!"

—*Newspeak*, with Billy Allen

COMMON EUROPEAN PARLIAMENT ADMITS SOVIET UNION

With only 53 dissenting votes out of 561 cast, and despite the bellicose and hollow threats continuing to emanate from Washington, the Common European Parliament courageously voted today to admit the Soviet Union to Common Europe.

"This is the greatest historical event since the end of the Great Patriotic War," President Dimitri Pavelovich Smerlak declared. "Indeed, historians of the next century may end up deeming it greater. The great wound down the center of Europe has at last been healed. Mikhail Gorbachev's old dream of a common European house has at last been realized—one Europe, from the Atlantic to Vladivostok! A golden future is spread before us!"

—*Tass*

X I

When Red Star, S.A., minitelled its invitations to the gala celebration, Sonya's was in the name of Sonya Ivanovna Gagarin, the usual signal that her American husband was persona non grata.

This time, however, she could easily understand why, nor would she think of subjecting Jerry to such an ordeal even if he *were* invited. An American at a celebration of the Soviet Union's entry into Common Europe would only be the object of triumphant gloating.

Nor would Jerry's presence aid in her endeavors to clear her political karma with the Moscow Mandarins, a cause that might at least be advanced in tonight's expansive atmosphere, where the champagne and vodka would flow freely and everyone would be happily speculating about how the Soviet entry was going to enhance Red Star's fortune and their own careers.

Ordinarily, she would have arrived with Ilya Pashikov, who would have left with someone else, an oft-used social convenience for both of them. She had her boss as her escort, and in return served as the perfect beard for the notorious lady-killer, since no one could think him a cad for leaving with a woman other than the one he arrived with as long as the woman he arrived with was married and strictly a business connection.

But that would be pushing things a bit now.

Ilya had called her in on the carpet first thing in the morning on the day after ESA sprang the fully funded design stage Grand Tour Navette program on the Soviet negotiating team.

"You knew about this, Sonya, didn't you?" he said by way of greeting when she arrived in his office. "It wasn't true that your husband knew nothing."

Something about the way he was looking at her told her that denial would be worse than futile. "No, Ilya Sergeiovich, it wasn't," she was forced to admit.

"Then why didn't you *tell* me?" Ilya whined with as much petulance as anger. "Believe me, they're not exactly impressed with our department now back in Moscow!"

"I . . . I haven't put your position in danger, have I . . . ?" Sonya asked woefully, realizing for the first time that not reporting Emile Lourade's strategy to Moscow through Ilya would indeed reflect rather directly on him.

"No, no, no, of course not," Ilya said irritably. "But if we *had* delivered up the information, the Paris economic strategy department, which is to say you and me, Sonya Ivanovna, would have come out looking like the state of the art."

He peered at her speculatively. "You knew all this, Sonya," he said. "So why didn't you do what was right?"

"I *did* what was right, Ilya," Sonya found herself declaring somewhat forcefully.

Ilya leaned back in his chair. "You would perhaps not mind explaining how this is possible . . . ?" he said in a strange soft voice.

Sonya tried. She told him what Emile Lourade had done to Jerry. And how he had nevertheless signed Franja's admission papers. "After that, there was no way I could do anything that he might see as yet another betrayal, and whether he ever found out about it or not was entirely beside the point."

She looked at Pashikov, who was eyeing her most peculiarly now. "Not that I really expect you to understand, Ilya. . . ."

"Why not? Am I some nikulturni peasant from the tundra?" Ilya said quite indignantly. "Do you suppose that just because I wear Italian suits I lack a Russian heart?"

"You're not angry?"

Ilya shrugged, and in that moment his patrician airs seemed to become the genuine versions of themselves, and Sonya could see what all those other women must see in this man aside from the long blond hair and the cossack good looks.

"How could I be angry?" he said. "You did as your heart commanded, like an honest Russian wife, if you will forgive my Slavic phallocracy. I admire you all the more as a woman for it."

Then the moment passed and he became her boss again. "This, however, will not be what appears on both of our kharakteristikas. Instead of heroes of socialist entrepreneurship, Sonya," he said, "if the Moscow Mandarins were to be told *this* explanation of our failure, we would both be written off as hopeless bourgeois romantics, so we had just better let them grumble about our incompetence for a while and forget it."

It wasn't quite clear whether they *had* forgotten about it in Moscow, for while Ilya's anger had evaporated instantly, and while he was still friendly enough, he had been acting a little strangely around her, had become a bit more formal and closemouthed, as if, perhaps, more bureaucratic shit had flowed downhill upon him than he gallantly cared to admit.

So Sonya hadn't even thought to ask Ilya to escort her to

the celebration. She just left the office after work, slowly ate a platter of coquillage at a nearby brasserie to kill some time, and then took a taxi to La Decorusse by herself.

When Red Star decided that Paris should have a trendy place dedicated to Soviet Chic for it to show the corporate flag in from time to time, it had chartered a corporation in which it held 40 percent of the shares. The other 60 percent went to its French partners under the commission to create a hall that major corporations would be eager to rent for major corporate parties, thereby enhancing Red Star's prestige when it commanded the place for itself. And, of course, to make the style Russian, to make that style à la mode, and to do it at a profit.

Voilà, La Decorusse, which had spawned the style that was sweeping through Europe, and which Red Star subsidiaries were marketing unmercifully with everything from furniture to clothes to fast-food decor to food packaging to the new Place Russe Métro station. These days everything was Deco Russe.

The vanguard of this Soviet marketing invasion had been built on the Seine-side site of the sprawling old Renault factory as the centerpiece of the Place Russe, a new traffic circle that was accreting a trendy residential quartier around it in the traditional fractal Parisian fashion. On land that another Red Star partnership with well-connected Frenchmen had previously acquired at quite a reasonable price.

This icon of the Deco Russe style was modeled on traditional Russian church architecture and retrospective science fiction. An onion dome had been blown up into the entire structure, but it had been cunningly formed into a compromise between an Orthodox cupola and Flash Gordon's antique rocketship. Laser panels sent spirals of dopplering light up and around it, so that it looked like a combination of a church dome, some kind of Islamic flying saucer, and a rocketship about to screw itself out of the gravity well like a baroque Slavic phallus. Subtle it was not.

The inside of the dome was painted like a traditional outside, except that the brilliant spirals of colors rotated upward into interpenetrating double helices that spangled the ceiling with oddly curved diamonds of scores of different hues formed by the interference pattern.

The bandstand was a Lucite bubble suspended from the ceiling by a mirrored tube and speed-streaked with chrome eagle's wings like a cartoon satellite, and in it a quartet in rakish asymmetrically cut black tuxedos played subdued instrumental versions of transmogrified Russian folk songs on synthesizers and electronic balalaikas.

Buffets and bars had been set out around the periphery of the circular hall, with random scatterings of café tables inboard of them, leaving a large central area for dancing, which, though the place was crowded already, was being largely ignored.

The walls of the hall were not quite there. Holopanoramas circled the room, opening it out into a kind of generalized Soviet landscape, where bustling Tverskaya Street in the winter snow merged into a sunny Black Sea summer into spring sunset on the tundra into Tashkent sunrise into late afternoon on the Nevski Prospekt.

High above the floor and roughly on a level with the orbiting bandstand, a hodgepodge of walkways and little platforms were cantilevered out from a circumferential balcony; clear plastic, shining chrome, burnished steel, with railings and ramps of stylized space construction girders, giving the feeling of some kind of conceptual Cosmograd hanging overhead, with those who could take the vertigo perched on high and able to conceive of themselves as cosmonauts.

Nothing exceeds like excess, as somebody's old folk saying has it, Sonya thought as she wandered aimlessly around the party, sipping pepper vodka, nibbling at caviar canapés and cracked crab, drifting in and out of idle conversations, and counting the house.

Just about everyone from Red Star's Paris office above the level of secretary and janitor was there, including Ilya Pashikov, who was chatting up a ravishing young redhead, and whose sidelong glance and body language gave Sonya to understand that he wished the conversation to remain private and become as intimate as possible.

There were a lot of Embassy people as well, to judge from the presence of Ambassador Tagourski and his wife, who never attended such functions without an enormous entourage. There was a scattering of Red Army colonels and generals. There were a lot of people who might have been anything at all—security people, KGB, Tass, industrial representatives, Space Ministry people. Any Russian in Paris who was anyone seemed to be at the party.

And not much of anyone else, it would appear, for everyone seemed to be speaking Russian, and there was a certain Russian mood to the party that would not have persisted at an international reception, a looseness in the atmosphere, a loudness of voice and expansiveness of gesture, an easy disregard for personal body-space, a Slavic earthiness and exuberance bursting through the bonds of the formal clothing.

We are good Eurorussians all, Sonya thought, but tonight a bit more Russian than Euro. She found herself approving of the policy that had made this a basically Russian celebration. For while this was indeed a great day for all of the new Greater Common Europe, it was a day of special sweetness to a Russian.

"One Europe from the Atlantic to Vladivostok," if still a geographically confused slogan, was no longer a dream but a reality. The Soviet Union was now a member of the European family of nations, not as an economic charity case, but as the major economic, military, and technological power, first among equals.

And for the people here, for the Eurorussians of Paris, who had spent their careers outside Mother Russia helping to bring this reality about, it was a special kind of communal triumph.

We will not be any less the good Europeans for allowing ourselves to celebrate this one very special night together by ourselves as Russians, Sonya decided.

And so she wandered around the party, sipping vodka and not counting the glasses, chatting idly in Russian with people from other departments, with an office manager from Tass, with an economic officer from the Embassy, with a military attaché, with people from secretarial pools, with everyone in general and no one in particular, letting the traditional Russian sacrament melt her into the warm and exuberant communal glow.

And then she saw him.

Or thought she saw him.

Could it really be?

He was sitting at a little café table with a fellow who had the air and formal dress of a diplomat, and he looked a bit the diplomat himself in his black suit and white shirt. His hair was more gray than black now, and there were lines in his face, of course, but the eyes were the same, and the curve of the nose, and the ironic line of the mouth.

It was. It was Yuli. Yuli Markovsky. Here in Paris. After twenty years.

Sonya stood there on the spot, transfixed. Yuli hadn't noticed her yet. What should she do? How could she *not* speak to her old lover, the man she had been more or less engaged to, the road not taken? But on the other hand, it had all ended so badly that last drunken night in Moscow. . . .

Sonya edged closer to the table, hoping that Yuli would see her and take matters into his own hands, but he was deep in conversation with his colleague and didn't notice her. She went over to the nearest bar, got herself a fresh glass of vodka, and drank half of it down for courage.

When she returned, Yuli was alone.

Sonya shrugged. There was nothing else for it. She took another sip of vodka and approached his table.

"Yuli . . . ? Yuli Markovsky?"

Yuli looked up at her somewhat blearily with reddened eyes. He was obviously somewhat drunk. But tonight, by now, who wasn't?

"Sonya . . . ?" he said.

"May I?" Sonya said, pulling up a chair before he had nodded.

They sat there for a long moment just staring at each other awkwardly.

"You are still working for Red Star?" Yuli finally said.

Sonya nodded. "Assistant director of the economic strategy department here in Paris. And you?"

Yuli laughed strangely, and the ghost of an old familiar smile played across his mouth. "Well, as you may have heard, they have not made me Foreign Minister yet," he said. "But I am still in the foreign service, a middle-rank position in the Moscow bureaucracy, admittedly, but I still have my hopes. . . ." He frowned and sipped at his own half-empty glass. "Not under the present political conditions, of course," he muttered rather bitterly.

"Married . . . ?" Sonya asked, not knowing what else to say. This was all so incredibly formal and awkward.

Yuli nodded. "Three children. You?"

"Two," Sonya said, not caring to bring up the matter of her American husband.

"So, Sonya?" Yuli said.

"So, Yuli?"

"Have you gotten what you wanted out of life? Are you happy?"

"Good marriage, good children, a good life here in Paris," Sonya told him. "Perhaps my career might be advancing more rapidly. . . ." She shrugged. "And you?"

Yuli laughed again, but it did not seem like a particularly happy laugh. "La même chose, as they say in France," he said.

"And what are you doing in Paris?"

"Ministry business," Yuli said, in a tone of voice that made it clear he was not about to elaborate.

There was something truly horrible about this conversation that had Sonya wishing she had never noticed Yuli. Having once seen him, there had been no way she wasn't going to talk to him, but having begun talking to him, she found that she really had nothing of consequence to say, and neither, from the looks of it, did he. Their time together had been twenty years ago, it had not ended well, and they hadn't had any contact with each other since.

They were two other people, two strangers, attempting to make idle talk under extremely awkward circumstances, and Sonya found herself searching for a graceful exit line, when the music suddenly stopped.

Heads turned upward toward the bandstand as Ambassador Tagourski, of all people, looking a bit green around the edges with vertigo, emerged from the access tube and into the bubble, where he spoke with one of the musicians, who said something back to him, as conversations died into a pregnant silence.

"I have a rather unpleasant announcement to make, though I suppose the news is not entirely unexpected," the Ambassador's amplified voice said. "The President of the United States has signed a bill suspending interest payments on all government paper held by the governments of Greater Common Europe or private European citizens or corporations. These external debts will be converted into non-interest-bearing bonds redeemable only in blocked funds which may only be used to purchase manufactured goods and agricultural commodities within the United States. . . ."

Murmurs of confusion swept around the hall.

"For those of us unversed in these technicalities," Tagourski said, "what it means in plain Russian is that the Americans are abrogating their external debt, or at least the part owed in Common Europe, which amounts to something on the order of fifteen trillion American dollars."

"They've done it!" Sonya exclaimed as the place broke up into tumult. "They've actually gone and done it!"

"You expected otherwise?" Yuli Markovsky said cynically. "Believe me, this is only the beginning. Their next move is going to be the one that really hurts."

"Their next move?"

"Of course," Yuli said, "isn't it obvious? This is merely their vengeance on Western Europe, almost none of the loans they've just turned into toilet paper are in any way held by the Soviet Union. But when the expropriations begin—"

"Expropriations!"

"What a wonderful excuse for them!" Yuli said almost as if Sonya wasn't there. He took a sip of vodka and launched into the sort of semi-drunken declamation that she now found herself remembering all too well.

"No one quite knows just how much American real estate, stock, oil fields, coal mines, manufacturing facilities, and the rest is owned by European governments, individuals, corporations, and consortiums, but the Foreign Ministry's best estimate is that it is close to 30 percent of their national wealth, after all these decades of investment. What a boost for their moribund economy when they seize it all and sell it off to their own capitalists! Even at the discount prices the government will probably let it go for, they will net almost enough to pay off the Japanese component of their external debt in the bargain! One must admire their ruthlessness!"

"But that's outright theft!" Sonya exclaimed.

Yuli shrugged. "It's an honorable Third World tradition," he sneered. "Time was, the Soviet Union used to encourage it!"

"They can't possibly believe they can get away with such a thing!"

"Oh really?" Yuli said contemptuously. "Who is going to stop them? Certainly not *us!* While we were on our great peace offensive and turning ourselves into good little Europeans, *they* were making themselves militarily invulnerable. Their orbital lasers could destroy everything we or the Europeans have up there—the Cosmograds, Spaceville, every last satellite, perhaps even our Moonbase—in about as much time as it just took me to tell you about it. They've been deploying Battlestar America for decades, and the brute fact is that the damn thing works, or at least it works well enough to make them totally immune to the threat of force, as has been more than amply demonstrated by the way the world has had to stand aside while they do just as they please in Latin America."

"But surely, economic sanctions—"

Yuli laughed bitterly. "Oh, to be sure, Common Europe will no doubt nationalize American holdings here, such as they are, in retaliation, but the Japanese will do nothing for fear of giving the United States a handy excuse to nationalize *their* American holdings. Even a nation that doesn't play chess seriously can understand the advantage of trading a bishop for a rook and a queen!"

Sonya was appalled to say the least. "Is this mere conjecture on your part, Yuli, or . . ."

Yuli shrugged cavalierly. "A lot of it has been out in the open all along," he said. "When you add the necessary minimum of intelligence data . . . They mean what they've been saying, they're intent on turning the Western Hemisphere into a totally self-contained American economic empire, and no one can keep them from getting away with it. . . ."

Yuli continued to babble on, but Sonya was no longer listening. "They've got the resources to do it, coal, iron ore, copper, oil, more than enough farmland, uranium. . . ."

The professional part of her mind had taken over and was racing ahead to the pragmatic consequences.

Red Star, S.A., had no direct American holdings—Soviet investment had long been prohibited by American law—but it held hundreds of millions of shares in scores, perhaps hundreds, of Common European corporations that certainly did. And when the Americans expropriated those holdings, the prices of those stocks would plunge, there would probably be bankruptcies. . . .

"How much time do we have, Yuli?" she demanded.

"What?" Yuli said, blinking at her like someone emerging from a trance.

"How long before the Americans begin their expropriations?"

Yuli shrugged. "A matter of weeks, perhaps. They'll wait

for European outrage at the debt renunciation to peak, hoping for some stupid gesture from Common Europe, which no doubt will be conveniently forthcoming, and then they'll use it as an excuse to—"

"It's been interesting talking to you, Yuli," Sonya said, rising from her chair, "but I've got to get going now, you understand. . . ."

And she stormed off into the tumult in search of Ilya Pashikov. There was a nasty undercurrent that had taken the euphoric edge off the celebration, but from the passing snatches of conversation that Sonya overheard, it seemed to be mostly a matter of righteous indignation and besotted anti-American outbursts. It would seem that few if any of the people here had access to Yuli's intelligence, or if they did, were not yet clear-minded enough to draw the bottom-line conclusions.

She finally found Ilya still blithely attempting to seduce the same redhead as if nothing of personal significance had occurred. "If you will excuse us," she said, grabbing him by the arm.

"Sonya—"

"*Now,* Ilya!" Sonya insisted. "This is vitally important! We must find some place private to talk."

"This had better be good, Sonya," Ilya muttered petulantly. "*She* certainly was!"

"Oh it is, Ilya, it is!" she assured him, and muttering and glowering, Pashikov allowed her to lead him up onto the balcony, and out along one of the dizzying walkways to a clear Lucite platform where a small table and two chairs hung out in space high above the mob scene below.

"So, Sonya Ivanovna?" Pashikov demanded, folding his arms across his chest and staring fixedly straight ahead at her, as if in order to avoid looking down at all costs.

"So, Ilya Sergeiovich . . ." Sonya replied, and she told him what Yuli had told her, omitting the political rantings and sticking to the economic pragmatics.

"Yes, yes, all that sounds quite awful," he said when she had finished. "But why did you have to bother me about it *now?* It's not our department's responsibility, after all, and I was right in the middle—"

"Will you stop thinking with your prick for five minutes and use your head for a change, Ilya Sergeiovich!" Sonya shouted at her superior angrily. "Our department, meaning

you and me, has been in disfavor ever since . . . well, ever
since *you know* . . . has it not? Don't you see, this is our
chance to remedy all that! We are now in a position to save
Red Star billions of ECU!"

"We are?"

"Of course we are! We must pass this information to the
securities trading department at once! We have a week, two,
maybe three, to unload our shares in the companies that are
going to be affected before the bottom drops out!"

Ilya's eyes lit up. "Oh," he said simply. "Yes, of course
you are right. Well done, Sonya, well done!" And he
grabbed her by the hand, pulled her to her feet, and started
dragging her back along the walkway toward the balcony.

"What are you doing, Ilya? Where are we going?"

"To find Lev Kaminev!" Ilya told her. "He's down there
somewhere. . . ."

The party had ripened considerably despite the bad news,
or indeed, perhaps in part because of it. People had taken to
slugging back shots of vodka in the old traditional style
rather than sipping at it. The band had started up again, and
there were dancers out on the floor, including a group of
louts attempting to demonstrate their inebriated athletic
skills by doing the kazatski and laughing uproariously when
they fell on their butts. Ties were askew, jackets had been
discarded, and yes, there was terrible off-key group-singing
going on too.

It seemed impossible to find anyone in this melee, except
by random fortune, but once Ilya Pashikov was aroused, he
took the bit in his teeth, demanding the whereabouts of the
head of the trading department from all and sundry in a
loud commanding voice until they finally found Kaminev,
standing by one of the bars refilling his glass.

"A word with you, Lev, it's quite urgent," Ilya said, grabbing him by the arm.

Lev Kaminev's eyes were on the bloodshot side, but his
elegant powder-blue suit was still unwrinkled, his red tie still
neatly tied at the collar of his well-pressed white shirt, and
not a lock of his thinning gray hair was out of place. He
simply nodded and let Ilya lead him off to an empty table
near the circumference of the hall, where the holopa-
norama, all too appropriately, seemed to place them
squarely in the middle of the Siberian tundra.

"Tell him, Sonya," Ilya said, and Sonya did.

Kaminev's frown grew deeper and deeper as she went on, his lips began to tremble, and by the time she was finished, he had turned rather pale.

"What a nightmare!" he moaned. "We stand to lose billions!"

"Not if we act quickly," Sonya babbled at him. "Not if we start selling our shares at once, you must get to a terminal immediately and begin—"

Kaminev shook his head. "It's not at all that simple," he said. "If we just suddenly start dumping massive blocks of everything, we'll knock the bottom out before the Americans even do a thing. This has got to be done as slowly and subtly as possible. Buy puts where we can first. . . . Sell calls at market prices where it's feasible. . . . Then start unloading in reasonable-sized blocks gradually. . . . Keep the market from collapsing by trading options through dummies while we do it. . . . We can't be greedy and expect to come out ahead, or we'll start a panic ourselves, but maybe we can hold our losses under 20 percent, if . . ."

He ran his hand nervously through his carefully coifed hair, ruffling it into a scraggly rat's nest. "What a mess!" he groaned. "Our departments are going to have to work together on this, Ilya, and we're going to have to work day and night. We're going to have to model the whole damned situation and construct a trading program to get us out of it. . . . Lord, the variables involved . . . And if we're wrong, if we go ahead with all this, and the Americans *don't* expropriate . . ."

He looked over his shoulder nervously at the ersatz wastes of deepest Siberia, took a deep breath, and stared directly at Sonya. "If my department trades on this information and it turns out to be incorrect, the Supreme Soviet will reinvent the gulag just to have a place to ship us all to," he said. "You are *sure* this is not simply vodka talking?"

"Well . . . ," Sonya muttered uncertainly, contemplating the vista now herself and shivering. Yuli clearly *had* been drinking, and—

"The Ambassador is still here," Ilya said forcefully. "Put it to him in no uncertain terms! And if he hasn't been told about it, which would hardly surprise me, I will make some calls to Moscow in the morning. To people who will see to it that the Foreign Minister himself will be called on the carpet if need be. If they have been withholding information like this from Red Star—"

"Indeed!" Kaminev snapped. "That such information had to be winkled out by our own intrepid economic strategy department will be quite a black mark for them. If it's true, this may be just what it takes to get their obstructionism out of our hair for good and all."

He rose to his feet. "Keep this under your hats, you two," he said. "I'm going to go have a word with his Excellency. Can you get me a preliminary breakdown on our holdings in the affected companies by noon tomorrow, Ilya? Along with *their* holdings in the United States?"

"It'll take some doing," Ilya told him, "but we'll be on top of it!"

"I'm sure you will!" Kaminev said, and disappeared into the crowd in search of Ambassador Tagourski.

Ilya Pashikov sat there grinning at Sonya.

Sonya grinned back.

"You really *should* have my job, Sonya," he said.

"Who knows, if this goes well, maybe you'll get a nice promotion, and I will!" Sonya declared.

"Indeed!" Ilya exclaimed. "Why not?"

And he stood up, took her hands, pulled her to her feet, hugged her, and kissed her exuberantly on both cheeks. "If you weren't a married woman, I'd give you the kiss you really deserve for this!" he said.

He shrugged. He grinned. "On second thought, under the circumstances, why not?" he said, and planted a quick hard one on her lips.

A warm glow of excitement and accomplishment suffused Sonya from head to toe. Under the circumstances, it seemed no betrayal of Jerry to kiss him briefly back.

A PAGE FROM STALIN'S OLD BOOK

While it would certainly seem true that the United States has turned itself into a long-term pariah-nation by its massive expropriation of foreign property, unable to borrow on international markets or attract foreign capital for the foreseeable future, it is also true that with the stroke of a pen, the Americans have regained control of their own faltering economy, managed an indirect devaluation of the dollar in a manner politically acceptable to their own electorate, and made it abundantly clear that world opinion will no longer exercise even residual restraint over American policy in Latin America.

Thus, in a sense, did Stalin build the Soviet Union into a major industrial power by sheer act of national will. Thus did Hitler rescue Germany from a state of total economic collapse. Internal autarchy and external imperialism is an old realpolitik formula for short-term national renewal.

What happens later may be something else again. But when did American politicians ever look much further into the future than the next election?

—*Argumenty i Fakty*

X I I

A line of American Marines stood almost shoulder to shoulder on the sidewalk in front of the new cinder-block wall that had replaced the ironwork fencing on the Avenue Gabriel side of the American Embassy compound when Robert Reed arrived to pick up his American passport, the wall itself was crowned with rolls of razor-wire conspicuously wired for electricity, and there were neuronic disrupters mounted atop it at twenty-meter intervals. French Garde Républicain troops on horseback in the gutter cordoned the Embassy off from the park across the narrow street.

Even the passport office had been moved inside the compound for security's sake, and the security was heavy indeed. Bobby was gone over with a metal detector and a bomb-sniffer at the gate, then body-frisked before he was even allowed to join the line waiting to get into a temporary structure that had been thrown up to house the new passport office, and if there had been a place to do it conveniently, they probably would have made him drop his pants and looked up his asshole too.

Bobby could well understand the paranoia. The park between Avenue Gabriel and the Champs-Élysées was already filling up with people when he emerged from the Concorde Métro stop, many of them carrying furled banners, others carrying what looked to be the usual covered buckets of blood and shit and brandishing throwing sticks rigged out of broom handles and plastic bowls, and the few flics in evidence were conspicuously conversing with the assembling demonstrators.

Paris had been awash in anti-American demonstrations for the past week, ever since the United States had announced its expropriations of European assets, and the French police had done nothing more than hold it down to property damage; indeed, several cabinet ministers had even addressed more organized and semi-official demonstrations. Fortunately enough, examinations had just ended and the school year was over, so there were no arguments about whether or not it was safe for Bobby to attend classes, but Dad had backed up Mom in her insistence that the Dodgers jacket stay in the closet for the duration, and he had been told to stick close to home.

Bobby had gotten to the mail first this morning, as he had been doing for two weeks in anticipation, and when he finally saw the letter from the American Embassy, he pocketed it before anyone else saw it, for he knew that he would be forbidden to go down to the Embassy to pick up his passport if he was foolish enough to ask permission.

Everything else was set. He had been admitted to both UCLA and Berkeley, and since both were part of the California State University system, he had managed to bullshit them into giving him till August 25th to decide between them. He had an Air India ticket to New York for a week from Friday, and he even had a two-month prebought Air America travel card good for standby on all internal American carriers.

So he was not about to let the last detail hang in the air until his parents thought it was safe for him to go to the American Embassy, whenever that might be, if ever. Mom was already making noises about how maybe this might not be a good time to go to America, and he wasn't about to give her the chance to stop him by claiming it was too dangerous to pick up his passport until the departure date had passed.

He simply waited around till two o'clock, when Franja finally went out and left him alone in the apartment, and then took the Métro to the Place de la Concorde. Once he came back with the passport, he could just play innocent. If he never dreamed he had to ask for permission to do such a simple thing, Mom could hardly contend that he had disobeyed her, and even if she did, well, he would already have what he needed, now wouldn't he?

Bobby was not about to let a bunch of stupid demonstrations keep him from picking up the necessary papers, and from the scene inside the compound, it seemed that no other American still remaining in Paris had been scared away either.

The place was bedlam. The yard outside the passport office was mobbed with people, some of them actually lugging suitcases, demanding protection, demanding asylum, demanding to see the Ambassador or the commercial attaché, venting their spleen at the French, at the American government, at the Marines who body-frisked them, at each other, at the clerks trying to form them up into a line, all at the top of their lungs, and all at once.

It took Bobby at least an hour to get into the building, another hour on another line to exchange his letter for some kind of stupid authorization form, and then two hours on yet a third line before he could exchange *that* for his precious passport.

By then it was nearly seven o'clock, he was going to be late for dinner, Mom and Dad would already be home, and they had probably already stopped being worried and become furious. But at least he *did* have what he had come here for.

In a truly foul mood by now himself, fatigued by the endless waiting, irritated by the snarling mob scenes, and more than a little worried by what he was likely to catch when he finally got home, Bobby kneed and elbowed his way past the people clogging the temporary passport office, and out into the courtyard.

Something was very wrong.

There was a crowd of people clustered around the compound gate peering out through the heavy iron bars, and the gate was shut, with two Marine guards backed against it with their M-86s at port arms. There were more Marines inside the wall manning the remote control consoles wired to the neuronic disrupters atop it.

And then Bobby noticed what he had been hearing all along.

There was an immense roaring tumult coming from the other side of the wall, and the ragged rhythmic stamping of massed feet. Behind this, like the vocal track of a max-metal cut badly mixed to overemphasize the bass line, he could barely distinguish the words of the chant.

"AMER-I-*CAN*, AS-SAS-*SAN!* AMER-I-*CAN*, AS-SAS-*SAN!*"

Bobby shoved his way to the front of the mob around the gate, and what he saw through the bars made his stomach drop and his knees tremble.

The entire park across from the Embassy was clogged with people, all the way from the Champs-Élysées to the gutter of Avenue Gabriel, where the mounted Garde Républicain troops cordoned the mob off from the American Marines.

A sea of pumping fists and screaming mouths and reddened pop-eyed faces. An Uncle Sam effigy with a death's-head face hanging by a noose from a rude gibbet. An American flag on a pole, burning above the mob. A section of a long lettered banner he could not make out. Another banner that was a crude blowup of a thousand-dollar bill, smeared with blood and shit.

"AMER-I-*CAN*, AS-SAS-*SAN!* AMER-I-*CAN*, AS-SAS-*SAN!*"

Bobby had seen anti-American demonstrations before; indeed he had once marched in them himself. But he had

never felt anything like the wave of hate washing over the
Embassy wall. It went beyond politics, beyond economics,
beyond rationality. It was an outpouring of animal rage.

"AMER-I-*CAN*, AS-SAS-*SAN!* AMER-I-*CAN*, AS-SAS-*SAN!*"

Bobby was afraid. Bobby was ashamed. Doubly ashamed
—for America, and for the fantasy vision that flashed unbidden through his mind, an image of the American Marines
firing into that sea of angry people, blowing the nightmare
away with massed automatic-weapons fire.

"AMER-I-*CAN*, AS-SAS-*SAN!* AMER-I-*CAN*, AS-SAS-*SAN!*"

And then a glob of something came sailing in a lazy arc
over the wall and smacked up against the Embassy building,
smearing the gray stone with a patch of brown. And another, falling just short and impacting in the courtyard in
splatters of blood and turds.

A Marine sergeant came dashing up to the guards at the
gate, yelling something Bobby couldn't make out. "Cock-
suckers!" one of the gate guards shouted loud and clear.

More boluses of shit and blood came sailing over the wall
to splatter the Embassy. And then, for some reason, a great
cheer went up from the mob outside, and a massed fusillade
of ordure flew over the wall toward the building.

A moment later Bobby saw why.

The gate guards had leveled their M-86s at the mob outside. "Clear the gate! Clear the gate!" one of them shouted.
There was a clatter of horses' hooves on concrete. Marines
within the Embassy compound began herding the crowd
around the entrance away from the gate, and being none
too gentle about it.

Bobby had just a glimpse of what was happening before a
black Marine yanked him backward away from the gate by
the shoulders.

The Garde Républicain horsemen were trotting their
mounts up onto the near sidewalk and down the street to
the left. They were leaving the Embassy to the mob. There
was nothing between the wall and the mob now but the
cordon of M-86-toting Marines. . . .

Oh no, Bobby thought, they're going to have to fire into
the crowd! He didn't know who he loathed more in that
moment—the Americans who were about to gun down un-

armed people, or the fucking flics who had deliberately provoked them into doing it by leaving.

But it didn't happen.

Instead what happened was something that, at least for
the moment, made Bobby proud to be an American.

If the French had pulled the Garde Républicain in order
to provoke an American atrocity, the Americans weren't
biting.

The gate swung open, and two lines of Marines came
double-timing through it rapidly but in orderly file, their
weapons leveled at the mob to hold it back, but not firing.
The Marines were withdrawing into the compound.

It took only a minute at most to accomplish the maneuver. Then the gate guards withdrew, slammed the gate shut,
and threw a switch beside it.

With a triumphant roar, the mob surged forward to press
against the bars—

—and reeled backward, staggering and screaming from
the pain of the electric shock.

There was total chaos within the compound. The civilians
were dashing reflexively away from the wall as the roaring
mob pressed up against it, and a squad of Marines formed
up in front of the gate with their M-86s leveled just in case.
Some of the civilians were making for the safety of the Embassy building itself, but another squad of Marines had
formed up in front of the entrance to block them.

Fusillades of shit and blood splattered against the façade
of the Embassy and rained down into the courtyard. Bobby
stood there transfixed in the middle of it all, not knowing
what to do or where to run to, just trying to keep from being
knocked off his feet by the panicked people running around
in circles to no purpose.

"Look out!" someone shouted behind him.

Bobby turned toward the voice, but he turned the wrong
way, and besides, it was too late. As he turned, something
heavy and wet hit him on the left shoulder, splattering into
his hair and onto his left cheek. He staggered, almost fell,
righted himself, looked down at his windbreaker, saw it,
smelled it, gagged, and vomited all over his shoes.

The left side of his jacket was smeared with a congealing
mess of thick red blood and half-dissolved brown shit. The
stuff was in his hair and splattered all over his face. Spatters
of it were all over his pants.

He retched again, tore off the jacket, used the more-or-less clean part to wipe his face and neck, then toweled furiously at his hair, and tossed it away.

Blood and shit continued to smash against the Embassy building and pour down out of the sky into the courtyard. People were running around screaming. And, Bobby numbly realized, empty wine bottles and stones and bricks were now coming in over the wall too. . . .

"ATTENTION! ATTENTION! ATTEN-*SHUN!*" a great amplified voice shouted out above the chaos.

A black Marine officer had emerged from the building and stood at the Embassy entrance shouting into a bullhorn cranked up to maximum volume. "WE ARE GOING TO NEURONIC DISRUPTERS! WE ARE GOING TO NEURONIC DISRUPTERS! MARINES, INSERT YOUR PLUGS! CIVILIANS, BACK UP AGAINST THE BUILDING AND PRESS YOUR THUMBS IN YOUR EARS!"

Bobby forgot the blood and shit that was still splattered all over his pants and the puke drying on his shoes in his haste to get as far away from the wall and the disrupters as possible. He had never experienced a neuronic disrupter, but he, and everyone else crowding back up against the Embassy building, knew full well what was about to happen.

The neuronic disrupter cranked out a high volume of carefully chosen subsonic and ultrasonic frequencies that did extremely unpleasant things to the human nervous system. It stimulated a somatic panic response. It made it literally impossible to think. It vibrated the skull and the auditory apparatus to create one killer of an instant migraine. It loosened sphincter muscles, destroying bowel and bladder control.

It was the crowd-control weapon of choice of the American forces in Latin America, touted as noninjurious and humane by the United States, reviled as outrage against human dignity by the European media, who loved to show images of hapless Latin Americans clutching their guts, holding their heads, and shrieking in agony like animals.

Bobby himself had often enough shared in the conventional outrage, but now, terrified, infuriated, reeking of blood and shit and vomit, with his back up against the wall of his Embassy and his thumbs pressed tightly in his ears, it was another story.

"ACTIVATE NEURONIC DISRUPTERS!"

The disrupters were directional, but some backwash was inevitable, and even with his thumbs pressed tightly in his ears, Bobby felt a horrible vibration, as if a miniature jackhammer were at work on the top of his head. He found himself pressing harder and harder back against the building wall, fighting the urge to break and run. His bowels felt like shimmering jelly, and it took an enormous effort to keep from pissing in his pants.

It couldn't have gone on for more than five minutes, but it felt like hours. People around him fell to their knees. Some of them had wet stains about their crotches. What was going on on the other side of the wall, where the mob was getting it full blast, was difficult to imagine.

"DEACTIVATE NEURONIC DISRUPTERS!"

And all at once it was over.

The headache pain was gone, as was the urge to flee to nowhere in particular. His bowels firmed up, and he no longer had the overwhelming urge to piss.

And there was a strange hushed silence. No more mob noises. No more ordure and missiles sailing over the wall. People stood around numbly, smeared with filth, stealing sidelong glances at each other.

A Marine guard deactivated the charge on the gate. A sergeant formed up two neat lines of troops. The gate was opened, and the two files of Marines trotted out through it to reestablish their cordon.

"IT IS NOW SAFE TO LEAVE THE COMPOUND," the Marine officer said through his bullhorn. "PLEASE DO SO IN AN ORDERLY FASHION. REMEMBER—YOU ARE *AMERICANS.*"

And indeed, people who a few moments before had been running around and screaming in panic dutifully and politely formed themselves up into a rough triple line and filed out through the open gate quietly, without any pushing or shoving.

Bobby stood there in the street for a moment, surveying the wreckage and trying to sort out his feelings.

The gutter and the sidewalks were littered with debris—placards, banners, throwing sticks, overturned buckets of blood and shit, an Uncle Sam effigy that had been trampled underfoot, puddles of piss, rocks, bricks, broken bottles.

He shuddered as he imagined what it must have been like out here only a few minutes ago, thousands of people clutching their aching heads, shitting and pissing in their pants, fleeing in animal panic, just like the Latin Americans he had seen scores of times on television.

He crossed the street and began walking toward the Place de la Concorde Métro stop, past the line of Marine guards, who stood staring stony-faced straight ahead, at ease with their M-86s slung on their shoulders.

He paused. He looked up and behind him at the façade of the American Embassy.

It was encrusted with blood and shit.

And so was he.

But neither had been dishonored.

For despite it all, his American passport was in his pocket, and despite the terrible provocation, not a Marine had opened fire, not a rioter had died.

And the Stars and Stripes still waved in the breeze over the ordure-encrusted Embassy, transforming the blood and shit itself into a badge of honor.

And in this most unlikely of all moments, making Bobby prouder than he had ever been before to be an American.

CARSON TO RUN FOR SENATE

Representative Harry B. Carson today announced his candidacy for the Republican nomination for United States Senator and formed a Senatorial campaign committee.

Party leaders expect no serious opposition to nomination of the popular Congressman from Dallas who has claimed much of the credit for spearheading the Renationalization Act in the House. State Democratic leaders refused public comment, but the long faces at party headquarters told the whole story. A preliminary phone poll shows Carson favored over the strongest possible Democratic candidate by a margin of 27 percent.

—*Dallas Straight Shooter*

"Are we going to wait *forever?*" Franja groaned.

Sonya glanced across the dining room table at Jerry, who sat there stabbing nervously at his half-eaten pâté with his fork and staring into space. "Shall I, Jerry?" she said.

"What?"

"Shall I serve the salmon?"

"Jesus, how can you two think of food at a time like this?" Jerry snapped irritably.

Sonya shrugged. "We've waited over an hour already," she said. "We can sit here staring at each other or we can sit here and eat. What else can we do?"

When Bobby hadn't shown up on time for dinner, she had waited ten minutes and then angrily served up the pâté de canard, leaving his plate empty. Let him miss the entrée, it would serve him right!

Fifteen minutes later, when he still hadn't turned up, the anger had turned to worry. Now she had passed into a perverse state of mind where paranoia and anger mingled. Her mother's heart was filled with fearful fantasies of what might have happened to Bobby, but if nothing really *had* happened to justify this behavior, he was going to wish that it had when he finally got home!

"At least now that you and Pashikov have finally finished pulling off your stock market coup, I would have thought you might finally start caring about your family again!" Jerry shot back.

"Oh no, not that again!" Sonya moaned.

"Oh *yes,* that again!" Jerry said. "Or is that too much to ask from the assistant director of the economic strategy department of Red Star, S.A.?"

"I'm going to serve the salmon!" Sonya declared, and she stomped off into the kitchen, set the oven for two minutes of microwave rewarm, and slapped the ON button angrily.

It had been like this for weeks now. Kaminev had sworn them to secrecy, and Ilya had made it clear that that emphatically included Sonya's American husband. . . .

She and Ilya had been working endless days and evenings analyzing the holdings of every European company in which Red Star held an interest, preparing scores of economic-impact papers, and doing most of it themselves so as to minimize the possibilities of leaks to the staff, some of whom just might have started trading options on their own if they knew what was going to happen. It had been exhausting but exciting, and, in its way, a welcome escape from Jerry's endless depressive bitching and whining.

At least to hear him tell it, Boris Velnikov, the chief project engineer that the Soviet Union had imposed upon ESA, was strictly a bureaucrat who hadn't done any real hands-on work for years, and a Russian chauvinist with an open contempt for Americans in the bargain.

Jerry had been excluded from key meetings, they wouldn't give him a staff, and his access to the main project computer files had been limited to what Velnikov considered relevant to "maneuvering system design." Complaining to his old friend Corneau did no good, and Emile Lourade wouldn't even return his phone calls.

When Sonya *did* manage to get home in time for dinner, she was forced to endure endless tirades against Velnikov, and when she didn't, she had to suffer through whining complaints about how she was neglecting her own family.

It got to the point where she began catching dinner with Ilya after work even when they ended early enough for her to go home in decent time to eat with Jerry and the children.

Sonya was forced to keep her silence and take it. She even managed to hold her tongue when Jerry started insinuating that her evenings with Ilya Pashikov might not be entirely business.

The only thing that had kept her going was the work itself. Beneath the permanent exhaustion there was an exhilaration, the exhilaration of at last working at the full stretch of her powers on something that really mattered, that affected the destiny of her company and her country..

The best-case scenario always came up the same—Red Star, S.A., was going to lose about 18 percent of its net worth no matter what they did. But in the long run, there was indeed a way of coming out ahead.

Kaminev began selling stock in the companies that were likely to be bankrupted by the expropriation of their American assets—in modest-sized blocks through dozens of dummies on every stock exchange in the worldwide net. When the stocks dropped below a predetermined price, they bought big blocks of out-of-the-money calls, firming up the price of the underlying stock, enabling them to sell more shares and buy cheap out-of-the-money puts, shedding their holdings gradually as the prices ratcheted downward in a controlled manner. It was a losing proposition, but all the computer models showed that this scenario would minimize the damage.

Red Star also held stock in many companies that would survive the expropriations, and unloaded big blocks, driving the prices prematurely downward close to what the models said would be their post-expropriation worth.

When "Yankee Thursday" hit, and the European markets blew off 30 percent of their value in the panic, Red Star had already disposed of all its stock in the companies that were going to go belly-up, as well as a lot of the shares it had held in those the models said would survive.

At the bottom of the market, when sellers outnumbered buyers ten to one at any price, Red Star was sitting on a mountain of cash, and it spent most of the money buying up huge blocks of shares in the companies the models had identified as survivors.

Companies whose stock prices Red Star itself had driven down to their post-expropriation intrinsic worth *before* the panic drove them even lower. Which not only let them bottom-fish like bandits at artificially depressed prices, but let Moscow grandly announce afterward that it had stepped in to shore up the markets in the interests of Common European solidarity.

When the dust cleared, Red Star had sold off its shares in the companies that were going to fold at a net loss of about 22 percent, but had greatly increased its holdings in the survivors at cut-rate panic prices that were already bouncing upward, and the Soviet Union had come out smelling like a political rose in the bargain.

Yankee Thursday's trading had gone on long into the night, and Sonya and Ilya had cracked open a celebratory case of vodka for the staff afterward, so Sonya hadn't gotten home till after 3:00 A.M., riding high on euphoria, fatigue, and a certain amount of vodka, and she was surprised and delighted to find Jerry in bed but still waiting up for her. Now at last she could tell him the whole truth and clear the air between them, the perfect ending for a perfect day.

But Jerry was in an even fouler mood than usual. "Where the fuck have you been?" he demanded by way of greeting.

"At the office, of course," Sonya said calmly. "What a day!"

"*Day?*" Jerry snapped. "It's nearly 4:00 A.M.! What have you and Pashikov been doing?"

"Celebrating with the staff," Sonya told him as she started to undress. "Haven't you heard the news?"

"How could I miss it?" Jerry said sourly. "I've been catching shit all day. And now you come reeling home in the wee hours of the morning!"

Sonya kicked off her shoes, peeled off her blouse, stepped out of her skirt, and cuddled up to him on the bed in her bra and panty hose. "Poor Jerry," she cooed, throwing an arm around his shoulders. "Don't worry, things have turned out a lot better than anyone yet realizes. . . ."

"You're drunk!" Jerry snarled, pulling away from her.

"I may have had a few vodkas," Sonya admitted. "But believe me, I earned them."

"So you and *Ilya* tied one on together!"

"Oh really, Jerry, it was just a little office party! To celebrate!"

"The bottom falls out of the stock market, and you and your boss get shit-faced together to celebrate?"

"We made out like bandits, Jerry!" Sonya exclaimed happily. "That's what I've been trying to tell you!"

"Tell me what?"

"What Ilya and I have been working so hard to accomplish all these weeks!"

"Aside from a little hanky-panky?"

"Will you stop it, Jerry, you know that's absurd, I'm trying to tell you *why* I've had to spend so many extra hours at the office!"

"So tell me," Jerry said belligerently, folding his arms across his chest and regarding her skeptically like some KGB interrogator in a bad historical movie.

She did. But when she was finished, his expression still hadn't lightened. If anything, he seemed even angrier.

"All this time, and you didn't tell me a thing . . . ?" he said slowly in a tightly controlled voice.

"I couldn't, Jerry, I was under orders, and besides—"

"You let me sit here and stew in my own juices, imagining all the things you were doing with Pashikov—"

"—you might have blown the whole thing."

"Blown the whole thing! What did you imagine I would do? Tell the CIA? Mortgage the apartment to buy put options, or whatever the hell you call them? You think I give a good goddamn about any of this crap!"

"Then why are you so angry, Jerry?" Sonya asked reasonably.

Jerry's rage abruptly subsided into a sad sullen smolder. "Because my own wife didn't trust me," he said in a much smaller voice. "Because your loyalty to Red Star was more important than your loyalty to me. . . ."

"Oh, Jerry, Jerry," Sonya cooed, reaching out, trying to roll over onto him.

But Jerry pushed her away. "Not tonight, dear," he said sarcastically, "you're drunk, and I've got a headache." And he rolled over onto his side to face away from her.

And they hadn't made love since.

Jerry Reed sat at the table silently fuming. What a week this had turned into! While Sonya had made the world safe for Soviet stock market speculation, Velnikov had used the foul odor surrounding all things American to pressure Corneau into appointing a chief maneuvering system engineer directly above him.

"One can understand how Boris feels, n'est-ce pas?" Patrice had said with a little shrug when he finally called Jerry into his office. "Here he is with the title of Chief Project Engineer, and there you are, the engineer whose basic plans form the framework for the whole project. He has power, but no professional respect, while you are so to speak the Grand Old Man, the éminence grise. It is natural for him to want you as far out of the circuit as possible. . . ."

"What about *my* feelings, Patrice?" Jerry demanded.

"I know things are difficult for you now, Jerry," Corneau said. "But after all, we are in the early organizational phase, where there is really very little for you to do. Once we get down to actual design, things will be much different."

"Will they, Patrice?"

"Bien sûr!"

"With a chief maneuvering system engineer above me?"

"Ah, but you forget that this maneuvering system design consultant job description is just a fiction! Once the project is truly underway, you will be working directly with me, and on everything!"

"Velnikov will permit this?"

"*I* am in charge of this project, not Boris Velnikov!" Corneau declared, perhaps a bit hollowly. "He may be . . . connected, as they say in Moscow, but *I* am the project manager!" He pursed his lips. "Still . . . ," he said reflectively.

"*Still . . . ?*"

Corneau shrugged. "What with the recent American un-pleasantness, the political pressures on me to accede to Velnikov's demands in this matter are going to be pretty irresistible," he said. He favored Jerry with a sardonic little smile. "Peut-être, the wisest course might be to preempt him, n'est-ce pas? Let *you* step aside for the good of the project yourself, and be quite sure that everyone knows it. . . ."

"Just great!" Jerry had said. "You hand me the knife and ask me to slit my own throat."

"It is not like that, Jerry," Corneau had said somberly. "I am truly sorry you feel this way. At least do think it over."

And he had left things hanging like that. And Jerry had thought it over. Over and over and over again.

This was the sort of miserable bureaucratic politics that he hated and that Sonya was so good at. But the way things had been going between them, he hadn't even mentioned it to her. He had a feeling that he knew what she would say—go along with the inevitable, cover your bureaucratic ass, and at least rack up some Brownie points in your goddamn kharakteristika.

Or worse still, the way she and Pashikov were riding so high with Moscow after their great stock market swindle, she might try to go over Velnikov's head and have Red Star put pressure on him to back off. But that would mean doing it through the Golden Boy, in return for what Jerry didn't care to contemplate, for while his mind told him that the idea that she had been having an affair with Ilya Pashikov was pure paranoia, the thought of going to the son of a bitch for a favor through her made his stomach turn and his blood boil.

And now this thing tonight with Bobby—

Sonya came out of the kitchen with a sour look on her face and the big wooden serving tray in her hands bearing a dish of salmon steaks and roasted potatoes and a bowl of hollandaise sauce. She put it down on the table and dished out salmon and potatoes for the three of them, leaving Bobby's plate empty.

Where the hell *was* he? It just wasn't like Bobby not to show up for dinner like this. And I *told* him to stick close to home, what with all the anti-American—

"Oh, Mother, this fish is dry as dust!" Franja moaned.

"Well then put some of this hollandaise—"

The apartment door opened and then closed with a thump. And then Bobby came down the hallway and into the dining room.

"Bobby!" Sonya exclaimed.

Bobby stood there in his shirtsleeves. His pants were coated with a dried crust of what appeared to be shit, the left side of his hair was plastered to his head with what looked like more of the same, there was a smear of it on his forehead, and his shoes were splattered with something that looked very much like dried vomit.

"Where the hell were you, Bobby?" Jerry demanded. "What the hell happened to you?"

Bobby smiled at him stupidly. He fished something out of his back pants pocket and held it up like a protective talisman. "I . . . uh . . . went down to the American Embassy to get my passport," he said. "I . . . uh . . . got caught in this demonstration. . . ."

"You were in the riot at the American Embassy!" Sonya cried, not knowing whether to be furious or relieved.

"What riot?" Jerry said.

"Haven't you seen—"

"There was a peaceful demonstration at the American Embassy," Franja broke in, "but the gringos turned on their neuronic disrupters and turned it into—"

"That's a lie!" Bobby shouted. "They were charging the wall, they were throwing blood and shit and bottles and stones, and the Marines *had* to—"

"I saw it on the news!"

"I was *there,* and you weren't!"

"And I'll bet you really enjoyed it!"

"That's enough, you two!" Sonya shouted. "Robert, you go take a shower at once! We'll discuss this when you're decent!"

"About a century from now!"

"That'll be enough of that, Franja," Sonya said angrily. "Be quiet and finish your dinner, or leave the room!"

It was a tense ten minutes in the dining room while Bobby showered. Franja sat there silently gobbling up her salmon and potatoes. Sonya picked impatiently at her food, not speaking, obviously saving it up for Bobby.

Jerry didn't even bother with his food as he sat there dreading what was about to come.

Finally, Bobby returned to the dining room in a T-shirt, jeans, and his battered old Dodgers jacket, his hair wringing wet from the shower, bedraggled, but triumphant and defiant.

"You've got some explaining to do, Bob," Jerry said quickly, before Sonya could open her mouth or Bobby even had a chance to sit down. "You were *told* to stick close to home."

"But this was *important,* Dad," Bobby said as he seated himself. "I *had* to go get my passport, I'm leaving for America next week, after all, and I—"

"That's quite out of the question now!" Sonya snapped.

"What?" Bobby shouted.

"The Russian mission to the U.N. was ransacked by a mob! They've put Battlestar America on yellow alert! You've got Senators screaming for the seizure of Bermuda and Cayenne and Martinique and Curaçao under the Monroe Doctrine! The President himself is talking about annexing Baja California! The worst elements of the American ruling class are using the anti-American reaction in Europe that they provoked themselves to justify a new round of naked imperialist aggression!"

"So what?" Jerry said. "What does all that political crap have to do with—"

"So what!" Sonya shouted. "The entire country has gone mad! America is about as stable as one of its Latin American puppets! We cannot send our son into such chaos! It would be like . . . like blithely sending him off to college in Madrid right before the Spanish Civil War!"

"Or Budapest just before Khrushchev sent in his tanks to crush the Hungarian freedom fighters?" Bobby snarled angrily. "Kabul just before the Russians invaded?"

"Bob!" Jerry exclaimed. "Can't *you* at least leave politics out of it?"

Sonya stared across the table at her son, feeling the full brunt of his rage as he glowered back at her, and strangely enough, she felt a surge of love for him as he stared her down and swapped political insults like an adult and an intellectual equal.

"No, Jerry, Robert is right," she said, still looking straight at Bobby. "Politics *is* what this is all about. Yes, Bobby, the Soviet Union has done terrible things in the past, even as America is doing now. You're quite right, letting you go to America now would be just like sending you to Budapest or Kabul in front of the Russian tanks."

"That's not what I meant, Mom, and you know it!"

"I know you won't believe it, but I *am* doing this for your own good, Robert—"

"You lied to me!" Bobby shouted. "You never intended to let me go!"

"That's not true, Bobby!"

"How can you call your own mother a liar?" Franja cried indignantly.

"No one's talking to you, so shut your fucking face!" Bobby screamed at the top of his lungs, his face flushed red, his eyes bulging, veins standing out in his neck, as he bolted to his feet and slammed his fists down on the table.

"You're all the same!" he shouted. "All you fucking Russian liars! You'll do anything to get your own way! You'll cheat and steal and spy and scheme and lie to your own children!"

"That's enough, Bobby!" Sonya cried. "I'm still your mother, and I don't have to listen to this imperialist filth!"

"Oh don't you, Mom?" Bobby snarled at her. "Haven't you been going around bragging how you and Red Star pulled off your big stock market swindle? Some Common Europeans! The Soviet Union is in Common Europe for a month, and you're already screwing everyone! And you call *Americans* imperialists!"

"How dare you—"

"I've got my ticket and I've got my passport and I'm an American and I'm going to America and no fucking Russians are going to stop me!" Bobby howled in completely uncontrolled rage. And he stormed out of the dining room.

"So go to America and rot with the rest of the dirty gringos!" Franja shouted after him.

"That's enough, Franja!" Jerry shouted. "Go to your room! Your mother and I have some private talking to do!"

And Franja left, leaving Sonya sitting there vibrating with

adrenal backwash, alone with her husband, as he stared at her with a cold unreadable expression.

"The boy is right," Jerry said evenly, forcing himself to stay calm. "We gave our word, Sonya. It's a matter of honor."

"Honor!" Sonya snapped. "What about *duty?* What about parents' duty to their children, to protect them from danger, and if necessary from themselves? Would you really send your own son into danger over a *word?"*

"It depends on the word," Jerry told her.

"Phallocratic rubbish!" Sonya declared angrily. "For *this,* you'd let your son march off into a hornet's nest?"

Jerry thought of Bobby, standing there befouled and bedraggled, but holding up his American passport triumphantly. "If that's what it takes to let him become his own man," he said. "Better danger than giving up a dream."

"Honestly, Jerry!"

And Jerry remembered another young man with another dream, long, long ago, a young man who had given up everything to follow it, and the girl who had stood by his side and given him the courage to do it.

"You didn't always feel this way, Sonya," he said softly. "Don't you remember someone else who risked everything for love and a dream?"

Sonya's eyes softened. "Yes, I do, Jerry," she said, her hand creeping across the tabletop toward his. "You were very brave, and I do remember. But this is different. . . ."

Jerry was not quite ready to take her hand yet. "The dreams may be different," he said, "because they're our children's, not ours, but the courage to follow them, that never changes. . . ."

"Jerry—"

"*I* had a dream people told me I could never have, and if I hadn't chosen my dream over safety, I wouldn't be here now begging you to let our son choose *his.*"

Sonya's hand backpedaled across the table. "And if I don't?" she said.

Jerry thought about it. He thought about twenty years of marriage. He thought about his own endless travails and frustrations. He thought about Rob Post, dead now, with all his dreams unfulfilled. And he thought about Bobby, standing there with his passport in his hand, covered with blood and shit and vomit, but undefeated still.

He sighed. He hardened his heart. Now too was a moment that called for courage, not for himself, but for his son.

"If you don't, Sonya, I'm going to have to march him down to the American Embassy tomorrow and put him in their care. He's got a right to American citizenship, and they'll give it to him. And keep him in the Embassy until it's time to board the plane."

"You do this, and I'll leave you, Jerry!" Sonya blurted.

"You make me have to, and I won't care," Jerry shot back without thinking.

"It's blackmail."

"Call it what you like."

They stared at each other for a long hard moment.

Finally, Sonya sighed. "Over the summer, then," she said. "But in the meantime, he applies to the Sorbonne. And comes home in the fall."

"That's going to be up to him, isn't it?" Jerry said.

"He applies to the Sorbonne or he doesn't leave with my permission," Sonya said coldly.

"You drive a hard bargain."

"So do you, Jerry, so do you."

"I've learned in a hard school."

"Moi aussi," Sonya said. "Moi aussi."

And she rose from the table and left him sitting there with the wreckage of dinner in the empty room.

NEW ANTI-AMERICAN VIOLENCE IN BAJA

A mob of at least a hundred Mexicans, apparently under the influence of alcohol and marijuana, invaded the Sunshine Plaza Shopping Mall in Libertyville on the southern outskirts of Tijuana today, harassing shoppers and inflicting considerable property damage before being forcibly ejected by American security guards.

"The Tijuana police refused to do a damn thing about it," Elton Jarvis, Sunset Plaza's manager, complained angrily. "If the Mexican authorities refuse to protect American property, maybe it's time we Baja Californians got ourselves a government that will."

—Los Angeles Times

"What's wrong with you, Sonya?" Ilya Pashikov said. "You've been dragging around the place like something out of Dostoyevski for days now. Why the long face and the staring into space?"

"I'm sorry, Ilya," Sonya muttered. "I know I'm not getting much work done, give me a few days and I'll snap out of it. . . ."

Ilya shrugged. "Why not?" he said with a warm little smile. "Take a whole week if you want to. After this last month, who is to say we haven't earned it! And when you come back, *you* can cover for *me*, there's a lady friend of mine in Antibes who's been pining away for lack of attention. . . ."

"A vacation?" Sonya said in some surprise. "Just like that?"

When Ilya had called her into his office, she had expected a dressing-down, for she knew full well that she had not been working well since that awful confrontation with Jerry. She would drag herself into her office, shut the door behind her, shuffle papers aimlessly, drink endless cups of coffee, avoid dealing with anything she could put off, initiate nothing, and spend most of her time brooding over what had happened.

It wasn't so much that Jerry had gotten his way in the end, it was the *way* he had worked his will on her, and indeed, if she was honest about it, the way she had tried to work her will on him too.

You do this, and I'll leave you, Jerry!

You make me have to, and I won't care.

"Politics stops at the bedroom door," someone's old folk wisdom had it.

But whoever had said that had not peered inside *her* bedroom these past weeks! After almost twenty years of marriage, one could hardly expect the red-hot passion of courtship. But surely that did not mean that marriage was supposed to slide into this amatory Cold War?

They were polite to each other, too polite, perhaps, but she lacked the courage to reach out to him and break the ice for fear of rejection, and so, perhaps, did he. There was only one way to heal the wound that those terrible words had opened up in their marriage, but the wound itself seemed to keep them from touching, the lack of sexual contact seemed to feed on itself, the hurt feeding the celibacy, the celibacy feeding the hurt, the tension building and building into something too complex and convoluted for the simple straightforward resolution of a good uncomplicated fuck. . . .

"Cannes? Ibiza? Crete?"

"What?"

"Where will you go, Sonya?"

"Go?"

"On your vacation!" Ilya exclaimed. "From the look of you, you're a thousand kilometers from here already!"

"I'm sorry, Ilya," Sonya muttered. "I don't think this is the time for me to take any holiday. . . ."

"Why not?" Ilya said. "You're certainly not doing much good around here!"

There was no censure in his voice when he said it, only Ilya's usual lighthearted bantering tone, and when she rose up out of her funk to take a really good look at him, she saw that beneath it there was a genuine warm concern. She felt a surge of emotion as she looked into his honest blue eyes, a longing she could not quite define.

"I just can't go off and leave Jerry and the children right now, Ilya," she said equivocally, wondering why she could not quite meet his gaze.

Ilya leaned across the desk toward her. "Trouble at home?" he said softly. "Is that what this is all about?"

Sonya bobbed her head.

"Want to tell me about it?"

"Oh, Ilya," she moaned. "I just *can't*. . . ."

"Of course you can," Ilya said. "What are friends for?"

Now Sonya did look up at him and face him honestly. The finely tailored mustard-colored suit, the romantic Tartar features, the long flowing golden hair, the perfect lady-killer who made no bones about it. But behind and beneath all that, there was something else, the something that she now realized she had been responding to.

Ilya Sergeiovich Pashikov *was* her friend. Perhaps the only real friend she had.

Ilya rose up from behind his desk, went to the door, and locked it from the inside.

"Ilya! What do you think you're doing!"

"Breaking the rules," he said. "I won't tell if you don't." He came back to the desk, opened a drawer, withdrew two shot glasses and a bottle of buffalo-grass vodka. "As the old

Russian-American folk saying has it, 'When the going gets tough, it's time to get drunk!' "

Ilya took the vodka over to the office couch, sat down in the left-hand corner, patted the seat beside him. "Come on, Sonya, have a few and get it all off your chest."

Sonya found herself walking over to the couch and sitting down on the opposite end. Ilya poured two glasses and handed her one. "Drink up!" he commanded.

Sonya slugged down the tepid, pungent, oily stuff, and grimaced. "It's warm," she said.

"Is it?" Ilya said, studying his glass. He bolted it down, muzhik-style. "You're right," he said, pouring two more. "We'd better have another quickly, so we won't notice the taste."

Sonya laughed and drank up. Ilya poured another round. And another.

"So?" Ilya said. "What's the problem?"

A wan warm glow suffused Sonya's limbs, like the strangely satisfying fatigue that had come toward the end of so many of their long days working on the impact reports and company analyses together, the loose-jointed feeling that came from sharing hard and exciting labor, the feeling of tired comradeship that had come after the sun went down, when they had staggered out to the nearest brasserie for a bottle of wine, a quick dinner, and an idle discussion of the day's work.

Somehow, she found the vodka dissolving her back into that special time and place that she and Ilya had shared, and she started talking, not about impact statements and scenarios, but about Bobby, and Jerry, and what had happened that awful evening, with the same end-of-the-day ease, with the distance of a tale told to an old and trusted friend, to a workplace comrade far, far away from the scene of domestic strife.

Ilya, for his part, just sat there listening, saying little, nodding his head and bobbing his long golden hair, pouring more vodka when their glasses got empty. Somewhere along the line, Sonya's shoes had been kicked off, and her legs had become tucked under her on the couch, and the room began to whirl a little, and she found herself next to him, cuddled in his comforting masculine aura, not touching, but physically closer, somehow, than she had been in bed with Jerry all these weeks.

"Ah, but you are punishing yourself needlessly, Sonya, I think," Ilya said expansively, leaning a bit closer himself, and seeming to weave in her vision woozily, though whether she was woozing, or he was woozing, or both of them were sharing a friendly little wooze together, it was hard to tell.

"How so, Ilya?" Sonya said, gazing into the depths of his somewhat bloodshot blue eyes.

Ilya shrugged, and in so doing, managed to lean even closer, so that she could smell the aroma of him, compounded of cologne, and talc, and his warm vodka-perfumed breath. "You do not really wish to leave your husband, do you?" he said. "And he does not really wish to leave you, da?"

"I suppose not," Sonya said. "But things have been very hard, Ilya, very hard indeed. . . ."

Ilya reached out and patted her hand. A thrill went through her, unbidden. This man, this beautiful man, who was a veritable human octopus with other women, though certainly a suave and not unwelcome one, had never touched her flesh *this way* before. "Poor, poor Sonya," he said. "Perhaps the problem is that things have not been . . . hard enough, n'est-ce pas?" he drawled.

"Oh, Ilya!" she cried, and pushed him away with a gentle shove to his chest, but not without a girlish little giggle.

Ilya threw his arms up and back, letting himself loll in languid ease against the couch. "No, seriously," he said. "I am not exactly a world-class expert on marital discord myself, not having succumbed to the traps and snares of conjugal bliss thus far—and with a little luck and some help from my lady friends, hopefully I never will. However, when it comes to the discontent of other people's wives, let us say that I am not unacquainted with what the Americans would call the 'seven-year itch,' in your case, a decade and more overdue, I should say. . . ."

"Should you, Ilya?"

"Probably not," he admitted. "But on the other hand, I am decently drunk enough to throw such cautions to the wind, as it were, or even as it were not, so to speak. Which is to say . . . Which is to say . . ." He scratched his head. "Which is to say *what?* I'm afraid I've forgotten what I'm talking about."

Sonya laughed. "Knowing you, it was probably sex," she said.

"Sex? Ah yes, no doubt you are right! Now there is a subject concerning which I indeed have some expertise!"

"Do tell!"

"About whom? A gentleman never tells, you know, and that is what I am, good Communist or not!"

"What a beast you are, Ilya Sergeiovich!" Sonya cried.

"Moi?" Ilya said superciliously. "Far from it! I have never forced my attentions on any woman!"

"Only because you haven't had to!" Sonya told him.

"Ah, but this is not so, not so at all!" he declared. "Oui, it is true, I am never without the amorous attentions of the multitude, but that does not mean I have never manfully refrained from plucking forbidden fruit!"

"Oh really? Like whom?"

"Like you, Sonya Ivanovna," he said.

"Me?" Sonya said in a tiny voice. Dust motes seemed to hang and sparkle in the air before her. A delicious fear blossomed in her breast and spread down her stomach and between her thighs, where it became a treacherous dissolving warmth.

"Surely you have noticed?" Ilya said, prying his upper torso shakily off the couch, leaning forward, and staring deep, deep into her eyes.

"Noticed what?" Sonya whispered, leaning closer herself.

Ilya glanced down at his crotch, where a telltale bulge strained against the fabric of his tightly tailored pants.

"Oh really, Ilya," Sonya said softly. And she reached out her hand to push him away again. But when her palm touched his chest, something, some trick of gravity, or vodka, or she knew not what, made it linger there, feeling his heartbeat.

"I have fucked at least three hundred women," Ilya said, staring into her eyes. "I have been a noble stakhanovite of sex. I have fulfilled my five-year plan a hundred times over like a true hero of socialist labor. Fucking for me, it is nothing. I flit from flower to flower, as it were, floating like a butterfly, stinging like a bee, as the gringos would have it. But truth be told, never have I bedded a woman whom I truly respected as I respect you, my good and true friend."

"Oh, Ilya, as the gringos would also say, you are so full of shit that it is coming out of your ears!" Sonya said. But she found herself putting her other hand on his shoulder.

"No, no, no, it is true!" he declared. "We have worked

together, we have shared meals together, we have drunk together, we have smelled the sour sweat of each other's fatigue. We have shared every intimacy save one. . . . So what does it matter? Who is to know?"

"You are quite drunk, Ilya Sergeiovich!"

"And you are quite shit-faced yourself, Sonya Ivanovna."

"Who am I to deny it?"

"Well, shall we get it over, then?"

"Get what over?"

"The cosmic inevitable," Ilya said, and he swept her up into his arms, and he pressed his lips against hers, and thrust his tongue deep into her mouth. And that was the end of thought.

Why the pull-back on Wall Street? The conventional wisdom is that we're just seeing the inevitable profit-taking after the big Renationalization run-up. But if you look at where all the cash being pulled out of stocks is going, you get a different picture, amigo. Institutional investors, flush with the profits they've taken, are gobbling up Baja California real estate like there's no tomorrow, inflating land values to the point where there are few real bargains left.

But adventurous investors can still cash in by buying secondary regional bank stocks. The majors are already in up to their eyeballs, leaving the smaller banks to write the loans for the Johnny-come-lately small-fry speculators in a lenders' market. True, a lot of this action is highly leveraged, and it's not for the weak-hearted.

For conservative investors, defense stocks remain the most prudent play, particularly the California-based majors.

—*Words from Wall Street*

XIII

As the ancient pickup truck began climbing up out of Boulder and into the majestic fir-covered foothills of the Rockies, Robert Reed finally began to feel that he was really in the America of his dreams—hitchhiking west across the Continental Divide toward fabled California, just like the beatniks and Oakies and hippies in all the old novels he had devoured in Paris. On the road at last!

Behind lay Denver, and New Orleans, and Chicago, and Miami, and Washington, and New York, and a ghastly ten days that had disabused him of most of his preconceptions, including his original plan to use his Air America pass to hop from city to city, seeing the country as he zigzagged across it in the general direction of Los Angeles.

New York was everything the legends said, and worse. Hundreds of soaring towers rising right out of crumbling rat-infested ruins. Elegant restaurants and sidewalk vendors selling what looked suspiciously like rat-kebabs. The Statue of Liberty, where they ran you through metal detectors and bomb-sniffers before they let you climb the long spiral staircase to the crown. The Empire State Building with its magnificent view of the city from on high and its hundred floors of foul crash-cubicles within. Central Park, with its tent cities, patrolled by armored cars. Beggars and prostitutes on Wall Street, right in front of the famous Stock Exchange.

It was like some dreadful living political cartoon of the injustices of American corporate capitalism, and after a day, and a sleepless night, and another day wandering the savage streets, Bobby had had more than enough, and he caught a shuttle flight to Washington on an ancient 767 that lost an engine on the forty-five-minute flight from La Guardia airport.

Washington was not nearly as expensive as New York. The center of the city was ringed by relatively cheap and relatively decent tourist hotels, though from what Bobby saw on the bus ride in from the airport, the surrounding sprawl of slums was, if anything, worse, reminding him of nothing so much as the shantytowns surrounding some gleaming African government center, and just as thoroughly black.

But the nation's capital had geared itself to tourism, its only major industry besides government, and what festered

outside the gleaming alabaster centre ville was kept at bay
by an army of police, who were constantly in evidence
checking the identity papers of anyone who was black and
did not dress up to their stringent standards of middle-class
civilization.

The center of the city had been turned into a kind of
patriotic Disneyland, and Bobby, like most of the rest of the
tourists, signed himself up for the two-day guided tour. He
was taken to the top of the Washington Monument, and
inside the House and Senate chambers. He saw the Lincoln
Memorial, and the Jefferson Memorial, and the White
House. His group was quick-marched through the Smithso-
nian and the National Aerospace Museum and the Library
of Congress—though the Pentagon, and the Vietnam memorial, and the Challenger monument were for some reason not on the tour.

And all the while he was subject to the most appalling
jingoistic blather from the tag team of guides, who sounded
as if they were all reading from the same script, and probably were.

The Washington Monument was an excuse to remind the
tourists of George Washington's warnings against entangle-
ments with effete Europeans. The Iwo Jima statue was the
occasion for the glorification of what the Marines were presently about in South America. The National Space Museum
was somehow a monument to the vision that had given the
country Battlestar America, which was now allowing it to
thumb its nose at a hostile world.

Bobby was mighty glad he was wearing his Dodgers jacket
as the citizens on his tour sucked all this up with avid agreement and choruses of diatribes against the evil Russians and
the perfidious Peens, for it was quite clear that the general
opinion was that Common Europe had sold out civilization
to Godless Atheistic Communism, that Europe richly deserved the economic hosing it had just received in return,
that American military might was the Last Best Hope of
Man, and that he had better keep his mouth shut and his
European birth to himself.

Washington was absolutely dead at night, and the guides
had made it clear that so were you if you strayed out of the
safe areas in search of fun and games, so Bobby spent his
two evenings there watching American TV in his hotel
room, or at least as much of it as he could stomach.

There were game shows, and soft-core porn, and endless episodic series in midstream, mostly tending toward glorification of past American military ventures in World War II and Korea and Cuba, a completely insane musical about Teddy Roosevelt, a science-fiction series featuring cannibalistic aliens who spoke with stage-Russian accents, and a Ronald Reagan film festival.

The news shows were even more puke-awful and frightening. To hear the commentators and the edited footage tell it, Europe was committing fearful atrocities against American citizens, the Soviet Union was seizing control of the Common European government, American troops were beating the bejesus out of the guerrillas in Venezuela and Argentina, and the Mexicans were brutally attacking American settlers in Baja California, and cruising for a bruising. Since the Mexican government was in the hands of European dupes anyway, the general consensus was that the Monroe Doctrine was about to be applied, and none too soon, for the purpose of which a naval task force was in the process of being assembled off Miami, and another off San Diego.

From Washington, Bobby caught a flight to Orlando. When he got there, he found that the Kennedy Space Center had been placed off limits to civilians and was surrounded by endless tacky suburbs servicing military and space personnel that sprawled all the way to the frontier of the Magic Kingdom.

This seemed somehow appropriate, for Disney World had decayed into a hideous parody of the ruins of an out-of-date future, where the amusement rides were clogged with drunken and swaggering military personnel, and the Epcot Center displayed the last century's scientific wonders, and creaky audioanimatronic robots sparked and jerked spastically. Mickey Mouse, Roger Rabbit, and Donald Duck waddled down Main Street in military uniforms, terrorizing Frenchie the Frog, Limey Dick, the Frito Bandito, and Ivan the bright Red Bear.

Miami was the most prosperous American city Bobby had seen, terrifying where New York and Washington had been merely depressing, filled as it was with soldiers, sailors, airmen, mercenaries, arms merchants, speculators, whores, drug dealers, political refugees—the major staging base for the U.S.'s military and paramilitary operations in Latin America and the Caribbean.

The drinking age seemed to be about twelve, and so Bobby was able to spend a night there bar-hopping, sipping truly dreadful tropical concoctions and listening to the local bar-talk with growing horror.

It was no secret here that a large naval task force would soon be on its way to blockade the Gulf Coast of Mexico. The bars were full of sailors from the ships taking their final liberty, paratroopers who expected to be dropped on Vera Cruz and Mexico City any day now, Marines and soldiers on R&R from Venezuela and Argentina full of gleeful war stories, all of them drunk out of their minds on booze and adrenaline, and eager to go out and kill some more spicks for God, country, and kicks.

What the denizens of the Miami bars were fantasizing about was a President with the balls to *really* enforce the Monroe Doctrine as God had intended, to kick the fucking faggot Europeans out of Bermuda, Curaçao, Cayenne, Martinique, and the rest of their Western Hemisphere territories and throw them all open for a big land grab like what was shortly going to come down in Baja, what a cakewalk *that* would be, real profitable too, and surely there must be some way to apply the Doctrine to Canada, the Canucks still were part of the British Commonwealth after all, now weren't they . . . ?

One night of this was more than enough, and so the next afternoon, once his hangover and upset stomach had subsided to the point where he could face another move, Bobby escaped the feral lunacy of Miami, shaking and sweating, on the first flight he could get, which turned out to be to Chicago.

Chicago was another New York, with a little less dirt and a lot more wind, and then on to New Orleans, which was decay dripping with verdigris in sweatbox heat, and another wide-open military pigpen, and from there to Denver, which at least was farther north and farther west.

Which was about the best that could be said for it. To a born-and-bred Parisian, Denver was hardly a city at all, more an endless collection of dull bedroom arrondissements with no street life.

Between Denver and Los Angeles, there was nothing, or, as the old American saying had it, "miles and miles of miles and miles." He could hop a plane to LA and fly over it, or . . .

Or he could hang out his thumb and try to find that other America that his heart told him must still be out there somewhere. The Rockies and the Great Desert. The Sierras and the Mojave. A thousand miles and more of empty spaces as cities were counted on the map, but the land of legend from another perspective, cowboys, and Indians, and cattle drives, and wandering hippie tribes, outlaws, and ghost towns, and timeless mystic landscapes.

So Bobby lettered the word "West" on a piece of cardboard, screwed up his courage, shouldered his backpack, walked to the nearest freeway entrance, stuck out his thumb, and waited.

He had waited in the hot smoggy sun for nearly an hour, while electric city cruisers, big long-distance fuel-cell haulers, and petrol-guzzling monsters buzzed by, quite ignoring him, before this old pickup truck, with its load of toilet bowls and plumbing fixtures, finally pulled up.

Bobby dashed to the passenger-side door and opened it. The driver was a burly gray-haired man in his sixties wearing a battered straw cowboy hat, mirror shades, and a set of filthy blue coveralls.

"How far west ya goin', bucko?" he said in what Bobby imagined was a perfect cowboy drawl.

"LA."

"Figures for a Dodger fan," the driver said, with a little laugh. "Bring your butt aboard, you like, get ya as far as Vail, anyway."

The driver's name was Carl. He thought it was real hilarious when Bobby asked him if he was a cowboy. "Figures the last of the hitchhikers make me for fuckass cowboy! Though them'd call me outlaw, thinkin' at it!"

"Outlaw?"

"Shithouse bandito, bucko, make it! Haw! Haw! Haw!"

"Huh?"

"Hey, Bob, I'm a *plumber,* make it, and when they get the bill, they're gonna shit in their pants anyway, haw, haw, haw, serve 'em right for buyin' them Jappo johns in the first place!"

Carl did a lot of talking on the way from Denver to Boulder, and Bobby kept his mouth shut for the most part, for most of it was about how the ol' US of A had been corned by the Jappos and the Peens for far too long now, and it had been about time *we* got down to doin' the screwin', and he should know 'cause he had done his time in fuckin' Nicaragua and Panama, was only luck they had made him a shithouse commando in the Army and taught him a trade still worth a fuck of a buck after all these years, or the spicks woulda iced him in the jungle, and if not, he'd probably be screwin' bolts in a factory fer nigger wages 'stead of screwin' the homesteaders, make it, that was the scoop they said about plumbers, really *was* a license to steal, haw, haw, haw . . .

It was a tense ride until they drove through Boulder and began climbing up into the mountains, and Bobby had started to hate this ignorant, hate-spewing, chauvinistic gringo.

But now that they were climbing up into the verdant green mountain fastness, a change had come over Carl the plumber. He ceased his jingoistic jabber, popped an actual *Beethoven* chip into the truck's player, and sat there, leaning back in his seat, holding the roof with one hand out the open window, steering with the other, taking an occasional deep breath of resinous pine-tinged air, with a dreamy smile on his face.

"Nothin' like this in Akron, bucko," he'd mutter from time to time. "Fuckin' God's country, yes . . . Love this drive . . . 'Magine what it was like when there was nothin' here but mountain men and grizzlies, hey . . ."

Higher and higher they climbed, into vaster and vaster mountains, where there was nothing to be seen but green trees and brown loam and outcroppings of gray granite, and it seemed to Bobby that the America of the past ten years was slipping away, in space and time, and some elusive understanding seemed to tease at the edge of his consciousness, and strangely enough, he began to feel a kinship with this plumber, this old veteran of the Central American wars, this former shithouse commando, for all of that seemed long ago and far away as they retraced the epic journeys of the long-ago pioneers through a landscape that the hand of man had scarcely touched since Columbus first set foot on the American shore.

The landscape changed as they drove higher, the trees thinned out and became scraggly, and then they were above the treeline, and there was nothing but rich brown earth and dark slate-colored rock.

"The fuckin' Continental Divide," Carl said softly. "From

here on in, the streams all flow west. It's the roof of the world, make it, the backbone of this great fuckin' continent. Made this drive a thousand times, still can't help thinkin' about it. Fuckin' pioneers crossed all this in covered wagons behind horses and mules, make it, bucko! Shit, they musta had balls the size of watermelons! Makes ya proud, don't it, Bob? Know what I mean?"

Bobby nodded, for in that moment he did understand, and something he had feared lost was all at once found, and he understood what he had been feeling. There was just him, and Carl, and the timeless grandeur of this immense landscape, as it had always been, as it would always be, and none of what lay in the cities and the lowlands could ever touch it.

"Yeah, Carl," he said contentedly. "Makes you proud to be an American."

Carl drove through Vail, a onetime resort town that had been overdeveloped into a miserable little industrial city that seemed obscenely out of place in this glorious mountain setting, then dropped Bobby off on the highway where a narrow feeder road wound back into the canyons, right in the middle of glorious nowhere.

Bobby stood there on the road all by himself in the high mountains, and not minding it at all, for the better part of an hour before he got picked up by a big empty flatbed hauler driven by a squat, ugly woman with crew-cut blond hair and wearing an ancient brown leather jacket, whom he at first took for a man.

"Esmerelda's the handle, believe it, not exactly butch, now is it, used ta call myself Erika back when I cruised the bars in Philly in neo-Aryan gear, brass swastikas and all, ya shoulda seen me, woulda creamed ya cojones, but when I came up here to blow all that, I took back the name ma mommy gimme, seemed only right, know what I mean . . . ?"

She laughed when Bobby goggled uneasily at her. "Hey, relax, boy, I ain't about to eat *you*, not my thing, I'm what they call a diesel dyke, though never drove nothin' but these fuel-cell haulers, now this time, it's a load of logs I'm pickin' up—'bout a hundred down the road for Salt Lake, so I can take ya as far as the turnoff. . . ."

Bobby got another hitch almost immediately after Esmerelda dropped him off, this time on a slow, full log hauler
driven by a black man named Duke who claimed to have
had a cuppa with the New York Yankees way back when,
went two for fifteen in the majors, you could look it up, but
just couldn't handle the split finger. Duke took him all the
way down into the corner of Utah, where the mountains got
lower and rockier, and things started to dry out, and he
could feel the warm breath of the approaching desert, and
taught him more about baseball than Bobby had dreamed
possible.

The sun was going down by the time Duke dropped him
off at a little rustic camp beside roaring river rapids, just a
tiny general store, a fuel station, and a few cars and tents
down by the riverside.

"Now you listen up, Bob," he told him. "You don't try to
go no further tonight, and tomorrow you don't take no ride
that don't get you all the way to Vegas, 'cause you *do not*
want your ass caught out there by the road in the desert!
And when you get to Dodger Stadium, spring for a seat in
the lower deck right behind the plate and see if you can pick
up the old split finger any better'n I could; you'll see why
I'm out here truckin' it, betcha!"

Bobby went into the store and bought himself packets of
some plastic-looking yellow cheese and rubbery pink
charcuterie, an apple, a small loaf of whole wheat bread,
and a can of beer, which was about all he could figure out to
put together for dinner out of the meager stock. The man
behind the cash register had long red hair, a bushy unkempt
beard of the same color, a big belly bulging out his T-shirt
over a wide belt, and all in all fitted perfectly Bobby's image
of what an old mountain man should look like.

"Uh . . . you wouldn't have a room to rent for the night,
would you?" he asked.

The storekeeper looked at him peculiarly. "This look like
a motel, Angeleno?" he said. "Too good to sleep out by the
river?"

"Uh . . . I don't have a tent or a sleeping bag."

"Huh?" The storekeeper seemed quite amazed by that.
"Watcha doin' way out here without campin' gear?" he demanded righteously.

"Hitching my way to California."

"Jeez!" the storekeeper exclaimed, his surprise tinged

with a certain awe, or so it seemed. He studied Bobby speculatively. "Ain't got no room, but I got an old bag I could lend you. 'Course this ain't free-lunch city."

"How much?"

"Got something else in mind, city boy. You afraid of a little honest grunt-work like the rest of 'em?"

"I can handle it, I guess. . . ."

The storekeeper took him around the back of the building and opened a door flanked by three big empty garbage cans. Inside was a musty storeroom piled with cardboard boxes of canned goods. Empty cartons, old tin cans, and general litter were scattered all over the dusty wooden floor.

"Shouldn't take you more'n an hour t'clean this mess up, and then you can have the sleeping bag for the night, or crash in here. 'Course if you ain't never slept out under the stars in *this* country, and from the looks of you you haven't, y'd be an asshole ta miss it!"

It actually took more like two hours for Bobby to get the job done, but he really didn't mind, it was the first time he had done physical labor for *anything*, let alone a simple place to sleep, and somehow it made him feel . . . connected to something he could not quite define, a part, somehow, of the mighty landscape, of this western country and its timeless slow-moving stream of life.

And of course, he opted for the sleeping bag and took it down to the riverbank, where he ate his cold meal and drank his beer staring into the foaming rapids, luminescent and scintillant in the brilliant mountain starlight.

Then he crawled into the sleeping bag, deliciously tired after the long eventful day, and lay there gazing up at the stars through the gently waving tree crowns.

Oh yes, he had been right to leave the cities and the airports behind him to ride his thumb along the open road, for an entirely different America had emerged from this ground-level perspective.

People here still seemed to be living off lumbering, ranching, farming, and servicing each other, as they had since other sons of Europe had first made their way west across this great continent to become Americans. The American West and its people had in some deep way not changed since the days of the cowboys and Indians and would in the same deep way remain as they were long after cities grew old on Mars.

Out here, drifting off to sleep by an American river under these brilliant American stars, Bobby was content for the first time since he had set foot on these shores. At last he felt that he had in some way come home. At last he had found a piece of the America of his dreams, an America he could truly love.

The next morning, Bobby canvassed the people in the tents by the river, trying, as per Duke's warning, to find a hitch that would take him all the way across the desert to Las Vegas. The best he could find was an old retired couple named Ed and Wilma Carpenter, on their way to Death Valley, where, they assured him, he should be able to catch a lift to Los Angeles even at this time of year; what with the Fuller Dome and all, it was a summer resort for Angelenos too, even with the heat.

"You can drive, son, can't you?" Ed Carpenter asked him. "Wilma and I, we're getting on a bit, and we could do with a bit of relief."

Bobby thought about lying about it, but he had already told them one about being a UCLA student on his way back to school from visiting his folks back East, and besides he had no idea whether he could fake it once behind the wheel.

"'Fraid not," Bobby said. "I never learned how."

Ed looked at him peculiarly. "You go to school in *Los Angeles,* and you can't drive a car?"

"Uh . . . I live in the dorms, and I've got a bike," Bobby said, giving him a good European explanation. "And . . . uh . . . my folks, they don't have much money," he added when Ed didn't seem to quite buy that for some reason.

Ed looked at Wilma. Wilma looked at Ed. They both shrugged.

"Well, why not?" Ed said. "The car just about drives itself, and there won't be any cops out there. Be good to have a young man to talk to. What you say, Bob, you want to try to learn how to drive? After all, you *are* a Californian, sort of. . . ."

"Oh, Ed!" Wilma cried. But she giggled, and the three of them climbed into the electrocruiser, Bobby in the backseat, and off they went, with Ed Carpenter at the wheel.

The car was a fuel-cell job with four-wheel electrodrive, air conditioning, plush bucket seats front and rear, a water-cooler, a little refrigerator, "our little living room on the road," Wilma called it.

Ed and Wilma had owned a furniture store in Golden, and after ten years in business, they had put aside enough to put a down payment on the building it was in. Never thought they'd make enough to retire, but then three years ago, a developer came around and bought up the whole block to put in a shopping mall, gave them a nice price, and after they closed out the mortgage, they had enough money to buy a life annuity which paid out enough so they could indeed retire and take these little camping trips, see Yosemite, the Grand Canyon, Zion, and now Death Valley. Their son Bill was a captain in the Air Force, flew Penetrators out of Edwards, and they were going to tool up there and pay him a visit later on.

They were a pleasant enough old couple, and as the car descended out of the western slopes of the Rockies into the dry and rocky high desert, they had exhausted their modest little life story and started quizzing Bobby about his.

Bobby had been dreading this a bit; it was going to be a long drive, and he didn't like the idea of spinning long elaborate lies for these honest, open people, but it was second nature by now, and besides he was fearful of revealing his European background to the parents of a captain in the United States Air Force.

So he made up a story about his mom and dad back in Akron, she was a schoolteacher and he was a foreman in a steel mill, just plain folks, but they had managed to save up enough money to send him to UCLA, what with a partial scholarship he had gotten, where he was presently majoring in world history, thought he might end up teaching too, maybe even at a university level, who knows . . . ?

"World history?" Ed said somewhat dubiously. "What are they teaching about that at *UCLA* these days?"

"Pardon?"

"I hear tell they got *Reds* teaching history to you kids out in California, or so Bill says. . . ."

"Reds? You mean . . . Communists?"

"Oh, Ed!"

"Now come on, Wilma, everybody's always hearing this stuff, now we've got a chance to really learn something about it from Bob here. What about it, Bob?"

"What about what?"

"Well, for instance, is it true that those European-loving chrome-domes are telling you kids that the Russians won the Second World War?"

"Well, they sure don't teach us that the Germans won it," Bobby replied uneasily.

" 'Course not! We went over there and gave that Hitler what for after the Peens all rolled up and presented their butts to the Krauts—"

"Ed!"

"And the Marshall Plan? They teach you how the Peens swindled us out of all those billions and never paid back a dime?"

"What?"

"See, Bill was right, Wilma, they don't teach these kids a damn thing!"

"Now you watch your swearing, Ed Carpenter!"

"Now what about Vietnam? What do they teach you about the KGB selling heroin to the hippies and starting those riots in Chicago?"

"Uh . . ."

"I thought so! Why I'll bet they don't even tell these kids how KGB agents in the Carter administration sold out the Panama Canal to the Communists in Panama! Or the way the English started the Civil War to grab our cotton fields. Or how Fidel Castro killed Jack Kennedy."

"Oh don't be silly, Ed, everyone knows all that!"

Even in the air conditioning, Bobby started to sweat as nice old Ed Carpenter poured out the most amazingly bile-filled crackpot version of fragmentary history that he had ever heard.

The Mexicans had forced America into the Mexican War by invading Texas. Communist agents had created the stock market crash of 1929 so they could elect themselves FDR, whose wife, Eleanor, was an agent of the KGB. A senile Ronald Reagan had been hypnotized by Mikhail Gorbachev, who was a secret graduate of the Pavlov Institute. The Soviet entry into Common Europe was the first step toward the creation of a Soviet world empire, and Spaceville was a front for the clandestine creation of a European Battlestar America, which would be used to force the United States to give back the property that America had just so righteously seized. . . .

"*That* what they teach you at UCLA?" Ed Carpenter demanded.

"Uh . . . not exactly," Bobby muttered dazedly. "I mean—"

"I thought not!" Ed declared triumphantly. "See Wilma, Bill was right, they don't teach these kids a goddamn thing!"

"I will not have you swearing in front of this boy!" Wilma cautioned crossly. "What kind of people do you want him to think we are?"

Bobby had to choke back his laughter at that one at the time, but as the drive wore on, he had time to ponder the question seriously, and it perplexed him sorely indeed.

They came out of the western foothills of the Rockies into the most amazing landscape Bobby had ever seen. The Great American Desert stretched out before him under a pitiless blue sky, a vast wasteland of naked rock and searing sand in washed-out tones of dun and gray, an immense and apparently utterly lifeless nothingness that seemed to go on forever.

Here the road was arrow-straight, the traffic was sparse, and after about an hour, Ed Carpenter pulled over to the side of the road.

"Why don't you take this stretch, Bob?" he said with a grin. "No way any cop can sneak up on us out here!"

And Bobby found himself driving the electrocruiser across the Great Desert at exhilaratingly high speed, while Ed, and when she could get a word in edgewise, Wilma, kept up a ceaseless patter.

Driving the car, even for a neophyte, was simplicity itself; there was power steering so forgiving you could take your hand off for five minutes at a time on a road like this, an accelerator pedal and cruise-control switch, a brake pedal, which Bobby never had to use once, a digital speed display, and that was about it.

The conversation, though, was deeply disturbing. One minute Ed Carpenter was expanding on the immensity of the landscape and the incredible courage of the pioneers who had crossed it in covered wagons, and the next he was ranting about the treacherous Peens who were befouling American Embassies and seizing American property. He would launch into quite a fascinating discourse on the creatures that lived in this wasteland, and then he would segue into a diatribe against the Mexican government, which was persecuting honest American homeowners in Baja, and which soon enough was going to get what it so richly deserved.

More disturbing to Bobby than the rabid jingoism, or the necessity of holding his tongue when the better part of him cried out to refute this vicious blather, was the fact that, despite what was being spewed forth, he *liked* Ed and Wilma Carpenter.

They had been kind to him. They were polite avuncular old folks with a feel for the country they were traveling through. Their love for America was genuine and somehow touching. They even let him drive their car.

Yet at the same time, they sincerely believed the most vile chauvinistic filth. Ed Carpenter's ravings were exactly the sort of stuff that the European media put in the flapping mouths of the worst sort of caricature Americans. What had happened to America to make them like this? How could good people like Ed and Wilma believe such stuff?

What was he supposed to believe about them?

Wilma took the wheel about fifty kilometers from the outskirts of Las Vegas, just as the billboards were starting to appear, and turned off onto a ring road around the city.

"We don't go through Vegas?" Bobby said, rather disappointed.

"Goodness no!" Wilma replied. "The traffic through the center is terrible, and besides, it's full of Japs these days, come to gamble away the money they've taken from us, and all sorts of prostitutes and perverted sex shows besides!"

"Not the sort of thing for a nice young man like yourself to see," Ed agreed. "The American Ginza they call it, and the Japs can have it! Now Death Valley, where we're taking you, *that's* something to see, you'll never forget it, I promise you that, Bob!"

Once they had skirted Las Vegas, a low range of sere mountains started to rise along the western edge of the road, and soon enough Wilma took a turnoff toward them, through a little town, and up the slope, to a view from the crest of the ridgeline that quite took Bobby's breath away.

Below them stretched a long desert valley beneath the towering peaks of the High Sierras, an elliptical dry lake bed, all salt and sand, shimmering in the waning afternoon sunlight like an immense mirage, like something that wasn't quite there. And flashing and gleaming in the middle of it like the faceted eye of a gigantic insect, a huge geodesic dome.

"Wow . . ." was about all that Bobby could manage to say. "It's like . . . it's like another planet!"

Ed Carpenter laughed good-naturedly. "Sure is something, isn't it?" he said. "It's the lowest piece of land on *this* planet, Bob, and hotter in the summer than the devil's backside." He pointed to a distant peak in the high craggy mountains on the other side of the Valley, where Bobby thought he could make out an actual frosting of *snow* near the top. "And yet there you have Mount Whitney," Ed said, "which is the highest point in the continental US of A!"

"You're right," Bobby said softly, "this is a sight I'll never forget, and I'll never forget you folks for showing it to me, either." And meant it.

The Carpenters were going to stay at Scotty's Inn, which, Ed told him, was a tiny hotel where you had to book weeks in advance, and "something of an old folks' home, Bob, you wouldn't like it anyway." The Dry Wells Dome was where the young folks went, lots of rooms he could afford, and it would be the best place to get a hitch to LA in the morning.

So they drove him down to the Fuller Dome in the center of the valley floor, and said good-bye in the air-conditioned car in the parking lot outside.

"Well, it was pleasant meeting you, young man," Wilma said. "Good luck to you in your studies."

"And don't you let those Reds in UCLA pull the wool over your eyes, you hear?" Ed Carpenter said as they shook hands.

"I won't, Ed," Bobby told him. "Traveling with you folks has sure been an education."

He meant it too, and not entirely sarcastically, either, for the Carpenters had taught him an important lesson. Which was that people could believe the foulest things and still be good folks at heart. A lot of the people who had thrown blood and shit on the American Embassy in Paris were probably just as sweet on a personal level as Ed and Wilma Carpenter.

"Politique politicienne!" he could hear his father saying, and for the first time, he thought he really understood what Dad meant.

Then he got out of the air-conditioned car and was nearly bowled over by the wall of heat. Talk about another planet! This was like stepping out of a spaceship air lock onto the surface of Venus. The cruel sun seared his unprotected eyes. He could feel it frying his skin. He could actually see the heat waves coming off the hot metal of the parked cars.

He stood there for a few moments, taking in the incredible experience and waving a last good-bye to Ed and Wilma as they drove off, and then trotted quickly to the Dome's main entrance.

The Dry Wells Dome was air-conditioned, of course, but they kept it at a balmy 80 degrees Fahrenheit to simulate an attenuated desert experience, and there were palm trees and desert succulents, as well as a big swimming pool fashioned out of some clever synthetic that mimicked frozen dunes of sand. There were rude cabins scattered among the trees, and a kind of main street reminiscent of Disney World, half a dozen restaurants, a drugstore, a liquor store, boutiques, a saloon, a small hotel, all done up like a brand-new mining town out of the Old West.

It was crowded inside the Dome, mostly with people in their teens and twenties, most of them with deeply bronzed skin and showing plenty of it, the men in bathing trunks or brief bikinis, the women parading around bare-breasted, Midi-style.

Bobby went over to the hotel to rent a room, but the guy at the desk, ludicrous in a tightly tailored cowboy suit and ten-gallon hat, told him that nothing was available.

"What am I supposed to *do?*" Bobby moaned.

The ersatz cowboy looked him up and down. "Wal," he drawled, "ya can stow your gear with me, partner, till you find yourself some pussy, good-lookin' young kid like you shouldn't have no trouble finding someone with an empty bed around here."

"Are you kidding?"

"Are you kidding *me,* partner? What else does anyone come to Dirty Death for?"

For want of anything better to do, Bobby checked his pack and wandered over to the saloon. There were certainly plenty of girls around here who looked unattached, but there were plenty of guys who looked like they were on the make, and back in Paris, Bobby had not exactly been a lady-killer. He wasn't a virgin, but he wouldn't have to take off

his shoes to count on his digits how many times he had
gotten laid, either. Of course it *was* warm enough in here to
sleep out under the trees if he could find a place where no
one would roust him. . . .

The saloon was done up like an Old West bar, more or
less. Rustic walls, and a wooden floor sprinkled with saw-
dust. A long wood-and-brass bar with stools in front and a
mirror behind it, staffed by three bartenders dressed to look
as if they had just stepped out of a cowboy movie. Round
wooden tables. A big crystal chandelier.

The bar was full of bronzed young men and bare-breasted
young women, eyeing each other, nuzzling each other,
drinking together, slow-dancing naked breast to naked
chest. Bobby felt like a boob in his jeans and Dodgers
jacket, like Holden Caulfield with a hard-on walking down
the beach at St.-Tropez.

Nervously, Bobby took a seat near one end of the bar, an
empty stool on either side of him, and ordered a beer. The
bartender gave him a funny look, but mercifully did not ask
him to produce an identity card. Bobby sat there nursing a
tasteless and watery American lager, stealing oblique
glances at all the tantalizing naked flesh, and miserably contemplating a night of sleeping on the ground.

He was staring down into the diminishing yellow depths
of his glass when he heard a female voice beside him say "A
kir."

A kir? He hadn't heard the word or seen the drink since
he left Paris.

"A what?" the bartender said.

"A *kir*, don't be so jingo, gringo!"

There was a girl leaning over the empty stool next to him,
her bare breasts dangling delicious centimeters from his
forearm. She had long, sun-bleached blond hair flowing
over her tanned shoulders, good average looks, she seemed
to be about his age, and she was close enough for him to
smell the bright sunny musk of her.

"How the hell am I supposed to make that?" the bartender demanded.

"Glass of white wine and a splash of crème de cassis,"
Bobby ventured.

The girl looked over at Bobby and flashed him a radiant
smile. "Dorky!" she exclaimed. "A man of the world in a
Dodgers jacket out here in the depths of gringoville!"

"I've . . . uh . . . spent some time in France," some instinct made Bobby say.

"You've been to *Europe?*" the girl practically squealed, sitting down on the stool next to him. "Make that two," she told the bartender. "One for me, and one for . . . monsieur in the Dodgers jacket."

"Bob," Bobby said.

"Eileen. God, Bobby, how did you ever manage to get to Europe, what with the exit-visa restrictions, and all?"

Bobby hesitated. This was the first time since he had gotten off the plane that anyone had expressed anything but loathing for things European. Well, what the hell, it had gotten him this far, now hadn't it?

"I was born there," he told her. "In Paris."

"Paris!" she cried, leaning closer, her eyes practically sparkling. "Oh yar! I never thought I'd get to fuck a Frenchman!"

"Uh . . . I'm not exactly a Frenchman . . . ," Bobby stammered. "I mean, my father is an American, and I don't exactly have American citizenship, but I do have an American passport, and—"

"Oh you'll do!" Eileen declared, brushing his forearm with her hard bare nipples. "Well, come on, Bobby, tell me all about Paris!"

And over three kirs, he more or less did, leaving out the parts about his Russian mother, and his sister going to Yuri Gagarin, and precisely *why* his father had left the country, and building up the parts about Paris nightlife, and trips to the Côte d'Azur, and his nearly nonexistent experience with sophisticated French girls.

"So what are you doing in boring old California, then?" Eileen asked. By this time they had crowded together on the adjacent barstools and she had one bare arm flung around his shoulder, and her cheek almost pressed against his.

"I'm going to college in the States," he told her. "UCLA or Berkeley, I haven't decided which."

"Fuck a Russian duck!" Eileen exclaimed. "*I'm* going to Berkeley! Forget UCLA! I grew up in LA, in fact I've been spending the summer at home with my parents, and I've been dating UCLA men. What a gang of gringos! You'd *hate* it there!"

"Well—"

"Hey, you want to buy me dinner and let me tell you about *me?*" Eileen said.

"Sure," Bobby said.

"Great!" Eileen told him. "And here's something to prove I'm gonna be worth it." And she took his head in both hands, pressed her lips against his, pried his mouth open, and suddenly plunged her warm wriggling tongue deep, deep, into his mouth.

They went to a nearby Chinese restaurant, and, over moo shu pork, lobster in black bean sauce, and egg foo yung, Eileen did most of the talking, with one hand pressed against his thigh under the table as she used her chopsticks expertly with the other.

Her name was Eileen Sparrow. Her father was a real estate agent and her parents had a house in Beverly Hills, in the lowlands below Wilshire, admittedly, but Daddy had taken a second mortgage to buy up this land in Baja, and soon enough they'd probably be rich enough to move up into the Glen, or even Bel-Air. Which was not to say that she herself was some kind of *gringo,* you understand, you couldn't choose your own parents, unfortunately, now could you? Not that she hadn't been the perfect little spacebrain jingo till she started at Berkeley last year, where she was majoring in English at the moment, and gotten in with the Reds, who weren't at all fooled by this crazed gringo jingo, and they'll just *love* a real Frenchman from Paris, *especially* if he's some kind of American too, I'm driving back up to Berkeley next Monday, you can stay in Tod's room till then, he's in the *Army,* can you believe it, we'll have to tell Mommy and Daddy that you're a classmate from school, they wouldn't like the idea of me bringing home some guy I picked up in Dirty Death, and for chrissakes *don't* tell them you've ever even *been* to Europe, Daddy *hates* the Peens, you just be sure to wear the Dodgers jacket, he just *loves* the Dodgers, what a mucho macho ducko schmuck . . .

"Okay," she said, over the almond cookies, "now you pay the bill so we can get out of here and go back to my room and fuck."

The room itself wasn't much—just a TV set, a bureau, two nightstands, and a water bed—but Bobby wasn't paying much attention to the decor. He was quite dazed, his cock was chafing impatiently against the zipper of his jeans, and his balls felt like they were about to explode.

The moment she closed the door, Eileen threw herself into his arms, thrust her tongue deep into his mouth again, and tumbled them onto the bed, where they rolled around groping and feeling each other until Bobby felt he was about to come in his pants.

At just this strategic point, Eileen disengaged herself, sprang up off the bed, leaned back up against the wall, and thrust her hand deep into her shorts. "Take off your clothes," she said huskily, running her tongue slowly around her lips, wriggling her ass against the wall, and working her hand inside her pants. "Do it nice and slow."

Bobby, in a red-hot trance, slowly undressed himself on the bed, while she stared straight into his eyes, rolling her head, wriggling against the wall, licking her wet lips, and masturbating herself.

"Stand up," she told him when he was finally naked. Bobby stood up.

"Lean back against the wall."

"Lean back against the wall?"

Eileen nodded, and sucked languidly on her own tongue. "This is really an important moment for me," she said. "I'm about to suck my first French cock."

I'm not really a Frenchman, Bobby was about to stammer, but he never got the words out, for suddenly she was kneeling on the floor before him, and her hands grabbed him by the buttocks, and her mouth slid all the way down his prick, and before he knew quite what was happening, he was getting the first blowjob of his life.

It was delicious, it was wonderful, it was better than anything he had ever imagined, and he wanted to make it last forever. But under the circumstances, it was a lost cause, and in no more than a couple of minutes, he exploded into a release that left him languid, and tingly, and quite limp, and more than a little embarrassed.

"Not bad," Eileen said, rising to her feet, licking her lips. "Kinda quick come, but not bad." She looked at him expectantly. "Well?" she said.

"Well what?"

"Well, now I've Frenched you, aren't you gonna French me?"

"Huh?"

"*Huh?* What kind of *Frenchman* are you?"

"I told you, I'm not exactly a Frenchman . . . ," Bobby stammered in embarrassed perplexity.

"Yeah, I know, but you're not gonna tell me you never . . . you know . . ."

"Know what?"

"Jeez, sucked a cunt!" Eileen exclaimed in exasperation. Bobby felt that he must be flushing scarlet. Eileen goggled at him for a moment, then a broad smile creased her moist lips. "You never have, have you?" she said softly. "This is going to be your first time. Oh yar! Too much! What luck!"

She pushed him back onto the bed on his back, and before Bobby quite knew what was happening, she was sitting astride his face, with her thighs clamped tightly around his head, and one hand in his hair, and the hairy quick of her pressed against his mouth.

Bobby had seen a certain amount of porn, and read a few cunnilingus scenes in novels, and had some vague notion of this most intimate feminine anatomy, but he had never been in this position before. Legend had led him to expect a certain odeur du poisson and a bad taste, but there was none of that, to his pleasant surprise; however, he did have a certain amount of trouble finding the target.

But Eileen Sparrow was a willing teacher—"Further down . . . no, a little higher . . . deeper . . . ah, that's it! Use the tip of your tongue! Harder! Faster!"—and once he started to figure out what he was doing, he found he quite enjoyed it, especially when she started moaning in pleasure, and reached behind her, and began stroking his cock in time to the rhythm of his tongue.

By the time she came in his mouth with a loud scream, Bobby's nervousness and trepidation were quite gone, and he felt relaxed, and manly, and confident, and ready for more.

He rolled her over onto her back and did it in the old traditional missionary position. This time she came long before he neared the top again, and he was able to give her yet a third orgasm before he spent himself.

Afterward, as they lay there side by side, he felt dreamily content, and proud, and macho, a man of the world at last indeed. Nevertheless, he found himself laughing.

"Hey, what's so *funny*, Bobby?"

"I was just thinking," Bobby said, "in Paris, all I wanted

to do was come to the States and learn how to be a real American. And now here I am, and what do I learn? How to be un vrai Français!"

"Oooh, you're so *cute!*" Eileen squealed, hugging him convulsively. "They're just gonna *love* you in Berkeley, my little gringo froggie!"

Billy Allen: "I don't get it, Senator—"

Representative Carson: "Not yet, Billy, the people of the great State of Texas don't get to elect me till November."

Billy Allen: "Well, Congressman, or soon-to-be Senator-elect, or whatever—Harry—why *did* we buy up a load of Mexican debt that everyone knows isn't worth its weight in toilet paper? How can you support such a crazy move, especially in an election year?"

Representative Carson: "It's bailed out a lot of banks and private investors who could have gotten into deep trouble otherwise, many of them in Texas."

Billy Allen: "At the taxpayers' expense! A lot of people think it's pretty outrageous to help out the same country that's harassing American citizens in Baja. A lot of people think the Mexicans will just default, leaving us holding the bag. I mean, didn't *we* just—"

Representative Carson: "We're not Common Europe, and Mexico's not the United States. If they can't come up with the cash, well, we can always take it out in trade . . . real estate, for example."

Billy Allen: "You mean invade Baja California?"

Representative Carson: "Oh, I wouldn't call it *invasion,* Billy. After all, if you hold the mortgage on a piece of property and the owners can't meet the payments, what else can you do to protect your investment but fore-close?"

—*Newspeak,* with Billy Allen

XIV

Eileen was appalled to learn that Bobby had no driver's license, not even a European one, which might not exactly be in his favor if they got chipped while he was driving, but which would at least make *her* legal. "Nosey joesy," she declared when he offered to take the chance and drive anyway, "that's a thousand-dollar fine and a three-month suspension, and Daddy would have me *executed!*"

So they drove up out of Death Valley with Eileen at the wheel of her snappy little two-seat Chevy electrosport, Bobby's hand in her crotch on the empty stretch of road running through the dry high desert, and she actually had him bring her off at 120 kph just before the road met the main freeway.

The six-lane freeway ran up over the San Bernardino Mountains toward the Los Angeles Basin through more arid empty desert country, at least for the first hour or so, but Bobby felt as if he had suddenly crossed an invisible frontier as soon as they hit it.

The traffic thickened, cars cut in and out aggressively, big heavy-duty long haulers rumbled along in the right-hand lane, many of them carrying ominous-looking loads concealed under khaki and Air Force–blue tarps, highway patrol helicopters buzzed overhead like angry dragonflies, and military aircraft cracked through the air high above at supersonic speed.

About forty minutes out of San Bernardino, the billboards started, and then the endless sprawl of low tract houses, industrial parks surrounded by wire fences, shopping malls surrounded by immense parking lots, and finally a heavy miasma of smog, dirty brown in the distance, sparkly blue-gray up close, washing out the landscape.

"Bienvenidos a Los Angeles!" Eileen drawled.

"This is LA already?"

Eileen laughed. "It might as well be. It's all like this from here on in."

And it was, only more so. The traffic got thicker and thicker until it was crawling along in stops and starts, and the wide-open western landscape was buried under tract housing, shopping malls, factories, parking lots, billboards, chemical plants, freeway interchanges, apartment blocks, and general unidentifiable industrial bric-a-brac.

And yet, even inside the car, Bobby could sense something new in the air besides the smog, something he had not felt in America before, a kind of manic energy, a sense of feverish motion, mad enterprise, tumbling and churning and smoking toward some unimaginable future in quick-time.

"This sure isn't like the East," he muttered.

Eileen laughed. "This is like *Southern California,*" she told him. "It's not like *anything.* It's not even on the same *planet.*"

"There's something in the air, and I don't mean the—"

"S-M-O-G?" she said. "M-O-N-E-Y!"

"Huh?"

"This is where the money is," Eileen said. "It's like someone picked up the country at the corner of Maine, and it all slid downhill to here. While the rest of the US of A was going broke and being bought up by the Peens and the Jappos, the Golden State just got more *golden.* Still grows everything and ships it everywhere. Still the world capital of show biz. And biotech that the gov never let the foreigners get their hands on. . . ."

She shot him an evil leer. "But most of all what makes Southern California golden is like *war!*" she declared. "Lion's loot of all the defense money the gov's been sucking out of the rest of the country's been shoveled into a tube that comes out *here* ever since good old Ronnie Reagan stopped making cowboy movies! Battlestar America! Edwards! Vandenberg! Penetrator bombers! Tanks! Napalm! Ammo! We crank it all out, and they ship it to Latin America, and they blow it all up, and they come back for more. Oh yeah, the Pentagon is Southern California's Bright Green Money Machine! This is where all the gringo jingo makes the pockets jangle!"

"That's horrible . . . ," Bobby muttered.

"*Tell* me about it! And you haven't even met *Daddy* yet!"

They finally drove out of the vast industrial sprawl and through downtown Los Angeles, then headed west through more industrial wasteland, turned north at another freeway interchange, and finally came out onto Wilshire Boulevard, smack into the middle of a monstrous traffic jam.

They crept past tall apartment blocks, office towers, indoor shopping malls, and then through the center of downtown Beverly Hills, past plush hotels, car showrooms, luxurious boutiques, and plastically elegant restaurants.

" 'The Miracle Mile,' they call it," Eileen told him. "It's a miracle if you can drive a mile in an hour. There's a subway from downtown under here, but no one would be caught dead in it—earthquakes, you know, we're still waiting for the Big One to knock all this down, and it can't come too soon for me."

Eileen finally turned south off Wilshire, and all at once they were in another world, a relentlessly rectilinear grid of tree-shaded streets, large well-kept houses in phony Spanish, Tudor, Midi, and even medieval styles. There was not a café or a tabac or a market for blocks and blocks, and hardly any people walking on the sidewalks.

"The only reason they have *sidewalks* in Beverly Hills," Eileen said, as if reading his mind, "is so they'll have something to *roll up* at nine o'clock at night."

They finally pulled up in the driveway of a truly bizarre house, a small-scale replica of some crazed children's book illustrator's concept of an English castle—two stories of phony Tudor white stucco and wood beams crowned with miniature tessellated turrets and parapets, nothing exactly a right angle or in a straight line, and a front door done up as a simulacrum of a raised drawbridge, replete with solid brasswork mimicking the winch and chains.

"Be it ever so humble," Eileen said, as she rang a doorbell concealed in the brasswork, "there's no home like *this*."

Big Ben chimes rang out lugubriously behind the door. A few moments later the door opened, and a middle-aged woman in an asymmetrically cut red-and-green tartan skirt and matching sleeveless blouse appeared in the doorway. Her arms and her face were tanned an even synthetic bronze and her blond hair was conked up into an elaborate crest that looked vaguely like a Roman helmet.

"Eileen!" she cried. "Kissy-kiss!" And she pecked her daughter lightly on the cheeks French-style. "Who's this?" she said, eyeing Bobby dubiously.

"This is Bobby Reed, a friend of mine from Berkeley, he's passing through town on the way from visiting his folks back East, and I'm giving him a ride back to school, so I told him it would be okay for him to stay with us until we leave, that's not like a *problem*, is it?"

"In Tod's room," Mrs. Sparrow said rather coldly.

"Oh, *Mommy!*" Eileen moaned. "It's not as if I were pretending to be a virgin—"

"In Tod's room!"

"That's okay, Mrs. Sparrow," Bobby said quickly. "Your house, your rules."

"What a nice young man," Mrs. Sparrow said, giving Bobby a rather plastic-looking dead smile. But she led the two of them into the house, through a foyer, and down into a sunken living room, where a man with a severely squared-off brown crew cut and dressed in a tan sleeveless bush jacket and matching jungle shorts sat on a big leather couch watching a videowall.

"Hi, Daddy, this is Bobby, I'm driving him back to school, and he's going to stay with us until then," Eileen said. "Bobby, this is Daddy."

Mr. Sparrow pried himself off the couch, shook Bobby's hand with a firm grip. He was tall, broad, athletic-looking except for an incipient paunch, and his soft-featured face, which appeared to have been tanned to match his wife's, seemed somehow out of place beneath his pseudo-military hairdo.

"Dick Sparrow," he said by way of greeting. "I'm watching the news, and it's getting good, don't mind if we see the end, do you?"

"Oh, *Daddy!*"

"Tawny, why don't you get us some tequila?" Dick Sparrow said, ignoring Eileen's protest and reseating himself on the couch. He gave Bobby a manly wink. "Might as well get used to it, right?" he said enigmatically.

Bobby sat down on the far end of the couch from Dick Sparrow, with Eileen between them. On the videowall, an announcer was staring solemnly into the camera and proclaiming in grave sepulchral tones.

". . . and given the Mexican government a month to secure the necessary foreign exchange in order to comply, or present an acceptable alternative."

"Acceptable alternative!" Dick Sparrow cried. "Yeah, right, like five trillion tons of frijoles!"

On the screen, an aircraft carrier was sailing into a dockyard, surrounded by destroyers and hovercruisers, while a big blimp hung with helicopter gunships floated overhead.

"Meanwhile, the redeployed elements of the Pacific fleet have reached San Diego, where, we have learned, they will take on an additional complement of Marines and a brigade from the 82nd Airborne Division. . . . While at El Toro Marine base north of San Diego . . ."

Shots of tanks churning over sand dunes, Marines jumping out of Ospreys, hitting the beaches from landing craft, low-flying tactical support fighters rocketing empty coastline.

". . . Operation Alamo continues . . ."

"What's going on?" Bobby exclaimed.

Dick Sparrow eyed him peculiarly. *"What's going on?"* he said. "Where you been, boy?"

"Uh . . . on the road . . ."

Sparrow shook his head, and returned his attention to the news. *"What's going on,"* he said, "is that we're finally going to go in!"

"Go in?"

"Are you for real, boy? We're finally calling in our markers. The gov's bought up the Mexican debt at twenty cents on the dollar, paid too much, you ask me, and now the beaners have to cough it up. And if they don't, which they won't, seeing as how they don't even have the cash to pay their own Army, we'll take Baja as compensation—"

". . . in Mexico City, the President refused comment, but the Minister of Defense declared that the territorial integrity of Mexico would be defended—"

"With a bunch of old junk!" Dick Sparrow shouted at the screen. "The beaners won't last a week, you can get six to four in Vegas!"

Tawny Sparrow returned with a tray bearing a bottle of tequila, shot glasses, lemon wedges, and a salt shaker.

". . . while in Strasbourg, the Common European Parliament passed a—"

"Fuck the Peens!" Dick Sparrow shouted. "They mix in, and they'll eat anti-protons!"

". . . and in the red-hot National League pennant race, Kazuo Konokawa hit a three-run homer in the bottom of the ninth to give Miami—"

Dick Sparrow hit a touchpoint on his remote and the screen went dead. He poured out four shots of tequila, licked the top of his hand, poured salt on it, tongued it, gulped down the contents of his little glass, bit into a lemon wedge.

"To Greater California!" he cried.

"Greater California?"

"Daddy's bought up acres and acres of desert north of Ensenada," Eileen said.

"You better believe it!" Dick Sparrow declared. "Say, your family got any money, Bobby? I can still get you a deal on a hundred acres only seventy miles from La Paz, but you've gotta move fast, I mean, the best stuff's already long gone, and when our boys move in—"

"Oh, Daddy!"

"Come on, boy, drink up!" Dick Sparrow said, handing Bobby a shot glass, a lemon wedge, and the salt shaker. "To the gallant boys who are about to make us rich! To Greater California! To bigger and better things to come!"

Bobby shrugged, salted his hand, licked it, gulped down the powerful, oily-tasting stuff, and bit into the lemon. The fiery tequila exploded in his gut like a small air-to-ground missile. Nor did he refuse when Dick Sparrow poured another round before dinner. Around here, he had the feeling he was going to need it.

Dinner was a huge salad full of strange tropical fruits, roasted chicken in a weird spicy brown sauce, a wedge of chocolate cake, and more appalling gringo jingo from Dick Sparrow.

After dinner, Tawny Sparrow showed Bobby his room on the upper floor, her son Tod's old room, the walls still festooned with posters and photos of American military hardware. Then the four of them watched a horrible film called *Freedom's War* on television—an alternate history shoot-'em-up in which the United States won the Vietnam War with the judicious use of tactical nuclear weapons—while Dick Sparrow continued to blather on about Latin American real estate deals, European perfidy, the coming age of American rebirth, what might ultimately be done to put the Jappos in their place, and the golden future of California.

Finally, after the news, and some talk show where the host pried into the sex lives of the guests with savage abandon, the Sparrows retired, leaving Bobby and Eileen alone in the living room.

"Fuck a Russian duck," Bobby muttered dazedly.

"Daddy's *something,* isn't he?"

"How do you *stand* it?"

Eileen laughed. "I don't," she said. "Why do you think I'm going to *Berkeley?*"

"Well, we're going to be in LA for the next three days, so I might as well show you around so you'll know what you're *escaping,*" Eileen told him after breakfast. "And I guess we should start with *UCLA.* . . ."

They walked up to Wilshire and took the subway. "Parking there's just *impossible* unless you've got a student sticker," Eileen told him. "It's only two stops, so we *probably* won't get caught in an earthquake."

They came out right in front of one of the main entrances to the sprawling campus—the idea had been to encourage the student body to use the subway, Eileen told him, but of course, no true Trojan would be caught *dead* commuting to school in anything but his car.

"Trojan?"

"The team's name. Some ancient Greek jingo, I think. Also a brand of condom, you know, what everyone put on their unclean *pricks* during the Plague Years, just *perfect,* don't you think?"

UCLA was an immense sprawl of low buildings and short towers, more like a huge industrial park than Bobby's vision of a college campus. Pedicabs pedaled by grim-looking middle-aged Mexicans ferried students back and forth between classrooms for a few dollars.

"This place is just so big . . . ," Bobby said. "Why don't the students use bicycles to get around?"

"Bicycles!" Eileen exclaimed. "This is Gringo Jingo Land, not the *Third World!*"

They spent the morning wandering around the campus, then had a horrible steam-table lunch at one of the college cafeterias. "An experience *not* to be missed if you still have any thoughts of going here," Eileen told him.

By then, Bobby was beginning to get the idea. Huge as it was, the campus still seemed crowded, something like sixty thousand people went to school here, Eileen told him, the majority of them Asians and Chicanos, clean-cut in pressed jeans, walking shorts, Trojan T-shirts, short, functional haircuts, with an air of grim earnestness as they marched in squads from class to class. There were an amazing number of men in military uniform; four years of free tuition in return for four years as cannon fodder was how a lot of people financed their education here.

"It's not exactly like I thought it would be," Bobby muttered.

"Which was . . . ?"

He shrugged. "I don't know," he said. "The Sorbonne with palm trees . . . This feels more like some kind of *factory* than a real university campus."

"That's *just* what it *is!*" Eileen told him. "A factory for turning out engineers and technicians and soldiers and general gringo jingo spare parts for the Big Green Money Machine!"

They took the subway back to the Sparrows' house; Tawny Sparrow was out shopping or something, so they were able to enjoy a long love-making session in Eileen's room, which brightened up the rest of the afternoon. But the thought of another dinner like last night's filled Bobby with dread.

"Well then, let's do the town, such as it is," Eileen said when he voiced his trepidations.

And they more or less did.

They drove down to Chinatown, a vast sprawl of souvenir shops, oriental boutiques, kitschy art galleries, holoshows, and Chinese restaurants, where they had quite a good meal in a place that looked like a fast-food joint from the outside and a Chinese palace straight out of Disney World on the inside.

They drove to the world-famous corner of Hollywood and Vine, and walked the length of Hollywood Boulevard, looking at the stars on the sidewalks. The Chinese Theater, the Egyptian one across the street, the Kyoto and the Angkor Wat down the block, Brown's Famous ice-cream parlor, the Hollywood Wax Museum, and the rest of the old landmarks were now built into the ground floors of immense high-rise office blocks, like the old Coupole on the Boulevard Montparnasse. Bobby got the eerie feeling that a whole section of the city had been turned into a Disney version of itself.

"No grand tour of la-la land would be complete without a session on Mulholland Drive," Eileen told him as she drove up Laurel Canyon Boulevard into the Hollywood Hills, a low range of mountains completely overgrown with weird houses and free-form apartment blocks that hung from every nook and cranny, many of them actually hanging out from the hillsides on frail-looking stilts.

Mulholland Drive, however, was something else again, a ridgeline road that ran all the way along the crest of the Santa Monica Mountains from east of here to the sea, Eileen told him, and one of the few areas in Los Angeles that the developers had been prevented from festooning with ticky-tacky, though she was sure Daddy was working on it.

Here, the houses were far apart and large, and they were set back off the road amid the rough natural chaparral, and when the car rounded a curve, Bobby was treated to a sight that quite blew him away. Eileen parked the car on a shelf of wheel-beaten earth that seemed as if it had seen generations of use, and they got out, and she just let him gape without saying a word.

The shadowy shoulders of the mountains tumbled down toward a long broad valley floor jeweled with millions of lights, a huge manmade star field that filled the valley completely and oozed up the slopes of the mountain range on the other side like a scintillant amoeba. Gridworks of glowing streetlights checkerboarded the vista, and rivers of red and white neon freeway traffic flowed through it. A golden aura seemed to hover over it, quite washing out the night sky, except for the running lights of airplanes and helicopters flitting above it like fireflies. It glowed, it shimmered, it wriggled with electronic motion, it seemed like some kind of huge man-made organism—vast and energetic and pulsating, and somehow eerily alive.

"Merde . . . ," Bobby whispered.

"And that's only *the Valley*," Eileen said behind him.

Bobby stood there gaping in wonder. And then he heard the sound.

Compounded of the chatter of passing helicopters and the drone of light planes and the far-off rushing roar of all the distant traffic echoing up the mountain slopes, and the bustle of all those millions of lives, the triumphantly artificial landscape seemed to be singing an electronic song that thrummed in his bones. Waves of energy pulsed up at him, sweeping him away on their electronic tide, into a place he had never been before.

In that moment, looking down from the roof of the world on what Americans had wrought on the edge of the continent, and feeling the artificial life's breath of Los Angeles surging up at him, Bobby felt himself awash in the sheer glorious unbridled crazy *power* of it all.

In that moment, Bobby somehow knew what it really meant to be an American, felt for the first time inextricably a part of this land's collective destiny, for better or worse, of the unknown future still unfolding in this once-lost homeland, where, however tormented, however twisted, some grand and mysterious spirit had not yet vanished from the Earth.

"Well, *come on,*" Eileen said impatiently, tugging him by the hand toward the car.

"Huh?" Bobby muttered in a daze.

"We're on *Mulholland Drive,* we're supposed to have the Mulholland *experience!*"

"What . . . ?"

"We're supposed to *screw* in the car, of course!"

"In *there?*" Bobby muttered, looking at the cramped interior of the two-seater. "I don't think we can really—"

"Of course we can!" Eileen insisted. "People have been doing it up here for at least *a hundred years!*"

As it turned out, she was right. It was uncomfortable, and difficult, and quick, but he managed to get it up, and get it in, and get her off, and he even managed to come himself. Nevertheless, it was an anticlimax.

"Well, now you've had the Mulholland experience," Eileen said afterward. "Something *else,* isn't it?"

In a way that Bobby doubted she could ever understand, she was right.

Saturday, Bobby talked Eileen into taking him to a ball game; they were leaving on Monday for Berkeley, and it was going to be the only chance he would have to see Dodger Stadium.

It was another endless crawl through traffic down to Venice to the ball park built out on pilings and completely surrounded by ocean under a clear azure sky, but, to Bobby, at least, it was worth it. It was one of only three parks left in the majors where the game was played on natural grass, and the Dodgers beat the Mets 8 to 6 in a wild slugfest that ended dramatically with a bases-loaded triple in the bottom of the ninth by Hiro Yamagawa, who last year had become the first .400 hitter in the majors in decades.

The crowd was something else too. In the prime lower-deck seats behind the plate that Bobby had sprung for, remembering Duke, there were well-dressed Anglos, stunning starlets, and actual TV stars, or so Eileen said excitedly as she pointed them out. Out in the bleachers, which were done up as a hillside park without seats, Chicanos and blacks, who seemed to have their own self-segregated sections, whooped and hollered with every hit. A whole section of upper-deck grandstand was filled with military personnel in uniform, who got in for half price. Another part of the upper deck was an organized cheering section, where thousands of people held up cards forming pictures—the Dodgers emblem, company logos, the American flag, even a stylized wing-flapping American eagle—on cues from the P.A. announcer.

There were vendors selling curried popcorn, burritos, beer, sushi, and steamed hot dogs, and all in all, it was the perfect American experience, the essence somehow, of LA.

Some guy she had gone to high school with had invited Eileen to a beach party out near Malibu on Sunday, and early that afternoon, they fought the freeway traffic for an hour and a half, managed to find a parking space, stripped down to the bathing suits they wore under their clothing in the car, and made their way down the jampacked sand to where a big red helium balloon floating high above the acres of bare flesh marked the scene of the party.

"Now remember, Bobby, not a *word* about Paris or Europe," she warned him. "I went to Beverly Hills High with most of these doofs, they're all a bunch of gringo jingos, and I don't want you to end up starting a *fistfight.*"

About twenty people were sitting on beach towels around a metal beer keg, sunning themselves, drinking, making out, eating take-out junk food, while awful martial-sounding max-metal music muttered unheard at medium volume from a portable chip deck.

A big blond surfer type with the ridiculous name of Tab greeted Eileen with a hug and a goose, got them beers, and he and Eileen introduced Bobby around while Bobby stuck to his well-rehearsed road story about returning to Berkeley from a visit back home to his folks in Akron.

And thus began a long lazy sunny afternoon that quite fulfilled Bobby's image of the archetypal Southern California beach party. He swam. He made a fool of himself trying to ride a motorized surfboard, falling off over and over again, until he had finally swallowed enough of the Pacific to give it up. He necked with Eileen. He played a spaced-out slow-motion netless version of impromptu volleyball with a big balloon filled with a mixture of air and helium.

And, like everyone else, he drank. By the time the sun started crawling down the perfect California sky toward the mirror of the Pacific, everyone was pretty well blotted, a few people had actually puked, no one was inclined toward further athletics, and the drunken bullshit began.

There was a lot of techtalk that bored Bobby speechless, as well as a good deal of pissing and moaning about teachers he didn't know. There was also a good deal of obscene banter about who was and was not fucking whom, about which he couldn't care less. It was all a lot of blather by people he didn't know or care about, and for the most part he just lay there on a beach towel next to Eileen, drinking whatever was passed to him, and zoning out into the deepening blue of the Malibu sky.

". . . hear Billy's goin' in with the 82nd . . ."

". . . get his dumb ass shot off!"

"Naw, my dad says the beaners'll go without firing a shot. . . ."

"Bullshit! Gonna be a duster. . . ."

"My ass!"

"*My* dad says they're gonna give Baja veterans forty acres, he's pissed at me for not joining up."

"Are you for real? The Big Boys got title on everything worth anything down there already!"

"Gonna be a duster!"

"Bullshit! Beaners can't last a week, and they know it."

"It's a Commie gov, ain't it?"

"So fucking what?"

"So they gotta be figuring the Rooshians—"

"Rooshians won't do dick, buncha pussies. Didn't save the Cubans' asses, did they? Didn't lift a missile! Too busy corning the Peens!"

"*We're* the ones that just corned the Peens!"

"Haw! Haw! Haw!"

"I *still* say gonna be a duster, war'll last at least six weeks!"

"Crappo!"

"Economics."

"What the fuck *you* know about economics, Butch?"

"*My* dad works for Zynodyne, he says the fix is already in. They won't *let* the beaners go without a fight."

"*They?*"

"Defense industry, asshole. Resupply contracts are already out. Biggo buckso. They're planning on using up a hundred bills' worth of ordnance on the beaners, min. Lots of overtime already, and they're looking to hire."

"Yeah? Short term?"

"Week to week. Hundred an hour, usual double time, *triple* for weekends. . . ."

"Hey, not a bad deal. . . ."

Bobby's appalled attention was slowly captured by this drift in the conversation. He had certainly heard enough of this cynical imperialist merde from Dick Sparrow and elsewhere, but to hear it coming out of the mouths of mecs his own age whom he had swum with, played volleyball with, drunk with, was somehow much, much worse.

"Think your dad could do me something?"

"Maybe. . . ."

"Hey, Eddie, your dad works for Collins, don't he? They hiring short-termers too?"

"Could find out. . . ."

"You guys can't really be serious!" Bobby finally blurted.

Butch, a big burly guy with short black hair, gave him an open friendly smile. "'Course I'm serious," he said pleasantly enough. "You want, I suppose I could put in a word for you too. . . ."

"La merde!" Bobby snapped without thinking. Eileen, lying beside him, punched him in the small of the back.

"What?"

"You can't really be serious about going to work in *munitions plants!*"

"*Bobby!*" Eileen hissed in his ear.

"Why the fuck not? Hey, *hundred an hour,* that's biggo buckso!"

"Making weapons to kill people who just want to be left alone!"

"*Left alone!* Hey, they ain't leaving the Americans who bought land in Baja fair and square alone, now are they?"

"It's their country, isn't it?"

"Bullshit! Everybody knows Mexico ripped off Baja during the Civil War, what's his face, Pancho Villa and his frito banditos! We got a right to take back what was ours, like it says inna Monroe Doctrine."

"Is that supposed to be some kind of joke?"

"What are *you* supposed to be, some kind of Communist?"

"Hey, Eileen, your boyfriend some kind of Berkeley Red?"

"Beaner-lover!"

There was a long moment of silence. People who had been lolling back and not paying much attention suddenly had their eyes on him. Oh shit, Bobby thought.

"Bobby's just a little *blotted,* that's all," Eileen said. "You're drunk, aren't you, Bobby?"

Bobby sat up, a little woozily. He tried a little smile and a shrug. "I'm not the only one," he said lightly.

"What do you mean by that?" Eddie said belligerently, his blue eyes more than a little bloodshot.

"Nothing," Bobby said. "Forget it."

But somehow things had already gone over the edge. Bobby found himself in the center of a whirlpool of hostile vibes.

"You some kind of *Communist?*"

"Fuckin' KGB's all over Berkeley, my dad says!"

"I'm no Communist!" Bobby insisted nervously.

"Then why you defending the fucking beaners?"

"Just people, is all . . . ," Bobby said lamely.

"They ain't *people,* they're *beaners!*"

"Bet the little doof's a Peen-lover too! What about it, *Bobby-boy,* the fuckin' Peens that stole half our fuckin' country and sold it to the fuckin' *Rooshians,* they just *people* too?"

"They ain't *people,* they're *Peens!*"

"Nuke 'em till they glow blue!"

"Let 'em eat anti-protons!"

"Let 'em eat *frijoles,* haw, haw, haw!"

Bobby felt the blood pounding behind his eardrums. His hands, unbidden, balled into fists. The angry pop-eyed faces in the mob outside the American Embassy in Paris swam through his memory, became the faces of these young Americans glaring at him under the open Southern California sky.

AMER-I-*CAN,* AS-SAS-*SAN!* AMER-I-*CAN,* AS-SAS-*SAN!*

The echo of the chant mocked him twice over. What was the difference between *those* jingos and *these?* Except that *these* assholes were starting to convince him that what he had thought was a lie might be the truth.

Eileen grabbed his hand, and he let his fist unwind into it. But a big part of him, the *better* part of him, could not let this merde go unanswered. He owed it to his parents, he owed it to himself, and somehow he owed it to America too.

"How can you believe this shit?" he shouted, bolting to his feet. "Don't you see that you're talking just like the gringo jingo bastards they say we are? Americans *can't* be like this! You just can't be!"

"What the fuck kind of American are you, you Peen-loving Commie!"

"Fuckin' Berkeley Red!"

And all at once, everyone was on their feet shouting drunkenly, and Bobby found himself surrounded by what was about to turn into another mob, or, somehow, the *same* mob.

"Boys!" Eileen moaned patronizingly. "Stop this juvenile horseshit! You're all *blotted* out of your minds! You're too *drunk* to have a fistfight! You'd just end up *puking* all over each other!"

Some of the other girls laughed and poked at some of the guys with mock punches, and the moment of physical tension receded a tad.

"Come *on,* Bobby," Eileen said, tugging him by the hand. "We've got to *go* now!"

Reeling, realizing how drunk he really was, and how close he had come to getting the crap beaten out of him, Bobby let her lead him away toward the car. Over his shoulder, he saw that her old high school friends had collapsed back onto their beach blankets and were already passing bottles, swilling more beer, and laughing among themselves.

"I *told* you what a bunch of gringo jingo doofs they all were! You could've gotten yourself *killed!"*

"What's *happened* to America?" Bobby sighed maudlinly.

Eileen shrugged. "You've met *Daddy,* haven't you?" she said.

Bobby managed a wan little laugh. Eileen pecked him on the cheek. "Come on, Bobby, snap out of it," she said gently. "I'll show you something better to remember la-la land by."

—

"And so we bid a fond farewell to scenic Los Angeles," Eileen said. "What a *zoo!* Still, it's beautiful from up here, isn't it, where you can pretend you don't know what's really going on. . . ."

Bobby had to admit that it was.

They had driven up the Pacific Coast Highway, then taken a long winding canyon road up into the sere brown hills beside the sea, way up to a shelf of land high atop the ridge-line. They had parked the car and walked out to the lip of a cliff, where they now stood, looking out over the Pacific and the beach and the city curving south around the wide bay.

By now, the sun, orange and umber under the purpling sky, was bisected by the mirror of a sea reflecting the blazing perfection of an archetypal Southern California sunset, rosy and violet through the smog.

The lights of the Los Angeles Basin were coming on, glowing up at them through the brown layer of the smog deck, a magnificent electronic enormity foaming up against the Santa Monica Mountains like a great luminescent breaker, sweeping away around the majestic curve of the bay toward San Diego, toward the Mexican border, toward things that seemed quite unreal from this lordly mountain-top vantage.

Bobby knew that the crazed city below was writhing in a superheated torment, that something had gone very wrong down there, that dark deeds were veiled behind the cloak of lights. Yet, like America, it was beautiful still.

As the sun was swallowed up by the ocean, and a tide of darkness slowly rolled across the surface of the sea toward the shore, the vast scintillant city, by some trick of the mind's eye, seemed to be rising triumphant out of the natural landscape to challenge the washed-out stars—like America itself, beautiful, prideful, a light that not so long ago had been the shining hope of the world.

Or was Los Angeles, like America, slowly sinking back into the primeval darkness, doomed to subside like legendary Atlantis into the oblivion of the sea?

In that moment, as Bobby stood there at the edge of the continent, at the last frontier of the dream, the issue, like the vista, still seemed ambiguous, still seemed in doubt.

A DELIBERATE INSULT TO
MEXICAN SOVEREIGNTY

No Mexican government can seriously consider the American offer to cancel our external debt in exchange for the cession of Baja California. Those who warn that this outrageous proposal is only a thinly veiled ultimatum are, of course, entirely right. But to suggest that the Republic of Mexico has no alternative but to accept the inevitable is treason, pure and simple. The Yankee aggressors may have the planes and the ships and the overwhelming military superiority, and they may indeed be able to work their will against us.

One hundred million Mexicans may be robbed of our land, as we were in 1845, but let it never be said that we were robbed of our honor. We must stand firm against all odds. We must fight to the death for every centimeter of our sacred national soil.

—*Noticias de Mexico*

X V

The drive up to the San Francisco Bay area was a big disappointment. Eileen wouldn't take the Pacific Coast Highway or even 101. "It'd take *twice* as long that way," she told Bobby, "and you can't do any of the driving." So there was no scenic seacoast road, no Big Sur, no Monterey, no Carmel.

Instead, Eileen took Interstate 5 through the San Joaquin Valley, an arrow-straight freeway through what she told him was the most productive farmland in the world.

Productive it might be, but scenic it wasn't as they drove for about three hours up the long flat valley floor, past endless fields of crops broiling under a pitiless sun, moistened by huge sprinkler systems, harvested by spidery-looking machinery, watched over by little observation blimps. It was more of a gigantic food factory than Bobby's romantic concept of farmland, or worse still, like some kind of military operation against nature itself.

The landscape finally began to change as they climbed out of the valley up into the low rolling hills to the north and west, where it was cooler, moister, and greener, but the improvement didn't last for long, as the traffic thickened, and big factories sprang up beside the road—mostly defense plants, Eileen told him—and then the usual sprawl of tract houses, shopping malls, fuel stations, car lots, fast-food joints, and billboards that seemed to be characteristic of the approach to California cities.

But then they crossed another range of hills, and quite suddenly they were crawling straight north on a clogged freeway with a stupendous view that quite took Bobby's breath away.

To the west, beyond a coastal sprawl of industrial crudland, San Francisco Bay was an immense sweep of blue water sheened golden toward its western reaches by the palpable rays of the late afternoon sun. White sails dotted the bay like a fleecing of scattered clouds, and the wakes of boats sliced the azure surface like the contrails of high-flying jets. Far to the northwest, Bobby could just make out the Golden Gate Bridge, ghostly within a bank of fog that was rolling through it and around it like an immense slow-motion breaker, pouring up the hills of San Francisco overlooking the narrow mouth of the broad bay, and wrapping the outlines of the buildings in the crystal mist of legend.

"Now *that's* what I call the *real* California!" Bobby declared.

"You can't mean *Oakland!*" Eileen said. "Ugh!"

Between the elevated freeway and the blue waters of the bay, enrobed in brown photochemical smog, was a truly repellent other vista that Bobby hadn't deigned to notice.

Piers, dry docks, and fuel tanks spread out from the shore, connected by mazeworks of gangways, railheads, and girder bridges, and overarched by cranes, power lines, and elevated conveyers. Inland of the docks were warehouses, big sheet-steel sheds, scruffy buildings, and big open lots surrounded by high razor-wire-topped fencing. Trucks and workers and forklifts were scurrying busily everywhere.

Tied up at the piers or enfolded by dry-dock scaffolding were the objects of all this intense activity. A big aircraft carrier with huge cranes loading helicopter gunships, jump-jets, Ospreys, and hovercraft onto its flight deck. Four destroyers. A heavy cruiser. Three big troop-carrying hover-craft being loaded with gunbuggies and hovertanks and artillery pieces. Assorted tankers and freighters with numbers painted on their battleship-gray superstructures, all taking on cargo. And waiting in the parking lots, more tanks, trucks, gunbuggies, mobile rocket launchers, gunships, and assorted major military hardware.

"Here too?" Bobby moaned.

"Better *believe* it!" Eileen told him. "Without the Navy Yard, Oakland would be even more of a basket case than it already is. But don't worry, no one ever *goes* there. Berkeley is another *world*."

The freeway finally ascended into the hills, where the trees and shrubbery masked what lay to the south and west from view, and when they came down into Berkeley itself, it did indeed seem like another and far more appetizing world.

They descended out of the hills along a tree-shrouded avenue lined with private homes and low apartment complexes, past a little square with a cluster of restaurants and shops that reminded Bobby of Paris. They drove down a main street, with a big university campus on one side, and bookstores, chain restaurants, video shops, chip-rentals, supermarkets, and Laundromats on the other, then turned left onto another main drag, but of quite a different character.

"Voilà, Telegraph Avenue!" Eileen proclaimed. "The center of the universe!"

Telegraph Avenue was relatively narrow, and the traffic crawled along it at a slow walk, giving Bobby plenty of time to soak up the ambiance and marvel.

Small shops lined both sides of the street—bookstores, computer equipment shops, clothing stores, chip-boutiques, weird little craft shops selling leather goods, jewelry, bric-a-brac. There were junk shops purveying old furniture and household goods. There were tiny little restaurants, bars, sidewalk cafés, a film theater, a little playhouse, porn shops,

liquor stores. Music played from cafés and clubs and portable chip-decks.

And the street was jammed with boulevardiers, almost all
of them in their teens and twenties. The majority of them
looked like the kids Bobby had grown used to seeing in the
rest of the States; mecs in jeans, T-shirts, walking shorts,
short-sleeved sport shirts, clean-shaven, with short, neatly
groomed hair, girls in more tightly tailored versions of the
same gear, or wearing halters, short skirts, spandex stretch
pants in bright primary colors.

But a third or a quarter of the strollers on Telegraph
Avenue looked like nothing Bobby had ever seen.

Mecs in asymmetrically cut jeans, one leg long, the other
short, embroidered, studded, painted in crazy random
rainbow patterns. They wore flowing medieval-looking
blousons, big floppy leather cowboy hats, Arab kaffiyehs
dyed in neon colors. Black leather jackets open over bare
chests. Wide belts with gigantic carved wooden buckles. Silk
sashes. Shaved heads tattooed or painted in complex designs. Brilliantly dyed hair done up in spikes and crests.
Long unkempt flowing locks that went down to their *asses*.
Oh yes, the circus was in town!

And the *girls* were something else again! The same profusion of wild hairdos. Tinted plastic blouses and halters that
seemed transparent. Skintight T-shirts with naked breasts
painted on them. Short asymmetric skirts and high patent-
leather boots in many colors that seemed to go all the way
up to their crotches. Long flowing skirts painted with landscapes and spacescapes and abstract patterns. Girls who
seemed entirely nude inside wrap-around capes patterned
like oriental rugs. Girls in brief Japanese happi coats festooned with flashing electronic jewelry. Girls who had it and
flaunted it, yes indeed!

If Telegraph Avenue reminded Bobby of anything, it was
the streets of St.-Germain, up around the Sorbonne and
down in the crowded maze of little streets off the Place St.-
Michel, but amplified, augmented, magnified, and somehow
gloriously Americanized.

He found himself falling instantly in love. With who, or
with what, he didn't know, but he felt the spirit of the street
calling to him, beckoning him, giving him the eye, like the
most beautiful girl he had ever seen smiling at him, crook-

ing her finger, seductively inviting him to come and lose himself in the carnival of her eyes.

Telegraph Avenue petered out rather abruptly into another area of tree-shrouded residential streets, the private houses old and crumbly looking, the low apartment complexes gone somewhat to seed, and only then did Bobby find his voice again.

"Where to now?" he asked Eileen. "Your place?"

"*My* place? I live in the *dorms*, you can't stay with me."

"But I thought—"

"Come *on*, Bobby, I mean I just picked you up in Dirty Death a few days ago. I mean I like you, and we can *date* and all, but it's not like you're my instant *boyfriend* or something. I mean I see lots of guys here, I don't want to, you know, *tie* myself up with a live-in regular, even if I could. . . ."

She gave him an all-too-knowing look. "Besides," she said, "from the way your *tongue* was hanging out on Telegraph Avenue, you don't either, now do you?"

Bobby had to laugh. "Ya got me," he was forced to admit. "But . . . what am I going to do? I really don't have that much money, and I don't know anyone here but you."

"Don't worry about it," Eileen told him. "I think I know a place you can crash real cheap, that's where we're going now, Little Moscow."

"*Little Moscow?*"

Eileen laughed. "That's what the *Gringos* call it, anyway," she said. "The people who live there don't call it *anything*. Except maybe Nat's place, when they want to tell someone where the party is. You're gonna love it, Bobby. And they're gonna love *you*."

Eileen parked the car in front of a ratty-looking old three-story woodframe house on a somewhat disreputable-looking side street full of similar houses, with overgrown lawns, unkempt shrubbery, peeling paint, rickety porches and front stairs.

The front door was open, and she led him straight inside without knocking, into a long hallway, past the doorless entrance to a big living room full of musty-looking old furniture, where half a dozen people were sitting around in front of a videowall, past a toilet from which he heard the sound of flushing, and into a big untidy kitchen.

There was a stove, a microwave oven, two old refrigerators, a big restaurant double sink piled high with dirty dishes and grimy pots, and a big redwood picnic table with two long backless redwood benches. A blond girl in a dirty white T-shirt and cut-off jeans was stirring a huge steaming kettle with a big wooden spoon. A guy with long black hair was ripping up salad greens at the redwood table and tossing them into a large old wooden bowl.

"Hi!" Eileen said brightly. "Where's Nat?"

"In his room marking papers," the mec said, without looking up from his kitchen chores.

Eileen led Bobby out of the kitchen back into the hallway, then up two flights of stairs to another hall that led past a series of doors, some of them open, revealing small bedrooms with people reading, or working at computer consoles, others closed, including the one at the far end of the hall, with a crudely drawn poster tacked to it. The poster showed a hand holding five playing cards, a royal flush, and in spades.

"Knock-knock!" Eileen yelled, banging on the door.

"Who's there?" said a man's voice from the other side.

"Uh . . . José. . . ."

"José who?"

"José can you see by the dawn's early light . . ."

A moment later, the door opened. The man who stood in the doorway looked to be about thirty, with thick curly black hair, a big, slightly hooked nose, wide lips, and dark brown eyes under heavy brows, eyes that seemed to flash and sparkle with some secret and highly amusing knowledge. He wore old black jeans, and a red-and-black lumberjack shirt bulging slightly over the hint of a paunch, sleeves rolled up past the elbows.

"You are . . . ?" he said in a rather rough voice. "You know what a putz I am with names, if you know me at all."

"*Eileen Sparrow,* Nat," Eileen said in some exasperation.

"This is?" Nat said, nodding toward Bobby.

"Bobby Reed. All the way from Paris."

Nat's eyebrows arched upward. "You want?"

"A place for Bobby to crash."

"You can pay?"

Bobby shrugged. "I've got *some* money," he said.

"What can you afford?"

Bobby thought about it. "Not much," he said, rather shamefacedly. "Three hundred a night?"

"Too much. Deuce, if I say okay."

"Great!" Bobby exclaimed in surprise.

"Not so fast. You willing to do your share of chores?"

"Sure."

"You really a Frenchman?"

"Not exactly. I mean, I was born in Paris, but my father is an American, and I'm thinking about going to college here, and—"

"You play poker?"

"Huh?"

"I asked you if you played poker, kid. Seven- or five-card stud. Jacks or better. Straight draw. None of this wild-card bullshit."

"Well . . . uh, no, not really, I mean I know the rules, but . . . ," Bobby muttered in something of a daze.

"You willing to learn?"

"Well, yeah, sure, why not?"

Nat gave a positively manic cackle, rubbing his big thick hands together. "Now *that's* what I like to hear!" he said. "First lesson after dinner. Spaghetti with meat sauce, or so they tell me, but what kind of meat, better you don't ask. Gotta get back to marking this shit now. What a bunch of assholes! About all these kids know about history is that Columbus seduced the Virgin Islands, and Ronnie Reagan had an extra prick under his armpit that he used on Congress. Well, what the fuck, half right ain't so bad!"

And he closed the door behind him.

"That's *it?*" Bobby stammered.

"That's *Nat Wolfowitz!*" Eileen told him, rolling her eyes toward the ceiling.

There were ten people at dinner that night, plus Bobby and Eileen, and over salad, served first in the American manner, spaghetti in rather watery meat sauce, and plenty of rough red California wine that presumed to call itself Burgundy, Bobby learned all about "Little Moscow."

"Why do they call this house 'Little Moscow'?" he asked ingenuously as the spaghetti was being served. "You people aren't really Communists, are you?"

There was a moment of dead silence along the big picnic table. A big black girl named Marla Washington gave him a rather hostile look. "What are *you*, some kind of gringo jingo?" she snapped. "You think we've got something *catching?*"

"Hey," Bobby shot back on instant impulse, "some of my best friends are Communists."

"Very funny," said Jack Genovese, who had made the salad.

"No, really . . . ," Bobby said. He paused. Well, what the hell, if he was really going to live here, these people were going to find out all about him sooner or later anyway. "My mother's a Party member, and my sister is gonna end up with a Party card too, I guess. . . ."

"You serious, kid?" Nat Wolfowitz said. "I thought the last American Communist went out with the dodo."

"My mother's a *Russian.*"

"A *Russian?*"

"I thought you were some kind of Frenchman," Wolfowitz said.

"Well, I was born in Paris, but my mother is a Soviet national, and my dad still has American citizenship, even though they lifted his passport, and . . ." Bobby threw up his hands. "It's kind of complicated," he said.

"Do tell," said Nat Wolfowitz. Eileen eyed him a bit peculiarly, suddenly reminding Bobby that he hadn't exactly told her all of this stuff. The rest of them studied him quite intently, though without apparent hostility, as if he were some kind of exotic creature suddenly dropped down from a flying saucer into their midst. Which, from their point of view, he realized, he was.

So, over spaghetti and a couple of glasses of bad red wine, Bobby told his life story, such as it was, and as he did, a strange thing began to happen.

He was one of the youngest people at the table, and he hadn't been in the house for much more than three hours, but here he was, holding the attention of all these college students; even Nat Wolfowitz, who was some kind of assistant professor or something, listened raptly, with a kind of respect, even. What was more, by the time he had finished, they were smiling at him, dishing him out more spaghetti, refilling his glass, making him feel more welcome, somehow, than he had ever felt anywhere before any time in his life.

"And so now here I am," he finally said. "*Now* will you guys tell me why they call this place 'Little Moscow'?"

"Because we're all *Reds!*" exclaimed Cindy Feinstein the spaghetti maker, and everyone but Eileen broke up into raucous laughter.

"Then you *are* Communists?"

More laughter.

"Explain it to him, Nat," said Karl Horvath, a pudgy kid in a Donald Duck T-shirt. Wolfowitz poured himself another drink, leaned forward on his elbows, and rattled it off in rapid fire.

"Berkeley, like Gaul, as in Charles de, is divided into two parts. Party of the first being the Gringos, who you may have noticed, clean-cut all-American boys and girls, techheads for the most part, noses to the grindstone, eye on the main chance, namely a good job in biotech or better yet the defense industry, jingo assholes who study hard, give boring parties, blot themselves on beer . . ."

"Boo! Hiss!"

"Balls to the wall!"

"Party of the second part being weirdos like us, who have no ambition to cog into the Big Green Machine, major in economically pointless shit like history and literature, are less than entranced with Festung Amerika, Pigs in Space, and our snatches and grabs in Latin America, and are not entirely convinced that the Peens are a treacherous gang of frog-eating faggots—"

"Real party animals!"

"Complete garbageheads!"

"Know how to wail!"

"Which, from the Gringo point of view, makes us all a bunch of un-American Peen-loving Commie degenerates who oughta be tarred and feathered and ridden out of the country on a rail, especially since we don't let *them* come to *our* parties. . . ."

"Hence, Reds!"

"Hence, Little Moscow, hotbed thereof!"

"Je comprends," Bobby muttered.

"Oooh, *French!*" Cindy moaned in good-natured mock admiration. "Très chic!"

Bobby laughed. A warm glow of contentment suffused his body, and not just from the wine and the heavy meal. For the first time in his life, he felt that he had found a group of people roughly his own age who truly accepted him for what he was, for *all* that he was, the first really like-minded people he had ever met, Americans in a kind of exile themselves, just like him, people whom he sensed could become a real circle of true friends.

How unexpected, and how sweet it was, that he had found them here, in the United States.

After dinner was over, Bobby learned the rules of the house. There were fourteen people currently in residence, meaning that he was responsible for the communal dinner one night in fourteen. One day in fourteen, he had to clean the living room and the halls. One day in fourteen, he had to do the bathrooms. And one day in fourteen, he had to do the dinner dishes, and since he was the new boy in the house, he might as well get started now. After he was through, he could join the poker game.

It seemed like a fair and not very onerous arrangement, and so Bobby took Eileen's phone number, promised to call, kissed her goodbye, and got down to doing the dishes that people had stacked in the sink, another house rule.

Bobby had never faced such a stack of dishes and pots in his life, indeed since he had grown up with a dishwasher in the kitchen, he had scarcely faced any dishes at all, but he set to work with a will, it really wasn't so bad, and after less than an hour, he had everything stacked in the drying rack —don't bother to dry anything was, fortunately, another house rule—and he was ready to join the poker game.

Wolfowitz, Marla, Jack, Barry Lee, a thin gangly Oriental with his hair done up in a red Mohawk, and Ellis Burton, duded out in asymetrical painted jeans and a leather vest, were already playing around a big round table in the living room, and since another of the rules was that Nat would not play poker with less than three or more than five hands, Bobby was told that he would have to kibitz until someone dropped out or was cleaned out.

"Don't worry, kid," Wolfowitz told him, "with these marks, that won't take long."

Bobby knew the basic rules of poker, but he had played very little; nevertheless, it didn't take him long to see what Nat Wolfowitz meant.

It was a low-stakes game with a ten-dollar-bet limit, and

one of the other rules was that you had to leave when you lost two hundred bucks. "I only play with these rubes for practice," Wolfowitz declared with an evil leer as he shuffled the cards. "From each according to their ability, which around here ain't Jack shit, to me according to my greed, which approaches infinity as a limit, but I don't take serious money from my friends, I save that for the Fat Men."

The game was dealer's choice, but only straight draw, five- or seven-card stud, and jacks or better were allowed, and Wolfowitz always opted for seven-card when he had the deck.

"Poker, like life, is at least as much luck as skill," he informed Bobby, "but seven-card stud gives skill more room to operate. It's what separates the men from the boys and the boys from their bucks."

But if poker was really half luck, then why did the bills pile up so consistently in front of Nat Wolfowitz? He seemed to win about every other hand of seven-card stud, often with mediocre cards, and when he won, he won big. If someone else opened up a game of jacks or better, he dropped out immediately unless it turned out later that he had been holding three of a kind or higher. At straight draw, he either took two cards or less, or folded. At five-card stud, he seemed to follow no pattern that Bobby could discern.

It didn't take much more than an hour for Marla Washington to lose two hundred dollars and leave the game.

"Lesson number one," Wolfowitz said as Bobby took her place at the table. "The secret of winning at poker is to avoid losing."

"That's number *two*," Ellis Burton moaned as he dealt a hand of straight draw. "Lesson number *one* is don't play with Nat."

Bobby had a pair of tens. Jack Genovese opened. Barry Lee raised. Wolfowitz dropped out. Bobby called. Ellis called. Jack took two cards. Wolfowitz shook his head. Barry took one card. Wolfowitz groaned. Bobby took three cards and got another ten. Ellis dropped out.

"Dumb," Wolfowitz said.

"Check," Jack said.

"Shit," Wolfowitz groaned.

Barry bet five dollars.

Bobby raised him five.

Jack dropped out.

"I don't believe it," Wolfowitz said.

Barry saw Bobby's five and raised him ten.

Hesitantly, Bobby called.

Barry Lee turned up four spades and the king of hearts. Bobby raked in the pot, feeling pretty damn proud of himself.

A dozen hands later and down a hundred and fifty dollars, it was another matter. "Children, children," Nat Wolfowitz said as he won yet another hand, this one at seven-card stud with threes over fives and nothing but a pair of fives showing, "wishful thinking is the opium of the poker-playing masses."

While Bobby thought he was beginning to understand what Nat Wolfowitz was saying in theory, when it came down to practice, the man was a poker-playing monster. He could babble on and on and on about how he was doing it, and *still* beat you consistently even when you thought you were using his own principles against him. How did he do it? Was it luck? Was he telepathic? Or was his line of bullshit somehow part of his game?

However Wolfowitz was really doing it, the only thing that kept Bobby from losing the limit was that he still had twenty dollars left when Ellis and then Jack were cleaned out by Nat, leaving only three players, and, under the rules, ending the game.

"Well, kid, you learn anything?" Wolfowitz asked him as he walked him upstairs to his room.

Bobby shrugged. "Not to play poker against you, Nat," he said.

Wolfowitz laughed as he opened the door to a spare little room. There was a bed, a bureau, a desk, a chair, a lamp, all old stuff out of the junk shops of Telegraph Avenue by the look of it.

"Righter than you think," Wolfowitz said. "Poker, like life, only *looks* like a zero-sum game. A real player doesn't play *against* the other guys, he plays *the cards*. This poor screwed-up country doesn't understand that anymore, that's why it's in such shit, even though it's got no cause to bitch about what it's been dealt. We ever learn what we once knew, and we'll be back on top of the game. You ever really understand what I'm telling you now, and you'll win consistently at poker."

"Even against you?"

Wolfowitz laughed. He shook his head. "You still don't get it, kid," he said. "*No one* wins by playing *against* a real player. You figure that one out, and you'll be a real player too. And that's the koan for tonight. Think about it, Bobby, and maybe you'll find you got your hundred and eighty bucks' worth."

PRESIDENT SMERLAK EXPRESSES
SOVIET SOLIDARITY WITH MEXICO

After a meeting with the Mexican Ambassador, Pedro Fuentes, President Dimitri Pavelovich Smerlak reaffirmed the support of the peoples of the Soviet Union for the territorial integrity of the Republic of Mexico.

When asked whether any concrete steps were being taken by the Soviet Union to forestall an American invasion of Mexico, President Smerlak announced that the Soviet Union would introduce resolutions condemning any such invasion in advance in both the United Nations General Assembly and the Common European Parliament, and expressed confidence that they would pass in both bodies by overwhelming majorities.

"That, a tortilla, and a cup of refritos would just about make a burrito," Ambassador Fuentes observed enigmatically.

—Novosti

The next week was a golden time for Bobby.

He spent long sunny afternoons cruising Telegraph Avenue and buying himself a proper outfit—asymmetrically cut blue jeans with red-and-white painted stripes, perfect Franco-American ambiguity, a black velvet blouson embroidered with a flaming California sun setting behind a silhouetted palm tree, and a pair of used tooled-leather cowboy boots.

He cooked a big pot of choucroute garnie for the communal dinner, which was well received—even though the charcuterie was hot dogs, knockwurst, chorizo, and something called Canadian bacon, which was all he could find in the supermarket, and the limp sauerkraut came out of cans —probably because he loudly proclaimed its French authen-

ticity and managed to come up with Dijon mustard and a
couple of jugs of cheap Alsatian wine.

He toured the bars and clubs and cafés of Telegraph Avenue with Ellis and Jack and a mec from New York named
Claude, met lots of people, heard strange retro music called
"Acid Rock" and bizarre Peruvian jazz played by a flute
band, and was introduced everywhere not as just the new
kid in town, but the Parisian sophisticate from France.

He cleaned the living room and the halls, which was
merely tedious, and the bathrooms, which was pretty gross,
but he didn't mind at all; somehow these domestic chores,
which he had never been forced to do at home, cemented
the feeling of belonging that he had never found anywhere
else before.

And he joined in the nightly poker games a few more
times, though he swiftly came to realize that he could hardly
afford to play every night. Once he even came out ahead,
thanks to a lucky run of cards, and thought that maybe he
had picked up something from Nat Wolfowitz, until the next
game, when, all too cocksure, he stayed in just about every
hand, bluffed wildly, and was cleaned out in less than an
hour.

Finally, after endless passed messages and missed connections, he got ahold of Eileen and persuaded her to take him
on a tour of the Berkeley campus. It seemed almost as big
as UCLA, the architecture and the sprawling layout weren't
that much different in style, and the place was thronged
with the same sort of Gringos he had seen on the Trojan
campus, but the Reds of Telegraph Avenue were everywhere in evidence too, lounging in groups on the lawns,
listening to soapbox speakers around the Telegraph Avenue
entrance railing against the coming invasion of Mexico, arguing with the Gringos, and that somehow made all the
difference in the world. UC Berkeley was alive in a way that
UCLA was dead, and it didn't take Bobby more than that
one afternoon to realize that this was surely the place for
him.

He took Eileen to dinner in a little inexpensive African
restaurant on Telegraph, and then back to his room at Little
Moscow for a couple of hours of love-making, after which
she insisted on going back to her dorm.

He protested gallantly, but the truth of it was that he
really didn't mind, for somehow, outside of bed, her com-

pany seemed to have paled beside that of his newfound circle of friends; by this time, he was feeling like a Little Moscow insider, and Eileen Sparrow, who lived in the *dorms,* who was hardly known by his housemates, who was a native of *LA,* a city despised by the Berkeley Reds as the citadel of the Big Green Machine and all it implied, and who, despite her political heart being more or less in the right place, *talked* like one, clearly was not.

Tomorrow was Saturday, and that was party night in Little Moscow, and while Bobby, as a member of the commune, took pride in being able to invite her and would hardly have been crude enough not to do so, his pleasure was tempered by a certain feeling of detachment, a desire to be there on his own, and he didn't offer to pick her up and escort her, nor was he disappointed when she didn't ask.

By nine o'clock, the house was pretty much filled up with people, and the party was well stocked with the bottles of wine and vodka and tequila that they had brought along, for one of the other rules of the house was that party guests were expected to contribute the refreshments, else how could the commune afford to throw these things every week?

Or, as Wolfowitz put it, "There may not be any such thing as a free lunch left in Festung Amerika, but *we* have figured out a way to keep ourselves well supplied with free booze."

Music played on the living room chip-deck—all sorts of stuff, since guests brought their favorite chips too—wine and liquor flowed, and there were even people smoking hand-rolled cigarettes that some guy in a black leather jacket claimed was *real marijuana,* smuggled past the interdiction inside *body bags* from the Venezuelan war zone.

Bobby wandered around the party waiting for Eileen to show up, but half hoping that she wouldn't, what with all the truly incredible girls hanging around, dressed to kill in brief electronic happi coats, see-through plastic blouses, shorts that were all but nonexistent, even with bare boobs artfully peeping out from shirts open to the waist.

They were more than willing to chat with the likes of him too if there was someone like Marla or Claude or Karl around to introduce him as the exotic import from Paris, and for the most part it wasn't dumb talk, either. What they wanted to hear about was life in Paris, what he thought about the Soviet entry into Common Europe, what he had learned in his romantic odyssey hitchhiking across the country, whether Common Europe was *really* going to break off diplomatic relations with the United States if Mexico was invaded, and, of course, the differences, if any, between European women and Americans like themselves.

Bobby found himself at the drifting center of really interesting conversation; girls, and mecs too, for that matter, moving in and out of his sphere of influence as he moved around the house, trailing an actual entourage for the first time in his life, and enjoying it hugely.

And more than mere ego-stroking pleasure, though there was certainly plenty of that, he found the sense of belonging he had found among his housemates in Little Moscow extending outward toward the Reds of Berkeley in general.

They too were Americans in a sort of exile, dreaming vaguely of a future American Renaissance connected somehow to Berkeley's long radical past, an America that would give up its Latin American adventures, kick down the walls of Festung Amerika, join with Common Europe, and again become the light of freedom that had once illumined the world.

The object of attention of all these fantastic and intelligent girls, spinning tall tales of a Europe he had in reality been only too glad to leave, Bobby Reed found that he had come home to a place he had never been before. Except in his most impossible dreams.

When he strolled into the living room feeling like the cock of the walk, he had half a dozen people trailing after him, first and foremost a truly stunning girl named Shandra, who had huge lustrous dark eyes, fine aquiline features, smooth coffee-colored skin, long black hair worn in wild unkempt ringlets, who wore a kind of rainbow-tinted translucent plastic body-cloak that made it clear she had nothing on under it, and who had been listening to him longer than any of the others, staring at him quite openly without saying much.

And when he found a seat in the crowded room at one end of a musty old couch, a handful of people seated themselves on the floor before him, including Shandra, who folded her long brown legs under her Indian-style, propped her elbows on her knees and her head in her hands, and sat there looking up at him raptly as he spun his war story about the riot at the American Embassy.

". . . I was there getting my passport when it started, they started heaving shit and blood over the wall, and—"

"They really threw *shit?*" exclaimed a mec in a cowboy hat.

"Shit and blood all mixed together, I got splattered myself, let me tell you, it was—"

"I thought that was a bunch of gringo jingo propaganda!"

"Hey, I was *there,* the Embassy was covered with blood and shit, the mob was charging the wall, they had to use the disrupters—"

"To defend the flag and all that jingo shit!"

"To defend the people trapped in the compound," Bobby insisted.

"Woulda been better if they had *sacked* the Embassy, woulda taught the jingos a lesson they'd never forget."

"You wouldn't be saying that if you were there," Bobby said. "Those people were out for blood, you should've seen the hate in their eyes. . . ." He shuddered, remembering.

Shandra, who had been sitting there silently the whole time just eyeing him, finally spoke up in a soft lilting voice that sent shivers down Bobby's spine. "Did *you* hate *them?*" she said. "I mean, while it was going on?"

Bobby looked deep into her big brown eyes, pondering— pondering what she really wanted to hear him say as much as the truth of his feelings at the time, and finding, somewhat to his surprise, that they were one and the same, or so at least it seemed.

"No," he said. "I was afraid, and I was angry too, maybe, but how could I really hate those people? I mean, they were *right,* weren't they, America had just given Europe a good hosing, and they had good cause to hate the United States."

"That is very wise," Shandra purred up at him, and although she really didn't move, she seemed to be leaning closer.

"Then why you defending the fucking Marines?"

Bobby shrugged, his gaze locked with Shandra's, searching for the words that would draw her closer, and all at once something that Nat Wolfowitz had said suddenly seemed to make sense. "The Marines were dealt a shitty hand of cards," he said. "They played them the best way they could.

The Embassy didn't get sacked, and no one really got hurt, either. Made you proud to be an American."

"Proud to be an American!" the guy in the cowboy hat sneered.

"Aren't *you* proud to be an American?" Bobby shot back, still staring straight at Shandra.

"Are you?"

"Proud of what we just did to Common Europe? Proud of what we're about to do to Mexico?" Bobby sighed. "Yeah, what America's been doing since before I was born isn't anything to be proud of," he said. "But *we're* Americans too, aren't we? We start hating America, don't we end up hating *ourselves?* Don't we leave our country to the jingos?"

There was a long moment of silence. Shandra slowly unwound herself from her squat, rose, sat down on the couch beside him. "You don't mind?"

"Not at all," Bobby said, beaming at her, feeling the warmth of her thigh pressed against his.

"You've actually hitchhiked across the country?" she said. "That was very brave, people just don't do that anymore."

"They don't?" Bobby said innocently.

Shandra laughed. She snuggled closer to him. "You really *are* a European, aren't you?" she said.

Bobby threw up his hands, shrugged, and in the process managed to drape his arm on the couch back around her shoulders without quite touching her. "I've spent my whole life trying to figure that one out," he said. "In Paris, I felt like an American, but in New York and Washington and Miami, an American was the last thing I wanted to be. . . ."

Shandra leaned even closer. He could smell the jasmine perfume of her, feel her heat. "And now that you're here in Berkeley?" she said, placing a gentle hand on the top of his thigh.

"Now that I'm here, I like it just fine," Bobby whispered, letting his arm slide down the couch back. Shandra fitted herself into the crook of his arm; without knowing quite when it had happened, Bobby realized that his entourage had melted away, leaving him alone with this gorgeous and apparently willing creature.

"You have a room here, do you not . . . ?" Shandra suggested.

"Hi, Bobby!" a female voice piped brightly. Bobby looked up and saw Eileen Sparrow standing over them. Oh shit!

"Uh, hi, Eileen . . . ," Bobby muttered guiltily.

"Don't let me *disturb* you," Eileen said dryly.

Jesus! "Uh, we were just . . ."

"So I see," Eileen said. "Cute, isn't he?" she said to Shandra, without a hint of malice. "And he gives pretty good *head* too, I taught him how."

Bobby felt that he must be turning scarlet.

Eileen laughed. "Where's your European *sophistication?*" she said, and laughed again.

Shandra laughed too.

"You . . . uh . . . don't mind?" Bobby stammered.

Eileen made a great show of gazing around the room and licking her lips theatrically. "With all these *men* here?" she exclaimed. "Come on, Bobby, this is *Berkeley!*" And she sashayed off, blew him a kiss over her shoulder, and was gone.

Though it took him four more days to nerve himself up to make the dreaded phone call home, the Sunday afternoon after the party was when Bobby Reed realized that he had long since decided that he was going to go to college here in Berkeley no matter what his mother said.

Shandra Corday had been wonderful in bed indeed, at least from his limited critical perspective, but that was not what caused Bobby's great revelation. Indeed, Shandra had made it quite clear to him afterward that this was just a nice little adventure for her, as, if he was honest, it had been for him; she was seeing three other men and was not at this point in her evolution looking for the love of her life.

"This is, after all, Berkeley," she told him in the morning, and they both had a friendly little laugh over that.

No, what did it, strangely enough, was the phone call from Eileen Sparrow that came while he was still in bed with Shandra. Marla Washington opened his door and, without raising an eyebrow or missing a beat, told him he had a phone call. Bobby pulled on his pants and took it in the kitchen.

"Hi, Bobby," Eileen's voice said brightly on the other end of the old-fashioned audio-only American phone. "Have a good time?"

"Uh . . ."

"*I* had a wonderful time, I met this guy with millions of muscles who *fucked my brains out!*"

"Why are you telling me this, Eileen?" Bobby stammered.

"Why to thank you for inviting me, of course!"

Bobby didn't know what to say to that.

But Eileen Sparrow, as usual, was not at a loss for words. "Well, that's not exactly the whole truth, Bobby," she said when he didn't reply. "I mean, you were *so silly* last night, I mean you acted like I was your *mother* or something! I just wanted to set you straight, I mean, I really wasn't pissed at you at all, truly, truly, I wasn't. Okay?"

"Okay," Bobby said, quite touched.

"I mean, you don't owe me anything, and I don't owe you anything, so please, please, just have a good time and don't be so *uptight* about it. We're young, we're horny, it's only like *natural,* and this is—"

"I know, I know, this is *Berkeley!*" Bobby said, and they both laughed.

"Well, I gotta go now, Bobby," Eileen said. "Mr. America has another *hard-on,* would you believe it?"

"Have fun," Bobby said, and, somewhat to his surprise, he realized that he meant it.

"Oh don't worry, I *will!* 'Bye!"

And that was the moment of revelation, as Bobby stood there in the kitchen, with Karl and Cindy pouring themselves coffee from the communal urn and Shandra Corday upstairs in his bed, and Eileen Sparrow off somewhere in bed with someone else, but enough of a real friend to have called him to set his mind at ease.

This was where he belonged. This was a time and a place and a feeling that he never wanted to leave. He would go to college at UC Berkeley. He would major in history, and maybe he could go to grad school here too, and get a job teaching at the university like Nat Wolfowitz, and with luck, he could stay here in Berkeley forever.

Finding the courage to call Paris was something else again. Mom would go through the roof. The deal was that he was supposed to come back to Paris and go to the Sorbonne in the fall, and Dad had had to get into some pretty bad stuff with her to get him even this trip. Things had not been so terrific between them when he had left, which was maybe one of the reasons he hadn't called home at all yet. And now . . .

Bobby put it off, and put it off, and put it off, but finally, late at night after another losing poker game, when he knew he would catch his parents at the breakfast table, and fatigue had fogged his brain sufficiently, he found himself walking into the empty kitchen and dialing Paris before he had complete awareness of exactly what he was doing.

Maybe they've left already, he told himself as the phone rang once, twice, thrice.

"Hello?" said his father's voice on the other end.

No such luck.

"Hi, Dad, this is Bobby."

"Bobby! Where the hell are you? We've been worried sick! Sonya, it's Bobby, pick up in the bedroom!"

"I'm in Berkeley, Dad, I'm sorry, but—"

"Robert!"

"Hi, Mom—"

"Where on earth are you?"

"He's in Berkeley, Sonya."

"Why haven't you called?" Mom demanded. "Not even a postcard!"

"I—"

"And what's wrong with the picture? Our screens are blank."

"This is *America*, Mom, ordinary homes aren't wired for v-phones, remember?"

"But the decent hotels certainly must have—"

"I'm not staying in a hotel, I've got a room in this great house, with wonderful people, it's real cheap, and I can stay here as long as I want, so it's hardly gonna cost you *anything* for me to go to UC Berkeley, except for tuition. . . ."

There, it was out, and done.

"Oh no you're not, Robert!" Mom snapped.

"Oh yes I am! My mind's made up, and you're not gonna change it. I'm going to Berkeley!"

"Not on our money, you're not, Robert," Mom said. "Not one ECU, not one ruble, not one dollar!"

"Sonya!" Dad exclaimed.

"He'll forget about this nonsense as soon as he runs out of money."

"Sonya, he's got a right to live his own life, we can't blackmail—"

"This is all your fault, Jerry Reed! I *knew* we should never have let him go to that madhouse in the first place! No money, Robert, you're coming home, and you're going to the Sorbonne!"

"Never!" Bobby shouted. "I'm staying here."

"We'll see how long you last supporting yourself and paying your own tuition. . . ."

"I'll . . . I'll get a job!" Bobby stammered.

"I'm sure there are endless jobs in California for eighteen-year-olds with no experience that pay enough to send you through a capitalist university," Mom said sarcastically.

"I'll . . . I'll join the Army! They pay for four years of college in return for four years' service."

"Bob!"

"Go ahead, Robert," Mom said knowingly. "That's one silly bluff I'm quite ready to call."

Bobby forced himself to think coldly. *Play the cards,* he told himself. *You don't have much showing, but they can't be sure what you've got in the hole.*

"Have it your way, Mom," Bobby said in as cool a tone as he could muster. "I can always deal *drugs,* they bring back marijuana in body bags from the South American war zones, did you know that? I know the guys who are doing it. No one goes broke dealing dope in Berkeley. . . ."

"Bob!" Dad shouted in a horrified voice. "For God's sake, don't do anything stupid! I'll get you the money one way or another, I promise!"

"Jerry!"

"Goddamnit, Sonya, you want your own son dealing *dope?* You want to see him rotting in some miserable jail for twenty years?"

"I won't have it, I won't have you blackmailing us like this, Robert!"

"Now the Politburo is calling the Supreme Soviet a bunch of Commies?" Bobby snapped back.

There was the sound of a receiver hanging up.

"Promise me you won't do anything foolish, Bob," Dad's voice pleaded. "Give me your number, and I'll call you back when I've convinced your mother to listen to reason. But please don't do anything stupid, let me handle it, okay?"

"Okay, Dad," Bobby said. "But I'm serious. I'll do whatever I have to to stay here. Do you believe me?"

"I believe you, Bob," Dad said woodenly. "Just wait for my call before you do anything."

And after Bobby gave him the number, he hung up, leaving Bobby alone in the empty kitchen in the dead of night, wondering what he would *really* do if his bluff was called.

Two days later, Mom and Dad called together. It was really strange. "The three of us have got to work this out as a family instead of fighting with each other," Dad said in a weird pleading tone of voice.

"Your father and I have worked out a compromise," Mom said, sounding strangely distant. "You come home to Paris for college, and you can spend your summers in America."

"No," Bobby said.

"Please, Bob," Dad pleaded. "You're making things very difficult."

"I'll spend my summers in Paris if you pay for me to go to Berkeley," Bobby countered.

"I *told* you this was futile, Jerry!" Mom snapped angrily.

"Bob, please, your mother and I—"

"I thought you were on my side, Dad! All that stuff you were always telling me about America ever since I was a little kid—"

"Bob—"

"—it was all a lie, wasn't it? You never believed a word of it!"

"You know that's not true! If it wasn't for me, you wouldn't be in America in the first place!"

"That's the first intelligent thing you've said in a week, Jerry Reed!"

"Sonya!"

"Don't Sonya me!"

"Please, Bob, can't you see that your mother and I—"

"Classes start here in ten days, and if I don't have the tuition money by Monday, I'm going to have to borrow the first installment from my dealer friends and start pushing drugs to pay it back or they'll stuff *me* in a body bag!"

And he hung up on them and let them think about it.

Finally, late Sunday night, Bobby got the long-awaited call from his father. Dad sounded weary, and distant, and strangely defeated.

"All right, Bob," he said tiredly. "I'll be wiring you the money tomorrow."

"Hey, that's great, Dad, that's just great!" Bobby exclaimed. "How did you manage to convince Mom?"

There was a long silence and then an audible sigh on the other end of the line. "That's . . . that's between your mother and me," Dad finally said. "You know . . . she really *does* love you, in her way. . . ."

"She sure has a funny way of showing it."

"Yeah, well . . . love isn't always easy, Bob," Dad said sadly. "Love isn't always right either. Sometimes, well, people who love each other hurt each other, like . . . like . . . Well, someday, if you're not so lucky, maybe you'll understand. . . ."

"Are you all right, Dad?"

There was a long pause. "Just terrific," Dad said hollowly. "Haven't a care in the world. . . . You take care, Bob."

"Uh, yeah, you too, Dad," Bobby said uneasily, and that was the way the conversation ended, with his jubilation soured, at least for the moment, by feelings of vague guilt for he knew not what.

Bobby's somber mood didn't last much past breakfast. He went over to UC Berkeley to fill out his matriculation papers, spent the afternoon wandering around the campus, went back to the house, called Eileen and Shandra to tell them the good news, and before dinner, the money arrived from Paris. He won forty dollars at poker that night, cashed the draft from his father the next morning, paid up his tuition in the afternoon, had dinner with Eileen, made love, spent the next night with Shandra Corday, and by that time, the strange way Dad had acted on the phone was quite forgotten.

Until two days later, when Marla Washington handed him a letter that had arrived in the mail. "All the way from Russia!"

It was from Franja. His Russian was still good enough for him to read the Cyrillic on the stationery. It was a Gagarin University envelope. The letter lay heavily in his hand like a very cold and very dead fish. Franja had never written him a letter before, and somehow he had the feeling that this was not going to be a pleasure. And when he took it up to his

room to read it in private, it was even worse than he had
imagined.

> *Dear Bobby:*
>
> *I do hope you are enjoying yourself in Gringoland,
> little brother. I suppose you're not very interested in
> what your vile little blackmail scheme has done to your
> own parents, but I'm going to tell you anyway.*
>
> *Father went out and wired you your tuition money
> without even telling Mother, did you know that? I only
> wish you had been there when he finally told her at
> dinner, it would have been only what you deserve. They
> screamed and yelled at each other for over an hour. It
> was horrible.*
>
> *They called each other all kinds of names, and when
> Mother finally ended up calling Father a fascist gringo
> unilateralist, Father actually accused her of having an
> affair with Ilya Pashikov. And the so-called conversa-
> tion ended with Mother shouting "Just maybe I will!"*
>
> *Mother ended up sleeping on the couch, and when I
> left they were barely speaking to each other.*
>
> *When you told Father to sign my admission papers to
> Gagarin, I made the mistake of thinking you might
> have some human decency, after all. Stupid me! You're
> no different from the rest of them, Bobby Le Gringo.
> You've wrecked our parents' marriage for your own self-
> ish purposes just as Washington is intent on wrecking
> international peace and prosperity in the service of
> American greed and envy.*
>
> *But then, you're actually* proud *to call yourself an
> American, now aren't you?*
>
> > *Three cheers for the
> > Red, White, and Blue,
> > Franja Yurievna*

Bobby stormed out of the house in a tearful rage and
jogged all the way to Telegraph Avenue. He knew just what
he was looking for. Half the stationery stores on Telegraph
Avenue were selling the hateful thing, and it was just the
perfect reply for sister Franja.

He bought one of the postcards, addressed it to her with

no message on it, and mailed it before he had time to think about it, wondering maliciously what the Soviet postmen would make of it.

On the postcard was a hideous bear wearing a big sombrero with a hammer and sickle on it in case anyone didn't get the message. It was bent over at the knees with a piteous expression on its face and its ass in the air.

Uncle Sam was buggering it with a laser-beam phallus.

Franja never answered back.

Eight days before classes started at UC Berkeley, there was a coup in Mexico City. Two days after that, the blatantly CIA-backed puppet regime ceded Baja California to the United States in return for cancellation of the Mexican debt. The next day, elements of the Mexican Army seized the capital and executed the traitors.

The day after that, an American aircraft carrier task force sailed into Vera Cruz harbor, Navy planes strafed the city, and Marines went ashore. Another carrier task force landed amphibious forces at Rosarita Beach, and two armored divisions crossed the border and occupied Tijuana. Yet a third carrier task force blockaded the Pacific coast of mainland Mexico.

The Gringos celebrated with enormous beer-busts all that weekend. There was no party at Little Moscow that Saturday. Everyone sat in the living room watching TV coverage from the war zones.

The Marines were wiping up the last resistance in Vera Cruz. The amphibious forces landed at Rosarita Beach had already linked up with elements of the ground forces that had taken Tijuana. The President went on the air and announced that the United States had no territorial ambitions in mainland Mexico. The President of the Soviet Union denounced American imperialism but promised nothing. The Common European Parliament passed a meaningless resolution of condemnation. The Mexican chief of staff had apparently ordered his army to disperse into battalion-sized units and begin guerrilla warfare.

It was all over but the shouting, which was still going on all over town.

"And in Berkeley, California, *this* . . . ," the announcer said.

"Hey, that's Telegraph Avenue!" Bobby exclaimed.

And so it was, the camera apparently mounted on a truck moving down the center of Telegraph, about two hours ago, by the look of the lighting, dollying slowly past sidewalks jammed with drunken jingo louts, waving beer cans, mugging at the camera, holding giant burning sombreros on the ends of poles, sticking up American flag posters on the windows of closed shops and restaurants, singing "God Bless America" in beered-out unison.

"Doesn't it make you proud to be an American?" Claude muttered bitterly.

"A peaceful victory demonstration . . ."

"By every drunken asshole in town!" Karl shouted at the screen.

". . . was disrupted by a small group of agitators . . ."

"Oh shit," Nat Wolfowitz moaned, as the camera suddenly zoomed down Telegraph Avenue into a tight shot on a small group of demonstrators, no more than two dozen of them, and Reds by the look of their clothing. They were carrying a black wooden coffin, and they were marching behind a big American flag hung upside down from a clothesline strung between two poles.

". . . believed to be members of an extremist Marxist group known as the American Red Army . . ."

"Bullshit!" Marla Washington shouted. "There's no such thing!"

"Tell me about it. . . ." Wolfowitz grunted.

The demonstrators marched slowly up the street beneath a hail of beer cans and paper cups. Some jerk in a white T-shirt and running shorts ran up to the front rank and spat in a girl's face. Then it all started to happen at once. Mobs of Gringos rushed the demonstration from both sides and the front. Fistfights broke out. Someone grabbed one of the poles holding the flag. Someone grabbed the other pole.

The camera reverse-zoomed, then the tape jump-cut to another angle. The jingos had the flag. A huge mob of them paraded down the sidewalk behind it, pumping their fists in the air and screaming.

". . . forcing patriotic Americans to rescue Old Glory from desecration."

"Those poor stupid brave bastards . . . ," Nat Wolfowitz said.

"And in New York, Lance Dickson pitched a no-hitter for

the New York Yankees against the Boston Red Sox, pulling them to within a game and a half of first place—"

"I think we can do without the fucking ball scores," Jack Genovese said, and turned off the videowall.

There was a long moment of silence. People just sat there staring at each other, saying nothing.

"Well, Bobby," Marla Washington said grimly, "you still want to go to college in good old Berkeley?"

"Yeah, maybe you oughta go back to Paris while you can."

"*You're* not stuck here in Gringo Jingo Land. . . ."

"Not yet, anyway. . . ."

"What about it, Bobby, you sure you wouldn't rather go home and be a Frenchman?"

"And take us with you?"

Bobby realized much to his surprise, and no little discomfort, that all eyes were now on him. Even Nat Wolfowitz was staring at him with the strangest expression on his face.

"What about it, kid?" Wolfowitz said. "You gonna fold this hand and go home to someplace sane like a smart player? Or stay here in the game like a sucker?"

Bobby realized that he had to say something. *What are you now, Bobby Reed?* they all seemed to be asking him. *You're the only one here who gets to choose. You still want to be an American?*

Bobby thought about what he had just seen. He thought about those agonizing phone calls with his parents, the last call from Dad in particular. He thought about Franja's letter, and the postcard he had sent in reply. He thought about his golden days with his new friends here in Berkeley. And in his mind's eye, he saw another mob, and the American Embassy smeared with blood and shit.

"So call me a sucker, Nat, 'cause I'm staying," he said. "I only wish I had been out there with them, marching behind that flag."

"Out there getting the crap beat out of you on television?" Marla said.

"Somebody had to do it," Bobby told her. "The goddamn jingos may have smeared blood and shit all over *our* flag, but when those people hung it upside down and marched up Telegraph behind it, they washed it clean, they made it something to be proud of again. They showed the world that there are still some *real* Americans."

"Now is the time for futile gestures?" Wolfowitz said sarcastically. But his eyes told quite another story.

"Hey, Nat," Bobby said, staring straight into them, "so it's a lousy hand we've been dealt. But these are the cards, and this is the only game in town, so we gotta play 'em."

Q: How many Russians does it take to shave the hair off a wild Bear?

A: One hundred thousand and three. Two to hold him down, one to wield the razor, and 100,000 to elect the result to the Supreme Soviet.

—Krokodil

HERO OF SOCIALIST PARKING

When Moscow police towed off Ivan Leonidovich Zhukovsky's brand-new Mercedes for triple-parking on Tverskaya Street, Ivan Leonidovich decided not to take things lying down. Instead, he stole a welding laser from his place of employment, broke into the police garage at 3:00 A.M., fused the transmissions of seventeen city tow trucks, turned himself in to the authorities after boasting of his exploits in a long drunken phone call to this newspaper, and demanded his right to a trial by jury under Soviet law.

"Let's see if the bastards can find a panel of patriots who will convict me!" he declared. "I'm guilty of nothing but what every red-blooded Russian motorist wishes he had the courage to do himself!"

—Mad Moscow

For better and for worse, life in the Soviet Union was not quite what Franja Yurievna Gagarin Reed had anticipated.

The better of it was that, with the Soviet Union now economically integrated into Common Europe, Moscow was already quite another city from what she remembered from her girlhood visits.

The bustle was still there, people still casually elbowed you aside in the Metro and the streets, there was still that feeling that this was the center of the world and everyone knew it, people still sold everything and anything on the sidewalks, but Moscow was evolving almost overnight into a truly European city; you could watch it happening, as all the spring flowers sprung up in neon profusion through the melting snow.

With all economic barriers lifted, the biggest new consumer market in the history of the world had suddenly opened up in the form of three hundred million Soviet citizens who were being offered easy credit for the first time in their lives. Consumer goods of every conceivable description were pouring into the Soviet Union as Common European companies fought for a piece of the action. To each according to his credit limit at 15 percent per annum, from each in small monthly payments.

Billions of ECU were lavished on advertising campaigns to sell everything under the sun, utterly transforming the Moscow cityscape with billboards and neon signs and videowalls and garish storefront displays. Every bus was festooned inside and out with advertising posters, cabs sold ad space, trees, walls, lampposts, were plastered with advertising stick-ups. A huge videowall had even been erected on the façade of the GUM facing poor Lenin's tomb across Red Square, and Tverskaya Street had been turned into a kind of scaled-down Champs-Élysées, with neon signs, instant sidewalk cafés, animated videowalls, lavish display windows, sleazy souvenir shops, fast-food restaurants, pickpockets, and gawking tourists from Japan and Central Asia.

The traffic jams were horrendous, and streets, alleys, and courtyard parking lots were jammed with parked cars, legal and otherwise, as every Muscovite's unfulfilled dream of a car or a moto was suddenly and instantly granted with no money down and easy monthly payments. The militia traffic wardens were to be seen everywhere, waving their white batons, mostly futilely, for the New Breed of Soviet motorist for the most part heeded not the old signal to pull over and meekly accept a ticket from a mere pedestrian official and had to be chased down by the new scooter police. Traffic signals seemed to be in the process of going up at every major intersection, and none too soon for anyone trying to cross against any driver's sacred right to make a right turn. The broad main avenues were fender-bending nightmares as automotive traditionalists persisted in attempting recently outlawed mid-block U-turns across multiple lanes of creeping cars.

Dozens of new movie houses, video rental stores, nightclubs, theaters, discos, saloons, and restaurants seemed to be opening up every week. Brand-new bookstores and art galleries were everywhere. Twenty new hotels had already been built and more were on the drawing boards. There was a casino near the Park Kulturi, and live sex shows around the corner from the Foreign Ministry on the Arbat Strip. The quantity of alcohol—hard liquor, wine, and beer—available was now limited only by the seemingly bottomless capacity of the populace, and the city was awash in drug dealers from all over Common Europe.

Hookers worked the crowds in plain sight of Lubyanka on Dzerzinski Square, and the Arbat had become a St.-Germain. You could get drunk on the sheer energy of the crowds around the Arbatskaya Metro station even at 2:00 A.M. with the system long closed, as club-crawlers continued their revelry en plein air amid peddlers and gambling games and street entertainers.

After over a century of lip service to dour socialist morality, Moscow was learning how to boogie openly, and taking the crash course in a mad effort to make up for all that lost time. It was Mad Moscow, indeed!

The worse of it was that Franja found little time to enjoy it.

Yuri Gagarin University had grown up around the old Yuri Gagarin Cosmonaut Academy at Star City, out in the banlieue, and while the Metro went straight from Star City to the centre ville, she found that a Saturday night now and again was about all the time she had to spare for fun and games in the city.

As a highly motivated teenager in Paris, Franja had been

a stellar student. Here, she was surrounded by thousands of other former star students just like herself, all competing for a comparative handful of openings in the actual Cosmonaut school.

The Soviet Union now had six Cosmograds in orbit and two more under construction. There was a permanent lunar base, and talk of establishing one on Mars. There were three launch facilities for heavy freight boosters, factories all over the Soviet Union building the hardware, satellite ground stations, data-processing facilities, development labs, and design centers.

The number of actual cosmonauts needed for this effort —Cosmonaut Pilots, Cosmonaut Flight Engineers, Cosmonaut Explorers—was only a few hundred. But the number of engineers, technicians, skilled workers, and assorted support personnel required to do the scut work was up there in the tens of thousands, and Gagarin University's task was to turn them out on a production-line basis.

For the first two years, everyone took the same basic courses, after which the top 5 percent, as determined by secret equation factoring in academic standing, physical condition, kharakteristika, and, of course, connections, was admitted into the Cosmonaut school.

Everyone else received a final year's training in some less exalted specialty—equipment maintenance, manufacturing, communications, ground control, computer programming, construction, data analysis and processing. After graduation, about 10 percent of the student body went on to graduate-level scientific studies, and the rest became the working class of the Soviet space program.

As a result, the competition was utterly ruthless. Classes ran six hours a day five days a week, and while the homework load was officially set at three hours a day, anyone who didn't put in at least four or five hours after class was not going to make it. Saturdays and Sundays were officially free time, but anyone who didn't volunteer his time for Komsomol activities was not considered motivated.

Students were required to live in the dorms, big ugly concrete housing blocks set up to "psychologically prepare students for Cosmograd life." Each student had a bed, a locker, a table, a chair, and a computer console in a large communal room divided by thin cardboard partitions. Bathrooms were communal and spartan. There were communal kitchens and commissaries, and students were required to do kitchen duty as well as keep the building shipshape. The dorms were co-ed, but what love-making took place had to be conducted quietly so as not to disturb the studies of the more diligent—apparently more "psychological training" in Cosmograd etiquette.

The work was the most intellectually demanding Franja had ever experienced, the hours seemed endless, but she had never been one to be afraid of hard work. Her fellow students might be dour obsessive grinds for the most part, but then so was she. What little dating she found time and inclination for consisted mostly of tours of the facilities, museums, and displays of Star City, a whole little metropolis given over almost entirely to the Soviet space program. What sex she indulged in was mostly quick, functional, and, of course, quiet, a matter of obtaining sufficient erotic exercise to keep one's mind clear for one's studies, a common attitude at Gagarin, where one's lover was also one's competitor.

All in all, she probably would have been happy at Gagarin, or at least too preoccupied to have any time to feel unhappy, were it not for the politics.

The President of the Soviet Union, as well as the Presidents of the constituent republics, were chosen by universal suffrage in multicandidate elections, as were the Delegates to the Supreme Soviet. But the politics of the Russian Spring had turned the Supreme Soviet into an unseemly bear pit of savage factional controversy.

"*The* Communist Party" did not exactly exist anymore. It had devolved into an uneasy confederation of factions and national communist parties, each one competing for votes on a local level with at least one overtly nationalist party, and each one, therefore, representing the chauvinistic interests of its constituency far more avidly than any central ideology.

The Russians themselves had become just another national minority, though still the largest by far and still in control of the central government, the central Party machinery, the economic apparatus, and the Red Army, to the point where the distinction between "Soviet Federalism" and "Great Russian Nationalism" was entirely lost on the Confederalists, aka the "Ethnic Nationalists."

The Ethnic Nationalists were a loose alliance of convenience of every national grouping with its own republic or even autonomous region. Nothing seemed to appease their appetite for independence—not popular election of their own national Presidents and Parliaments, not control of local taxes and national budgets, not even the formation of their own independent internal security forces, the so-called national militias.

The more they got, the more they wanted. Every concession, every step away from "Federalism" and toward "Confederation" was taken as a victory over "chauvinistic Russian hegemony." Ethnic Nationalist candidates won elections by outdoing each other in demanding greater and greater autonomy and lately even direct membership in Common Europe as sovereign national states.

Nor were the Russians themselves united. The so-called Eurorussians still dominated the Russian delegation in the Supreme Soviet, but in the Russian Republic, and even more so among Russian minorities in the other republics, an ominous sense of Russian nationalism had surfaced from the lower depths of society into the higher circles.

It could be as seemingly benign as the craze for neo-Czarist nostalgia or all the Russian Orthodox TV extravaganzas, as troubling as the profusion of mystics and faith healers in peasant blouses or the filth churned out by the Pamyat hard core, or as silly as the attempt to purge Western chord progressions from Russian rock 'n' roll, or as terrifying as the rhetoric of demagogues who proclaimed that the Soviet Union needed the strong hand of the Slavic master race in firm control of the "Asiatics."

Crude or subtle, it was all part of a Russian chauvinism that associated the threatened loss of Russian hegemony within the USSR with the entry of the Soviet Union into "degenerate bourgeois Common Europe."

These so-called Mother Russians might be a minority movement, but they were very much in evidence. On the streets of Moscow, this meant Uncle Joes—Pamyat street hooligans in Stalin T-shirts with mustaches to match—smashing the windows of foreign shops and fast-food stands, terrorizing crowds outside theaters and movie houses showing films and plays from the West, gang-raping "Westernized" girls, and roughing up people whose "Russian purity" they called into question. In the media, it meant things like an endless TV series idolizing Peter the Great, max-metal renditions of traditional Russian folk music, and gory comic books obsessed with the Great Patriotic War. In the Supreme Soviet, it meant Delegates in peasant blouses, cossack pants, and jackboots, foaming at the mouth for the benefit of the TV cameras and mercilessly heckling non-Russian speakers.

And in Gagarin University, it meant that someone like Franja Yurievna Gagarin *Reed* was constantly required to prove her Russianness.

Her light French accent might be considered chic among most of her fellow students, who fancied themselves modern Eurorussians and contemptuously referred to the Mother Russians as muzhiks, Bears, or worse, but there was a scattering of such unenlightened creatures on the faculty who tormented her for it.

"In *Russian,* please, Franja Yurievna," they would tell her, pretending they didn't understand her correct answers to their questions.

Being a Eurorussian repatriate with an effete French accent was bad enough, but when they found out that her father was an *American,* their attitude degenerated to a naked hostility that all too many of her classmates came to share.

And since marks were determined by a combination of grades and subjective evaluation of classroom performance, the disfavor of these miserable nikulturni reactionary Bears was enough to pull her overall average down to only a few points above the mean.

Worse still, she knew all too well that her kharakteristika, upon which her Parisian upbringing and her father's nationality were black marks enough already, and upon which any hope of getting into the Cosmonaut school also depended, was *also* being unjustly blackened by the Mother Russians among her teachers.

It was the bitterest of ironies. Franja was being discriminated against as an *American!*

Mother too, to judge from her letters, was suffering unjustly for the misdeeds of the American imperialists, not to mention Bobby's selfish insistence on attending college in the United States.

After the Great Stock Market Coup it had seemed that Mother must surely be due for a promotion to department head of something. Instead, after Bobby had entered the

University of California at the same time that the Americans were invading Mexico, the Party had called her on the carpet for a political review, and only the intercession of her good friend Ilya Pashikov had saved her Party card and with it her lowly position as his assistant.

Yet Franja also found herself empathizing with her American father, even though it was he who was the unwitting source of her torment. Just as he had turned his back on America in the pursuit of his dreams of space only to find himself unjustly shunted off into a dead-end job anyway because of his American birth, so was *she* being unfairly robbed of her chance to go to Cosmonaut school by an American birthright she had never wanted any part of.

By the time the results were in on her first year at Gagarin University, it was all too apparent that she had no chance of getting into the Cosmonaut school no matter what she did in the second year, and by the time she went home to Paris for the summer recess, she was seriously thinking of giving up and quitting.

Matters at home were not exactly conducive to lightening her despairing mood.

Father had grown quite bitter with the way things were going with his career at ESA. And it was all too painfully clear that Mother and Father were not getting along at all.

They still slept in the same bed, but what went on behind the bedroom door was something that Franja did her best not to imagine. They fought often in front of her, and frequently over the most stupid and trivial things, and when they weren't fighting, they seemed distantly polite but cold to each other, manifestly attempting to put on a good face for her benefit, which only made things worse.

The only bright spot was that the Americans had imposed extremely restrictive entrance visas as part of yet another tightening of their loathsome National Security Act, meaning that if Bobby wanted to come to Paris for the summer as planned, the chances were excellent that he would not get back in, something she was certain he would not risk, meaning that Franja was at least spared *his* presence at this tense and depressing family reunion.

But that was hardly enough. She spent two weeks moping fecklessly about the city, pondering her own problems without really being able to discuss them fully, without it degenerating into another of Father's anti-Russian tirades, and bearing horrified and helpless witness to the degeneration of her parents' marriage.

She found herself longing for the spartan dorms of Gagarin University, where she at least had more than enough hard work to keep her distracted, and once she found herself waxing nostalgic for *that* venue of torment, she knew she had to leave. Where she would go was something else again, but she had to get out. The Midi, maybe, or the Black Sea, anywhere where she could lie on a beach during the day, engage in meaningless sex at night, and try to sort out what she was going to do with the rest of her life.

It took her several days to get up the courage to tell her parents, but finally one night at dinner, when the entrecôte béarnaise had come out right, and the Bordeaux had been excellent, and they all had managed to get through the salad course and into a good chocolate gâteau and perfect coffee without any untoward event, she managed to ease into it.

"I think it would be a good idea for me to get away by myself for a while and find someplace quiet and sunny to think," she said. "I'll come back through Paris to see you for a week or so before I go back to Gagarin . . . if I go back. . . ."

"*If* you go back?" Mother said. "All this talking about quitting isn't really *serious?* So you haven't had such a good year academically, it's just a matter of getting down to work and trying harder."

"I *told* you a thousand times, Mother, I've been working as hard as I can, but I just can't fight the politics."

"You're *sure* you're not just using that as an excuse?"

"You know me well enough," Franja shot back in exasperation. "Am I a shirker? Have I ever been afraid of hard work?"

"No, but—"

"I've been right all along, Sonya," Father said bitterly. "First they do it to me, and now they—"

"Enough, Jerry! The question is, what are we going to do about it?"

"What *can* we do about it?"

"I can talk to Ilya—"

"The Golden Boy!"

"Ilya's well connected, he's certainly proven—"

"Far be it from me to deny that your *colleague* Pashikov is well connected with the shits in Moscow," Father shot back contemptuously. "But might I point out that a good word from *Ilya* would be the last thing in the world to improve Franja's situation?"

"Oh really?"

"Imagine how kindly these Bears or Mother Russia Fuckers or whatever they call themselves would feel toward our daughter if they get dragged onto the carpet on the word of some Westernized degenerate in an Yves Saint-Laurent suit like *Ilya Pashikov!*" Father exclaimed. "It'd be almost as useful as a personal letter of recommendation from the President of the United States!"

Mother glared at him silently. Franja wished she were somewhere on the Black Sea already.

"So what do *you* suggest, Jerry?" Sonya finally said.

"I could talk to Emile Lourade—"

"You can't even get him on the phone!"

"Well Corneau then . . . ," Father muttered weakly. "He owes me, Franja could transfer to the ESA program, and—"

"Corneau! You can't even get him to give you an office with a window!"

Father sighed. He looked so forlorn and defeated that Franja wanted to get up and hug him. For the first time she understood, really understood, what it must be like for him to see all his dreams defeated, to see his daughter's dreams defeated, and to be unable to do anything to help her either.

"I guess there's not much we can really do for you, Franja," Father finally said softly. "That's a bitter thing for parents to have to admit, you know. . . ."

"That's the truest thing you've said in months, Jerry," Mother said sadly. "We like to think we're in charge of our lives, but sometimes things and forces beyond our control . . ." She threw up her hands. "Sometimes it's hard to know when to start blaming others and stop blaming yourself. . . ."

A strange look passed between her and Father, a ghost of a smile, a sad recognition of something private between them. But in the next moment it seemed to have passed, as Father's face hardened, and he looked away from Mother, and stared directly into his daughter's eyes.

"But that's no excuse for giving up," Father said. "Stick it out. And if you can't get into the Cosmonaut school, take whatever you can get that will give you time out of the gravity well. You're young, and the golden age of space exploration is just beginning, and when the Grand Tour Navettes become operational, they're gonna have to dig deep. Get up there, Franja, get up there however you can. And someday, you'll see, it'll be you and me, out there on our way to the Moon, to Mars, even. You and me, Franja, they're not gonna make it easy for us, but we're gonna do it. You believe that, don't you? Don't you, Franja?"

Franja's eyes filled with tears. "You're such a space cadet, Father," she stammered. "You only believe all that because you're a hopeless romantic."

Mother's eyes seemed to moisten too, and she looked directly at Father with a wistful tenderness that Franja had not seen between them for the entire two weeks she had been home, now, ironically enough, on the very eve of her departure. And indeed, she sensed, because of her imminent departure, somehow.

"I won't give up," Franja blurted hastily in the wan hope of preserving the moment. "I promise," she said. "Because I believe it too."

Which, of course, she did not, but it didn't take her more than a few days thinking about it on the beach near Nice to realize that there was really nothing else for her to do.

Besides, she *had* given her word, and lightly made or not at the time, she found that a promise to her parents at this sad pass between them was not something that she had the heart to break. If Bobby had been the cause of this rupture, she had to do what she could to heal it, and under the circumstances, not disappointing them, while not very much, was all that she had in her meager power to do.

So at the end of the summer she went back to Gagarin University and threw herself into her studies as if even harder work would be enough to overcome all obstacles. But although her grades did improve somewhat, at the end of the year, when the names of those who had been admitted to the Cosmonaut school were announced, hers was not among them.

She was in a foul mood indeed when she went in for her appointment with Vassily Yurovets, the so-called Career Guidance Counselor, the meeting that would decide the course of her final year at Gagarin, for whatever that would be worth, which at the moment did not seem like much.

Yurovets was a beefy red-faced man in his early fifties with receding blond hair and a body that seemed held together against a tendency to fat by rigorous exercise and iron will. He had been a Cosmonaut Pilot himself, until the onset of high blood pressure had forced his permanent grounding, and the walls of his office were decorated with photographs of Cosmograds, Mars ships, old comrades, and himself standing in a spacesuit on the surface of the Moon with the Soviet lunar station in the background.

"So . . . Franja Gagarin Reed . . . ," Yurovets said, punching up her records on his terminal. He frowned, he shook his head. "What a name!" he said. "You are related to *the* Yuri?"

"No, I'm not," Franja said. If I was, she thought sourly, I'd probably be on my way to the Cosmonaut school now.

Yurovets glanced back at the screen, then studied Franja speculatively. "It says here that your father is an American named Jerry Reed . . . ," he said.

Oh no, Franja thought miserably, please don't *you* be a damned Bear too!

"This would not be by some wild chance *the* Jerry Reed?" Yurovets said.

"*The* Jerry Reed?"

"The American defector who created the Grand Tour Navette concept . . . ?"

"That's my father," Franja admitted grudgingly. "You've heard of him?"

"Of course I've heard of him!" Yurovets declared. "I read the original magazine article back before . . . well, back when I was still a cosmonaut. What an inspiration! And now that we are actually in the process of fulfilling his vision . . ." He frowned. "You, ah, will pardon my indelicacy, but your father, he is still alive?"

Franja nodded.

"Then why is he not directing the project?" Yurovets demanded.

"That, Comrade Yurovets, is a long sad story," Franja told him cautiously. "A rather political one . . ."

Yurovets nodded his head, pursed his lips. "I see . . . ," he muttered. "So the bastards are everywhere, even in ESA. . . ."

"Comrade Yurovets?"

Vassily Yurovets seemed to snap back into focus. "Well, we are not here to discuss your father's glorious past, but his daughter's future," he said briskly.

"Such as it is," Franja muttered disconsolately.

Yurovets cocked an admonitory eyebrow.

"That is to say," Franja stammered quickly, "what I really want to be is a cosmonaut, but—"

"An entirely admirable ambition," Yurovets said. "But these grades . . ."

"I know—"

"And this kharakteristika, and what's this, you're not even a Soviet citizen! What a mess!"

"I plan to take Soviet citizenship as soon as I reach my legal majority," Franja told him.

"But why not already? Surely you realize—"

"Surely I do, Comrade Yurovets!" Franja declared. "But my father—"

"Won't sign the papers because he won't have any part of his daughter becoming a Soviet citizen because the Russians are preventing him from achieving his own ambitions?"

"There you have it," Franja said miserably.

Vassily Yurovets drummed his fingers on the desktop. "I begin to see the vector," he muttered. "Let us dig a bit deeper. . . ."

He spent several minutes playing with his keyboard, staring at his screen, muttering under his breath. Finally he looked at Franja, steepled his fingers, seemed to hesitate before he spoke.

"This must go no further, you understand, and I will strenuously deny that the following conversation ever took place . . . ," he said.

"Comrade Yurovets . . . ?"

"I have compared your class grades with your examination marks, and in many instances they do not properly correlate at all," Yurovets said. "And as for the instructors in question, their proclivities are all too well known. . . ."

"Proclivities . . . ?"

"Let us not mince words!" Yurovets said angrily. "They are all a gang of Russian chauvinist Bears! The bastards! It makes my honest Ukrainian blood boil! Do not think that you are the only one who has suffered injustice at the hands of these swine! Whole peoples writhe under their yoke!"

Franja did not quite know how to take this outburst, but for the first time in a long while, she allowed herself to feel a glimmer of hope.

"So let us speak with brutal frankness," Yurovets went on. "While you probably would not have achieved the grades necessary to enter the Cosmonaut school anyway, the fact remains that you have been the victim of unreconstructed Russian chauvinism as much as any Ukrainian, and against the daughter of *Jerry Reed*, at that. The honor of this institution, the Cosmonaut corps, and what the Soviet Union is *supposed* to be demands that this imbalance be redressed somehow. . . ."

His anger subsided somewhat, and he threw up his hands. "Not that there is all that much that I am in a position to do," he admitted. "However . . . Speak from the heart, Franja Reed—what is it that you *really* want?"

"To be a cosmonaut!" Franja said.

Yurovets sighed. "Admission to the Cosmonaut school is out of the question," he said. "But perhaps there is another path . . . difficult, true, problematic as well, but . . . How badly do you want to be a cosmonaut? What sacrifices are you willing to make? What chances are you willing to take?"

"Name them!" Franja declared.

"What this meeting is supposed to be about is your area of specialization for your final year," Yurovets told her. "Students are allowed to choose on the basis of their class standings until the quotas for the various specialties are filled, and since, despite the machinations of the Bears, you *are* in the top half of your class, your choice is a fairly wide one. Nevertheless, I advise you to select a specialty that is considered among the least desirable. Equipment maintenance technician."

"Maintenance technician!" Franja moaned. "Glorified dockhand!"

"Just so," Yurovets said. "Few students volunteer for that! But it *will* get you out of the gravity well, and let me tell you as a cosmonaut, that five or ten years from now, when the Grand Tour Navettes are operational, there will be a need for crews that the graduates of the Cosmonaut school will not be able to completely fill. And believe me, when we are forced to pluck people out of the ranks, they will be people with experience in space, however lowly, not a bunch of groundlings with fancy degrees!"

Franja goggled at Vassily Yurovets in amazement. "My father told me much the same thing!" she said.

"Did he?" Yurovets exclaimed. He positively beamed at her. "What an honor!" He laughed. "Great minds, it would seem, run along the same channels after all!"

He grew more serious, somber, even. "Perhaps in the future these things may change, but right now your kharakter-istika is a dreadful mess, and what you sorely need is a great big gold star, so to speak, which I will gladly inscribe in your records if you agree . . ."

"Agree to what?"

"If you take my advice and train as a maintenance techni-cian, I will, shall we say, embellish the record a bit," Yurovets said. "The way it will read is that you marched in here like a good little Stakhanovite, eyes gleaming with pa-triotic fervor, and before I could get my mouth open, you positively *demanded* the honor of becoming a maintenance technician for the good of the Motherland, knowing all too well that the unfortunate bourgeois egoism of too many of your less idealistic classmates has led them to eschew such vital honest proletarian labor in favor of cynical self-serving careerism. Or words to that effect."

Franja could not help bursting into laughter. "Would any-one actually believe such nonsense?" she said.

Vassily Yurovets shrugged. "People who can believe that Joseph Stalin was anything but a madman and a monster or that Russians should rule this great nation of ours forever by right of blood are fully capable of believing *anything!*" he declared. "Even that a girl like you could be as much of a self-righteous ass as they are!"

ARE WE STILL REALLY ALONE?

Some may find it peculiar that the unequivocal discov-ery of some sort of extraterrestrial civilization on the fourth planet of Barnard's star has done so little to trans-form our own. A certain excitement, the sending of messages, and now the Barnards have been pretty much forgotten by the general public. More than forgotten, perhaps, deliberately put out of mind.

All of us now living will, after all, be dead before an answer from the Barnards, if it ever comes, can possibly reach us. Most people don't like thinking about that. It's too much a reminder of our own mortality. And those of us who do think about it are frustrated by a great mystery whose answer we know we will never live to learn.

One wonders whether the Barnards will feel much the same when they receive our messages. But that too, alas, is a question whose answer those now living are fated never to learn.

Those of us who do care are fated to die knowing we were born out of our proper time.

—*Space and Time*

X V I I

Franja had flown in Concordskis on regular flights between Paris and Moscow, but *this* was something else again.

She was bussed to the Star City airport, along with half a dozen other newly graduated maintenance techs, and loaded on the plane with no waiting and no formalities. This Concordski was a Space Ministry job, with a cabin that had been chopped in half to make room for extra cargo in the rear. The overhead video screens that replaced the windows on commercial Concordskis were absent, and nobody bothered with the familiar safety and oxygen mask instructions.

The door was sealed, the plane began to move, it stopped, shuddered as the turbofans went through their run-up, and then it took off. There were about forty passengers on the flight, reading books and magazines, passing flasks of vodka, or just catching a snooze. It should have been a boring, claustrophobic, and depressing experience.

But it wasn't. For this was not a flight to Paris but to orbit, to Cosmograd Sagdeev; at long last, the year's tedium was over and Franja was on her way up out of the gravity well.

The best that could be said about her year's training as an equipment maintenance technician was that, after what she had gone through in her first two years at Gagarin, the work was easy, the competition nonexistent, and the instructors quite indifferent to both her background and her accent.

Her fellow students were the dregs of the University—dullards who considered themselves lucky to have gotten this far or slackers who spent most of the time cursing their misfortune. The instructors were mostly middle-aged ex space techs whose primary concern was familiarizing the students with the tools and the equipment, true working-class types uninterested for the most part in politics, who considered themselves fortunate to have retired into these sinecures, held their indifferent students in equally indifferent contempt, and were somewhat pleased, not to say bemused, by Franja's diligence and enthusiasm.

But now all that was over, and the great adventure was beginning!

Franja's only disappointment was that she was being denied the glorious view and had to content herself with imagining it in her mind's eye: the blue sky purpling to black and the Earth falling away as the Concordski's main engines took over with a satisfying slap of the seatback against her body, the planet's surface curving and the stars coming out as the plane rose faster and faster through the upper atmosphere, the judder, the hesitation, and the sudden change in the music of the vibrations as the Concordski's engines went to internal oxidizer for the final kick to orbital velocity, and then—

The vibrations stopped and the plane glided along in perfect silence as Franja felt a sudden slightly queasy floating sensation. She loosened her seat belt and felt herself rising up off her seat against it. She wormed her hand between the seat and her butt and squealed in delight as it fitted loosely into the gap.

"Free fall! We're weightless! We're in *orbit!*"

"What?"

Her seatmate, a middle-aged man who had spent the whole time reading, finally looked up from his book at her.

"I said, we're in orbit!"

"Since this is a flight to Sagdeev, that should hardly be surprising," he said owlishly. "This is your first time?"

"Yes!" Franja declared excitedly.

"Well, don't worry about it, you'll get used to it. But if you *are* going to throw up, please remember to use the vomit bag. Globules of puke floating all over the cabin would definitely be considered nikulturni."

And he reburied his nose in his book.

There was a series of little chuffs and judders as the Concordski fired its maneuvering jets, then a long silent glide, then more chuffs and judders as it matched orbits with the Cosmograd. Franja felt a little queasy, but she was not going to vomit, there was no question of giving the bookworm such satisfaction. There was a series of little *poings* against the hull as technicians attached the cable, and then just a hint of acceleration as the Cosmograd reeled the Concordski toward the air lock.

More clangs and poings and a rather unseemly bang as they mated the spaceway to the plane's door lock. Then the door slid open, Franja's ears popped as the pressure was equalized, and the passengers undid their seat belts and, pushing and bouncing off seats, floor, walls, and occasionally each other, swam awkwardly toward the exit.

Franja grabbed onto the first of a set of rings set into the top of the short tubular spaceway and pulled herself hand over hand through it and into the Cosmograd.

The first thing that she noticed was the smell, a faint rank odor of old sneakers, natural armpits, boiling cabbage, and a chemical tang vaguely reminiscent of toilet disinfectant.

She found herself floating near the center of a large round chamber about fifteen meters in diameter, its "walls" coated with peeling sky-blue paint. The mouths of five passageways led off into the rest of the Cosmograd, and a three-dimensional cross of ropes led from the center of the chamber to the lines of hand-rings that crisscrossed its surface. Franja managed to clutch onto one of the ropes as disembarking passengers brachiated along them, grabbed onto handholds, and pulled themselves into the passageways and out of the debarkation chamber like a cageful of gibbons, leaving her and her six fellow novices floating about in confusion, wondering what to do.

"Where are the new monkeys? Ah, there you are, how could I tell?"

A burly woman in a green sleeveless jumpsuit had pulled herself into the chamber from the passageway "below" Franja and hung upside down by one hand from a ring like an inverted ape.

"I'm Melnikov, your temporary keeper, and I'm supposed to show you to your cages, so stick close, try not to trip over your tails, and let's go," she said, and pulled herself back into the passageway.

After a certain amount of bumping, confusion, and cursing, Melnikov managed to assemble all of them in the passageway behind her, a dull green tube with the ubiquitous line of handholds down the center of an arbitrary ceiling and blue, green, red, black, and yellow lines painted down an arbitrary floor.

"Welcome to Cosmograd Sagdeev, such as it is," she said. "We're going to crew quarters now, that's the yellow line in case you get lost, red goes to command and control, blue to the air locks and freight ports, which you'll be seeing plenty of, green is science, of which there is not much, and black is equipment, repair, and construction, which will be your main bed of pain; save your questions for later, and follow me."

Melnikov led them down the passageway toward another, smaller spherical module with more passageway branches, down another passageway, through another intersection module, following the yellow line as the others branched off, until, after more swerves and turns than Franja could hope to remember, they reached a spherical module where all the passageways were marked with only the yellow and big white numerals.

"From here all roads lead to the monkey cages," she told them. "Remember the number of your dormitory module, there're only five, you can count that high, can't you?" She fished a little clipboard out of a jumpsuit pocket. "Lermitskovski, Bondarov, follow me, the rest of you stay here and wait your turn."

She led two of the recruits off down passageway 1, returned a few minutes later, and read off two more names. "Khukhov, Reed . . ."

Franja found herself brachiating down passageway 2 close behind Melnikov, with Khukhov, a small dark-haired woman who looked a little green around the gills, trailing

after. A series of round doors ran down two arbitrary sides
of the passageway, each marked with a big white numeral.

"This one's yours, Reed," Melnikov said, hanging from a
ring by a door marked "4." "Orientation in half an hour, go
down to the end of this passage and follow your nose toward
the commissary. Borscht and Hungarian sausage—don't
worry, you can't miss it. Well, come on, Khukhov, you can
puke later, on your own time!"

Franja pushed open the unlocked door and hauled herself
through into a cylindrical room painted pale yellow. A
round gray plastic table was bolted to the arbitrary ceiling
above her along with four matching chairs equipped with
seat belts. A row of four clothes lockers lay along the arbitrary floor. There was a small canvas cubicle on the right-
hand wall through the open flap of which a toilet bowl could
be seen projecting out from the wall at a right angle. There
was a bigger tent affair on the left-hand wall, this one rub-
berized, with nozzles and some strange kind of drainpipe.
There were hand-rings all over the place.

The far half of the cylinder was divided up into four equal
slices by green canvas partitions. There were privacy flaps
across the openings and one of them was snapped shut. Two
of the cubicles were empty, and in them Franja could see
rubber sleep-nets fastened to the bulkhead and flexible
gooseneck reading lamps.

In the fourth cubicle, a man in a green jumpsuit was
snugly secured between two sheets of net-webbing, reading
a magazine with a naked lady on the cover.

"Hello . . . ?" Franja said uncertainly.

The man looked up, unsnapped his top sleep-webbing,
vaulted out of the cubicle, drifted over to her upside down,
gave her a gentle shove toward the "ceiling."

"You must be the new monkey," he said. "Have a seat.
I'm Sasha Gorokov."

"Franja, uh, Gagarin," Franja said, catching hold of one
of the chairs, pulling herself up, or was it down, into it, and
buckling the belt across her lap. With a series of seal-like
motions, Gorokov seated himself and buckled in, and all at
once they were seated across a table from each other on the
floor like proper human beings, or so at least for the moment it seemed.

Gorokov looked her up and down quite frankly. "Not

bad," he said. "The last one was built like a bear, with armpit hair to match. You *do* shave your armpits don't you?"

"*What?*" Franja exclaimed.

Gorokov laughed. He had an unkempt mop of thick black
hair, lazy brown eyes, and a rather supercilious grin. "I really don't like to fuck girls with hairy armpits," he said. "I
mean, they'll do in a pinch, but—"

"If you think—"

Gorokov laughed again, harder this time. "Yes, yes, I
know, I'm a vile crude muzhik, and you wouldn't touch me
with a fork, but don't worry, you'll get used to it. We're all
monkeys here, with sex lives to match. Wait till you try it
hanging from the rings by your feet! I could show you now,
if you'd like."

"Certainly not!"

Gorokov shrugged. "No offense, there'll be plenty of time
later, believe me. Let's have a drink."

So saying, he unbuckled his belt, brachiated over to a
locker, came back with a plastic squeeze-bottle with a built-
in straw, sucked on it, smacked his lips, handed it to Franja.
"Go on, try it, it's been aged in plastic over a week!"

For want of anything better to do, Franja gingerly took a
sip, and spat it out in a fine spray of droplets that immediately began drifting around the room. It seemed to be about
150 proof and it tasted like kerosene.

"Don't worry," Gorokov said, "you'll get used to it."

"I have to go now," Franja said frostily. "Would you at
least tell me which cubicle is mine?"

"Why the one next to mine, of course!" Gorokov said.

"But they're *all* next to each other!"

Gorokov gave her a lubricious wink. "You're beginning to
get the idea already!" he said. "Cozy, isn't it?" And he
broke up into raucous laughter.

In his way, Sasha Gorokov had been right. It was quite
amazing what you could get used to when you had no
choice.

Cosmograd Sagdeev was cobbled together out of five basic module types and various add-ons. The dormitory modules were reconfigurable to contain scientific workstations,
control rooms, tool lockers, and workshops. The big spheres
of the type that served as the so-called passenger debarka-

tion lounge were also used to house the two commissaries, the library, the crew lounge, the main command center, the two gymnasiums, and the single observation deck, and served as bulk storage facilities as well. There were six working air-lock modules for spacewalks, and one outsize air lock which could be opened, clamshell-like, to swallow satellites for repair. There were docking facilities for lunar shuttles and Mars ships outside, as well as antenna complexes, solar panels, clusters of sensors, station-keeping thrusters.

All this had evolved rather randomly over the years, and it was all connected by passageway modules and crossroads spheres. From the outside, Sagdeev looked like something put together by a committee of schoolchildren playing with an antique Tinkertoy kit. On the inside, it was a crazy maze, navigable only via the color-coded lines, and by smell.

Sagdeev was not one of the glamorous Cosmograds devoted to science or Earth observation. It was basically a repair, maintenance, and occasional construction depot in Low Earth Orbit, servicing satellites, heavy-lifter upper stages, GEO sat sleds, lunar shuttles, freighters on their way to Spaceville, and the occasional Mars craft, which was to say a glorified repair and refitting garage in space.

What this meant for its complement of one hundred space monkeys was endless grunt labor, lightened only by the fact that some of it involved spacewalking, which was every bit the magnificent soul-stirring experience that Franja had imagined, when she had the time to think about enjoying the view, which was seldom. Even EVA, which was certainly considered the best duty, was mostly a matter of tedious hand labor through clumsy suit-gloves or even more recalcitrant waldoes.

What it also meant was that Sagdeev's living quarters were allocated according to a class structure as rigid as anything that had existed under the Czars or the Brezhnev bureaucracy. The Cosmograd commander, his immediate subordinates, and the occasional cosmonaut VIP had whole dormitory modules to themselves. Supervisors bunked two to a module with a bulkhead between them for privacy and their own toilets and showers.

Monkeys slept four to a module, sharing each other's snores, toilet sounds, and farts, of which there were plenty, thanks to the food, which would surely have been relegated to the hog trough by the lowliest Bulgarian peasant. Rationed as they were to a three-minute shower every third day, they had plenty of intimacy with each other's body odors too.

For reasons it took Franja several weeks to fully comprehend, the monkey cages were sexually integrated. Aside from Sasha Gorokov, she shared hers with Boris Waseletski, a muscular blond sexual athlete who seemed to have a different woman between his webs every twenty-four hours, and Tamara Ryamskolya, a rather homely and sloppily built woman for whom the "docking maneuvers," as she called them, were an improbable dream come true.

Monkeys worked eight-hour shifts and then had sixteen hours off in order to maintain the terrestrial cycle, which meant that for sixteen hours of every "day" there was little to do but sleep, eat the vile food, do your mandatory workouts in the gym, read, watch TV in the crew lounge, swill the foul rotgut distilled on the sly from better-you-don't-ask, and screw.

Things being what they were, and her fellow monkeys being what *they* were, drinking and screwing were the main leisure-time activities.

Everyone fucked everyone else like, well, like a cageful of bored monkeys. Privacy being virtually nonexistent, Franja grew accustomed to the sight of the bodies of her cagemates quicker than she would have ever believed possible groundside. The sight of naked pricks became quite routine. So too did she become rapidly inured to the sounds of fucking on the other side of the canvas partitions.

Where privacy was impossible, nudity taboos would be ridiculous, and any futile attempts to honor them only a source of tension and frustration. Healthy men and women closely confined with plenty of time on their hands and not much else to do with it were going to have sex anyway, and since there was so little opportunity to do it in private, it made sense to ignore what was going on in the nets next door.

So too was the indiscriminate and frequently drunken nature of space-monkey sex a necessary adaptation, and one that the authorities had wisely encouraged by bunking men and women together. In such tight and closed quarters, passionate romances and deep relationships would only lead to jealousies, rivalries, angst, feuds, fistfights, and explosions.

Sex in Sagdeev was more like sport than an expression of

personal affection or even lust. Zero gravity opened up a whole new world of possibilities, and the premium was on inventiveness, on the most bizarre configurations possible, rather than the simple act itself.

One could simulate groundside sex by doing it inside the webbing, but nobody was much impressed with that. One could do it up against a bulkhead easily enough, head to toe or crosswise, for variety's sake. Doing it floating in the middle of a chamber, using countervailing thrust vectors alone, was a more advanced configuration that frequently led to scrapes and bruises when it tumbled out of control. Real experts could screw themselves around a module in a controlled trajectory.

Franja grew accustomed to all these sexual athletics long before she became enough of a true monkey to indulge in them herself, for monkey-cage sex also tended to be a *spectator* sport, especially when enough "space vodka" had been consumed. Couples showed off their latest moves or tried out experimental configurations before the critics. There was even a certain amount of wagering on the sidelines. Would orgasm be achieved before the configuration lost its stability and began to tumble? Could a twosome screw itself across a module in under two minutes?

At first Franja had been appalled by this behavior and never imagined she would sink low enough to indulge in it herself. But the work was tedious, the TV and the library boring, she was simply not one to drink herself into oblivion, she was going to be here for a year, she was a healthy young woman with normal urges, any kind of meaningful relationship was entirely out of the question, and slowly but inevitably she began to face the fact that sooner or later she too was going to have to make the final adaptation to Cosmograd life.

Franja had certainly not gone without offers, but monkey etiquette, scrupulously observed by even the coarsest of louts, frowned heavily upon excessive insistence, and as long as she refrained from rising to gentle and humorous baiting, she was more or less left alone.

Boris Waseletski was recommended by all the women, and a Hero of Zero-Gravity Sex from what she had seen of his public performances; she was just about the only woman in the cages he *hadn't* screwed yet, and he made it perfectly obvious that he was eager to complete his collection.

But for that very reason, not to say the fact that Boris was a nikulturni lout, Franja decided that she would be better off with Sasha Gorokov. Sasha might be crude, but he was no cruder than the average monkey, and at least his crudity was leavened with a certain good-natured sense of humor.

So when a time came that they happened to be alone together in the dormitory module, Franja asked him for a drink of the stuff he always had in his locker. Sasha raised a surprised eyebrow, but otherwise made no untoward reaction as he fetched a squeeze bottle, and then they were strapped in across the table just as they had been that first day aboard, what now seemed half a lifetime away.

This time, however, Franja forced herself to slurp down an impressive quantity of the vile stuff, determined to get as drunk as possible as quickly as possible and get this over with. With luck, they might be able to get in and out of the webbing before anyone else showed up to watch.

"I *told* you you'd get used to it," Sasha finally said when her head was really reeling and she could stomach no more of it.

"Yes, maybe," Franja muttered, "I guess since I'm here for the duration, I don't have much choice."

"We'll make a real monkey out of you yet."

Franja giggled drunkenly. "I think I've made a monkey out of myself already, thank you," she woozed dizzily.

"Not yet you haven't . . . ," Sasha said slowly.

"I'm *getting used to it,* am I not?"

"Is that what this is all about?"

"Oh the hell with it!" Franja declared. "Let's just screw like good honest monkeys! It's time I got used to that too, is it not?" She unbuckled herself, floated across the table, threw her arms clumsily around his neck, fumbled with his seat belt, freed him, kicked off the table, propelling them toward the sleep cubicles, mightily relieved to finally be getting this business over with.

"Wait a minute!" Sasha said, disengaging himself. "For your first time, we really should do something special."

And he took her by the hand, and, brachiating with the other, led her out of the dormitory module, into the maze of passageways, bumping and reeling, to the big satellite repair air lock.

The work-bay was empty now, except for the Octopus. This was the latest piece of equipment to be boosted up to

Sagdeev, and was still in the process of being evaluated. It was an EVA work-pod with six waldo arms, flexible cylinders ending in clusters of grippers and tools that did indeed resemble segmented metallic tentacles. Three people could work inside the thing at once in a shirtsleeve environment; it had its own maneuvering system, and a big bubble canopy with internally heated double-glazing to prevent cold-burns from random contact.

"What say we give the Octopus a workout?" Sasha said. "The poor stupid bastard certainly needs one!"

Franja grimaced. The Octopus had proven to be a nightmare to the space monkeys. Three people could in theory work inside it at once, but the tentacles were forever interfering with each other, and the geniuses on the ground had neglected to provide any of the waldo control panels with an overriding master control system.

"The Octopus!" Franja cried. "That damned thing is entirely useless for any real EVA work. . . ."

"Quite so," Sasha said, "but it's perfect for fucking!"

So saying, he popped the bubble canopy, they crawled inside, resealed the Octopus, and opened the clamshell air lock. Sasha fired the Octopus's main thruster, and they rose up out of the air lock and into the starry blackness.

The Octopus might not be exactly spacious by groundling standards, but since the pod was designed for a work crew of three, it was roomy enough with only the two of them inside. There were three seats one could strap into, three sets of waldo controls, and the maneuvering console; other than that, it was mostly empty space, though Franja could see no comfortable surface free of angles and protuberances against which they could perform the act, and not much room for free-fall drifting, either.

Sasha maneuvered the Octopus well clear of the Cosmograd, then rolled it over so that the view beyond the bubble canopy was truly magical.

The Earth hung overhead, an immense curve of blue, green, and brown, fleeced with snowy swirls of cloud, illumined brilliantly around the edge where the sun seemed to be setting behind it, the limb of the planet glowing in the Gegenschein. Thousands of multicolored stars peered down upon them unblinkingly from the velvety blackness.

With Cosmograd Sagdeev eclipsed by the body of the Octopus, the illusion was complete. There they were, weightless, seemingly alone in the immensity of space, soaring free above the Big Blue Marble. It might almost be called romantic. . . .

Sasha peeled off his coveralls, and Franja did likewise, and they floated nude in the center of the Octopus, heads upright, looking out at the Earth and the stars. Being monkeys, and dormitory mates at that, the sight of each other's naked bodies was not exactly novel, and hardly arousing in and of itself, at least as far as Franja was concerned, though Sasha, good monkey that he was, had no trouble raising an immediate erection.

"Well, now what?" Franja said uncertainly, glancing about the interior of the work-pod for a place of comfortable purchase.

"Now I will show you a whole new meaning for the phrase 'going down,'" Sasha said, and grabbing her frankly by the breasts, shoved her upward, so that the velocity carried her up and back against the transparent and heated bubble canopy.

Perspective underwent a sudden shift. Suddenly Franja seemed to be floating in the starry blackness itself, with the Earth *below* her. A moment of reflexive fear and vertigo overcame her, for with her back up against the glass, vision told her that she was falling backward down through the void toward the planet, with nothing visible between her and the big drop to reentry.

Sasha laughed when he saw her expression. "Don't worry," he said, "the canopy is designed to take a hundred-gram meteorite impact, it'll certainly stand up to what we have in mind, so just lean back and enjoy it."

So saying, he swam beneath her, pried her legs open wide, and forthrightly buried his face between them.

When Franja snaked a hand in his hair and looked at him floating between her thighs as the tingling waves of pleasure began, perspective shifted again, and *down* became Sasha's direction. Now she seemed to be floating light as air on the tip of his tongue, purchased on a point of pleasure, lifted upward and outward into the heavens surrounding her, rising like a goddess toward the stars on a wave of ethereal energy.

She threw back her head and let herself dissolve into the sensation, gazing up at the Earth floating above her, like the queen of the world riding up and out into the infinite blackness, until a tremendous orgasm took her in an explosion of stardust.

Loose-limbed, dreamy-eyed, creamily content with no further sensation of up or down, she opened her arms, and her legs, and, luxuriating back against the bubble canopy, took him into her, and they coupled there naked in the vast emptiness between the stars like true space monkeys.

"That was . . . that was . . . ," Franja muttered afterward as they quite literally came drifting down from the star-spangled ceiling.

"Cosmic?" Sasha suggested with a grin. He laughed. And then, quite unaccording to normal space-monkey etiquette, he leaned forward and planted a little kiss on her lips.

"What was that for?"

Sasha laughed again. "For a special moment," he said. "At last, Franja, you are a true space monkey!"

And so, at least for a time, she was. After that, Franja went through a period of several weeks when she was determined to try everything and everyone.

She had never been very promiscuous, indeed, for someone born well into the post-AIDS Second Sexual Revolution, she had been something of a prude, channeling a good portion of her libidinal energies into her studies and her single-minded pursuit of a life outside the gravity well.

But now, here she was, after all, a space monkey in Cosmograd Sagdeev, and for the first time in her life, there was no real reason not to loosen up.

However, after she had screwed her way through about twenty of her fellow monkeys, after she had learned how to do it floating free in the center of a module, after she had relaxed to the point where screwing in front of an audience seemed neither perverted nor particularly arousing, after there finally was nothing much new or novel, nothing that she hadn't done already, even space-monkey sex palled as an escape from the boredom of Cosmograd life, and she found herself spending more and more time wrapped in her own thoughts.

She would spend hours just floating freely in the observation deck, staring out the big bubble canopy at the Earth and the stars, her thoughts too drifting along freely in zero gravity.

This experience was, after all, what she had spent her whole previous life pursuing, and now here she was, with all the time she wanted and then some to commune with the stars, with the Earth as seen entire from on high.

She would stare at the Earth; huge, luminous, and with its green forests and savannas, its blue oceans, its ever-changing swirling white cloud patterns, palpably alive, the only living thing in all that cold black immensity. She would watch the lights of its cities sparkling in the darkness behind the terminator as the Cosmograd's orbit swept it around the planet.

And then she would turn her back on the Earth and look out at all those stars and imagine each of them as a potential abode of life, each of them another Sol, another Barnard's star.

She imagined them circled by living planets, each the home of a civilization as rich and complex as the one that lay behind her, and, orbiting on some space station like this around them, beings much like herself, gazing out at a different configuration of these same stars, at the unknown distant Earth, at *her,* and thinking these very thoughts.

That was the dream that had drawn her up out of the gravity well, that was the dream that she and her father shared, that was the vision toward which the best in the species was yearning—to cross that daunting immensity, to meet those fellow beings out there among the stars, to peck through the eggshell of the solar system and be reborn into a grander and wider realm.

But the more she stared out at the distant stars, the more she realized that was a future she really had no hope of living to see. She would never even live to hear the reply to the messages being sent to Barnard's star, if indeed the Barnards ever answered. The distances were so immense, present human technology was so puny in the face of that immensity, that the best she could hope for was to play some small part in these early stages of the great adventure and then be gone.

In her lifetime, humans were never going to walk the surface of another living planet, breathe the exotic intoxicating air of an alien atmosphere, explore an unknown biosphere, meet the citizens of a whole new world. The Moon was dead. Mercury and Venus were infernos. If there was life in the clouds of Jupiter or the superheated ocean of

Uranus, it could never be touched and smelled. At best, she might live to walk the surface of Titan in a bulky suit and see living things through a helmet-glass darkly.

And Mars was a bitter tantalization. Life had started there when the planet was wet and young—proof, like the discovery of the Barnards, that life on Earth was no improbable chain of coincidence—but long gone now, leaving humans alone in this solar system.

No, in her lifetime, it was all going to be like Sagdeev, cramped little contained environments, long hours of boredom, frail bubbles of life floating in a deadly immensity, submarines in a cosmic sea.

When she tried to share these thoughts with her fellow monkeys, what she got were glazed stares, sexual advances, jokes, the offer of a squeeze bottle of rotgut to lighten her mood. It was contrary to space-monkey etiquette, perhaps of necessity, to consider these things, or at least to voice them aloud, and she soon gave up trying.

More and more, she found herself alone with her thoughts, alone with her doubts. All her life had been focused on getting here, but now, she had found, as the old saying had it, that there was no *here* here, only dull labor, boredom, and mindless screwing, nor could she see an end to it in her allotted span.

More and more, she found herself looking down on the Earth and wishing she were there. There was more life and excitement in the Mad Moscow she had hardly known than up here in any of these tin cans. The stars were cold and dead and unreachable, but the Earth hung huge and alive and eternally tantalizing before her.

Behind the terminator, the Earth too was a galaxy of stars shining in the darkness, but each star was a city—Beijing, Tokyo, Jakarta, Rio, hundreds of them, thousands of places she had never seen—teeming with life, bright with possibility, beacons of adventure. Compared to that, what was a lifetime spent confined in these miserable little submarines in space?

Day after day, Franja came to the observation deck to look down on the living Earth, longing for something as deeply, in the end, as ever she had longed to be where she was now.

She had fought her way up out of the gravity well seeking some sort of magical transformation. And now that she had found it, it had turned out to be something quite different from what she had imagined it would be.

Up here on high, she had seen the Earth from a new perspective, and it would never seem the same again. *That* was the transformation. She had sought a new land of wonder and adventure. And there it was, shining in the darkness before her, where it had been all along.

It took a long time for her to admit it, but finally she knew that she wanted to go home, home to a world that the woman she had now become had never seen before. And she started counting the days and the weeks and the months till her release.

CARMELO TO CHALLENGE MICHAELSON

State Assemblyman Albert Carmelo (D-Berkeley) announced today that he would seek the Congressional seat now held by Republican Dwayne Michaelson. "Berkeley has a long Democratic tradition," Carmelo declared, "and without Presidential coattails to help my opponent this time around, I feel confident that I have a good chance of unseating him."

—*Oakland Express*

XVIII

In Robert Reed's junior year at UC Berkeley, Nat Wolfowitz decided to run for Congress. He announced this in the middle of a poker game, right after he had raked in a pot at seven-card stud with nothing better than tens and sixes.

"You're out of your mind, Nat," Bobby told him. "You'd be lucky to carry Telegraph Avenue."

"I bluffed you out of this one on the sixth card with nothing but a lousy pair of sixes showing, didn't I?" Wolfowitz said.

"That's not exactly the same thing!"

"Isn't it?"

"Come on, Nat, you're not really *serious!*" Marla Washington said.

She was the only person in the game who had been living at Little Moscow when Bobby had arrived in Berkeley, and she had never been too terrific at poker. The other two hands, Johnny Nash and Frieda Blackwelder, were relative newcomers whose skill did not at all match their enthusiasm, and while Bobby was still no match for Wolfowitz, and knew he never would be, he had long since learned that by playing defensive poker behind Nat and not getting greedy, he could win modest amounts more or less consistently enough to augment the modest living allowance he was getting from his parents in Paris.

"Depends on what you mean by *serious,*" Wolfowitz said. "It's not as if I expect to *win.*"

"Huh?"

"Of course I don't have a chance of winning," Nat said blithely. "The district takes in a big chunk of Oakland as well as Berkeley, the whole economy is dependent on the Navy Yard, even Berkeley is more Gringo than Red, most people are not gonna like what I'm saying at all, and even if the Democrats and Republicans split right down the middle, I don't have a prayer of sneaking in."

He laughed. "Who the hell wants to live in Washington anyway?"

It was Bobby's deal. "Straight draw," he declared cautiously, not wanting to deal with anything more complicated while Nat was running this little psyche-out. If that was really what it was. Nat had the strangest look on his face, devilish and ironic, yes, but also somehow dreamy and faraway. He couldn't *really* be serious, could he . . . ?

"Come on, Nat, what are you *really* up to?" Bobby said as he dealt the cards.

"Teddy Roosevelt, Jesse Jackson," Wolfowitz said. "Writ small."

"What *are* you babbling about?" Marla said.

"Was Teddy Roosevelt who called the Presidency a bully pulpit," Wolfowitz said. "Jesse Jackson was this radical black preacher back in the 1980s and '90s who kept running for President over and over again even though he knew he had no chance of winning."

Bobby checked his cards. King high, without even a pair or a three-card flush. "Because *running* for President was also a bully pulpit?" he said.

Frieda checked. Johnny bet fifty dollars. Marla raised fifty. Wolfowitz glanced at his cards and folded. Bobby locked eyes with him for a moment and then dropped out too. Frieda called. Johnny called.

Wolfowitz beamed at him. "You're getting it, kid," he said.

Frieda took one card, probably pulling to a straight or a flush. Johnny took three, probably holding a pair. Marla took two, three of a kind, no doubt.

Bobby lost interest in the hand as they bet and raised each other, and so did Nat Wolfowitz. "I've won enough in the big games to finance a couple thousand posters, a few radio spots maybe, and we could start charging a few bucks' admission to the Saturday night parties. Enough to generate a little free press coverage, if I keep saying the same outrageous thing."

"Which is?"

"The United States has to do whatever it takes to get into Common Europe," Wolfowitz said.

Marla looked up from her hand. "That's crazy, Nat!" she said.

"We all know that it's true," Wolfowitz said.

"Yeah, but *we're* a bunch of Reds!"

"Bet, will you, Marla!"

"Yeah, play *poker*?"

"Uh . . . call . . . ," Marla said distractedly, shoving another fifty into the pot.

"What about you, Comrade Eurocrat?" Wolfowitz asked Bobby. "Does it look so crazy from your perspective?"

Bobby, by now, was one of the senior members of Little Moscow, and his European background gave him a certain intellectual cachet. So he felt that he really had to say something intelligent; it was necessary to his mystique.

The so-called Western Hemispheric Common Market gave America an enormous captive market and raw materials at artificially depressed prices. But this kept Latin America impoverished, and with the United States frozen out of Greater Common Europe, Africa a basket case, and the Japanese pretty much in control of Asian markets, Latin America was the only export market America had.

The endless guerrilla wars all over the hemisphere kept the American defense industry humming and unemployment at a politically tolerable level. But, having stiffed Common Europe, the United States had firmly established itself as an international deadbeat, leaving no way to finance deficits overseas.

Domestic spending had to be cut to the bone, but the federal budget still ran a deficit, which meant floating rubbery paper inside the United States, which meant high interest rates, which meant inflation, which meant higher interest rates, which meant more inflation . . .

The only things that kept the economy from collapsing were cheap raw materials from Latin America, cheap food prices generated by unexportable surpluses, and government pressure to keep wage increases below the inflation rate and profit margins above the prevailing interest rates.

So the standard of living kept drifting downward, but not dramatically enough to rock the slowly sinking boat. Especially with Europe and Japan and guerrillas in Latin America to blame for the American people's misfortune and the ever-tightening strictures of the constantly amended National Security Act to silence anyone unpatriotic enough to voice the awful truth.

"Sure, Nat, *we* all know that getting into Common Europe is the only way out," Bobby finally said. "But *how?* They won't even let in our exports. How do you propose to get them to even think about letting us join?"

Marla turned up three eights. Johnny and Frieda groaned as she raked in the pot.

"Pay them back what we owe them," Wolfowitz said.

"You're talking about trillions and trillions of dollars!" Bobby exclaimed.

Wolfowitz took the cards. It was his deal. He cut the deck

and began shuffling the cards with his usual gambler's flourish. "It'd be an offer they couldn't refuse," he said.

"Yeah, sure, but where would we get the ante?" Bobby replied. "And even if we could, how on earth would you sell such a thing to an electorate of Peen-hating jingos?"

Wolfowitz shrugged. "I haven't figured that one out yet," he admitted. "But then, I'm not going to be elected, so I don't have to worry about such petty details, now do I?" he said. "All I want to do is to force people to at least start *talking* about it."

"The bully pulpit? Bully-*shit,* you ask me!"

Wolfowitz shrugged again. "How does that make me any worse than the Democrats and the Republicans?" he said. "Seven-card stud, suckers, the ante in *this* game is only fifty dollars, so pony up, surely you guys can come up with *that much* somehow!"

Wolfowitz kicked off his campaign with a big Saturday night party. Bobby and the other inhabitants of Little Moscow pasted posters up all over Telegraph Avenue and the campus, and Wolfowitz mailed out a press release that got him a short item in the college paper and a brief mention on one FM radio station. "Nathan Wolfowitz for Congress—Now Is the Time for a Futile Gesture," the slogan went.

It was hard for Bobby to take the whole thing seriously, but much to his surprise, the house was jammed to the rafters by nine o'clock Saturday night, with people spilling out onto the front porch, the lawn, even the junk-strewn backyard, despite the chill fog rolling in off the bay. Wolfowitz had decided against charging admission, at least for tonight, in order to maximize the crowd, but he had Bobby and the others going around with bowls and baskets and hats to solicit contributions, and amazingly enough, in small bits and pieces, the money came pouring in.

It was too much of a mob scene for Nat to do anything like make a big speech, but that would have been redundant anyway, Bobby realized after an hour or so of listening to snatches of conversation while he passed the hat.

The Reds of Berkeley, those of them who still dared to show their true colors and risk the wrath of the Gringos who had ruled the streets ever since the night of the infamous Flag Riot, were longing for something like this. It could have been Wolfowitz or it could have been anybody. Now indeed was the time for a futile gesture, as far as the Reds of Berkeley were concerned, and futile or not, Bobby had not seen such political energy and even crazy hope since the annexation of Baja.

Bobby kept having to empty his hat onto the ever-growing pile of small bills and coins on Wolfowitz's bed, and his pockets were stuffed with bits of paper scrawled with the names and telephone numbers of people eager to work in the campaign.

It was exhilarating to be sure, at the very least it made for one hell of a party, and some of the phone numbers in his pockets were those of interesting girls who had already been impressed by his residency at Little Moscow, his European background, and his proximity to Nat.

But he also found it all rather disturbing. All these people, all this money, all that energy, all that hope, and the truth of it was that Nat Wolfowitz didn't have a ghost of a chance of being elected to Congress, or even dogcatcher for that matter, even in Berkeley. That all these people had managed to convince themselves that it *was* possible, that they were willing to invest their time and even their money in the "Futile Gesture," well maybe that wasn't so bad, it gave them hope, direction, something to do that could make them feel they were really accomplishing something.

What really troubled Bobby was that Nat himself didn't even pretend to believe it. He went around talking about getting the United States into Common Europe and the need for an "American Gorbachev," namely himself, and all the while openly calling the whole thing a futile gesture. Yet he did it with the sly grin he always used to convince the marks that the garbage he *seemed* to be holding was going to be the winning hand when he turned up his hole cards.

But Bobby knew damn well that in *this* game, Nat had nothing better than a four-card flush in his hand, and there was something about *that* that made him seem like, well, like something of a four-flusher.

"You're Bobby Reed, aren't you?" a girl said as she dropped a bill in his hat as he was making his way down the hall to the staircase to dump another full load on Wolfowitz's bed.

She was of medium height with short straight mousy brown hair, and she was wearing a bulky blue sweater and a long loose red denim skirt that gave little indication of what might lie beneath. But there was something about her face . . .

"The one and only," Bobby admitted.

"The guy who moved here from France . . ."

"Bien sûr," Bobby drawled.

There was a sparkle of intensity in her green eyes that was almost frightening. She had a cute little snub nose like a cartoon rendering of the all-American college girl, but the line of her mouth seemed about ten years older and harder. For the life of him, Bobby couldn't figure why, but it was turn-on at first sight.

"The world-famous froggy make-out artiste?" she snapped, her face suddenly becoming a mask of anger. "You think you're gonna talk yourself inside *my* pants with your suave European sophistication?"

"What . . . ?" Bobby stammered.

"Nosey josey, don't go getting the wrong idea," she said, as she handed him a crumpled piece of paper. "I want very badly to work in this campaign, but not badly enough to become another notch for you to cut into your dork."

"If I'm such a notorious lady-killer, where do you come off believing I'd be interested in the likes of *you?*" Bobby snapped back.

She suddenly underwent another instant transformation. "Hey, come on, where's your Gallic sophistication?" she said with a sly little smile. "Don't you know when someone's putting you on?"

"Huh?"

"Not that you don't have quite a reputation. You think you can go around screwing half the women in Berkeley without the rest of us knowing your line and the length of your prick down to the millimeter?"

Bobby felt himself blushing scarlet. His head was reeling. Yet somehow he found himself becoming more and more entranced.

"What's your name, anyway?" he demanded.

"Sara Conner."

"Well, look, Sara Conner," Bobby snapped, "if you're really serious about working in this campaign, then you'd better learn some manners, I mean, all we need is someone who thinks it's cute to insult people she's never even met."

Sara Conner's demeanor changed yet again. "Hey, I'm

sorry," she said, with what seemed like genuine sincerity. "Really. I just wanted to see how you'd react. Maybe I got carried away a little, people do tell me I come on a little strong—"

"That I can believe—"

"—but I really *do* want very much to work for the Wolfowitz campaign, so please, please, have a sense of humor, and don't hold it against me."

And she stood there looking all nervous and eager with a pleading expression on her face.

"Maybe we should start this conversation over?" Bobby suggested. "Come on upstairs with me, and—"

"To your bedroom?"

Bobby rolled his eyes upward. "To *Nat's* room!" he groaned. "I've got to empty this hat so I can come back for more!"

Sara laughed, and this time Bobby, beginning to catch on, managed to laugh with her.

Sara's eyes widened when she saw the pile of money on Wolfowitz's bed. "Wow," she said, "this is really serious funding!"

Bobby dumped his hatful of money on the pile. "Not really as much as it looks, just a big pile of small bills," he said, staring at the money, at the concrete evidence of all those vain hopes downstairs. At the moment, it reminded him of nothing so much as another poker pot that Nat was raking in with a hand that no one had been willing to pay to see.

"What's the matter?" Sara said, apparently sensing his mood.

Bobby sighed. He sat down on the edge of the bed. "Nat's a good friend of mine, and I'm certainly not saying that all this is a con, but . . ." He shrugged. "You *really* don't think he has a chance of winning?"

"No. So?"

"*So?*" Bobby exclaimed, waving a hand over the untidy heap of money. "So *this!*"

"You think he's going to *keep* the money?"

"Of course not. He'll spend every dollar of it, and probably all his poker winnings besides, but—"

"But what?"

"But he can't win! He knows he can't win! It's just not right!"

"*I* know he can't win and some of that money is mine,"

Sara said. "*You* know he can't win and yet you've spent all night collecting it."

"And not feeling too terrific about it," Bobby admitted. "I mean, look at it, a huge pile of loose change we've bull-shitted out of hundreds of people. It's not so much the money, it's . . . it's . . . it's the emotional con job, the damn futility of it all. . . ."

"You have a conscience!" Sara exclaimed.

"Is that supposed to be another insult?" Bobby muttered sourly.

"No, no," Sara said quite earnestly, sitting down on the bed beside him as if to prove it. "I understand how you feel, and it's really quite . . . commendable. But you've got it all wrong."

"I do?"

Sara bobbed her head up and down. "All wrong," she said. "Nobody's bullshitting anyone. I know Wolfowitz is not going to win, most of the people who've tossed their money on this pile know he's not going to win, hell, *he* knows he's not going to win, and he admits it openly. It's not winning the election, it's—"

"Oh no, please don't say it's how you play the game!"

Sara did not laugh. "It's *changing* the game!" she declared passionately. "Back in the days of Thomas Jefferson, there was one party called the Democratic Republicans, and now it's all come full circle, there hasn't been a meaningful election in this country since before we were born. The Democrats say 'so's your mother,' and the Republicans say 'you're another,' and they both agree not to bother anyone with the real issues, because they're both really the same, and every two years one team or the other wins the pennant and nothing changes and the country keeps sliding down, and even people who can see what's happening don't do anything, because the way the game's set up, they don't see anything they can possibly do . . ."

Bobby stared into the depths of her fiery green eyes in amazement. She was hunched over, positively vibrating, her hands balled into fists. He was taken aback, entranced.

"Don't you see, Nathan Wolfowitz is out to change all that! He's saying the unsayable. They're gonna call him a Commie and a Peen-lover and a traitor, and he's going to lose. But while they're calling him names, they're gonna be forced to talk about what *he's* talking about to do it. He's going to be *news*, at least in the Bay Area. He's going to lose big, but he's going to lose *loud!* And all the louder because he's shouting into a vacuum."

"So what?" Bobby said. "Berkeley Red Runs for Congress! Man Bites Dog! Pig Farmer Kidnapped by Flying Saucer!"

Sara shook her head. "You know what the significant thing is about a talking dog, Bobby?" she said.

Bobby cocked an inquisitive eyebrow.

"Not how *well* it talks, but that it's *talking* at all!"

Bobby laughed. He found himself leaning closer. Sara didn't even seem to notice.

"Now *is* the time for a futile gesture!" she said. "My great-grandfather was an IRA terrorist. My grandmother was one of the people who managed *not* to get hit when the National Guard started shooting at students at Kent State. My grandfather was a goddamn Weatherman! And even if my father *is* an insurance salesman and my mother a kinder-garten teacher, I've got a long heritage of futile gestures to uphold."

"You're talking about *revolution?*" Bobby exclaimed. "Bombs and assassinations and riots in the street?"

"I'm talking about *doing something!* Anything, win or lose! Acting on what I believe in, instead of just sitting on my ass talking about it! *That's* why I want to work for Wolfowitz. That's why there's all this money lying on this bed. People here want to *do something!* Don't you understand that, Bobby Reed? Don't you feel it? Haven't you ever wanted to do something like that yourself?"

Bobby found himself forced to really think about it, as much by the passion of Sara Conner's convictions as by the logic of her words. He thought about his boyhood dreams of America. About his long campaign to get here. And about how ruthlessly he had fought to stay. He remembered sitting in the living room here the night of the Flag Riot, watching it all on TV. And he remembered remembering in that moment another riot, in Paris, and an American Embassy smeared with blood and shit.

And finally he remembered the words he had said when all eyes were upon him that night, even as Sara Conner's eyes were measuring him now.

I only wish I had been out there with them marching behind that flag. The goddamn jingos may have smeared blood and shit all over our flag, but when those people hung it upside down and marched up Telegraph behind it, they washed it clean, they made it something to be proud of again. They showed the world that there are still some real *Americans.*

And he had stayed. He had stayed in the States to do he knew not what. And he hadn't left since for fear they would never let him back in. He had been a real American himself that night, but what had he done since? What had anyone done but bitch and moan and complain?

Those had indeed been real Americans out there behind that upside-down flag, making their futile but necessary gesture, and he understood that better now than he ever had before. Those were real Americans, and they had made him proud, given him a moment of courage.

And the girl sitting beside him on the bed heaped with money was surely another. And so, somehow, had she.

"Yeah," he said quietly, "I have wanted to. Thanks for reminding me."

Sara Conner smiled at him for the first time, a little soft smile, but in Bobby's eyes it was radiant. "It's Wolfowitz we should both be thanking for giving us the chance to try," she said.

Bobby wanted to gather her up in his arms and have her right there atop Nat's campaign funds. But he knew better than to try. "I guess I'd better get back to passing the hat, then," he said instead.

He picked up his empty hat, stood up, extended a hand. She took it and let him help her to her feet. At least that was something.

"Uh . . . can I . . . ah . . . call you sometime?" he said awkwardly.

Sara Conner eyed him warily. "As soon as you've got some work here for me to do," she said, artfully begging the real question.

"You really *are* a hard case, aren't you?" Bobby said, softening it with a smile.

"Maybe," she said. "But then, these are hard times, aren't they?"

Bobby quite impulsively raised her hand to his lips and

gave it a quick kiss. Sara Conner yanked it back as if it had been scalded.

"What the hell was that?" she demanded angrily.

Bobby stared her down. He shrugged. "What else?" he said with a little laugh. "It just seemed to be the time for a futile gesture."

She stared at him stonily for a long moment, but he could see the crinkles forming at the corners of her mouth, and then she couldn't contain it anymore and favored him with a short reluctant chortle.

And so it began.

Donna Darlington: "Aren't you afraid that all you're going to accomplish with this so-called futile gesture is to insure the reelection of Dwayne Michaelson by pulling votes away from Carmelo?"

Nathan Wolfowitz: "You really think I'm gonna get enough votes to do that?"

Donna Darlington: "Don't *you?*"

Nathan Wolfowitz: "I don't know and I don't care."

Donna Darlington: "Then why *are* you running for Congress? Just to see yourself on television?"

Nathan Wolfowitz: "You got it, Donna! I'm here, ain't I?"

Donna Darlington: "Just a dumb ego trip!"

Nathan Wolfowitz: "Not a *dumb* ego trip. *Dumb* is what my airhead opponents are saying."

Donna Darlington: "And what *you're* saying isn't? That the solution to all our economic problems is to join Common Europe?"

Nathan Wolfowitz: "Anybody got a better idea? Certainly not the pinheads running against me!"

Donna Darlington: "But the Europeans hate us! And we owe them trillions of dollars!"

Nathan Wolfowitz: "So we pay them back."

Donna Darlington: "With what?"

Nathan Wolfowitz: "You expect me to have *all* the answers?"

Donna Darlington: "That's the most irresponsible thing I've ever heard."

Nathan Wolfowitz: "So what? I'm not going to be elected, am I?"

Donna Darlington: "This is all a stupid stunt so you can babble your left-wing Peen-loving garbage on television!"
Nathan Wolfowitz: "Doing pretty well, ain't I?"

—*Bay Area Newsmakers,*
with Donna Darlington

Little Moscow became the headquarters for Nathan Wolfowitz's campaign. There were fund-raising parties every Friday and Saturday night, the living room was filled with desks and telephones, people kept coming and going at all hours, there were ugly jingo demonstrations outside from time to time, the poker games were canceled for the duration, the communally cooked meals were replaced by hastily gobbled junk-food take-out, there was noise at all hours that made sleep problematic, and all in all, life in the house was swiftly transformed into permanent exhausting chaos.

But Bobby didn't mind. The first person he had called when the extra phones were put in was Sara Conner. As he had expected, she proved to be a demon of a telephone campaigner, pulling in the contributions, persuading people to register, hassling hostile voters unmercifully without letting them get a word in edgewise, who knows, even persuading a few fence sitters, if such there were, to vote for Nat, and going at it every single day after classes, from five till midnight.

Which was to say he got to share a quick meal with her during her break every night, got to listen to her talking on the phone, got to bask in her aura, and got not much else, for a solid ten days. He had never met a woman like this. When it came to politics, she was the traditional Berkeley Red and then some, but when it came to the free-and-easy sex which was just as traditional to Berkeley, she acted like some kind of anachronism out of the AIDS era before the Second Sexual Revolution.

When he gallantly offered to let her share his bed so she wouldn't have to drag herself home to the dorms late at night, she gave him looks that would melt glass. But she continued to share her quick meals with him. On day five, when he gave her a good-bye kiss on the cheek on her way out the door, she favored him with a smile. But when he tried to kiss her on the lips the next night, she pulled away.

Bobby couldn't understand it. She was friendly, she was quite willing to talk, she even sought him out for meals, but she continued to play the Ice Princess. Her behavior was quite beyond his experience.

He had certainly encountered his share of girls who were simply not interested. But in every way but one, Sara Conner acted as if she *was* interested. So why in the world was she torturing him like this?

It became something of an obsession. He lost interest in other girls. He was horny all the time. And he found himself trying to impress her in the only way that seemed possible.

He threw himself into the Wolfowitz campaign, at least when Sara Conner was in the house, taking his turn at the phones, beside her when he could manage it, stuffing envelopes, counting receipts, pep-talking the other campaign workers, writing P.R. copy, and in general working his ass off to prove his dedication to the Futile Gesture.

Weirdly enough, he found himself perversely *enjoying* it. Sitting there in the living room beside Sara with an aching hard-on and making phone calls. Rapping enthusiastically with campaign workers while feeling her eyes on the back of his head. Eating pizza and barbecue and hamburgers across the kitchen table from her, discussing politics and fantasizing about her enigmatic body. The sexual tension was enormously frustrating, but there was also something, well, sexy about it, energizing in some crazy way.

And despite his better judgment, he found himself actually becoming dedicated to the Wolfowitz campaign, as if the act he was putting on to impress Sara Conner had turned him into a Method Actor, as if in the process of convincing her, he had convinced himself, as if, somehow, all the political discussions he had with her while possessed of a raging hard-on had transferred all that frustrated sexual energy from his dick to his brain.

No, Wolfowitz was not going to win, the early polls gave him about 10 percent, and it was not going to get much better, but the campaign itself, the hustle and the exhaustion, the frenzy and the superheated atmosphere, even the jingo demonstrations outside the house, and the bomb threats, and the crank phone calls, and the snide media coverage, along with the feeling of taking part in some foredoomed but noble adventure, were like some kind of drug, a permanent adrenaline high.

He had missed being part of the Flag Riot. He hadn't gotten to march behind that upside-down flag. But he was marching behind it now, and if he knew all too well that this too was going to end up being a futile gesture, the spirit of the effort was something he wouldn't have missed for the world.

And Sara Conner's weird behavior had given it to him. Which only made him want her more.

One morning when they happened to be having a cup of coffee alone together out on the front porch, he voiced his frustrations to Nat Wolfowitz.

Nat laughed. "The phenomenon is not unknown in the literature, kid," Nat told him. "The technical term is 'cock-teaser.' "

Bobby grimaced. "Tell me something I don't know, Nat," he said. "Like *why* is she doing this?"

Wolfowitz shrugged. "You won't know that until you see her hole cards, you should pardon the expression," he said.

"And when is that going to happen?"

"At the end of the game, of course. Unless you fold first, in which case, you'll never know. Life is like poker, kid, you gotta pay to see. And that, it would seem, is what she's making you do now."

"Jeez, Nat, what am I supposed to do?"

Wolfowitz laughed. "These are the cards kid," he said. "Play them, or drop out of the hand."

Bobby sighed. "Which should I do?" he asked.

"That depends on what *you're* holding," Wolfowitz said.

"What I'm holding is my *prick*, Nat!" Bobby groaned.

Wolfowitz laughed again. "Seems to me you've already got too much in this pot to drop out now."

"That's the best advice the American Gorbachev has to offer?"

"Well . . . ," Wolfowitz said slowly. "You might try a futile gesture. Think about it, kid."

Bobby thought about it. He thought about it long and hard. Yeah, sure, try a futile gesture! But what the hell was that?

And then, on day ten, during the dinner break, when they were both in the kitchen grabbing slices of pizza, it suddenly came to him, and when it did, he realized it had been obvious all along.

What was the most futile gesture he could possibly make under the circumstances?

Turn up his hole card, of course! Come right out and tell her exactly how he felt. Then, at least, she'd *have* to show him her hand, and one way or another, the game would at least be over. Wolfowitz had been right all along, these after all *were* the cards, and if he wasn't going to fold, he really had no alternative but to call.

"Uh, could we eat out on the porch, Sara?" he said. "There's something I should discuss with you in private."

"Something to do with the campaign?"

"Uh, yeah, sort of," Bobby told her. Though not exactly the one you think, he thought.

They went out onto the rickety front porch and sat down on two old folding chairs. Across the street, a handful of pickets paraded back and forth carrying signs that read "Stick It Up Your Peen," "Fuck Communism," "Traitor Wolfowitz," and "Eat Anti-Protons, Peen-lovers." Two bored-looking cops stood at either end of the police-line sawhorses. The jingo jerks yelled across the street at Bobby and Sara for a minute or two when they first appeared, but then quickly lost interest.

It was not exactly romantic, and yet, in a certain sense . . .

"Well, what is it, Bobby?" Sara said, biting off the tip of her pizza slice.

Bobby took a deep breath, felt a hollow blossoming in his stomach, hesitated. Ah, the hell with it!

"I really want to go to bed with you, Sara," he said. "Surely you've noticed."

Sara, surprisingly enough, didn't react at all. She didn't even look at him. She took another bite of pizza and chewed it down slowly before she even spoke to him.

"I've noticed," she finally said.

"So?" Bobby demanded.

"So what?"

"Jesus Christ!" he groaned. "So yes or no, already!"

Sara finally looked up at him, but her face was quite unreadable. "Why do you want to go to bed with me?" she said.

"Because you turn me on, damn it, why else?"

"What about me turns you on?"

"Come on, Sara, give me a break, you think this is easy?"

A ghost of a smile creased her lips. She slowly licked a glob of pizza sauce off of them with the tip of her tongue. "No," she said. "Why should it be?"

"You're enjoying this, aren't you!" Bobby cried.

Sara laughed knowingly. "Aren't *you?*" she said. "Haven't you been? Don't you have a hard-on right now?"

Bobby flushed. "Sara!"

"Answer my question and then I'll answer yours," Sara said. "What about me turns you on? My tits? My ass?"

"Will you be serious!"

"This is *very* serious to me, Bobby," Sara said earnestly. "I want you to be honest with me. I want you to be honest with yourself. Why do you want to fuck me?"

Bobby sighed. He thought for a long moment about what he was supposed to say next, and then gave up. All right, he decided, give her what she wants, speak straight from the heart.

"The way you dress, I don't even know what your tits and ass look like, so it can't be your fantastic body, I guess," he said. "Maybe it's your eyes, I mean, there's something there that . . ." He threw up his hands in exasperation. "I don't know how to say any of this right," he admitted. "I just feel different around you, you know, I act different, I think different, I'm a different person somehow. . . ."

Sara smiled at him softly. "Do you like it?" she said quietly.

"Of course I like it!" Bobby snapped. "But I can't say I'm too entranced with what's going on now!"

Sara laughed, then grew suddenly serious. "Are you in love with me?" she said.

Bobby sat there transfixed. No one had ever asked him that before. "Are you in love with *me?*" was all he could manage to say.

"I asked first."

Bobby shrugged. He sighed. He looked down at his shoe tops. "I've never been in love with anyone before," he muttered, "so how the hell should I know if that's what I'm feeling?"

"Me too," Sara said, and broke into a smile that was positively radiant.

"So?" Bobby said.

"So I guess after we get off tonight, we'd better find out," she told him. And she leaned over, pressed her lips against his, and opened her mouth. The pickets across the street hooted and jeered. He could taste the pizza on her tongue. But none of that mattered. Somehow, it only served to make the moment sweeter.

Far out in Berkeley, long known for leftist loonies, comic candidate Nathan Wolfowitz is getting laughs with his independent campaign for Congress. Wolfowitz, a UC Berkeley assistant professor of history and notorious card shark, advocates American entry into Common Europe and openly admits that his campaign is primarily financed by poker winnings.

"Why not?" declares the self-styled American Gorbachev. "At least I'm not dealing marked cards from the bottom of the deck, which is more than you can say for what the Democrats and Republicans are doing to the American people!"

—*Time,* "People"

They went up to Bobby's room at 12:30. Bobby had been fantasizing about this moment endlessly, but now that it had finally come, he found his mind quite empty when it came to an opening move. They sat down on the edge of the bed together awkwardly, not touching, not saying anything, just staring at each other for what seemed like an agonizing eternity.

"This is weird . . . ," Bobby finally managed to say.

"Uh-huh. . . ."

"So . . . ?"

"So . . . ?"

And then, somehow, all at once they were in each other's arms and kissing, and once that finally managed to happen, it was another world. They rolled each other around the bed, and groped each other clumsily, and fumbled with their clothing, all the while keeping their mouths tightly locked, tasting each other's tongues, hot, and awkward, and not at all fastidious in the sudden release of all the endlessly prolonged sexual tension between them.

Somehow, they managed to get their clothes off without breaking the long, long kiss, and then, at long, long last,

Bobby lay naked in his bed atop the naked body of Sara
Conner.

He propped himself up on his hands and took a long look
at what was now finally revealed. Her ribs showed a little
beneath small breasts with large, erect pink nipples. Her
pubic hair was black and thin, and there was a small mole
just to the southeast of her belly button.

In truth, it was a rather ordinary female body, and Bobby
had seen much better, but, in that moment, under the circumstances, the sight was nevertheless magic.

He kissed her on the belly, deep inside each thigh, he
sucked on one nipple, then the other, gave her a long kiss
on the mouth, and then slipped his prick easily inside her.

It had been simple and basic up until that moment, but
then it became something quite unlike anything he had experienced before. As he fucked her, Sara stared straight
into his eyes, moaning, and sighing, but hardly blinking, and
finally, when he had built her up to a peak, she took his
head in her hands, and pulled him down into an open-
mouthed kiss, so that when she bucked, and screamed, and
came, she breathed her orgasm, her spirit, her essence, deep
inside him.

And then, a moment later, with her hands kneading his
balls, she broke the kiss, and he found himself looking deep,
deep, deep, into her green eyes as he came, and when he
did, she smiled, and ran her tongue slowly across her lips,
and kissed him ever so gently in the moment afterward.

"So?" she said with a contented sigh.

"So . . . ?" he answered.

"So is this the beginning of a meaningful relationship?"

Bobby rolled off of her and snuggled her into the crook of
his arm. He leaned over and kissed her tenderly on the lips.
"Could be," he said. "Tell you one thing, it certainly wasn't
any futile gesture."

Billy Allen: "And why do you call yourself the American
Gorbachev?"

Nathan Wolfowitz: "Because he's my hero. He took a
country that had had a terminal case of economic and political constipation for seventy years, held his nose, and gave it
the enema it so desperately needed. Sound familiar, Billy?"

Billy Allen: "Please! We're on *national television!*"

Nathan Wolfowitz: "And so are the atrocities we're committing every day in Latin America, Billy—seen any good neuronic disrupter footage lately?"

Billy Allen: "Roll the damn commercial!"

—*Newspeak*, with Billy Allen

Nathan Wolfowitz's Congressional campaign did turn out to be a Futile Gesture, as promised, though the Election Night party at Little Moscow was hardly a wake. For once, the drinks and the food were on Wolfowitz, not the guests—residents and campaign workers only.

Sara Conner was more or less both by that time; she hadn't exactly moved all of her stuff into Bobby's room, but she did stay over every night after the campaign work was over, and she had moved in three or four changes of clothes, as well as her computer.

The phones and the desks had been removed from the living room, and everyone gathered around the videowall to watch the returns. Even though the outcome was never in doubt, Wolfowitz waited till after midnight before making his formal statement.

By then, 98 percent of the precincts were in, and the final numbers would not vary by more than a percentage point or two at most. Michaelson, the Republican, had won with 48 percent of the vote. Carmelo, the Democrat, got 39 percent. Wolfowitz finished way behind with 13 percent.

"Well, at least we prevented the bastard from getting an absolute majority," Sara said to Bobby as they sat there on the couch holding hands and watching the inevitable. "Not too bad for a futile gesture."

"And maybe cost Carmelo the election . . . ," Bobby muttered.

"So what? It's all the same anyway. At least we gave them something to think about."

Nathan Wolfowitz got up from his armchair and turned off the videowall. He stood there for a moment, letting everyone wait to hear his words of wisdom. The room fell silent. Everyone sat there feeling washed out and somber.

"Well, it's all over but the shouting, isn't it?" Wolfowitz finally said. He spread his arms. He threw back his head.

"Aaargh!" he shouted at the top of his lungs. "Okay, kids," he said, "now it's over. Anyone for poker?"

"Jesus, Nat, is that all you've got to say?" someone shouted.

Wolfowitz shrugged. "We anted up, we played the cards, we lost the hand," he said. "What else is there to say?"

"You gonna run again next time, Nat?" someone else shouted.

"For Congress?" Wolfowitz said. "Forget it. The next election is a Presidential year, right? So let me be the first to announce my candidacy for President of the United States."

There was a good round of laughter.

"No, I'm serious," Wolfowitz declared. "Dead serious."

"Sure you are, Nat!"

"Think about it," Wolfowitz said. "We just passed the hat around this time and financed the whole thing out of that and my poker winnings. And we *still* managed a few sound bites on the national news, didn't we? Shit, I even got five minutes on the goddamn Billy Allen show before they pulled the plug! Well, there's the possibility of *federal matching funds* in a Presidential race. Who knows, with a little trick accounting, next time I might even be able to campaign at a *profit*. Running for the Presidential nomination could be a whole new career. Beats trying to teach history to assholes, anyway, don't it?"

"Yeah, *which* nomination, Nat?"

Wolfowitz shrugged. "Does it matter?" He fished a Ronald Reagan ten-dollar piece out of his pocket. "Tails, I'm a Democrat, heads I'm a Republican," he said, flipping the coin high in the air and catching it with a slap of his palms.

"Well, fuck a duck," he said when he looked at it, "I guess I've just become a Republican! Now come on, *this* campaign has just about cleaned me out, so let's play some poker, suckers!"

Bobby didn't join the poker game. Instead, he went out into the backyard with Sara. They stood there holding hands amid the garbage cans and cardboard boxes full of old computer printouts and assorted campaign detritus.

"Well, it's over," Bobby said.

"The campaign, you mean?"

"Yeah. It was something, wasn't it?"

"Uh-huh."

By now Bobby knew her well enough to know that he was

going to have to say it. "But it *is* over," he muttered. "I guess you'll be moving back to the dorms now. . . ."

Sara turned to face him. By now her eyes were quite readable, and what Bobby saw there sent his spirit soaring. "Is that what you want?" she said.

"You know it isn't."

"So?" she said, looking down at her feet and kicking one sneaker with the other.

"So . . ."

"Say it, Bobby. . . ."

Bobby found himself staring at his own feet. "So I love you, Sara Conner," he said, "and I've never said that to anyone before. Stay here with me."

Sara reached out, took his chin in her hand, lifted his head, and kissed him. "I thought you'd never ask," she said dryly.

Bobby laughed. "No you didn't," he said.

Sara laughed back at him. Her eyes seemed to sparkle. "I guess ya got me," she said.

"I guess I do. . . ."

"So?"

"So . . . ," Bobby said, and hugged her to him.

HOW DEAD IS MARS?

While no living organism has yet been found on Mars, the fact is that cosmonauts have only explored the smallest fraction of its surface. The absolute negative is a most difficult case to prove. And if the visionary plans to someday terraform the planet with water ice from the moons of Jupiter should ever come to fruition, the question might prove to be of more than academic interest.

Aside from the ecological morality of destroying the remnants of any Martian life by altering the environment, there is the unsettling question of what might emerge from beneath the permafrost if such life existed and proved capable of adapting to a warmer and wetter environment. Might we unwittingly loose terrible plagues upon our Martian colonists in the very act of preparing the planet for shirtsleeve habitation?

—*Argumenty i Fakty*

XIX

Six months into Franja's tour on Cosmograd Sagdeev, they began the assembly of the *Nikita Khrushchev,* the ship that would carry the next expedition to Mars, and she found herself, like most of the other space monkeys, spending most of her work shifts outside the Cosmograd in a spacesuit working on its construction.

The *Khrushchev* was being cobbled together out of Cosmograd modules. First a framework had to be assembled. Then one of the big spheres was secured to the leading end to serve as the command center. Four dormitory modules were then slung behind it to luxuriously house the crew of eight for the long two-and-a-half-year mission—only two to a module!—and connected to the command module and each other by standard passageway modules. Another sphere behind the dormitory cluster became the crew lounge and gymnasium. Behind that came two more dormitory modules which would be outfitted as scientific workstations. Behind the science modules, a cluster of four of the big spheres to hold oxygen, water, food, supplies, and the life-support machinery.

Fourteen more spheres were slung behind *that.* Four of them would be filled with liquid hydrogen and liquid oxygen for the conventional thrusters and maneuvering rockets. The other ten would hold the reaction mass for the ion drive. A hundred and fifty meters down the central spar a nuclear reactor was secured, and finally, behind that, the rockets and the ion drive.

Connecting up all these modules and spars and main components was straightforward if tedious and strenuous labor, but once the basic ship was assembled, the nightmare for the space monkeys really began.

There were kilometers and kilometers of wiring, fuel lines, oxidizer lines, and air lines that had to be strung, connected, tested, and retested, around this maze of modules, passageways, and spars in order to turn the assemblage into a working Mars ship; all of it had to work perfectly, and most of the work had to be done in spacesuits, with the supervisors constantly yammering in one's earphones.

Important work it might be, but fun it was not, and Franja, like the rest of her long-suffering fellow monkeys, soon came to loathe the *Khrushchev*, and refer to it as The Bastard, which, in terms of *their* humble part in the grand adventure, it most certainly was.

Franja still spent hours and hours staring longingly out the observation deck bubble canopy at the Earth, but now the view was occluded by the ungainly sight of The Bastard, tethered to Sagdeev in a matching orbit a quarter of a kilometer "below," as were her thoughts.

On the one hand, she was even more fed up with the confinement and tedium and boredom of the Cosmograd and counting the days till the end of her tour and escape. But on the other hand, there it was, The Bastard, blocking her clear view of the promise of the living planet below, and at the same time, tantalizing her with the vision of what might have been.

Unlikely as it might seem, that ungainly mess was going to *Mars,* and if things had turned out differently, she might be one of the lucky few to make the voyage on it, to stand on the soil of another planet beneath alien skies, to see the towering immensity of Mons Olympus, to look down into the huge dry canyons where once water had flowed, who knows, to even be the one to discover the living remnants of the extinct Martian biosphere which some scientists still believed might yet be found in some isolated pocket ecosphere.

For *that,* she might still be willing to endure a year on the way to Mars in an environment even more cramped than Sagdeev, and another year on the way back, and six months in yet another series of tin cans on the Martian surface. Instead, she was condemned to another six months in this miserable Cosmograd, suffering much the same boredom and working her ass off besides, with no grand adventure to show for it at the other end.

She found herself wishing that The Bastard would just go away, disappear, leave for Mars and be done with it already, and stop tormenting her with a dream that had already died.

But of course it didn't. The Mars Excursion Vehicle was boosted up in pieces by heavy lifters, and the monkeys had to assemble the damn thing in orbit, then horse it into place and secure it below the main assemblage of The Bastard.

The cabin had to be mounted to the internal framework, and then the engines and control systems and freight module. Then the balloon with its hydrogen tank and the main fuel and oxidizer tanks. Finally, and worst of all, the metal skin had to be glued to the framework, panel by tedious panel.

The MEV would enter the Martian atmosphere as a hypersonic glider, using atmospheric braking to slow it down enough for the huge balloon wing to be deployed that would soft land it by the station on the surface. Six months later, the balloon would lift it into the upper atmosphere just as smoothly, the engines would fire, and the MEV would rendezvous with the *Khrushchev*.

Oh yes, the MEV was an elegant triumph of Soviet technology, and Franja could not help feeling a surge of pride as she floated in the observation deck watching a team of monkeys mounting the finished product below The Bastard. The endless hours of her own tedious labor that had gone into it were, however, another matter. All that tedium, all that sweat, all that fatigue, and for what? So eight other people with better connections could get to ride it.

Is this what it really feels like to be a Hero of Socialist Labor? she thought sourly.

Five days after the MEV was mated to The Bastard, a real celebrity came up to Sagdeev on a Concordski—Colonel Cosmonaut Nikolai Mikhailovich Smirnov. Smirnov had already been to Mars. Smirnov was a Hero of the Soviet Union. Smirnov was the future commander of the *Nikita Khrushchev*, and he was going to stay on Sagdeev for the next month, overseeing the final outfitting of The Bastard before his crew came aboard and the Mars ship departed.

Nikolai Mikhailovich Smirnov was also, well, a stunning figure of a man. Sagdeev was, after all, the smallest of small towns, and Franja, like every other woman aboard, had plenty of occasion in the next few days to look him over. Tall, slim, elegantly muscular, angularly featured, with piercing blue eyes, Nikolai Mikhailovich looked every inch the cossack Prince, an impression he did nothing to dispel with his tightly tailored uniforms, his lustrous black shoulder-length hair, and his outrageously dramatic handlebar mustache.

"Comrade Cosmonaut Movie Star," the female space monkeys called him. "The Count" was the least disparaging thing the envious male space monkeys called him, the rest being obscene speculations on his manhood or the lack thereof, and indeed Franja herself began to wonder, for even after a week, not one woman aboard had yet bragged about getting between the nets with him, and, monkey-cage sex being what it was, one could be sure that where there was no smoke there had certainly been no fire.

Franja herself, not being made out of stone, certainly would not have turned down the opportunity if it offered itself, but she was not about to engage in the demeaning simian antics of her fellow monkeys to tempt "Comrade Cosmonaut Movie Star" to prove his questionable manhood, which obvious tactics had, at any rate, proven entirely futile. As a visiting cosmonaut, Nikolai Mikhailovich had a whole dormitory module entirely to himself, and when he wasn't eating, or suited up and hovering around the final work on The Bastard, or working out in the gym before a slavering audience, he selfishly kept it all to himself.

It was quite a surprise, therefore, when the Object of All Desire started a conversation with *her*.

When the magic moment happened, she was holding onto a ring and floating in the observation deck, as she so often did, staring out at the Earth past the untidy bulk of the Mars ship, watching the white swirl of the cloud deck, the lights of the cities in the darkness behind the terminator, just letting her thoughts drift aimlessly as the Sagdeev orbited round and round the planet, lost in the procession of brilliant blue seas, sere dun desert, verdant rain forest, defiantly artificial night lights, the whole living world enormous and complex rolling tantalizingly beneath her in the cold hard blackness while—

"Yes, it is quite beautiful," a deep mellow male voice said behind her.

Franja started, turned awkwardly, still holding onto the

ring, her body flipped sidewise at an oblique angle by the quick motion of her head and shoulders, and there he was, above her and looking down, floating freely behind her, standing in midair with his arms folded across his chest and those piercing blue eyes looking right at her and a strangely wistful smile creasing his wide full lips.

"How long have you been there watching me?" she demanded, quite flustered.

"Oh, quite a while," said Nikolai Mikhailovich Smirnov.

"Do you usually spy on people like that? Is that what you do for amusement?"

He frowned. "I'm sorry," he said. "I just saw you there, contemplating as it were, and it didn't seem right to disturb you, and then . . ."

He shrugged, and the motion sent him drifting up toward the top of the bubble. He turned a midair somersault, kicked his legs, swam downward, grabbed a ring, and righted himself beside her, a display of space-monkey aerobatics quite dazzling in its lithe and casual ease.

"And then I realized that, after all, I *had* been watching you, and it seemed rather nikulturni not to make my presence known, so I felt I had to say something," he said. "But it *is* beautiful, and believe me, I *do* understand how precious a little solitude can be up here, so if you wish, I will now make my apologies and leave you to it. . . ."

"No, please don't go," Franja found herself saying, quite charmed by his careful and thoughtful manners, so different from the space-monkey etiquette she had become all too used to, and different too from what she would have expected from a high and mighty Colonel Cosmonaut.

"You're sure?" he said. "You're not just saying it to be polite?"

Good Lord, Franja thought, could that be it? Has Comrade Cosmonaut Movie Star failed to avail himself of what he's been constantly offered simply because this beautiful creature is actually an old-fashioned *gentleman?* So it would seem, for up this close, some instinct told her in no uncertain terms that this man did not have a gay bone in his body!

Franja smiled at him. "Where *did* you learn such old-fashioned manners, Colonel Smirnov?" she said. "In Cosmonaut school?"

Nikolai laughed, sending a thrill through her. "Not quite . . . what did you say your name was?"

"I didn't. It's Franja Gagarin Reed, Colonel Smirnov," Franja fairly gushed.

"Please call me Nikolai," he said. "We don't address each other by rank where I learned my manners. Not out there, we don't. . . ." And for a moment he seemed to be looking past her, not at the Earth, or at his ship, but to the side, straight out into the starry blackness.

"Out there?"

"Mars," he said, "or rather perhaps on the voyage there and back. . . ." He seemed to return from some vast distance. "A year there, six months on the surface, a year back with the same few people . . . It's a trip that changes anyone who makes it, Franja. At the very least, we Martians learn to be very, very polite to each other. Manners, as you call it, become an absolute necessity. Sometimes it gets . . . it gets . . ." He frowned, he shrugged, he seemed quite at a loss for words.

"And *sex?*" Franja could not keep from saying. "I mean, two and a half years . . . I've always wondered . . ."

"Not like here," Nikolai said quite somberly. "It simply can't be tolerated, a few people in such close quarters. To tell you the truth, it's something we haven't figured out yet, if we ever will. Mixed crews of single people have not worked well. Four couples would be best, but the chances of assembling such a crew are minimal, and if some people are having sex and others aren't, well . . . So now we're back to trying an all-male crew, and it has nothing to do with outmoded Slavic phallocracy."

"But what do you *do* for two and a half years?"

"We suffer, we masturbate," Nikolai said evenly.

"For two and a half years?"

"For centuries sailors and explorers were forced to do just that. . . ."

"But sailors . . . well, you know . . ."

Nikolai grimaced. "If anyone tried *that,* we'd shove him out an air lock!" he declared.

"It all sounds quite horrible."

"It isn't," he said, "or perhaps it is, but it's the price we have to pay for something wonderful."

"Something wonderful . . . ?"

Nikolai Mikhailovich Smirnov grabbed hold of a second hand-ring and seemed to chin himself up on the two of them, looking straight out into the infinite depths like a boy into a sweet-shop window. He didn't even seem to notice as Franja swiveled around to float close beside him, close enough to smell his lilac cologne, close enough to feel the heat of his body, or so to her it seemed.

"The voyage itself is mostly privation and boredom," he said. "And there is a slow subtle kind of terror too, when the Earth no longer shows a disc, and you're out there in a hard cold nothingness that goes on and on and on quite literally forever. And then that passes, and you feel something impossible to describe, a hideous kind of ecstasy perhaps, what the Buddhists and the Hindus must feel when they confront the reality of the Great Void, you are all alone, tiny beyond insignificance, and yet . . . and yet . . ."

A shudder went through his body. Franja found herself inching closer.

"And yet you are somehow also a part of something vast and eternal . . . ," Nikolai went on in a dreamy voice. "And then Mars begins to grow, and grow, and you feel an enormous sense of relief, somehow, just to see another planet, any planet, though somehow there is a sense of loss too, and then before you know it, there is the excitement of making orbit, and the crazy flight through the atmosphere, and then you are floating down toward another world. . . ."

Hesitantly, Franja put an arm around his shoulder, not daring to actually touch him, just letting it float there behind him, unseen, unfelt, apparently unnoticed.

"Another world!" Nikolai exclaimed. "True, you can never breathe the open air, but in the Martian summer, at noon, in light atmosphere suits, there are times when you can feel the distant warmth of the sun, and the wind, and you stand out there on alien soil, looking down, perhaps, into some great dry river valley where water once flowed, where life once began, and you realize in the pit of your stomach, in your lungs, and your heart, and your balls, that you *really are* standing on another world entire. And on the long voyage home, you look out at all those stars, and you think that somewhere out there there are people, yes, call them that, *people,* looking back at you, and someday, somehow . . ."

He stopped. He turned. He gave her a foolish, boyish grin that went straight to her heart. "Well, you shouldn't get me started like this," he said with endearing embarrassment. "That's a Martian for you, we can't help getting all mystical over it; despite the realities of Dialectical Materialism, I suppose we're all still romantic old Slavs at heart. . . ."

Franja could not help herself. She threw her arms about his neck, and, hanging there, kissed him.

"What . . . what was that for?" Nikolai Mikhailovich stammered.

Franja looked downward, rather mortified herself. "I . . . I . . . I've never met a real hero before," she said.

"Oh come now, don't be ridiculous!"

Franja looked up into his wide blue eyes. And what she saw there was a man who had gazed upon vistas that would have withered her spirit—or transformed it into she knew not what. What she saw was a man who had endured unspeakable loneliness and isolation and sexual frustration in the service of something vast and oceanic and beyond her understanding, and who would soon bravely commit himself to the same adventure again. What she also saw was a little boy who was quite touchingly embarrassed to see a woman mooning over him like this.

"No, it's true, Nikolai Mikhailovich," she said. "And if you don't see it, why that makes it all the more real. You're a real hero, in the best and finest sense."

"What rubbish!" he said, averting his gaze.

"Not at all," Franja insisted.

"I'm no hero. Just an ordinary man who's been quite fortunate to have been granted an extraordinary experience. . . ."

"Is that so?" Franja said, screwing up her courage. "Well, since you so strenuously deny being a hero, perhaps the hero's code will not prevent you from accepting my modest gift. . . ."

"Gift? What gift?"

"Something to think about all the way to Mars and all the way back," she told him. "If you are going to spend two and a half years masturbating, let me give you a memory worth masturbating over."

Colonel Cosmonaut Nikolai Mikhailovich Smirnov blushed quite scarlet.

Franja laughed. "Surely a Hero of the Soviet Union who has braved the cosmic vastness does not lack the manly courage to do what gallantry demands under the circumstances?"

"I really shouldn't . . ."

"Oh yes you should!" Franja insisted. "The honor of the Cosmonaut Corps demands no less!"

"Well, if you insist on putting it that way . . ."

Nikolai was quite nervous as Franja dragged him through the maze of passageways toward the big air lock feeling, no doubt, that all eyes were upon them, which, no doubt, they were. He was properly scandalized when she proposed that they commandeer the Octopus for their own amorous purposes, but in the end, she had her way, for when it came down to such matters, the Colonel Cosmonaut was really quite the little boy.

As Sasha Gorokov had done so many months of tedium ago, Franja maneuvered the Octopus so that the canopy looked out upon the unsullied starry blackness.

Once this was accomplished, she found herself floating in the pod with a rather flustered-looking cosmonaut hero who did not at all seem prepared to make the first move. Well, modesty and shyness certainly hadn't gotten her this far!

She undid the clasps of her jumpsuit, wriggled out of it, and, kicking off a hand-ring, propelled herself toward the top of the bubble canopy, where she spread-eagled herself against the heated glass, presenting what she hoped was an irresistible image of naked flesh haloed in glory by the glittering star field.

To judge by the way Nikolai floated there beneath her, gazing upward with his mouth hanging open, she had achieved the desired effect, but he made no move to either take off his uniform or join her.

"Well?" she demanded.

"Well!" he sighed uncertainly.

"Well, take off your clothes and come on up here, or *down* here, if you prefer to see it that way. . . ."

Without taking his eyes off her, Nikolai managed to peel off his clothing, rather awkwardly for someone who had demonstrated such casual skill at zero-gravity aerobatics. His nervousness, however, she was relieved to see, had not prevented him from achieving quite a firm erection.

He kicked off the edge of a console and floated up toward her. She reached out, caught his hands, and pulled him down on top of her.

Once this docking maneuver was successfully completed, he became quite another man, kissing her roughly, kneading her breasts, and thrusting himself into her almost immediately, as if all those months of sexual frustration and careful politeness in space had served to make him quite lose control at the first touch of feminine flesh.

As indeed it would seem that it had, for after no more than a dozen long hard strokes, he groaned, and spasmed, and spent himself within her.

Immediately afterward, he withdrew, and rolled away from her, and half curled himself up into a ball, and floated there, staring out into space unable to meet her gaze, with the most miserable expression on his face.

"I—"

She stopped him with a gentle finger to his lips. "Don't say anything," she told him. "I understand. . . . You poor man. . . ."

Though in truth, when he did turn to face her, she found herself staring into the eyes, not of a heroic Colonel Cosmonaut, but of an acutely embarrassed little boy. Nothing could have moved her heart more.

"We have plenty of time, Nikolai," she said softly. She reached out and embraced him and gave him a long lingering kiss.

Then, remembering what Sasha had said and done, she rolled him back against the canopy, grabbed him by the knees, pried his legs open, smiled up at him, and said: "Let me show you a whole new meaning for the phrase 'going down.'"

And she did. She floated beneath him, and took his limp flesh in her mouth, and perspective reversed, and there she was, floating *above* him light as air, while he lay back against the bubble, rising up out of the cosmic vastness itself like a god of space, his long black hair seeming to roll and break like the waves of the starry sea, a dark corona haloing his perfect hero's face.

Soon enough, indeed perhaps sooner than she might have wished, his manhood rose too between her lips, and he reached down, snaked his hands in her hair, and pulled, dreamy-eyed and smiling, pulled her face up into a truly tender kiss.

Then he kicked himself clear of the canopy as he gathered her up in his arms, and entered her again, surely and gently this time, and, hugging himself tightly to her, he made love to her, truly made love to her, floating freely in the air, softly and gently, keeping them clear of the canopy, and the consoles, and the floor with deft little kicks whenever they drifted close.

It was quite an incredible experience, perhaps the most incredible experience of Franja's life. At this zero-gravity maneuvering, Nikolai was quite the master, and with nothing beneath either of them to react against but each other, their motions were slow, and lingering, and tender of necessity, their rhythms quickly melding into the most intimate synchrony, and staying there for a long, long time.

Franja's pleasure built slowly and reached a plateau that seemed to go on forever in space and time, flying there weightless as a cloud in the infinite and endless stellar vastness in Nikolai's arms, melded together, dancing in the air, in the vacuum, in the ecstasy, and when she finally crested into orgasm, it seemed quite literally shattering, stars flashing within and without, as she soared up over the top to dissolve into the universal sea.

They floated in each other's arms silently for quite a while afterward, catching their breath, quotidian and cosmic, before Franja came back close enough to the here and now to speak.

"Where did you learn to do *that?*" she whispered.

Nikolai turned in her arms to face her, positively glowing, with the most affectingly boyish grin on his lips, his blue eyes looking down, then up into hers. If there had been a floor beneath them to do it against, no doubt he would have shuffled his feet.

"Right now," he said. "Right here, with you."

And he took her hand, and together they floated there naked, two tiny frail creatures of flesh and blood, looking out into the cold and glorious vastness of the infinite cosmos.

CARSON INTRODUCES BILL TIGHTENING EXIT VISA RESTRICTIONS

Senator Harry Carson (R-Texas) has introduced legislation that would allow the Central Security Agency to refuse exit visas on the broader grounds of "national interest" rather than requiring the CSA to show "national security" grounds for such restrictions as the National Security Act now calls for.

"Sure, changing one word seems like bureaucratic nit-picking," Carson admitted, "but the way the law reads now, unpatriotic polecats are getting the benefit of the doubt. We need to untie the hands of the CSA by giving them much broader discretionary power. Sometimes one little word can make a lot of difference."

—AP

"Are you really serious about this relationship, Bobby?" Sara Conner said in bed one night toward the end of the spring term.

"Of course I'm serious," Bobby declared without thinking.

"Well, if we're going to stay together, we should have our own apartment," Sara said with her familiar firmness. "I'm getting pretty fed up with living like this. Aren't you?"

Bobby thought about it. They had been living in his room at Little Moscow for over five months now, and he had to admit that it was pretty damned cramped, crammed as it was with books, papers, chips, discs, files, underwear, cosmetics, socks, and endless assorted junk, and there was always crap to be cleared off the bed every night and no place left to dump it but the floor.

True, they didn't do anything in the room but sleep, study, and make love, and true too that it was rather amazing that they didn't get on each other's nerves more than they did, especially with Sara being Sara, but he had to admit that the room was something of a pigpen, nor did he much like having to clear the bed of debris every time they wanted to fuck.

But an *apartment?* That was really a serious step. And besides . . .

"But how can we afford it?"

"I've already found a place we can afford," Sara told him. "It's not much, a pretty tiny one-bedroom, but we can swing it."

"You have? We can?"

That Sara, having already decided what she wanted, had gone out and found an apartment already was by now not so

surprising. Bobby had long since learned that she was like
that, and indeed, he suspected, she had really gone out and
gotten *him* when she wanted him in much the same self-
contained and even Machiavellian fashion.

"We're only going to be living in it over the summer and
for another two terms till we graduate," she told him. "With
what you're paying here, plus the living allowance my parents send me, plus what I've already saved up by moving out
of the dorms, we can handle it with what we can both make
working over the summer."

"You've got it all worked out, haven't you?" Bobby said, a
bit perturbed, but not without admiration.

"Yup."

"I had hoped we could go to Paris this summer to meet
my parents . . . ," Bobby muttered rather disconsolately.

"Oh, *Bobby,* we've gone over that a thousand times, don't
you even read the papers?" Sara moaned.

Bobby sighed. That was another thing about Sara that he
had learned to accept and even admire. Not only had her
family been political for generations, she was a journalism
major with a firm career goal in mind, to become a political
reporter, on a newspaper if she could, on TV if she had to.
More to the current point, for Sara the personal and the
political were inseparable.

Even when it came to *his* own name.

"Bob is such a *jingo* name," she told him. "It makes me
think of birdbrained jocks in gym shorts, swilling beer from
cans. But when I call you *Bobby,* it makes me think of Bobby
Kennedy, the last politician this country produced that was
worth a damn. Living with a man I can call *Bobby* makes me
feel, I don't know, like something's still alive. And Bobby
Reed, well . . ."

She wanted to know if he was any relation of *John* Reed.
Bobby hadn't even known who John Reed was, much to
Sara's exasperation.

"You and he have a lot in common," she told him. "John
Reed was an American journalist who went to Russia to
cover the Revolution and stayed there out of conviction.
And you *chose* to be an American the way he chose to become a Soviet. For God's sake, Bobby, you should at least
see *Reds!*"

She dug out a tape of the old movie, and while Bobby
found the sad story of political idealism betrayed depress-

ing, the love story was something else again, something that became a secret bond between them, and after that, he found that he didn't mind being called Bobby anymore.

That was Sara. She could take his common old American name, run it through her political sensibilities, and hand it back to him as a special gift with whole new meanings.

But those same political sensibilities had quite convinced her that Paris was out of the question.

Under the current political conditions, the provisions of the National Security Act, her family background, and the dossier she was certain existed in some Central Security Agency computer in Washington, Sara was sure there was no way she could be granted an exit visa to visit Common Europe.

And she was equally convinced that if Bobby ever left the United States, given his father's history, his mother's nationality and employment, his own ambiguous nationality status, and the dossier she was sure the CSA had on *him,* there was no way he would ever get back in.

Which was to say there was really *no* way he could leave the country and count on getting back in to be with Sara.

And that was something he was not about to risk, despite all Dad's pleading on the phone.

So . . .

So Bobby went with Sara to look at the apartment she had found in a crumbling old building on a back street off of Shattuck. It was tiny, barely thirty square meters, and the toilet didn't flush quite right, and the Pullman kitchen equipment was ancient, and he did spot a roach or two, but compared to the room at Little Moscow it was enormous, and there *was* a door they could shut between the small living room and the even smaller bedroom, plus two closets, and Sara *had* worked out the numbers, so in the end, they took it.

Bobby managed to get a summer job through the University translating dull French history papers for academic journals, and Sara held her nose and took a job as a waitress. The money wasn't much, but by the end of the summer, they had enough saved up to pay the rent through the end of their senior year. After that . . .

Well, Sara had her own firm ideas about that too, and, as was her way, had waged a campaign to convince him, and by

the time the fall term had arrived, had pretty much succeeded.

"Sure, Berkeley is wonderful," she told him, "but we can't
live like this forever. You don't want to end up like all those
people who go straight from graduation into grad school
and from grad school into a teaching job at the University
and end up never leaving, thinking that the rest of the world
is just something out there somewhere south of Oakland
that they don't have to pay any attention to. . . ."

"I don't?" Bobby said. For the truth of it was that before
he had met Sara Conner, that had indeed been pretty much
his life plan.

"No, you don't," Sara kept insisting. "Certainly *I* have no
intention of ending up a campus wife in Berkeley! I want to
be out there in the *real world* doing something that matters,
with you or without you; I can't live my life like an ostrich
with its head in the sand!"

It was quite a bit for Bobby to handle. The oblique refer-
ence to marriage was the least of it, somehow; their lives
and their finances were currently so intertwined that in a
sense he felt married to Sara now, and one more document
in a life that had so long been papered with passport and
visa and nationality red tape did not seem all that significant. Indeed, the thought of living without Sara seemed like
divorce already.

And *that* was what got to him. He loved her, and the
thought of losing her was intolerable. He was convinced that
she loved him too, but he was equally convinced that he
would have to fit his career choice into the life she wanted
to lead if he was to retain her love past college.

And what Sara wanted was to be out there in what she
called the "real world," *doing something*, which, Sara being
Sara, meant doing something to change the world, or at
least something that could give her that illusion; being a
political reporter somewhere, not languishing in the protected groves of academe with a professor of history at UC
Berkeley.

Far from resenting this, it made Bobby love her all the
more. Indeed, he even found himself envying such an idealistic passion, for he knew damn well that he had nothing like
it himself.

But Sara being Sara, she also understood all this, and
instead of threatening or browbeating him, launched a cam-

paign to fire him with her own ardor, to convince him intellectually, to present a vision that they could truly share.

"You could do so much, Bobby," she insisted. "You have perfect French and more Russian than you're willing to admit. You've got a decent background in history, and you've lived in Europe, and you can write better prose than I do. You'd be a terrific reporter, a foreign correspondent even, if some paper wanted you badly enough to hassle the visas. . . ."

Bobby, in the end, wasn't all that hard to convince. All the translating he had done over the summer had shown him that he could write facilely enough in English. There weren't many American reporters fluent in French and possessed of passable Russian, and fewer still who had grown up on the other side of the Great Atlantic Divide. He could make good money as a journalist, better than anything he could hope for as one of a horde of teaching assistants struggling up the academic ladder. . . .

"You owe it to yourself and your country, Bobby!" Sara also insisted. "The media's so hopelessly jingo, and you've got a really unique viewpoint to contribute. It would be just awful if you wasted all that vegetating in an academic hothouse like Berkeley, when you've got what it takes to *do something,* to be someone who really matters!"

Bobby would have liked to believe that *that* was what convinced him to change his major to journalism at the beginning of his senior year. But Sara had taught him how inseparable the political and the personal could really be.

He was choosing a higher-paying career that would take fuller advantage of his experience and skills, he was choosing a career that might indeed allow him to better the world, to be someone who mattered.

But above all, he was also choosing to make a life together with the woman he loved, the woman who had pushed him into this more adventurous and idealistic career in the first place, and that was surely a textbook example of *enlightened* self-interest.

ANOTHER EXTRATERRESTRIAL CIVILIZATION?

Soviet astronomers say they may have discovered another extraterrestrial civilization, this one much more advanced than that of the fourth planet of Barnard's star. Lunar-based astronomers have detected an object about five thousand light-years away toward the galactic center that could be a so-called Dyson sphere, a star entirely enclosed by an artificial shell in order to capture its total output of energy.

Gravity-wave perturbations indicate an object of about half a solar mass, stellar occlusions suggest a solid body with a diameter approximately that of the orbit of Jupiter, and infrared studies indicate a surface temperature in the liquid water range.

"If this is not a Dyson sphere," a spokesperson for the Soviet Academy of Sciences said, "it must be something even stranger. Unfortunately, there is no way of obtaining any kind of visual image at this range."

Sending a radio message would not be a practical means of resolving the mystery either, since a round-trip communication would take a minimum of ten thousand years.

—*Science News*

Franja's affair with Colonel Cosmonaut Nikolai Mikhailovich Smirnov was the talk of Cosmograd Sagdeev and something of a scandal as well. Needless to say, she was the envy of every woman in the monkey cages, but, space-monkey etiquette being what it was, that would have resulted in nothing worse than obscene good-natured banter if she had played it by the unstated rules.

But she didn't. While she didn't move her clothing or personal effects into Nikolai's module, since moving out of one's assigned quarters was a clear violation of the official regulations, she did spend all her sleep periods alone between the nets with him, and that was a violation of the unwritten space-monkey code.

Not that sex between monkeys and supervisors or even command personnel was frowned upon; those privileged to bunk two to a module or to have a module all their own were human too, and hence fair game. However, using such liaisons to enjoy entire sleep periods in such luxurious quarters smacked of using sex as a commodity of exchange; class treason, whoredom, and that was considered nikulturni indeed.

Worse still, far worse, Franja and Nikolai were conducting a private and monogamous affair. Neither of them would fuck anyone else. They wouldn't even fuck *each other* before an audience. In short, they had established a *relationship,* and that was the worst transgression of space-monkey etiquette conceivable. Relationships meant passion, jealousy, envy, and who knew what other powerful emotions that could cause only trouble in such close confined quarters.

Indeed, it skirted perilously close to violating actual regulations, and only Nikolai's lofty status as a Colonel Cosmonaut, Mars expedition commander, and Hero of the Soviet Union kept official displeasure at bay.

Franja could not help knowing all this on a certain level, but frankly, Comrades, as the old American saying had it, she didn't give a damn. She had enough trouble keeping herself from falling in love.

She had never met a man like Nikolai. She had never met anyone who had come even close. That he was a gorgeous physical specimen and that his prowess at zero-gravity aerobatics made him a fantastic lover was the least of it, which was not to say it wasn't plenty.

That he had been to Mars, that he was a Colonel Cosmonaut, might be part of it, not because of his exalted status, and probably not even because he really was what she had once dreamed of becoming, but because of what his experiences had made him.

In a curious way, Nikolai reminded her of her father, of a younger, stronger, somehow more innocent Jerry Reed, who had had all the right connections, who had gotten all the right breaks, who had gotten to live his dream in the real world, and who therefore had never lost the sweetness and purity of the boy he had once been, building his own telescope, devouring science fiction, gazing up at the stars, and voyaging across the blackness in his mind's eye.

Nikolai was a boyish idealist whose innocence had never been crushed. Nikolai was a mature man with a mystical vision. Nikolai was a man of courage and dedication, willingly undergoing incredible privation and sexual frustration in the service of what he believed, which made fucking him as often and as long and as well as possible an honor as well as a pleasure.

"Hero of the Soviet Union" was an honorific that most people sneered at these days, and Franja herself had always pictured such a personage as a stiff figure in a uniform bedecked with silly medals. But Nikolai Mikhailovich Smirnov gave "Hero of the Soviet Union" new meaning for her.

Nikolai was the real thing.

That actually might have been intolerable if Nikolai hadn't also been, well, *Nikolai*. His sweet manners were real. He was a considerate lover. He was not without humor. When they weren't working or making love or working out in the gym—Nikolai was a stickler for that—they spent hours and hours gazing out at the stars together, talking of Mars and the chances of finding living remnants of the vanished Martian ecosphere, of what might lie beneath the clouds of Titan, the atmosphere of Jupiter, the Uranian ocean, of the mysterious Barnards, of the destiny of consciousness in the universe, of where it all might have come from, and what it was evolving toward.

Nikolai rekindled in her dreams which had been deadened by the boring months aboard Sagdeev. Nikolai gave her the spiritual courage to long once more after things she might never have. Nikolai showed her the secrets of her soul.

How difficult it was not to fall hopelessly in love with this man!

But what a disaster it would be if she allowed it!

Within a month, Nikolai would be on his way to Mars, and he would not return for two and a half years. Any thought of a life together beyond his departure was quite hopeless. Unless . . .

Unless . . .

It was foolish, it was foredoomed and she knew it, but somehow she knew she had to try anyway, and ten days before the *Nikita Khrushchev*'s departure date, as they snuggled together in the nets, she did.

"Nikolai," she said, "I want to go to Mars with you."

Nikolai laughed. "And I want you to come to Mars with me too," he said lightly. "I would also like to live to be two hundred and command the first expedition to Barnard's star. . . ."

"I'm serious!"

"So am I!"

"Nikolai!"

"Franja, please!"

"You're well connected," Franja purred. "You're the expedition commander. And didn't you tell me your sister was married to Marshal Donets?"

"Ah, I see, it's all quite simple," Nikolai said dryly. "All I have to do is tell my brother-in-law the Marshal that I wish to bump a crew-member who has been preparing for the expedition for years in favor of taking my girl friend along on an otherwise all-male expedition to Mars. And of course, he will make a phone call to the President, and our story will quite melt his romantic Slavic heart. . . ."

"Well, when you put it that way . . ."

"That's the way it is, Franja, and we both know it," Nikolai told her gently.

Franja sighed. "Well, you can't blame a girl for trying," she said, and strangely enough she felt rather relieved, knowing that at least she had, and it was over.

Nikolai kissed her softly on the lips. "I really do wish I could leave you with something to remember me by," he said. "And I *am* a Colonel Cosmonaut and a Hero of the Soviet Union, and I *do* have connections, and Marshal Donets *is* my brother-in-law. . . . Make another wish, Franja, something a bit more realistic, and I promise I'll do what I can to grant it."

"What did you have in mind?"

"What do you want out of life, Franja?"

Franja thought about it long and hard, and with Nikolai, she had learned to do her thinking out loud. "I grew up wanting to be a cosmonaut like you, and I worked so hard to get into Gagarin, and when I was there, I worked so hard to get into Cosmonaut school, and when I didn't get in, I allowed myself to be talked into becoming a space monkey in the hope that someday . . ."

"Someday what?"

"Someday, somehow, having experience outside the gravity well, however lowly, would get me into the Cosmonaut Corps when the Grand Tour Navettes became operational and the Corps needed to expand rapidly. . . ." she told him. "But after a few weeks in Sagdeev, I knew I didn't want to spend my life in a succession of submarines in space, and all I wanted was to go home, and what I was going to do back on Earth after this tour I didn't even think about, and . . . and . . ."

She kissed him on the cheek. "And then I met *you*, Nikolai," she said, "and now I find myself, much to my surprise, dreaming of Mars, and Titan, and places beyond, but there doesn't seem to be any real hope of that, and . . . and I'm really quite confused. . . ."

"Hmmm . . . ," Nikolai muttered. "Well, I can tell you one thing, and that's that the Grand Tour Navettes *are* eventually going to mean a big need for more personnel," he said. "There'll be more Cosmograds, a city or two on the Moon, a Mars colony, many expeditions farther out. . . . But what they're going to come looking for is not so much space monkeys as pilots."

"Pilots?"

"To be specific, Concordski pilots. After all, the Concordski is a sort of spaceship already. It goes ballistic even at the apogee of terrestrial milk runs. It goes into orbit and rendezvous with Cosmograds. It goes all the way out to Spaceville in GEO. Anyone who has Concordski wings could easily enough learn to pilot a GTN in a few weeks. If you're really serious, you should get yourself Concordski wings. With a Concordski rating and a year's zero-gravity experience as well, you'd be right up there at the head of the line when the time comes."

"How could I manage to do that?" Franja said.

Nikolai laughed. "*That much,* at least, Marshal Donets would be willing to arrange for his brother-in-law, the Hero of the Soviet Union," he said.

FIRST HAT IN THE RING

Nathan Wolfowitz, UC Berkeley professor and former independent candidate for Congress, became the first announced candidate for the Republican Presidential nomination at a press conference held in a Las Vegas casino.

"Sure it's a little early, but I've got a name-recognition problem," Wolfowitz told reporters. "And it's never too early to start raising money, not for someone like me who can't count on the usual fat cats, and wouldn't if he could."

When asked why he had chosen such an unusual venue for his announcement, the candidate replied that he intended to raise money via a series of high-stakes fundraising poker games, and invited bemused reporters to participate in the first such event immediately following the press conference.

According to highly unofficial sources, the candidate emerged ten hours later as the big winner.

—*People*

When Bobby started applying for journalist jobs two months before graduation, he found himself running up against an unexpected stone wall. His marks were good, he had hundreds of pages of good prose to show in the form of all the translations he had done, three years as a history major counted in his favor, as did his knowledge of French and Russian, and even his European background, at least in certain circles.

But the answer was always the same. "We'd like to hire you, Mr. Reed, but we simply can't. You're not an American citizen."

Under federal law, no company that paid federal taxes could hire a noncitizen who did not have a federal work permit. And the unemployment situation being what it was, Green Cards were simply not being issued, except in rare cases where a national security need could be established, which certainly did not apply to reporters.

On a certain level, Bobby had known this all along, but he had avoided confronting the reality as long as possible.

The only way he could work in the United States was by surrendering his Common European passport to take American citizenship.

But as an American citizen, he wouldn't be able to leave the country without an exit visa. And what with his father's questionable status, his own European birth, his background as a Berkeley Red, and the way they were arbitrarily enforcing the National Security Act these days, they might never grant him one.

"It's a big commitment," he told Sara over dinner. "If I take American citizenship, there's a good chance I'll never be able to see my parents again."

"If you don't," she pointed out, "you'll never get a job, and that's not just a good chance, it's a dead certainty. You really don't expect me to support you for the rest of your life . . . ?"

"No . . . ," Bobby muttered miserably. "But . . ."

"Look at it this way," Sara said. "It's only a problem because of things like the damned National Security Act, and that's the kind of thing we're committing ourselves to work to change, isn't it?"

"So . . . ?"

"So your mother's a Marxist, isn't she? Wouldn't she approve? Wouldn't she consider it a perfect example of enlightened class self-interest?"

"You don't know Mom . . . ," Bobby said. "And Dad—"

"Jesus Christ, Bobby, your father *defected* so he could work for what he believed in, didn't he? You're telling me he's a total hypocrite?"

"No, but . . ."

"And what about *me?*" Sara snapped. "*I've* made a commitment to you, haven't I? We simply can't live a life together unless you become an American citizen, that's the bottom line, and we both know it."

Bobby sighed. "Yeah," he said. "Yeah!" he declared much more firmly. "Okay, Sara, I'll do it. But only if you'll make the same commitment to me. Let's . . . let's get married!"

Sara dropped her fork into her plate. She stared at Bobby. "I thought you'd never ask," she said.

"Did you?"

Sara laughed. "No," she said, "but I did think it might be slightly more romantic."

"What could be more romantic than this?" Bobby declared forcefully, realizing, to his surprise, that he meant it. "Here I am, maybe trapping myself inside this fucked-up country forever to commit myself to changing it and to stay with the woman I love! Way I see it, that's a hell of a lot more romantic than violins and flowers!"

Sara broke into a radiant smile. "When you put it that way, how can a girl say no?" she said, and she leaned across the table and kissed him.

And so a week later, Bobby filled out his citizenship application, and a month later the papers came through. A week after that, they were married before a municipal judge. After the ceremony, Bobby kissed his new bride, and then took the Oath of Allegiance.

COSMONAUTS TO BARNARD'S
STAR?

Dr. Vassily Igorovich Yermakov, of the Space Studies center of the Soviet Academy of Sciences, has suggested that it might be possible to someday send a manned mission to Barnard's star using no more than an advanced version of the Grand Tour Navettes now under development.

Such a starship might take centuries to arrive at its destination, but the ship could be piloted by an Artificial Intelligence, and the cosmonauts would travel in an electronically induced state of suspended animation or, better yet, in cryogenic suspension.

"Both the Americans and ourselves are working on the early stages of developing such techniques," Yermakov pointed out. "What a pity that we cannot be pooling our efforts."

—*Izvestia*

The observation deck was crammed with onlookers as the *Nikita Khrushchev* warped slowly away from Cosmograd Sagdeev, but once more, for the last time, Nikolai Smirnov had pulled strings for Franja, and she was allowed to watch the departure in blessed solitude, alone, suited up, clinging to the framework of the Cosmograd, out in the starry vastness that was about to swallow up the only man she had ever loved.

Tears clouded her vision, and there was no way to wipe them away inside her helmet, nor, really, did she want to, for they glazed the sight of the departing Mars ship with a gauzy and merciful curtain of glittering crystal highlights, softening the stars, romanticizing the sorrow.

There had been a lot of back and forth between Nikolai and Marshal Donets this past week, but Nikolai had fulfilled his promise. His brother-in-law the Marshal was going to get her into the Concordski pilots' school in Central Asia, and there was nothing left but the paperwork and the formalities.

There had been a lot of frenzied love-making and a few tears, but no sad drama, for after all, he was a Hero of the Soviet Union, and she was a jaded space monkey, was she not, and they had both known that this moment was inevitable from the beginning. They were star-crossed lovers in every conceivable meaning of the term.

Franja turned away for a moment to gaze down at the Earth, to which she would soon be returning, and the new life that awaited her there now was also a departing gift from Nikolai, a purpose, a career, a dream restored. He had done the best that he could to leave her better off than he had found her, and even now, with tears in her eyes, Franja still was able to marvel at how well he had succeeded.

The *Nikita Khrushchev* was five kilometers from the Cosmograd now, and suddenly, silently, a tongue of blue flame erupted from the main thrusters, steadied, became a solid beam of blue light, and the Mars ship began to accelerate, pulling away from her, setting out across the sea of space toward its far-distant destination.

Franja stayed out there in the vacuum watching it dwindle into the teary black mists until its exhaust was just another star, a pinpoint of blue light dwarfed by the immensity, but arcing slowly and bravely across it. Only then, for the first and last time, did she say it.

"I love you, Nikolai Mikhailovich Smirnov," she finally said, when there was no one else to hear it, when it no longer mattered.

Or perhaps when it mattered most of all.

RECORD WHEAT CROP IN UKRAINE

The Ministry of Agriculture has announced that this year's Ukrainian wheat crop is the largest in history. The new genetically engineered seed and improved farming techniques were given part of the credit, but Ministry agronomists admit that the global warming trend, which has brought longer and warmer growing seasons and more rain, was largely responsible.

"We do not believe this is an isolated event," a Ministry spokesperson said. "We are finally experiencing the begin-

ning of the climatic shift that has been predicted for decades."

—Novosti

X X

Sonya Gagarin Reed had been waiting in dread for the
other shoe to drop ever since Robert called to blithely announce that he had just signed his American citizenship papers and gotten married to someone they had never even
met. And to turn the screw a little further, Jerry had refused
to understand her ire, had taken it out on poor Franja in the
end, and they had been arguing bitterly ever since.

"How could you do such a thing without even consulting
us?" she had demanded, admittedly with a good deal less
than maternal enthusiasm.

"We love each other, Mom," Robert's voice said over the
phone.

"That's not what I'm talking about, and you know it!"

"No, I don't, Mom, I don't know what you're talking
about at all."

"I'm talking about taking American citizenship without
considering the consequences," she snapped.

"I certainly *have* considered the consequences! The consequences were that without American citizenship, I could
never get a job!"

"And what about *my* job, Robert?" Sonya shouted back.

In the afterglow of the Great Stock Market Coup, Sonya
had expected some kind of promotion. When it had not
been forthcoming, Ilya had assured her that it was only because they were saving her for *his* job when the time came
for him to move up. After all, he had pointed out, it would
be foolish to promote her sideways to director of some
other department, where her experience would not be
nearly so valuable.

But a year and a half later, when Ilya Pashikov was made
Director of the Paris Office of Red Star, they brought in a

bitch on wheels from Moscow named Raisa Shorchov to fill his old job above her.

The night he told her, Ilya took Sonya out to an expensive dinner at La Mer Noire, filling her with champagne, Sevruga caviar, baked sturgeon, Pouilly-Fuissé, raspberries Romanoff, and ancient Cognac, and he didn't work up the courage to say it until the second after-dinner drink, leading her to believe all the while that this was by way of some kind of celebration.

As, for him, it was.

"Well, as the old American saying has it, there's good news, and there's bad news," he said when he was finally drunk enough. "The good news is that I've been promoted to Director of the Paris Office—"

"Oh, Ilya, that's wonderful!"

"The bad news is . . . ," he muttered, studying the bottom of his Cognac snifter.

And he told her.

Sonya sat there stunned, motionless, not even able to cry.

"I did everything I could, believe me, I came perilously close to losing my own promotion over it, I mean, we *have* been discreet, but once I started making calls over people's heads to Moscow, well, even what's left of the KGB can still manage to put one and one together if you rub their noses in it hard enough. . . ."

"But *why?*" Sonya demanded. "I've more than earned it!"

Ilya sighed. He shrugged. "What it all seems to boil down to is that the Moscow Mandarins just don't consider you politically pure enough to hold such a position. With a son going to university in America, and Jerry forever trying to go over Boris Velnikov's head to his French friends at ESA . . ."

"It's just not fair!" Sonya exclaimed, holding back her tears.

Ilya reached across the table and took her hand. "I quite agree," he said. "You know I do. But the Bears are taking bites out of other people's asses too, you know. . . ."

"You went too far trying to help me, didn't you?" Sonya said softly.

Ilya smiled ruefully. "Do you know what I say to that?" he said. He held up the middle finger of his right hand. "I say *this* to that!" he declared. "And as for going too far—in the end, it will be the miserable chauvinist bastards who go too far! In the glorious words of Nikita Khrushchev, we will bury them, you'll see!"

"Oh, *Ilya*," Sonya sighed.

And in the end, she had gone off with him to his apartment for solace after dinner that night too. He was such a true friend. And if she was going to have a lover, who better than Ilya Pashikov?

Ilya, with all his other women, was entirely undemanding. The thought of falling in love with such a man and doing something irrevocable and foolish was ridiculous, as Ilya himself often enough took pains to point out. Ilya was a true comrade in the best and truest sense of the word. And if she knew all too well that having sex with him was a betrayal of Jerry, well, at least, it was a betrayal with a friend who knew its limits.

So too had Ilya done his best to make her durance vile under Raisa Shorchov as bearable as it could be under the circumstances. Shorchov was ten years her junior, which was humiliating enough. Shorchov, unlike Ilya, treated Sonya like a subordinate instead of a colleague, indeed, seemed to delight in lording it over an older woman with so much more experience. Perhaps this was because she was an incompetent capable of doing little but collecting reports and projections, signing her name to them, and passing them on to her superiors as her own work.

Shorchov was, in fact, a political appointee who seemed to have been shoved down Red Star's throat by the Bears in Moscow. Her idea of economic strategy seemed to be theirs, namely that Red Star should serve as an instrument of Russian policy, and that Russian policy should be to seize control of as much of Common Europe's industrial apparatus as quickly as possible, and never mind what it did to the balance sheet.

Shorchov was forever babbling on about Slavic Destiny, and she made it quite clear that she considered her sojourn in Paris an exile to be endured on her way to bigger and better things in the future, once she was safely back on sacred Russian soil.

It was only Sonya who kept the morale of the economic strategy department from completely falling apart under such titular leadership, and Ilya virtually refused to meet with Raisa Shorchov without Sonya's presence. "Comrade Director of the economic strategy department" was what he called Shorchov to her face, and the real input from the department into Red Star policy decisions came from private conversation with Sonya.

But while this kept Sonya functioning instead of throwing up her hands and doing something foolish, it certainly did little to endear her to her superior, and she knew full well that Raisa Shorchov would seize the first available opportunity to have her removed from the assistant directorship. Which was why when Robert so cavalierly informed her that he had taken American citizenship, which might just finally be the edge that Shorchov needed, Sonya had indeed, to a certain extent, lost control.

But that certainly didn't justify the way Jerry had treated Franja when she called all the way from Cosmograd Sagdeev two days later to give them her good news.

Being a call from orbit, there had been no video, but when she had put the call on the speaker so they could both listen to their daughter's excited voice, Sonya didn't need a video hook-up to picture Franja's happy face as she burbled on about the good turn in her fortune.

Some cosmonaut friend of hers, a lover by the sound of it, had prevailed upon an apparently well-connected relative to get her into Concordski pilots' school at the end of her tour on Sagadeev.

"Isn't it wonderful?" Franja exclaimed. "With Concordski wings *and* a year's experience in orbit, I'll be first in line when your Grand Tour Navettes open up all those new positions, Father, Nikolai agrees with you entirely on that!"

Sonya saw Jerry wince at the phrase "your Grand Tour Navettes."

"We're both very happy for you, Franja," she said quickly to cover Jerry's silence, glad for once that there was no video link to show Franja the look on his face. "You're sure everything has really been arranged?"

"No problem, Mother," Franja assured her. "Marshal Donets has already presented my application personally, and as soon as my citizenship papers—"

"Your *what?*" Jerry snapped.

"My Soviet citizenship papers," Franja said. "They've already been processed in Moscow, but until copies arrive at the pilots' school, they can't formally—"

"You just went ahead and did it without even asking my permission?" Jerry said thickly.

"I'm a legal adult, and I no longer need your permission, Father!" Franja snapped back. Then, in a much more conciliatory tone, "Besides, a Marshal of the Red Army could hardly walk an application through for someone who wasn't even a Soviet citizen. He'd look ridiculous, or worse, and—"

"You did this to avoid embarrassing some fucking Russian general!" Jerry shouted.

"I . . . I thought you'd be pleased, Father," Franja said, more in pain than in anger.

"Pleased! Pleased that you've taken Soviet citizenship to kiss some Russian general's hairy ass!"

"Stop it, Jerry!"

"Pleased that I'm at least going to have a chance of being aboard one of your Grand Tour Navettes after all, maybe even as a pilot," Franja said, her voice an unsteady mixture of hurt and controlled anger that she had somehow managed to modulate into an attempt at conciliation. "You and me together on a GTN to the Moon, Mars even, just like you told me, Father. . . ."

Even as she heard her daughter say it, Sonya knew that Franja, with the best of intentions, was saying the worst thing possible, for Jerry was quite irrational on the subject these days, and this was certain to do nothing but set him off.

But the vehemence of his tirade stunned even her. Jerry's face reddened, tears welled up in his eyes, his hands balled into fists, veins stood out in his neck, and he went quite out of control.

"*My* Grand Tour Navettes!" he shouted, his voice breaking up into sobs. "The goddamn Russians have stolen the whole fucking project away from me! I'll *never* fly on a Grand Tour Navette, thanks to the fucking Russians! I'll never live to see the Moon! I'll never even get up out of the gravity well! The goddamn fucking Russians have taken my whole life away from me! You disgust me, Franja! You make me want to puke!"

"Jerry—"

"Father—"

And he had stormed out of the living room into the bedroom and slammed the door behind him.

And now, here they were, sitting in the living room continuing yet another dinner-table argument over Robert and Franja long after the second cups of coffee had grown as cold as their marriage bed. Sonya sat on the big blue leather couch where there was plenty of room for two, but Jerry had pointedly taken up his usual position in the armchair on the other side of the coffee table.

"*Please,* Jerry," Sonya insisted yet again. "You've *got* to make your peace with Franja, you can't just disown your own daughter!"

"Like the peace you've made with Bobby?" Jerry snapped.

"I told you, Jerry, I'll call Robert and try to smooth things over as soon as you apologize to Franja," Sonya said. "If you agree to do it afterward, I'll even call him first."

"She's the one who should be apologizing to me!"

"For what?" Sonya demanded. "For doing what she had to do to get into pilots' school?"

"How is that any different from what Bobby did?"

Sonya sighed. "It isn't," she admitted. "I was wrong too, and I *am* willing to do the right thing. You're just being stubborn, Jerry, and you know it! You're furious at Boris Velnikov, and you're just taking it out on the easiest available Russian, who unfortunately happens to be your own daughter. Not to mention—"

The phone rang.

"Saved by the bell," Jerry said dryly, and punched the accept button.

A Soviet flag appeared on the screen, immediately replaced by a young woman's face.

"Somehow I think this is for you," Jerry said, and he got up out of the chair next to the phone and let Sonya sit down within range of the camera.

"Sonya Gagarin Reed?"

"Yes. . . ."

"I am required to inform you that your presence is required at the office of Ivan Josefovich Ligatski, assistant counselor to the deputy director of the political section, at the Soviet Embassy this Thursday at 3:00 P.M."

"Are you . . . are you required to tell me what this is all about?" Sonya stammered.

The young woman glanced down at something off camera, or at least pretended to. "Review of Party status," she said.

"Review of Party status?"

"That's what it says here," the functionary said. "It would not do to be late." And she hung up.

Sonya sat there staring numbly at the blank screen.

"What was that," Jerry said blithely, "more red tape?"

Sonya looked up at him, and as the expression on his face changed, she saw mirrored there what he had seen on her own.

"It's serious?" he said softly, peering down at her with an expression of real concern, a concern for her that she had not seen for a long, long time.

"Very serious," she said somberly. "I have a terrible feeling that this is just what I was afraid of when Robert became an American citizen. I *knew* that Shorchov would try to use it against me somehow, but this . . ." She shuddered.

Jerry came closer. He actually placed his arm across the back of the chair, not quite touching her shoulders.

"You're . . . you're not in trouble with the KGB?" he said.

Sonya would have laughed if the situation were not so grim. "I only wish that was it," she said. "The KGB is in no position these days to intimidate high Red Star circles. Ilya could make a few phone calls, and they'd be forced to go away. But this . . . this is much worse . . ."

Review of Party status? Assistant counselor to the deputy director of the political section? In the bad old days, they used to have a more straightforward term for that—commissar.

"Worse than the KGB?" Jerry said nervously. "What could be worse than the KGB?"

His anger had quite evaporated. Real worry was plainly visible on his face. Was it possible that he really did still care?

"Anything to do with a review of Party status," she told him. "Shorchov would like nothing more than to see my Party card lifted. . . ."

"They'd really do that?"

Sonya shrugged. "Probably not," she said. "Probably they're just calling me in on the carpet. But review of Party status is an official proceeding, and it will appear on my kharakteristika. And that's bad enough, what with all the black marks I have already. . . ."

Jerry's arm touched her shoulder. "You're really this worried about that kind of bureaucratic bullshit?"

Sonya looked into his eyes, bobbed her head. "Yes," she said, "I am."

Jerry looked back, and she could see the pain in his eyes when he said it, feel the shame of it knot her own gut, knowing what it must be costing him. "Surely your good friend the Golden Boy can take care of it, can't he?" he said with no irony in his voice.

"Not this," she said. "If he tried, that in itself would be a black mark on *his* kharakteristika too."

"And you wouldn't want to risk that, would you?" Jerry shot back, and all at once she could see him withdrawing, sense that a moment that might have been was already past.

"I couldn't, it wouldn't be fair," she told him from the other side of the wall that, after all, still lay between them.

CONGRESS OF PEOPLES CONVENED IN PARIS

Delegates from separatist movements from all over Common Europe opened their four-day meeting at Port Maillot today, designed to draw up a charter for an ongoing Congress of Peoples which will promote the rights of so-called national minorities. Groups represented include Basques, Scots, Ukrainians, Walloons, Slovaks, Welsh, Bavarians, Uzbeks, Corsicans, Catalans, and Bretons.

While there seems to be no general agreement on ultimate goals, there does seem to be a consensus that those European nationalities that do not have their own nation-states within the Common European framework must band together to bring about structural alterations that will further de-emphasize the already-diminished sovereignty of the member states in favor of building what a huge banner hung inside the meeting hall calls "A Europe of Peoples, not Nations."

—Le Monde

Oh how Jerry Reed hated this prison cell of his dreams!

When Corneau had assigned him the low-status windowless office, Jerry hadn't really cared, even though he knew what it implied in the pecking order, for he had no interest in such bureaucratic games. He had a desk, a chair, and a computer terminal, and as far as he was concerned that was all he needed to do his work.

While everyone else was tied up in endless meetings during the set-up phase, he was able to spend his time at the computer turning his old conceptual renderings into blueprints for actual hardware. By the time the maneuvering system section had been set up without him, under Steinholz, he already had plans detailed enough to break up into hardware specs for subcontractor bids.

Rather than slap Steinholz in the face with them, he had taken them directly to Patrice Corneau. "I can see you haven't been wasting your time, Jerry," Patrice had told him. "It's possible we can use some of this. I'll pass it along to Velnikov and ask him to have Steinholz take a look."

"What are you talking about, Patrice? These are complete plans for the maneuvering system, ready to let out for bid. We can save months!"

The project director shook his head. "That's really being naive, Jerry," he said. "We can't start subcontractor bidding until *all* systems and components have been firmed up into hardware specs. Your maneuvering system specs look very good in isolation, but how can we know how well they will integrate with the specs for the other systems until those specs exist?"

Reluctantly, Jerry had been forced to agree, and in the months that followed, as he continued to design his own versions of various sub-systems in isolation, he watched, via his terminal, with a galling mixture of personal anger and professional satisfaction, as Steinholz's team slowly and meticulously duplicated his own work at a snail's pace, making only minor modifications to justify their existence.

But when he showed Corneau preliminary specs for the framework and propulsion systems, Patrice had shaken his head. "This is all quite elegant, Jerry," he said. "But it's all pretty irrelevant."

"Irrelevant? What do you mean, irrelevant?"

Corneau shrugged. "For the most part, you're simply duplicating work that others are already doing. Some of it is quite parallel, some of it goes off at a tangent, none of it's integrated with the overall design. What good are specs for a framework designed in isolation from the fuel balloon or the cabin? What's the point of designing a propulsion system without a fix on the overall payload?"

"Well then, damn it, Patrice, why don't you give me access to the main data banks so at least I can know what the hell is going on?" Jerry said irritably. "You just admitted that I have a need to know."

Jerry's terminal gave him access to the maneuvering system section's data banks, but he was locked out of the data banks of the other design sections. Patrice was forever muttering vaguely about "access on a need-to-know basis" and promising to rectify the situation when "the time came."

Surely what Corneau was telling him was that the time was *now*.

Corneau shrugged and avoided his eyes. "I'm afraid I can't do that, Jerry," he said.

"What do you mean, you can't do it? You're the project director, aren't you?"

Patrice still wouldn't look at him. "It's a political position, after all, you know . . . ," he muttered.

"No, I *don't* know! What's that supposed to mean?"

Corneau sighed. "It means that Velnikov would go through the ceiling if I allowed you general access," he said.

"Velnikov! Who's the project director, Patrice, you or that Russian bastard?"

"Let us say that Velnikov . . . has routes outside the normal chain of command," Corneau said. "There's a lot of Russian money in this project, and he's, well, he's Moscow's man. I don't like it any better than you do, but there we have it."

"We'll see what Emile Lourade has to say about this!" Jerry snapped.

"This comes from Emile, Jerry," Corneau told him. "The way things are set up, he's answerable to Velnikov in certain matters too. . . ."

"Like my access to the main project data banks?"

"There you have it, Jerry," Patrice admitted.

"Goddamn it, Patrice, you *promised* I'd have access to the whole project through you!"

"*Input,* Jerry, not *access.* And I'm not going back on that. I'll put these specs into the main data banks where the frame and propulsion teams can consult them as much as they want to. And I'll do the same with anything else you turn in."

"Big deal!"

"That's the best I can do," Patrice said sadly. "That's all I can do. I'm sorry, Jerry, really I am."

So for want of anything else to do, Jerry continued to develop his own Grand Tour Navette hardware specs, dumping the results blindly into the main data banks and printing out his own hard copies, papering the walls of the office with them, even making fumbling and amateurish attempts to construct models, which by now filled most of the shelf space.

What would happen to him when the design phase was finished he did his best not to think about, just as he tried to avoid thinking about the son he might never see again, and Sonya's affair with Ilya Pashikov.

There would hardly be a place in the project for a "maneuvering system design consultant" when the construction phase began, and it seemed certain that Velnikov would not allow Corneau to make him the head of any hands-on engineering team. Beyond the end of the design phase, the future was a featureless black void into which he dared not peer too deeply.

So too did he dare not confront Sonya directly. He knew that she was screwing the Golden Boy from time to time, and he let her know that he knew often enough, but she refused to acknowledge that he knew, and he would not force her to. For what would happen if he did was another void in his future he knew better than to gaze upon directly lest it turn his present to stone.

He could precipitate a crisis any time he chose by simply confronting her openly. And she could easily enough force him into it. But she didn't. She never spent the night anywhere but their apartment on Avenue Trudaine. Just as he confined himself to oblique put-downs of Pashikov, she never went beyond defending him as a "good friend."

And in some strange way, he managed to convince himself that she was playing the game this way because she still loved him somehow. Pashikov, after all, was well known for screwing every woman he could get his hands on, and Sonya herself joked about it. Perhaps that was her way of telling him that this affair was a thing that could never go any further, that she had chosen Pashikov for an occasional lover because he was safe, because a relationship with him was impossible, and hence he was no real threat to what was left of theirs. Indeed, he might even be keeping them to-gether.

Did *he* still love her? That was another thing he dared not confront openly.

And yet . . .

And yet, agonizing as it might be, the configuration was stable. Life without Sonya was quite literally unimaginable, as unimaginable as life without his work, futile or not. They were the two poles of his existence, they were all he had. And if both were beds of frustration, somehow each made the other bearable; that was a stable configuration too, and he dared not disturb it, for he could conceive of no other.

But though the end of the project's design phase might be vague years in the future, last night's call from the Soviet Embassy, and Sonya's reaction to it, had in the end filled him with dread too.

But why was he *afraid?* What was he afraid of?

Although he could put no face on it, he could feel it coming. Something was rushing down the timeline toward him at hypersonic speed, silent and invisible until the moment of impact like an incoming missile, something that could shatter the fragile stability of his life's configuration as surely as the end of the project's design phase.

But this was not something that lay inevitably but safely in the vague future like the end of the design phase or the moment of death. It might be faceless and formless, but it would arrive at ground zero on Thursday.

While the bumper wheat crop in the Soviet Union has depressed current prices on the international market, wheat futures prices have actually risen due to the drought in the Midwest. The thinking seems to be that Washington will resist pressures to allow the sale of Russian grain in the American market, and the insurgents will diminish the harvest of the big crop coming to maturity in Patagonia.

But some contrarians are shorting wheat futures, looking to the new fields in mid-Canada to weigh in heavily in the next few weeks.

We say that the smart thing to do is stay out of wheat futures entirely. The apparent climatic shift has created too many uncertainties. There's no reliable data base on the new northern Canadian fields, and the Patagonian guerrillas just may let the crop be harvested in order to gain local support and wreak economic havoc in the Chicago exchange. It's all too much of a crapshoot. Stay away and wait for things to shake down.

—*Words from Wall Street*

Ivan Josefovich Ligatski did not look like the fictional version of a typical Chekist thug out of the bad old days, usually portrayed as a burly balding brute in an ill-fitting blue suit, nor did he look like a fictional Party martinet, thin, ascetic, with old-fashioned wire-rimmed glasses and prim bloodless lips.

His suit was a rakish light gray and tailored well enough, he had curly medium-length black hair, an ordinary build, full lips, and rather large brown eyes unadorned by glasses.

But there was a full mustache above his lips, and while it was hardly one of the Stalin handlebars affected by Uncle Joe street hooligans, in place of a standard shirt and tie, he wore a stylized white peasant blouse with an off-white brocaded collar, and together they made the point, subtly perhaps, but unmistakably enough for Sonya's heart to sink as she entered his office.

Ligatski was a Bear, and he didn't care who knew it.

"Sit down please, Comrade Reed," he said without rising from behind his desk. Using her American married name instead of calling her "Sonya Ivanovna" was another bad sign, and "Comrading" her did not seem designed to put her at her ease either. Or was she just becoming paranoid? Or was making her paranoid the intended effect in the first place?

Get ahold of yourself, Sonya, she told herself as she sat down on the hard plastic chair in front of Ligatski's standard-issue metal desk. You are the assistant director of the economic strategy department of Red Star, S.A., and, judging from his title and this office, you outrank this petty functionnaire, at least from a certain perspective.

The office had a window, but no real view, cheap beige carpeting, a computer terminal on the desk, no couch, no coffee table. There was, however, a rather fancy electrified antique samovar and tea service on a small banquette. And a color photo of Lenin. And good Lord, that was an *icon* sitting on top of the bookcase.

Ligatski did not offer tea, and that bit of boorishness certainly *was* significant, especially on the part of a neo-traditionalist like this.

"I will come directly to the point," Ligatski said. "You have brought your Party card of course?"

"Of course," Sonya said frostily. Assuming a low posture, as the Japanese would say, would do no good when dealing with a character like this.

"Let me have it."

"What?"

"Have you been here so long that you can no longer understand a polite imperative construction in Russian?" Ligatski said archly. "I will try something less complex, then. Give me your Party card, Comrade Reed."

Trembling with fear and no little rage, Sonya took her wallet out of her purse and extracted the familiar plastic-laminated Party card. Instead of handing it to Ligatski, she slapped it down on the desktop midway between them. Ligatski eyed her narrowly for a moment, then picked it up, glanced at it, then back at her. He tapped it edgewise on the desk three times, then held it there, pressed upright between his fingertips and the desktop.

"This lists your nationality as Russian," he said.

"Of course," Sonya said coldly. "As Russian as you are."

"Oh really? *I* am not the sort of Europeanized cosmopolitan who would choose to endure twenty years and more living in self-imposed exile from the land of my birth!"

"As a loyal Soviet citizen and Party member, I gladly serve my country wherever my country requires me to serve," Sonya told him evenly.

"And I suppose marrying an American was an expression of Russian patriotism as well?"

"That is not Party business, and you know it!" Sonya snapped back angrily.

"The *Party* decides what is Party business and what is not, Comrade Reed," Ligatski replied frostily.

Control yourself, Sonya, control yourself, she reminded herself. The fact of the matter was that Ligatski was all too correct. "Very well, Comrade Ligatski," she said evenly. "If the *Party* deems it proper to drag my marriage into these proceedings, I must point out that the Party was far from displeased with my action at the time. Indeed, it was discreetly suggested that I would be doing my country a service by marrying Jerry Reed. Surely that is in my kharakteristika."

"What is also in your kharakteristika is that you used the Party's need to secure yourself a transfer from Brussels to Paris," Ligatski said.

"From each according to her contribution, to each according to her need," Sonya replied dryly.

Ligatski scowled. "Very clever," he said. "Perhaps you can also misquote Lenin to explain how your son's defection to the United States may be construed as service to the Party as well?"

"Robert didn't *defect* to the United States. He was entitled to claim American citizenship under American law."

"He was also entitled to Soviet citizenship under Soviet law," Ligatski snapped. "Why did he choose American citizenship instead?"

Sonya found her ire overcoming her fear, and perhaps her bureaucratic good sense. "He's an adult," she said. "He made his own choice. And it's no business of yours!"

"It's *Party* business, Comrade Reed," Ligatski shot back. "As a Party member, you should have raised your son properly as a boy so that as an adult he would have freely made the right choice. Failing to do so is construable as dereliction of Party duty as well as the maternal role."

Sonya's mouth fell open at that. She could find no words that would not make matters much worse if she dared to utter them. It figured that a Bear like this would be an archaic Slavic phallocrat too!

"Well, Comrade Reed, what do you have to say for yourself?" Ligatski demanded.

"What do I have to say for myself?" Sonya stammered. "About all I can think of to say at this point, Comrade Ligatski, is will you please get to the point, whatever it is!"

"The point, Comrade Reed, is that you are unfit to hold membership in the Communist Party," Ligatski said, and he palmed her Party card, opened a drawer, slipped the card inside, and slammed it shut with a metallic thunk.

"You cannot do this!" Sonya shouted, bolting to her feet. "It is a violation of every principle of Socialist Legality!"

Ligatski was on his feet shouting too. "You are a fine one to lecture the *Party* about Socialist Legality, Sonya *Reed!*

You call yourself a Russian? Corrupted entirely by twenty years in the West! Married to an American! With a son who has defected to the United States! Conducting a sordid affair with a superior in the bargain and using him to protect yourself from the consequences of your disloyalty!"

"So that's it, is it? This is the work of Raisa Shorchov!"

"Raisa Shorchov is a loyal Russian patriot, which is more than can be said for you!"

"I demand that you return my Party card at once! You have no authority to do this! There have been no legal proceedings. I demand my rights under Soviet law."

Ligatski sat down again and crossed his arms in front of his chest. "Party membership is a privilege, not a right," he said. "And I am fully authorized to revoke your membership. You do realize what that means?"

Sonya knew what it meant, all right. She sank back onto her chair with most of the fight knocked out of her.

Obviously, Raisa Shorchov had finally found a way to get rid of her. Obviously, she had used Robert's taking of American citizenship to go around the Red Star bureaucracy to her friendly Bears in the Party apparatus. At the very least, being thrown out of the Party would mean Sonya's losing her job in Paris and being offered something dreadful back in the Soviet Union, probably east of the Urals too.

And if she refused whatever they offered, no major company here was about to offend Red Star, S.A., and the Soviet Union to the point of hiring someone they had blacklisted.

She would be unable to secure anything but a menial position in Paris, and if she capitulated and returned to the Soviet Union, she would never see Ilya again, she would have to leave Jerry, and she would be stuck all alone in some terrible job in some miserable provincial city, perhaps for the rest of her life.

"I don't suppose there's anything I can say to change your mind?" she moaned miserably.

"Nothing whatever," Ligatski said. "If it were personally up to me, someone like you would be tried as a traitor and given a good long term of internal exile as far above the Arctic Circle as possible."

"There is no longer such a thing as a gulag," Sonya pointed out.

Ligatski frowned. "Unfortunately, at the moment that is true," he admitted unhappily.

Sonya rose shakily to her feet.

"Sit down, Comrade," Ligatski said.

"What for? There is no longer any point in enduring your abuse, now is there, seeing as how you've made it quite clear that there's nothing I can do to alter the situation. Indeed, as long as I've got nothing left to lose, I might as well tell you what I think of you and your—"

"Sit down, Comrade, we're not through!" Ligatski said more forcefully.

"We're not?"

"No, we are not. My personal feelings are not the issue here. My duty is to speak for the Party whether I like the realities or not." And all at once, he seemed to become furtive, embarrassed.

He got up, went to the samovar, drew two glasses of tea. "Have some tea, Comrade Reed," he said, amazingly enough, and handed her a glass.

Sonya's bureaucratic instincts filled her with sudden hope. Was all that had gone before merely the opening move of the game the Americans called "Bad Cop, Good Cop," with Ligatski forced, for some unfathomable internal reason, to play both roles against his will?

"Speaking for the Party now, not myself, I have been authorized, or if you prefer, required, to offer you a means by which you may prove your loyalty to the point where your Party card will be returned and all mention of this meeting stricken from the records," Ligatski said, fidgeting and squirming as if his anus were impaled upon a stake.

"Do tell . . . ," Sonya said quietly, sipping at her tea.

"Unfortunately a situation has been created from which the Party requires your assistance in extricating itself," Ligatski told her fatuously. "Your daughter's application for admission to Concordski pilots' school has been forthrightly championed by Marshal Donets himself, a . . . well-connected personage in the Red Army. The Marshal interjected himself into the process before your son assumed American citizenship and before Comrade Shorchov reported your affair with Ilya Pashikov to the Party apparatus. The Party was unaware of what Marshal Donets was doing, and the Marshal was unaware that your Party membership was about to be revoked. . . . You understand the situation . . . ?"

"Not in the least," Sonya told him truthfully.

Ligatski sighed. "There are, shall we say, ideological differences of opinion, within both the Party and the Red Army, and, ah, political groupings which cross organizational lines. . . ."

"Eurorussians and Bears. . . ."

Ligatski scowled. "If you *must* be crude about it, yes," he admitted grudgingly. "Marshal Donets is one of the staunchest Russian patriots in the Red Army—"

"An unreconstructed old Bear—"

"—and is an important ally of high officials in the Party of like mind who for obvious reasons would not wish to see him embarrassed by this breakdown in communication between the Party and Army structures."

"Embarrassed by *what?*" Sonya said, quite unable to imagine where all this was going.

"By you and your daughter, of course."

"What *are* you talking about?"

"Do I have to draw you a picture?" Ligatski snapped. "Donets went way out on a limb to get your daughter into the pilots' school without any idea that your Party membership was about to be revoked. It's completely out of the question for someone whose mother has been thrown out of the Party for cause to attend pilots' school, and quite frankly, Donets will look like a fool or worse when her admission is revoked."

Sonya lifted her glass to her lips and savored a sip of tea. "I see," she said, smiling over the rim of her glass at Ligatski. "So this has all been a charade. You *can't* really lift my Party card because it would create a situation that would embarrass a prominent Red Army Bear!"

"No, you do not see!" Ligatski snapped. "This process has gone too far to simply be buried without a gesture on your part. It would then become ammunition in the campaign of the degenerate Westernized elements in both the Party and the Red Army to discredit the integrity of patriotic forces! There are unprincipled creatures within both structures who would leak the whole mess to the yellow press and create a public scandal in order to further their struggle against patriotic renewal."

"And we wouldn't want *that* to happen, now would we?" Sonya purred. Better and better! It would seem that it was *she* who had *the Bears* over a barrel! No doubt that was the reason for these desperate scare tactics in the first place!

"Certainly not!" Ligatski declared. "That is why this affair must have an outcome that will serve as an exemplary lesson in Russian patriotism should it ever be publicly revealed! That is why realpolitik requires, against all justice, that you are to be allowed to retain your Party membership in return for making a gesture that will draw an ideologically correct moral out of the story should it ever see the light of day. That is why you must divorce your husband, Jerry Reed."

Sonya sat there silently, unable to even think, as if she had been banged on the top of the head with a mallet, as Ligatski babbled on.

"If you obey the Party's orders, you will retain your Party card, your daughter will be permitted to attend pilots' school, you will keep your job in Paris, and you will be promoted to Raisa Shorchov's position when she is recalled for her part in stupidly creating this whole unfortunate situation in the first place."

"This is monstrous!" Sonya cried. "You can't be serious!"

"Believe me, Comrade Reed, this is no joke!"

"It's insane!"

"Not at all," Ligatski said. "By divorcing your American husband, you purge yourself of responsibility for the actions of your son and prove your Russian patriotism. We both know that your marriage is a hollow shell, but still, the notion of choosing country over love will appeal to the best instincts of the romantic Slavic soul, which is to say, should the story come out, we will paint you as a patriotic heroine. You might even get a medal. Only we will know the sordid truth."

"You're bluffing!" Sonya cried. "I won't do it!"

"Then you will be stripped of your Party membership and posted to Alma-Ata," Ligatski said. "Needless to say, your husband will not be permitted to join you, assuming that you could even persuade him to do so. Your marriage will effectively be over in any case, while you endure all these penalties and reap none of the benefits that patriotic cooperation would bring."

"I'll . . . I'll stay here in Paris with Jerry and get another job!"

Ligatski shrugged, smiled sardonically. "Technically

speaking, that is an option, I suppose," he said. "Of course, if you take it, that will mean that Marshal Donets will be severely embarrassed—"

"Screw Marshal Donets!"

"—and if Marshal Donets is embarrassed, all that will be left to us is to take vengeance, and you may be sure that that vengeance will be total and complete. We will make it known that you were dismissed from your position for conducting an affair with your superior in order to protect yourself from the consequences of having used internal Red Star information to make a killing on the bourse during the panic of Yankee Thursday."

"That's a lie!"

"Entirely beside the point," Ligatski said airily. "The point is that we will make quite certain that no European company of any consequence will hire you."

"Jerry makes a decent enough salary, the children are grown, we could get by. . . ."

"Vengeance, as I have said, will be total and complete. Your husband may not be so willing to support you when your affair with Pashikov becomes a public scandal. And in any case, he will be unable to do so after Moscow demands that the European Space Agency dismiss him as an American mole. Pashikov himself will suffer a severe enough loss of credibility that his friends in Moscow will not be able to prevent his reassignment to Novosibirsk. And of course, your daughter's hopes of getting Concordski wings will be dashed too, as well as her hopes of ever being admitted to the Party."

"You'd really do all that . . . ?" Sonya whispered.

"No, Comrade Reed, *you* would be responsible for ruining the lives of your husband, your daughter, Pashikov, and yourself, not the Party," Ligatski said. "The choice is yours. Pashikov can retain his present position, your daughter can become a Concordski pilot, your husband can remain at ESA, and you can become Director of the economic strategy department of Red Star, S.A., in Paris. You may even maintain a social relationship with your husband as long as the papers go through and you do not share the same domicile. Or you can bring everything crashing down on everyone's head."

Ligatski favored her with a wintry smile. "Let it not be said that I lack a romantic Russian heart," he told her. "You are authorized to discuss as much or as little of this conversation as you wish with your husband." He shrugged. "If he is a reasonable man, he must agree to accept the inevitable. If not, well, what will you have lost?"

"You're saying that all that is required is a legal divorce and separate domiciles?" Sonya said, grasping at straws. "We can still see each other? We can still spend time together in each other's apartments?"

"Why of course, Comrade Reed, we are not heartless monsters, we are not made of stone, we want to make this as easy for you as is consistent with the needs of the Party," Ligatski oozed ingenuously. "Think it over. Talk it over with your husband. I am sure you will see reason. Take your time. You have till next Tuesday at 3:00 to give me your answer."

STATUS OF FORCES LEGISLATION STILL BLOCKED IN STRASBOURG

Backstage negotiations have once more failed to produce a compromise to break the deadlock blocking the Status of Forces legislation introduced by Germany and backed by most of the smaller member states. France, Britain, and the Soviet Union still refuse to merge their armed forces under a command structure directly responsible to the Common European Parliament.

The Russians cite internal security needs, the British and the French raise the bogeyman of American adventurism, but in reality it seems more a matter of preserving obsolete tatters of so-called national sovereignty, an outmoded concept that dies hard in military circles.

The British *have* offered to place their nuclear forces under a Common European command, but it seems to be merely an empty gesture aimed at currying favor with the nonnuclear members, for they know full well that neither the French nor the Russians are having any of it.

—Die Welt

Sonya was sitting on the couch in the living room with a bottle of vodka on the coffee table before her and a large half-full tumbler of it in her hand when Jerry returned home from work. She was not disheveled and she didn't really seem drunk, but the way she looked at him was enough to tell him that the worst, whatever that might mean under these circumstances, had indeed happened.

"Well . . . ?" he said.

Sonya looked away from him, down into the depths of her glass. "Well, they lifted my Party card . . . ," she muttered. "And that's the *good* news. . . ."

"Why?" Jerry said, sitting down on the edge of the couch beside her.

Sonya gulped down a slug of vodka. "That's the *bad* news," she said. "They lifted my Party card so they could blackmail me into doing what they want me to do in order to get it back."

"Which is . . . ?"

Sonya sighed. She took another drink of vodka. She wouldn't meet his gaze. A shudder wracked her body. "I just don't know how to tell you this, Jerry," she said. "But I must . . . I must . . ."

She got up, went to the sideboard, got out a wineglass, sat back down on the couch, filled the glass to the brim with vodka, and handed it to him. "Better have this first," she said. Now she did look directly at him, and he could see that her eyes were filling up with tears.

"Jesus, Sonya, what is it?" Jerry demanded.

"The worst thing in the world," Sonya said.

"Will you stop playing games?" he snapped. "Whatever it is, you're making it ten times worse."

"Have a drink first, Jerry," Sonya pleaded. *"Please. . . ."*

"You're really serious, aren't you?" Jerry said.

Sonya just nodded. And Jerry could feel a cold pressure on the back of his neck, the shock wave of whatever it was that he had dreaded, about to fall upon him with ballistic inevitability and shatter the fragile stability of even the poor sad thing that his life had become.

He lifted his glass to his lips and took a long harsh gulp of warm acrid vodka. It seared his throat on the way down and exploded in his stomach with a blast of bitter bile.

When Sonya had left the Soviet Embassy, it had all seemed horribly simple. In the cold clear light of bureaucratic logic, she could even rationalize what she knew she had to do. Ligatski had left her no choice. She had to divorce Jerry to save Franja and Ilya and Jerry himself, aside from anything they might do to her; the moral responsibility for this despicable necessity therefore lay with the Party, with the Bears, with Ligatski, with Donets, not herself.

Besides which, their marriage *had* long since become a hollow shell. If she sacrificed Franja and Ilya and herself and what was left of Jerry's career to save it, what, after all, would be preserved but an empty formality?

But then, sitting alone in the living room, in the apartment where they had spent twenty years of their lives, sipping at warm vodka, and waiting, and waiting, and waiting, the memories of all those years came flooding back, and all that cold logic had been quite dissolved away.

How could she *really* do such a thing? How could she let *the Party* make such a decision for her? In what way could she delude herself that she was something better than Ligatski if she did?

"Well, Sonya, spit it out already, will you?" Jerry said.

She sighed. She bolted down an enormous gulp of putrid raw warm vodka. He was right. There was nothing else for her but to puke up the whole vile story.

"So you can keep your goddamn *Party card!*" Jerry screamed. "So some fucking Commie bastard general doesn't get *embarrassed!*" He bolted down the rest of his vodka and threw the glass across the room, where it bounced off the wall and fell to the carpet without shattering. "Cocksucking motherfucking son of a bitch!"

Sonya sat there on the couch beside him, her head hanging limp between her hunched shoulders. "I had to tell you, didn't I?" she muttered miserably. "Oh, Jerry, Jerry, what are we going to do?"

I can't believe what I'm hearing! he thought. Though on another level, of course, it was easy enough to believe that the Russian bastards who had frozen him out of his own project were ruthless and unprincipled enough to pull something like *this* if it served their vile purposes.

But that Sonya hadn't simply told them to take it and stick it . . .

"What do you mean, what are we going to do?" Jerry shouted at her. "You're not telling me that you'd really divorce me over a fucking piece of paper! You can't really be seriously considering going along with this shit!"

Sonya still wouldn't look at him. "I know this is difficult for you, Jerry," she stammered, "but you've—"

"Difficult!"

"—got to calm down and really think."

"I am really thinking!" Jerry snapped. "I'm really thinking of going over to the Russian Embassy and beating the living shit out of Ivan Ligatski!"

Now Sonya raised her head slowly and did look at him. Her eyes were red and teary, but the cold expression on her face chilled him to the marrow. "You've got to stop reacting and start thinking," she said in a grim mechanical voice. "We've got to consider the options."

"Options!" Jerry sneered. But all the force had gone out of his voice. An enervating coldness seemed to be radiating from the pit of his stomach, along his limbs, up his neck to his brain. Dust motes seemed to sparkle in the lamplight. Everything seemed to be happening at a distance. A sour backwash of vodka seared the back of his throat.

"This isn't about my Party card," Sonya said. "This is about you and me and Franja. They're not bluffing, Jerry, they have no reason to bluff. They'll throw Franja out of pilots' school. They'll fire me for cause and see to it that the only place I can ever work again will be on the other side of the Urals."

She forced a bitter false laugh. "The way they've set it up, if I *don't* divorce you, we won't have anything left but our marriage license. They'll yank me back to the Soviet Union and we'll never see each other again."

"Fuck 'em!" Jerry stammered. "The mortgage here is just about paid off. The kids are grown. I can support us on my ESA salary. We can make it. . . ."

"Haven't you been listening? If I don't divorce you, you won't *have* a job at ESA, they'll accuse you of being an American spy and force ESA to fire you, *deport* you, maybe. . . ."

"They can't get away with that!" Jerry cried. "Emile Lourade is still my friend, he'll protect me—"

"Like he's protected you from Boris Velnikov all along?" Sonya snapped. "Face it, Jerry, you're still legally an American citizen. You've got an office full of plans for the whole GTN project—"

"*My* plans, not theirs!"

"How could you prove it? They'll break in and film everything, copy everything you have on disc. They've probably done it already. And they don't have to prove anything, just provide ESA with a fig leaf. It's politics, Jerry. The Soviet Union provides 40 percent of the financing for the Grand Tour Navette project, remember? Even if Lourade tried to protect you, which he wouldn't, he'd be replaced by someone who would see things their way. No one's going to risk offending the Soviet government just to protect you."

"Jesus . . . ," Jerry moaned.

"Besides, this isn't just about us," Sonya said. "What about Franja? Three years at Gagarin slaving away for nothing. A year on some miserable Cosmograd. And now she's finally gotten a chance to make some kind of life for herself. And if we defy them, they'll take it all away."

"You've really got this all figured out, haven't you?" Jerry said bitterly.

Sonya turned away from him, slumped forward, hung her head. "*They've* got it all figured out," she said softly. "I've had hours to sit here and try to think of a way out. And I can't find one."

She raised her head slowly and looked directly into his eyes. "Can you, Jerry?" she said pleadingly. "If you can, please tell me! I don't want to do this, really I don't!"

"But you will, won't you?" Jerry snapped.

"I leave it up to you, Jerry," Sonya said. "You decide. I'll do whatever you say."

"Bullshit!" Jerry cried. "You've already decided. You're just trying to fob it off on me!"

"No, I really mean it. Tell me what to do."

Jerry glared at her.

He thought about how their marriage had begun, how the goddamn Russians had wanted her to marry him in the first place to insure that he would take the ESA job, to get their hands on the American sat-sled technology; what bitter but perfect irony that they were now ending what their own machinations had begun. He thought about that piece of shit Boris Velnikov who had slowly but surely broken his dream just as the same breed of shit in the Pentagon had destroyed Rob Post all those years ago. He thought about the son he had raised in exile whom he might never see again. He thought about his Russian daughter, the daughter who had shared his dream, who had been forced to betray him to the fucking Russians to pursue it.

And he tried to think of a way out. He tried, and he tried, and he tried, and he came up empty. And the harder he tried, the more furious he became. At Ligatski. At the Party. At the Soviet Union. At Sonya. And in a way that would not bear direct examination, at himself.

"Well, Jerry?"

Jerry threw up his hands. He sighed. "You tell me, Sonya," he finally said. "You tell me. . . ."

Sonya looked down again. "Look at it this way," she muttered in a small voice. "It doesn't have to be anything more than a legal formality. All that's really required of us is a divorce and separate domiciles. We can still see each other. We'll keep our jobs. Franja can go to pilots' school. Marshal Donets won't be embarrassed. Sooner or later the whole thing will blow away and the Party will lose interest, and then we can live together again as man and wife in all but name. . . ."

Man and wife in all but name! That inversion of the lie they were already living finally tore it. That was finally a level of self-deception that what was left of his manhood would no longer let Jerry maintain. That was *really* rubbing his face in it!

"Like we've been doing ever since you met Ilya Pashikov?" Jerry shouted. "And in the meantime, you can fuck him whenever you like! How convenient for you, Sonya!"

Sonya stared at him wide-eyed, and it all came pouring out. "You really think I'm a complete imbecile? You really think I don't know you've been screwing the Golden Boy ever since . . . ever since you spent all those long nights with him working on the great stock market scam? Oh yes, Sonya, I've known all along! And you've known that I've known, and I've known that you've known that I've known, and the plain truth is that neither of us had the guts to admit it!" Tears burned Jerry's eyes. A bubble of nausea exploded in his guts. Red rage seethed behind his eyeballs. His hands balled into fists.

"What's the point, anyway, Sonya?" he shouted. "We're man and wife *only* in name! What's the point in throwing everything else away over a *legal formality* like that? Go ahead, kiss the Party's hairy Red asshole! Get your goddamn divorce!"

And he found that there was a part of him that welcomed

this final release of the endless awful tension, this bursting of the angry boil, this outpouring of poisonous pus. "I'll make it easy for you," he said in a colder, harder voice. *"I'll* file! I've got plenty of grounds, now don't I?"

And in those words, he knew, was the real end of their marriage, the true divorce. And at least he had found the courage to do it himself.

Senator Carson: "In a way, this Wolfowitz has a point, I mean besides the one on the top of his head."

Billy Allen: "How so, Senator?"

Senator Carson: "Well, he's right about one thing, Billy——a big part of our economic problems stems from the fact that our exports are being frozen out of the biggest and richest market in the world."

Billy Allen: *"You're* not suggesting that we join Common Europe too?"

Senator Carson: "Hell, no! And anyway the damn Peens wouldn't let us in in the first place. But . . . if something should happen to break the whole damn thing up . . . if the Europeans could be made to realize that it's all part of a Russian master plan to take over the world . . . Well, then it'd be a whole new ball game."

Billy Allen: "But *how*, Senator?"

Senator Carson: "I figure *that* one out, Billy, and maybe *I'll* run for President!"

—*Newspeak*, with Billy Allen

It took two weeks of looking for Jerry Reed to find an apartment. He did his searching after work, and somehow the long hours of hassling real estate agents, trudging around Paris, and looking at an endless succession of too-expensive apartments kept him together, kept him from thinking. He would eat his petit déjeuner at the little hotel, take the Métro to work, immerse himself in the job, spend the rest of the evening apartment hunting, eat a grim and lonely dinner, with a full bottle of wine, at some brasserie, reel back to the hotel drunk enough to crash out, then wake up the next morning to begin the cycle over, running mindlessly on automatic.

Indeed, perhaps, he was prolonging the process deliberately, for in the end he rented a small one-bedroom that was no larger and no cheaper than a dozen others that he had seen. Perhaps too there was something masochistically perverse in his final choice, for the apartment was on the Île St.-Louis, only two blocks from the apartment where he and Sonya had spent the early happy years of their marriage.

That apartment had been sunny and airy, with a magnificent view north across the Seine, across the city, into the brightness of the future, the perfect place for a pair of young newlyweds about to embark on a life together. This apartment was cool and shadowy and had a view of an old and musty stone courtyard, and that too seemed somehow appropriate for *this* stage in his life.

By the time he had rented the apartment, gotten the videotel, and gas, and electricity turned on, gotten a sparse suite of furniture moved in, and gotten his clothing out of Avenue Trudaine, the divorce papers had come through.

He insisted on waiting for Sonya to sign them before he went to the lawyer's office himself, so as to avoid the sight of her. That was on a Thursday. He took off work on Friday, laid in a supply of Cognac, and finally allowed himself to fall apart.

He drank and drank and drank for the next two days, sealed in the cell he had imprisoned himself in, staring mindlessly out the living room window, down at the old gray stone of the courtyard, thinking fragmented thoughts of California, and outer space, of twenty years of marriage, and twenty years of dreams and hopes, and that last terrible night when his world had ended.

Sunday at about noon, he awoke, sick to his stomach, with a raging headache, and quite famished. Without bothering to shower off two days' worth of grundge or shave off two days' growth of beard, he dragged himself out of the apartment into the cruel eye-killing sunshine of the Quai de Bourbon.

For those with the spirit to enjoy it, it was a glorious sunny Parisian day, with the tour boats plying the Seine, and the streets filled with people, and the amateur painters out in full force. Jerry slouched his way to the west end of the Île and collapsed onto a chair by a sidewalk table outside a brasserie near the Pont St.-Louis overlooking Nôtre-Dame.

He ordered an omelette parmentier and a café double

from a waiter, who looked quite askance at his disheveled appearance, and sat there eating his lunch and drinking his coffee and watching the world go by like a man from Mars, alone, abandoned, letting the French babble of the other patrons and the passersby wash over him like a wave of Muzak.

And at last he allowed himself to really think. His marriage was over. His daughter was a Soviet citizen, and he had turned his back on her. His son had built a life for himself in America, and America, the country that had betrayed him, might as well be on the far side of the Moon. His Grand Tour Navette had been taken away from him, and he was never going to get it back.

What was left to him? What was he supposed to do with the rest of his life?

A distant roar made him look up. There, in the cloudless blue sky over Paris, the contrail of a Concordski wrote a clean white line across the heavens; a flight in reality, no doubt, on its way to Rome, or Tokyo, or Melbourne, but in his mind's eye, he saw the silver dot at its point rising toward the clear cold blackness, toward orbit, toward Spaceville, toward the Moon, and beyond.

Toward where he still longed to be.

Up, and up, and up it rose, pure and hard, a bright silvery focal point drawing the vapor of the atmosphere behind it, no longer Earth-bound, shrugging off the ties of the planet, and at last he knew, at last he could see the ballistic trajectory of his life, shorn of all terrestrial illusion.

Up there was where he belonged, up there where there was no gravity to tie his flesh to the world's pain and illusion. *That* was what was left to him, to ride into the up and out, to float free of the bounds of the atmosphere, of the leaden constraints of gravity, up there in the cold, pure, black vacuum, where his spirit dwelled already, where his heart had always been.

That was what was left to him. That was the dream that had brought him to this pass in the first place, all those years ago. Sonya, Franja, Robert, America, they all seemed like a dream now, ghosts, phantoms, stations of the way.

Only one thing was real now. Only one thing mattered. Before he died, he would get there somehow. He would float free and clear and weightless above the wreckage of his life. He would see the Earth entire from on high.

Whatever it took. Whatever the price. Had he not paid everything he had already?

Europe. America. The Soviet Union. Words on a map. The past. Up there, that was the future.

"L'addition, s'il vous plaît," he told the waiter.

Whatever it was, he was ready to pay it.

PART THREE

AMERICAN SPRING

CNN: "Mr. President, President Gorchenko has charged that the presence of so many American media consultants, pollsters, and campaign experts in the Ukraine is blatant interference in the internal affairs of the Soviet Union . . ."

President Carson: "I thought the whole question of the campaign was whether or not the free people of the Ukraine wanted to continue to be dominated by the Russian oppressors."

CNN: "You haven't answered my question."

President Carson: "Sure I have. Kronkol promises to take the Ukraine out of the Soviet Union, so if he wins, who he hired to run his campaign is no business of Moscow's, and if he loses, well, what's Gorchenko got to bitch about?"

San Francisco Chronicle: "But Gorchenko has also charged that the Ukrainian Liberation Front chose Vadim Kronkol as their Presidential candidate on the advice of American media advisors they had hired beforehand and not the other way around. After all, he was a TV personality with no previous political experience."

President Carson: "So what? Way I see it, the ULF had the right to hire anyone they wanted to. And American campaign experts just happen to be the state of the art. Most of the Latin American politicians use them, the Israelis use them, even the Chinese use them, so why should the Ukrainian Liberation Front be any different?"

New York Times: "Vice President Wolfowitz has charged that Kronkol was picked by the CIA as the most rabid secessionist candidate they could find who knew how to sell himself on television. . . ."

President Carson: "That's a better description of Nathan Wolfowitz himself than it is of Vadim Kronkol."

(Laughter)

Atlanta Constitution: "But the Vice President also charges that it's all a CIA-run plot to break up the Soviet Union—"

President Carson: "The Vice President, as usual, is full of crap."

(Gasps)

Houston Post: "But you wouldn't be sorry to see the Soviet Union disintegrate, would you, Mr. President?"

President Carson: "Like the rest of the American people, I'd cry great big crocodile tears all the way to the bank."

(Laughter)

—Presidential Press Conference

X X I

As usual, Jerry Reed awoke long before the alarm went off. He crawled out of the grimy bedclothes, and, as was his habit, staggered naked to the bedroom window, parted the raggy curtains, and looked down into the courtyard.

Though it wasn't quite raining, the old gray stones were slick with moisture, and the small slice of sky visible beyond the rooftop across the court from this angle was gray and dirty in the wan early morning light. But nothing could dampen his enthusiasm for today's big event.

He stumbled over dirty laundry into the water closet, took a piss, then went into the living room, opened a window halfway, blinking himself fully awake in the cool blast of humid air, and forced himself to go through his daily exercise regime.

Twenty-five deep-knee bends with five-kilo weights in either hand. Fifty jumping jacks with the hand weights. Twenty-five sit-ups. Twenty-five push-ups. Ten minutes running in place with the weights.

One did not even pull 3 g's on a Concordski boost to orbit, and zero g did not exactly require the body of an athlete, but even though commercial flights took rich invalids to the Spaceville retirement modules every week, ESA still required a fairly high standard of fitness of its own space-certifiable personnel.

The official rationale was that ESA personnel had to be in shape to *work* when they got up out of the gravity well, and, unlike the invalids headed for Spaceville to spend the rest of their extended lives in zero g, had to be able to survive the transition back to leaden Earth-normal when they were finished.

Jerry suspected that it had more to do with maintaining the ancient outmoded tradition of physical machismo that had really meant something when cosmonauts and astronauts had ridden into the up-and-out atop huge brute-force booster rockets rather than anything currently pragmatic.

But those were the rules, and there was no arguing with them, and if all this daily grunting and panting and sweating was the price a middle-aged man had to pay to keep his ESA certificate, he would pay it willingly in the same grimly pragmatic spirit with which he had renounced his American citizenship for Common European nationality when it became clear that he would have to do so in order to get the position that made all this exercise necessary in the first place.

It had been a long hard grind, but in two weeks it would all be worth it. The dream of his lifetime would finally be realized. He would ride a Concordski up out of the gravity well into the Low Earth Orbit where the assembly of the first Grand Tour Navette was at last nearing completion. He would spend ten days aboard supervising the final installation of the maneuvering system, and then he would be there to monitor its performance on the shakedown cruise to the Moon and back.

It wouldn't be a long cruise—two and a half days to the Moon and two and a half days back. He wouldn't actually set foot on the lunar surface—the GTN would make two lunar orbits and then return. But he *would* at last float free of the constraints of gravity. And see the Earth entire from on high. And experience the cold unwinking brilliance of the firmament from beyond the haze of the atmosphere. And see the Moon itself from as close as two hundred kilometers.

"You can walk on water, kiddo," Rob Post had told him all those long years ago. "You'll have to give up everything else to do it, but you can walk on water."

Jerry believed in the truth of that now, more fully if more bitterly than he ever had before, but the thing of it was, he had finally learned, you had to be damned sure of precisely what you meant by "walking on water" first.

On that awful hung-over morning after his long drunken binge to mourn the death of his marriage, with Sonya gone, and the children continents and oceans away, and even the pathetic remnant of his career seemingly about to be taken away from him when the project's design phase ended, when, much against his will, everything else that he had ever lived for had indeed been stripped from him, the contrail of an ascending Concordski had written a clean message across the sky of Paris, a pure white line pointing with ballistic inevitability to where he belonged.

As he had sat there at a sidewalk café drinking his coffee and watching the Concordski dwindle, he had remembered at last what he *really* meant by walking on water. One way or another, he was going to get up there before he died.

The first order of business was to pull himself together. He cleaned the Cognac out of his apartment. He started working out. He refused to see Sonya and kept their phone conversations brief. He quite lost contact with Franja. He spoke to Robert on the phone occasionally, but kept his emotional distance. He ate, he slept, he worked out, he went to work. He spent his unwelcome idle hours reading science fiction and technical journals. His personal life became nonexistent.

It didn't matter. He was going to walk on water. He had already given up his country, his marriage, his family, and his project to do it, and he was more than willing to give up what little else remained to distract him from the purity of his obsession.

The second order of business was to somehow persuade Patrice Corneau to keep him on after the design phase ended. And if he had to give up what little was left of his pride to do it, he was ready now to do that too. He went to the project manager who had been his protégé and friend back when such things mattered and pleaded shamelessly for Corneau to find him something, anything.

"What do you have in mind, Jerry?" Patrice said when he was finished invoking past emotional debts and present open desperation. "You haven't had any hands-on experience in years and years, nor have you led an équipe. What am I supposed to do with you?"

"Come on, Patrice, I've got twenty years' experience, I

know this project inside out, surely you can find *something*," Jerry insisted.

Corneau sighed. "You are forcing me to be painfully blunt, Jerry . . . ," he said unhappily.

"Go ahead, Patrice, after what I've been through, I think I can take it."

Corneau shrugged. "You're a designer, a concept man, Jerry, and all that is about to be finished," he told him. "As a working engineer, you were merely competent, and your experience is years out of date—"

"Goddamn it, Patrice, it's my project you're managing, and you know it! What about something in your office, assistant manager, or something? Can't you create a position for me? I'm begging you, Patrice, and I admit it!"

"I'd like to, Jerry, but my hands are tied. You are simply politically unacceptable for anything on that level, and we both know it . . . unless . . ."

"Unless?"

"I hesitate to even mention this, but . . . Perhaps I could make you . . . Assistant Project Manager for Design Integration. . . ."

"What the hell is that?"

Corneau laughed. "Who knows?" he said. "Something to keep you on the project for old times' sake. We'd have to make it up as we went along. But . . . but you'd have to pay a heavy price."

"Name it!" Jerry declared.

Corneau would not quite meet his gaze. "You'd have to renounce your American citizenship and become a Common European national," he said uneasily. "That's the only way Emile and I could force the Russians to swallow it. They'd never accept anyone without Common European citizenship on an administrative level." He sighed. "Believe me, I would enjoy shoving this down Velnikov's throat!" He shrugged. "But after all these years, knowing how you feel . . ."

"I'll do it!" Jerry said immediately.

Corneau's eyes widened in amazement. *"Now?* After all these years? Merde, Jerry, if you had only done it in the first place!"

Boris Velnikov objected strenuously, but Emile Lourade backed up Corneau, and Patrice moved Jerry to an office adjoining his own, no bigger than his old one, but much closer to the action. Jerry really didn't have much to do except attend endless meetings and serve as Corneau's messenger boy.

The project manager found it quite useful to let his assistant project manager for design integration deliver his decisions when someone's toes were going to have to get stepped on. It allowed him to play Good Cop to Jerry's Bad, and Jerry, the Grand Old Man of the Grand Tour Navette to this generation of senior engineers who had been the last to remember what it was like to be out-of-favor Space Cadets, was just the figure to resolve disputes with minimum ill will.

Everyone knew that he had designed a whole alternate vehicle, working in isolation. Everyone knew he had been obsessed with the project before there *was* a project. Everyone also knew that he had neither a vested emotional interest in any subsystem design nor a political ax to grind. He was the ideal messenger, the one least likely to get his head chopped off for delivering bad news.

He was also an excellent club with which to batter down Velnikov when the chief project engineer began delivering his spirit messages from Moscow. When Patrice Corneau suspected he was going to hear something he didn't want to hear, he found ways to make himself unavailable, and Velnikov, much to his displeasure, found himself forced to communicate through Jerry.

Velnikov knew exactly what Corneau was doing, but he was stuck with it. Jerry tried to avoid rubbing it in as much as possible, rather than further antagonizing someone who had already proven to be enough of an obstacle.

Patrice Corneau had cunningly set things up so that they could not afford to be enemies. And if their relationship was cold to say the least, at least it became more or less civilized.

Still, Jerry was quite amazed when Boris Velnikov actually suggested that they have a drink or two together after a late afternoon meeting. Utterly bemused, he let Velnikov pile him into a cab and take him to Les Deux Magots, the historic old café on St.-Germain across from the church itself, the legendary haunt of long-gone superstar intellectuals, preserved in amber for the delectation of intellectual tourists, at outrageous prices, for about a hundred years.

Velnikov sat them down at an inside table, ordered Cognacs, and came right to the point. "We have never exactly approved of each other, Reed, but big changes are coming at ESA, and it occurs to me that our mutual interests might best be served by an alliance of convenience. We don't have to like each other to serve our own class self-interests."

"Spare me the dialectical materialism, will you, Boris?" Jerry said. Although Velnikov always called him "Reed," Jerry took a perverse pleasure in calling him "Boris" as if that was his natural bureaucratic privilege as Corneau's assistant.

Velnikov allowed himself a scowl, nothing more. He was a thickset balding man who wore artfully cut loose suits that managed to make him look powerful rather than corpulent, the archetypal boss, and when he scowled like this, it was usually the prelude to an attempted browbeating.

But not this time. "My contacts in Moscow tell me that Emile Lourade is soon to become Common European Minister of Technological Development," he said in a rather strangely conspiratorial tone.

If Jerry was supposed to be impressed by this inside information, he wasn't about to show it. "What's that got to do with our mutual interests?" he said diffidently.

"Corneau is almost certain to be named Director to replace him," Velnikov said, and that did give Jerry pause. Who would replace Patrice as project manager when he moved up? How long could he expect to remain "Assistant Project Manager for Design Integration" when that fancy title was just a bureaucratic euphemism for his personal relationship with Corneau?

Velnikov, of course, had no trouble reading the obvious in his mind. He smiled grimly. He nodded. "Yes, the whole Agency is going to be thrown into a state of flux, Reed. You have much to lose, and I have much to gain."

"How nice for you, Boris," Jerry said dryly. He frowned in some confusion. "It's all too obvious what I have to lose," he said, "but what do you think you have to gain?"

"I intend to replace Corneau as project manager," Velnikov said.

Jerry took a sip of Cognac and swallowed hard at the thought of that. If Velnikov became project manager, Jerry's ass was already out the door. What was the bastard trying to tell him?

"I can see that you do not find the prospect pleasing," Velnikov told him with a hideous smile.

"They'll never allow a Soviet project manager, and you know it, Boris."

"I want the job very badly, Reed," Velnikov declared with a force that bordered on anger.

"I wanted it too once, Boris," Jerry told him. "You'll pardon me if I don't get too upset to see you standing in my shoes for a change."

But Velnikov held himself under tight control. "Point taken, Reed," he acknowledged, rather manfully, Jerry was forced to admit. "But that is the past. The question is, what do you want now?"

"What do you care what *I* want?"

"Because I'm prepared to give it to you in return for services rendered," Velnikov said. "You're close to Corneau. When the time comes to recommend a successor, he'll talk it over with you. . . ."

"And you actually expect me to put in a good word for *you*, Boris?" Jerry exclaimed in amazement.

"Yes," Velnikov said blandly.

"Why the hell would I do that?"

"Tell me what you really want, Reed, and I'll tell you why I know you'll do whatever you can to help me become project manager."

"You're really serious about this, aren't you?"

Velnikov just nodded briefly.

"I want to go up there, Boris," Jerry told him. "I want to get at least as far as GEO. I want to see Spaceville floating out there in the darkness. I want to see the Earth from space. I want to feel it, I want to be there, I want a ride in my own creation."

Velnikov cocked his head to one side and stared at Jerry narrowly. "That's really all you want?" he said distrustfully. "You do not demand a higher executive position? You do not even require that you retain your present one?"

"Politique politicienne," Jerry said scornfully. "Shit for the birds. You want my help, you get me up there. Nothing more, nothing less."

Velnikov studied him silently for a long moment. "I believe you, Reed," he finally said. "I do not understand you, but I believe you. Very well, I make to you this promise. When I become project manager, I will quite literally give you the Moon."

"The Moon . . . ," Jerry said softly. "What do you mean, the Moon?"

Velnikov smiled a vast smug smile. "If you are serious about what you say, it will not be so difficult," he said. "Not if you are really willing to take a demotion to get there, all the way down to chief propulsion and maneuvering system engineer."

"Subsystem engineer!" Jerry exclaimed. What irony! The very position that Velnikov had kept him from having all these years! The very reason that he had had to con Patrice into creating this phony job for him in the first place!

But this time Boris Velnikov seemed to have misread him entirely. "Yes, I know, it seems unthinkable, but the position *would* require you to supervise the system integration on the prototype in orbit and monitor it during the shakedown cruise," he said. "And current thinking is to create a big splash by taking the GTN as far as lunar orbit. You can't expect to stay part of management, there won't be anyone aboard except operational personnel."

"How do I know that I can trust you?" Jerry said. "We've been, well, enemies so long. . . ."

"I've never been your enemy, Reed."

"Oh come on, Boris!"

"No, it's true. I've certainly never liked you, and I've never trusted you, and you've been a thorn in my side, but I've never blocked you from anything out of personal pique. Everything I've done was done for sound policy reasons, and believe me, not always policies set on my level. I've taken no particular pleasure in it. You've been a security risk and a political embarrassment, but now the situation has changed, and we can be useful to each other. Our self-interests are no longer in conflict, it's as simple as that."

"Simple to you, maybe . . . ," Jerry muttered.

"Oh come on, Reed, what do you have to lose, after all?"

Nothing I haven't lost already, Jerry was forced to realize.

"Okay, Boris," he said, "so *if* you make project manager, I'll take the job. But beyond that, I don't promise anything."

Velnikov sipped at his Cognac. "You don't have to, Reed," he said. "It's merely a matter of following your own enlightened self-interest. That's the reason we can trust each other—precisely because we don't have to."

Jerry clinked glasses with the Russian. "You know, Boris," he said, "for once I think I know just what you mean."

And by the time Patrice Corneau finally called Jerry into
his office to tell him the inevitable, Jerry had just about
decided to play Velnikov's game. It was, after all, from his
point of view, the only game in town.

After the congratulations were over, Patrice leaned back
in his chair and smiled. "Of course, as Director of ESA, I
have to appoint a new project manager for the Grand Tour
Navette, subject of course to the usual review process," he
said. "I'm in a bit of a quandary. The logical choice, in terms
of the project, is, I'm afraid, going to be rather hard to make
the politicians swallow. What do you think, Jerry, should I
have a go at what might be a futile gesture, or play it safe
and nominate someone like Clark or Steinholz?"

"This may sound strange coming from me, Patrice," Jerry
told him, "but I think you *should* go ahead and try to appoint Velnikov."

"*Velnikov!*" Corneau exclaimed. "I'm not talking about
Velnikov, I'm talking about you!"

"Me?" Jerry stammered.

"You've often enough said that you should have had the
job instead of me, and I've agreed from the beginning, as
you well know," Corneau said. "No one knows the project
better. You've been right in the middle of everything as my
assistant. The engineering staff respects you. It could be
good pub. Rationally speaking, there isn't any other logical
choice. Don't you agree?"

"Of course I agree!" Jerry exclaimed in an utter daze.
"But . . . but . . ."

Jerry's brain was reeling. He found himself struggling for
psychic purchase. "My God, Patrice," he said, "after all
that's happened, what makes you think you can get away
with appointing me?"

Corneau leaned forward and stared into Jerry's eyes with
the strangest expression. "I have a *chance* of getting away
with appointing you now, Jerry," he said. "You've taken
Common European citizenship, and that helps. You've been
functioning more or less as my deputy. How *much* of a
chance?" He shrugged. "That is certainly one of the im-
ponderables. Perhaps only a slight chance. But the good of
the project and simple justice points right at you, old friend.
I may very well fail. You may be publicly embarrassed.
That's why I'm leaving it up to you, Jerry. What do you say,
should I go ahead and try?"

"But . . . but Velnikov—"

"Wants very much to be project manager, oh yes, I know," Corneau said, leaning forward now and frowning. "And Moscow wants very much to foist him on us. But a Russian project manager would be unacceptable to Strasbourg."

"And you think there's a chance in the world that the *Russians* would accept *me!*"

"They just might if Velnikov became Deputy Director of ESA as a quid pro quo," Corneau said. "They'd have their man higher placed than expected, and as my deputy, the bastard would be effectively out of the operational circuit."

Patrice smiled at him. "Well, Jerry, one old Space Cadet to another, do I go ahead and try?" he said. "What do you say?"

What did he say? Jerry didn't even know what to think.

Wasn't Velnikov's offer what he really wanted? Hadn't he long since decided what he really meant by walking on water? Hadn't he given up everything else for it already? Should he really throw away all that for what was likely to turn out to be Patrice Corneau's futile gesture?

Round and round it went in his head, and it did not revolve smoothly. There was a missing piece in all this, he didn't know what it was, but he could feel it grinding painfully in his brain like a gear train with a missing tooth on a cogwheel. Something here just did not compute.

"I don't know what to say, Patrice," he finally said cautiously. "This is such a shock. . . . You've got to give me time to think. . . ."

"Naturellement," Corneau said. "But unfortunately, we're on a tight timetable. In order to prevent confusion and weeks of political infighting, it has been decided to announce all three appointments simultaneously—Emile as Minister of Technological Development, me to replace him as Director, and a project manager to replace *me.* So nothing happens until we have a project manager to announce. I can let you sleep on it for two days, Jerry, but I'm afraid you'll have to give me your answer before the weekend."

Jerry staggered out of the project manager's office and went straight home even though it was only four o'clock. He needed to be alone to think. But after hours of sitting on the hard black leather couch in his disheveled little living room, staring into space, he was as confused as ever.

Or worse. He had the eerie feeling that there was something lurking beneath the surface of all this that he didn't
understand. That perhaps he was simply unequipped to understand. Something churning around like a hidden serpent
deep within the bowels of the deepest dirtiest levels of what
he had always scorned as politique politicienne.

He desperately needed to talk this over with someone
who understood these dirty bureaucratic games, someone
who could tell him whatever it was that he sensed Corneau
would not.

Velnikov? He was certainly a bureaucratic weasel, and he
certainly had deep connections in Moscow. But of course he
couldn't talk to *Velnikov* about any of this!

He knew only one person in the world whom he could
turn to for useful help now.

She had spent her whole life playing bureaucratic hard-
ball. The Golden Boy was at least as well connected as
Velnikov, and Red Star had real clout in Strasbourg too.

And she owed it to him, didn't she? She owed him more
than she could ever pay. She owed him his life back at the
very least.

But how could he call Sonya? He hadn't seen her in over
a year. He hadn't spoken to her on the phone for something
like six months. And for over three years, their occasional
phone conversations had been painful, and businesslike, and
coldly brief. How could he face ripping open that deep
old wound by crying out for her help now?

You'll have to give up everything else to do it. . . .

Everything?

Even this?

Even this, kiddo, Rob Post's voice seemed to whisper in-
sinuatingly in his ear.

He poured himself a small Cognac, slugged it down,
poured himself another, and without letting himself think
any further about what he was doing, he sat down in the
armchair in the videotel camera's field of vision and
punched in the number of the apartment on Avenue
Trudaine.

Sonya answered on the third ring. She was close to the
camera. All he could see was her head and the collar of a
plain white shirt. She looked older than he seemed to remember, it had been a year, but had she really looked as old
as this? There were lines in her face where he had thought it

would be smooth, and something different about the set of her mouth, and a severity to the ear-length cut of her hair. And her eyes seemed so world-weary and cynical.

He tried not to think about what *his* videotel camera must be showing *her*.

"Hello, Jerry," she said, allowing only her raised eyebrows to show surprise.

"Hello, Sonya," Jerry stammered. "Uh . . . how've you been doing?"

"Surviving," she said coolly. "And you?"

"I need your advice, Sonya," Jerry blurted. And, having spat it out and gotten directly to the point, "You owe me that much."

"Of course I do," she said with unexpected tenderness. "It was never my idea to drift apart."

It was never my *idea to divorce you!* Jerry was about to snap back. *Screwing Pashikov was never my idea either!*

But the face on the screen had softened and let a sadness show through, and his heart would not let him say what his mind told him was presently entirely beside the point.

"It wasn't either of our ideas, was it, Sonya?" he said instead. "Our lives just got ground up in the political machinery. There's no point in blaming each other for it now, is there."

"I'm glad you've finally come to that sad wisdom, Jerry," Sonya said, and the professional bureaucrat's mask went back up. "So tell me your problem, and I'll gladly do whatever I can to help you."

Perhaps that was for the best. At any rate, he found himself pouring out the story, not so much to the memory of his wife as to the mature detached professional bureaucrat on the screen, to the Director of the economic strategy department of the Paris office of Red Star, S.A.

Sonya's face didn't show anything as he told her of his cynical deal with Boris Velnikov, nor did she react to the news that Emile Lourade was becoming a Minister and Patrice Corneau was moving up to ESA Director. In her position, she probably had known it was coming before he had. But when he told her that Corneau had offered to put him up for project manager, her mouth fell open, and by the time he had finished, she was shaking with rage for some unfathomable reason.

"That's loathsome!" she declared, her nose puckered up in an apparently sincere expression of disgust.

"Loathsome?" Jerry exclaimed. "What's loathsome about trying to do the right thing?"

"Merde, Jerry, how can you be so naive? Patrice Corneau knows damn well he has absolutely no chance of being allowed to appoint you project manager! Don't you see what's really behind this?"

"No, I don't," Jerry said simply, "That's why I had to call you."

"Corneau is *using* you, Jerry," Sonya said with angry passion. "Moscow badly wants Velnikov as project manager, and we have enough clout to veto whoever they put up until they break down and capitulate to end the deadlock. Our negotiators still come equipped with a good set of iron underpants. But if Corneau nominates you and refuses to put up anyone else until we withdraw Velnikov, it will be a clear signal that they're serious, that the deadlock can only end with the appointment of a compromise. Once that happens, you may be sure that Moscow will demand your head on a platter for serving as Corneau's dupe, and he'll give it to them."

Laid out as nakedly and angrily as all that, it had the instant ring of the disgusting bureaucratic truth. It was also, upon the briefest reflection, the only theory that accommodated all of the data.

"It's fuck-your-buddy time, isn't it?" he said.

"It's always fuck-your-buddy time, Jerry, when are you going to face up to that? It's the second law of bureaucracy."

"Well, what the hell am I supposed to do?"

"Apply the first law of bureaucracy," Sonya told him, "cover your ass."

"How am I supposed to do that?"

Sonya's face hardened, and when she spoke, it was the middle-aged survivor of the bureaucratic wars speaking, not his angry ex-wife, or the girl he had been enthralled by, or even the woman who had walked out on him to save her Party card.

"Give Corneau what he so richly deserves. Give Moscow what it wants."

"What?"

"Let Corneau propose you for project manager. Let the

process become good and deadlocked. Then you step aside
in favor of Velnikov, in the interests of the project, European solidarity, world peace, and humanity's future in
space; don't worry, Tass will write a stirring speech for the
press release. They'll have no choice, not when the Godfather of the Grand Tour Navette magnanimously steps aside
and kisses Velnikov publicly on both cheeks."

Jerry goggled at the hard-eyed mature woman on the
screen. Was the woman he had married really capable of
this?

Was he?

"And why should Velnikov live up to his end of the bargain?" Jerry said, realizing as he said it that he had made
the moral decision already.

"Because, despite what you think, Russians are not unprincipled swine whose word of honor is worthless!" Sonya
snapped at him. Then, more coldly: "Besides which, Red
Star will see to it that promises are kept. When the time
comes for you to withdraw in favor of Velnikov, you will
approach Moscow through Red Star, through me, they'll
certainly find that credible enough. And Ilya will transmit
your offer directly to the Red Star Tower. And the Director
General of Red Star himself will call President Gorchenko,
who will order Tass to set up the public announcement. And
all along the line, everyone will know what Velnikov promised you. Your ass will be plated with bureaucratic gold,
Jerry. No one is going to sour such a triumph for Red Star
on that level with a cheap double-cross if we have anything
to say about it, and after we, not any government or Party
apparatus, deliver Velnikov as project manager, believe me,
we will!"

"And the Golden Boy will come out looking even more
golden, won't he?" Jerry muttered. And instantly regretted
it. Sonya's face seemed to grimace for just an instant, as if it
was merely a glitch in the transmission, her eyes flared angrily at him for a longer moment, and then her expression
became more distant, somehow, not so much cold as
strangely wooden.

"His standing will certainly not be diminished," she said
evenly.

"And neither will yours, will it?" said Jerry. "You two are
still . . . a team, aren't you?"

"In a manner of speaking," Sonya said tonelessly.

"What do you mean by that?"

"Let's not get into that," Sonya said wearily. "Can't we just try and be friends?"

"I don't think I can really be your friend after all that's happened, Sonya," Jerry told her. But he did let it be.

"I want to be your friend, Jerry, if you'll let me," Sonya said. "You came to me for help, remember . . . ? So at least let me give it to you. Don't trust Patrice Corneau. Trust me."

Jerry sighed. "I guess I really have no other choice," he admitted. "But it certainly feels strange climbing into bed with all these goddamn Russians. . . ."

And then he nearly bit his tongue off when he saw the look on her face. Her mouth twisted into a snarl even as tears welled up in her eyes.

"I'm sorry, Sonya, it just came out."

"I'm sorry too, Jerry, I'm sorry for a lot of things. So if we can't really be friends, then just let me be your ally in this, okay?"

"Okay, Sonya," Jerry said. He stared at her image on the screen trying to think of something else to say, anything to end the conversation on anything but this oh-so-civilized level. But nothing would come.

Sonya stared back at him apparently just as blankly. "I'll stay in touch, Jerry," she finally said lamely.

"Yeah, you do that," Jerry said, and they broke the connection.

Afterward, Jerry had just sat there in his tiny living room for a long while, staring at the dead screen, at the piles of journals spilling off the coffee table, at the science-fiction novels overflowing the bookcases and mounding up against the walls, at the clutter of chips and printouts surrounding the computer station, at the dust and the dirty glasses, at the physical evidence of what his life alone had become.

Somehow, something had made him clean up the entire apartment before collapsing that night, piling up the books and magazines as neatly as possible, straightening up the computer stand, changing the linen for the first time in two weeks, washing the mounds of dirty dishes, scrubbing the sink and stove, even making a pass at the bathtub and the toilet bowl.

That had been a long, long time ago, and he had never done anything like it since, but from that day on, he had never let things devolve to the point they had reached before. The living room had pretty much reverted to its primitive state, and the bedroom still had its pile of laundry, and the bedclothes were usually stale, but now, on the morning of the final static firing tests, the kitchen was at least bearable when he turned on the coffee machine, and the bathtub was more or less clean when he showered off the sweat of his workout.

The shaving mirror was more or less clean too, and the face in it, though the hair was now streaked with gray, and the skin a bit more than finely wrinkled, and the eyes hollowed by incipient bags, looked somehow younger today than it had before that call to Sonya, before Velnikov became project manager, before he became chief propulsion and maneuvering system engineer, before he had been able to look forward with concrete assurance to riding his Grand Tour Navette to the Moon. Older in years, in wrinkles, bags, gray hair, salt-and-pepper stubble, it was younger around the eyes and mouth, hopeful, and almost relaxed where it had been tense with frustration and bitter with ancient defeats.

By the time he had finished shaving and dressing, the coffee was ready, and he took a big mugful into the living room along with a somewhat stale pain au chocolat, and had his quick petit déjeuner sitting on the couch and thinking about today's test.

The main engines were already certified and waiting on the pad atop a dumb freight rocket for tomorrow's boost to orbit. All that was left was routine static firing of assorted maneuvering system rockets, certainly nothing exciting in and of itself.

But then, once the rockets were certified, they would be taken down, and crated, and flown to Tyuratam, and boosted into orbit, and that would be the end of his work on the ground. Next stop—orbit, assembly, and then the Moon.

What his life would be like after his fifteen days in space was something he hadn't really thought about until now. What do you do after you've finally walked on water? He was too old to seriously hope for any crew position when the fleet of Grand Tour Navettes became operational, too old to dream of exploring Mars, unqualified for anything in the bases on the Moon.

But after he had stepped aside for Boris Velnikov, things

had changed for him at ESA. Patrice Corneau might have become distant and cold and certainly no longer his patron as Director of the Agency, but much to his ironic bemusement, Jerry had become rather the pet of the Russians.

Velnikov had not only delivered as promised, he had actually managed to get Jerry a raise. It would seem that Velnikov's friends back in Moscow had never informed him that Jerry's move had been concocted by Sonya and Ilya Pashikov in the Paris office of Red Star. They hadn't even prepared him for the Tass announcement. The morning after it had all broken in the press, Velnikov had showed up in Jerry's office with a rather dazed expression on his face and a bottle gift-wrapped in gold foil.

"I don't know what to say, Reed . . . *Jerry,* if I may," he said. "I must admit that I feel like a bit of a fool . . . all these years· . . ." He shrugged bearishly and slapped the bottle down on Jerry's desk. "Here," he said, "a poor gesture, perhaps, but . . ."

Jerry unwrapped a fifth of brown liquor with a fancy label lettered in elaborate Cyrillic and festooned with gold and silver medallions.

"Genuine Russian potato vodka," Velnikov told him. "Produced for export. One hundred proof and aged in Cognac casks for seven years. I have it on reliable authority that it is the best vodka in the world."

"Thank you, Boris," Jerry said, quite touched despite his cynical knowledge, for it was plain that Velnikov's emotion was innocently genuine.

"Thank *you,* Jerry," Velnikov said. "To tell you the truth, I still find it hard to believe what you've done for me. We were never exactly friends."

"And I was never exactly going to be project manager, we both know that," Jerry told him honestly.

"But neither was I, or so I had thought until yesterday. They were using each of us to block the other." Velnikov hesitated, studied Jerry's face for a moment. "Would you mind telling me why you *really* stepped aside for me?"

"We had a deal, Boris, remember?"

"Of course! And you may be sure that I will live up to my end of the bargain! But still . . ."

"You wanted something, and I wanted something, Boris," Jerry said, "and when I was forced to really look at it, I realized that I didn't want to give up what I wanted to get what you wanted for yourself. So partly it was just a smart tactical move. But . . . well, the way the bastards had things set up, we were both going to get screwed. And whether I liked you or not, I could see that when it came to what that felt like, we were really standing in each other's shoes. Know your enemy, right? But when you really do, well . . ."

"It's hard to stay enemies, yes," Velnikov said. "May I?" he said, reaching for the bottle. "Shall we?"

Jerry had nodded, and Velnikov opened the vodka, and they shared a drink of the smooth, pungent, powerful stuff out of plastic coffee cups.

"What you have done is going to put you in a certain disfavor with Agency circles answerable to Strasbourg," Velnikov had told him afterward. "They won't be able to do anything overt, of course, but it will be there. So I want you to know that circles answerable to Moscow will see to it that you still have a future with the Agency after the Grand Tour Navettes become operational. I've cost you the patronage of Corneau, but for what it's worth, I want you to know that you'll always have mine."

And Velnikov had been true to his word. He had appointed Jerry chief propulsion and maneuvering system engineer and appointed a Russian manager over him named Igor Kalitski who was young, and eager, and deferential, and whose concept of his job was to keep paperwork and bureaucrats away from Jerry Reed and let him get on with the real work.

Lately Boris had intimated that Jerry could be promoted up to Kalitski's job when he came back from the shakedown cruise; the section would still be active until the whole fleet was operational, and by that time, perhaps, ESA would be ready for a Russian Director, namely himself, and Jerry could finish his career as Deputy Director of the European Space Agency in the best of all possible worlds.

Jerry finished his coffee and left the apartment without bothering to put the empty mug in the sink. Was that what he wanted? To become a sub–project manager and then Deputy Director? They'd never make him Director after what he had done, but it would certainly be a decent capstone to his career.

For some strange reason, a frisson of depression flashed through him as he descended the stairs, a shadow of gloom entirely inappropriate to this day of all days. For the first time in years and years, the future ahead of him seemed empty somehow, occluded, unfocused, and thoughts were leaking in around the edges of his mind that he fought to push back.

But the sun was actually starting to break through the overcast when Jerry reached the street. People were bustling along the narrow sidewalks of the Quai de Bourbon toward the Pont St.-Louis and the St.-Michel RER station. A hydrofoil bus cleaved the river with twin white contrails, heading east toward the Porte de Bercy. The morning traffic jam on the Quai de la Tournelle had already built up by the time Jerry reached the Left Bank. Horns honked, pedestrians jabbered, cabdrivers cursed, dogs shat on the sidewalk, and Jerry found himself absorbed into the energy of the dawning day.

Worries about what his life would be like after his ride to the Moon seemed meaningless and far away, an artifact, no doubt, of the gray beginning to what was turning into a sunny day.

After all, he told himself, if what everything he had been told and had read was true, the man who went up would not be the man who came down.

The RER, of course, was jammed, but it was only a short ride to the Gare du Nord to catch the new express line to the ESA complex at Le Bourget, and the train was always mostly empty out of Paris in the morning, going against the commuter tide into the city from the banlieue.

At first, Jerry endured the crush in good humor. Soon enough, he would be up out of the smell, and the noise, and the Earthbound press of bodies, and the bonds of gravity itself, up there where it was cool, and clear, and clean, and the starry brilliance went on forever.

Afterward, well . . .

It didn't bear thinking about right now.

But standing there in the packed RER car with bodies pressed all around him, Jerry suddenly found himself thinking about it anyway. Maybe it was the odor of massed humanity. Maybe it was the press of the flesh. Maybe it was the young lovers kissing passionately in the middle of it all and who gave a damn. Maybe it was all he had given up to walk on water crowding suddenly in on him, now that he was about to actually do it, now that the countdown to the moment he had always dreamed of had really started, now that the fulfillment of a lifetime's obsession was only two weeks away.

"You're a real space cadet," Bob had told him. "You ought to be a citizen of Mars."

And that was what he suddenly felt like, right there in the RER, pressed up against the bodies of these strangers, like a Man from Mars. He suddenly felt his own weirdness. The years of friendless celibacy. The obsessiveness of his existence. The vast distance between what he had willed himself to become and the ordinary humans, with their ordinary loves, and lives, and children, pressed against him in this RER car.

A chill went through him. The truth of it was that he had turned himself into a creature with no personal life at all. Politics had taken his son away from him and caused him to disown his own daughter and destroyed his marriage. And he had done the rest.

Oh yes he had! Hadn't Sonya asked to be his friend on the night she had given him back his life, *this* life, that in some deep way, he could now not keep from knowing, was rushing blindly toward its triumphant conclusion? And hadn't he turned her down? Why had he done that? Why had he still insisted on keeping all contact between them to the barest minimum? Why hadn't he even accepted her offer to celebrate together at a neutral restaurant when their scheme had succeeded? Why wouldn't he see her even now, after the Golden Boy had finally been promoted back to Moscow and out of their lives?

Why was he thinking these grim thoughts now, of all times, riding the damned RER toward his last Earthbound task before leaving all this stuff far, far behind him?

What was he suddenly so afraid of?

He had given up everything to walk on water. He had turned himself into a Man from Mars.

What do you do *after* you've walked on water?

Rob Post hadn't told him the answer to that one.

But he was going to find out.

As surely as what went up sooner or later had to come down.

Art Collins: "But when you come right down to it, Mr. Vice President, who gives a damn? Wouldn't it be a good thing if the Ukraine secedes from the Soviet Union? Wouldn't other captive peoples be encouraged to do the same thing? Wouldn't every American like to see the Soviet Union fall apart and maybe take Common Europe with it?"

Vice President Wolfowitz: "I certainly wouldn't."

Art Collins: "Why not? Wouldn't it mean the new access to the world's largest export market that we so desperately need? Wouldn't it make America the world's number one economic power again?"

Vice President Wolfowitz: "Like the rest of the country, Art, you've been listening to too many speeches by our pinheaded Commander in Chief, and the only bottom line Harry Carson understands is the one he hangs his dirty laundry on. What about the trillions and trillions of dollars we've stiffed them for? Oh, yeah, all we have to do to convince them to welcome us with open arms is use our media muscle to destroy the economic and political structure they've spent decades building!"

Art Collins: "President Carson believes—"

Vice President Wolfowitz: "Harry Carson is a schmuck."

Art Collins: "That's pretty strong language!"

Vice President Wolfowitz: "If it talks like a schmuck, runs the country like a schmuck, and surrounds itself with other schmucks, it probably *is* a schmuck, even if it wasn't cruising this poor screwed-up country for another international bruising like the biggest schmuck of all."

—*Newspeak*, with Art Collins

XXII

It was going to be a busy day as usual for the Director of Red Star's Paris office.

In the morning, there would be the usual briefing from the economic strategy department, plus the monthly cash-flow report to approve before transmittal to the Red Star Tower, and then she would have to deal with the matter of the failure of the chromium shipment to arrive in Lyon on time. Over lunch and no doubt a healthy sample of the product, she would have to haggle with the President of the Bordeaux Wine Merchants' Association over the ridiculous prices they were demanding for what inside information said was a mediocre year. In the afternoon, there would be the matter of the Crimean oranges, the transmission deal with Renault, the purchase of Midi Hydrofoil, and the fusion torch co-development deal with the French and the British, which was still hung up over the budgetary split. On top of that, she would have to fit in an essentially pointless meeting with the visiting producer from Sovfilm who had the ridiculous notion that it was her job to get him major French distribution for some big-budget epic about the Spanish Conquest of Mexico that they had shot in Uzbekistan on German money with a cast of Tartars and Italians.

Still, as she sat in her big corner office sipping a cup of coffee as she contemplated the day to come, Sonya Ivanovna Gagarin found herself thinking of Jerry.

She hadn't given much thought to her ex-husband since she had maneuvered his appointment as chief propulsion and maneuvering systems engineer on the Grand Tour Navette. That had been the true divorce settlement, the discharge of her debt to him, and her final freedom from the years of pain and guilt.

The divorce had been merely a pragmatic necessity, or so she had put it to him at the time, a mere legalism; their relationship could continue, eventually they could even live together again, it would be a divorce in name only.

What *had* she been thinking?

In fact, of course, their *marriage* had been what had long since come to exist in name only. What a phantasm it had been to suppose that they could maintain a friendly relationship after the divorce, let alone remain lovers!

Had her affair with Ilya Pashikov been cause or effect of the estrangement between her and Jerry? A natural outcome of an intimate working relationship with an attractive man whom she really had more in common with than her bitter space-obsessed husband? Or a tawdry seeking after what she had stopped getting at home?

The thought that *she* had divorced *him* after what he had endured to preserve what was left of their marriage filled her with self-loathing.

Perhaps that was why she had tried to convince herself that she really was in love with Ilya. On some level, it made what she had done seem less cold-blooded. If she could convince herself that she had been in love with Ilya all along, that Ligatski's blackmail had simply provided her heart with a convenient excuse to follow its own dictates, it would ease the guilt that tormented her.

Then too, she had found herself living alone for the first time in over twenty years, rattling around in the big empty apartment where she had raised a family. Jerry might not have been much of a companion for a long time, but at least he had been a human being to come home to.

So what had been for so long a matter of casual and occasional after-work sex became, at least on Sonya's part, the beginning of a potential relationship. She was now a free woman, after all, and Jerry refused to have anything to do with her. And Ilya Pashikov had always been a free man. And now that Ilya had become Director of the Paris office and she had become Director of the economic strategy department, and their working relationship had become less full-time and intimate, were they not freer, somehow, to pursue their affair of the heart?

Ilya, at least at first, had been everything a friend and lover should be. He took her to dinner three or four nights a week. They spent the night together in each other's apartments on a more or less regular basis. There were weekend trips to London and Rome and the Midi. Ilya was a better lover than Jerry had ever been. Ilya was a sophisticated man of the world. Ilya was someone she never grew tired of talking with.

But Ilya was . . . *Ilya*.

He was theatrically handsome, a dashing dresser, and younger than she was. Women couldn't keep their eyes or their hands off of him, and he was hardly the sort to dissuade them. Ilya was ambitious, he dreamed of being Director of Red Star itself someday, and sooner or later that meant promotion back to the Red Star Tower in Moscow. For these reasons, and no doubt more, Ilya Pashikov had always steered well clear of monogamous relationships, serial or otherwise.

In retrospect, what was amazing was not that Sonya failed in the end to make this beautiful leopard change his spots, but that Ilya remained more or less loyal to her for the better part of six months, at least as far as she cared to let herself know, out of friendship.

Indeed it was Sonya herself who unwittingly forced him to disabuse her of her illusions.

They had taken a TGV to Amsterdam for the weekend and rented a two-room suite atop a small hotel overlooking a canal. The suite was done up more like a little apartment than a set of hotel rooms. The bed, with its gaudily quilted comforter, was a weathered old walnut antique, and there were nightstands and a wardrobe to match, along with scattered bric-a-brac and an oil painting of a windmill. The sitting room had an overstuffed couch and armchair, a fireplace, a small set of chairs and table out of somebody's grandmother's kitchen, a set of Delft china locked behind the glass of a breakfront, and a bookcase filled with crumbling old volumes in Dutch and English.

It all seemed so cozily romantic in a homey sort of way as they sat there at the kitchen table sipping Genever and gazing idly out at the crazily leaning narrow buildings across the canal like an old married couple. It reminded Sonya of the early days with Jerry in their old apartment on the Île St.-Louis; not the place, and not the man, she told herself, but the feeling. A feeling of really belonging somewhere with someone that she had not felt for a long, long time, that she had thought was quite gone from her world.

"Have you ever thought about making a life with someone, Ilya?" she mused somewhat woozily. "Settling down? Getting cozy? Even getting married?"

Ilya froze in mid-sip with the expression of someone who had just discovered the hard way that his glass was filled with piss. He looked across the table at her and shook his head slowly, then forced a smile.

"Merde, no!" he said lightly. "What a disaster I'd be as a husband!"

"Not with the right woman," Sonya told him. "You're kind, you're sensitive, you're—"

"A hopeless philanderer, and we both know it!" Ilya declared. "And what is more, I enjoy it. Then too, I am a good Communist. From me according to my ability, which has not failed me yet, to the women of the world according to their need, which is boundless!"

"Oh, Ilya, you're not really the shallow creature you pretend to be!"

"Oh yes I am!" he insisted. "Believe me, Sonya, I'm just another pretty face."

"You haven't been that way with me," Sonya said. "You've been kind and understanding and gentle, and you've helped me through a bad period like a true friend. You've been a prince."

Ilya rolled his eyes upward, still trying to make light of everything in his usual manner. "First you accuse me of being husband material, now I'm a Czarist reactionary!" he said in a tone of forced gaiety. "Next thing I know, you'll be down on your knees with a ring and a rose proposing marriage!"

"Would that be so bad?" Sonya said softly.

Now Ilya's expression finally did become serious, somber even. "You're serious . . . ?" he said.

"I could be if you wanted me to be," Sonya said truthfully.

Ilya sighed. "You are forcing me to be serious with you, Sonya," he said, "and it's entirely out of character. Why, after all, do you suppose I'm such a philanderer in the first place?"

"Because you're constantly tempted?" Sonya suggested.

"Because despite all appearances, I do not wish to be a swine. I do not wish to create illusions that are doomed to be shattered. I am not out to break hearts."

"You could have fooled me," Sonya said dryly, beginning to sense that she had pushed something too far, and trying to lighten up.

But Ilya's mood had changed. He had become deadly earnest, maudlin even. Suddenly he looked ten years older, which was to say for the first time he really looked his own age.

"I'm a careerist, Sonya, and I freely admit it," he said. "I am determined to become Director of Red Star, and who

knows what after that. Which means that I will go where
Red Star posts me. Which means that any wife of mine
would have to trail along behind me like the good little
victim of Slavic phallocracy. And such a woman I could
never respect. So if I am to be true to myself and not become a domestic tyrant, I must go through life alone and
console myself with the abundance of feminine distractions
that the luck of my genes has fortunately provided me
with."

"And when you are old and gray . . . ?" Sonya said
softly. It all sounded so sad.

"When I am old and gray, I will content myself with old
gray women, no doubt," Ilya said.

"Like me?" Sonya blurted. "Widows and spinsters and
lonely divorcées?"

"You are neither old nor gray, Sonya," Ilya said, reaching
out to take her hand. "You are a comrade and a colleague
and a friend. And you are more like me than you care to
admit. You are precisely the kind of woman I would want to
spend my life with. And precisely the kind of woman I dare
not seek to have."

"I don't understand. . . ."

"Oh yes you do!" Ilya said knowingly. "You're a careerist
just like me. If you weren't, you'd still be married to Jerry
Reed. If tomorrow I were posted to Moscow and asked you
to come back with me and be my bride, would you give up
your life in Paris and your career to be at my side?"

Sonya could not meet his eyes.

Ilya patted her hand. "We are birds of a feather," he told
her. "That is why we are true friends. That is also why a
marriage or an exclusive liaison between us would be a disaster. Sooner or later we would have to part or crush each
other's spirits. Or both."

"Oh, Ilya . . . ," Sonya moaned miserably.

"Oh, Sonya!" Ilya cried, visibly forcing himself back into
character by an act of will. "It is stupid to be sad! For now,
we have a true friendship, and we enjoy each other in bed.
Is it really such a sad thing to have a true comrade to fuck?
How many people do not even have that? Come on, ma
chère, we're just two lugubrious old Slavs who have had too
much to drink, let's just forget this maudlin conversation
and go on as before."

And he had swept her up into his arms and dragged her

into the bedroom and done his considerable best to prove
the point. But after that, things had changed. Ilya continued
to take her to dinner, but now it was only one or two nights
a week. They continued to be lovers, if that was the word,
but their assignations became less frequent. And Ilya made
a point of attending some receptions with other women.
And going off for the weekend with them.

In the end, their relationship settled into something not
unlike what it had been when she was married to Jerry,
shorn of the guilt. In the end, she would even accompany
him to receptions and stand by without tears if he left with
someone else.

It might not be much, but it made her life stable. If she
was not exactly happy, she could persuade herself that she
was content. She had the job she had always wanted,
she had a tolerable sex life, she had a friend and confidant
ready at hand, and from time to time, she had a visit from
Franja, a daughter who on the one hand was living a
strangely similar life, and who on the other reminded her of
a younger version of herself.

Upon graduating from pilots' school, Franja had taken a
job as a Concordski pilot with Aeroflot, flying international
milk runs. She had a boyfriend in Moscow with whom she
shared an apartment in the Arbat, another Aeroflot pilot
named Ivan Yortsin, and, at least to hear Franja tell it, they
had an arrangement that was a more passionate and intimate version of Sonya's friendship with Ilya.

With anywhere no more than ninety minutes from anywhere else by Concordski, pilots flew two or three hops a
day four days a week, sometimes spending their days off
back in Moscow, sometimes in a city a continent away. With
Franja and Ivan both keeping the same kind of crazy trans-
continental schedule, their times together in Moscow were
random and occasional, and a scrupulously monogamous
relationship would be entirely insane.

So they confined their monogamy to Moscow and did
what they pleased elsewhere, which was to say that her
daughter would seem to be living much the same carefree
existence that Sonya herself had enjoyed long ago, when she
was a card-carrying member of the Red Menace tripping the
European life fantastic on her weekends off, only compressed and enhanced by the perpetual hypersonic speed on

the one hand, and anchored by a kind of dynamically stable relationship on the other.

On Franja's brief and occasional layovers in Paris, they talked more like girl friends than mother and daughter. Franja told tall tales of her adventures, sexual and otherwise, and Sonya told similar war stories of her wild days as a member of the Red Menace newly arrived in the West. Franja talked about Ivan from time to time, and Sonya made perhaps a bit more of her affair with the glamorous Ilya Pashikov than there really was.

They avoided the painful subject of family matters, but every time Franja hopped in and out of Paris in those years, Sonya, much against her will, was left with thoughts of Jerry, the void at the center of their chatter when her daughter was there, the ghost in the apartment on Avenue Trudaine when she left.

It was then that Sonya started using her connections to follow the progress of his career.

She was surprised when Jerry renounced his American citizenship in favor of Common Europe. That was certainly not the Jerry she had known, who had adamantly refused to do the politic thing for twenty years out of twisted loyalty to the country that had betrayed *him*.

She was dumbfounded when Patrice Corneau hired Jerry as his deputy. The Jerry she had known would have been an utter disaster in such a bureaucratic position. Had the divorce really changed him that much?

But when word began to come through to her of the manner in which Corneau was using him, the situation started to become disgustingly clear.

Boris Velnikov was a bureaucratic threat to the project manager, and Corneau was forcing Velnikov to deal with him through Jerry. It was both a clever bureaucratic ploy and a nasty piece of personal vengeance. As a tactic for tormenting Velnikov and keeping his influence minimized, Sonya had to admire it.

But as a cynical use of an old friend as expendable cannon fodder in the bureaucratic wars it was a good deal less admirable, and it made her fearful for what would happen to Jerry when Velnikov moved up.

And Velnikov *was* going to move up, if Moscow had anything to say about it.

Forty percent of the GTN budget was being provided by

Moscow, but only 27 percent of the subcontract money was coming home, and both the Bears and the Ethnic Nationalists were cynically using the issue as a club with which to batter President Gorchenko. Gorchenko was even under pressure from his own faction to do something about it.

Since the contracts were already let out, economic adjustments were out of the question. Gorchenko needed *something* to keep the lid on, and under the circumstances, that could only come from a symbolic change in personnel.

Sooner or later, Emile Lourade was going to move on to bigger things, and when that happened, there would be a shake-up.

Getting Velnikov appointed Director was out of the question; the inevitable choice would be Patrice Corneau. That would leave the GTN project manager's job open. Velnikov was the logical choice, and Moscow would insist on his appointment, claiming, with justice, that failing to appoint him could only be due to anti-Russian discrimination.

If that happened, the Bears would demand a suspension of Soviet participation in the financing of the project, public opinion would be on their side, and real damage would be done to both the Eurorussian cause in the Soviet Union and the Soviet position in Common Europe.

So Moscow was going to push very hard for Velnikov's appointment when the time came. There was going to be a very nasty power struggle, and poor naive Jerry was once more going to be ground to pieces in it. If Moscow lost, the whole project could fall apart. And if Moscow won and Velnikov became project manager, his vengeance on Jerry would surely be swift and merciless.

Sonya monitored the developing situation with growing helpless horror, but there was nothing she could see to do about it until word came through from Ilya's connections in Moscow that Emile Lourade was up for appointment as Common European Minister of Technological Development. It was starting to happen. If she was going to do anything, she had to do it now.

"We've got to do something to protect Jerry," she told Ilya. "His job is all that he's got left."

Ilya shrugged. "I understand how you feel," he said, "but believe me we're going to have enough trouble getting Velnikov appointed. They're going to fight it tooth and nail."

"Could they succeed in blocking Velnikov?"

"They would seem to think they can; they don't seem to understand the domestic Soviet situation, or if they do, they simply don't care," Ilya told her. "Me, I don't think so. Gorchenko has much more riding on this, politically, than the Western Europeans. He can't afford to back down, even if it means killing the whole project. They can, and they'll have to, but it could take them a long time to face up to the situation."

"Isn't there *something* we can do?"

Ilya grimaced. "About the only thing you can do is persuade Jerry to make his peace with Boris Velnikov," he said.

"Jerry won't even talk to me. And besides, he hates Velnikov. And the feeling would seem to be mutual."

"Hmmm . . . ," Ilya muttered thoughtfully. Then his eyes lit up and he smiled his best bureaucratic grin. "Perhaps *Velnikov* could be persuaded that it would be in his best interests to make his peace with Jerry Reed!"

"What?"

"Jerry has the ear of Corneau. What's more, he's a sort of transnational symbol these days, a real live Europeanized American. I could speak to Velnikov. I could tell him that you still have some influence with Jerry. And that Red Star therefore has reason to believe that Jerry could be brought over to his side. That the support of someone like Jerry Reed might be at least marginally useful. I could even intimate that I was transmitting the opinion of higher circles, as it were."

"But Jerry would never do anything to help Boris Velnikov!"

"He might if Velnikov offered him the right quid pro quo . . . perhaps the job of chief project engineer, if and when Velnikov moves up to project manager. . . ."

"You'd go out on a limb like that for me, Ilya?" Sonya said, quite moved. "For Jerry?"

Ilya shrugged. "Who am I to deny that I am in some small way responsible for his misfortunes?" he said. Then the bureaucratic grin came back. "Besides, should *Moscow* believe that I had some small hand in getting Velnikov's appointment through, it will look very pretty in my kharakteristika."

Ilya had his talk with Boris Velnikov, and Velnikov had his tête-à-tête with Jerry, an apparently successful meeting, or so Velnikov had reported back to Ilya, and Sonya had felt more at peace than she had in years.

She had discharged a debt of honor. She had written the happiest ending possible to the long chapter of her and Jerry's life together that she could under the circumstances, and now she could consider it closed.

Or so she had thought till the night that Jerry had telephoned her and plunged her right back into the middle of the whole mess.

He had looked perfectly dreadful; old, and tired, and distracted, and perhaps a little drunk. Nor, after all these months with no contact, did he waste much time on small talk.

She smiled inside when he told her of his deal with Velnikov, but when he told her that Corneau had offered to put *him* up for project manager, her heart sank, and she was quite amazed at the depths to which his so-called friend was prepared to sink.

How much can I tell him? she asked herself. Certainly not that this is about to destroy everything Ilya and I have done for him! Certainly not why Corneau's cynical ploy is almost certain to fail! But he *has* to be made to understand what Corneau is really up to. . . .

"Corneau is *using* you, Jerry," Sonya had told him angrily. And she told him how. But she didn't tell him why it wouldn't work, nor how *Ilya Pashikov* had put himself on the line to protect Jerry's interests.

Instead she let him think that Moscow would have his head as Corneau's dupe if the Velnikov appointment did not go through. But how to walk him through the bureaucratic mine field without telling him things he was simply not prepared to hear . . . ?

And then it came to her. It was perfect!

"Let Corneau propose you for project manager," she had told him, and laid the whole thing out. It would be marvelous! Not only would it put Corneau and the Western Europeans in an impossible position when Jerry stepped aside and endorsed Velnikov, it would be a demonstration of transnational solidarity on the part of a Europeanized *American,* and that would give the Bears a good solid P.R. kick in the pants!

She told Jerry that she would keep in touch and there were a few necessary and awkward phone conversations be-

tween them while the wheels were turning, but after
Velnikov was appointed project manager, and Jerry became
chief propulsion and maneuvering system engineer, that was
really the end of it as far as she was concerned, nor did Jerry
seem very eager to have anything further to do with her.

She had gotten Jerry what he really wanted most in life,
hadn't she? He was going to get his spaceship ride. It was *he*
who had destroyed the heart of their marriage with this
childish obsession, wasn't it? It was this obsession that in the
end had driven her into the arms of Ilya Pashikov. She had
only been forced to write a legal end to the hollow specter
of their marriage, and that too had at least been partially
done to preserve his adolescent dream.

Jerry was going to get what he wanted most in the world,
more than he had ever wanted her, if the sad truth be told.
And she had gotten it for him twice over, hadn't she? There
was no more reason for guilt. All that was dead. All that was
past.

Sonya sighed and finished the last of her coffee. It was
10:30 and time for the briefing from the economic strategy
department.

She had gotten what she had always wanted too, or most
of it, hadn't she? When Ilya was finally promoted to Assistant Vice President of Red Star and transferred back to
Moscow, thanks in part to his role in the successful outcome
of the Velnikov affair, she had gotten his job in Paris.

And if she could not quite delude herself that she didn't
miss him, well, their so-called affair had cooled down to a
mere understanding long before he had left, and she had
always known that Ilya would have to leave Paris for her to
sit in this office.

And so here she was, Director of Red Star's Paris office, a
mature bureaucrat at the pinnacle of her career. She had
her work. She had her visits from Franja. She had all the
money she would ever need. She had a life in the West that
need never end. She had everything that a young girl in
Lenino had ever dreamed of and more.

Didn't she?

Nevertheless, after Ilya had left, she had once more taken
to following Jerry's career from afar. A hobby, idle curiosity,
no more, she told herself, something to fill some of the
empty hours. . . .

It was going to be another standard busy day for the Director of the Paris office of Red Star, S.A., and it was time to get down to it.

But across the city and out in the banlieue, she knew that this was going to be a very special day for Jerry Reed, and she couldn't help thinking about it.

This was the last day he was to spend ground testing his rockets and the first day of the countdown to the fulfillment of the dream of his lifetime. In two weeks, he would ride a Concordski into space, up there at last, where he had always belonged.

Sonya sighed. It really *was* time to begin her working day.

But she knew that she would never have a day in her life like the day Jerry must be having now. She would never feel what he was going to feel at the apogee of his Concordski ride, never ride a dream into the up and out.

In a superficial way, their lives had turned out quite similarly. They were two lonely people with nothing left but their work. But today she knew that Jerry had something that would never be hers.

She was a professional bureaucrat, it was an honorable calling, and here she was at the top of her career. By all objective standards, her life was a success story.

He was a spacecraft designer who had never gotten to work at the full stretch of his powers, never received the just fruits of his labor, and by all the usual objective standards, his career was a tragic failure.

But by some other, more elusive, more absolute standard, it was Jerry whose life in the end had the higher meaning. He was a man with a vision, and soon, at long last, against all odds, and via the aid of the woman who had divorced him, the man who had made him a cuckold, and a country that he loathed, he would live to experience a fulfillment of that vision, a completion of the spirit, that the successful bureaucrat could never know.

And at last Sonya admitted it to herself.

She envied Jerry his incomprehensible vision.

Perhaps she always had.

THE UKRAINIAN REAGAN

Ironically enough, it was Vice President Nathan Wolfowitz, the self-styled "American Gorbachev," who hit the nail on the head when he called Vadim Kronkol the

"Ukrainian Ronald Reagan." While Reagan might have been a mediocre actor and Kronkol one of the Soviet Union's most successful television personalities, both were political nonentities before they were chosen to run for office by backstage political forces, and both were chosen for their proven ability as TV salesmen, Reagan for the General Electric Company, and Kronkol for Ukrainian nationalism.

And while Kronkol may have never gone so far as to co-star with a chimpanzee, his antics as the presiding ringmaster over the circus called "Tonight in the Ukraine," with its bizarre mélange of ethnic nationalism, faith healing, traditional entertainments, and Ukrainian Catholic preachments, could have taught Mr. Reagan himself a thing or two about monkey business.

And indeed, the horde of American political mercenaries now running Kronkol's Presidential campaign are busily working away applying some of the very same techniques that made "the American Kronkol's" campaigns so ruthlessly effective.

—*Mad Moscow*

Thus far, everything had run smooth as glass, not that Jerry Reed had really expected otherwise. Clones of these components had been tested over and over again, and all the design flaws and glitches had long since been worked out, so today's work was merely a matter of static firing all the actual motors that would be boosted up to the Grand Tour Navette being assembled in orbit.

There were quite a few rockets to be static tested, of various sizes and thrust ratings, and they had been set up on test stands all around the ESA complex.

The biggest motors were the actual vectoring thrusters, capable of altering the GTN's trajectory even while the main engines were firing. There were four of them, to be mounted in a cross halfway down the boom between the body of the GTN and the main engines. They would be hooked up to the main fuel supply in the balloon and work in concert, and they were capable of being throttled up or down to produce anything from subtle course corrections to a swift one-eighty virtually on a dime with the main thrusters off.

This meant that they had to be static fired on the big outdoor test stand used to handle the main thrusters. It was the first test of the day, and by far the most dramatic. The vectoring thrusters were set up side by side on the outsized test stand, and Jerry and the team ran the tests from inside the remote blockhouse.

When the vectoring thrusters were installed in their cross configuration on the GTN, with the nozzles pointing outward, course changes could be made by punching numbers into the maneuvering computer, but Jerry had designed the system so that the GTN could also be flown by the seat of the pants with a computer-controlled joystick. There had been a lot of argument about that one, but every prospective pilot in the program, as well as everyone else with a pilot's license, had endorsed it a thousand percent.

So when Jerry test-fired the vectoring thrusters, he had the silly pleasure of doing it first with the joystick. The four directions of control fired each of the line of thrusters in sequence, and the distance the stick was displaced from the center point throttled the thrust up and down.

Some comedian had brought a chip-deck into the blockhouse and dropped in the *William Tell Overture,* and while the recorded orchestra played the music, Jerry improvised to it on the "rocket organ." As the music changed in pitch, he switched from one thruster to another, trying at the same time to match volume with thrust level. Little gouts of flame, full shattering blasts, medium notes, danced crazily up and down the line of thrusters to the kitschy music, while the techs laughed and cheered and beat time against the control panels.

When the overture was finished, and Jerry had taken his ironic bows, they punched in the preprogrammed test sequence and let the control computer take over. Jerry doubted that he would ever be a maestro on the rocket organ, but everything tested out perfectly to the fifth decimal place.

After that, things became more routine. The automatic station-keeping jets were quite small, designed as they were to simply keep the GTN in a stationary position with all other maneuvering rockets inactive. There were dozens of them which would be affixed all over the spacecraft, and they were set up on a series of six indoor test stands, and it took Jerry the rest of the morning to run through these sequences.

After a short lunch over which no one really wanted to linger, Jerry went over to the hangar where two dozen of the warping jets were set up side by side on a long test bed. This was the system that would maneuver the GTN in proximity to Cosmograds, space stations, Concordskis, lunar shuttles, and Martian excursion vehicles. Delicacy was what was required here, and so there were four dozen very low-powered thrusters in the system. On the actual spacecraft, they would be gimbal-mounted in a computer-controlled ring around the boom, in lateral banks along both sides of the main framework, and fore and aft of the cabin, so that the GTN could maneuver with pinpoint precision at velocities as low as a meter a minute.

With these low-power rockets, safety required no more than a steel partition with a viewing window between the test bed and the control console, and when Jerry arrived and began the test sequence, the sounds of the rockets firing were no more than fairly loud hisses, and the exhausts were barely visible. The instruments told the story, and through the first seventeen tests, everything was boringly nominal.

But when Jerry threw the eighteenth switch, the rocket failed to fire.

"Merde!" mutted Albrecht, the team head.

Jerry opened the switch and closed it again.

Still nothing.

Jerry turned around and cocked an inquisitive eyebrow. Albrecht shrugged. "Probably just a loose connection between the panel and the test bed," he offered lamely.

Jerry was not amused. There was an untidy mess of electronic spaghetti running from the control console, across the hangar floor, and to the test bed. He nodded toward the cables. "It could take all day to find a short in all of that," he told Albrecht unhappily.

"Could just be the switch," Albrecht suggested hopefully.

"Assume it is and replace it," Jerry snapped, and he fidgeted for twenty minutes while a technician removed the suspect switch and installed a new one.

When Jerry threw it, nothing happened.

"Fuck!" he exclaimed.

"I hope it's not the motor . . . ," Albrecht said uneasily.

"You and me both!"

"What now?"

Jerry thought about it. If they started screwing around with the wiring now, the test bed could be down for hours if they were lucky, and all day if they weren't. If it *was* a bad motor . . . well, he didn't even want to think about it.

"We'll test the rest of the motors first and then worry about it," he said. "Waste a lot less downtime that way."

"Makes sense," Albrecht agreed, and they fired the remaining six rockets. Everything went nominally.

"Now what?" Albrecht said.

"We'd better have a look at the motor," Jerry sighed. "If that's the problem, we're fucked, but it'd take a lot longer to find a short in the wiring if that's all it is, so we'd better eliminate the possibility of the worst news first."

"I guess you're right," Albrecht said unhappily. "Shut down the panel, we don't want to take any chances while we're out there if there *is* a short in the wiring," he ordered his crew. "And I don't think I have to tell you that this is *not* a smoking break!"

He and Jerry stepped out from behind the safety partition and threaded their way across the wiring to the test bed. "Well?" he said as they stood over number eighteen.

"First thing to do is remove the cowling and check the fuel and oxidizer lines," Jerry told him.

Albrecht nodded, took a wrench out of a coverall pocket, and carefully loosened the series of bolts securing the top half of the cowling to the interior framework of the small motor assembly. He lifted off the oval piece of sheet metal, handed it to Jerry, leaned over, and peered into the guts of the mechanism.

"Well . . . ?" Jerry said, holding the cowling over his head with his right hand, and leaning forward impatiently to peer over Albrecht's shoulder at—

"Scheissdreck!" Albrecht shouted, leaping backward, colliding with Jerry, knocking him off balance. "The hydrogen line's loose, we've got to get—"

Jerry staggered back, threw up his arms in a futile attempt to regain his balance, and the cowling flew loose from his right hand as he spun around and started to fall—

—as the cowling came clattering down on the rocket motor assembly—

—there was a soft whooshing explosion—

—something slammed into the base of his skull—

THE MEDIA BLITZ ROLLS ON

Vadim Kronkol, having purchased another hour of airtime on an American broadcast satellite with money that went in one pocket as it went out the other, made yet another rabble-rousing speech that seemed to have gone through several rewrites in both Washington and Hollywood, invoking everything from the Stalinist genocide against the Ukrainian kulaks to Catherine the Great's alleged predilection for stallions to demonstrate that Russians were nikulturni barbarians and perverts who regularly ate innocent Ukrainian babies for breakfast.

It was quite a vintage performance by the Ukrainian Rasputin, next morning's polls showed he had improved his lead over the nearest voice of reason another five points, to 69 percent. This time, the American satellite targeted Moscow and Leningrad too, where there certainly are no votes to be won for the Ukrainian Liberation Front, as if to provoke Russians into providing riot footage.

Which unruly mobs in both cities dutifully did, led by Uncle Joe hooligans, but joined by many of their Russian nationalist elders who certainly should have known better. And of course the American media wizards have now taken the choice footage of Uncle Joes smashing restaurant windows and beating up supposed Ukrainians and cut it up into the sixty-second commercials that are now saturating the Ukraine.

The next step is all too predictable. Kronkol's next televised speech will have been given a good excuse to be even more hydrophobic, the Americans, as rumored, will no doubt blanket all of Russia, leading to even better atrocity footage from which to cut yet more inflammatory commercials for Kronkol.

The hairiest of Bears are being used like Hollywood extras by these mercenary American media-masters. Have no rational illusions. These people could sell dehydrated water in the Sahel desert and they can sell a raving atavism like Vadim Kronkol to the Ukrainians.

After all, they sold Harry Burton Carson to the Americans, didn't they?

—*Mad Moscow*

Sonya had been in a meeting with the Renault people when some nameless ESA functionnaire had telephoned Red Star, and the first call hadn't gotten through to her. It took a second call, this one from Boris Velnikov himself, to get the switchboard to break into the meeting, and then ESA had told her that a car and a police escort were already on the way. They were there within fifteen minutes, but le rush had already started, and it took an hour to get through the traffic even with a motorcycle escort.

All Velnikov had been able to tell her was that there had been some kind of accident, a hydrogen explosion or something. Jerry was alive, but he was badly injured, some kind of brain damage. They had helicoptered him to the nearby airport hospital, which, Velnikov assured her, was the state of the art when it came to head-trauma cases.

Velnikov was waiting at the entrance when she finally arrived at the hospital, along with a gray-haired woman in doctor's greens, whom he introduced as Hélène Cordray, the chief of the neurosurgery unit.

"How is he? What happened?" Sonya demanded as they hustled up the stairs and into the building.

"Your husband's condition has been stabilized, and his life is in no immediate danger, Madame Reed," Dr. Cordray said.

"There was an accident on the test bed," Velnikov told her, "a hydrogen leak, a small explosion—"

"—a small piece of metal was embedded in his medullary cortex, we were able to remove it quickly and keep the damage localized, but there has been significant trauma and a permanent loss of function—"

By this time they had reached a bank of elevators. One of the doors opened, Dr. Cordray ushered them inside, hit the button for the third floor. "I'll be able to explain it more fully in my office—"

"I want to see him," Sonya told her. "Now."

The doctor looked at Velnikov, shook her head.

"It's *my* husband, not his, and you'll take me to him *now,*" Sonya snapped angrily.

"Very well, Madame Reed, if you insist," the doctor said without rancor, and she hit the button for the fifth floor.

They rode up to the fifth floor in silence and walked rapidly down a green corridor smelling of disinfectant and synthetic lilac, past a series of heavy metal doors and large windows, through which Sonya could not keep herself from catching unsettling glimpses of patients lying in hospital beds in various states of unwholesome infirmity, hooked up to IV stands, computers, ominous-looking banks of life-support machinery.

"Your husband is in a sterile chamber, so we can't go inside," Dr. Cordray told her, as they stopped by one of the windows.

"Merde . . . ," Sonya whispered as she peered through the glass.

There was a bed in the room, all but hidden by banks of machinery, and a nurse at the foot of it, sitting on a chair before a series of monitors. Jerry lay in the bed with his eyes closed and his skull swathed in white bandages. There were IV lines in both of his arms and another catheter in the bandages near the top of his skull. Two electrical cables led from the back of his head to a pair of consoles about the size of large television sets that looked something like mainframe computers. There were electrodes taped all over his bare chest with leads running to yet more bulky devices. A transparent oxygen mask fit over his nose and mouth.

"The brain areas that control respiration and heartbeat have been destroyed," Dr. Cordray said softly. "We're using computers to simulate the lost function. There has been no deterioration of the higher brain centers, and we believe that motor control, excretory, and sexual functions have not been lost. Barring unforeseen circumstances, we believe he will make a full recovery."

"A . . . a full recovery?" Sonya stammered.

"Except for what has already been lost. He will always require computer assist to maintain heartbeat and respiration, of course. . . ."

"He'll have to spend the rest of his life like *this!*" Sonya cried. "You call that a full recovery!"

"This is only temporary, Madame Reed, please try to control yourself, there are other patients—"

"Equipment is being flown in from Star City," Velnikov said, "and it's far more sophisticated than this."

"From . . . from Star City . . . ?" Sonya stammered.

"I wanted to discuss the prognosis before you subjected yourself to this sight, Madame Reed, but you insisted on seeing the worst immediately," Dr. Cordray said soothingly. "I assure you the situation is not as hopeless as it currently seems. Now please let us go to my office where we can discuss matters much more calmly."

Numbly, Sonya let herself be led back to the elevator, down to the third floor, along a corridor to a small spare office, where the doctor sat down behind a plain metal desk and she and Velnikov perched on hard metal chairs before it.

"The Soviets are flying in a new piece of equipment," Dr. Cordray said.

"It's an experimental device we've been developing for really long-duration space travel," Velnikov told her. "The idea is to slow down respiration and heartbeat to produce an artificial state of hibernation, but the software can easily enough be modified to induce normal heart and lung function."

"With your permission, we will keep your husband under sedation and implant permanent electrodes in his brain and then seal the incision," the doctor said. "The Soviet device needs no physical connection, it uses external electrodes that complete the circuit through electromagnetic induction. This prevents the probability of infection through a permanent opening in the skull and fascia."

"And since it has been designed for use by cosmonauts, where weight counts, it has been highly miniaturized, and the power requirements have been reduced to the point where it can run on a twelve-volt battery."

"Your husband will have considerable mobility, Madame Reed."

"Considerable mobility . . . ?" Sonya said, looking back and forth between the two of them distractedly. "Highly miniaturized . . . ?"

"It weighs only eleven kilos with the battery," Velnikov said. "It's about the size of a portable television set, and we can mount it on a cart for mobility. The connecting cable can be as long as you like, so Jerry will be able to move freely around a room without moving the controller."

"It all sounds quite horrible," Sonya said. "Isn't there something else you can do? A brain transplant, maybe?"

Dr. Cordray shook her head. "Only the Americans are working on anything like that, and they're at least five years away, and by that time . . ."

Velnikov shot her a dirty look. But it was too late.

"By that time, *what?*" Sonya demanded.

The doctor's eyes became furtive.

"Tell me!" Sonya insisted. "I have a right to know!"

Dr. Cordray sighed. "The Soviet device can only *approximate* normal hindbrain function, of course," she said. "Also, there will be an enzyme debt from the loss of brain tissue that will be difficult to compensate for with artificial supplements. Eventually, there will be accumulated vein and artery damage, mini-strokes, perhaps full-bore cerebral hemorrhages, slow emphysema. . . ."

"I see . . . ," Sonya whispered. "How long?"

"Two, perhaps three years, at the outside," the doctor said. "Of course, by that time, there could be new advances, you never know. . . ."

"You're talking about two or three years of . . . of . . . of a slow horrible deterioration toward . . . toward . . ."

"I'm sorry, Madame Reed, it's the best we have to offer," Dr. Cordray said. "A year ago, there would have been nothing at all."

She reached into a desk drawer, pulled out some printed forms and a pen, and handed them to Sonya.

"What's this?" Sonya stammered.

"Permission forms. Since this certainly qualifies as heroic life-extension measures, we need the permission of next of kin to implant the electrodes. We also need permission to keep him on the present life-support machinery beyond ninety-six hours."

"You mean if I don't sign these papers, you'll just turn it all off and let him die?"

"That *is* the law. As his wife, you *are* legally next of kin."

"*Ex*-wife," Sonya blurted.

Dr. Cordray glanced at Velnikov. "I thought . . . ?" She looked back at Sonya and frowned. "This is rather ambiguous, legally," she said. "Is there someone else who could sign quickly? A son? A daughter?"

"Our son is in America. Our daughter is an Aeroflot pilot, and I have no idea where she is right now."

Dr. Cordray frowned. She grimaced. "This does present legal problems," she said. She drummed her fingers on the desktop. "The devil take it!" she finally exclaimed. "I'll take your signature as next of kin, and let the law argue about it later. I'll not stand by and let someone die over such a minor technicality."

"Assuming that I'm willing to sign . . . ," Sonya said.

"There is no other alternative, Madame Reed."

"Oh yes there is, Dr. Cordray."

"You're not thinking of . . . ?"

But Sonya was. Jerry would never live to take his space-ship ride. He would probably never even be able to work again. He would be tied to an eleven-kilo piece of machinery for what little remained of his life. And what would remain would be a slow but steady physical deterioration. Perhaps mental degeneration as well. And he would be alive and aware the whole time to watch his own decline. Wouldn't it be more merciful if he never awoke?

He would be an invalid, with no one to take care of him, no—

A wave of self-loathing washed over her as she thought it. That's it, Sonya, isn't it? she told herself in disgust. There's no one but *you* to take care of him, is there? No one but you to sit around and watch him slowly die and listen to his complaints and his anguish and his self-pity on the long way out.

For over twenty years, she had lived with this man. They had raised a son and a daughter together. She had watched as his life had narrowed down to a single obsessional point, an obsession that now lay forever beyond his grasp. She had betrayed him. She had divorced him. She had broken his heart.

And now, rather than face a few sad short years of taking care of him, she had been willing to let him die.

Let him die?

No, Sonya, nothing so passive as that. If you don't sign these papers, if you're not willing to do what must be done, what no one else can do in the time left to him, you're not letting him die, you're *killing* him. As surely as if you pulled the plug with your own hand.

Sonya sighed. She took up the pen. "No, of course not," she said, "we've got to do what little we can."

THEY FROZE TESSA TINKER'S BRAIN!

An exclusive source close (very close!) to Hollywood sex queen Tessa Tinker, who died last week of injuries sustained when her Maserati-Mercedes smashed into a Beverly Hills garbage truck at 75 mph, has told us that her brain has been preserved by a process derived from hush-hush military work by a funeral home in wacky Northern California. Someday it may be revived and transplanted into a new body cloned from the dead actress's flesh, to star in another thirty-three pant-and-groan epics.

If the revived actress's future performances run true to previous form, brain damage won't be much of a problem as long as her new body is faithfully reproduced by the cloning process, silicon implants and all.

Look for *Return of the Zombie Sex-Queen* to appear sometime within the next two hundred years!

—*The National Enquirer*

KRONKOL GOES TOO FAR, PRESIDENT GORCHENKO DECLARES

President Constantin Semyonovich Gorchenko has strongly repeated his declaration that the Ukraine has no such legal basis for seceding from the Soviet Union after Vadim Kronkol, candidate of the Ukrainian Liberation Front for the Presidency of the Ukrainian S.S.R, declared that he would consider his election a referendum on Ukrainian independence.

"We may have no legal basis under Soviet law for preventing American agents from foisting off Kronkol on the Ukrainian people," the President admitted. "But neither would his election constitute a legally binding secession referendum under the constitution, and Soviet law provides ample means for keeping him from leading the Ukrainian people into an act of open rebellion, up to and

including mobilizing the Ukrainian national militia and placing it under Red Army command," he warned the Ukrainian revanchists.

—Pravda

X X I I I

A dull throbbing ache, a scratchy feeling, a pressure,
emerged from the void. The ache slowly localized itself at
the back of his head. The scratchy feeling was a raw dry
throat. The pressure was the weight of his body in a supine
position. Images began to drift across his mind's eye—a big
bowl of Häagen-Dazs chocolate ice cream covered with
chocolate syrup, the living room of the apartment on Avenue Trudaine, a figure in a bulky old spacesuit walking in
slow motion on the gray surface of the Moon, the clean
white contrail of a Concordski cleaving the blue sky over the
Île St.-Louis, a bank of rocket engines throttling up and
down in a musical sequence, a crowded rush-hour RER car,
his hand toggling a switch back and forth, Dieter Albrecht
handing him a motor cowling, a floor coming up at him as
he fell, a soft whooshing explosion, blackness—

Jerry Reed realized that he was awake. And conscious.
And alive.

Not without effort, he blinked open gummy eyelids,
winced as a cruel light blinded him, blinked again rapidly,
squinted his eyes, slowly let them adjust to the slitted light,
then opened them wide.

He was in a small white-walled room. Lying in a bed. He
tried to bring his hands to his face to wipe his eyes clear of
tears and found that his arms were restrained. He swiveled
his head left, right, saw that his forearms were tied down to
handboards, saw the IV needles in the pits of his elbows,
looked down the length of his body and saw the electrodes
taped to his bare chest.

Hospital room. A lot of bulky electronic equipment

around his bed. He wriggled his toes. In working order. He blinked rapidly several times, and his vision slowly cleared.

There were two people sitting by the foot of the bed. In green smocks. Women. One of them seemed to be staring at something hidden by the bulk of an electronic console. Watching TV? The other was reading a newspaper.

The woman reading the newspaper was . . . was . . .

"S . . . Sonya?" he croaked weakly against some kind of peculiar resistance.

The woman started, rose, tossed aside the newspaper, rushed to the head of the bed. "Jerry!" she cried. "You're awake!"

It was! It was Sonya! Looking ashen and drawn, but smiling down at him.

"So it would seem," Jerry managed to say. But the words did not come easily, somehow; he seemed to be fighting the rhythm of his own breathing.

"I'll get Dr. Cordray," the other woman said, a nurse no doubt. "You'll want a few minutes alone."

"Sonya . . . I feel kind of strange. . . ."

There were tears in her eyes. "There was an accident. You were hurt." She paused. She hesitated. Her lower lip trembled.

She leaned over and kissed him on the cheek. "But I'm here to take care of you, and you're going to be all right."

"Take care of me . . . ?"

"They say you can leave the hospital in a few days, and I'll be taking you home."

"Home?"

"Avenue Trudaine, remember, Jerry?"

"But we . . . but you . . ."

Sonya wiped tears from her eyes with the back of her hand. "You're going to need someone to take care of you . . . while you . . . recover," she said. "And who else is there? You don't want to spend weeks in the hospital by yourself, now do you?"

"But you and me . . . it's been years. . . ."

Sonya laid a finger on his lips. "Not now, okay, Jerry?" she said softly. "We'll have plenty of time to talk all that out later."

And she replaced her fingers with her lips. "For now, let me just be glad you're alive," she said after she had kissed him. "Let's not worry ourselves just yet about the past."

Jerry's mind was still fuzzy, but not so fuzzy that he didn't realize something must be very wrong, or Sonya would not be here, crying like this, kissing him, and telling him she was going to take him home and care for him after all these years.

"What's wrong with me, Sonya?" he demanded. "What's happened?"

"You were hit in the head by a piece of metal from the explosion," Sonya said. "There was . . . there was . . ." She seemed to be choking on something she couldn't bring herself to spit out.

It could be only one thing.

"Brain damage?" Jerry whispered.

Sonya looked down and nodded.

Jerry wriggled the fingers of his right hand, then his left. He tried out his toes again. He moved his arms against the restraints. He kicked his feet under the bedclothes. There was nothing wrong with his vision or his hearing. He was thinking clearly now. He could smell the acridly chemical hospital odor, the thin tang of ozone from the electronic equipment surrounding him, Sonya's jasmine perfume.

"I seem to be in full working order . . . ," he said.

"You are, Jerry, you are."

"Then—"

At that moment, the nurse returned with a gray-haired woman in medical greens.

"This is Dr. Cordray, Jerry," Sonya told him. "She'll explain it all to you better than I can."

Sonya shot a hard sidelong glance at Hélène Cordray as the doctor approached the bedside, a reminder not to violate the agreement they had come to after the electrode-implant operation.

There was no reason to make things worse by telling Jerry the whole truth. It would be needlessly cruel to let him know that what awaited him was two or three years of slow physical and mental deterioration toward an inevitable death. Better to leave him with hope.

"I am not in the habit of lying to my patients," Dr. Cordray had protested.

"I'm not asking you to lie, Dr. Cordray," Sonya told her. "Tell him all about his injury in full detail. Tell him all about the device that's keeping him alive—believe me, he'll be fascinated, and he'll probably understand the technology better than you do. Just don't tell him all the gory details about what's going to happen to him, and don't tell him he's only got two or three years left. That's not a lie, really, since you don't really know. In two years, anything could happen. A year ago, there wasn't even this."

"But if he's so technologically knowledgeable—"

"He's a visionary, Dr. Cordray. He reads science fiction. They're just now building spacecraft that he designed over fifteen years ago. The present and the future are the same things to Jerry in ways that you and I can never understand. All you have to do is make a full recovery seem *possible* to him, and believe me, Jerry Reed will do the rest himself."

Dr. Cordray had shrugged. "Very well, Madame Reed, I will try," she had said. And then she had looked Sonya in the eyes, woman to woman. "Divorced or not, you still love this man very much, n'est-ce pas?" she had said, stepping quite outside her professional persona, and Sonya had had nothing to say to that.

"Well, Monsieur Reed, how are you feeling?" Hélène Cordray said.

"Okay, I guess," Jerry told her. "How long have I been out?"

"Approximately seventy hours—but a good part of that was because we had to do a second operation."

"*Second* operation?"

"A piece of metal had to be removed from your medulla, and we decided to keep you under anesthesia until we could do the electrode implant. . . ."

"Electrode implant? What's happened to me?" Jerry said fearfully.

Dr. Cordray gave him a cool bedside smile. "Your . . . wife tells me that you are a technologically knowledgeable person," she said. "So if you will have a little patience, I will give you the full details."

And, to the extent that she had agreed upon with Sonya, she proceeded to do so.

Jerry had a terrible sinking sensation in his gut when the doctor told him that the brain centers that controlled heartbeat and respiration had been permanently destroyed. And when she showed him the wheeled console next to his bed, and the cable leading from it to the induction electrode taped to the back of his skull, there had been a queasy feeling of disorientation, tinged, perhaps, with a kind of disgust.

But once she started trying to explain how the thing worked, he found himself becoming rather fascinated, amused even, for he had read a bit about what the Soviets called the "hibernautika," enough to know that he understood it better than she did, enough to realize that what he was hooked up to was not the complete version of the device they were trying to develop. The full-bore hibernautika was supposed to be able to induce both hibernation and sleep, not merely control heartbeat and respiration rates, and to control full-spectrum brainwave function as well. In theory, at least, it would make interstellar voyages possible at sub-light speeds.

He hadn't thought they were this far advanced on the project, and what she was describing was only a piece of the device. Still, the degree of miniaturization was impressive, and there was something somehow fitting about the fact that he was being kept alive by a piece of space-technology spin-off that hadn't even been fully developed yet, but that in its completed form might someday allow men to go to the stars. And if it was a piece of *Soviet* technology, well, he had long since made his peace with that.

"Is this version programmable for other functions?" he asked.

The doctor cocked an eyebrow at him. "Other functions?"

Jerry studied the console by his bedside. It was a matte-finish aluminum box about the size of a small television set. There were two knobs and two liquid crystal readout panels but no keyboard, and from this angle, he couldn't see whether it had an interface port on the back.

"What you've described is a partial version of something called the 'hibernautika,'" he told her. "The full device is supposed to have other functions. Alpha-wave control. Sleep induction. Selective muscular stimulation. Can I program this thing for any of that?"

"I haven't the faintest idea, Monsieur Reed," the doctor said, "and in any case, I would not at all advise tinkering with the circuitry!"

And she exchanged strange glances with Sonya, who then shook her head and broke into a warm but ironic little smile.

"How much mobility will I have?" Jerry asked nervously.

"Quite a bit, really. The present cable is only temporary; you can have a much longer one on a reel. And it even has a self-contained power supply for travel away from mains."

"I can travel?"

"After a fashion," Dr. Cordray told him. "Stairs, of course, will be a barrier, and you certainly can't use the Métro or buses. Nor risk walking down crowded streets. But automobiles should present no problem."

"What about the Concordski? What about zero g?"

"You are talking about *airplanes*, Monsieur Reed?" the doctor exclaimed. "You are talking about *space travel?* This is a joke, oui?"

Only then did it really hit him. He was alive, yes, but his real life was over. He would never ride his Grand Tour Navette. They wouldn't even let him on a short-hop airplane, let alone a hypersonic Concordski pulling almost 3 g's. He probably wouldn't even be allowed to go back to work on the ground.

This was the end of everything he had ever lived for.

Better I had never woken up to face this living death.

He shook his head. He rolled his eyes up at the ceiling. He burst into sobs and he didn't give a damn who saw. "I can't take this, Sonya," he cried. "Why don't you just do me a favor and pull the plug?"

"It isn't hopeless, Jerry!" Sonya said. "You won't be tied to this thing forever! Isn't that right, Dr. Cordray, there are new developments right around the corner, aren't there?"

He had been so brave while the doctor told him of his condition that it had made her want to cry. And when he had started babbling on enthusiastically about the machinery that was keeping him alive, she had wanted to hug him to her—that was the crazy, innocent, eager, overgrown little boy with whom she had fallen in love, long, long ago.

And she was not about to let that Jerry roll over and die.

She fetched Dr. Cordray a swift kick in the ankle. Hélène Cordray, to her credit, and Sonya's everlasting gratitude, did not allow her face to show Jerry a response.

"Well, yes, this is perhaps only a temporary expedient," she said. "You know better than I do, Monsieur Reed, that what weighs eleven kilos now could weigh a few grams later. With sufficient miniaturization, we could implant the whole device. . . ."

Jerry turned his head on the pillow to look at her. Sonya could see him composing himself by act of will. "Atomic level switching . . . ," he muttered. "That could certainly get the circuitry down by two levels of magnitude. . . ."

"An implantable isotopic power core such as we use in pacemakers would then make you entirely mobile," Dr. Cordray said, bless her heart.

"Be better off with a replaceable external module," Jerry mused. "Easy enough to use induction to power the implant from outside . . ."

"If you say so, Monsieur Reed."

"What about an organic solution? A brain implant?"

"Not beyond the realm of possibility, though it would be rather difficult to make the neuronic connections. . . ."

"Maybe not, if it was cloned from my own genome. . . ."

"There is that . . . I have heard that the Americans have succeeded in cloning the entire brain of a rat. . . ."

"To use as a missile guidance system, but the software problems don't seem to have been licked yet. . . ."

Sonya's intellect was quite lost as they proceeded to drift off into realms of technobabble far beyond her ken. But her heart was filled to bursting as she watched Jerry talk himself up from the blackest of pits, as he became more and more animated, as he dragged himself back into the world of the living by his own bootstraps.

"Well, Monsieur Reed, this has certainly been a stimulating conversation," Dr. Cordray finally said. "But it is really time you got some rest."

And she took Sonya by the arm, nodding toward the door.

"I'll be back tomorrow," Sonya said, blowing Jerry a kiss.

"Well, I guess I'll be here, won't I?" he said, and he smiled, and he winked, and Sonya's spirit soared.

"Not for long, Jerry," she said. "Soon we'll be going home."

"Mon Dieu, what a man!" Hélène Cordray exclaimed out in the corridor. "What a mind! What courage! You will pardon an old woman for saying this, but I could easily enough have fallen in love with him myself! How lucky you are! How ever could you have let a man like that slip from your grasp?"

"*I* divorced *him*," Sonya told her.

"Incroyable! Why on earth did you do that?"

Sonya sighed. "Je ne comprends pas," she admitted.

"But you love him still, do you not?"

Sonya nodded. "C'est vrai," she said softly. "I do believe I do."

HEROIC UKRAINIAN DEFIES MOSCOW

Ukrainian Presidential candidate Vadim Kronkol scoffed today at Russian President Constantin Gorchenko's threat to absorb the Ukrainian national militia into the Red Army and use it to crush the independent Ukrainian Republic that he plans to declare unilaterally after he is elected.

"I'd just like to see Gorchenko try to put patriotic Ukrainian soldiers under Russian command," the defiant Kronkol told reporters at a press conference in Kiev. "Does he really think he can use our own boys against us? The latest Gallup and Roper polls both show that the Ukrainian national militia supports Ukrainian independence by a margin of four to one!"

—*New York Post*

After the usual unconscionable forty-minute crawl in the taxiway stack, they were finally at the top of the runway with takeoff clearance from the clods in Narita tower. Franja ran up the turbofans, got the high sign from her flight engineer, nodded to her co-pilot, released the brakes, and the Concordski accelerated down the runway. When her ground speed showed 289 kph, she pulled back on the yoke, and the Aeroflot flight from Tokyo to Paris was at last airborne, fifty-one minutes late, quite exasperating, considering that the flight itself would last only ninety minutes.

In fact . . .

She thumbed on the cabin intercom. "This is Captain Gagarin speaking. Aeroflot wishes to apologize for the delay in takeoff, which was due entirely to airport congestion. Since we will be flying a ballistic trajectory at maximum suborbital velocity, I'm afraid it will be impossible to make up the lost time. Our flight time will be ninety minutes, about half the time we have spent on the ground waiting for a takeoff slot. We hope you enjoy the flight."

Constantin Bulanin, the co-pilot, laughed. "Not exactly according to regulations," he said.

"Next time I may just pipe it through the tower frequency too," Franja said dryly. "It's as close as we can get to really giving those numbskulls a piece of our mind!"

When the airspeed reached 620 kph, Franja ignited the main engine, killed the turbofans, and felt the soul-satisfying kick of the 2.7-g acceleration pressing her back against the padded seat as the hydrogen-burning scramjet quickly took the Concordski up to hypersonic speed on atmospheric oxygen.

And that, alas, was the end of manual flying until the approach to De Gaulle. She keyed in the preprogrammed flight sequence for Paris, and the computer took over the con. The climb-angle steepened to 63 degrees, the sky outside the small windshield quickly deepened from azure to purple to black, and then, at 130,000 meters, when the stars were beginning to show and the atmospheric oxygen had become too thin to sustain combustion, there was a slight judder, and then a little surge of added acceleration as the engine went over to internal oxidizer.

The burn continued for another five minutes, until the Concordski's speed was just 1,000 kph under orbital velocity at an altitude of about 30 kilometers, and then the engine shut down, and the plane went into its silent, weightless glide up to the apogee of its ballistic parabola, and that was it.

Franja loosened her harness and let herself float a few centimeters clear of the seat. From here on in, till the end of the reentry sequence about half an hour away, there was really nothing to do but monitor the instruments and watch the small slice of starscape visible through the narrow windshield.

The life of a Concordski pilot was not exactly thrilling when it came to the flying itself. You fidgeted endlessly on the ground as you advanced slot by slot toward the top of the runway, you took off, you went hypersonic, you turned the plane over to the computer, you waited, you took over again after reentry, flew circles in the holding stack, and landed.

So much for the romance of the air! Even her work aboard Cosmograd Sagdeev had been more exciting than this, with its spacewalks and the bizarre feeling of power that came from manually moving large masses around in zero g.

But though she still chafed at the thought that it would take two more years of seniority before they would start giving her orbital flights to Cosmograds, and two more before any hope of the choice assignment to Spaceville runs, and though Mars, or even the Moon, was still a vague distant dream, Franja seldom found herself regretting the decision to trade life as a space monkey for a career of flying milk runs for Aeroflot.

For while flying Concordskis from city to city was nothing to write home about, once you landed, why there you were! Four days of flying, then three days off. What with the ninety-minute hops, you ended up flying two or three legs a day, and what with the ability to swap flights with fellow pilots via the international Aeroflot bulletin board, with a little horse-trading, you could take your three days a week off just about anywhere. Paris! Rome! Tokyo! Sydney! London! Leningrad! Kiev! Munich! Amsterdam! Vienna!

You might not see any more of space than a slice of star field through a small windshield, but you certainly saw the world!

While Franja still just might have traded the life of a Concordski pilot for an expedition to Mars or Titan, she certainly would not have traded it for anything else on Earth. Concordski pilots were citizens of the world. Time zones had no meaning for them, nor did the days of the week. Via the bulletin board, you could always find an open apartment to stay in in a choice location in any city where Aeroflot flew. Or a ready-made playmate for the long weekend if that was what you chose, and your three days off were *always* the weekend in the Concordski Club.

And then there was Ivan. Theirs was a relationship that only a Concordski pilot could really understand.

Franja had been determined to live in the Arbat from the moment she learned she was going to be based in Moscow, for while the district's wild nightlife had been tamed somewhat into a more refined version of itself in the service of enhanced real estate values, it still stood for everything she felt she had missed as a dedicated student during her years in Yuri Gagarin.

Unfortunately, she was not exactly the only Muscovite with the same desire, which was why the Arbat was becoming so gentrified, and why no single person could afford the outrageous rent on even an Aeroflot pilot's salary while tripping the lavish life fantastic around the world.

When Franja sought out a prospective roommate on the Concordski Club bulletin board, she certainly hadn't expected a man to apply, but Ivan Fedorovich Yortsin was handsome and charming, there was instant sexual chemistry between them, and when he pointed out that a one-bedroom was the most two Aeroflot pilots could hope to afford in the Arbat, that both of them would have a better time sharing a bedroom with each other than with some platonic roommate, and proved it to her complete satisfaction, that was the clincher.

Especially when he pointed out that each of them would have the apartment to themselves as often as not, given the realities of Concordski pilots' schedules, and explained the working rules of the Concordski Club, of which he was a veteran member.

So they rented a one-bedroom one block off Arbat Street, and they scrupulously followed the code of the Club. For a former space monkey, it was hardly the depths of degeneracy that the Mother Russia bluenoses delighted in calling it.

When both were elsewhere, the Arbat apartment went on the bulletin board. When either of them was alone in Moscow, the apartment was exclusively that person's. When they were both in the city together, they always partied together and were never so gauche as to go home with someone else. But what they did when they were in separate cities, by mutual agreement, happened to two different people on another planet.

The scandal sheets and the sex magazines and the yellow media could say what they liked about the notorious love lives of the Concordski Club, and they never tired of doing so, but the code of the Club worked.

Like the flight profile of the plane itself, the life of a Concordski pilot was mostly a long, weightless, high-speed glide.

But now the flight was descending from its apogee, and

the computer had turned the nose down, and a slice of the planet was barely visible at the bottom of the windshield, and it was time for Franja to tighten up her harness again and prepare herself for reentry, into the atmosphere, into the Earthbound cares and travails of the real world.

Ordinarily, she welcomed the return to another turn at manual flight, looked forward with eager anticipation to coming down into the excitement of another city half a world away.

But not this time.

She had been en route from Lisbon to Melbourne when the accident happened, and by the time Mother had called there, she was already on her way to Vladivostok, and by the time word got there, she was in Peking. Mother had finally caught up with her in Singapore, but she was scheduled to fly to Tel Aviv, and it was too late to find a trade-off to Paris.

In Tel Aviv, it had taken endless complex trading to get her on this flight to Paris at the beginning of her next four-day shift. She had managed to trade her scheduled flight to Vienna for a hop to Kiev, where she connected with a flight to London that enabled her to take a hop to Barcelona, where she managed to get herself a flight to Tokyo, where she was forced to spend three days on the ground before the regulations would allow her to fly this run to Paris.

And all the while, via phone conversations with Mother, she learned what had happened in disjointed fragments. In Singapore, she had learned about the explosion, Father's head injury, that he was on life-support machinery, that some sort of permanent machinery was being flown in from Moscow.

By the time she spoke to Mother from Tel Aviv, electrodes had been implanted in Father's brain, he was hooked up to a permanent portable life-support device, and his life was out of danger.

And before she had left Tokyo, Mother had told her that they were about to release Father from the hospital, and he would be there at Avenue Trudaine with her when Franja arrived.

The computer fired the Concordski's control jets with a series of chuffs and judders, flipping the plane head for tail, so that it was falling backward. The main engine fired up for three minutes, killing velocity, then the computer turned the craft again, so that it was descending belly-first with its nose in the air.

Once, twice, thrice, the Concordski skipped through the upper reaches of the atmosphere, bleeding off more velocity with atmospheric braking, and then it eased into a shallow downward hypersonic glide.

When it was deep enough into the atmospheric envelope for the scramjet to run on external air, the computer fired up the main engine again, and returned the Concordski to manual control, flying at 4,000 kph at 100,000 meters, descending directly toward Paris at a shallow glide slope of 20 degrees.

Franja pulled back on the yoke, flew a tight downward spiral with the nose in the air, throttling back the main engine, until the airspeed was down to 2,000 kph. Then she shut off the scramjet and continued to fly high-aspect spirals until the airspeed dropped to the point where the turbofans could endure the airstream.

Then she retracted the turbofan intake cowls, fired up the conventional jet engines, and voilà, the Concordski was a conventional airliner descending into the holding stack over De Gaulle at subsonic speed.

And for once, she was not displeased when the tower told her that there would be a twenty-minute delay for a landing slot. For once, she was in no hurry to be on the ground.

For in their last conversation in Tokyo, Mother had pleaded with her to stay with them on her layover in Paris. And Mother had already prevailed upon Aeroflot, via the Red Star Tower, to grant Franja four days of emergency leave.

It would have been heartlessly cruel to insist upon staying in a Concordski Club apartment against Mother's wishes under these dire circumstances. She was committed now to four days with the two of them en famille at Avenue Trudaine. With a mother who had assumed responsibility for a man she had not lived with for the better part of a decade. With a father who had disowned his daughter years ago.

What sort of family mise-en-scène *that* was going to be did not bear thinking about.

Franja sighed as she banked the Concordski yet again into another circle around the holding pattern. The acceleration might be negligible, but the pressure was there, gently pushing her into the padded seatback.

The weightless floating freedom of free-fall was long gone.

The Earthbound ties of gravity had returned with a vengeance.

CONGRESS OF PEOPLES TO DELAY VOTE ON KRONKOL REQUEST

Ian MacTavish, Secretary of the Congress of Peoples, told a press conference today that no action would be taken on Vadim Kronkol's request that the Congress declare its support for Ukrainian independence.

"While we have welcomed the Ukrainian Liberation Front as a member organization, and while there is overwhelming support for their position among the other nationless peoples of Europe, if we vote such a resolution before the Ukrainian election, we will only open ourselves to the usual charges of subverting national political processes," Mr. MacTavish said.

"After the election is over, and Mr. Kronkol is able to resubmit his resolution as the duly elected President of the Ukraine, you may be sure the Ukrainian people will then receive our fraternal endorsement," he added.

—*The Guardian*

"Hello, Franja," Jerry said, not knowing what else to say to the daughter he had not spoken to in years.

"Hello, Father."

To say that this was an awkward moment would have been the understatement of the century, Jerry thought. There he was, sitting on the couch in the living room, where Franja had not seen him in years, and there she was, standing before him, cold and aloof and justifiably so he had to admit, unsuccessfully trying to hide her shock at the sight of what he had become.

He found himself feeling sorry for *her*. What *was* she supposed to feel? How *could* she react? Here she was, confronting the father who had disowned her, and instead of being able to express the anger, the bitterness, even the hate, that she must surely feel, all that had been instantly consumed by the pity he could see in her eyes.

Jerry knew what a pathetic sight he must be, with the induction electrode secured to the back of his skull by a cross of tape and a wide rubber band looped around his head over it for safety's sake, with the cable leading from his head to the reel atop the hibernautika console beside the couch.

He saw it constantly in Sonya's eyes, in the way she had babied him these past two days back in the apartment, fetching him coffee, bringing him pillows, speaking nothing but soft tender words, treating him like a frail old man.

Now she stood there beside Franja, her lower lip trembling, her eyes all misty, paralyzed like the two of them, unable to find the words to break the long awkward silence.

Jerry sighed. He had been forced to do a lot of unaccustomed thinking since he woke up in the hospital, still more in these two days in the apartment that had once been their home.

There was only one reason why Sonya had taken him back into her life, and that was because there was no alternative. He simply couldn't take care of himself. It was this, or a nursing home. And Sonya could not have lived with the guilt of leaving him to that.

If this was love, it was strictly a love born of pity, a love that stuck in the back of his throat. It was shameful, it was unmanning, and for the first time in his life, he had been forced into endless introspection.

Riding to work on the day of the accident, he had suddenly felt the distance that he had opened up between himself and ordinary human emotions. He had given up everything to walk on water, and in the process had turned himself into a Man from Mars.

The accident had changed all that. He could no longer afford to remain a Man from Mars. Now he was dependent on Sonya for everything, and he had to find what ways he could to give her something, anything, back. Or else be nothing but a burden, a guilt, an object of pity, a thing, not a man.

And so it was up to him to say what needed to be said to break this silence now.

"Look, I want to thank you for coming here at all,

Franja," he blurted out. "I know what a shitty father I've been, and—"

"Please, Father, not now!" Franja shot back. "I mean—"

Jerry forced a grin. "I know, I know," he said. "It's quite a shock seeing your own father turned into a cyborg."

"Father—"

"And a Russian cyborg at that!" Jerry said, patting the console beside the couch. "I've got a bunch of Soviet circuitry replacing a part of my brain, who knows, give it enough time, and maybe it'll turn me into a good Marxist." And he managed a laugh at his own stupid joke.

Franja's frozen face actually cracked into a ghost of a grin. Sonya's eyes filled with tears. "I'll go put on some coffee," she said awkwardly, and left the two of them alone.

Jerry stared silently at his daughter for a long moment, once again not knowing what to say. Franja stared back, looked away, then sat down on the opposite end of the couch from him.

"So . . . so how do you feel?" she said, looking away from him across the room.

"Okay, despite all appearances," Jerry told her.

Another long silence.

"Look, Franja, I know how difficult this must be for you . . . ," Jerry finally said.

"And for you too, Father," she replied coolly.

Jerry sighed. There was nothing else for it. And after all, it really *was* up to him.

"I know how lame this has to sound after all these years, but I really am sorry," he said. "For everything."

Franja looked down at the carpet.

"I was wrong," Jerry told her. "I was so wound up in what Russian meddling had done to *my* career that I couldn't see that you had to do what was necessary for yours. You were just doing what you had to."

"What I *wanted* to do, Father!" Franja snapped, looking up at him angrily. "I always wanted to be a Soviet citizen, and I'm proud to be one now!"

"And I'm proud of you, Franja," Jerry told her. "I used to hope that it would be Bob who . . ." He winced at the thought of Bob, stuck inside America by the damnable National Security Act, and who even now, under *these* circumstances, could not get an exit visa for a simple visit home.

"But here you are," he managed to go on, "with Concordski pilot's wings, and someday, it'll be you who gets to go where I . . . where I . . ."

Franja's face softened. "Please don't talk about that now, Father," she said. "I know how much it must hurt you to . . . to . . ." And she looked away again.

"I . . . I only wanted to tell you how proud of you I am . . . ," Jerry stammered.

"You've taken a long time to say so, Father!" Franja snapped, looking back at him with hurt in her eyes. Then, more softly, "I'm sorry."

"I don't want your pity, Franja, but I do want us to try and be a father and a daughter to each other again," Jerry told her. "I can't honestly tell you that I'm going to try and make it up to you, because I can't. But . . . but can we start over?"

Franja looked into his eyes. "I don't know, Father, I really don't, it's been so long, and so much has happened. . . ."

"Can't we at least try?" Jerry begged her. "For your mother's sake? You know, it's not easy for her, suddenly having me back here again like . . . like this. She's . . . she's going to need your support. At least, let's try to be civil to each other for her sake, okay?"

Franja's expression softened. She studied his face narrowly, as if looking at someone she had never seen before. And perhaps she is, Jerry thought, perhaps she is.

"All right, Father, if you put it that way . . . ," she said quietly.

Jerry reached hesitantly across the couch and touched her hand. Franja's face showed no reaction. But at least she didn't pull away.

Los Angeles Times: "Mr. President, what will you do if the Russians use the Red Army to suppress a Ukrainian secession by force?"

President Carson: "Support the Ukrainian freedom fighters."

NBC: "With what?"

President Carson: "With all my heart and soul, like any other freedom-loving American!"

CBS: "With arms?"

CNN: "With American advisors?"

New York Times: "With military support?"

President Carson: "Wait a minute, wait a minute, who said anything about getting into a shooting match with the Russians?"

Houston Post: "*You* did, Mr. President! You just pledged your full support for the Ukrainian freedom fighters!"

President Carson: "Oh no I didn't!"

NBC: "Now you're saying you'll stand by and do nothing while the Red Army invades the Ukraine?"

President Carson: "Who did you say you represented, Bill, *Tass?* Of course I support the Ukrainian freedom fighters, but I'm fully confident that they'll be able to make the Russians see reason without any American military intervention."

CNN: "How can you say a thing like that, Mr. President? How can the Ukrainians hope to hold off the Red Army on their own?"

President Carson: "Because Gorchenko won't dare send in the Red Army."

San Francisco Chronicle: "Why not?"

President Carson: "Uh . . . ah . . . let's just say we have intelligence data that lead me to . . . uh . . . believe that . . . ah . . . the Ukrainian freedom fighters have what it takes to . . . stand up to Russian aggression."

—Presidential Press Conference

"How can you submit yourself to this, Mother?" Franja said as they sat across the dining room table from each other over coffee, late that night, after Father had gone off to bed. "Have you really thought out what it's going to be like?"

Mother sat there with her shoulders hunched over, staring down into her coffee cup. Franja had to admit that the evening had gone far better than she had feared. Mother and Father hadn't fought at all. Dinner had been quite civilized. Mother had even seemed rather cheerful, though Franja suspected it was a bit forced.

And Father . . . She had to admit that this had not been the man she remembered. He had forthrightly apologized to her. He had tried to make his peace as best he could for Mother's sake. He seemed quite different now. Perhaps the years had mellowed him, or more likely, the accident had changed him. After all, she hadn't seen him for years.

But still . . .

"There isn't anyone else to take care of him, Franja, you know that," Mother said. "What would you have me do, put him in a nursing home for the rest of his life?"

Franja sighed. "But what kind of life are you going to have like this?" she said softly.

"He can take care of himself during the day. I'll be going back to work on Monday."

Franja reached out and took her mother's hand. "I'm not being hard-hearted, really I'm not," she said. "I can certainly understand how you must feel now. But two years from now? Five? Ten? Twenty?"

A sob wracked Mother's body. And then she burst into tears.

"Mother . . . ?"

Mother continued to cry, her head hanging limply from her shoulders.

"Mother, what is it?"

Mother choked back her tears, rubbed her eyes, looked up at her. "He's dying, Franja," she said. "He'll be *gone* in a year or two. That thing isn't perfect, it only approximates what he's lost. There'll be little strokes, cerebral hemorrhages, emphysema, mental deterioration. . . . He's going to die slowly and horribly over the next couple of years, aware, and awake, and watching himself slip away . . ."

"My God!"

". . . I can't let him go through that alone, can I? Locked away in some nursing home, some hospital, all by himself, with no one by his side, no one to love him, nothing to do but sit around and feel himself rotting away."

"But . . . but he seems so . . . *cheerful* . . . so . . ."

"Brave?" Mother said. "Oh yes, he's been very brave, it's enough to break your heart."

"You haven't told him, have you?" Franja blurted numbly.

"Of course not! How could I do a thing like that? And you're not going to tell him either, Franja! We can't let him die like that, we can't take away his hope."

"But sooner or later . . ."

"Better later than sooner!" Mother declared. "We've got to give him at least that! It's all that we can do."

"Of course," Franja said. The walls seemed to be pressing in on her. First the accident, then a painful and awkward reunion with the father who had not spoken to her for years, and now . . . this.

"I know you've got your own life to live, Franja, but please, please help me!" Mother pleaded.

"Of course," Franja muttered. "But what can I do?"

"Make your peace with him, Franja. Come home whenever you can. Be a daughter to him. Let him be a father to you. Forgive him, Franja, everything he's ever wanted has been taken away from him, and now . . . now it's his life."

Franja stood up, walked around the dining room table, threw her arms around her mother's shoulders and hugged her. "You can count on me, Mother," she said. "I won't let you down."

Mother rose shakily to her feet and threw herself into Franja's arms.

"Oh God, I hope so!" she cried. "Oh, Franja, I really need a friend! And you're the only one that I have!"

GRAND TOUR NAVETTE
MAIDEN FLIGHT PERFECT

Patrice Corneau, Director of the European Space Agency, has announced that last week's shakedown cruise of the first Grand Tour Navette went almost perfectly. No significant problem with any system was discovered on the four-day cruise around the Moon. The flight was a complete success.

"This is the dawning of a new age in space for the human species," Corneau declared. "Grand Tour Navettes will make lunar cities a real possibility, allow us to establish a permanent base on Mars, turn Spaceville into a money-making concern at last, take us to Jupiter, Saturn, and perhaps even beyond. Columbus discovered America and Magellan circumnavigated the Earth under sail, but it took

the advent of the steamboat to begin to build a society
that was truly global. That's where we are in space now."

—Agence France-Presse

X X I V

When Sonya went back to work, Jerry had little to do but
watch television, read science fiction, and play with his computer. He had always hated TV dramas, the news these days
was mostly about some election in the Ukraine that had all
of Europe in an uproar, and the occasional item about the
delays in the maiden voyage of the Grand Tour Navette.

And when, at last, he was constrained to sit alone in the
living room and watch the main engines of *his* Grand Tour
Navette fire up on television, watch the great ship gloriously
and majestically warp out of orbit toward the Moon without
him, watch it dwindle slowly into the starry blackness until
all that was visible was the pale blue point of light of the
exhaust moving like a man-made star across the firmament,
that was more than he could bear of watching television.
Nor could he endure the bitter thought of reading any more
science fiction.

So after that, he disappeared into the bits and bytes, using
his computer to access every data bank he could, research-
ing the literature on cloning of brain tissue and implantable
electronics, hoping to ferret out something along the cutting
edge that would be applicable to his own condition.

There wasn't very much. When it came to electronics, the
hibernautika itself was the state of the art. No one was even
working directly on the implantable electronics he needed
to live a real life. Given six months or so of intensive research in the field, he might very well be able to design the
circuits he needed himself—and he certainly had nothing
but time on his hands—but the level of miniaturization
needed to produce practical implants seemed about a decade away.

Cloning of brain tissue was another matter, and, in its

way, even more frustrating. The Americans were still way ahead in biotechnology—that and the endless elaboration of space-weapon technology were about the only areas in which the United States was still on the cutting edge—but the latest wrinkle in the endlessly exfoliating National Security Act barred access to American data banks to users outside the United States, he could find no way to break through the blocks, and the only way to even get hints about what was going on in the States was from vague secondary and tertiary sources limited to what was published in the popular press.

The Americans had succeeded in cloning whole rat brains, but as part of some ghoulish military program. What they seemed to be doing was cloning brains from rat genomes, then immediately subjecting them to some kind of polymerization process, which preserved them in amber, as it were, so that they needed no biological matrix. The dead brains—if they were ever biologically viable in the first place, a point that seemed deliberately obscured—could then, at least in theory, be used as highly miniaturized circuit boards for complex missile guidance systems.

It didn't seem very applicable to his own problem, and in any case, it was all under a military security lid. Still, if and when the work was duplicated in Europe, there might just be something to it. The ability to clone rodent brains implied the ability to clone human brain tissue. And even if the product was not biologically viable, if it could indeed be polymerized and programmed, it certainly would lick the miniaturization problem, the lost brain tissue could be replaced by a polymerized and programmed clone of itself.

It wasn't much, it might be at least a decade away, but it was something. And it was the only hope he was able to find, however vague and distant, in all his weeks of research.

And the knowledge of it forced him into the one area he had dreaded exploring.

His heartbeat for the most part had seemed regular and normal, and he really had no problem breathing. He experienced no discomfort, and he felt strong and healthy. But there were moments . . .

Sometimes when he spoke long sentences rapidly and loudly, he felt a certain tension between his voluntary breath control and the forced breathing rhythm of the machinery. And if he forced his way through it, and built up a carbon dioxide surplus and oxygen debt, there was a lag before the circuitry increased his involuntary breathrate to compensate, leaving him out of breath and dizzy for a few moments.

Once in a while, he awoke from a nightmare with his heart racing. Sometimes he seemed to feel the blood rushing behind his eardrums. Erections tended to make him feel light-headed, they were short-lived, and he was afraid to do anything with them. If he stood up too abruptly, he experienced a frisson of vertigo. When he tried a little aerobic exercise—a few jumping jacks—his lungs seemed to be working too hard and his heart too little.

The hibernautika was good, but the circuitry had been designed to control the heartbeat and respiration of cosmonauts in a steady state of rest, indeed in hibernation. The programming had been modified for normal activity, but he suspected that the complex natural feedback-loops between heartbeat and respiration were less than perfectly modeled.

How good *was* the hibernautika? How well would his health hold up over decades?

Jerry avoided looking into this question as long as he could, but once he had found out everything possible about implantable electronics, the future of miniaturization, the cloned and polymerized rat brains, once he had a picture of the long-term possibilities, there was nothing for it but to at last learn what was known about his present situation.

There was nothing at all in the literature about the long-term biological effects of the hibernautika. If the Russians had done any such experiments, they were under a tight security lid.

But after all, the hibernautika was only a miniaturized version of the much bulkier life-support equipment they had used in the hospital, that machinery had been around for years, and there would be no security lid in that area.

Brain damage like his was quite rare, and the machinery had mostly been used to keep bodies of massively brain-damaged victims going to supply organs for transplants, or as a temporary expedient during operations or recovery from cerebral edemas.

Extensive search yielded only seven cases similar to his, where the machinery had been used as a permanent means of maintaining the lives of otherwise viable patients.

None of them had survived past twenty-two months.

The case histories were chilling.

Blood clots. Weakened arteries. Aneurysms. Emphysema. Cerebral hemorrhages. Arrthythmias.

Two of the patients had died of massive strokes, suddenly, and comparatively mercifully. They were the lucky ones.

The others had slid downhill slowly from accumulated ministrokes, minor heart malfunctions, progressive emphysema, and blood-vessel damage. They had suffered successive small episodes of brain damage, loss of bowel and bladder control, slow deterioration of higher cerebral functions, they had gone out as mental vegetables, but not before they had endured months of slowly watching their own minds decay. Those were the only two prognoses.

If he was lucky, he would die quickly of a massive stroke.

If he was not, what he had to look forward to was under two years of a slow wasting away in physical and mental agony.

He turned off the computer and sat there in front of the dead screen for a long, long while, not even thinking, hardly even feeling, as if he had become a human vegetable already.

Then he began to cry. That went on for a long time, as he just sat there, wallowing in self-pity, devoid of all coherent thought.

Then, finally, he was able to feel anger.

The goddamn doctors had lied to him! They had treated him like a child!

What right did the bastards have to lie to me like that? What right did they have to lie to Sonya?

Sonya . . .

Of course.

Suddenly all the rage went whooshing out of him. No, the doctors had not been cruel, they had been merciful after their fashion. He was a man, he had endured disappointment, despair, and frustration all of his life, he had lost his country, and his son, and his marriage, and his dream. He could take it. He was taking it now, wasn't he?

But Sonya . . .

No, the doctors had been right not to tell Sonya. She would fall apart. She would go to pieces. All the guilt of her affair with Ilya Pashikov, of the divorce, of the success of her life and the ultimate tragic failure of his, would come crashing down upon her, would bury her in despair and self-loathing.

Jerry sighed. Face it, he told himself, she only took you back home out of a sense of guilty responsibility; this has been no passionate romantic reunion. We sleep in the same bed, but we don't make love. I'm a patient, not a husband.

And yet . . .

And yet wasn't *this* an expression of love, love of a pale, attenuated kind? And if she knew the truth, would not even that be turned entirely into an unbearable pity?

Unbearable, in the end, to both of them.

Sonya must never know.

And if in the end that was really going to be impossible, well, at least let her keep the illusion of hope as long as possible, let the months of despair be comparatively few, let what little time they had left together be as easy for her as he could contrive to make it.

He owed her that much, didn't he? A last act of love on the way out.

So by the time Sonya came home from work, Jerry had pulled himself together. He wiped all mention of the truth from his computer's memory, just in case. He greeted her at the door, he kissed her, he smiled, he even helped her prepare dinner as he used to long, long ago.

He nodded pleasantly all through dinner as she went on about the details of her day's work, and he even tried to at least seem to be paying attention to her babble about the Ukrainian crisis.

Sonya had been pleased, if a bit bemused, at his uncharacteristic interest in political affairs, but she seemed to suspect nothing, and after dinner, when she asked him about *his* day, he made up some nonsense about research he had been doing on wormholes and cosmic strings, which made about as much sense to her as the politics had to him, and the evening glided smoothly by.

Indeed, by the time it was time to go to bed, Jerry had managed to talk himself up out of the pit, and he drifted off to sleep quickly.

But in the middle of the night, he dreamed he was floating freely in space at last, orbiting the Earth weightlessly, watching the cloud deck and the continents drift by, swimming through the vacuum effortlessly and joyfully in his spacesuit like a cosmic porpoise, walking on water at last. . . .

And then there was some kind of suit malfunction, and his air was cut off, and the icy cold of space poured in, and the breath was sucked from his lungs, and—

He awoke in bed gasping for breath, his heart beating slowly and stupidly in his chest. It took only a few moments for the hibernautika circuitry to regularize his heartbeat and respiration, but in those moments the vision was cold and cruel and clear.

He was going to die, and soon.

In that moment, the confrontation with his own impending mortality was realer than it had been all day, the terror of it was quite overwhelming.

But as he lay there in the darkness, he found a source of strength in it too. For once you face the inevitability of your own death, really face it, there is a power that comes to you.

For life itself was the last thing that anyone had to give up. And once you know for a certainty that you have to give up that too, why it all becomes crystal clear, as clear, and as hard, and as sharp-edged as the stars seen from beyond the mists of the atmosphere.

What do you do when everything else is gone? When you know you literally have nothing left to give up?

You walk on water.

If only for a moment at the very end.

KRESKOV CALLS FOR ELECTION LAW REFORM

Delegate Piotyr Andreiovich Kreskov of Novosibirsk introduced a resolution calling for election reform into the Supreme Soviet and then withdrew it after Ethnic Nationalists and Eurorussians alike shouted him down.

"With all the attention fixed on the impending Ukrainian Presidential election, it somehow seems to have escaped everyone's attention that the present system, which allows constituent republics to choose the dates for their own elections, is going to result in a hideous mess," Kreskov pointed out. "If, as seems inevitable, Vadim Kronkol is elected President of the Ukraine, we're going to end up right in the middle of the worst crisis since the Great Patriotic War, with an election campaign for this body and the Soviet Presidency going on! If the Supreme Soviet would pass a law synchronizing these elections, we could be spared the paralysis this is certain to bring."

After Ethnic Nationalist delegations shouted their outrage at this latest attempt by centralist Great Russian hegemonists to usurp the sovereign powers of the constituent republics and Eurorussian delegates wrung their hands in despair at this clumsy provocation on the part of the well-known Bear, Kreskov rather lamely explained that he was not suggesting that anything could be done about it now, but that the present crisis had merely pointed to a flaw in the constitution that needed to be addressed once it was over.

"He knew just what he was doing," many Eurorussian delegates charged afterward. "It was a clear attempt to incite chauvinistic outrage between Russians and Ethnic Nationalists, and it certainly succeeded."

—Novosti

"He's been living on the phone, Franja, he's got them all roped into this crazy scheme," Mother said. "I don't know how to stop it, I don't know what to tell him, I'm at my wits' end."

It had been five days since Franja had been able to get back to Paris, and during that time Father would seem to have been as busy as the maniacs in the Ukraine. The last time she had been home, all this had seemed like a harmless fantasy, indeed Mother herself had even been more or less encouraging it as a way to keep his spirits up, and Father had certainly seemed like his old space-obsessed self, minus the bitterness, and the anti-Soviet tirades.

He had babbled about it endlessly during every meal, and Mother had just sat there, and smiled, and let him rave on.

The shakedown cruise of the first Grand Tour Navette had been such a complete success that they were already starting to boost components into orbit with which to assemble the second. The news coverage had been extensive, it had been the ideal diversion from the impending crisis in the Ukraine, and there had even been a rather long feature interview with the Father of the Grand Tour Navette that had been carried on *Vremya*.

Franja had caught it back home in Moscow. Ivan was in

town at the same time for once, and he had been complaining of late that she had hardly spent any time at all with him since her father's accident, taking off-days in Paris she could have spent in Moscow with him. He had actually started to act *jealous* of the attention she was lavishing on her invalid father—at his expense, or so at least Ivan seemed to be beginning to see it. So she had made sure they watched the interview together, hoping that it would somehow make him understand, smooth the troubled waters.

And it had.

Ivan had fidgeted and cursed under his breath during the inevitable lead story on the Ukrainian election, but when Jerry Reed's image appeared on the videowall—a full establishing shot of Father sitting on the living room couch with the hibernautika console conspicuously in evidence—his broad strong face had softened, the frown lines smoothed out, and he had taken her hand and squeezed it.

The interview itself had been rather a tearjerker, with the English interviewer spinning out an elaborate and overcomplex metaphor comparing Father to Moses looking down from afar, after forty years of wandering in the wilderness, upon the Promised Land he was destined never to see, intercut with images of the Grand Tour Navette orbiting the Earth, approaching the Moon, the triumphant return.

The interviewer had tried to squeeze the maximum bathos out of Father's present condition, but Father, smiling rather dreamily and bravely, seemed to be fighting her every inch of the way, going on about the wonderful Soviet device that was keeping him alive, how fitting it was that it was a piece of space-program spin-off, how symbolic it was of the transnational spirit of the European Space Agency, how grateful he was to have played a part in this epic moment of human history, almost as if Tass had written his lines for him.

"I hope those bastards in the Ukraine are watching this!" Ivan said. "An *American* going on like this about transnational solidarity! But you always told me that your father *loathed* the Soviet Union . . . ?"

Franja couldn't understand it either. "He always used to," she said. "I guess it took a hard hit on the head to bring him to his senses."

"Hmmm . . . I wish Gorchenko had the balls to apply the same therapy to the blockheads in Kiev. . . ."

"And finally, what do you see for the future, Mr. Reed?" the interviewer said, as the camera moved in for a concluding close-up on Father.

But Father had not taken the opportunity to present his vision of mankind's destiny as a space-going species. Instead, he had stared directly and dreamy-eyed into the camera, and smiled a sad little, brave little, quite heartrending smile.

"This marvelous Soviet device that has been keeping me alive was developed to enable cosmonauts to someday go to the stars in a state of hibernation," Father had said instead. "So there's really no reason why it can't enable *me* to go as far as Spaceville, or the Moon. So what I see for the future is not a Moses forever barred from his Promised Land, but myself, up there on a Grand Tour Navette, on my way to the Moon. As just a tourist, maybe, but getting there just the same. And if there are those who say that's an impossible dream, well, that's what they were saying about the Grand Tour Navette twenty years ago, wasn't it? We live in the golden age of space travel. Formerly impossible things are happening every day."

"And you told me that your father couldn't cope with politics?" Ivan had said softly. "If it was a question of a popular vote, he'd be on his way now. What a man! You are *sure* he's an American? He has the heart of a true Russian!"

On Franja's next trip back to Paris, Father had been bubbling with enthusiasm, totally absorbed in his hopeless fantasy, going on and on about the letters he was receiving from all over Europe, about how, after all, Spaceville was full of retirees in far worse shape than he was, about how it was his *right* to ride the Grand Tour Navette.

And Mother, for her part, had kept up her smiling front and just let him go on, encouraging him even. Only when she was alone with Franja did she let her heartache show through.

For course the whole thing was out of the question. Even if there was some way to persuade the European Space Agency to give him his Grand Tour Navette ride, the strain of a Concordski boost to orbit, if it didn't kill him, would accelerate the accumulated brain and lung and blood-vessel damage he was already suffering. He wouldn't even be allowed aboard a short-hop airplane; the cabin pressure changes would be too much for the hibernautika to properly handle, and no commercial carrier's insurance would cover him.

"But why do you encourage him then, Mother?" Franja had asked.

And Mother had shrugged and sighed. "It keeps his spirits up. It's like his own little science-fiction story. I think he really knows it's impossible himself, but . . . What am I supposed to tell him, anyway? The truth? That he's dying? That it's breaking my heart twice over to hear him go on like this . . . ?"

And she had broken into tears then, and collapsed into Franja's arms, sobbing. But by breakfast the next morning, she was all smiles and enthusiasm again when Father displayed the latest packet of letters. And so the visit had gone.

But that was then, and this was now.

By now, so it seemed, Father had been busy putting pressure, moral and otherwise, on his friends and colleagues at ESA. All during dinner, he had gone on and on about what he had already accomplished.

Patrice Corneau, at least to hear Father tell it, had agreed to let him ride the second Grand Tour Navette on its shakedown cruise as an "honorary observer," provided that he was authorized to do so by a resolution of the Common European Parliament. Emile Lourade had agreed to endorse such a resolution, provided it was introduced by the government of a member state. Boris Velnikov had promised to take the matter up with his nebulous contacts in Moscow.

Mother had kept up her smiling façade throughout all this, but Franja could see how plastic it was, and now Mother for the most part kept her silence. She seemed drawn, and wan, and vibrating with unreleased tension, and toward the end, over dessert, she even slipped to the point where a certain anger had shown through.

"Of course I doubt if Velnikov is as connected as he likes to pretend," Father had said. "He's got some real influence, but it would certainly help if there was some pressure from the Red Star Tower—"

"I've told you a hundred times, Jerry, Red Star has no influence on—"

"—but it has plenty of influence with the contractors, and the contractors—"

"Have nothing to do with government policy!"

"But Tass does, and the Paris bureau would love a story like this, wouldn't they, what with—"

"The tail does not wag the dog!"

"But *Red Star* is one big dog, and you're the Director of the Paris office! You're an important bureaucrat here, Sonya, there have got to be other important bureaucrats who want favors from you, you can trade them back and forth till you get a Foreign Ministry stamp on a request from Velnikov, and then—"

"It just doesn't work that way, Jerry!"

"You can at least try!"

"I told you, I *am* trying! But I simply can't promise you the results you want! It's no easy matter for the Director of Red Star's Paris office to commandeer the services of the central governmental apparatus!"

"I'm not asking you to do anything like that!"

And Mother had taken a deep breath, and calmed herself, and spoken in a much more soothing tone of voice. "Yes you are, Jerry," she said softly. "And I really am trying. Just please, please, don't expect me to work miracles overnight."

"Impossible things are happening every day," Father had said more quietly, and Mother had nodded, and smiled, and the moment had seemed to finally glide past.

But after Father had gone to bed, Mother had taken Franja into the living room, and poured them both Cognacs, and let her anguish and her ire come out.

"I don't know what to do, Franja, they're all encouraging him shamelessly—Velnikov, Corneau, Lourade—they're all just telling him whatever they think he wants to hear."

"But don't they know, Mother, about . . . I mean . . . ?"

"Of course they do!" Mother snapped angrily. "They're all just stringing him along and passing the responsibility for saying no to someone else! Corneau tells him, of course, all I need is a resolution of the Common European Parliament. Lourade tells him, sure, I'll back the resolution as soon as a member state introduces it. Velnikov says, sure, I'm on your side, but my connections in Moscow . . . It's the oldest bureaucratic game in the book. No one wants to say no, no one can say yes, so they just toss the responsibility back and forth until it gets caught by someone who has no one to pass it along to."

Mother sighed, took a long sip of Cognac. "And the way the cowards have set it up, at least in Jerry's eyes," she said, "that's me."

Franja took a sip of Cognac herself. As Mother had asked, she had tried to be a real daughter to her father. There had been no further recriminations about the past. She had been cordial, she had been friendly, she had been sympathetic. At first, it had been something of an act, playing the role of dutiful daughter to a father who had betrayed her. But Father had been cordial too, gentle, wistful, and what had begun as a favor to her mother had perhaps slowly transmuted into the real thing.

For this was a different man from the father who had disowned her, and perhaps it had been Ivan who had shown her the truth of that. "What a man!" Ivan had declared. "He has the heart of a true Russian!"

And so he did, Franja admitted to herself now. Like a true Russian, her father was a dreamer, a romantic, a brave spirit who defied the fates, who was ready to dare anything to fulfill what he saw as his destiny, even in the face of death. How could she deny her love to such a man?

And for the first time in many a year, she found herself thinking of her old lost love, Nikolai Smirnov, out there somewhere now beyond Mars. Nikolai would understand what she felt even better than Ivan.

Nikolai would understand why now, at long, long last, she felt so proud to be the daughter of Jerry Reed.

"Perhaps . . . perhaps you should do what Father asks?" Franja said. "You could, couldn't you?"

"Do what?" Mother said. "Help him kill himself?"

And Franja saw her mother for the first time through different eyes. Saw a woman quite different from herself, a woman who would never understand what she and her father shared. "To write his own happy ending," she said.

"Franja!" Mother cried. "What *are* you saying?"

"Nothing, Mother," Franja said, staring down into her glass.

Perhaps you have lived in the West far too long, she thought.

Perhaps you have forgotten what it means to have a Russian heart.

KRONKOL BY A LANDSLIDE

Final election returns from the Ukraine show that Vadim Kronkol has captured 69 percent of the Presidential vote. The Ukrainian Liberation Front has won 221 seats in the 302-seat Ukrainian Parliament.

President Harry B. Carson, on behalf of the American people, has congratulated Mr. Kronkol on his smashing victory, referring to the Ukrainian leader as "a fellow freedom fighter" and the "George Washington of his country."

The American Vice President, Nathan Wolfowitz, an avowed political enemy of President Carson who was put on the Republican ticket by desperate party leaders in what both men freely admit was a pragmatic deal to break the long convention deadlock, was quick as usual to distance himself from the head of his own government.

"That grinding noise you hear is the Father of Our Country gnashing his wooden choppers in the grave," the Vice President declared. "What scares me is the thought that he's going to have a lot more new company if Harry Carson keeps shooting his mouth off without thinking, like the flannel-mouthed demagogue he is."

—*The Times* (London)

It was all so frustrating, so near, and yet so far. He had convinced Patrice Corneau to see things his way, he had convinced Emile Lourade, he had even convinced his old enemy Velnikov; why couldn't he convince his own wife?

Sonya, for all her talk, was really doing nothing. She was treating him like an invalid, like a piece of fragile glasswork to be kept in cotton batting, something to be carefully preserved against all possibility of risk.

Not that Jerry couldn't understand why. The doctors had led her to believe that if he was careful, if he took good care of himself, if he took no risks, he could survive indefinitely like this, or at least long enough for a brain transplant or an electronic implant to become possible.

He had to admit that, from her point of view, she was doing the right thing.

And the only way he could see to change it would be to tell her the truth.

But he couldn't do that, he just couldn't. He might be

willing to give up everything to walk on water, including what little was left of his life, but when it came down to it, he realized that the one thing he couldn't do was take away Sonya's hope. He just didn't have the ruthlessness or the cruelty to go that far.

And that left Franja.

Franja shared the dream. She had been up there herself. At least Franja would understand what he felt. Perhaps she could convince Sonya without having to tell her . . . without having to tell her . . .

He badly needed an ally. Perhaps just as badly, he needed someone to confide in. But that would mean telling Franja the full truth.

Could he do that?

Was there anything else he could do?

Jerry sighed. He got up off the couch, went to the breakfront, poured himself a big Cognac, downed it all in one long fiery gulp. There was nothing else for it. Sonya was at work, Franja was in the kitchen making lunch, if he was going to do it at all, he might as well get it over with.

He reeled up his cable snugly, grabbed the handle of the hibernautika, and walked into the kitchen, wheeling the damned thing along with him.

Franja stood by the wooden countertop, buttering slices of bread for sandwiches, the tomatoes, ham, cheese, and red onions already sliced and ready.

"It'll be ready in a few minutes, Father," she said without looking up. "Want to open some white wine?"

Numbly, Jerry opened the refrigerator, pulled out a half-full bottle of Bordeaux, pulled the cork with his fingers, fished two wineglasses out of the dishwasher, filled them, gulped down a glass, refilled it, and held out the other glass to Franja.

"Just put it in the dining room and I'll be right in," she said without looking at him.

"Drink it now, Franja," Jerry said, shoving the glass at her.

"Father?" Franja said, looking up, finally, and eyeing him peculiarly.

"There's . . . there's something I've got to tell you, Franja . . ." Jerry stammered. "And . . . and it's not going to be easy . . . for either of us."

He handed Franja the glass. She shrugged, took a small

sip. Jerry stared at her. She stared back. Neither of them spoke for a long moment.

"Well, Father," Franja finally said. "For God's sake, tell me!"

Jerry sighed. He took another gulp of wine, screwed up his courage, and did.

"I . . . I've got a good reason to ride the next Grand Tour Navette, Franja," he began shakily. "I . . . I've got a good reason to get myself up there as soon as I can. . . . Your mother . . . she doesn't . . . The fact is that I'm dying, Franja, I've got maybe a year or two, that's all, and it's not going to be pleasant. . . ."

"Why . . . why are you telling me this, Father?" Franja said in a strange cool voice.

"Because I don't want to go through it, Franja! I want to trade a year or two of slow agony for a few bright shining hours! I want to die happy, is that so hard to understand? Wouldn't you, Franja? Wouldn't you?"

Franja stared at her father, not knowing what to say, not knowing what to do, but knowing how cold and hard she must seem to him now, standing there dry-eyed in the face of this awful revelation. She tried to bring tears to her eyes by an act of will, but failed utterly. For she had known all this too long, she had cried herself out with Mother when she had told her.

And Father had known all along after all! Of course he would, she realized in retrospect. She should have known that Jerry Reed would plunge into the data banks as soon as he was able. And Mother should have known too. He was that kind of man, he always had been.

And just as Mother was the kind of woman who would shield him from the truth, so was he the kind of man who would shield *her*.

And that, finally, was indeed enough to bring honest tears to her eyes. "I do believe I would," she said softly. "But why tell me?"

"Because I need your help, Franja," Father said. "I have no one else to turn to. I certainly can't tell your mother. I'm telling *you* because you've got to help me find some way to convince her to do what we both know is right without telling her the whole truth and breaking her heart."

Franja looked at her father through new eyes. There he stood, with an electrode fastened to the back of his head, wired to a device that was keeping him alive and slowly killing him at the same time, facing the end of his life with a bravery she doubted she could ever have summoned up.

Here he was, still, in some sense, the same overgrown little boy that he had always been, ready to pursue his vision to the very end with the same open heart, yet unwilling, even now, to break Mother's to do it.

Perhaps this man has misjudged me in the past, she thought. Perhaps he has done me injustice, even cruelties. But he gave me his dream, did he not? And now, in his moment of need, who does he turn to?

How much more have *I* misjudged *him?*

And now, here *she* was, with the hardest decision of her life facing her. Should she do what she knew her mother would want her to do and hold her tongue? Or speak the truth and put an end at last to this beautiful but foolish dance of loving deceit?

She sighed. She reached out and took her father's hand.

Oh yes, he had a Russian heart!

And so did she.

"Mother already knows," she said.

Father stared at her without reacting for a long, long moment. Then he put his glass down on the countertop and took her in his arms.

"Asshole that I am, I love you very much," he whispered into her ear. "What a fool I've been, what a blind stupid fool."

Franja burst into tears. "Moi aussi," she said, burying her face in her father's neck. "Moi aussi."

No one greeted Sonya at the door when she returned home from work, and when she went into the living room, Jerry and Franja were sitting on the couch together, side by side, their thighs almost touching, closer than she had ever seen them sitting since Franja had left home, and with strangely identical solemn expressions on their faces.

The sight of the two of them sitting together like that, like a loving father and daughter at last, should have warmed her heart, but the hardness in their eyes, the determined set of their jaws, filled her instead with a foreshadowing frisson of dread, and she somehow knew before Franja opened her mouth.

"Father knows," Franja said. "He knows everything."

"You told him!" Sonya cried angrily. "Franja, how *could* you!"

"*I* told *her*," Jerry said quietly.

"You . . . you told her?" Sonya stammered. "You . . . you knew all along?"

"Of course I knew," Jerry said. "You really think I'm such a fool? You really thought I wouldn't research the literature?"

"Why didn't you tell me, then? Why did you let me . . . ?"

"Why didn't *you* tell *me*?" he said softly, not at all in an accusatory tone.

"Because . . . because . . ." Sonya's eyes filled with tears. And she could see that Jerry was on the brink of crying too.

"Exactly, Sonya," he said. "You couldn't tell me, and I couldn't tell you. What a pair of fools!"

"*Loving* fools, Jerry, loving fools . . . ," Sonya whispered.

"You'd better sit down, Mother," Franja said, and she squirmed her way along the couch away from Jerry, leaving room for her to sit in between.

Sonya sat down on the couch between her husband and her daughter, feeling the warmth of their bodies beside her, the comfort of them, feeling more truly at home in her apartment—in *their* apartment—than she had in years and years. Now, only now . . .

"Now what?" she sighed.

"Now we face reality like a family of adults," Franja said with quite undaughterly firmness.

"My lungs are going to fill up with fluid, and my arteries and veins are going to decay, and there'll be heart arrhythmias, and little strokes, and—"

"Jerry! Please!"

"It's the truth, Sonya. You can't do anything to save me. Nobody can."

"You can't give up hope like this, Jerry!"

"I haven't given up hope, Sonya," he told her. "I've got

all the hope in the world for something wonderful, something you *can* help to—"

"Oh no, Jerry, for God's sake, not *that* now!" Sonya cried. "You can't be serious!"

But one look at his face told her how serious he really was.

"I'm . . . dead serious," he said. "It's now or never. I ride the next Grand Tour Navette, or I die without ever having my moment, for nothing, as the buffoon in a stupid farce. Is that what you really want for me? Is it, Sonya?"

"Jerry . . ."

"Spaceville is full of people in worse shape than I am," he went on relentlessly. "I've done my homework. Hell, I designed the GTN, remember? The Grand Tour Navette will take me all the way to the Moon and back and I'll never even pull more than half a g." He gave her a foolish little smile. "In fact, it'll be healthier for me up out of the gravity well than it would be down here on Earth."

"I . . . I've done some homework too, Jerry," Sonya admitted. "The reentry strain . . . the cabin pressure differential . . . and you'd be under nearly three g's on the trip up to orbit. It'd cut months off your life, a year maybe. . . ."

"So what?" Jerry said coldly. "I'll have been there."

"I won't do it!" Sonya said. "I won't let you just give up and die! In the months you're talking about throwing away, *anything* could happen!"

"My God, Sonya, what do I have to do to convince you to help me?" Jerry said angrily. "Get down on my knees and beg?"

"Tell him, Franja!" Sonya cried. "Tell him how insane this is!"

"I can't do that, Mother," Franja said. "You're wrong, and he's right."

"What?"

"He's going to die, Mother. And nothing we can do is going to save him."

"I just can't accept that!" Sonya sobbed.

"You have to, Sonya! I have!"

"How can you sit there and . . . and . . . ?"

"Because I've still got a dream," Jerry said. "I don't want to spend what's left of my life doing nothing but sitting around and watching myself die. A few months of pain and agony for a chance to have what I've always wanted. Can't you see that *not* making that trade-off is what's insane?"

"No, Jerry, I can't, I just can't. . . ."

"Because it's not your dream, Mother, that's it, isn't it?" Franja said. "You've never understood it. You don't know what it means."

And she looked at Jerry as she spoke now, speaking to him, speaking for him, as Sonya had never heard her speak before.

"To feel the power of those engines fighting against gravity, against the bonds of the Earth, to feel the planet itself resisting your will . . . And then, suddenly, it's over, and there's silence, and you're weightless, and you look out, and there's the Earth, shining out there in the darkness, immense, and beautiful, and wonderfully alive. And the stars, more of them than you can count, and you know that there are planets out there around them, other living worlds, and on them, creatures like yourself, looking back across the light-years, across the centuries, and it all goes on forever, worlds and time without end . . ."

Franja sighed. She turned to face Sonya. "It's like . . . it's like nothing else there is, Mother. It's . . . it's everything there is, and you know your place in it. And you feel grand, and you feel tiny, and somehow . . . somehow you know what you're for. People have died for much less, Mother. For much, much less. Let him have it. Let him go."

There were tears in Jerry's eyes now. He reached across Sonya's lap and squeezed his daughter's hand.

"Listen to me, Mother," Franja said. "I'm my father's daughter, and I *know*. I've been there."

And Sonya almost saw it then, this vision that could never be hers, like what one experienced among true believers in the church of a religion whose faith you could not share.

She envied the two of them that vision. And loved them for it. And felt the bite of jealousy too. And the happiness of being part of a true family again. And the pain of standing a pace apart from its heart.

If only . . .

She raged at the injustice of it all. I am a Soviet bureaucrat, she thought. I am a good Marxist and a dialectical materialist. But just this once, I would like to believe in God. I would like to believe that you are out there listening to me, you miserable phallocratic bastard! I would like to

believe that you are able to hear me telling you what a
sadistic brute you are!

But no voice from the whirlwind answered back. There
was only Jerry and Franja holding hands across her lap,
regarding her silently with the same infinite vista in their
eyes.

Sonya sighed. She reached out and took their hands. The
touch of the two of them warmed her heart. She had never
felt closer to them and yet never more far apart. It was the
best moment of her life and the worst.

"I just don't know," she said. "What you're asking is so
hard. . . ."

"I know it is," Jerry said softly. "Really I do. . . ."

"You've got to give me time . . ." Sonya said miserably.

"I'd like to," Jerry said. "I'd like to give you anything you
want. I'd like to give you all the time in the world."

He shrugged. He smiled oh so bravely. "But I just don't
have that much time to give," he said tenderly. "It's just not
in this hand of cards."

VADIM KRONKOL TO ADDRESS
UNITED NATIONS

Despite the strenuous efforts of the Soviet Union to
prevent it, Vadim Kronkol, the new Ukrainian President,
will be allowed to address the United Nations General
Assembly next week, and is expected to use the opportunity to declare Ukrainian independence.

In 1945, when the U.N. was founded, the Soviet Union
demanded 15 General Assembly seats, one for each of its
constituent republics. The United States offered to accept
this position providing it was given 48 General Assembly
seats, one for each state. The eventual compromise gave
the Soviet Union 3 seats, one each for the republics of
Russia, Byelorussia, and the Ukraine.

In practice, the Byelorussian and Ukrainian delegates
have always been selected by the central government of

the Soviet Union, but when Yegor Shivlets resigned, the credentials committee was left no choice but to accept the credentials of the duly elected Ukrainian government over strong Soviet protest.

United Nations legal experts have pointed out, however, that, since the Ukraine has held a U.N. seat since the organization's inception, this is not an implied recognition of Ukrainian independence.

"The Russians can't have it both ways," a high U.N. official who asked not to be identified pointed out. "They've always maintained the position that the Ukraine was a quasi-sovereign state for representation purposes, the Kronkol government was duly elected under both Soviet and Ukrainian law, and so there is no legal basis whatever for questioning its delegation's credentials. The Soviet Union did this to itself, way back in 1945."

—Robert Reed, StarNet

X X V

"It's your father again, Bobby," Sara called out from the living room.

"Jesus Christ . . . ," Robert Reed muttered under his breath. "Tell him I'll be there as soon as I wipe the shaving cream off my face!" he shouted.

What a morning to call! This was the day that the shit was going to come down for sure, and for once some big news was going to be made at the United Nations, Bobby was actually going to get his byline on a lead story, and his head was thoroughly involved with the impending crisis.

Vadim Kronkol was scheduled to address the General Assembly at eleven o'clock, and it was no secret that he was going to use it as the forum for a Ukrainian declaration of independence from the Soviet Union.

What would happen after that was anyone's guess and everyone's. What would the Russians do? Present a rival Ukrainian delegation? Walk out? Send in the Red Army?

More to the point, what words would that pinhead Harry Carson put in the mouth of the American delegate, Reagan Smith?

That was going to be the real story. Everyone knew that Kronkol was going to declare Ukrainian independence. Everyone knew that the Soviets would not accept it.

But no one knew what President Carson would do. How could you predict the next move of a maniac?

Carson had certainly made it quite clear that he would recognize an independent Ukraine the moment it was formally declared. But how far would he really go in backing the Ukrainians against the Russians?

Would he threaten to supply arms to the Ukrainians if the Red Army moved? Was it true that there were American arms in the Ukraine already? Would Carson threaten to send in American "advisors"? An expeditionary force? And would he back up his words with deeds if the Russians called his bluff? Or was he just pounding his chest like the gorilla he was?

With Harry Carson, anything was possible. Bobby didn't envy the Russians.

The United States had sealed the Western Hemisphere and turned it into a series of economic fiefdoms. Resistance in Latin America had been reduced to the point where it was being handled by local proxies led by a handful of American advisors. And while this made the endless endemic guerrilla warfare far more politically popular, now that local cannon fodder was doing most of the dying, it was lousy for the armaments industry which kept the arteriosclerotic American economy going.

The result was that trillions of dollars were still being poured down the bottomless rathole of Battlestar America. By now the Pentagon probably didn't even know how much ordnance was deployed between Geosynchronous Orbit and the atmosphere. Anything and everything that the defense industry could dream up to sell to the Pentagon had been procured in overwhelming numbers and more had to be dreamed up every year to avoid a depression.

And all this was now in the hot little hands of President Harry Burton Carson.

Everything that the Russians and Europeans had in space between here and the Moon was hostage to Battlestar America. One word from Carson, and it could all be vaporized in about five minutes—satellites, Cosmograds, Spaceville, even Lunagrad, everything, trillions and trillions of ECU in capital investment, thousands of lives.

Even if Carson sent American troops into the Ukraine against the Red Army, the Russians might not dare go beyond opposing them with conventional weaponry. For if they went to tactical nukes, Carson could retaliate by destroying everything in cis-lunar space that wasn't flying the Red, White, and Blue. And even then, it was highly unlikely that the Soviets would dare to respond with a strategic nuclear attack on the United States. Some of their missiles would no doubt get through, but Battlestar America would swat down something like 95 percent, leaving the Soviet Union at the nonexistent mercy of an enraged America still bristling with ICBMs, submarine missiles, Penetrator bombers, hypersonic cruise missiles, and the new nearly unstoppable Slam-Dunkers.

Conventional wisdom was that it was all a monstrous game of bluff, with the United States holding all the hole cards. Russia wouldn't dare risk a nuclear confrontation with a lunatic like Carson, and Carson knew it. If the Red Army invaded the Ukraine, it might end up fighting Ukrainian troops armed by the United States, but as long as the Soviets didn't go nuclear, there would be no direct American involvement.

But it was Sara's paranoid theory that Harry Carson actually *wanted* to get American forces involved in an endless conventional war in the Ukraine.

"From his loathsome viewpoint, it's just *perfect,* Bobby. A nice big capital-intensive land war that would burn up more expensive weaponry in a week than all the guerrillas in Latin America manage to take out in a year. And there'll be more independence movements, in the Caucasus, Central Asia, God knows where, to back up with American product. Latin America all over again, only this time with a string of new governments running up the debt in place of the American taxpayer. It would keep the arms industry humming along in high gear for decades, and when it's finally over, if it ever is, the United States will own half of what used to be the Soviet Union!"

True, Sara was a political extremist even by Bobby's standards, and of course her theory was paranoid, cynical, and depraved.

But on the other hand, so was Harry Carson.

And today was likely to be the day that the world found out just how demented President Carson really was.

Today was the day that Bobby's miserable U.N. assignment was finally going to give him something important to write about instead of the usual meaningless round of impotent Third World rantings.

It had taken Bobby years to land this job, years of covering stupid city politics in Santa Barbara and stupider state politics in Sacramento, years of rewriting Tass and Reuters and Agence France-Presse to fit the jingo politics of a crummy rag in San Diego, while Sara wrote her free-lance pieces for little or no money for any disreputable shit sheet that would print them, while coming down on him for selling out to the jingo press in order to make the money that kept them from starving.

He had jumped at the chance to take the U.N. job with StarNet, even though it meant living in New York, paying more than half of his salary for a so-called one-bedroom apartment in a security compound on East Ninety-third Street. It had seemed like the opportunity of a lifetime, covering the United Nations, covering *world politics,* for the second largest newsnet in the United States.

Worth pauperizing himself to live in a tiny apartment in Manhattan, in an island of high security surrounded by a sea of squalor that made the Third World look like his memory of Paris. Worth enduring the steam-bath summers. Worth the claustrophobia and the cockroaches. Worth paying double for every meal in a restaurant and every bag of groceries.

After all, he was the U.N. correspondent for StarNet, wasn't he? His stories would appear in a hundred newspapers, some of which would even run his byline, would be mouthed by TV newscasters all over the country.

Even Sara, who had long since stopped being enthusiastic about anything he did, who had never had anything good to say about New York, had excitedly urged him to take it.

"God, Bobby, it's a chance to really do something that matters!" she had said the day he got the call from StarNet. "A chance to say things that matter about something that *counts!*"

Of course, in practice it had turned out to be nothing quite so glorious. The United Nations had long since degenerated into a forum for Third World bitching and moaning. Most of the Latin American seats were held by revolutionary governments in exile. The Africans begged money which was not forthcoming. The Chinese condemned Caucasian economic imperialism. The Latin Americans railed against the United States. And the real players, the United States, Common Europe, and the East Asian Common Market, just yawned, went about their unilateral business, and ignored the rest of the world's cries of agony.

In the beginning, Bobby had actually tried to cover the endless futile speechifying with insight and passion. But after the umpteenth story was killed or rewritten into total blandness, Bobby finally got the message that his fellow American U.N. correspondents, as cynical a bunch of time-servers as he had ever seen, had been trying to give him all along.

No one in the United States gave a shit what happened in the United Nations. No one cared what happened in the Third World. Someone had to cover the U.N. for the major newsnets and papers simply because it was there. But it was strictly filler material for the back pages or the tag end of newscasts, on a par with science news, flying-saucer sightings, agricultural statistics, and man-bites-dog.

Until now.

Now Vadim Kronkol was going to use the U.N. as a forum to declare Ukrainian independence from the USSR.

It was Bobby's golden opportunity. If he could put his own spin on it, he had a shot at putting his byline on a story that would make his reputation, that could break him out of the pack.

No doubt all his so-called colleagues were now thinking the same thing, but they had long since lost their edge. This was his chance to shine before the world.

But to do that, he had to have his wits about him today. He had to be focused. He had to be sharper than he had ever been before.

Bobby groaned as he quickly ran his razor over the rest of his face and wiped off the remains of the shaving cream without bothering to brace himself with aftershave.

What a day to have to deal with another of Dad's phone calls on his way out the door!

He simply *couldn't* leave the country. In the beginning, it had been because he feared he could never get back in, but that was before the Central Security Agency had really clamped down, and now he couldn't even get a *one-way* ticket out.

Not with a sister who was a Soviet national and a mother who was a ranking officer in Red Star. And certainly not with a wife who insisted upon maintaining open involvement in every crazy radical group on the Central Security Agency's admittedly catholic shit list.

He had known all this before Dad's accident, it was what had kept him from working as a foreign correspondent, yet he *had* tried to get an exit visa after the accident, he had been willing to risk not getting back in.

Or had he?

Wasn't *that* the real source of his guilt? He had tried to get out only because he was sure he would fail, in order to make himself feel less guilty about his true priorities of job and wife. And that *was* something to feel guilty about.

That was the real guilt that overcame him when he spoke to Dad on the phone.

He had known all along that he would never really have risked everything for the sake of his father, and Sara had known it too. She had certainly objected when he went down to apply for the exit visa, but her objections had been as pro forma as the futile gesture itself.

Indeed, she had even made light of it when he had come home afterward and told her what had happened.

"Well, Bobby, I suppose you could try to get through to Nat Wolfowitz," she had said sardonically. "After all, he *is* the Vice President of the United States. Maybe he'd remember you."

Bobby groaned.

Nathan Wolfowitz, true to his word all those years ago back in Little Moscow, had indeed made a career out of campaigning futilely for President. The first time out, he had run for the Republican nomination and gotten about 900,000 votes. As soon as the election was over, he announced that he was now a Democrat, and declared for the Democratic nomination four years hence.

He continued to call himself the "American Gorbachev," and ran once more on a program of "Bringing America Back Into the World" that called for repealing the National Security Act, dismantling the Central Security Agency, pulling out of Latin America, slashing the defense budget by 70 percent, and using the money to pay back the old abrogated foreign debt over a twenty-year period in return for an immediate entry into Common Europe.

Sensible as this might be, it was about as generally popular as a fart in church, but it *did* make him great talk-show filler, the archetypal "Man You Love to Hate," and the endless TV exposure did give him recognition value.

After four years of this, he actually managed to qualify for matching federal campaign funds in the Democratic primaries, and he pulled almost three million votes. He went into the convention with something under two hundred delegates, but as the only candidate willing to violate the ancient tradition of not appearing on the convention floor till after the nomination, he was the media star of the otherwise dull event.

Immediately after the general election, he announced that he was now a Republican again and started running for the nomination. By now he was a familiar figure in a crowded field, dominated on the one hand by Creighton Laxalt, the candidate of the established money, and on the other by the fire-breathing Senator from Texas, Harry Carson.

The television debates swiftly degenerated into a series of over-the-top shouting matches between Carson and Wolfowitz. There was something perversely refreshing, after so many decades of meaningless blather, about a Presidential campaign in which two of the candidates openly hated each other's guts.

Carson went into the convention ahead of Laxalt, but about two hundred delegates shy of the nomination, after having earned the undying enmity of the also-rans. The convention remained deadlocked through twenty-three ballots.

The party brass locked all of the candidates in a smoke-filled room for twelve straight hours. What went on in there was mercifully lost to history, but what came out was surely the slimiest and most amazing back-room deal in the history of American politics.

Nathan Wolfowitz had gotten to the convention a distant fourth, with 281 delegates.

But that was enough to put Harry Carson over the top.

And somehow, the party leaders had managed to break the deadlock by getting the two of them to share the same ticket.

When dumbfounded reporters asked Wolfowitz how he could possibly have agreed to run for Vice President with *Harry Carson,* Wolfowitz had leered into the camera and shrugged.

"The real job of the Vice President is to sit around hoping the President will drop dead," he said. "At least now the American people know they've got themselves a candidate for the job with his heart in his work."

Carson and Wolfowitz never campaigned together. Wolfowitz spent the campaign making the same speeches that had regularly goaded Carson into televised rage. Carson never even mentioned Wolfowitz's name.

Vice President Wolfowitz occasionally presided over the Senate, but Carson wouldn't even send him to a funeral unless it was his own. It seemed to suit the Vice President just fine. He spent most of his time attacking his own administration and suggesting that Harry Carson could best serve the nation by doing himself in.

"Wolfowitz! Wolfowitz couldn't even fix a parking ticket."

And Sara had just shrugged and smiled. That she had suggested that Bobby try to get *Wolfowitz* to help him get an exit visa was her strange way of forgiving him, of telling him that she had really known that he had never been serious about leaving her to be with his father in the first place.

Bobby loped into the little living room, still naked, took the phone from Sara, sat down on the couch. "Hello, Dad, how's it going?"

"Getting there, Bob, getting there. But I need your help." Oh no!

"I told you, Dad, there's no way I can get out of the—"

"There's something you can do for me in the States, Bob."

"There is?" Bobby said. Sara brought him a cup of coffee and a toasted bagel from the kitchen area. Bobby checked the clock—8:36! Jesus, and he wasn't even dressed!

"Could you get me my clothes from the bedroom?" he asked Sara. "I've got to be out of here in five minutes." Sara nodded and departed.

"I want you to check out an outfit called Immortality, Inc., in Palo Alto," Dad said.

"Check out *what?*"

"They've supposedly developed a death-suspension technique, Bob."

"A what?"

"I've only been able to extract a sketchy description from the data bases here. They take a tissue sample and freeze it in liquid nitrogen, and they also back it up by recording the genome in software. Then they record your instantaneous consciousness somehow and polymerize your brain."

Sara came back into the living room with his suit, a shirt, shoes, socks, tie, a pair of Jockey shorts. "I'm not following you, Dad," he said as he pulled on the shorts.

"It seems pretty sound. Lots of redundancy. They'd clone a new body from the genome, then either fix what's wrong with my brain and transplant it, or just dump the software into a new one."

"Do *what?*" Bobby exclaimed as he managed to wriggle into his shirt without dropping the phone.

"Bring me back to life," Dad said.

"Sounds like science fiction to me, Dad," Bobby blurted. "They can't really do that, can they?"

"Not now, of course," Dad said. "Later, when the technology has progressed. Five years, ten, a century, it doesn't really matter, not if my genome is properly recorded and my personality software is preserved."

Bobby buttoned up his shirt and stepped into his pants, trying to figure out what to say to *that.* It all sounded quite crazy, but how could he say that to his father, to a man facing his own impending death? It wasn't any worse than a belief in heaven or nirvana, was it? But then again, it wasn't any better either. . . .

"Bob? Bob? Are you still there?"

"Yeah, I'm still here, Dad, but I've got to get going soon. I . . . I . . . Look, Dad, you . . . ah . . . you really take this . . . uh . . . seriously? I mean, you really believe . . . ?"

"What counts is what we can make your mother believe," Dad said sharply. "If she believes I have a chance to live again, then maybe we can finally convince her to do what she has to do to get me on the Grand Tour Navette."

Oh Christ! Bobby thought as he sealed his fly and buckled his belt. What the hell is going on back there? They said that there would be progressive brain damage. Had it started already?

"And you, Dad?" he said, pulling on his socks. "Do you really believe this stuff?"

There was a long pause on the other end of the phone. "It doesn't matter what *I* believe," Dad finally said softly.

"It does to me," Bobby told him, stepping into his shoes. *I'd like to know whether you've gone completely round the bend.*

Another pause. "Well, at least it's better than just being dumped in a hole in the ground," Dad finally said.

Bobby sighed. There was no refuting the logic of *that.* The scheme might be crazy, but Dad was sane. He had been dealt a handful of crap, and everything he had was in the pot, so what else could he do but pull to that inside straight?

8:44! Shit, I've got to get out of here!

"Look, Dad, I'm running real late," Bobby said. "Just what do you want me to do?"

"Go to Palo Alto. Find out everything you can about Immortality, Inc. And get ahold of whatever promotional material you can get out of them. Tell them you're doing a feature story."

"Fly to California! Look Dad, in case you haven't noticed, there's a big crisis about to—"

"Ninety minutes there, ninety minutes back, a couple of hours in Palo Alto, is that so much to ask, Bob?"

"They don't fly Concordskis in the United States, remember?" Bobby reminded him. "It's an all-day trip here, and I'll get back zoned out of my mind right in the middle of the biggest story I've ever gotten to cover."

8:50! Bobby had been trying to fasten his tie with the phone in one hand, and it was proving impossible. And he should have been out of here ten minutes ago!

"It's my life, Bob," Dad said plaintively. "It's everything I've ever lived for. I'm begging you, Bob, you've got to do this for me, and you've got to do it soon."

Right, Bobby thought, *this is your father, and he's got about a year to live, and now you're about to brush him off because you don't want to take a day out of your own life for fear of screwing up a story!*

I could take a red-eye Saturday night and fly back Sunday afternoon. Nothing ever breaks on Sunday, not even the end of the world. . . .

You certainly owe him that much, now don't you?

"Okay, Dad, okay, I'll do it, and I'll call you Sunday," Bobby said. "Now I've really gotta go."

"Do what?" Sara said when he had hung up the phone.

"Fly out to California and back this weekend," Bobby told her, knotting his tie clumsily without bothering to waste time going to a mirror.

"For what?" Sara demanded.

"You wouldn't believe me if I told you," Bobby said, slipping into his jacket and snatching up his computer. And he pecked her on the cheek and dashed out the door.

EURORUSSIANS SLIDE FURTHER IN POLLS

While the fragmented field running against him all but insures Constantin Semyonovich Gorchenko's reelection as Soviet President, the Eurorussians continue to slide in the polls, the latest results of which indicate the election of a Supreme Soviet almost equally divided among Bears demanding an immediate invasion of the Ukraine, Ethnic Nationalists supporting Ukrainian independence, and Eurorussians like President Gorchenko, prevaricating and chewing their fingernails down to the quick.

In other words, unless something totally unexpected happens, we are likely to elect a President who doesn't seem to know what to do and a Supreme Soviet so thoroughly deadlocked that it would probably prevent him from doing it if he knew what it was.

—*Argumenty i Fakty*

Like everyone else in Moscow, and no doubt all across the Soviet Union, Franja had stayed home to watch the disaster unfolding on television, wishing very much that Ivan was here to hold her hand, or even that she was back in Paris with her mother, for this was no time for a Russian to be alone.

Vadim Kronkol's fateful U.N. speech had gone more or less as expected until the very end. The Ukrainian President, still decked out in his television costume—black cossack boots and pants and a floridly embroidered peasant blouse—had ranted on about Stalin's genocide against the Ukrainian kulaks, the outlawing of the Ukrainian Catholic Church, Khrushchev's atrocities, continuing Great Russian economic and cultural hegemonism, and so forth, working himself up into the usual towering rage before he got to the point.

With his long black hair, thick black beard, and piercing blue eyes, he looked the perfect incarnation of Rasputin, and indeed, *Mad Moscow* claimed, perhaps even seriously, that the American media advisors had actually chosen him by programming Rasputin's physical and personality parameters into a computer and running that against the Ukrainian national data bank.

Watching him in his hour of glory, Franja could well believe it. Certainly Kronkol's performance could not have been more perfectly crafted both to appeal to the worst depths of centuries of jealous Ukrainian hatred of the Russians and to inflame the Bears' most rabidly chauvinistic image of the treacherous race of ingrates who had sold out to the Nazis in droves during the Great Patriotic War.

Which was precisely what the *real* Rasputin, the one in Washington, no doubt intended.

"The free people of the Ukraine therefore are left with no real alternative but to throw off the yoke of Russian oppression once and for all and reclaim their rightful place in the community of sovereign nation-states," Kronkol finally roared. "Now is the hour! This is the moment that the Ukrainian people have waited for through centuries of religious, economic, political, cultural, and linguistic subjugation! As duly elected President of the Ukrainian people, I hereby declare complete and total Ukrainian independence from the Russian Empire! The Ukrainian Soviet Socialist Republic is dead! Long live the independent Republic of the Ukraine!"

Actually hearing the Ukrainians declare independence might still be a shock to the nervous system, but Franja had known it was coming, and the actual moment came as almost a relief.

What really counted would be the speech of the American delegate, and the reaction of President Gorchenko.

If Gorchenko let the Ukraine secede without following the tedious and lengthy process adopted during the Pribaltic crisis to prevent just such actions, how many other republics would try the same thing? Worse still, the Ukraine was the second most populous republic in the Soviet Union, and without the Ukrainians, who had been the ambivalent allies of the Great Russians for centuries, the Russians would be outnumbered by the Asiatics.

What was at stake was nothing less than the survival of the Soviet Union as a multinational state, as the Eurorussians saw it, or Russian control of that state, as the Bears saw it.

But if Gorchenko sent in the Red Army, the resulting bloodbath would surely polarize every other ethnic minority in the Soviet Union into irreconcilable anti-Russian hatred, increasing the strength in the Supreme Soviet of Russian and Ethnic Nationalist chauvinists alike, at the expense of his own Eurorussian faction. And what a madman like Carson would do did not bear thinking about.

So Gorchenko's only course would be to prevaricate through the election, hold the Red Army in check while the Bears ranted for action, and, by playing them and the Ethnic Nationalists off against each other as extremists, assume the vague statesmanlike middle ground. It wasn't much, but it was all that Gorchenko could do under the circumstances.

But then Kronkol dropped his bomb.

"As the President of the independent Republic of the Ukraine, I am now submitting our formal application for admission as a new member state in Common Europe to the Common European Parliament," he declared with the wickedest leer. "And in so doing, I express solidarity with oppressed stateless peoples everywhere! Let the courage of the heroic Ukrainian people inspire you all to seek your own destinies! I not only ask you to vote for our admission, I ask you to join us! Side by side, we will build a new Europe, a free Europe, a Europe not of nation-states but of free and independent peoples!"

What an uproar that had started on the floor of the General Assembly, as Kronkol marched down from the podium and out through the center aisle to boos and cheers and the waving of fists, grinning like an ape at his own masterstroke of devilment!

"A Common Europe of Peoples, not Nation-States," as Vadim Kronkol had known all too well, was the slogan of the Congress of Peoples, the umbrella organization of the ethnic nationalist movements that permeated Common Europe. Basques. Bretons. Scots. Welsh. Bavarians. Slovaks. Serbs. Croats. Flemings. Frisians. Lapps. Catalans. Macedonians. There was hardly a member state in Common Europe that was not an ethnic mosaic, that did not contain minorities who spoke their own languages, professed their own culture, considered themselves a subject people.

And now the damnable Ukrainians had incited a whole new level of this transnational tribalism. Ethnic nationalists throughout Europe had long been campaigning for various forms of local autonomy, but none of them had dared to unilaterally declare their independence from a nation-state and apply for membership in Common Europe.

By forcing the issue in the Common European Parliament, the Ukrainians had transformed their cause from an internal Soviet matter into a transnational debate on the nature of Common Europe itself in which ethnic nationalists all over Europe would be their rabid allies.

And the worst was surely yet to come.

The President of the Assembly rapped his amplified gavel for order, and the tall, elegant, silver-haired figure of Reagan Smith, the American Ambassador to the United Nations, slowly paraded down the center aisle to the podium.

"We now recognize the delegate from the United States," the President said, and Franja held her breath, no doubt along with the rest of the world, as Smith ascended to the podium, and the camera moved in for a head-and-shoulders shot, and the shouting died away into a terrible, pregnant silence.

Smith slowly drew a single piece of paper out of the breast pocket of his suit jacket, placed it before him, took out an old-fashioned pair of wire-rimmed reading glasses, and put them on, as if to distance himself personally from the official nature of what he was about to say.

"I am authorized to read the following statement from the President of the United States," he said in a strange flat voice, as if he were trying very hard not to choke on his words.

"The government of the United States hereby formally recognizes the sovereign and duly elected government of the Republic of the Ukraine and takes great pleasure in welcoming the formerly oppressed people of the Ukraine into the community of free nations. And in keeping with our long and honorable tradition of protecting the national integrity of threatened peoples from the depredations of Soviet imperialist hegemonism, the government of the United States hereby formally notifies the government of the Union of Soviet Socialist Republics that the Republic of the Ukraine has been placed under the nuclear shield of Battlestar America. Any nuclear attack upon the Republic of the Ukraine will be tactically regarded as a nuclear attack upon the territory of the United States and dealt with accordingly with the full defensive resources at our command."

Franja goggled at the videowall as pandemonium broke loose in New York. What on earth did they mean by placing the Republic of the Ukraine "under the nuclear shield of Battlestar America"?

How far would they go if Gorchenko called their bluff? Would they merely use their defensive weapons to neutralize incoming Soviet missiles, or would they launch a strategic strike themselves? And what would they do if the Red Army simply marched on Kiev and Lvov and Odessa?

As the screen cut to a shot of the Soviet delegation, Franja saw that the representatives of her own government seemed just as confused as she was. Whispering heads crowded around Malinin, the Soviet Ambassador, who in turn kept shrugging, and grimacing, and turning his head back and forth like a distracted spectator at a tennis match.

Finally, he rose rather shakily to his feet and asked for the floor. And when the President of the Assembly recognized him and he walked slowly down the central aisle like a man on his way to the chopping block, the dreadful silence was heart-stopping.

"The Soviet Union regards Vadim Kronkol's speech as an act of treason and not only does not recognize the existence of any such thing as an independent Ukrainian state, but no longer recognizes Vadim Kronkol as the legal President of the Ukrainian Soviet Socialist Republic. The Soviet Union is perfectly capable of resolving this internal matter without resort to nuclear force, rendering the bellicose threats of the United States meaningless. Nevertheless, the Soviet Union warns the government of the United States that any use of American military force to interfere with the legal suppression of an internal insurrection may be regarded as an act of war by the Soviet Union and dealt with accordingly."

And that was *all* that he said. He stepped down from the podium leaving every meaningful question unanswered, and the coverage shifted to some studio in Moscow, where a general, a Eurorussian delegate, a notorious Bear, and two television commentators had been assembled to babble foolishly into the vacuum.

Franja turned off the TV and just sat there facing the blank screen with an equally blank mind for several minutes. The walls of the apartment seemed to be closing in. The silence was terrifying.

What she needed was to be among people, Russian people, her people, lots of them, and the more anonymous the better. Somehow, what she needed now was to be out in the street.

It was a clear early spring night in Moscow, and there was a bite of cold in the air. Though the fashionable restaurants of Arbat Street were closed, and the clubs and bars, normally still buzzing at this hour, would have been pretty much empty as people sat at home to watch the disaster on television, Franja was surprised to find the wide pedestrian street thronged with people.

But this was not the usual permanent Arbat crowd, milling back and forth, up and down, bar-hopping, eyeing shop windows, haggling with street peddlers, clotting around street musicians.

Bundled up in coats and hats against the chill, moving in clots, in schools and shoals, or as solitary individuals like Franja, everyone seemed to be heading up the street toward the end of the strogat, toward its confluence with Kalinin Prospekt at the Arbatskaya Metro station.

The mob scene around the Metro station was if anything more packed than usual. The street merchants and musicians were still there, but no one was buying or listening. From the underpass came the rantings of a Pamyat agitator, but the pedestrian flow-through seemed unhindered by his efforts to draw an audience.

Most of the people seemed to be either headed down Kalinin Prospekt or trying to elbow their way through the crush into the Metro station.

Franja thought she understood, for the Metro was still running, and Marx Prospekt was only two stops away, and the same impulse was drawing her to the center of the city, toward the symbolic heart of the country, toward Red Square.

But somehow the last thing she wanted was to be crammed into a crowded Metro carriage deep underground. Besides which, it really wasn't that much of a walk. So she turned away from the Metro station crowd and crossed over onto the north side of Kalinin into another, this one moving east along both sidewalks, a spontaneous procession elbowing and shoving its way in true Muscovite fashion toward the centre ville.

A huge immobile traffic jam extended down the center of Kalinin Prospekt as far as she could see, but, despite the gridlock, the horns were eerily silent, as if simply being there in your beloved car, under the circumstances, was quite enough.

Though the stores and boutiques were long since closed, and even most of the gaudy neon and wall-screen displays had been turned off, the sidewalks were even more crowded than they usually were on a warm Saturday afternoon on this glittering avenue of commerce and consumption. But while the sidewalks were packed, the pedestrian traffic was moving along unimpeded by the usual eddies and cross-currents, for everyone seemed to be moving spontaneously and unanimously in the same direction—inward, homeward, somehow, toward Red Square.

Franja could feel it as she walked through the concrete canyons in the river of people, past the darkened shops and auto showrooms, the office buildings and the huge blank wall screens, the restaurants and cafés, the movie theaters and the magazine kiosks and the bookstores, down this street that seemed to symbolize all that the new Russia had become, all that had been gained on the long journey through time from the first stirrings of glasnost and perestroika to this full glorious flowering of the Russian Spring.

But now, with dark doings half a world away in Washington and New York blowing on a cold biting wind, Kalinin Prospekt also seemed to symbolize all that Russia stood to lose.

She could see it in the faces of the people, young people like herself in trendy European clothes, old babushkas who seemed like refugees from another time, workers in jeans and black leather, the odd soldier, even the hooligans with their Stalin mustaches, all moving silently and somberly down the street like some kind of timeless Christian procession toward Red Square, backward in time to the days of Brezhnev, Khrushchev, Stalin, the Czars, the boyars, to something vast and immobile, to a sense of belonging, inward to the center of the Russian heart.

And she could feel it in herself too, truly feel it for perhaps the first time, this sense of belonging, this wordless sense of communal oneness, this submergence of the individual into the Slavic soul that had been Russia's strength and its curse. That had defeated the Tartars and the Poles, that had built a nation and an empire, that had fostered a Communist Revolution and allowed a monster to rule it for decades, that had defeated the Nazis and sought to impose itself on the world and first put men in space, and seemed to have vanished into the bright new morning of the Russian Spring.

But now, with a long shadow once more lying across this ancient and tragic and long-suffering land, something primeval, something gloriously and terribly and essentially *Russian* seemed to have reemerged in this spontaneous pilgrimage back to Slavic roots, back to the basics, back to the center, back to Red Square.

At Marx Prospekt, Muscovite pedestrians had even managed to somehow shove Muscovite drivers out of their path, for here, amid the stony old government buildings and the glass towers of commerce, they had taken over the gutters as well as the sidewalks, a sea of people pressing inward toward the entrances to Red Square.

Tverskaya Street, Kalinin, Mira Prospekt, they all dead-ended into this innermost ring around the Kremlin, and Franja could well imagine people pouring inward down them all, for surely the people of the Arbat were not the only Russians drawn toward the center of their world tonight.

Franja found herself fighting her way through it all, using her hands and elbows with the best of them, but when she finally managed to shove her way past the old Moscow Hotel and as far as the Kremlinovski Prospekt entrance to the Square, she saw that she could penetrate no farther.

Red Square was a solid mass of people. Lenin's tomb was dwarfed by the distance, the honor guard completely hidden by the crowd. Beyond it, there were scattered lights in the windows of the government buildings behind the Kremlin wall, and floodlights illuminating the interior of the compound.

From where she stood, Franja could see that most of the people were looking toward the Kremlin, toward the big red stars still shining reassuringly high above its battlements, toward Lenin's tomb, as if waiting for someone or something to make a dramatic appearance atop the tomb, or even atop the wall, as if they were waiting for Gorchenko himself, waiting for *any* leader to emerge and give voice and words to their formless feeling, waiting to be inspired and reassured and brought together and given a common purpose, waiting for a Lenin to stand above them at the railway station and stir their Russian hearts.

And indeed, as she stood there, half waiting for such a figure to appear herself, Franja realized that the crowd wasn't merely waiting, it was demanding.

There was some kind of commotion immediately in front of the tomb. The noise of the crowd was angry and expectant. Voices were shouting things she couldn't hear. And people were waving Soviet flags and portraits of Gorbachev and Stalin, modern-day icons of the Eurorussians and the Bears. Bottles were starting to fly. She could sense fistfights breaking out at the front of the crowd. Someone was holding up an effigy of Uncle Sam dangling from a noose, someone else a fiery American flag.

And still no one appeared from inside the Kremlin wall. And Franja realized that no one would. What could Gorchenko say? What could anyone say that would focus the energies surging through the crowd, that would bring them all together, Eurorussians and Bears, the fearful and the furious, the old Russia and the new, the dark past that lived in even the most modern of hearts, and the hopes for the future that seemed about to be extinguished by forces beyond any Russian's control?

In that moment, it seemed to her that all of Russia had somehow been gathered together here in the center of the world. Eurorussians and Bears, the present and the past, the hopes and the fears, all gathered together in Red Square in the dead of night, on a spring evening with a cold wind blowing.

Then she began to notice that many people were not looking toward the Kremlin; older people for the most part, but young ones too, were staring along some other vector down the length of the square, with a different sort of expression, a strange timeless quietude that seemed far older and stronger than the Kremlin's red brick walls.

And as she followed their gaze with her eyes, she understood what had transfixed them.

Across the sea of people, far away on the other side of Red Square, the onion-dome fantasy of St. Basil's was brilliantly illuminated by floodlights, the ·gaudy gold and red and turquoise arabesques floating above the tumult like an eternal icon, like the shining symbol of the immortal Slavic spirit, like a Russia of the heart beyond the reach of history and time.

But as she gazed at the beautiful unreality of the ancient church, glorified by the electric magic of the modern age, her eyes were lifted upward into the night sky by the sweep of the domes and spires.

And there, among the stars, paled by the glow of the city, points of light were moving, and in her mind's eye, she could see what lay behind them.

Battle stations. Missiles. Orbital lasers. Anti-proton busters. Burning mirrors.

St. Basil's below, beautiful and precious, the perfect baroque image of the Russian soul, glorious, romantic, but oh so fragile beneath the transparent black sky.

And above it, orbiting the planet, Battlestar America, peering down from the darkness, circling like a cloud of carrion crows waiting for something warm and tender to die.

WOLFOWITZ CALLS FOR IMPEACHMENT

Vice President Wolfowitz, at a press conference called on the Capitol steps, has demanded that Congress immediately impeach President Carson.

"Grounds? You want grounds?" Wolfowitz shouted at outraged reporters. "He's fomented a revolution in a foreign country, which violates any number of laws that no one has paid attention to for thirty years, and now he's unilaterally involved us militarily in a potential nuclear confrontation without even bothering to get a Congressional resolution. If we don't get rid of Carson forthwith and use that as a fig leaf behind which to back out of this lunatic commitment, the idiot is liable to blow the whole world to atoms. Grounds for impeachment? There's enough

grounds to put him in a rubber room forever and throw
away the key!"

When asked for the President's reaction, Presidential
Press Secretary Marvin Watson said that the President
had nothing to say that was remotely fit to print.

—AP

"Uhhh . . . ?" grunted the voice on the other end of the
line.

"Dad? It's me. . . ."

"Bobby . . . ? Jeez . . . it's—"

"I'm calling from Palo Alto, Dad."

"And . . . ?" Dad grunted.

"Well, Dad, there really *is* an outfit here called Immortality, Inc.," Bobby said, "and they do offer so-called death
suspension, but, well . . ."

There was a long pause at the other end of the line, as
Dad no doubt struggled to full wakefulness, for while outside the motel room window Bobby could see people sunning themselves around the pool in the bright California
sunshine, in Paris it was the middle of the night.

Immortality, Inc., had turned out to be a low concrete
building behind a brick wall in a lightly wooded grassy compound, indistinguishable from the biotech labs, electronic
plants, and defense industry spook-shops that formed the
main economic base of the Palo Alto area.

Bobby had been met in the reception area by a Dr. John
Burton, a smooth smiling type with long blond hair who
looked like a surfer who had incongruously encased himself
in a very expensive gray silk business suit.

Burton had taken him into a slick office filled with tropical plants, where he had explained the operation to the "reporter from StarNet," his blue eyes sparkling with the
intensity of the true believer, or maybe that of a star used-
car salesman.

"You'll find out sooner or later, Mr. Reed, so I might as
well admit up front that we are operating under a funeral
home license," Burton told him.

"A *funeral home license?*" Bobby exclaimed. "This place
doesn't exactly look like a mortuary to me."

"It isn't," Burton said. "But under present California law,
we've had to get death suspension certified as a legal form

of burial in order to operate at all. Needless to say, it's something of an embarrassment. And unfortunately, it means we are not allowed to process a client before legally certified clinical death, which we do not believe is the blue max."

"Blue max?"

"Polymerize before brain death to minimize the chance of cerebral deterioration. The blue max for sure. Catch the brain before the hardware has a chance to erode."

"You mean *kill* them?"

"Come on, man, don't be ghoulish! We're talking about clients in a terminal state!" Burton shrugged. "But the law's the law, and we're stuck with it right now," he said unhappily. Then he brightened again. "Of course in the long run," he added hastily, "it's not anything we won't be able to get around."

"The long run?"

"Years, decades," Burton said expansively. "We know how to preserve our clients, but of course we still don't know what tech we'll need to revive them. That's why we go for so much redundancy—tissue samples *and* genome recording, brain polymerization *and* chip storage of instantaneous electrohologrammic patterns."

His eyes seemed to become a bit furtive. "And since we are talking about indefinite preservation of biological material and data storage, as well as covering the cost of the necessary continued research, which could take decades, we are forced to require a fee of two million dollars."

"Two million dollars!" Bobby exclaimed. Even in today's rubber money, that was more than the whole family could possibly afford.

"Sure it's a lot of money," Burton said airily. "That's why we've got a deal with the banks to treat it as a mortgage situation. Given an acceptable credit profile, you can get a pre-need contract for as little as 20 percent down on a twenty-year loan at only 6 percent above prime."

Bobby choked on that one. What did the banks do if you failed to meet the payments, repossess the brain? But he held his tongue, nodded politely, and let Burton take him on a tour of the facilities.

At least to Bobby's scientifically untrained eye, Immortality, Inc., seemed to be impressively funded and lavishly equipped. There was a complete operating theater and whole rooms full of computers. There was a storage chamber where tissue samples were kept in liquid nitrogen cooled by superconducting refrigeration units able to function independently for four months in the event of external power failure. There were research labs. There was a room full of arcane electronic equipment that supposedly recorded the "instantaneous hologram of consciousness" on chip.

Burton showed him the brain-storage unit. This was the only part of the facilities that at all reminded Bobby of anything like a mortuary. It was a modest-sized hermetically sealed room with what looked weirdly like ranks of filing cabinets lining the long walls, row after row of small steel drawers from floor to ceiling.

"Would you care to see one of our clients?" Burton said.

"You mean you've actually . . . uh . . . processed people already?" Bobby exclaimed in some surprise.

"Hey, we did Tessa Tinker, it was in all the papers. And we've done another twenty-three clients already. With pre-need contracts with about a hundred more, some *very* heavy people whose names I am not at liberty to divulge. You might be interested in a pre-need plan yourself."

"Pre-need plan . . . ?" Bobby stammered. The whole thing was getting more and more ghoulish by the moment.

"We take a tissue sample and record your genome right now. Your instantaneous hologram of consciousness too. And free updates as often as you can get here for them. When the time comes, your brain gets polymerized as soon as it becomes legal to do so, so you retain all your long-term memories, and we dump everything up until the time of the last hologram update into the hardware when we install it in the clone."

And as if *that* wasn't ghoulish enough, Burton opened one of the drawers and let Bobby look inside. There, cradled in Styrofoam like an enormous egg, was a human brain tightly packaged in some kind of clear shrink-wrap.

"Jesus . . ." Bobby muttered.

"Go ahead, touch it, man," Burton said.

Bobby goggled at him.

"Just to make a point," Burton said, smiling.

Gingerly, Bobby reached out and tapped the brain twice with his knuckles.

It was hard as a rock.

"No longer meat," Burton said. "Polymerized hard as a rock and twice as chemically inert. You could dunk it off a backboard and you wouldn't hurt it. Needs no refrigeration or special conditions. It could survive like that for centuries."

That was the capper of the guided tour, after which Burton took Bobby back to his office, gave him a large packet of lavishly illustrated promotional material, and asked if he had any questions.

Bobby, quite dazed by now, could think of only one question, and that was the only one that mattered. "Look, Dr. Burton, you'll pardon me for being brutally frank, but are you really *serious* about all this? Do you seriously think that someday you'll actually be able to clone bodies, depolymerize brains, and bring these people back to normal life?"

Burton just smiled his wide-open surfer's smile. "Can we really bring back dead people? Well, that's a philosophical question, man. Will they be the same people, or only feel like the same people? Depends on your beliefs about the soul. . . ."

He shrugged. "We don't have *those* answers," he admitted. "But you want certainty, why then you can always have yourself stuffed in a hole in the ground."

Bobby had planned to wait till a decent hour in Paris before he called his father, but by the time he got back to the motel, his head was reeling from the most macabre experience of his life, his sense of reality was slipping, and he needed to dump it all on someone *right now.*

So he had gone straight to the telephone and woken Dad up in the middle of the night.

"So tell me about it, Bob," Dad said, after a long pause, now, apparently, more or less fully awake. And Bobby did.

"Well, Bob, what do you think?" Dad said when he was finally finished.

"Hey, Dad, I'm no technical expert. . . ."

"But you *are* a journalist. Tell me what you feel. Is this a fly-by-night outfit or are they substantial?"

"Seemed pretty gilt-edged to me."

"Do you think these people are sincere or is this a fraud?"

Bobby had to think long and hard about that one. "Both, I think," he finally said. "As far as I'm concerned, it's all an expensive set for a high-budget science-fiction movie, but if it's bullshit, I think they've really sold it to themselves too."

"Good enough for me," Dad said immediately.

"Dad, I just got through telling you—"

"If these scientists have convinced themselves they're really onto something, then we can certainly convince your mother, she wants so much to believe. . . ."

Bobby groaned. "That's it, isn't it, Dad?" he said wearily. "You just want to use this to convince Mom to help you get your spaceship ride. I dragged my ass all the way out here with the world coming apart just to—"

"You've got to get to Paris, Bob! Together, I know we can convince her, the mere fact that you believe it enough to finally—"

"Jesus, Dad, you know that's impossible! Especially now! Don't you have any idea of what's going on in the world? That asshole Carson has put Battlestar America on yellow alert! Red Army units are moving toward the Ukrainian border! All flights to Europe have been suspended. *No one* can get in or out of the country now, let alone the likes of me!"

"You've got to try, Bob, you've got to try!"

"I have been trying, Dad, you know I have," Bobby told him guiltily. "Maybe when all this is over, if we haven't all been blown to bits . . ."

"Soon, Bobby, soon, I haven't got that much time."

Maybe none of us has, Bobby thought somberly.

And as he thought it, he at last understood his father's single-minded obsession with the wisdom of a sympathetic heart.

The whole world was staring death in the face now, just as Dad had been ever since the accident. The only difference was that he knew for a certainty when and how.

As he sat there in the sunny California motel room, Bobby found himself suddenly envying his father his inspired madness, his vision of something worth throwing away what was left of his life over. He even could find some empathy with the crazy schemes of John Burton.

Millions of lives might soon be thrown away for nothing more worthwhile than the fanaticism of the Ukrainian nationalists and the reckless stupidity of the imbecile in the White House.

Including his own.

Only now did that awful reality seep into his bones and his gut, only now had it really become something more than a hot news story. Time might very well be running out on everyone. This macabre conversation with Dad had suddenly made that theoretical truth terrifyingly personal.

He could die at any moment, he could be vaporized with no warning. The things that might be left undone, the debts that might be left forever unpaid, the words that he might never get to say . . .

"You're a lunatic, Dad," Bobby said tenderly. "You're a real space cadet. But I love you very much."

"Does that mean you'll help me, Bob? Does that mean you're on my side?"

Bobby sighed. "Yeah, I'm on your side," he said, and found somewhat to his surprise that now he really meant it. The dream might not be his, but the feeling behind it was now all too comprehensible. "I'll do what I can."

CARSON DEMANDS
WOLFOWITZ RESIGNATION

After days of official silence, President Harry Carson has finally responded to Vice President Wolfowitz's call for his impeachment.

Speaking to a group of selected reporters in the Oval Office, President Carson, whom those present described as flushed, and tense, and barely controlling his fury, demanded that the Vice President resign.

"If he doesn't, we'll see who impeaches who!" the President declared. "That s.o.b. is a traitor, he always has been, and now he's gone and proven it! He oughta be tarred and feathered and run all the way to Siberia on a rail in his underwear, not just impeached."

The President said that he had summoned the Vice President to a Cabinet meeting tomorrow to tender his resignation or face impeachment on charges of treason.

When reached for comment, Vice President Wolfowitz said that he would "accept the invitation." As for resigning, the Vice President said that he had no intention of stepping down unless the President resigned simultaneously.

"I hope he *does* try to impeach me," Vice President Wolfowitz declared. "At least it would force the House to debate the real issues instead of just clicking their heels

and screaming Heil Carson on cue. So go ahead, Harry,
do it, get your feeble little rocks off. Go ahead and make
my day."

       —San Francisco Chronicle

The tension in Prague had been so thick you could cut it
with a knife, and while the Americans were still considered
the main villains of the piece, and the Czechs certainly had
nothing good to say about the Ukrainians, there had been a
big demonstration in Wenceslas Square by Slovak nationalists supporting the admission of the "Republic of the
Ukraine" to Common Europe behind the banner of "A
Common Europe of Peoples, not Nation-States," there had
been a strident anti-Russian undertone, and Franja had
been glad to get airborne on her way back to Moscow.

According to the news, it was the same all over Europe. A
broad coalition of Basque, Breton, Scottish, Catalan,
Slovak, Corsican, Flemish, Welsh, and Lapp delegates had
sponsored a resolution in the Common European Parliament calling for the admission of the Ukraine, and while
they clearly did not have the numbers to push it through, it
seemed likely that they would be able to force a formal vote.

It was becoming quite clear that the Americans were aim-
ing not only at the dismemberment of the Soviet Union but
at the destruction of the unity of Common Europe itself, by
championing, through their puppets in the Ukraine, the
worst sort of jingoistic tribalism, turning national minorities
against their nation-states, nation-states against their national minorities.

The "Republic of the Ukraine" was loudly proclaiming its
"solidarity with the oppressed peoples of the Soviet Union"
and inviting them to join it in building a "Liberated Common Europe of Free Peoples." There had been demonstrations of support in Uzbekistan, Byelorussia, Armenia,
Azerbaijan, and for the first time in Franja's memory, riot
police had been sent in with water cannon and neuronic
disrupters to break them up.

But other than that, and a futile paper attempt to put the
Ukrainian National Militia under Red Army command,
President Gorchenko had done nothing. Like this flight to
Moscow, which had been stuck circling in the stack for

twenty minutes now, he seemed trapped in a holding pattern.

As she sat in the cockpit, flying endless circles, Franja found that, despite the deteriorating situation, she could sympathize with Constantin Gorchenko. What, after all, could the poor bastard do?

He certainly couldn't accept Ukrainian secession. But if he sent in the Red Army, there was no telling what the maniacs in Washington would do. So all he could do was mass more and more troops along the Ukrainian border, insist that it was all an internal Soviet matter, and use the impending national election as a handy excuse to "wait to hear the voice of the Soviet People."

But what seemed certain to emerge after the election, assuming Gorchenko could really hold off the catastrophe until then, would be a Supreme Soviet bloated with Bears and Ethnic Nationalists, where no one could put together a working majority, leaving Gorchenko himself, elected by default against fragmented opposition, sitting on an even hotter stove.

What would happen then was something not even *Mad Moscow* cared to speculate on in public print.

As for Franja—

Suddenly her co-pilot, Lentski, let out a wordless whoop.

Franja instantly snapped out of her trance of boredom. "What's wrong, Sasha?" she said, scanning her instruments at the same time and seeing that nothing was amiss.

Looking at Lentski, she saw that he was grinning from ear to ear like a foolish ape.

"It just came in on the radio, and we're ordered to inform our passengers immediately," he said. "Harry Carson is dead. He suffered a massive stroke during a Cabinet meeting, according to Tass. Apparently in the act of screaming obscenities at Vice President Wolfowitz, though that part's not official."

"Carson is dead?" Franja stammered.

"As a parboiled pig. You're to announce the sad news immediately."

Now it was Franja's turn to break into a simian smile and not care who saw it. "I'll try to keep my tears in check," she said as she switched her mike to the cabin speaker system.

"A sad moment, isn't it?" Lentski said, and burst out laughing.

"Comrades, your attention please, this is Captain Gagarin speaking. It is my . . . ah . . . solemn duty to tell you that we have just been informed that the President of the United States, Mr. Harry Carson, is dead. It would seem that his brain exploded in a fit of rage. I repeat, Harry Carson is dead. We will give you details as we have them."

Even through the cabin door, the applause from the passengers was quite thunderous. For of course Harry Carson was loathed by Bears and Eurorussians alike; the former because his threat to use Battlestar America to protect the American puppet regime in Kiev was preventing the Red Army from giving the Ukrainian traitors what they so richly deserved, the latter because his reckless adventurism was responsible for the crisis which threatened to sweep the Eurorussians out of the Supreme Soviet and destroy the Russian Spring itself.

Only the Ethnic Nationalists had anything but loathing for Carson, and if there were any of them aboard, they knew enough to keep their big mouths shut.

And now the architect of the impending catastrophe was dead, and Nathan Wolfowitz, Carson's bitterest enemy, the self-proclaimed "American Gorbachev," was apparently President of the United States.

It was almost enough to have a good Marxist believing in a just God.

WHO'S IN CHARGE HERE?

While the world hardly has cause to honestly mourn the sudden death of Harry Burton Carson, it has little cause to welcome the ascension of Nathan Wolfowitz to the American Presidency either.

With the Soviet Union and the United States seemingly on the brink of a nuclear confrontation, the White House is now occupied by a man who has vigorously opposed the policies that have brought us to this pass. That would be cause for guarded rejoicing, were not the new American President a man who has never held any position of responsibility.

Worse still, all the calculated leaks emanating from Carson Administration figures still in place in the so-called Wolfowitz Administration seemed designed to convey the impression that the new President will be the political prisoner of his Cabinet, the Pentagon, the Central Security Agency, and the CIA. If this is true, who will really be running the American government during the worst crisis since World War II?

And if it is not, how will a governmental neophyte like Nathan Wolfowitz cope with a hostile Cabinet, military, and security apparatus? Under the American constitution, he has the power to dismiss these disloyal officials, but the Congress must approve any replacements he nominates, and, judging by the impeachment talk already emerging, should he attempt to purge his administration of these Carson holdovers, we could end up with no government in Washington at all.

—*Le Monde*

X X V I

It had been a decade since Bobby had seen Nathan Wolfowitz in the flesh, but this seemed like neither the man he had played poker with nor the media image he had watched age on television, and not just because Wolfowitz was now wrapped in the aura of the Presidency.

Wolfowitz did not at all look like a man who had suddenly been granted the impossible dream of a lifetime by the hand of fate. Wolfowitz did not look like a man whose worst enemy had just dropped dead.

Wolfowitz looked like shit.

His thick salt-and-pepper hair was an uncombed mess. His Presidential blue suit looked as if it had been slept in. The knot of his tie was crooked. His face was drawn and ashen, and his eyes looked positively haunted.

And his performance was a good deal less than reassuring to both those who had voted for the "American Gorbachev" and the supporters of the Carson Administration, whose unwholesome apparatus and nightmarish policies he had so suddenly inherited.

Bobby had expected Wolfowitz to be nervous. He had a hostile Congress, an even more hostile Cabinet, a nonplussed Pentagon, a rebellious Central Security Agency and CIA, and there he was, with Battlestar America on yellow alert, and the borders sealed, and the Red Army massing on the Ukrainian border, and America already committed in the vaguest terms to defending the Ukraine.

But neither the poker wizard Bobby had played against in Berkeley nor the fast-talking shoot-from-the-hip Nathan Wolfowitz of a thousand and one television appearances had ever looked as freaked-out as this, would have been constitutionally capable of all this mealy-mouthed evasion, even with nothing showing and only a pair of deuces in the hole.

Bobby had moved heaven and Earth to get StarNet to send him here to Washington to cover President Wolfowitz's first press conference. He had bullshitted his superiors shamelessly about his "personal relationship" with the new President.

For now Sara's previously sardonic suggestion that he appeal to Nat Wolfowitz to get him an exit visa had new meaning. Wolfowitz was no longer a Vice President in political purdah. He was in charge of everything. He could do it with a word, with the stroke of a pen. All Bobby had to do was get to him.

And now here he was, in the middle of a crush of White House reporters, wondering what the hell he had been thinking. How was he *really* supposed to get close enough to Wolfowitz to ask him for anything? What made him think the new President would even remember someone he had played poker with a decade ago?

From the way Wolfowitz was behaving, it seemed like a minor miracle that the man had been able to remember to seal his fly.

"Mr. President, what does it really mean that the United States has placed the Ukraine 'under the nuclear shield of Battlestar America'?"

"Uh . . . Moscow's guess is as good as mine at the moment. . . ."

"You mean you don't even know what the policy is!"

"I mean that the previous policy died with Harry Carson, and I haven't had time to figure things out."

"But Mr. President, just what will the United States actually do if the Red Army invades the Ukraine?"

"Ah . . . I'm sure Mr. Gorchenko would like the answer to that one too. . . ."

"Mr. President, do you support independence for the captive peoples of the Soviet Union?"

"Er . . . it would be undiplomatic of me to make any comments that might be construed as an attempt to influence the current election campaign in the Soviet Union."

On and on it went, nonanswers to every question, and all the while, Wolfowitz's eyes darted back and forth frantically, his lips working nervously, his hands kneading the edge of the lectern.

Wolfowitz looked like a man who had bet the farm on an inside straight only to see the card he needed to fill it turn faceup on the sixth deal in someone else's hand. And he sounded like a man who had just learned some horrifying secret, something awful enough to turn him into a stammering mealymouthed politico.

It reminded Bobby of a book he had read in Paris as a kid, called *The Curse of the Oval Office.* In it, Timothy Leary, the acid guru of the 1960s, had hypothesized that there was some kind of curse on the Presidential office that drove otherwise sane men mad upon occupying it. Leary had pointed to Lyndon Johnson and the Vietnam War, Richard Nixon and Watergate. Bobby had thought it pretty humorous then.

It didn't seem so funny now.

"Mr. President, are you in contact with the government of the Republic of the Ukraine?"

"Uh . . . no comment. . . ."

"Mr. President, do you plan to discuss this crisis directly with President Gorchenko?"

"Uh . . . I'm ready to talk to anyone about anything that might get us out of this mess. . . ."

Jesus, what a disaster! Bobby thought. What's *wrong* with the man? Wolfowitz had started glancing back over his shoulder down the corridor behind the podium after every

question, as if hoping that someone would appear to yank
him off the stage.

Long tradition had it that these press conferences were
ended not by the President, but by the senior White House
correspondent, with a firm "Thank you, Mr. President." But
neither that worthy nor the rest of the press corps seemed in
any mood to end the embarrassing agony anytime soon. The
faces of the reporters were getting more and more surly,
waves of dismayed murmurs swept around the crowded
room after every answer, some of the reporters were even
cursing under their breath.

Bobby had long since given up any idea of trying to ask a
question himself, since the only one that came to mind was
"What the fuck's wrong with you, Nat?" Instead, he started
snaking his way through the crowd toward the podium, not
so difficult with everyone else jumping up and down and
waving their arms. He wasn't quite sure what he was going
to do, but he wasn't going to leave without at least *trying* to
get a word with Nathan Wolfowitz somehow.

"Mr. President, don't you think you at least owe the
American people some kind of coherent statement of what
policy you intend to follow to prevent a nuclear holocaust? I
mean, frankly, Mr. President, you really haven't said a
damned thing!"

There was a collective gasp and then a sudden silence at
that one. Something of the old Nathan Wolfowitz finally
seemed to flare up in the eyes of the distracted figure behind the lectern bearing the Presidential Seal.

"What the hell do you expect me to say?" Wolfowitz
snapped. "The world is on the brink of a catastrophe, and
I've just inherited the policies of the maniac responsible!
You really expect me to shoot my mouth off like an idiot
before I've even had time to think? Well, like it or not, I'm
not Harry Carson. Don't you think there's been enough irresponsible bullshit out of here already?"

The words of the President utterly stunned even the veterans of the White House press corps. No President had
ever called his immediate predecessor an idiot and a maniac
in public before the body was even cold. No President had
ever said "bullshit" on national television. And no President
had ever actually admitted he needed time to think.

For a long moment, no one moved, no one made a sound.
Then, finally, the voice of the senior White House corre-

spondent mercifully shouted out the magic words "Thank you, Mr. President," and pandemonium broke loose.

Everyone started shouting at once. Reporters broke for the exits. Other reporters surged forward and started trying to shout more questions at President Wolfowitz over the tumult as he stood there uncertainly on the podium, looking stunned, and distracted, and not knowing quite what to do.

Three Secret Service men emerged from the corridor behind the President. One of them took him lightly by the elbow, another said something to him, and they started leading him away.

Without thinking, Bobby shoved his way through the melee, and burst around the podium, screaming "Nat! Nat!" as Wolfowitz, his back to the room now, was about to disappear down the corridor with his escort.

Everything happened at once.

Arms grabbed him from behind. The President whirled around at the commotion. For a moment, their eyes locked.

"Nat! Nat! Please! I've got to talk to you!" Bobby pleaded at the top of his lungs as they started to drag him away.

Was that a ghost of recognition in the President's eyes? "Little Moscow! Berkeley! Bobby Reed!" Bobby shouted desperately. "Now is the time for a futile gesture, remember, Nat?"

"You're telling me!" the President groaned enigmatically, and he almost seemed to smile.

Two Secret Service goons had Bobby's arms pinned behind him in a double hammerlock. The President's escorts stepped in front of him, shielding him with their bodies.

"Nat! Please! I need your help!"

President Wolfowitz shoved himself between two of his Secret Service guards. "Stop!" he shouted. "I want to talk to that man!"

"Mr. President—"

"Do it!" Nathan Wolfowitz shouted. "You!" he ordered, pointing at the men restraining Bobby. "Bring that man here!"

No one moved for a moment. One of the President's guards tried to step in front of him again. Wolfowitz shoved him back angrily. "I'm the fucking President, ain't I?" he snapped. "You do as I say, or you can kiss your pensions good-bye!"

Bobby was shoved forward, with his arms still pinned behind his back. The President's escorts had their hands inside their jackets. Wolfowitz turned on his heel, led the procession about ten feet down the corridor, turned, looked at Bobby, grinned strangely.

"That was crazy," the President said. He studied Bobby narrowly. "I *do* know you, don't I?" he said slowly. "Little Moscow . . . ? Berkeley? The Flag Riot . . . ? You're . . . you're . . ."

"The kid from Paris, remember, Nat?" Bobby said. "The Congressional campaign? The—"

"Bobby!" the President said, grinning. "I never forget a mark! You're Bobby . . . Bobby . . ."

"Reed."

"Right, Bobby Reed," the President said. And he actually laughed. "Well, kiddo," Nathan Wolfowitz said, "what's a nice boy like you doing in a place like this?"

Bobby heaved an enormous sigh of relief. He almost started laughing himself. This was the real Nathan Wolfowitz, the man who had once been his friend.

"I'm desperate, Nat," Bobby babbled. "My father's dying in Paris, and I can't get an exit visa, and you're my only hope. Can I talk to you, Nat, just five minutes of your time, please, please. . . ."

"Let him go," the President said.

The Secret Service men made no move to release Bobby.

"I said let . . . the . . . man . . . go," the President said slowly and distinctly, as if talking to a small child. "I'm getting sick and tired of having to tell you people everything twice."

Finally, reluctantly, the Secret Service men released Bobby's arms.

"Okay, Bobby," Nathan Wolfowitz said, "five minutes."

"Mr. President, you have to—"

"What I have to do is take a piss!" the President said. "Where's the nearest john?"

"Mr. President . . . ?"

"The *toilet,* goddamnit! We both have to take a piss, don't we, Bobby?"

"My bladder's bursting, Mr. President," Bobby drawled.

The Secret Service men escorted them down the corridor, turned a corner, led them up another corridor to a men's room door. One of them opened the door for the President, who gestured for Bobby to precede him. Bobby walked into the toilet, with the President following behind. As Wolfowitz started to close the door behind himself, one of the Secret Service men stepped halfway through the doorway, blocking him.

"Where do you think you're going?" the President demanded.

"We're not supposed to leave you alone with—"

"I think I can manage to hold my own prick, thank you," the President snapped. "Now get the hell out of here and let us pee in peace!"

"Jesus, I've hated thugs like that all my life," Nathan Wolfowitz said when they were alone in the toilet, "and now they're all over me like flies on horseshit!"

He loped over to a urinal, unsealing his fly as he went. "I really *do* have to take a leak," he said. "So tell me your sad story, Bobby. I only wish I could tell you mine."

And so there, in a White House men's room, Bobby unburdened himself to the President of the United States while the President unburdened himself into the urinal.

"Let me get this straight," Nathan Wolfowitz said as he resealed his fly. "Your father is dying in Paris, you've got to get there to convince your mother to help him get his last wish by bullshitting her into believing that some funeral home in Palo Alto can revive him after they polymerize his brain, and the Central Security Agency won't give you an exit visa. . . ."

"I know it sounds pretty crazy, Nat, but—"

"Crazy!" the President exclaimed. "You think *that's* crazy?" His eyes seemed to unfocus, as if he were staring off into somewhere else, as if he were seeing something that made him shudder, made his shoulders slump. "I could tell you *real* crazy, Bobby," he muttered. "But I can't . . . I just can't. . . ."

"Will you help me, Nat?"

President Wolfowitz seemed to snap himself back into focus by an act of will. He gave Bobby a sickly smile. He waved his hands like a stage magician.

"Consider it done," he said. "I'll get you a diplomatic exit visa to Montreal, you can catch a plane to Paris from there, I'll make one of those Secret Service gorillas deliver the papers personally, yeah, I'd enjoy that. . . ." He smiled strangely. "How am I doing?" he said. "Is that Presidential enough for you?"

"Oh God, thank you, Nat," was all that Bobby could manage to say.

"Mr. President! You're already late for the Cabinet meeting!"

"Jesus Christ, can't you guys even learn to knock?"

A Secret Service man had entered the toilet unbidden and stood there tapping his right foot nervously. "Mr. President . . . ?"

"Coming, Mother," Nathan Wolfowitz drawled. He shrugged, turned, walked toward the door. He paused, looked over his shoulder at Bobby.

"By the way," he said, "you might be interested to know that they've actually polymerized *Carson's* brain," he said. "Not that it hasn't been dead for years anyway. I'm thinking of using it as the guidance system on the first missile we fire at Moscow, serve the bugger right. Though come to think of it, knowing Carson, the bastard would probably enjoy it."

And with that exit line, he was gone.

SOVIETS CHARGE CLANDESTINE
SHIPMENT OF AMERICAN ARMS TO
UKRAINE

—Reuters

KRONKOL DEMANDS RESTATEMENT
OF CARSON PROMISE

—Agence France-Presse

AMERICAN AIRPORTS SEALED BY
PENTAGON

—Le Monde

CONGRESS OF PEOPLES VOTES
SUPPORT OF UKRAINIANS

—Libération

AMERICAN EMBASSY SACKED IN
BUDAPEST

—The Times (London)

Deposits and payments are subject to verification. Those made after 2 P.M. may be applied on the following business day.

EAB®

Where you belong℠

370/0331 NOV 88 (LR 12/89) 2000 PKG.

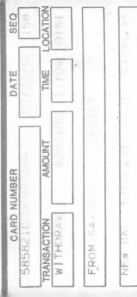

EAB Money Card Banking®

SEQ 158

DATE 7/29/9_

LOCATION 0151

TIME 11:0_

CARD NUMBER
5858210_

AMOUNT

TRANSACTION
WITHDRAW_

FROM SA_

NEW BA_

RETAIN FOR YOUR RECORDS

UKRAINIAN MILITIA SEIZES RUSSIAN
OFFICERS

—Die Welt

Bobby had never been on a Concordski before, and it was all a bit temporally disorienting. It had taken him five hours to fly from New York to California and two days to get to Montreal, with all flights out of the United States still grounded, and now here he was, less than three hours later, after having breezed through customs at De Gaulle, riding the RER into a Paris he had not seen since he was a teenager.

Things went from bad to worse after President Wolfowitz's disastrous press conference. The jingo press came out with a story that he had tried to fire the secretaries of State and Defense and the Attorney General, only to be told by the Congressional leaders of both parties that if he did, impeachment proceedings would begin immediately. There were leaked demands from the Pentagon that he declare an emergency under the National Security Act and place the country under martial law.

Vadim Kronkol publicly demanded a policy statement from Washington on the "imminent Soviet invasion of the Ukraine." Some maniac in Tbilisi declared Georgia an independent republic at an illegal rally in a restaurant, and a wild mass demonstration rampaged through the streets. Riot troops broke it up in a few hours, and hundreds of people were arrested, but not before the "Republic of Georgia" had been formally recognized by the "Republic of the Ukraine."

Nevertheless, less than two days after the press conference, Bobby learned, somewhat to his amazement, that a President staggering through a nightmare had not been too distracted to keep a promise to an old friend.

He and Sara were having dinner when a Secret Service agent showed up at their apartment with a sour expression and an envelope bearing the Presidential Seal.

In it was Bobby's two-week diplomatic exit visa to Montreal. There was none for Sara. There was also a handwritten note on a plain piece of paper.

Sorry. Best I could do with the mess I've been dealt.
Believe me, this hole card no one wants to pay to see.
I just hope the guy across the table is no better at
reading a bluff than you were.

Nat

Sara's whole attitude had changed when she read it. "I
guess this means you're going, huh, Bobby?" she said quietly.

"I have to, Sara. I've got no excuses left."

"I wish I could go with you. . . ."

"I know. . . ."

And she sighed, and smiled wanly, and reached out across
the table to take his hand. "It's okay, Bobby," she said
softly. "I do understand."

"You do? But I thought . . ."

"That was when Carson was President. If you'd gotten out
then, they would have never let you back in, but now . . .
we can trust Nat Wolfowitz, there's going to be an end to all
that fascist shit now. . . ."

"If there isn't an end to *everything* first," Bobby blurted,
and was instantly sorry, as Sara's face darkened. "I mean
. . . if I go, we might never . . ."

"Don't say it, Bobby! We'll get through it. You'll go to
Paris for a couple of weeks, and by the time you get back,
it'll all be over." Sara gasped and squeezed his hand. "I
mean . . . I mean I trust Wolfowitz to see the whole thing
through. . . ."

"After that press conference, you can still say that?"

"Come on, Bobby, you know that Nat Wolfowitz will
never start pushing the red buttons, no matter what."

"Yeah," Bobby agreed sincerely, "but if Gorchenko does,
the Pentagon's liable to yank them out of his hands."

"Gorchenko won't do it either. Why should he? The Red
Army certainly doesn't need nuclear weapons to walk all
over the Ukrainians!"

"True enough," Bobby said. "But if they do invade, we're
committed to—"

"We're not committed to do anything now!" Sara declared forcefully. "That crazy bastard Carson's dead, remember! Wolfowitz isn't committed to anything."

"Maybe you're right," Bobby had said, and he really had felt better about leaving her alone. "But . . . but you weren't there, Sara, he was so . . . he seemed so trapped, so off center, so . . . so terrified himself. . . ."

"Who wouldn't be? Only an asshole like Harry Carson." And Sara had smiled a brave little smile that went straight to his heart. "There's something to be said for a President who's willing to stand up there freaked-out like any sane person would be and tell the American people in words of one syllable that it's time for the bullshit to stop, now isn't there?" she had said.

They had both managed to laugh at that, and Sara had been a rock to the end. She didn't even cry when she saw him off at Grand Central Station. She smiled, and she kissed him, and she waved good-bye from the platform with the same fixed smile on her face as the train pulled out.

And Bobby had ridden the train to Montreal and the Concordski to De Gaulle with hope in his heart. Sara, after all, was right. It was Harry Carson who had brought the world to the brink in the first place, and Carson was dead. Wolfowitz had just been in a state of shock at the press conference, that's all. He had been the old Nat Wolfowitz in the toilet, more or less, hadn't he?

It was a whole new hand of cards now, and who better to have playing them than the old poker master himself?

But now, sitting in the RER, glancing at the haggard faces of his fellow passengers, and reading the European version of the situation in *Le Monde, Libération,* and *Europe Today,* Bobby found that hope beginning to evaporate again.

Things looked much darker from this perspective. The Europeans were not under the umbrella of Battlestar America. If American missiles fell on the Soviet Union, Europeans were going to catch the fallout.

And even if a war was somehow averted, enormous political damage had already been done to Common Europe. If Gorchenko did not suppress the Ukrainian secession, the Soviet Union would disintegrate, and every ethnic minority in Europe would start declaring independence from the stable nation-states.

Libé had a story about clandestine American arms shipments through Odessa, yet at the same time quixotically supported Ukrainian independence in the name of popular

democracy. *Le Monde* actually supported a Soviet invasion
of the Ukraine as necessary to maintain European stability.

What everyone here seemed to agree on was that the
whole thing had at least begun as an American plot to
destabilize Common Europe and fragment the world's dominant economy. And while no one in Europe mourned the
death of Harry Carson, no one seemed to take Nathan
Wolfowitz seriously either.

From the European point of view, a maniacal adventurer
had been replaced by a cypher who was a captive of the
Pentagon, the CIA, and the Central Security Agency, which
had been running the United States for years anyway. C'est
normal, was the attitude. C'est l'Amérique. C'est la même
merde.

Left, right, and center, the hatred of America now
seemed far worse than anything Bobby remembered from
his boyhood. When he changed to the Métro at the Gare du
Nord, he saw anti-American graffiti scrawled everywhere.
The magazine covers on the kiosks were more of the same.
The faces of the people on the Métro were grim and angry-
looking, staring into space, more like a New York crowd
than his memory of Parisians, and such was his paranoia,
that it seemed to him that everyone could see the American
passport tucked into his jacket pocket.

Avenue Trudaine was much as he remembered it, the
boucheries and the pâtisseries, the vegetable stands and the
tabacs, the flower stalls and the brasseries, the smells of
fresh bread and roasted coffee and the elusive ozone tang of
Paris itself, the joie de vivre of an uncannily ordinary Parisian day.

As a boy, he had never quite felt truly at home here, and
now, returning as a man after all these years, the charm
seemed somehow false, unreal, the Disney version of an
eternal Paris where the butcher and the baker, the flower
seller and the vegetable vendor, the corner newsdealer and
the shoppers with their net bags and their carts, would be
there like this forever, untouched and immortal no matter
what happened to the real world outside.

Or perhaps it was something far more personal. Perhaps,
Bobby thought as he took the little elevator up to his parents' apartment, it's stepping back into a reality that's been
no more real than voices on a telephone for all these years.
The divorce, the years of separation, the accident, the rec-

onciliation, if that was what it was, he had been there for none of it. It was a story told to him by people who had long since become strangers.

And he felt very much like a stranger himself as he rang the doorbell, a stranger from another land, an American, which, just now, did not seem to be something of which to be proud.

Mom answered the door. She looked older, but not as old, somehow, as he had expected her to look. Her face had networks of fine lines around the eyes and the mouth, but her chin was still firm, and her hair ungrayed, though that might have been dye. What was most different from his memories was the haunted look in her eyes, that, and the indefinable sense of maturity she exuded, the aura of a woman who had been touched by tragedies and travails, but who was long accustomed to wielding authority. A professional bureaucrat at the height of her powers.

They stood there studying each other silently for a long awkward moment. "So you've finally come, Robert," Mom said, and she kissed him on both cheeks French-style, though there seemed to be no warmth in it.

Dad was sitting on the couch in the living room. The sight of him was a dreadful shock that Bobby tried his best not to show. He was thinner than Bobby remembered. His face was sallow and gaunt. His hair was half-gray now and receding around the temples. And there was a feverish, too-bright look in his eyes.

And the machine . . .

Dad had described it on the phone often enough, but nothing could have really cushioned Bobby from the first sight of his father, with an electrode fastened to the back of his head by some kind of outsized rubber band, with a cable leading from it to a reel atop the gray metal console that was keeping him alive, which sat beside the couch.

The only vital thing about him was those eyes, still fixed upon vistas that other men could not see, and that told Bobby that he had been right to fly to Palo Alto and back in the middle of the crisis, that he had been right in risking all to get here, that he had been right to accost the President of the United States in the midst of a disaster, that he was right in what he was going to do now.

Dad rose up off the couch and walked across the living room toward him, the cable unreeling smoothly behind him

from the hibernautika console. He didn't say anything. He
just reached out his arms and took Bobby into them. They
hugged each other for a long time before anyone spoke.

"Good to see you, Bob," Dad finally said awkwardly.

"Good to see you too, Dad."

They stood there just looking at each other across the gulf
of years. Mom stood to one side, watching the two of them,
seeming sadly apart.

"I'll . . . I'll go get us some lunch," she said coolly.
"We've got a lot of catching up to do."

"Did you bring the material from Immortality, Inc.?"
Dad asked anxiously the moment she was gone.

"Yeah, yeah, I've got it in my bag," Bobby said, half exasperated, half amazed, at his father's single-mindedness, and
yet somehow also deeply touched.

Ten years of separation later, hooked up to this life-support machinery, slowly dying while the world itself was
threatening to come apart, Dad was still the same old space
cadet. It was as if Bobby had gone out to the pâtisserie for a
loaf of bread and come back ten years later, with, in some
weird way, no time at all having passed.

EURORUSSIANS AT NEW LOW IN POLLS
—Izvestia

UNLEASH THE RED ARMY, MARSHAL BRONKSKY DEMANDS
—Tass

Jerry fidgeted fretfully all during the agonizingly stiff
lunch, waiting for an opening. They talked for what seemed
like forever about endless this and that. Slowly, ever so
slowly, as the small talk wound down, Sonya began to warm
up to Bob, at least to the point of letting her mask of frosty
politeness drop and her real emotions show.

"Things have not been so easy here, you know, Robert, if
only you could have come sooner. . . ."

"I explained all that, Mom," Bob said in a carefully controlled voice. "They weren't about to issue an exit visa to

RUSSIAN SPRING   559

someone whose mother was a ranking Red Star bureaucrat."

"Surely things could not really have been—"

"Oh yes they were! For chrissakes, Mom, *Harry Carson*
was President!"

"I still—"

"Let him be, Sonya!" Jerry said. "The important thing is
that he's here now." And, suddenly sensing the opening he
had been waiting for coming out of his own mouth, added:
"And he had to go all the way to President Wolfowitz to do
it!"

"Believe me, Mom, if it wasn't for Nathan Wolfowitz, I
still wouldn't have been able to get here," Bob told her.

Sonya's face softened. "You really knew this Wolfowitz in
college, Robert?" she said in a somewhat less hectoring
tone. "He *is* different from Harry Carson?"

"Night and day, Mom."

Sonya frowned. "He did not seem very impressive on television. And the things the man said! At any rate, he is not
really in charge, is he? The CIA, the Central Security
Agency, the Pentagon, and Carson's old Cabinet, they are
still running things, are they not?"

Bob shrugged. "I think he's still fighting for control," he
said. "You should have heard him yelling at the Secret Service."

"He seems like such a . . . such a clown."

"You never played poker against him. Don't underesti-
mate Wolfowitz."

"And President Wolfowitz told Bob something wonderful,
Sonya," Jerry broke in.

"He did?" Sonya said.

Bob looked at Jerry perplexedly.

"Carson's brain," Jerry said.

"What on earth could be wonderful about that madman's
brain?" Sonya exclaimed. "Except, perhaps, that an autopsy
showed that he actually *had* one."

Bob glanced at Jerry. Jerry shot him a glance back and
kicked his ankle under the table. Bob shrugged. "It's been
polymerized, Mom," he said, somewhat hesitantly.

"It's been *what?*"

"Bob and I have a surprise for you, Sonya," Jerry said.
"Something quite wonderful. Tell her, Bob."

"Jesus, Dad," Bob moaned.

"We have to talk about it sooner or later."

Sonya glanced back and forth between the two of them. "What *have* you two been up to?"

"*You'd* better tell her, Dad," Bob said. "You understand this stuff a lot better than I do."

Jerry took a sip of wine, gathered up his courage and his wits, and did.

PRESIDENT GORCHENKO CALLS FOR CALM

——Pravda

MAY DAY PARADE TO BE HELD AS USUAL DESPITE CRISIS

—Mad Moscow

"The whole thing sounds insane," Sonya said when Jerry had finished his preposterous story. "Record your mind and your genome in software! Polymerize your brain! You can't be serious!"

"The science is sound," Jerry insisted. "They've already cloned rat brains."

"You are not a rat, Jerry Reed! You have a mind! A . . . a soul!"

"There might be some data loss, but when they clone me a new body, transplant the depolymerized brain, and dump the stored hologram into it, it *will* be me."

"Surely you are not saying that that is all there is to a man, to a soul, to a human spirit!"

Jerry leered at her wolfishly. "I thought *you* were the dialectical materialist," he said.

Sonya looked at Robert, who had said nothing during all of Jerry's mad presentation. "You believe this is possible too?" she said incredulously. "You really believe it?"

"Well . . . ," Robert muttered uncertainly.

"Show her the literature," Jerry said sharply.

Robert nodded, went into the living room, returned with a thick packet of papers contained in a folio embossed with the logo of Immortality, Inc.

It was certainly a slick presentation. There was an introduction that explained the process in layman's terms, lavishly illustrated with a photo layout on the labs and facilities. There was a long section of technobabble filled with formulas and diagrams and graphs and equations. And there was a balance sheet that indicated that the corporation was heavily capitalized, ran a small cash-flow surplus, but spent most of its income on research and development.

All in all, it reminded Sonya of a thousand such presentations that she had seen as the Director of Red Star's Paris office, all designed to convey soundness, seriousness, fiscal stability.

"It all looks quite impressive," she finally admitted. "But then so would a presentation for a well-designed fraud."

"They've already processed President Carson," Jerry said. "Bob got that straight from President Wolfowitz."

"So what?" Sonya snapped. "*His* brain was mummified before he ever took office, and if they ever bring *him* back to life as a zombie, no one will be able to tell the difference!"

Jerry shot a quick glance at Robert. Robert shrugged.

"Dad *does* have a point," he said. "Carson *was* the President, meaning that the Central Security Agency must have checked the whole thing out."

Slowly, the whole crazy idea began to take on a certain solidity for Sonya. It was hard to believe that a fraud would have gotten past the Central Security Agency.

Still . . .

"You really believe in this, Jerry?" she said softly.

Jerry looked right into her eyes. There he was, wired to the machinery that was keeping him alive, with his pale skin, his emaciating body, slowly wasting away, day by day, week by week, with only his eyes still bright and fully alive. He didn't have long to live, and he knew it. And so did she.

Jerry sighed. He shrugged. He hesitated, and when he spoke, Sonya knew that this time he was speaking the hard truth straight from his heart. "I *want* to believe in it, Sonya," he said. "So it's a long shot, so it's a big leap into the unknown. So maybe it's just whistling in the dark. But at least it's a hope, isn't it?"

Tears welled up in Sonya's eyes. He had been so brave since the accident, far braver, she realized, than she. And suddenly she realized what all this was *really* about. He wanted her to believe in death suspension so badly not just to relieve her anguish, but because if she did, it would remove the last excuse she had for not helping him to get his probably fatal spaceship ride.

That's how important it really was to him. It was quite literally more important than her grief or his own life itself. At last she understood that deep in her gut. It awed her. It filled her with a strange sort of envy. And it made her love him again in a way that the accident and these last weeks together never really had.

He was her crazy space cadet. And if he wanted to die as he had lived, who was she to deny it to him? What kind of love was that?

Sonya sighed. She smiled wanly at him. She reached out and took his hand. "I can't say I'm really convinced, Jerry," she said, "but God help me, I want very much to believe in it too."

BEER-HALL PUTSCHES, EVERYONE?

If it weren't making an already grim situation that much worse, the current mania for beer-hall declarations of independence would make a great musical comedy. We've already had independent republics declared by drunks and rowdies in Tbilisi, Alma-Ata, Minsk, Tashkent, and Baku, and reportedly, even at an Eskimo village above the Arctic Circle, and each and every one of them has been instantly recognized by the Republic of the Ukraine.

We're thinking of declaring an independent republic ourselves, citizenship available by subscription only.

—Mad Moscow

In a perverse sort of way, Franja was sorry she was not going to be in Moscow to witness the May Day parade in person, but realistically, she knew all too well that it just might turn out to be a piece of good luck that Ivan was in London and she was here in Paris on her way to her parents' place, even if it was going to mean being forced to share the same apartment with Bobby.

There was a bad wind rising in Moscow, with the election still two weeks away and Gorchenko sitting on his hands, while the Bears in the KGB and the Red Army openly demanded an immediate invasion of the Ukraine.

In desperation, Gorchenko had publicly appealed to the

American President to restrain the Kronkol clique, and Nathan Wolfowitz had replied with the bizarre statement that "the United States will be the last to use nuclear weapons, but we will certainly use Battlestar America to prevent anyone from gaining any satisfaction out of being first."

Grasping at straws, Gorchenko had actually praised this gibberish as "statesmanlike conduct." The Ukrainians, of course, took it as a statement of American support and praised Wolfowitz for his "solidarity with the Ukrainian people in their hour of need."

The Eurorussians sunk to new lows in the polls and the Defense Minister, Marshal Bronksky, openly called for Gorchenko's resignation.

Ominous rumors had been sweeping through Moscow for days. Gorchenko had tried to cancel the May Day parade but had been blocked by the Red Army. Gorchenko would make a dramatic speech of resignation from atop Lenin's tomb. There would be a military coup. Gorchenko would use the occasion to send the Red Army into the Ukraine in an attempt to salvage his position.

The parade would have already started back in Moscow as Franja left the Anvers Métro station, and she double-timed through the streets to the apartment building on Avenue Trudaine, waited impatiently for the agonizingly slow descent of the elevator, and thumbed the doorbell repeatedly till Mother appeared to let her in.

She dashed into the living room with Mother trailing behind her, where Father rose to greet her, and where Bobby sat frozen on the couch, looking anywhere but into her eyes.

"Hello, Father," she said, giving him a brief hug and a peck on both cheeks. Then she broke the embrace, loped across the room, turned on the wall screen, and tuned in the Tass channel.

A huge formation of schoolchildren in bright white peasant blouses, brilliant red pants, and black felt boots was marching past the reviewing stand atop Lenin's tomb. On a big float in the midst of the formation, a huge robot cossack danced with a giant robot bear.

"Jesus Christ, Franja," Bobby snapped, "I don't expect you to pretend to be glad to see me, but this is hardly the time to watch television."

"Shut up, Bobby, I have to watch the May Day parade!"

"Franja!"

"You too, Mother, something terrible is about to happen, I just know it!"

A squad of Olympic athletes, dressed only in red shorts and competition T-shirts despite the apparent chill, paraded past the camera behind ranks of Soviet and Olympic flags, the privileged few bearing giant papier-mâché replicas of their medals.

"Yeah," Bobby said, "we're all gonna be bored to death."

"Come on, Franja, is this really necessary?" Father said. "You haven't even said hello to your brother, whom you haven't seen for ten years!"

Franja glanced away from the TV long enough to glare at Bobby for a moment. "Hello, brother," she said poisonously, and then returned her attention to the parade coverage.

Behind the Olympic athletes came a huge formation of cossack horsemen in a film version of the traditional costume, with long red cloaks, black fur hats, and waving outsized swords in slow lazy circles above their heads while the prancing hooves of identical black chargers beat a staccato thunder as they trotted across the stones of Red Square.

Behind them came a unit of the Red Army. The front rank was a squad of hovertanks, their rotors roaring like an endless rocket blast inside their armored skirts, their turrets swiveled around backward so that the long guns seemed slung over their metal shoulders at the same angle as the combat rifles of the infantry in full-dress uniform that entered the square after them. Behind the infantry was a rank of self-propelled rocket guns, tracked all-terrain vehicles with huge clusters of revolving barrels mounted like telescopes atop them, each capable of firing ten mini-rockets a second.

"Screw you too, Franja!" Bobby said.

"Please!"

The tanks came abreast of Lenin's tomb. Gorchenko, standing in the center of the reviewing stand with Marshal Bronksy at his side in a uniform festooned with comic-opera medals, saluted. Only when the hovertanks had gone well past the tomb and the infantry was parading before it did the Marshal bring his own hand to the brim of his cap.

The hovertanks stopped. They cut their engines and came to rest on their skirt supports. The sudden silence came like a thunderclap. Slowly, almost majestically, and in smart unison, the turrets rotated, and the cannon swiveled to aim their barrels directly at Lenin's tomb.

"My God, what's happening!" Mother shouted.

"What do you think, Mother?" Franja muttered, sinking to the floor in front of the wall screen.

At the other end of Red Square, the self-propelled rocket guns also had the tomb squarely focused in their point-blank field of fire. The infantry formation marched in place for a few beats, then did a parade right to face the tomb. On the next beat, they unslung their combat rifles. On the beat after that, they sank to one knee, and brought their weapons up into firing position.

"Holy shit . . . ," Bobby muttered behind Franja's ear.

Marshal Bronksky said something to President Gorchenko. Gorchenko seemed to somehow melt back into the crowd of dignitaries behind him. Bronksky stepped up to the microphone on the central podium. The camera did not move in for a close-up. It held a long shot centered on the tiny figure atop Lenin's tomb as it spoke with a thunderous and echoing amplification.

"Citizens of the Union of Soviet Socialist Republics! In order to preserve the territorial integrity of the USSR and protect Socialist Democracy, I have been authorized by the Central Red Army Command to place the nation under conditional martial law for the duration of the current election campaign. The Presidency is hereby declared vacant for the duration of the election campaign. When the Soviet people have spoken, control of all government functions will be returned to their duly elected representatives."

"Conditional martial law?" Bobby muttered. "What the hell's that?"

Glancing behind her, Franja saw that her brother was kneeling on the floor before the wall screen now, close behind her, and looking at her with a dismay on his face that almost seemed to match her own.

"Quiet, Bobby, please," she pleaded.

"During the interim period, all civilian functions will be carried out by the officials presently in place and all Soviet citizens will retain their full rights under Soviet law. Full responsibility for military and foreign policy will be assumed by the Red Army Central Command."

Now the camera finally did move in for a head-and-shoulders shot of Bronksky, a solemn broad-featured man in middle years, whose face, somewhat to Franja's surprise, did not betray any pleasure in what he had just done. It seemed like the face of an honest Soviet citizen quite convinced that he was doing his painful patriotic duty.

That is, until he spoke again. Then a certain fire flared in his eyes and a certain wolfish satisfaction creased his lips.

"And the first official act of the Red Army Central Command will be to end the treasonous insurrection against Socialist Legality in the Ukraine. If the Kronkol clique surrenders itself to the Red Army Central Command within forty-eight hours, they will be permitted, despite their crimes, and in the interests of peace, to take political asylum in any country willing to bear their presence. If they fail to accept this magnanimous offer within forty-eight hours, their rebellion will be crushed at once by the full force of the Red Army."

The screen flickered, and then a tape loop of a Soviet flag waving gloriously against a bright blue sky replaced Marshal Bronksky. They played the "Internationale" through once, and then Moscow went off the air.

Sonya sat there staring at the dead screen without reacting for a long moment. Then she staggered over to the couch and let herself collapse onto it beside Jerry. "I can't believe this is happening . . . ," she stammered. "Fifty years of progress blown away just like that . . . A general issuing ultimatums from the top of Lenin's tomb . . ."

Jerry took her hand. Franja got up from the floor, sat down beside her, and put her arm around her shoulders, and the two of them huddled against each other as mother and daughter, as fellow Soviet citizens, as forlorn lost children of the Russian Spring.

Bobby got up and turned off the television set. He stood there across the room staring uncertainly at the three of them. No, at the *two* of them, Sonya could see it in his eyes. He was looking at two Russians, and Franja was glaring back at an *American* with naked hatred in her eyes.

"Just don't say it, Bob-bee," she snarled. "Just keep your big gringo mouth shut!"

But this was a different Bobby now. This was not the unhappy little boy writhing under the insults of his big sister who would miss no opportunity, let alone one as rich as this, to hit back. This, Sonya saw, with pride in her heart and tears in her eyes, was a mature man. A son to be proud of.

He didn't rise to the bait. He didn't snap back. Instead he walked slowly over to the couch and looked down at his sister with no anger in his eyes.

"Believe me, Franja," he said, "no Russian alive can hate what Harry Carson has gotten the world into more than I do. Not even you."

Franja looked back at her brother with open amazement. "You can say that now? This is not your moment of glory, now that it is *we* whom the whole world will hate and fear, as they did in Stalin's day, for what the Red Army has done and the catastrophe that the Bears are about to bring about?"

Bobby shook his head slowly. And then he knelt down in front of his despised sister. "Now maybe you understand what it was like for me when we were kids together," he said. "Now maybe you understand what it means to love a fucked-up country that the rest of the world hates. Now maybe you know what it feels like to be ashamed of the country you love. And love it still."

Then Sonya thought her heart would burst as he reached out to lay his hand gently upon his sister's.

Franja wouldn't take it, but she didn't pull away.

"Hey, Franja," Bobby said soothingly, "let's not let all the assholes do to us what they're doing to the rest of the world."

"Politique politicienne," Jerry muttered.

"You listen to Dad, Franja," Bobby said. "He's a crazy space cadet, but that's one thing he's been right about all these years. Politics has to stop somewhere. Can't we stop it here? Can't we stop it now? Can't we be some kind of half-assed family again?"

"Now you *do* make me ashamed, little brother," Franja said. And she squeezed Bobby's hand tightly, closing a circuit that Sonya had never thought to feel completed again.

The four of them touching, flesh to flesh to flesh to flesh, heart to heart to heart to heart.

What a golden tender moment it was!

How bitter and how sweet!

How bitter that it had taken a family tragedy and an imminent global catastrophe to bring it about!

How sweet that such a thing could happen at all!

Yet Sonya was certain that unlikely reunions like this
must be taking place now all over the world. In her mind's
eye, she could see this scene repeated in a million varia-
tions, as feuds were buried in tearful reconciliations and
black sheep were hugged back into the fold, and long-lost
lovers embraced, as all over the city, all over Europe, all
over the world, families huddled together fearfully and
reached out for the touch of reassuring flesh, finding out in
the hardest possible way what really mattered as they held
hands and waited for the end of the world.

". . . and in Geneva, a spokesman for the Congress of
Peoples announced that its delegates would immediately
submit a resolution calling for the expulsion of the Soviet
Union from Common Europe on the grounds of blatant
violation of the treaty of admission . . ."

—BBC

X X V I I

Though Mother's distractedly prepared linguini à la Romanoff was about the most glutinous version of that loathsome
dish that Franja had ever been subjected to, she forced herself to pretend to eat the mess with relish; this was certainly
no time to complain about the cooking, not with the world
coming apart and Father spinning out his incredible fantasy
of having himself "polymerized."

". . . in Rome, the Pope announced the beginning of a
prayer vigil that he vowed not to end till the crisis was
past. . . ."

Franja could not decide which seemed more unreal—the military coup in Moscow and the imminence of nuclear war, the discovery of a brother who seemed like quite another person, Father's plans for his own death, or the fact that all of this was going on while they sat around the dinner table together for the first time in ten years, eating Mother's linguini à la Romanoff.

". . . estimated at twenty thousand demonstrated outside the Soviet Embassy . . ."

To make matters even more bizarre, Mother, of all people, had insisted that the portable TV be set up on the sideboard, Mother who had always barred TV at the dinner table as barbaric and nikulturni.

But no one wanted to be far from the newscasts that were blanketing all channels, for at any moment, the news could come that the missiles had started to fly.

So while they sat there in the insanely normal process of eating a family dinner, while Father kept blathering about genome recordings, tissue samples, brain polymerization, and how they were going to come up with the money, there the TV sat, muttering darkly at low volume, haunting what should have been this most intimate and personal reunion like an evil electronic icon of the greater forces now controlling everyone's lives.

"We could take out a new mortgage on the apartment, that should get us close, and maybe we could even persuade ESA that this should be covered by my medical insurance. . . ."

". . . denounced the military coup in Moscow as a betrayal of Europe's faith in the dedication to democracy of the Soviet . . ."

"Assuming there's an apartment or an ESA left by tomorrow morning," Mother blurted, then bit her lip in dismay at her own lapse into the subject they had strenuously avoided all evening. "I mean, it seems so strange to be sitting here eating dinner and planning for the future when . . ."

There was a long uncomfortable silence only made worse by the muttering of the TV set.

Franja broke it by heroically forking a big glob of linguini à la Romanoff into her mouth, pretending to savor it, and saying, "If we are all going to be vaporized, I prefer to go with a full stomach."

Bobby actually laughed, picked up his own fork, and did

likewise. "And Mom's linguini à la Romanoff always was our favorite dish, wasn't it, Franja?" he said dryly. Even Mother was able to crack a smile at that one.

". . . was meeting with the National Security Council . . ."

"And as for planning for the future," Father said earnestly, "well, what have we got to lose? If they don't blow us all up, we'll have to get on with it afterward, and if they do, well at least we won't go out staring at the TV like zombies and doing nothing."

That sucked the momentary jocularity right out of the atmosphere.

". . . called for the expulsion of the illegal Soviet regime . . ."

"Oh, Jerry, aren't things bad enough, without having to dwell on . . . on . . ."

". . . declared that he would give the Red Army his answer within the hour . . ."

"On death?" Father said quite calmly. "No one likes to talk about it. No one likes to think about it. And no one really believes it's going to happen to him. But I've *had* to think about it. And now the whole world is being forced to think about it. The difference is that I've had plenty of time to consider the options."

". . . apparently refused another request by the Pentagon to place the United States under martial law . . ."

"*Options?*" Mother cried. "How can you talk about options?"

"There are always options," Father persisted. "You can kid yourself that it's never going to happen to you, or you can face reality and make the best of it."

"Make the best of it!"

"If you face the fact that the story of your life is going to have a beginning, a middle, and an end, well, then you know that what really counts is whether you can write the story that you want to in the time you've got."

"These are the cards, kiddo, all you can do is play them," Bobby muttered.

"What?" Franja said.

"Something Nat Wolfowitz used to say at the poker table, Franja."

". . . agreed to broadcast the Ukrainian leader's speech worldwide despite Moscow's protest . . ."

Somehow Franja found herself taking a certain comfort in the thought that Nathan Wolfowitz had the same vision of reality as her father, for Father's courage in the face of his own death was not at all macabre or morbid. *Everyone* was in Father's position right now, and they all had something to learn from the way Jerry Reed was facing it.

In that moment, she found her father reminding her of Nikolai Smirnov. What a shame that these two real heroes had never met. How well they would have understood each other!

"For God's sake, Mother, can't you see that he's right?" Franja found herself saying. "What are we supposed to do, sit around pretending none of this is happening, or try to do the best we can for each other in however much time we have left?"

"Franja—"

"Listen to Franja, Mom, she's making good sense," Bobby broke in unexpectedly with words that Franja had never expected to hear. And he actually put a supportive hand on her shoulder.

"All his life, Father has wanted to build his Grand Tour Navette and see the other side of the gravity well," Franja went on, feeling an unexpected strength and clarity filling her at the touch of Bobby's truly brotherly hand.

"Well, they took his project away from him, and then the accident took away his spaceship ride too. And it's in your power to give that much back to him, or at least to try. He's not your child, Mother. He's got a right to live for his own dream. Or if it comes down to it, to die for it."

"I don't want him to die!" Mother cried. "How can you expect me to let him kill himself?"

"But I won't be killing myself," Father said. "I'll have my happy ending, and then I'll just go to sleep for a while until it's time for the sequel."

Mother sighed. Her eyes grew cooler and her voice hardened a tone. "You really think I don't know what the three of you are doing? None of you really believes in this death-suspension nonsense! You're all just pretending you do to make me believe it! It's all just a silly conspiracy!"

"It's not nonsense, Sonya, it's scientifically—"

"No, Dad," Bobby said, "let's stop insulting each other's intelligence. It's a long shot in the dark, it's pulling to an inside straight, it's the only hope there is, but that's *all* that it is."

His face softened, became tender, as he smiled at Mother with a gentleness of which Franja would never have believed he was capable. "Yeah, it's a conspiracy, Mom, but it's a *loving* conspiracy. Things being what they are, don't you really think it's time you joined it?"

My God, little brother, Franja thought, you really *have* become a man!

Mother's face softened, her eyes misted over, she sighed, she shrugged. "You three just believe in this because you're crazy," she said softly. Then she smiled a faint little smile. "So all right, all right, now you can call me crazy too."

"You'll do it, Sonya?" Father said. "You'll really do it for me?"

"I'll start talking to Tass about it tomorrow," Mother told him. "If there is a tomorrow . . ."

"I could try to contact StarNet, there's a good feature story in this, and maybe we can sell them the—"

". . . live, from Kiev, where Vadim Kronkol is about to reply to the Soviet ultimatum. . . ."

Bobby froze. They all did. For Vadim Kronkol's face had appeared on the tiny TV screen, a sudden sinister apparition from the world outside.

"Oh my God, this is it!" Mother cried.

"Turn it up!"

Father reached out and turned up the volume, and they all pulled their chairs closer to the TV set.

". . . have shown their true faces . . ."

Horribly enough, there was no fear at all visible on the Ukrainian President's face; instead his fierce blue eyes blazed defiance, his full lips seemed to be savoring each word as he spat it out.

"The people of the Ukraine will not be denied their national destiny by a cabal of generals in Moscow! It is time the Russian imperialists learned the limits of their power. It is time they finally understood the determination of the Ukrainian people to free themselves once and for all from the rule of the Russians."

"Jesus Christ," Bobby moaned, "he's foaming at the mouth!"

"We defy the generals in Moscow! We defy the Red Army! We defy the Russian imperialists!"

Kronkol stared silently and grimly into the camera for a moment, glowering and grimacing like the fascist maniac that he was, like someone who could feel the hatred he was calling down upon himself and was fattening his ego on it like a vampire toad.

And then his lips parted in the most chillingly triumphant smile.

"But before they think to defy *us*," he said, "let them see what will happen to Moscow and Leningrad and their beloved Russia the moment the first Red Army boot desecrates sacred Ukrainian soil! Let them see what our American friends have given us in our hour of need!"

Suddenly there appeared on the screen the silhouette of a sleek slim missile. The camera pulled back as it slowly panned down it.

The missile stood erect in some kind of parkland. The camera panned around to show two more missiles on either side of it, revealing, as it moved, the shapes of buildings ringing the missile site.

The coverage cut to another missile site, this one in a church courtyard. And another in the middle of a traffic circle. And another and another and another.

"Oh no," Father muttered.

"What is it, Father?" Franja said. His face had turned ashen. He looked like he had just seen the end of the world.

"Those are Slam-Dunk missiles!" Jerry moaned. "They're fucking Slam-Dunk missiles!"

God, they were elegant, the latest triumph of an American aerospace technology long since given over to the black science of destruction.

The details were secret, but Jerry knew the conceptual design, and the concept, he had to admit even now, was brilliant.

There were five warheads on the bus atop the Slam-Dunk missile. Small ones, maybe two hundred kilotons apiece. These weren't city-killers, they were decapitation weapons, designed to take out command centers, government bunkers, selected missile sites, system control radars, launching facilities.

First-strike weapons, designed to penetrate defenses before anyone even knew they were coming.

In terms of throw-weight, the boosters were vastly over-powered to sprint the payload up to about fifty miles at blinding speed, giving less than a three-minute window to boost-phase interceptors. At the apogee of this steep, short parabola, the warhead bus separated. The bus itself was powered, blasting itself along the suborbital curve just under escape velocity until it was in position for separation, moving too fast for orbital interceptors to lock on.

It didn't matter that this moved the bus up to about a hundred miles before the warheads separated, for the warheads were *also* powered. They didn't just reenter the atmosphere and jig and jag as they fell onto their targets at mere terminal velocity. They came straight down at incredible speed—protected from incineration by their own shaped shock wave and by an ablative superconductor-cooled heat shield—with enough kinetic energy to vaporize twenty feet of concrete even if the detonator malfunctioned.

". . . ten missiles, each with five two-hundred-kiloton fusion warheads . . ."

"What's wrong, Jerry?" Sonya cried. "A minute ago, you were all brave talk, and now you look like you've seen your own ghost."

"Those are Slam-Dunk missiles. Starblitz weapons. They go up like a bat out of hell, and they come down at a thousand miles a second."

"What does that mean?"

"It means we can't stop them, Mother," Franja told her.

"That's right," Jerry said. "The Russians have nothing that can stop them. There's no time for a boost-phase detection-intercept cycle. Once the warheads separate, it's only seconds to impact. The only chance is to get the bus between injection and separation, and between the Ukraine and Moscow, that's maybe a sixty-second window. Battlestar America, just maybe. What the Russians have, never."

". . . as assurance to the world that these missiles are strictly defensive, and as proof positive to the Russian imperialists of the dedication of the Ukrainian people to their national destiny, we have placed these missiles in the midst of our major population centers, where any attempted preemptive nuclear strike at these purely defensive missiles will result in the deaths of millions of our own people. . . ."

"Shit, that's diabolical!" Bobby moaned.

"The man is crazy!"

"Like a fox," Sonya said grimly.

". . . to die for our national independence if need be! We will fire these missiles at Russian population centers if and only if the Red Army crosses our border. We say to the generals in Moscow, we have made our decision, now you must make yours. Invade the Ukraine at the cost of millions of Russian lives. Attempt to preempt us and bring on a general holocaust. Or let us have our freedom and accept us as a member of a fraternal Europe, not of nation-states or empires, but of free and independent peoples!"

Vadim Kronkol held a heroic pose for a long moment to let it all sink in, and then he spoke again, this time in much lower tones of sly insinuation.

"In the interests of peace and humanity, and in order to make the best effort possible to prevent a nuclear catastrophe that nobody really wants, we have sacrificed one tenth of our national deterrent to arrange a nonlethal demonstration. At eleven fifty-six tomorrow morning, Moscow time, we will launch a missile carrying five warheads containing not nuclear explosives but honest Ukrainian pig manure. At approximately noon, Moscow time, our fraternal donations of fertilizer will be delivered to Red Square."

Kronkol smiled sweetly at the camera. "We invite the generals in Moscow to get in some target practice at our expense. We have given you the launch time and the trajectory. Let's see how well you do in ideal conditions against dummy warheads. It should give you some idea of how you will fare if you force us to use these weapons in earnest."

". . . still no further word from the Red Army Central Command, while in Washington, President Nathan Wolfowitz still refuses to clarify the bizarre response to the Russian ultimatum that has so shocked an already-stunned world."

—CNN

"What do you think, Dad?" Bobby said. "Is there any chance at all?"

Dad shook his head. "If they get one out of five, it'll be a miracle," he said.

They had all stayed up till late in the night, transfixed by the wall screen. At any moment, the Russians might attempt a nuclear strike on the Ukrainian missile sites. Or the Russians might capitulate. If Dad was right, and when it came to this stuff, it was hard to believe he could be wrong, Bobby certainly knew that *he* would do one thing or the other if he were Marshal Bronksky.

But all during the world's long night vigil, neither had happened. Bronksky issued a short statement accusing the United States of nuclear blackmail. He demanded to know what President Wolfowitz was going to do when the Ukrainians fired their missile. He warned that if Kronkol was lying and live warheads exploded on Soviet territory, it would be taken as an act of war on the part of the United States and "dealt with accordingly."

Nearly two hours of talking heads later, Nathan Wolfowitz had used a photo opportunity to give a one-sentence answer that only seemed to make matters worse.

"Mr. President, Marshal Bronksky wants to know what you're going to do when the Ukrainians fire their dummy warheads at Moscow!"

Nathan Wolfowitz had smiled sardonically and shrugged his shoulders. "Like the rest of the world," he said, "I think I'll just sit back with a six-pack and watch the big game on television."

The reporters had been appalled, and so had everyone else, to judge by the rest of the night's commentary, but Bobby had been mightily relieved, though he couldn't make anyone who hadn't known the man understand why.

That was the real Nathan Wolfowitz, playing the awful hand he had been dealt with a perfect poker face.

Bobby didn't envy Wolfowitz the hand of cards he had to play one little bit. But still less did he envy the marks who were now playing against him.

And now here they were again, gathered in the living room before the wall screen, with a long-range TV camera far away atop a Tverskaya Street skyscraper holding a panoramic shot on Red Square while a white digital insert ticked off the minutes and seconds till noon.

The huge square was eerily deserted under the bright noontime sun. Nothing moved but a flag waving above the empty buildings behind the Kremlin wall and pigeons too stupid to realize they were scavenging on ground zero.

11:56

"Ignition and lift-off," Dad droned, just as he always had when he watched live coverage of an ordinary space shot. His eyes were bright and fixated on the wall screen, and there was a weird little smile on his lips. Even *now*, Dad was still the same crazy space cadet, no doubt in some twisted way, he was enjoying this.

11:58

"Insertion and warhead bus ignition."

11:59

"Warhead separation and—"

A blinding white light washed out the video image, followed immediately by an unguessable sound that blasted the audio into static. Another and another and another, too rapid to separate, and then the screen resolved into a fireball rising through a rolling gray cloud like a miniature nuclear mushroom and then five enormous overlapping thunderclaps as the microphones cleared to carry the secondary shock waves.

The cloud rose rapidly, dissipating quickly, raining debris across the screen for a few moments before the awful results could be seen.

Where the onion-domed church had been at one end of the square there was now a jagged ruin. The Kremlin wall was a line of rubble. The center of the square was a huge irregularly shaped crater. Lenin's tomb had had one of its corners blown off, and the stonework was a crumbling spiderweb of cracks, but, miraculously, it was more or less still standing.

Franja could not quite transfer the image of what she was seeing from her eyes into her brain. St. Basil's destroyed. The Kremlin wall smashed to rubble. Lenin's tomb cracked and crumbling. An enormous hole gouged in the center of the Russian heart. It was like a physical blow to her own breast. It took her long moments to catch her breath before she could even feel the pain.

"Well, it's good to see that Vladimir Illyich, at least, still knows how to be a survivor," Mother stammered.

It was an idiot remark, but Franja understood it. What else was there to say at a moment like this?

Those vicious cretins in Kiev had no doubt sought to humiliate the Russian people, to terrorize them, to break their hearts, by choosing as a demonstration the obliteration of the center of their world and their spirit and their history.

But if the Ukrainians thought that would cow Russia into submission, they had made a fatal error that the whole world was about to pay for. No one who had been in Red Square the night of the Ukrainian secession could doubt that fear, reason, or even the dictates of sanity itself, would allow this evilly brilliant attempt at psychic castration to go unavenged.

"I would not want to be in Kiev or Odessa right now . . . ," Franja said savagely, feeling the impulse to retaliate herself, even while knowing it was madness. But the generals of the Red Army, with the power to really do it in their hands, with Red Square a smoking ruin—

"Here comes the end of the world . . . ," Mother whispered as Marshal Bronksky's face replaced the awful spectacle. Bronksky himself looked like death in both senses of the term. His face was pale and drawn, his eyes blazing with fury, his jaws clenched tight in a futile attempt to choke back his obvious rage.

"We regard this unspeakable outrage as an act of war by the United States against the Soviet Union," he growled in a voice hoarse with contained emotion. "We demand that the United States forthwith remove its missiles from the Ukraine. If it fails to accomplish this within forty-eight hours, we will launch a nuclear strike against both the Ukrainian missiles and the United States, aimed not at military targets, but at population centers."

"The man's gone crazy!" Bobby exclaimed.

"On the contrary," Mother said grimly, "under the circumstances, this is quite an impressive degree of statesmanlike restraint."

Franja knew just what she meant.

ALL SOVIET FORCES ON FULL RED
ALERT
AS WORLD AWAITS RESPONSE
OF PRESIDENT WOLFOWITZ

—Tass

Nathan Wolfowitz did not wait for forty-eight hours to reply to the Russian ultimatum. Bobby had to admire his timing, and somehow it also gave him hope. Wolfowitz waited till 6:00 P.M. Paris time, 8:00 P.M. in Moscow, right at the top of the prime-time *Vremya* news, when it was noon in New York and 9:00 A.M. on the West Coast. Meaning that Nat was timing it to hit his maximum *European* audience.

"Ladies and gentlemen, the President of the United States."

Nathan Wolfowitz sat behind his desk in the Oval Office. He was wearing a tan sports jacket with leather patches on the elbows and a white turtleneck. His hair was neatly combed. His eyes sparkled with the unreadable amusement, feigned or not, that Bobby had faced a thousand times across the poker table.

"I will dispense with the usual formalities," President Wolfowitz said in a dry, cool voice. "In fact, I think I might as well dispense with *all* the formalities. In the name of the people of the United States, I apologize profoundly to the Soviet people before the world for the reckless stupidity of my pinheaded predecessor."

"Incredible!"

"That's Nathan Wolfowitz," Bobby said, and somehow found himself heaving a sigh of premature relief.

"I convey the condolences of the American people for the damage done to the heart of their capital, and offer to rebuild it under Soviet supervision entirely at American expense."

"He's . . . he's a genius!" Mom exclaimed.

"Now, I suppose I have to answer Marshal Bronksky's ultimatum," Wolfowitz drawled in quite another voice. "Well, unfortunately, I'm afraid there's no way I can do that, seeing as how there's no way I can retrieve Harry Carson's missiles from the Ukrainians without starting World War III myself."

He shrugged. He threw up his hands. "What can I tell you, Marshal? I guess you're just going to have to go ahead and launch your first strike against our population centers."

"What?"

"The man's gone mad!"

Nathan Wolfowitz's eyes grew harder than Bobby had ever seen them. For the first time he realized deep in his gut that his one-time friend really *was* the President of the

United States. And he suspected that much of the world felt the same. This was no Nat Wolfowitz that he had ever known. The game had changed the player.

"But *do* remember that we *have* bankrupted ourselves building a missile defense system with all the bells and whistles that our poor taxpayers' money could possibly buy and then some. And after we swat down most of your missiles, we're gonna be licking our wounds with most of our own strategic forces still intact, and everything neatly in place between here and the Moon."

Wolfowitz leered theatrically at the camera, just as he had leered at Bobby when he was sitting on a full house and didn't care who knew it.

"And we will *not* be amused," Wolfowitz said. "Think about it, Marshal Bronksy. And, oh yes, do have a nice day."

"This has been an address by the President of the United States, speaking from the White House in Washington, D.C."

"And you better believe it!" Bobby cried jubilantly.

WOLFOWITZ FIRES HEAD OF CENTRAL SECURITY AGENCY, VOWS NEVER TO APPOINT ANOTHER
—*New York Times*

WOLFOMANIA SWEEPS EUROPE!
—*News of the World*

NAT CANS DEFENSE SECRETARY, APPOINTS CHAIRMAN OF JOINT CHIEFS TO SILENCE JINGOS IN CONGRESS
—*New York Post*

XXVIII

It was Bobby's most improbable boyhood dream come true. Within a week, the long-despised Americans had become the heroes of the hour and the toast of Paris, and he had become StarNet's star reporter.

Nathan Wolfowitz had done the impossible. He had faced down the Russian ultimatum and stabilized a situation on the very brink of nuclear war, while committing himself to nothing at all.

Four hours before the Soviet ultimatum was due to expire, Marshal Bronksky announced that the deadline would be extended through the Soviet election in order to allow the Soviet people to express their opinion on this grave matter of national survival. Under the circumstances, it was the best face he could put on things.

Nathan Wolfowitz praised his action and archly professed a policy of noninterference in the Soviet election, interfering quite artfully in the act of doing so.

"Anything I said now would be entirely counterproductive," he declared. "It would only fan the flames of bug-brained nationalist passions and encourage the election of precisely the kind of irresponsible assholes who have gotten us into this mess in the first place. In the interests of sanity and world peace, I think I had better keep my opinions to myself, encourage like-minded Soviet citizens to vote early and often, and sit this one out."

The Eurorussians went up seventeen points in the polls.

The Red Army moved more troops up to the Ukrainian border as a continued show of force. The Russians also detached a task force from their Baltic fleet and sent it steaming through the English Channel toward the Strait of Gibraltar.

It made for an impressively bellicose spot on each evening's news, but optimists pointed out that the fact that it would take the task force ten days to arrive in the Black Sea off the Ukrainian coast could be taken as proof of Bronksky's temporary restraint, since its arrival on the scene would be neatly timed to coincide with the date of the Soviet election.

Constantin Gorchenko praised the American President

lavishly in a campaign speech in Leningrad as "a man after our own hearts" and "an American Gorbachev indeed."

When asked to comment, President Wolfowitz shrugged his shoulders, smiled, and praised his "friend Constantin Gorchenko" for his "good taste."

The Eurorussians went up another five points.

Wolfowitz T-shirts were everywhere. The most popular one showed the American President dressed as a matador, holding his cape behind him with one hand as he turned his back on a transfixed Russian bear, one finger of the other hand resting lightly on its fire-breathing nose.

Loathsome concoctions billed as authentic American cocktails appeared at fancy prices on the cartes of even the lowliest tabacs in Paris. Everyone wanted to eat hamburgers and Tex-Mex barbecue. Little American flag stick-ups went on sale all over St.-Germain and were plastered all over walls and lampposts and Métro hoardings. The Baseball Club de Paris made the national news. Someone pumped out a max-metal version of "God Bless America," and it zoomed up the charts, followed closely by a rerelease of Jimi Hendrix's notorious old cover of "The Star-Spangled Banner."

"Gringomania," as *Libé* dubbed it, had taken Paris by storm. There was hardly anything else in the newspapers. Serious intellectuals discussed it endlessly on talk shows. Restaurants and bars and novelty manufacturers cashed in big.

And so did Bobby. With the borders of the United States still sealed and all flights in or out still grounded, he was one of only a handful of American journalists in Paris, and the only one StarNet had.

They ran him deliriously ragged covering everything from pointless speeches by government officials to pro-American Métro graffiti, from the riot at the Russian Embassy to Harry's New York bar.

It was exhilarating, exhausting, and wonderful, but there was also something unsettlingly unreal about it. Here he was, zipping all over Paris to cover Gringomania, and here were the people of Paris, having, for all appearances, a high old time, as if they had been reunited with a long-lost lover, and all the while the clock was still ticking away toward midnight.

For despite the heady mood in the streets and cafés of

Paris, despite all the Gringomania, when you really thought about it, not that anyone wanted to, President Wolfowitz had solved nothing.

The Ukrainians still had their missiles. The Russians gave no indication of backing down. Wolfowitz had really done nothing more than freeze-frame the crisis just as the wave of destruction had been about to crest, in the manner of the famous Hokusai painting, but the tidal wave of nuclear destruction still hung there towering over everyone's head, waiting to come crashing down when the frame was unfrozen by the Russian election.

It was Gringomania indeed, or so it came to seem to Bobby, for it was not so much the real United States that Paris was feting, but the mythic America of his own boyhood longings, the America that had once been a beacon of light in another of Europe's darkest hours, as if by believing hard enough in that long-lost America of the heart's desire, the America that had liberated this land from the Nazi nightmare might be called forth from the mists of legend to roll back the night once more.

Bobby could feel it everywhere, immersed as he was in covering the amorphous story through human-interest features, and man-on-the-street interviews, and reports on demonstrations and politicians' speeches. Whenever he identified himself as an American, he was kissed on both cheeks. Politicians' press attachés whisked him inside for interviews the moment he flashed his StarNet badge. People bought him drinks.

It finally began to turn a little sour on Bobby. Were not these the same Parisians who had made his boyhood miserable? Who had burned the American flag and splattered the American Embassy, and indeed himself, with blood and shit?

> *"It's Tommy this, an' Tommy that*
> *An' Tommy go away . . ."*

And now here they were, with "God Bless America" at the top of the charts when the going got tough.

"But it's thank you, Mr. Atkins,
When the band begins to play!"

It was with an eerie sense of déjà vu and a strange feeling in the pit of his stomach that he went to cover the march on the American Embassy.

As another such demonstration had so many years ago, this one also began assembling within sight of the main entrance to the Embassy compound, but that was where the similarity ended.

That demonstration had taken place in the afternoon. That crowd had been a surly mob, and the flics had stood aside and tried to become invisible.

This demonstration had started assembling in the early evening. In place of the throwing-sticks and shit buckets and anti-American banners, there were posters of Nathan Wolfowitz, dozens of large American flags, and tens of thousands of little paper ones in the hands of the demonstrators, which, according to some sources, had been distributed by the Embassy itself.

Those demonstrators had assembled in the parkland between the Champs-Élysées and Avenue Gabriel, but for this one, the French government had actually closed the Place de la Concorde, and the vast concrete expanse was wall-to-wall people.

Ceremonial Garde Républicain horsemen in their dress uniforms, complete with sabers, shiny brass helmets, and long riding cloaks, lined the Place between the Champs-Élysées and the Avenue Gabriel, even their horses held at stiff attention. In the center of the formation, two cavalrymen held French and American flags flying from ornate bronzed standards.

And Bobby arrived on the scene, not by Métro, but riding atop the camera truck that StarNet had rented for the occasion, a van with a platform atop it for Bobby, his French cameraman, and the satellite uplink disc. The StarNet logo had been postered to the sides of the van, and an American flag flew from a tall whip antenna above it. The American Embassy, which it seemed these days could arrange anything, had assured StarNet that this would get its crew instant red-carpet treatment from any French police agency, on orders issued by the Première and the Mayor of Paris themselves.

When the StarNet truck found itself blocked by the crowd at the Rue de Rivoli entrance to the Place, far across it from what would be the main photo opportunities, Pierre Pham, the loan-out producer from Antenne 2, inside the van, made a quick call to somewhere, and less than five minutes later, four Garde Républicain horsemen made their way through the unprotesting throng, bracketed the van, and escorted it slowly but surely across the square to the scheduled head of the march, ushered along by a sea of waving flags, and wild cheering.

"This is Robert Reed in Paris, and what an incredible scene this is in the Place de la Concorde, as what Paris police estimate as at least half a million people gather here to show their support for the United States and President Wolfowitz," Bobby began when the uplink was established.

The flics, so it seemed, had actually been waiting patiently for the cue from his own producer, for the horseman at the right front corner of the van leaned down toward the open window, said something into his wrist radio, and the line of equestrian troops blocking the entrance to the square moved out up the Champs-Élysées at a slow ceremonial canter behind their twin flags.

The crowd began marching up the avenue behind them, waving their American flags, unfurling banners, throwing flowers, hats, paper cups, Wolfowitz buttons in the air, shouting, and screaming, and chanting incoherently.

"Lay back a little and let the front ranks get ahead of you," Bobby heard Pham tell the driver through the inter-com circuit. "I want this from over the heads of some crowd."

The van stopped for a few minutes to let the head of the procession get about a hundred meters ahead of it, then inched forward at walking speed into the Champs-Élysées itself.

Before Bobby, the crowd filled the broad avenue and overflowed the sidewalks, thousands of little paper flags turning the Champs-Élysées into a rolling river of red, white, and blue.

And then there was a sound all too familiar to Bobby from his stay in Los Angeles, but one he never thought to hear in Paris, where all overflights were long forbidden—the deep bass dragonfly drone of approaching helicopters, a sound made utterly ominous by endless footage from the Latin American war zones.

Four helicopters flying loose formation like gunships dodging ground fire swooped low over the marchers and up the Champs-Élysées at a walking pace, scattering something that looked like silvery confetti.

"What the hell?" Bobby muttered into his open mike. His visceral reaction had been to a cloud of rockets and gouts of napalm, but instead he was seeing fairy dust.

"Get a shot of those choppers!" he screamed at his cameraman.

"Je ne suis pas un imbécile!" the cameraman shouted back.

Bobby glanced down at his monitor to catch the zoom-shot. In the shaky close-ups, the insignia on the helicopters were clearly visible as the cameraman panned across them in sequence. The StarNet logo, looking as if it had been stenciled on quickly at the last minute. The French Air Force. French National TV. And, incredibly enough, the colors of the United States Marines.

And what they were dropping, Bobby realized a moment later when the strains of the "Marseillaise" began to play at an ear-killing tinny high volume, was a huge cloud of "mouches du pub," tiny self-contained radio receivers and speaker systems about the size of a ten-franc piece that were usually used to torment crowds at street festivals with commercials.

But now the damn things were being put to a far less obnoxious use. The French national anthem, as played by a full orchestra, was being broadcast into thousands of mini-speakers scattered all along the line of march, and the crowd was picking it up, an immense collective voice belting out the words from the bottom of their hearts.

"I don't know if you can hear me over all this," Bobby shouted into his mike, "so I had better just shut up and let the people of Paris speak for themselves."

Up the Champs-Élysées for a long block, and then a crush at the head of the procession as it turned onto the narrower Avenue de Marigny, and oozed around the corner onto the even narrower Avenue Gabriel, reversing direction as it approached the American Embassy.

The Marine guards, who had been so conspicuously in

armed evidence around the compound wall before that other demonstration, years ago, were now nowhere in sight, and as the head of the march reached the street outside the Embassy building itself, and the van took up a camera position in the middle of the crowd, Bobby realized, in some befuddlement, that the flagpole above the Embassy was empty.

When Bobby glanced at his monitor to catch the overhead shot from the StarNet helicopter, he gasped in the throes of an emotion he could scarcely contain. It might be corny, it might be cleverly engineered for the benefit of the TV audience, but it still took his breath away.

The crowd had piled up for the length of the Avenue Gabriel. It stretched clear around the corner of the Avenue de Marigny, down the Champs-Élysées, and back into the Place de la Concorde itself. The entire area was one vast sea of people. From overhead, the little American flags were a pointillist ripple of red, white, and blue. Half a million voices and about as many mini-speakers joined in a rendition of the "Marseillaise" that rocked him to his kneecaps.

"There must be half a million people out there," Bobby babbled into his microphone. "Oh, God, this is incredible, I've never seen anything like this before, you can feel the energy coming up at you in waves, the emotion is enormous, ladies and gentlemen, the whole city has gone crazy. . . ."

It seemed to go on forever, the shouting, the singing, the flags waving. There was no thought of any opportunistic politician trying to stand up and make a speech in the middle of this.

And then the "Marseillaise" slowly began to die away. In a few minutes, there was an eerie pregnant silence.

And then, another song began to play on all those mini-speakers, and after the first few bars, half a million voices were singing the words to the revived golden oldie.

The song at the top of everyone's chart, the max-metal version of "God Bless America."

Bobby's eyes filled with tears as he heard the people who had once scorned him welcoming him home.

"God bless America,
Land that I love . . ."

People in the crowd were turning on flashlights, thousands of brave little beacons waving in the darkness that surrounded the eternal City of Light.

> *"Stand beside her*
> *And guide her . . ."*

Flashlight beams converged toward the Embassy building, toward the empty flagpole. Most of them were consumed by the darkness, but enough of them were high-powered halogen beams to bathe the void at the top of the pole in a perfect Hollywood spotlight.

> *"Through the night*
> *With a light from above. . . ."*

The crowd was singing it in a mighty collective French accent that at any other moment would have been quite ludicrous, but now, to Bobby's ears, it was the sweetest sound he had ever heard.

And then, slowly, majestically, the Stars and Stripes began to ascend the flagpole, unfurling in the breeze as it rose against the dark sky.

> *"From the mountains,*
> *To the prairies,*
> *To the oceans white with foam . . ."*

Bobby didn't even realize he was singing into an open mike, as the American flag ascended to the top of the flagpole, as rockets exploded star shells over the centre ville, Roman candles whooshed up out of the crowd, a million firecrackers went off, as the people of Paris and Bobby himself bore witness to the impossible event that they themselves were creating as they sang the long-lost light back into the world.

> *"God bless America,*
> *My home, sweet home . . ."*

Oh yes, the cynical journalist in him knew that it was hokum, kitsch, a set piece written and produced by whomever Wolfowitz had hired as his media advisor in cooperation with his fellow flacks in the French government, something that would have made Bobby puke in Berkeley.

But even that couldn't make it any less real.

For Bobby, and, he suspected, for anyone who had been here this night, or even watched the StarNet coverage on television, this was a moment beyond the ability of the pros to create without the heartfelt collaboration of the audience. This was the real thing. This was magic. This was the true return of his country to where he had always longed for it to be in the eyes of the people who had scorned him as a gringo, and the true healing of the deepest wound that *this* country had inflicted on his own heart.

> *"God bless America,*
> *My home, sweet home!"*

And so it was.

Mais Paris aussi, mes amis, Paris aussi.

And now, for the first time in his life he found he could do it and really mean it.

"Vive la France!" Robert Reed shouted to the whole wide world via his satellite uplink as the song ended. "Ladies and gentlemen, I'm sorry, I just couldn't help it, I've never felt like more of an American in my life, but tonight I'm feeling like a Frenchman too! Aren't you?"

GRINGOMANIA!

Last night's demonstration at the American Embassy may have been carefully staged and lavishly produced by the American media-masters, but what happened afterward was truly spontaneous. When the semi-official event ended with the raising of the American flag, a hundred thousand people at the least poured up the Champs-

Élysées, gathering strength from onlookers, and staged a wild party in, around, and atop the Arc de Triomphe that didn't wind down till the early morning.

Dozens of similar demonstrations took place all over Paris. It was impossible for an American to pay for a drink anywhere in the city, and indeed, many Parisians were to be heard putting on American accents in English and getting free drinks too. Paris has seen nothing like it since the liberation of the city from the Nazis. Gringomania may be just that, and in the end, Nathan Wolfowitz may not save the world from nuclear holocaust, but at least it has served as the excuse for the wildest night of partying this city has seen for a hundred years.

—Robert Reed, StarNet

It had been impossible for Sonya, even as the head of Red Star's Paris office, to get through to the head of the Tass bureau on the videotel. Everything was in turmoil, and Tass wasn't speaking to anyone.

She could well imagine what was going on there, which was to say the same thing that was going on at Red Star and, no doubt, in the offices of every Soviet organization in Paris, only that much worse. The sense of isolation was terrible, from the hostile country in which they now found themselves, and from Moscow itself.

It would be worth your life to speak Russian on the streets now, and a Russian accent was enough to get you barred from a half-empty restaurant. French associates were frostily polite on the videotel. Business was at a standstill.

Moscow itself, when it spoke at all, spoke in a babble of conflicting directives in which one could easily enough read the state of panic as the powers that be in the Red Star Tower, that notorious collection of Eurorussians, attempted to do what they could to save the Russian Spring, while trying to cover their asses as best they could in case the Eurorussians lost the election, while the military government, and all that it implied, glared ominously over their shoulders.

How much worse for the poor bastards at Tass, who were charged with both reporting the bad news and putting the best possible public face on it!

So it was not so surprising that even Sonya couldn't get

Leonid Kandinski on the videotel. If *she* were the head of the Tass bureau, she would be doing her best to find a hole to crawl into and pull in after her.

Finally, she went over to Tass herself and bullied her way through the death-house gloom into his office. Kandinski, a balding, heavyset man in his early fifties, looked as if he had slept in his suit. His eyes were red, his face was stubbly, and his desk was littered with empty Styrofoam coffee cups, the big onyx ashtray overflowing with cigar butts. The place stank of stale tobacco smoke, sweat, and paranoia.

"Well, what do *you* want, Sonya?" Kandinski demanded. He fished a cigar out of a drawer, bit off the end, spit it on the floor, lit up, and actually inhaled off the vile thing.

"I've got a story for you, Leonid," Sonya said.

"Wonderful!" Kandinski moaned. "Just what we need!"

"You'll like this one," Sonya told him.

"Of course I will!" Kandinski drawled sarcastically. "I'm a modern Soviet journalist, aren't I? Nothing like another hot little item to brighten up my day! Don't tell me! Let me guess! What is it this time? Another passionate demonstration of support for Nathan Wolfowitz? Another shit-throwing incident at the Embassy?"

"It's a human-interest story," Sonya said.

"A human-interest story?" Kandinski babbled. "How marvelous! We're always interested in stories about humans! They're so much more newsworthy than animals!"

"Good Lord, Leonid, get hold of yourself!"

"Get hold of myself? Oh, I'd love to get hold of myself, Sonya, if only people would let loose of my lapels and stop shouting in my face! You have no idea what it's been like around here! Those ursine bastards in Moscow keep demanding more positive coverage, and of course it won't do to tell them there's nothing positive happening to cover! And the KGB has resurrected itself from the slime pits of history to threaten dire consequences if we don't toe the Party line. But no one knows what the Party line is. And now here you are, with a *human-interest story!*"

Sonya resisted the impulse to slap the man across the face. What an appalling spectacle!

"You *will* like this story, Leonid," she told him instead. "It's a chance to crack the news with something that will make us look good for a change."

"It is?" Kandinski said a shade less shrilly. "How is that possible?"

"By riding along on the Gringomania ourselves."

"You're serious? You've really got an angle to put our own spin on it?" Kandinski said.

"A mutual gesture of goodwill between ourselves and the Wolfowitz Administration."

"All right, all right, so tell me; we could certainly use a good laugh around here. . . ."

And Sonya did. She had thought all this out carefully, and after the incredible scene at the American Embassy, she had thought it all out again with Bobby. Bobby could do no wrong now, as far as StarNet was concerned, and they were all too willing to run a human-interest feature on Jerry, or anything else that would keep Bobby happy. They were even willing to sell the Russian rights to Tass for a price, nuclear crisis or not.

"Tass can run the feature simultaneously with StarNet," she told Kandinski. "The Soviet Union offers to fly the American Father of the European Grand Tour Navette into orbit on an Aeroflot Concordski and sponsors a resolution in the Common European Parliament to let him ride in his own spaceship, as a gesture of peace and European solidarity!"

Kandinski had sat there puffing on his cigar intently as she laid the whole thing out. Now he ground out the butt in his ashtray. He shrugged. "If it was up to me, I'd do it in a moment, we're dying for something like this," he said. "But you're talking about something that requires a policy decision from the government in Moscow. And no one even knows what that is now!"

"So why not have the Eurorussian delegates to the Common European Parliament sponsor a resolution that *Common Europe* itself requests the Soviet Union to supply the flight to orbit on Aeroflot? Think of it, Leonid, all those good Eurorussians asking Common Europe to request a gesture of goodwill from their own government for the sake of an *American!*"

"The Bears will hate it!" Kandinski said. "It'd seem like Gorchenko was behind—"

"Precisely."

"Oh," Kandinski said, and he actually smiled.

Two days later, with the election only a week away, it was

Kandinski who showed up unannounced in *her* office. His suit was freshly pressed, he was clean-shaven, and he seemed quite in control of himself.

"Well, as the damnable Americans would have it, there's good news and bad news," he told her. "The good news is that Gorchenko himself *loved* the idea and is more than willing to publicly order his faction in the Common European Parliament to sponsor your husband's resolution. The bad news is that he requires that Nathan Wolfowitz himself publicly request that he do so."

"What?" Sonya exclaimed.

Kandinski shrugged. "It's certainly an open secret that Wolfowitz is doing everything he can to get Gorchenko re-elected short of getting on the Trans-Siberian railway and kissing babies for him. The way Gorchenko sees it, I think, is that publicly acceding to a heart-stirring and entirely apolitical request from the American President should be good for a million votes minimum."

"And all I've got to do is convince President Wolfowitz to do it?" Sonya moaned in dismay.

Kandinski's eyes narrowed. "That may not be as difficult as it seems," he said. "The military may be controlling the international phone lines, but one gets the feeling that Wolfowitz and Gorchenko are communicating with each other obliquely in the media. This could be another spirit message, as it were. . . ."

"But how am I supposed to communicate all this to Nathan Wolfowitz?" Sonya cried. "Do they suppose in Moscow that all I have to do is pick up the phone?"

"Apparently we Eurorussians still have our moles in the KGB," Kandinski told her. "And the KGB knows all about your son's connection with Nathan Wolfowitz. He is to be the spirit messenger."

A EURORUSSIAN MAJORITY IN THE SUPREME SOVIET?

It seemed impossible a week ago, but now the latest polls show that Constantin Semyonovich Gorchenko is certain to win the Presidential election, and while this may have been a foregone conclusion all along due to the token nature of the opposition to the official candidate of

the Communist Party, the reverse in fortunes of Eurorussian candidates for Delegate is breathtaking.

Comrade Gorchenko, it would seem, has managed to
grow what the Americans call "coattails." Two weeks ago,
it looked like the Eurorussians would be lucky to capture
20 percent of the seats in the new Supreme Soviet. Now
they seem assured of a plurality, and have at least pulled
within striking distance of an actual working majority.

What the Americans have taken away in the Ukraine
election with one hand, they now seem to have given
back in the national election with the other.

But before the Eurorussians begin planning their victory
celebration, let them ponder the day after.

Will the Red Army Central Command *really* return
control of the government to the same man they took it
from at gunpoint?

—*Mad Moscow*

The new Bobby never ceased to amaze Franja.

Here he was, an American in a city that had suddenly
fallen in quite desperate love with the United States, and
there she was, just where she had imagined he had always
wanted her, with her country despised and its dream in
ruins, while he and his country had their shining hour.

She had expected him to lord it over her with his old
spiteful relish. But instead of tormenting her, he was endlessly solicitous—tender, even. Instead of rubbing it in, he
had become an understanding friend to talk to.

She hadn't really trusted him until that night when he had
come home late and drunk from covering the demonstration at the American Embassy.

Mother and Father were already in bed, and Franja was
alone trying to read in the living room, her mind utterly
distracted by the spectacle she had seen on television, a
spectacle that seemed contrived by the Americans specifi-
cally to torment her.

"We have to talk, Franja, we really have to talk like
brother and sister," Bobby said as he sprawled unbidden on
the couch beside her, reeking of wine, his eyes bloodshot.

"You're drunk, Bobby!" Franja snapped testily.

"As the proverbial skunk! It was incredible! People just
kept shoving bottles in my face! Everyone wanted to buy a

drink for any American they could find, and there just weren't enough to go around!"

"How wonderful for you!" Franja said sourly.

"Yeah, it was wonderful! You can't imagine what it felt like! The last time I went to the American Embassy, I came back covered in blood and shit, God, Franja, remember what I stunk like, and tonight we're all fucking heroes! Tonight I'm finally really proud of my country!"

"Tonight you are at last a true gringo," Franja replied dryly.

Bobby's face darkened. His drunken mood shifted precipitously. "You have no right to call me that, Franja, you never did!" he snapped. "You don't even know what the word really means! I've spent my whole adult life hating the fucking gringos! The gringos are the bastards who turned the United States into an armed camp and made it hated all over the world and screwed over our own father! Don't you dare call me a gringo!"

"I only meant—"

"I know what you meant, Franja," Bobby said softly, his mood changing abruptly again. "I'm not a gringo, and I never was, and there are millions like me, and fuck the gringos who smeared blood and shit all over our flag! Tonight I saw that flag going up with the shit washed off it by the guy who taught me how to play the cards, and I heard people cheering, and I thought of you."

"Me?" Franja said softly.

"I thought of all the shit you gave me for wanting to be an American. And I thought about what I've been watching you go through now. . . ."

"I knew you'd be getting around to rubbing it in sooner or later!" Franja snapped.

"No, no, no," Bobby soothed, patting her hand woozily. "I loved a country I couldn't feel proud of. I loved a country that was doing things that made people hate it and rightly so. I loved a dream that had died."

"A dream that had died . . . ," Franja muttered, and a terrible sadness came over her.

For tonight she could understand what being an American in Paris must have been like for her poor little brother. Tonight, she understood what it was like to feel ashamed of your country, and to love it just the same. Tonight it was she who still loved a dream that had died.

"Yeah, Franja, I do know how you feel," Bobby said. "So
that's why I had to talk to you. That's why I had to tell you
not to hate your country, big sister. Don't give up hope. For
seventy years, your country was under the thumb of bastards
like Stalin and Brezhnev, it was a long hard winter, but then
you had a spring. . . ."

Franja's eyes started to water. Bobby squeezed her hand.
"Hey, Franja," he said softly, "don't let it get to you. What I
learned tonight is that there's no winter so long that there's
never a spring. It'll come again for you too, big sister, you'll
see. What goes around, comes around."

He smiled at her. He winked. "It's an old American saying," he told her. "There must be something like it in Russian too."

Now Franja did quite burst into tears. "Oh, Bobby," she
cried, "what a terrible sister I've always been to you! You
make me feel so ashamed!"

"Hey, Franja, we were a couple of kids then," Bobby told
her, "we're not those people now."

And he had hugged her protectively to him like the big
brother she had never had.

And now here her little brother Bobby was, browbeating
the bureaucracy in the American Embassy.

"Yes, *that* Robert Reed, asshole, the one at StarNet who
gave him ninety seconds of prime time two days ago, and I
don't care if he's *taking a shit,* you pull him off the pot and
get him on the horn, or *you're* gonna be the one held responsible if I don't feel so generous next time!"

The four of them were gathered in the living room,
Mother and Father holding hands on the couch, Franja sitting in one armchair out of the field of view of the videotel
camera, watching the screen obliquely, Bobby in the other
in front of it.

The Seal of the United States blanked the screen for a
few minutes and then it was replaced by the face of the
American Ambassador, a thin ferret-faced man who had
contributed heavily to Harry Carson's campaign and been
given Paris as his payment.

"I'm sorry to disturb you, Mr. Ambassador," Bobby said
smoothly, "but I need you to convey a message to President
Wolfowitz."

"You need me to do *what?*" the Ambassador said.

"It's kind of a communication from Constantin Gorchenko."

"Kind of a communication from Gorchenko, Mr. Reed? What's that supposed to mean?"

"It means Gorchenko has indicated his wishes to Tass who told my mother, the Director of the Paris office of Red Star, to talk to me so that I could have you convey his message to Nathan Wolfowitz."

"An authentic communication from Constantin Gorchenko?" the Ambassador drawled sarcastically. "Wouldn't it have been easier to throw a piece of string across the Atlantic and hold tin cans up to their ears?"

"Gorchenko would like President Wolfowitz to ask something of him, so that he can make a gesture," Bobby pressed on. "He wants to make a gesture, but he has to be asked publicly."

"A gesture?" For the first time, there was a hint of interest in the Ambassador's voice.

"He wants the President to ask him to have his delegates in the Common European Parliament introduce a resolution to request that the Soviet Union fly an American into orbit on Aeroflot and then allow him to ride the European Grand Tour Navette to the Moon and back."

"You're not making the least bit of sense, Reed. Aeroflot isn't flying, and Gorchenko isn't President of anything now. And before this is over, the chances are excellent that there'll be nothing left in orbit but Battlestar America and Russian rubble."

"Not if Gorchenko is elected, Mr. Ambassador. Don't you see, he's asking Wolfowitz to treat his reelection as a fait accompli, and in return, he'll make a gesture. It'll show the world in some small way that it's at least possible for the two of them to make a deal."

"And just who is supposed to be the beneficiary of all this glasnost in the media?"

Franja could see Bobby hesitate, she could feel his chagrin, for she could well imagine how this was going to sound in the American Ambassador's ears.

But Bobby sighed, and then told him manfully and simply. "My father, Jerry Reed, the man who designed the GTN in the first place."

"Your father! Good day, Mr. Reed, it's been ever so—"

"Harry Carson's brain!" Bobby shouted before he could

hang up. "I know just what happened to Carson's brain, because I got it straight from Nat Wolfowitz while we were taking a piss together."

"What?" the Ambassador said, still on the screen, his hand frozen above the disconnect button.

"If you do know what I'm talking about, you know that puts me a lot closer to Nat than you'll ever be, and if you don't, la même chose, n'est-ce pas. . . ."

"I . . . I don't know what you're talking about . . . ," the Ambassador stammered. But Franja noted that he was no longer in any hurry to hang up.

"All I'm asking you to do is your duty. Pass on what you've heard with no comment. I'm not asking you to stand behind it yourself. Just get this on Wolfowitz's desk is all. The first law of bureaucracy is cover your own ass, as my mother always says, right?"

"I'm not promising anything, Reed," the Ambassador said weakly.

"I'm not asking you to," Bobby said, and then it was he who broke the connection.

"That was really masterful, Bobby," Franja said, truly filled with admiration for her brother, and for once more than willing to admit it openly. "But do you think it'll work?"

"It will if we can get through to Wolfowitz," Bobby told her.

"Just because the man was once your friend?"

"Because I'm pretty sure Wolfowitz wants something like this as much as Gorchenko does. They've been blowing kisses at each other all along. It wouldn't even surprise me to know that Gorchenko has gotten this through by other channels already."

"Politique politicienne," Father muttered.

"Don't knock it, Dad," Bobby told him. "This time, for once, it's gonna be working *for* you."

AN OPEN LETTER FROM PRESIDENT NATHAN WOLFOWITZ TO CONSTANTIN GORCHENKO

It has been brought to my attention that Jerry Reed, the American responsible for the creation of the European Grand Tour Navette, suffered a severe accident prior to the first cruise of the GTN, which prevented him from going along as planned.

Now he is being told that he can't fulfill the dream of his lifetime because his medical infirmities prevent him from being certified as an insurable passenger on a commercial flight to orbit.

Mr. Reed left this country many years ago in order to pursue that dream when the American space program was going nowhere but military hardware. For many years, he worked in secondary positions in the European space program, prevented by anti-American discrimination from working to the full extent of his considerable capacities. In the end, he was forced to surrender his American citizenship to gain his personal goals.

Somehow, Mr. Gorchenko, this is the story of our times, a story that I am sure you and the Soviet people wish to see have a happy ending as much as I do.

And at least in this small matter, you have, or I trust soon will have, the power to write it. So I appeal to you, Mr. Once-and-Future President, to give an Aeroflot ride to this son of America, up to a European Grand Tour Navette of his own design, and write a happy transnational ending to what has thus far been the same old unhappy international story.

Let it serve to light one small candle between us, in a world grown so dark. Together, let us show the world that, despite our present difficulties, our two great peoples share the same human heart.

> —AP, UPI, Tass, StarNet, Agence France-Presse,
> Reuters, USIA, Novosti

Jerry Reed had never imagined he would be watching so intently as election returns rolled in, let alone the results of an election in the Soviet Union. But Bobby had been right, for once the doings of the politicians running the world had indeed worked for him.

There had never been any confirmation from Washington or the Embassy that Bobby's message had gotten through to Nathan Wolfowitz. But two days before the Russian election, a White House spokesman had released the text of what he called an open letter to Constantin Gorchenko from the President of the United States.

"He's gone all the way," Bobby exclaimed, after they had read through the text in the *Herald Tribune* a second time. "He's actually used this to openly endorse Gorchenko. He's betting the farm on a Eurorussian victory and he wants the world to know it. What have those two guys been cooking up together?"

But Jerry hadn't paid any attention to the political message in the Wolfowitz letter, though the commentaries in all the papers were full of it. Even the hope that he might now get his chance to walk on water after all, if the world survived, was emotionally distant in the face of the strange emotion that brought the tears to his eyes.

For the first time in his life, he found himself loving a politician, a man he had never met, and not just because Nathan Wolfowitz was championing his cause. For the President of the United States had spoken for the justice of that cause, and while Jerry understood that his statement had been carefully crafted to serve his own political ends, his words rang true, they had been written from the heart. He was using his power to right a wrong, and he was taking genuine pleasure in it.

And that was a thing to love in a man, politician or not. Was this what politicians meant by real leadership? Was this why all of Europe loved this man? Was this why the world believed beyond all reason that Nathan Wolfowitz would see them through?

Perhaps it was. And perhaps that was why, in that moment, Jerry had the entirely irrational feeling that Nathan Wolfowitz had done it already.

A feeling that grew even stronger when Constantin Gorchenko answered the President during a final televised campaign rally in Leningrad on election eve.

Gorchenko spoke from the very railway station where Lenin had proclaimed the Bolshevik Revolution, there was a big Soviet flag behind him, and either a breeze or a wind machine dramatically ruffling his thinning gray hair. He wore a sharply tailored black suit and a white peasant blouse and looked like a Hollywood actor playing an old farmer, in short, like the Russian version of an American media-consultant's tailored image of a political winner.

And like an American politician, he went on and on, in rolling, roaring Russian simultaneously translated into florid singsong French.

They all sat there in the living room while Gorchenko recited his version of the entire history of the Soviet Union as an epic struggle for social democracy and political freedom—the overthrow of the Czars, the fight to survive as the first socialist state in a hostile capitalist world, the perversions of Stalin, the lost new beginning of Khrushchev, the dawning of glasnost, the flowering of the Russian Spring, the fraternal entry at long, long last as respected equals in the community of Europe.

Finally, he worked himself up to the climactic election-eve pitch.

"Is all that our parents and our grandparents and our great-grandparents worked and bled and died for to be swept away by primitive chauvinistic passions that have no place in a society that would live up to the transnational idealism of Marx and Lenin and Gorbachev?" he shouted at the top of his lungs.

"What kind of Russian patriots are willing to see Mother Russia herself devastated in the name of Russian honor? In what manner does the illegal action of the Red Army serve the principles of Socialist Legality that have at long last allowed the people of the Soviet Union to stand hand in hand with the rest of the civilized world?"

And then Gorchenko had lowered his voice and spoken in a much softer tone. "Two days ago I received a request from my good friend President Wolfowitz asking me to assist in getting an American a ride into orbit on a Soviet Concordski. A simple request, easily granted by the next duly elected Soviet President, and one which I shall certainly honor if the Soviet people choose to make me that man.

"I promise this because I know it will make me more popular. Oh yes, I'm a politician, and our sort of animal wants to be popular, even with people who cannot vote for us. But a *responsible* politician wants to be popular for doing the right thing. And just now, the world needs a Soviet government that can be popular for doing the right thing. And the world needs to see what truly lies in the Russian heart. So I stretch out my hand to Mr. Reed, as I stretch it out to President Wolfowitz. Let this be the first of many candles we light together in the dark."

"Jesus, the same exact phrase, that can't be an accident!" Bobby exclaimed. "They're talking to each other in some kind of code, we've been part of some elaborate put-up job!"

But Jerry didn't care if he had been a pawn in the game of politique politicienne this time. He had certainly been screwed by it often enough before, but this time he was going to come out a winner if anyone did, and this time, it seemed the players really did seem to be trying their best to make sure it wasn't a zero-sum game.

And so here he sat with his half-Russian, half-American family, watching the election returns from the Soviet Union and actually rooting for a Eurorussian victory harder than he ever had for the Dodgers or the Lakers or the Rams.

For in rooting for Gorchenko's team, he was rooting for his own team too, for Franja's chosen country and for Bobby's, for Sonya's homeland and his own, and, like any rabid rooter watching breathlessly from the stands, for himself too.

There was only one home team now.

They smiled together as the early projections showed the Eurorussians way out ahead. The smiles grew broader when early returns began to confirm them. They started slapping each other on the back when CBS and Agence France-Presse and StarNet called the election, giving the Eurorussians at least 67 percent of the seats in the new Supreme Soviet.

"Th . . . th . . . th . . . that's all, folks!" Bobby said when Gorchenko went on the air to claim victory, and he turned off the wall screen.

Sonya went into the kitchen for a bottle of champagne.

It foamed all over the rug when she popped the cork, but no one gave a damn. She filled the glasses, and they all stood there in front of the dead wall screen holding them high.

"To Nathan-fucking-Wolfowitz!" Bobby shouted.

"To Constantin Gorchenko!" said Franja.

"To the Russian Spring!" Sonya declared.

"To the Soviet Union!"

"To the United States!"

"Down with the gringos!"

"Down with the Bears!"

They all laughed, and then they all looked at Jerry, who had offered no toast.

And Jerry looked back at them. At the wife he had found

again at the end of his life. At the son who had come home to him against the odds in his hour of need. At the daughter who had understood a foolish father's dream.

He was dying. They all might die before he had the chance to live that dream. But they were all together now, as they had never been before, and out there there were men of goodwill fighting not to destroy each other but to keep hope alive.

"To the impossible come true," he said. "To walking on water!"

They clinked glasses, and downed their champagne. Tonight was a night when everyone could drink to that.

Sonya found herself unable to fall asleep that night. She lay in bed beside Jerry, thinking of all that had come to pass. A son returned to her as a man to be proud of. A daughter and father reunited. A world pulling back from the brink of nuclear war. A Russian Spring not yet extinguished by the winter frost. A dream that might yet be fulfilled before it was too late.

Was she happy? It was hard to know. Gorchenko might never be allowed to take office. Jerry would probably not live out the year. What right did she have to be happy?

Perhaps it was the champagne, though she hadn't drunk that much, but, yes, she did feel happy, whether she had a rational or moral right to that happiness or not. And she felt something else, something that she had never thought to feel again.

"Jerry, are you awake?" she whispered. And then, when he didn't answer, louder. "Jerry, are you awake?"

"I am now," he said.

"Jerry, I love you," she said.

"I love you too, Sonya," he muttered groggily.

"No, I really love you," she said, and reached out to touch his thigh.

"What is it, Sonya?" Jerry said in a clearer voice.

"I don't know, Jerry," she said, "but I want to make love to you. Maybe it's because I'm happy. Maybe because I'm afraid the world could still end tomorrow. Maybe because I've just remembered what it felt like. Maybe because . . . because I know I'm going to lose you."

For a long moment, she could hear nothing but his

breathing beside her in the darkness, breathing that would not even be possible were it not for the machine beside the bed. In her mind's eye, she could see nothing but a mysterious stranger across a dull and stupid party. A bedroom in their first apartment on the Île St.-Louis. A comatose figure in a hospital bed. A distant face on a videotel screen. The father of her children. The man whom she had betrayed. The love of her life.

"Wot do ya say, ducks, ya think we can still do it?" she said in a hokey English accent. "I've always wanted to have a bit of the old in-and-out wiff a bloody cyborg."

Jerry felt his heart racing as the hibernautika tried to cope with the blood rushing southward from his head. He could feel himself losing capillaries, he could imagine brain cells starving for oxygen, but that didn't prevent his long-dormant manhood from rising to the challenge.

He hadn't had a real sexual thought since the accident, and indeed, he had not felt anything that could really be called desire since Sonya had left him. But accident or not, whatever it was costing him, he had a hard-on now.

He could feel the blood humming behind his eardrums. He could feel his breath going short. He knew that what he was going to do might cost him weeks of life span, but he didn't care.

"Don't mind if I do, luv," he said, and carefully unreeled a loop of his life-support cable and draped it over the nightstand, to give himself slack to move.

Then he rolled over onto his side and hugged her to him, kissing her gently, and let her guide him home.

They lay there side by side, only their hips moving, and it was very slow and easy, and it took a long sweet time to happen, but still, when it did, it left him gasping for air, with his heart thumping and a million stars occluding his vision, and he could feel brain cells dying and blood vessels popping, and a little bit of his life spurting out of his cock.

But it didn't matter. He had been willing to give up that and more to walk on his own water alone.

And tonight a dying space cadet and the girl who had been his English porn star, against all the odds, and with the whole world against them, had walked on water together again too.

WILL DEAL ONLY WITH GORCHENKO, WOLFOWITZ DECLARES

The American President, Nathan Wolfowitz, has warned the Red Army Central Command to fulfill its promise to return the government of the Soviet Union to full civilian control.

"I will deal only with Constantin Gorchenko, the duly elected President of the Soviet Union," he declared. "The United States may have been supporting tin-pot military dictators all over Latin America for longer than anyone cares to think about, but as long as I'm President of the United States, this country is going to stand up for what we profess to believe in, namely democratic governments elected by the people, throughout the world. The peoples of the Soviet Union have elected Constantin Gorchenko President, and that's good enough for me. And if it's not good enough for the Red Army, well, don't call me, Marshal Bronksy, and believe me, I won't be calling you."

—Tass

RED ARMY CENTRAL COMMAND RETURNS POWER TO PRESIDENT GORCHENKO

With a tersely worded memorandum, the Red Army Central Command has returned full control of the Soviet government to the Administration of President Constantin Semyonovich Gorchenko.

"We have fulfilled our duty to preserve peace and order through the election, and now that our stated mission has been accomplished and the Soviet people have made their democratic choice, we relinquish all control of governmental functions to the duly elected representatives, as promised," the short communiqué declared. "The Red Army now awaits its orders from the Soviet President to do its patriotic duty in a normal manner, and as quickly as possible."

—Tass

XXIX

Sonya, despite all the dire speculation, had seen it coming all along, and so had most of the Russian bureaucrats in Paris.

How could the Red Army be expected to hand back power to the very man it dragged off Lenin's tomb at gunpoint in the first place?

How could it not?

To a Soviet career bureaucrat, the move was inevitable. Just as Harry Carson had painted America into a corner—and then died before he had to face the consequences—so had Bronksky and the generals painted themselves into their own corner by issuing a toothless ultimatum that Nathan Wolfowitz had thrown back in their faces.

They might have used the election to save face by delaying the inevitable, but now that it was over, they were still sitting on the same hot stove.

If they sent the Red Army into the Ukraine, the Ukrainians would launch missiles at the fleet off their coast and the invading troop formations. If they attempted a preemptive strike at the Ukrainian missiles, the chances were excellent that the Americans would use Battlestar America to thwart it, while the Ukrainians made a nuclear strike at Russian population centers. After which, the Americans might even launch a preemptive strike at the Soviet Union themselves, thanks to Bronksky's stupid threat to launch a strategic strike at *them* if the Ukrainians launched any of their American missiles.

But if they backed down, if they spinelessly acceded to the Ukrainian secession, other nationalities would only be encouraged to declare their own Soviet Socialist Republics independent sovereign states, and the Soviet Union would disintegrate within months or even weeks.

Whatever happened, the consequences would fall on the heads of whoever was in power. Surely rather than die their way out of it like Carson, the generals would much prefer to drop the mess they had made back in the lap of Constantin Gorchenko. If he failed, well, no one could blame the Red Army, could they? And if he somehow managed to avert catastrophe, why they could all give themselves medals for their patriotic dedication to Socialist Democracy.

The Red Army Central Command, was, after all, a bureaucracy, and even generals understood the first law thereof—cover your own ass!

Nathan Wolfowitz, however, not being a career Soviet bureaucrat, had perhaps never heard of the first law of bureaucracy, or at any rate had obviously been unwilling to leave things to chance. His support for Socialist Legality had dispelled any lingering thoughts of clinging to power on the part of the Red Army, and made him an unofficial Hero of the Soviet Union, but Sonya could not imagine what his own bureaucracy and his own people must be calling him now.

"What an amazing man this Wolfowitz is!" she declared as they all sat before the wall screen waiting for Constantin Gorchenko's fateful first address to the Supreme Soviet since his restoration to power. "Never have I heard a politician use such blunt language or admit so openly to his own country's crimes!"

"What about a guy named Gorbachev, Mom?" Robert reminded her.

"He calls himself the 'American Gorbachev,' doesn't he, I had forgotten that," Sonya said. "But even Gorbachev never got *this* far out ahead of public opinion in his own country. Won't the jingo press and the American majority that voted for Carson crucify Wolfowitz for disowning their own criminal acts in Latin America, especially at a time like this?"

"Nat Wolfowitz never did give a shit about what people like that said about him," Bobby told her. " 'The opprobrium of assholes is a badge of honor,' he told me one time."

Constantin Gorchenko approached the outsized podium to the thunderous applause of two thirds of the Delegates. The Bears quite literally sat on their hands as a gesture of contempt while the Ethnic Nationalists sat there staring stonily into space.

Marshal Bronksky met Gorchenko at the foot of the podium, said a few words to him, actually shook his hand, and then departed, looking less like a dictator surrendering power than a small boy who had just escaped punishment for his misdeeds by the skin of his teeth.

Gorchenko himself looked grimly determined as he mounted to the speaker's stand, but there was an ashen cast to his features visible even on television, a certain bloodlessness that gave Sonya a sudden chill, that made her wonder to what extent Gorchenko was really his own man, and to what extent he would be speaking words that the Red Army had put in his mouth.

"Citizens of the Soviet Union, Delegates to the Supreme Soviet, I thank you for the confidence you have placed in me, and I wish to assure you that I shall not waver in dedication to the task before us, which is to secure, once and for all, the territorial integrity of the Union of Soviet Socialist Republics and the unity of our great community of peoples against internal insurrection and the nefarious meddling of external powers."

"What?" exclaimed Franja, as loud boos and hisses erupted from the Ethnic Nationalist seats, as the Bears stood up and applauded, and the Eurorussian majority sat there staring at each other in horror and befuddlement.

As Franja was staring at Sonya.

"What's happening, Sonya?" Jerry said. "What's gone wrong? You two look like you've seen Joe Stalin's ghost."

"Perhaps we have," Sonya muttered. "It would appear that the Red Army has exacted a heavy price for its dedication to Socialist Legality."

As Gorchenko's speech continued in much the same bellicose vein, as he ranted against Kronkol and his cabal of traitors, and vilified the shade of Harry Carson, and denounced the genocidal machinations of the CIA, what had happened became all too horribly obvious.

The Red Army might have given civil power back to the elected President, but he in return had had to cede control of the military situation to them, accept public responsibility himself for whatever they did next, and deliver this horrendous chest-pounding speech, the text of which no doubt had been negotiated with the generals word by word.

When Gorchenko had worked himself up into a sufficient synthetic frenzy, he paused, took a sip of water, and stared straight ahead like an animated corpse as he delivered the dreadful words that the generals had put in his mouth.

"As President of the Soviet Union, I demand that the United States remove its missiles from the Ukraine. Since no sovereign Ukrainian state exists, we can only regard these weapons as being in the hands of employees of the CIA on Soviet territory, and as such, an act of war against the USSR."

"Oh no . . . ," Franja gasped. "What's he *doing?*"

"What he's been told to do, I'm very much afraid," Sonya said somberly.

"If the United States does not agree to remove its missiles within forty-eight hours, we . . . we . . ." Gorchenko seemed to be choking on his own words. "We . . . we will be forced to act accordingly."

There was a dreadful silence in the chamber. Not even the hairiest of Bears seemed ready to applaud that.

"But we will do so in a responsible manner," Gorchenko went on much more firmly, as if this was one part of the speech that had at least been a negotiated settlement. "We will not be the first to use nuclear weapons. We will let the Red Army settle matters with the Kronkol clique by conventional means on the ground. But should a single nuclear warhead explode on Soviet territory, our retaliation will be swift and total against everyone concerned."

"Jesus Christ," Robert groaned, "it's the same damn ultimatum!"

"It's the same damn situation, after all," Sonya told him. "It's one thing to hope for a miracle, but it's another to expect it."

Constantin Gorchenko paused for a sip of water again, paused to change faces, and now he seemed to be the real Gorchenko, not the reader of someone else's script.

"But let us not speak only of the gathering darkness," he said, "let us speak of lighting candles . . ."

"What?"

"There it is again!"

Sonya leaned forward intently. There was no doubt about it, this was another enigmatic message to President Wolfowitz, coded in a language they had developed from afar, somehow, a language only the two of them seemed to understand, a language that enabled them to communicate something over the heads of their bureaucracies and military commands.

"I call on you, President Wolfowitz, to light the first candle, to immediately announce the withdrawal of the Ukrainian missile sites from the protection of Battlestar America as a gesture toward peace," Gorchenko said. "Show the traitors in the Ukraine that they now stand alone. And in return, I will light the second candle, and soon enough there will be no more dark."

And with that enigmatic statement, incredibly enough, he left the podium.

"Second candle?"

"*What* second candle?"

"I don't know," Sonya muttered. "But somehow I earnestly hope that President Wolfowitz does."

WILL LAUNCH NUCLEAR ATTACK AT MILITARY TARGETS IF RED ARMY INVADES, KRONKOL DECLARES

—Reuters

UKRAINIAN MISSILE STRIKE WILL BE RESPONDED TO AS AMERICAN NUCLEAR ATTACK, BRONKSKY WARNS

—Tass

JOINT CHIEFS REPORTEDLY DEMAND PREEMPTIVE FIRST STRIKE

—New York Times

WILL LAUNCH ON WARNING, SAYS RED DEFENSE MINISTER

—New York Daily News

POPE BEGINS FAST FOR PEACE

—L'Osservatore Romano

SOVIET UNION ORDERS URBAN POPULATION TO SHELTERS

—Agence France-Presse

COOL NAT REFUSES TO DECLARE NATIONAL EMERGENCY, WILL ADDRESS THE WORLD

—*New York Post*

"What can he possibly do now, Bob?" Dad said.

"Something that no one could ever imagine," Bobby replied, repeating the very words Sara had left him with the last time he had managed to get a call through to New York.

"Like what?" Franja said.

Bobby sighed. "*I* can't imagine what either," he admitted.

"But you played poker with this man . . . ," Mom insisted. "What would he do now if this were a poker game? Not that it isn't!"

Bobby shrugged. "If I had ever been able to figure that out," he said, "he wouldn't have kept cleaning me out."

He could see that he had bucked up their spirits with this professed confidence in the card-shark magic of Nathan Wolfowitz, but Bobby couldn't really see how Nat could turn up a winning hand with what he now had showing.

Especially since Vadim Kronkol had raised wildly like a man who knew he was sitting on an ace-high straight flush.

Only two hours before Wolfowitz's scheduled speech, Kronkol had issued what he called his "final position," without, apparently, any recognition of the sardonic graveyard humor implied.

The Red Army now had twenty-four hours to pull back fifty kilometers from the Ukrainian border. If it didn't, he would launch three missiles, each armed with five unstoppable nuclear warheads, at the troop formations, and another at the fleet off the coast. If the Soviet Union attempted to attack Ukrainian population centers, which was to say his own missile sites, he would launch everything he had at Russian population centers. If the Americans did not use Battlestar America to destroy any incoming Soviet missiles, the blood would be on their hands too.

"That is how ready we are to die for our national independence," he had declared coldly. "Who is ready to die to take it from us?"

Bobby had seen Nat play this kind of hand many times before. The kind of hand where some mark had a four-card straight flush showing and was raising as if he had the missing card in the hole. If Wolfowitz was still in the game by the sixth card, it meant that he was sitting on it himself and therefore knew the raiser was bluffing.

But this time, no matter what he was holding, Nat couldn't drop out and wait for the next hand. If he didn't win this one, there wasn't going to *be* a next hand.

"Ladies and gentlemen, the President of the United States, speaking to you from the Oval Office in the White House, in Washington, D.C."

Nathan Wolfowitz wore a forest-green blazer, a white dress shirt, and a black string tie. He looked like a self-satisfied riverboat gambler about to rake in the pot, his eyes sparkling with that royal-flush glow. There was no doubt about it. No doubt at all.

"You can relax now, folks, it's all over but the shouting," Bobby said, grinning from ear to ear.

"How can you possibly say that?" Mom demanded.

"Easy enough if you've ever had the misfortune of seeing that look across a poker table," Bobby told her. "When he looks like that, it means he's sitting on the winning hand and doesn't care who knows it. The man has the cards."

"The Red Army has demanded that I retrieve our missiles from the Ukraine," the President began, dispensing with the formalities in the style to which the world had become accustomed. "Believe me, I would if I could, but I can't, so I won't."

The President threw up his hands. "I'm not about to defend the policies of my not-so-illustrious predecessors. Thanks to the bird-brains we elected, we wrote the biggest rubber check in history, passed it off on our sometime-friends, and then stiffed them for it like the international deadbeats we now so notoriously are. We then pissed away the loot building ourselves a chrome-plated white elephant called Battlestar America, dropping ourselves right back in the economic black hole we thought we had welshed our way out of. We've been propping up our hollow economy with a huge defense industry, and we've justified it all, at least on the funny-money balance sheet, by using our nuclear shield to hide behind while our bloated military machine found gainful employment propping up a series of puppet states and stooges in Latin America."

"I can't believe he's actually saying this!" Dad exclaimed.

"Why not?" Bobby said grimly. "It's the truth, isn't it?"

"But . . . but he's the *President of the United States!*"

"So he is," Bobby whispered. "So he is . . ."

Wolfowitz shrugged again. "What can I tell you?" he said. "Our leaders have been a collection of boobs and unprincipled charlatans for two generations, and we elected them, starting with a former straight man to a chimpanzee, and ending up with the late lamented Mr. Carson, who dealt this mess."

Bobby's head was spinning. Nat Wolfowitz wasn't saying anything he hadn't said a million times in Berkeley, he wasn't saying anything that hadn't been common table talk in Little Moscow. But this wasn't the guru of Little Moscow, or the man who had run an impossible campaign for Congress because it was time for a futile gesture, or the perennial futile Presidential candidate.

This was the President of the United States.

But he was talking like the Nat Wolfowitz Bobby had last talked to in a White House toilet.

And that, Bobby suddenly realized, was the source of the Wolfowitz magic. He didn't *care* about his Presidential image. He didn't have one. He wanted everyone to know that the guy sitting in the Oval Office *was* the guy who pissed in the White House toilet.

And that was the most cunning Presidential image of all.

President Wolfowitz's eyes hardened. "And now here I am, forced to play the hand they've dealt me, just as Mr. Gorbachev was forced to play what *he* was dealt by seventy years of bad road, just as Mr. Gorchenko is forced to pick up the crap that *he's* been dealt," he said.

"There ain't no justice in this world, folks, except the justice that we make. So all we can do is forget the past, play the cards, and try to light some candles."

"And you're sitting on the winning hand, aren't you, Nat?" Bobby muttered aloud to the screen. He couldn't see how, but he could see quite clearly that Wolfowitz knew the pot was going to be his. The look was unmistakable as he spread his hands palms down on the desktop and leaned toward the camera.

"President Gorchenko has asked me to light the first candle," Wolfowitz said. "He has asked me to place the Ukraine outside the nuclear umbrella of Battlestar America. That I could do. But it wouldn't stop the Ukrainians from using their Slam-Dunk missiles against the Soviet Union and the Red Army, and if that happens, general nuclear hell will break loose."

Wolfowitz paused, made a show of scratching his head, and frowning, as if studying his cards and feigning perplexity. "So rather than just call, I think I'll raise the ante high enough to separate the men from the boys and the boys from their toys."

"Here it comes, oh God, here it comes . . . ," Bobby muttered.

"Who am I to deny the protection of Battlestar America to anyone?" the President said. "I hereby extend it to cover the entire world, including the entire territories of the Soviet Union and the Ukraine. As of now, any missile launched against anyone anywhere in the world will be vaporized. And if anyone doesn't think we can do it, they're welcome to try. We've got enough ordnance in orbit to turn Mars into a parking lot, we've never had a chance to use it, and we've got a lot of good ol' boys up there with twenty years' of itchy trigger-fingers, just dying for a little target practice. And, oh yes, Mr. Kronkol, we *are,* after all, the people who programmed your guidance systems."

"My God, that's brilliant!" Bobby cried.

"Brilliant?" Mom said. "It guarantees that the Red Army will invade the Ukraine!"

"As for what the Russians and the Ukrainians will now do to each other out in the nonnuclear alley, that's not my job," the President said. "Far be it from me to get in the middle of two other people's divorce proceedings. But as a friend of the family with no further national interest in the outcome, I am tempted to offer some free advice."

He cocked his head to one side, shook it sadly. "Why are the two of you going to beat each other to bloody pulps?" he said. "Who wins what in the end? If the Ukrainians succeed in gaining their independence through glorious battle, they will then find themselves confronted with a Russian national state three times their size and in effective control of their transport net to the rest of Europe and controlled by outraged Bears in no mood to be friendly. If the Russians succeed in occupying the Ukraine by force, what they'll have on their hands is what we've been doing to ourselves in Latin America."

He leaned back in his chair and looked at a point in space above the camera. "We've been trying to make Latin Americans love us by military force for a long time now, and what's it gotten us? You go in thinking you're gonna make out like a bandit with cheap raw materials and cheap labor and a captive market whose economy you control, but the cost of the occupation eats up all the profits, and the resistance eats holes in the local infrastructure, and you end up taking endless casualties for the privilege of subsidizing basket cases in the name of manifest destiny. Sound familiar? Isn't that why Gorbachev cut the purse strings to his red-ink slave empire long years ago?"

"He cannot really be this disingenuous, can he, Robert?" Mom said. "Surely he realizes that this is an essential matter of national sovereignty!"

"So it really all comes down to the last recourse of the nation-state scoundrel, breast-beating noises about the sanctity of absolute national sovereignty," the President said.

Mom gasped.

Bobby laughed.

"Well, it no longer exists," Nathan Wolfowitz said, smiling sweetly. "I've just taken it away."

He paused to let that sink in. "The United States of America has already eliminated the absolute sovereign right of any nation to use nuclear weapons against any other. We've got the power to do it, and we will, and that period of history is dead as the dodo. What the new world is to become, Mr. Gorchenko, is up to you now. I've lit my candle, now it's time for you to light yours."

"*Again?*" Franja groaned. "He can't leave it like this, can he?"

"We're all going to have to let go of some national sovereignty to save our asses," Wolfowitz said. "Seems to me pissing contests over absolute national sovereignty are what got us where we now are. I ask the Russian and Ukrainian peoples to work themselves out a no-fault divorce by separating economic interdependence from national identity. I ask the Soviet government to give the Ukrainians enough national sovereignty to gain independent admission to Com-

mon Europe, and I ask the Republic of the Ukraine to cede
enough economic sovereignty to some kind of central authority to keep from shooting itself in the economic foot.
The petty details I leave up to you to work out. Just do it,
okay? Make me happy."

"What?"

"What on earth is he saying?" Mom muttered. "He's asking for the impossible!"

"And you *do* want to make me happy," Wolfowitz said.
"Because if you do, the United States of America will give
up a piece of *its* own sovereignty to provide an example for
the rest of the world. When, and only when, the Ukraine is
admitted into membership in Common Europe via a resolution introduced by the Soviet government, the United States
of America will apply for admission itself."

"That's what he's always wanted . . . ," Bobby exclaimed. "That's what we've all dreamed of."

"But it's an impossible dream, Robert, America owes
Common Europe far more money than it can ever repay!"

"And you *will* want to admit us very badly indeed,"
Wolfowitz went on. "Because upon admission, the United
States of America will cede control of Battlestar America to
the Common European Parliament. We've just taken away
everyone's sovereign power to launch nuclear missiles, and
we are ready to surrender *that* power to a community of
nations, for neither are sovereign powers that the world can
afford to have any single nation retain."

"They'll never let him get away with this," Dad stammered. "He's . . . he's giving it all away!"

"Not if I know Nat Wolfowitz," Bobby said.

Wolfowitz leaned back in his chair and crossed his arms
over his chest. "Of course there will be those who will demand that we cover the biggest rubber check in the history
of the world as the price of admission."

He shrugged. "Well, what can I say, we don't have the
money," he said. "And even if we did, we can't afford to
pauperize ourselves any further. It's hard to say how much it
all comes to, just as it's hard to tote up the complete bill for
Battlestar America. But I'll bet the figures aren't all that
different."

Wolfowitz grinned, his eyes sparkled like a flush in diamonds. "So let's just be mensches about it, shall we?" he
said. "Let's not nickel and dime each other like pikers. Let's

just say we hand over Battlestar America, and you forget about the abrogated debt, and we call it even. Isn't that an offer you can't afford to refuse?"

He actually seemed to be choking back laughter.

"I mean, after we've bankrupted ourselves to build the damn thing, you didn't expect us to just *give* it away!"

Bobby broke up. He laughed and laughed and laughed. He laughed until his sides ached. He laughed until he could laugh no more. He laughed as if the whole world was laughing with him.

"This has been an address by the President of the United States—"

"—speaking to you from the men's room in the White House in Washington, D.C.," Bobby declared, and broke himself up all over again.

SUMMIT PRODUCES AGREEMENT IN PRINCIPLE, BUT NO DETAILED ACCORD

The Strasbourg summit meeting has adjourned with agreement on the general principles of an overall settlement, but no detailed language for a treaty, which will be written by working committees established at the meeting, who will probably take at least six months to complete their draft.

Soviet President Constantin Gorchenko has agreed to introduce a resolution into the Common European Parliament calling for the simultaneous admission of the United States, the Ukraine, and any other Soviet Socialist Republic that decides to seek direct admission via national plebiscite. American President Nathan Wolfowitz has agreed to place Battlestar America under control of the Parliament as part of the eventual treaty of admission, and the leaders of the other present member states, after much heated discussion, have agreed to consider all old American debts to their governments, central banks, and private financial institutions formally canceled.

It was further agreed that all representation in the new Common Parliament shall be by direct election from districts of roughly equal population under a single statute to be enacted by the Common Parliament, that district lines shall be drawn and adjusted every five years by the Common Parliament, and that any legally qualified citizen of the whole may stand for any district without regard to the old national boundaries.

Member states will retain national military forces on an operational level, but these will be placed under a unified mixed command appointed by the Common Parliament, which will also directly control all nuclear forces as well as the Battlestar America defense system, whose personnel will be chosen according to a national quota system yet to be determined.

No name for the new transatlantic order has yet been agreed upon. "Union of Terrestrial Nations," "Union of Terrestrial Peoples," "Atlantic Confederation," "Northern Confederation," and "United States of Earth" have all been suggested, but none of these has met with general approval.

It would seem that the new order we are now embarking upon is as yet too fluid in its emerging nature, too much of a break with the past, too unforeseen in its eventual consequences, at present, even to have found its proper name.

                              —Robert Reed, StarNet

X X X

It seemed to take forever to get the Tass and StarNet crews settled in their seats, but at long last they had finally secured their equipment, Franja had her takeoff clearance, and the Aeroflot Concordski was at the top of the runway.

It wasn't stretching a point all that far to say that the

negotiations for the coverage of this flight had been more difficult and tortuous than what had gone on at the Strasbourg summit.

Tass had wanted this flight to depart from Moscow; this was, after all, an Aeroflot Concordski, and they had been the ones who'd put the whole thing together, hadn't they? Mother, and the doctors, had put their feet down on that. The medical risk had to be minimized, and that meant no prior flight from Paris to Moscow, and certainly not a grueling train ride. So it was agreed that the flight would leave from De Gaulle.

Tass then demanded exclusive coverage of the flight to orbit, and StarNet hit the ceiling. This was as much their doing as Tass's, they had a right to equal coverage. Tass then countered by offering shared coverage of the flight to orbit in return for an exclusive on the Grand Tour Navette. Agence France-Presse and Reuters screamed at that one— the GTN was a *European* ship, wasn't it?

Finally, StarNet agreed to pay Tass a handsome sum for the right to cover the flight to orbit for the American market, with Tass getting its exclusive in the rest of the world. The GTN trip would be covered by a press pool of all the major news agencies, one correspondent each, and a common cameraman, and each of them would have the right to sell their version on the open market.

Once the contracts had been signed, though, Tass took over and cut through red tape like a knife through butter. Jerry Reed's daughter was an Aeroflot pilot with a Concordski rating? Perfect! We'll have her fly her own father into orbit! Why not have her accompany him around the Moon? Good way to get our own spin on it for the folks back home!

At the last moment, they had even decided that Father should sit beside Franja in the co-pilot's seat. Aeroflot officials had protested that that violated any number of safety regulations, but the Tass people had made a quick call to Moscow, and now here Father was, sitting beside her as she ran up the turbofans, the hibernautika console lashed to the co-pilot's seat behind him, and an automatic camera taped over the instrument panel to catch the shot.

"I'll try to make this as easy on you as I can, Father," Franja told him.

"Don't worry about me, Franja," Father said, grinning

from ear to ear like the smallest of boys. "I'm not about to die on you now!"

"Of course you're not, Father," Franja said uneasily, and she gunned the engines, released the brakes, and the Concordski roared down the runway.

A MODEST PROPOSAL

The Americans, the Europeans, and the Soviets are presently in a quandary over the choice of a name for their new grouping, but from our perspective, the perspective of the majority of the world's struggling population on the outside looking in, the choice is obvious.

Why not call it the Caucasian Union and be done with it? For is it not a union of and for the developed white nations of the Northern Hemisphere, a consolidation of the economic and military power of the First and Second Worlds without regard for the welfare of Third World peoples?

If the rumored Japanese application for admission is ever accepted and that name becomes too racially offensive, "The Union of the Haves" would be an even better name, for that is just what it is.

—*Times of India*

Sonya stood alone with Robert on the tarmac, far away from the press and the official mob, and her heart skipped a beat as the Concordski lifted off the runway, tucked its landing gear into its belly, and seemed to leap into the sky.

"Bon voyage, Jerry," she muttered softly, and then she began to cry.

Bobby put his arm around her. "Come on, Mom," he said, "that's our crazy space cadet up there, and he's going where he's always belonged."

"He's killing himself, Robert," Sonya said. "You know that as well as I."

Bobby didn't say anything for a long while, as the Concordski dwindled away to a silvery glimmer still climbing up into the bright blue sky.

"Robert?"

"Let it be, Mom, let it be."

"I'm trying, Bobby, really I am!"

"I know, Mom, you've been very brave."

"Not as brave as he is!" Sonya wailed.

"Not many people are."

"Oh, Bobby, Bobby, I don't want to lose him now that I've really found him! Is that so selfish? Is that so wrong?"

"Of course it isn't," her son told her. "But don't think about losing him now. Think of him up there at last, where he's always wanted to be. Don't think of what we're losing. Think of what he's finally found."

Sonya tried, she really did. She stood there with Bobby's arm around her shoulders until she had entirely lost sight of the Concordski rising toward the stars, and she tried with all her heart to feel what Jerry must be feeling now, going home at last to his dream in the sky.

And she almost made it, her heart was almost glad, as she saw a tiny point of fire way up there as the main engine ignited, as Jerry rode it up and out to a place where she couldn't follow. She tried to be happy for him, even as a sad lorn part of her knew she was saying good-bye.

AN END TO AN ECONOMY OF LIMITS

Third World nations may have a moral and political right to their protests against the emerging new Northern Hemispheric order, for in the short run, and perhaps in the medium run as well, what has indeed emerged is a world in which a union of the rich northern developed nations will even more fully dominate the impoverished and fragmented peoples of the Third World.

But in the long run, the vast amounts of capital released by the consolidation of the military programs of most of the world's major powers, and the technological synergy among the American, Soviet, and European space programs, will result in the transformation of our present global economy of scarcity into a solar system—wide economy of abundance, with open-ended resources of raw materials, energy, and perhaps even land.

In such an environment, exploitation of Third World nations for cheap raw materials and labor will no longer make pragmatic economic sense, and while it would be too much to expect the developed nations to donate the lion's share of the benefits to lifting the rest of the world out of poverty, the era of economic imperialism will at least be over, and capital resources released for mutually advantageous development.

The slices may not be more equitably divided, but the pie will get bigger and bigger every year. In the long run, this rising tide will indeed lift all boats.

—Financial Times

Jerry's breath was quite literally taken away when the main engine fired and the g's pressed him back into his seat. It was like a sock in the stomach that went on and on and on, a mountain crushing his chest, as the hibernautika tried to stabilize his straining heart. His field of vision was filled with sparkles, and it kept threatening to go black. He seemed to feel capillaries bursting, his head rang like a hollow gong, and he could feel the rush of blood behind his eardrums.

"Are you all right, Father?" Franja's voice said thickly beside him.

"Yeah, yeah," he managed to wheeze, "I'm doing okay."

But of course he wasn't, and he knew it. He was blacking in and out, he was struggling to keep his head above water in an inky sea, and every so often, a wave broke over it, and he was no longer there, he was drifting down, down, down, into the darkness, where it would be so easy to just let himself float forever . . .

. . . floating upward like a cloud riding a thermal, upward like a dolphin rising for air, and bursting suddenly into the bright blue sunshine . . .

The boost was over. Brilliant white sunlight flooded the cabin through the windshield, and he was awake, and aware, and alive.

He could still feel his heart beating febrilely in his chest, and he still didn't seem to be getting quite enough oxygen, but his breathing had stabilized, and his vision had cleared, and his body was as light as air.

"Father? Father? You were unconscious there for a while, are you all right?"

Jerry loosened his harness, pushed with his feet, lifted his butt off the seat cushion, and floated there three inches above it, just as he had always imagined, laughing in delight.

"I feel wonderful, Franja!" he declared. "I've never felt better in my life!"

He was dizzy, he was weak, he could feel his heart beating abnormally, and he had a raging headache, but it was nothing but the perfect truth.

"The best is yet to come, Father," Franja said in a much-relieved tone of voice. "The best is yet to come."

She fired a series of attitude-control thrusters, and the Concordski rolled gently out of the sunshine like a basking whale.

And, oh God, there it was! Immense and glorious, glowing like a living jewel against the black velvet of the void.

He had seen this sight reproduced on film and video at least ten thousand times. He had dreamed of it, he had imagined it, all of his life. There had never been a moment when it was far from his mind's eye. But nothing had really prepared him for the authentic experience.

The seas glowed with a blue intensity that seemed to go all the way down into the core of the planet. The continents paraded by like great shaggy beasts. The cloud decks painted slowly moving shadows across the surface, swirling and whirling with the visible breath of the atmosphere. The whole Earth was restlessly, palpably, majestically alive.

And he was floating weightlessly above it like a dolphin at the apogee of its leap. He was looking back at where he had struggled up from like the first lungfish to climb gasping up the beach to gaze back in wonder at the mirrored surface of the sea.

The Concordski's orbit carried it past the terminator, or rather the Earth below seemed to turn beneath him to proudly display the lights of its cities, spangled sparsely across the great continents, gathered along the coastlines into nebulae, into stellar clusters, and it seemed as if the galaxy itself were mirrored down there, the promise of the true golden age of space to come, when the cities of man would spread themselves out among the stars.

And if he would never live to see that age, if he had been born far too soon to walk the streets of unknown cities on planets circling far-distant suns, well, he had lived long enough to have *this* moment. To sit here with his daughter and see *this* planet entire, to look back on the Earth, on the cradle of that far-distant galactic future, at the moment of its birth.

The Concordski continued along its ballistic orbit, and the sun rose again, baleful and beautiful, a fast, hard, orbital sunrise, sharp and sudden as a halogen lamp turned on in a darkened room.

"There it is, Father, there it is!" Franja cried, pointing at a mote of light shimmering in the actinic glare.

Yes, there it was, defining itself as they approached it, the silvery oval of the fuel balloon, the long needle of the central spine, the spidery framework, the passenger module slung beneath it.

The Grand Tour Navette shining there in the darkness, brilliantly lit by the orbital sunrise.

Franja began firing thrusters, and soon enough had matched orbits, and there he was, floating weightlessly, looking out at the true wonder of what he had wrought.

Sunlight gleamed on the silvery surface of the great fuel balloon, so like an outsized blimp from this perspective, like a whale of the stellar seas. Below it, the windows of the passenger module glowed with internal life, like the cabin lights of a great ocean liner seen from a dinghy at night.

It was indeed a true *spaceship*, the first of its kind. Not a "module" or a "vehicle" or a "space capsule," but a true ship of space, right off the cover of one of his father's old science-fiction magazines.

Flash Gordon would feel right at home. Buck Rogers would not be disappointed. Captain Kirk would be proud to take command.

He had done it. He had built himself a real spaceship, and he was going to ride it before he died.

And as Franja warped the Concordski closer to the Grand Tour Navette, as a spaceway reached out from the passenger cabin to mate with the plane's air lock, as thrillingly ordinary as a jetway rolling up beside an airliner outside the terminal, Jerry thought of Rob.

Rob Post's words echoed in his heart. "You're going to live in the golden age of space travel, it's up to you, kiddo, you can be one of the people who makes it happen."

And it was true. He was.

And it tasted just like a huge bowl of Häagen-Dazs chocolate ice cream swimming in deep, dark Hershey's chocolate syrup.

And you were another, Uncle Rob. Thank you for the ice cream.

Franja was too busy with final maneuvers to see him cry. But the camera above the instrument panel caught it all and broke the world's heart.

CONGRESS OF PEOPLES TO
REASSESS POSITION

The Congress of Peoples opened its meeting in Vienna today amid considerable division and confusion.

Did the arrangements worked out at the Strasbourg summit by the existing nation-states move far enough in the direction of a "Europe of Peoples" for the Congress to support it? Or should the nationless peoples unite in Parliament to either oppose it or modify it? And if the latter, modify it to what? Should the Congress of Peoples reform itself as a transnational political party? Or should it consider its work done and disband in triumph?

"This promises to be a long and complex session," Ian MacTavish said. "The Congress of Peoples has long been oriented toward a long hard struggle. Now we find ourself unexpectedly coping with a sudden partial victory."

Perhaps Slovak delegate Gustav Svoboda put it best: "The real question is whether there will be enough government left on a nation-state level to be worth fighting. Or whether we should just sit back, hold our peace, and let this obsolescent layer of largely ceremonial function just wither away."

—*Die Welt*

Father had suffered more damage during the boost to orbit than he had ever allowed to show. Franja should have realized that when he blacked out during the burn, but he had been so happy, and she had been busy maneuvering the Concordski, and she didn't see how bad it had really been until they were in the spaceway.

Three crew members came brachiating up the rings to greet them, just like space monkeys, and Franja had reflexively grabbed a ring herself. But Father just floated there at the end of the spaceway, waving his arms weakly in a futile attempt to stabilize his position, staring down the tube uncertainly, his face pale, his chest heaving, his eyes narrowed against the pain.

"I . . . I don't think I can manage that," he admitted grudgingly, as the crewpeople whipped up the spaceway toward them, then hung one-handed from the rings.

And they had had to ease him and the hibernautika down the spaceway into the Grand Tour Navette, just like a team of space monkeys unloading fragile cargo.

The cabins in the passenger module might seem like stark spare broom closets to anyone who had never been a space monkey on Cosmograd Sagdeev, but to Franja, they were the lap of space-going luxury. They were as big as a four-monkey bunkroom, but there was only one set of nets, and it had a blow-up headrest so that you could read comfortably in bed. There was a desk and a chair you could strap into. The clothes locker had drawers. The toilet was completely enclosed. And there was actually a small round porthole through which to see the stars.

They put Father in a cabin beside hers. He had wanted to tour the ship immediately, and the press pool was all too eager for it, but Franja had insisted that he rest, and once they had him in the nets, he lost consciousness almost at once.

Jerry awoke to the sight of Franja's face peering down at him with worried eyes. There was a young man floating beside her, above his sleep net, studying him with a more professional concern, glancing at some hand-held instrument.

Looking across his chest, Jerry saw that his shirt had been unbuttoned, that there were electrodes pasted above his heart, circuited through a tiny transmitter taped in the center of the cluster.

"Just a checkup, Father," Franja said all too reassuringly. "Dr. Gonzalez has been running some routine tests."

"How am I doing, Doctor?" Jerry demanded. "How long have I been out?"

Franja and the doctor exchanged quick uncertain glances.

"The truth, Doctor!" Jerry insisted.

Franja sighed. "Tell him," she said.

"Well, Mr. Reed, you did suffer some anoxia during the acceleration, and there has been some deterioration of heart function, and you may notice some minor problems with motor control . . . ," Gonzalez said slowly.

Then, much more rapidly: "But you have slept for nearly

ten hours, and the zero gravity seems to have improved your condition, or at least stabilized it."

"Can he move about, Dr. Gonzalez?" Franja asked.

Gonzalez seemed to ponder that for a long moment. "I suppose so," he finally said. Then he forced a ghastly phony smile. "That *is* what you've risked your life for, isn't it, Mr. Reed?"

"They're about to break orbit, Father," Franja told him. "They want you on the bridge for the big moment. Think you can make it?"

"Or die trying," Jerry declared, and he managed to laugh, feeling a pain in his chest as he did that quickly subsided. No one else thought it was very funny.

The doctor removed the electrodes, and Jerry managed to button up his own shirt, though his fingers felt a bit numb and wooden. They got him out of the nets, the doctor velcroed his oscilloscope to the bulkhead and took hold of the hibernautika's handle. Franja took Jerry's hand, and, brachiating along the rings easily with the other, towed him like a great frail balloon out of the cabin and up the central corridor to the bridge.

The standard bridge crew was four—a pilot, a co-pilot, a flight engineer, and the captain—though they had followed Jerry's original design and provided three extra couches for observers at the rear, well away from the instrument panels and controls.

One of these was occupied by the press-pool cameraman, who lay there in his nets swiveling his camera endlessly as Jerry was introduced to the French captain, the German pilot, the Russian co-pilot, and the British flight engineer.

But Jerry had little attention left for the formalities, he scarcely heard what anyone was saying, including himself, for his being was transfixed by a vision, and the vision that transfixed him was that of the vast curve of the Earth through the big observation bubble that formed the prow of the passenger module.

There had been endless argument about that bubble. It compromised structural integrity. It added to the cost. It was entirely superfluous, a wall screen and cameras would have afforded a much more complete selection of views.

But in the end, the romantics had won out, and there it was, the naked reality itself, palpable and massive in the crystalline vacuum, awesomely *present* as no video image could have been.

After the preliminary footage had been shot, they fastened Jerry into the couch beside the cameraman, Franja crawled into the nets of the one on the other side and took his hand, a shot that had the cameraman straining awkwardly in his restraints to get the close-up.

The bridge crew returned to their couches and the short countdown began.

"Sixty seconds . . ."

"All systems green."

"Thirty seconds . . ."

"Firing sequence initiated . . ."

"Ten seconds . . ."

"We have a commit."

"Zero . . ."

"Ignition confirmed," the co-pilot said, but it was entirely superfluous, as Jerry felt a subtle but unmistakable pressure squeezing him gently back against the padding of the couch. It was barely noticeable as the main engine overcame the GTN's massive inertia, but as it built up delta v, the pressure began to build up too, his lungs started to strain. His heart was racing in his chest by the time the curve of the Earth began to fall away.

Jerry knew that what he was experiencing was no more than a half g acceleration, but after the long hours of zero gravity, his body seemed to weigh twice, not one half, of what it had on Earth. It was like being plunged back into a suddenly unfamiliar and hostile element, like vaulting out of a long float in a heated swimming pool up into the sudden chill of the naked air.

It seemed as if he were trying to breathe some viscous fluid. Spiderweb tingles radiated from his chest down his arms. His head felt as if it were stuffed with broken glass. Tiny sparkles teased at his field of vision.

Oh please, please, don't let me black out now!

The Earth slid out of the observation bubble's field of vision as the Grand Tour Navette executed a roll, and now the transient sparkles were quite overwhelmed by thousands of hard bright stars glaring unwaveringly in the perfect darkness.

I won't! I won't!

He squeezed Franja's hand with what was left of his

strength and felt her strong young grip squeezing back. His field of vision seemed to narrow so that all he saw was the glorious star field drifting majestically across it from left to right. His body was pressed hard against the couch padding, as if a great hand on his chest were seeking to thrust him away from the vision before him, down, down, down, into the inky black waters. . . .

And then a brilliant silvery ball pushed back the circling darkness with a hard white actinic light as it swam majestically across the observation bubble.

The Grand Tour Navette juddered from the rapid firing of clusters of small thrusters and then it was centered in the bubble, in his fading field of vision, pulling him toward it, not down, down, down, but up, up, up, into the bright white circle of light mottled with faint gray dapplings, up a long narrow dark tunnel toward the glorious promise at the other end, toward the Moon.

He smiled, he sighed, and he let it take him up, up, and away.

After Father had lost consciousness on the bridge, Dr. Gonzalez had insisted that he rest in his cabin as much as possible and had given him a sedative to keep him asleep.

"I'm afraid the prognosis is not good," he told Franja. "Medically speaking, this has been a very foolish venture. He's worse than he was when he boarded. He showed some improvement after hours in zero g, but even this mild acceleration now . . ."

"The prognosis was always terminal, Doctor," Franja said grimly. "We all knew that, and so did he. But will he make it? Will he make it to the Moon?"

Gonzalez had shrugged. "That, I think, is not an entirely medical matter. His heart has been damaged, his respiration is becoming labored, and he's probably sustained scattered cerebral damage already. He could suffer a major stroke or heart attack at any time, or survive like this for weeks."

But then he had stepped out of his medical persona. "As a doctor, all I can say is that the flesh is deteriorating rapidly," he said. "But as a man . . . Well, the spirit is impressively strong. And he *deserves* to make it. And barring a major incident, that should count for something. All we can do is give him all the rest we can and pray to God for justice."

"I wish I could do that sincerely, Dr. Gonzalez, but I'm afraid I have a great deal of difficulty believing in God, just or otherwise. I'm afraid I'm not quite up to praying for cosmic justice."

And Gonzalez had smiled a strange little smile. "But I do, Señorita Reed," he told her, "so, con su permiso, I will."

And so Father slept most of the time, and Gonzalez prayed, and Franja found herself alone for most of the forty-four-hour voyage, eating in the commissary, sleeping in the nets, fending off the unwanted attention of the press-pool reporters, who refused to let her alone in the absence of their star performer, and spending most of her waking hours in the small observation bubble in the nose of the salon module, watching the imperceptible approach of the Moon.

It looked so cold and pale at first, a hard white disc of reflected sunlight, baleful and indifferent in the cruel black darkness, nothing like a planet, nothing like the living Earth she had spent so many hours regarding with wonder and longing as a space monkey on Cosmograd Sagdeev.

It seemed like a painted backdrop, a special-effects shot from some sleazy film; distant and flat, a foolish thing indeed for which to throw one's life away. What was it after all but a cold colorless rock whose only hint of life, the semblance of a human face that the eye constructed from the patterns of the mares and the craters, was a mere optical illusion, a perceptual denial of the lifeless reality?

Only as it grew larger and larger, only as the GTN could be perceived as actually speeding toward it, did it wax into a true sphere in her mind's eye, and loom into psychic focus as another planet, with a true geography cast into shadowed relief, with its own dusty version of mountains and valleys, desiccated and stillborn, but still truly another world.

Only then did the vision become real, become personal. Only then did it even occur to her that *she* too was about to experience the fulfillment of a teenage dream. Only then did she feel the impact.

She was going to the Moon.

How strange that she had never thought of it that way before! She had never thought of it as anything but *Father's* trip to the Moon. She had quite forgotten, somehow, that this was something that she too had dreamed of—as a girl listening to Father's stories, as a student in the lycée working so hard for admission to Yuri Gagarin University, at Gagarin itself, working night and day to bring a moment like this about, aboard Sagdeev, and in pilots' school too.

Only in these last years hopping from city to city, immersed in the newfound wonders of a *living* planet, had the dream of space lost its clear hard-edged purity and faded into some vague future possibility, become the memory of a dream dreamt long ago by someone else.

Only fortune, and indeed what had seemed like bad fortune at the time, had confined her to one planet and taught her to love the wonders of the Earth. She had never sought to be the woman she had become.

And only Father's misfortune had gifted that woman with the fulfillment of the lost girlhood dream she had inherited from him. Only now, when she had quite forgotten that goal in her total concern for him, was she about to receive what she had once so single-mindedly sought.

There was some kind of justice in that.

For only now was Father's last gift truly deserved.

And by God, Father deserved it too.

Franja did not believe in God, still less in cosmic justice.

But as she looked out on the dead white surface of the Moon, she thought she could see a tiny sparkle, the Lunagrad half-burrowed into the surface of this world that had never before known life, and she imagined cities spangled over the once-dead surface in some far-distant age, cities as teeming with life and complexity as any on Earth. And that too would be the fulfillment of the great human dream in the face of a cold and uncaring void.

Even a dead world could become what life chose to make it.

And she found herself remembering something Nathan Wolfowitz had said in the midst of a crisis that had threatened to scourge that life from the Earth in a paroxysm of human stupidity.

There ain't no justice in this world, the American President had said, *except the justice we make.*

Or in any other, she thought.

No, she couldn't bring herself to pray to a God she didn't believe in for cosmic justice. But just now she found herself envying those who could and did.

632   N O R M A N   S P I N R A D

AN OPTIMIST'S VIEW OF THE
GREAT SILENCE

Before the discovery of the Barnards, the pessimists took our failure to detect signals from extraterrestrial civilizations as proof that no one was out there. Now that we know that there is, now that we even have hints of unthinkably advanced civilizations toward the galactic core, the pessimists take our continued failure to detect interstellar broadcasts as proof that these civilizations are hostile or indifferent. Or even engaged in a Darwinian battle of tooth and claw we should seek to hide from.

But from an optimist's viewpoint, this failure to communicate may be seen as potential good news. For if it is possible for civilizations at a sufficient stage of advancement to engage in easy interstellar chatter, to *travel* easily to other stars, why would they bother? Why cope with a communications delay measured in decades and centuries when you can meet face-to-face? Who knows, civilizations much in advance of our own might even acquire the ability to travel faster than light, by worm-hole tunnels created by artificial black holes, for example, or more likely by something we cannot even imagine.

The pessimists look out at the stars, and they fearfully see the very chauvinisms we now, finally, seem to be in the process of overcoming writ large and eternal in a galactic behavioral sink.

But we optimists look out at the stars and hopefully see a galactic main and the ships of many peoples sailing its immensity, and we say perhaps they have avoided contacting us for the best of reasons. Perhaps they've just been waiting for us to grow up, put the strife and dangers of planetary adolescence behind us, hoist our own sails, and set forth to join them, not as the buccaneers we once were, but as a mature and worthy civilization.

—*Science*

Occasionally, Jerry found himself rising up to the surface of a sea of warm liquid blackness into a world of pressure and pain and sparky occluded vision. Sometimes Franja was there, sometimes the doctor, but most of these moments of conscious lucidity were endured alone, lying in the darkened cabin, feeling the breath being squeezed out of him, the edge of vertigo and nausea, the pains radiating out from his chest down his limbs, the headache that fragmented thought, the fetid metallic taste of his own death in his mouth.

A part of him would recoil and try to drift back into the comforting nothingness, but the stronger part of him fought to retain consciousness even of this, fought to remain awake and alive, fought not to die like a whimpering creature in the dark, used the pain, the struggle itself, as a goad to awareness.

Not yet! Not now!

Always the darkness was stronger, always his last thought was of being dragged back down beneath the surface, but always he came rising up again, and now he felt himself surfacing once more, into the pain, into the ceaseless pressure, into . . .

He blinked his eyes in wonder. There were still floaters in his field of vision, but he was seeing much more clearly now. And thinking more clearly too, he found himself realizing. He was fully awake. There were still tingly pains in his chest and limbs, but the pressure was gone. And so was the crushing weight of gravity.

His head still ached and he was still quite dizzy, but the black tide had receded from his mind, and his consciousness was clear and sharp. Gasping to breathe the attenuated air, he felt like a dying fish that had been tossed back into the water, reprieved and reinvigorated by a sudden return to his natural element.

As zero gravity was now.

And then he realized what had happened. The main engine had been shut down for the insertion into the lunar orbit. He had made it! They were there! They had reached the Moon!

But then he remembered that there was one ordeal yet to come.

They would use gravitational braking to let the Moon close the parabola of their flyby into an elliptical orbit, but they had to lose velocity first to do it, and that meant one more burn, a short, hard hot one at a quarter g, with the main engine thrusting against the forward vector.

First they would turn the ship. . . .

And the GTN began to jerk and judder as scores of little control thrusters brought it about. Then there was a long terrifying stillness as the computers verified the burn parameters.

And the ship shook and a great fist slammed him back into the padding, knocking the breath out of him, sending lightning bolts of pain across his chest and down his limbs, pounding him back into the inky waters, pushing him under, dragging him away, down, down, down . . .

Not yet, goddamn you! Not now!

Jerry ground his fingernails into the flesh of his palms. He bit down gingerly on his tongue. He would not let the darkness carry him away this time, he would not trust that he would rise to the surface again, he would damn well wait this out, he would not lose consciousness now!

Not yet, motherfucker! Not now!

It seemed to go on forever, and then, all at once, it was over. The main engine shut down, the fist on his chest disappeared, and he came bobbing weightless like a cork up out of the depths of the suffocating sea.

After the acceleration, the return of zero gravity was like a burst of exhilarating energy, a return to natural life. His breathing was labored, the pains in his chest and arms were worse than before, there was an unsettling numbness in his fingers and toes, but his vision had cleared, the darkness had receded, and he was very much awake and aware.

Indeed, everything seemed to have a special sharpness, a newness, a wonderful clarity. Slowly and awkwardly, he managed to disengage himself from the nets, and let himself float upward like a cloud toward the arbitrary ceiling. He just let himself drift like that for a while, exulting in the weightless freedom, until a ring came within his feeble grasp.

He was hanging there from it in a standing position when they came to get him, floating on his feet like a man, like a new man, like a man of the future who was going to the Moon.

Franja's eyes widened in amazement. The doctor frowned. The cameraman caught it for posterity.

"Well, well, Mr. Reed," the man from Tass said in English, with a smile of relief, "good to see you up and about."

Jerry insisted on making his own way to the bridge, hand over hand out of the cabin and down the central corridor, with Franja lugging the hibernautika behind him, and the cameraman brachiating awkwardly backward in front of him to get the shot. It seemed to require no strength at all, once you got into the rhythm of it and just let it happen in liquid slow motion, it was like some kind of effortless aerial dance.

You're a real space cadet, Bob had told him often enough. *You ought to be a citizen of outer space.*

He grinned as he brachiated down the corridor, weak as a kitten, still in pain, intimate now with his own approaching death, but flying weightlessly like a bird through its natural element just the same.

Now I am, Bob, now I am!

Franja said good-bye at the entrance to the bridge. There were only three free positions inside, and this was a moment that the press pool, robbed of so much human-interest coverage by Jerry's weakened condition, refused to cede to familial togetherness.

She handed the hibernautika over to the Tass reporter, whom the luck of the pool schedule had given this slot, and the bridge door opened. The cameraman backed awkwardly inside, and then the correspondent, beckoning for Jerry to follow.

Jerry grabbed the last ring in the corridor and vaulted feet first inside. The Russian co-pilot was there to catch him, hugging him about the waist, like a man tenderly catching a small child in his arms.

Through the observation bubble, the Moon was enormous, and the Grand Tour Navette was falling toward it as it approached the line of the terminator, descending toward the pearlescent gray surface just as the Eagle had in those televised images an entire lifetime ago.

But there it was, no longer an image on television, no longer a childhood dream, no longer a flat white circle but a great gleaming curve of a planet rising up to greet him.

The co-pilot released him, took him by the hand, and towed him gently to his own empty couch at the front of the bridge.

"We thought you might like to log a little flight time on the controls," the young Russian said tenderly. He grinned at Jerry. "Our way of saying thanks for the joystick," he said as he fastened the harness. "Thanks for giving us the fun of flying her by the seat of our pants!"

"Hold the joystick please, Mr. Reed," the Tass reporter said. "What a wonderful shot!"

The Grand Tour Navette sped across the sunlit surface

toward the line of the terminator, toward the dark side of the Moon, with the joystick control in Jerry's right hand, and his ship approaching lunar perigee.

The GTN crossed the terminator and swung around the darkened hemisphere into brilliant starry darkness, up and around toward the apogee of its elliptical orbit, and there it was, rising from behind the limb of its satellite, the globe of the Earth, huge and luminous and alive, and there Jerry was, at long impossible last, rounding the Moon, and looking back on all of cis-lunar space from the apogee of the spaceship's orbit, hanging weightless at the apogee of his own life.

Did he see those sparkling motes moving out there between the Moon and its planet, or were they more floaters in his field of vision, projection in his mind's eye? It didn't really matter, for he *did* see them, and they *were* there, the satellites and the Cosmograds, the battle stations and Spaceville, the lights of the present and future celestial city of man.

"There will be a short retroburn now to circularize our orbit," the captain said behind him. The ship juddered as the maneuvering thrusters fired, and it turned end for end, turned the observation bubble away from the Earth, away from the Moon, away from the birthplace, toward the face of the infinite vastness of the future, toward the unthinkably distant stars.

Surely *these* moving points of light had to be artifacts, visual distortions, projections of the heart's desire, but he *did* see them, as clearly as if he had been granted a vision of the far future that he would never live to see—Grand Tour Navettes moving out toward Mars and Jupiter and beyond, starships headed for planets circling far-distant suns.

The retroburn crushed him back into the padding, his breathing became labored, his heart seemed to flutter wildly, and pain shot down his legs and arms.

But it didn't last long, and he scarcely noticed it, for he was walking on water, soaring out among the stars, out into the future, out where he had always belonged.

They turned the ship again, and once more the Moon lay beneath him, but now the GTN was in a low circular orbit, sweeping majestically across the landscape of another world, great sharply shadowed craters and jagged uneroded mountains, pockmarked wastelands, and desert dusts, pearlescent in the hard sunlight, oh so *real* in the unnaturally sharp focus of the airless void.

They crossed the terminator again, swept over the nightside, then back over the sunlit surface.

And as they completed the full orbit, Jerry could see it down there on the surface below, and this was no illusion, this was unmistakable, the flash of the great solar mirror, the tiny sharp shapes outlined against the pearly brilliance, the round dot of the red circle they had painted on the surface to proclaim "Here we are!"

Lunagrad. The permanent human settlement that man had planted on another world.

It didn't matter that that ensign was red, that those were Russians down there. They were humans, and they were living their lives on another planet, and from this vantage, that was all that mattered, they were humans, they were walking on water, and so was he.

"Take the conn, please, Mr. Reed," the captain said.

"Fly her?" Jerry muttered, unable to take his eyes away from the vision before him.

"Just follow the captain's marks," the pilot said. "The computer will do the rest."

The joystick felt strangely cool and glassy in Jerry's grasp.

"On my mark," the captain said as they sped toward the sharp nightside divide.

"Mark!"

They crossed into darkness, and the stars came out, and Jerry pulled straight back on the joystick, and felt the main engine fire. But this time the pressure and the pain seemed to be happening to someone else, for he was riding a mighty rocket, he was in command of its vast forces, he was flying his own spaceship around another world.

"Ten seconds . . ."

The joystick was like a huge cold bowl of chocolate ice cream in a child's hands.

You're too young to understand what you're going to see tonight, but you're not too young to understand a whole pint of Häagen-Dazs. . . .

"Twenty seconds . . ."

The strange pearlescent television-gray lunar landscape coming up under the lander camera . . . The hollow descending hiss of the retro-rockets through the bulkhead . . .

The Eagle has landed . . .

"Twenty five . . ."

The bulky figure descending the ladder in slow motion . . .

"Shutdown."

The foot coming down on the gray pumice and changing the destiny of the species forever.

Jerry recentered the joystick and floated upward into a sparkly starry dark, but as the Grand Tour Navette rounded the limb of the Moon, a brilliant blue globe appeared at the end of the narrowing black tunnel, the Earth seen from beyond the gravity well, from beyond the onrushing darkness, looking back at him from where it had all started, looking back at him from the future he would never live to see.

But he had lived to see *this*.

That's . . . uh . . . one small step for mankind, one giant leap for a man.

"Mr. Reed? Mr. Reed?"

Jerry's vision was growing blurry now, the inky waters were rolling over him, all that he could see was a brilliant blue circle opening up before him, all he could feel was the wonderful chocolate taste in his mouth.

"Mr. Reed? Mr. Reed? Can you tell the world what it feels like to have finally made it? To fly to the Moon?"

"Like the biggest bowl of chocolate ice cream in the world," Jerry said into the microphone quite clearly before he sighed and let it carry him up and away.

"What a sight this is! Who would have believed such a thing was possible a few short dark weeks ago? But here it comes, a Russian plane, an Aeroflot Concordski, touching down on the runway at San Francisco Airport to bring a dying American hero home!

"The plane is turning toward the terminal now, the engine of the ambulance helicopter is already running. It is reported that Jerry Reed's condition has deteriorated further in the last few hours, the planned press conference has been canceled, and he will be taken directly to the hospital and placed in intensive care. . . .

"I have a feeling the world will long remember these pictures, ladies and gentlemen. I have a feeling this is like the

first shot of a mushroom-pillar cloud, or the very first footage of the Earth as a planet rising over the surface of the
Moon. That shot of the first Aeroflot flight to touch down
on American soil in a generation is an image that will forever
mark the border between an old world and the new."

—NBC

The strain of reentry had been far too much, they had
almost lost him, and after an hour of circling and messages
back and forth between Washington and Moscow, the Soviet
Concordski had finally been allowed to land at the San
Francisco airport.

That had been a glorious, and terrible, and infuriating
moment for Bobby, the cheers, and the lights, and the cameras, Dad's ashen face as they lowered the gurney from the
plane, the mad dash wheeling him through the press of reporters to the helicopter, the microphones shoved in his
face . . .

Too much had gone on too fast for Bobby to really have
time to feel anything, and now, locked in an awful deathwatch in a hospital room in Palo Alto, he found himself
almost wishing the press, with its noise and lights, would
find this place and burst into the room waving microphones
and cameras.

Anything to break this deathly stillness.

Franja stood beside him, numb and stony-eyed. Mom,
who had long since cried herself dry, sat by the bedside. Dr.
Burton stood at the other side of the bed, watching the life-
signs monitors expectantly, a sunny blond vulture in medical
greens. Sara hung back at the rear of the room, looking
rather lost.

Dad lay in the bed, breathing shallowly, and Bobby tried
to convince himself that his father was feeling no pain, that
he was just finally slipping away into a dreamless sleep.

He had been conscious only three times on the trip back
from the Moon, and, according to Franja, he had not really
been coherent, babbling things she could not understand.

"But his face, Bobby," Franja told him, "you should have
seen it. I never saw him look so happy."

Dad had been at the edge of death by the time they had
helicoptered him to Immortality, Inc., but he rallied tanta-

lizingly under intensive medical care, hanging on for three days now, neither quite dead, nor truly alive.

"If only we could blue-max him," Burton had fretted. "But no, we have to wait for clinical brain death, it's the damn law!"

And so the awful deathwatch had begun, and continued, and dragged, on, and on, and on, until now Bobby could only stand there, wishing for it to be over, wishing for his father to finally die.

"Sonya . . ."

Dad's eyes were still shut, but they were moving fitfully beneath his eyelids like those of a man in a dream, and his lips were moving weakly, and out of them came a dry whispery sound.

"I'm here, Jerry!" Mom said, squeezing his hand.

Dad's eyes slowly opened, swept weakly around the room, closed again. "I did it," he whispered, "I walked on water."

Bobby shot a glance at Burton, who nodded and departed. Then Bobby took Franja's hand, and they knelt down by the bedside.

"Yeah, Dad," he said softly, "you really *are* a bona fide citizen of outer space now."

Dad's eyes opened again and looked right at him for what Bobby knew would be the last time. And there was something in them, something brave, and crazy, and somehow satisfied, that almost let him make his peace with that.

"It's okay, Bob," Dad told him, as if reading his heart. "I've been there, I've seen it, it's not the end, just the end of the beginning . . ."

"Father—"

"What a life you're going to have, Franja!" Dad said. "You're going to live in the golden age of space travel. You're going to be one of the people who makes it all happen. Someday you're going to sail one of our little canoes into the harbor of a great galactic city. I know it. I've seen it. It's out there waiting for us, you and me, Franja, you and me. . . ."

Franja burst into tears. Bobby hugged her to him.

Father smiled. "You two go now, please" he said. "I think your mother and I would like to be alone. Take care of each other. Let me remember you like this at the end."

"Oh, Father!"

"Let it be, big sister, let it be," Bobby said, and he led her away.

"Sonya . . . I want you to do something for me," Jerry whispered, his voice growing dimmer with every syllable, his eyes closing heavily at the very end.

"Anything, love . . . ," Sonya said, leaning closer. "Jerry? Jerry?"

Slowly Jerry's head rolled over on the pillow toward her, slowly, even more slowly, he fought to open his eyes one last time. And then they were looking right at her, and were it not for what she saw there, she would have quite fallen apart.

But Jerry's eyes were bright and strong, and his dry cracked lips were creased in a faint smile. "Don't cry, Sonya," he whispered. "I've been there . . . I've seen it . . . starships sailing through the darkness like great ocean liners toward cities circling far distant suns . . . that's where we're all going, Sonya, won't it be grand . . . ?"

Sonya didn't know whether to rage or laugh or to cry.

Even now! Even at death's door! Still her urban spaceman to the very end! Never had she loved him more.

She had always thought she had loved him in spite of this.

Now she finally understood that this was the heart of everything she had loved him for.

"Sonya . . . Sonya . . ."

"Yes, Jerry, I'm here."

"I want you to do something for me."

"Anything, love."

Jerry's eyes looked down at the hibernautika sitting by his bedside, back into her eyes. "Turn me off," he said.

"Jerry!"

"Turn me off, Sonya!" he said much more strongly. "Let me go!"

"Don't ask me to do that!" Sonya cried. "You know I can't!"

"Sure you can, Sonya," Jerry told her. "It'll be just like going to sleep. Like Rip van Winkle. And I'll wake up in a brand-new world."

"Oh, Jerry," she cried, despite herself, "how can you talk like that even now?"

"Because I believe it, Sonya."

"You really believe it?" Sonya sobbed.

"Of course I do. I've seen it. I know it. This is the beginning of the golden age of miracles. Impossible dreams are happening every day. You're the one who's always telling me to read the papers, Sonya."

"Oh, Jerry, I just can't stand the thought of losing you!" Sonya moaned. "Is that so wrong?"

Jerry's lips creased in a weak little smile that his eyes made absolutely radiant. "Then let's not lose each other, Sonya," he said. "Live a good long happy life," he told her. "Think of it as a nice long separate vacation. But when it's over—"

"Jerry—"

"—when it's over, you come home to me."

"Oh, Jerry!"

"Let them put you in the time machine too, Sonya. Promise me you'll do that."

"Oh, Jerry, Jerry . . ."

"Promise me, Sonya!"

"I promise, love," Sonya said, willing to say anything to avoid saying the final good-bye.

Jerry sighed. He squeezed her hand one last time before his strength failed him. His head rolled away from her with a heartbreaking smile, and he stared at something he saw on the ceiling, smiling still.

"I've got a wonderful idea, Sonya," he whispered. "Have them put it in our contracts. Let's not let them wake us up for five hundred years. Let's not wake up until we can take the grand tour together again, let's begin our new lives with a long second honeymoon out among the stars. Wouldn't you like to do that, Sonya?"

"More than anything else in the world . . . ," Sonya said quite truthfully.

"Don't you believe that we will?"

"Yes, Jerry, I do," she lied.

"Then I'm ready to go there now," Jerry said. "Time to pull my plug." And he closed his eyes and spoke no more.

Sonya sat there by the bedside for a long, long time, listening to his agonized breathing falter away, watching his smiling tranquil face freezing into its final mask, crying and crying and crying, and waiting for some outside force to end this endless moment.

But nothing did.

Nothing would.

And somehow, she knew, nothing should.

Finally, she thought of the foolish promise she had made to him, to join him five hundred years after this moment was ended, a promise that had been made without belief, but now, she suddenly knew, not without a commitment of the heart.

And that had been his parting gift to her, a gift that she now saw had been hers for the taking all along if only she had made the leap of faith to seize it.

You can walk on water, Sonya, but first you have to find something worth walking on water *for*.

He had always had a dream like that and she never had. She had envied him that, and loved him for it.

But now he had finally succeeded in giving it to her. She could accept his most precious gift at last. She could believe it. She could feel it.

She could see them sitting there with a foaming bottle of champagne, toasting each other in a sidewalk café in another City of Light on a planet circling a far-distant sun, and looking back on this moment with a warm nostalgic glow as their true betrothal of the spirit.

"Let it be right," she whispered. "Let it be so."

And she reached out a loving hand and tenderly pulled the plug.